D0129816

Dick Francis Omnibus Two

RISK
FORFEIT
REFLEX

PAN BOOKS

Risk first published 1977 by Michael Joseph Ltd
and published by Pan Books in 1979
Forfeit first published 1968 by Michael Joseph Ltd
and published by Pan Books in 1970
Reflex first published 1964 by Michael Joseph Ltd
and published by Pan Books in 1976

This combined edition published 1999 by Pan Books
an imprint of Macmillan Publishers Ltd
25 Eccleston Place, London SW1W 9NF
Basingstoke and Oxford
Associated companies throughout the world
www.macmillan.co.uk

ISBN 0 330 39369 3

1 3 5 7 9 8 6 4 2

A CIP catalogue record for this book is available from
the British Library.

Phototypeset by Intype London Ltd
Printed and bound in Great Britain by
Mackays of Chatham plc, Chatham, Kent

RISK

To the memory of
Lionel Vick,
first a professional steeplechase jockey,
then a certified accountant;
always a brave man.
And my thanks to his associate,
Michael Foote.

CHAPTER ONE

Thursday, March 17th, I spent the morning in anxiety, the afternoon in ecstasy, and the evening unconscious.

Thursday night, somewhere between dark and dawn, I slowly surfaced into a nightmare which would have been all right if I'd been asleep.

It took me a good long time to realize I was actually awake. Half awake, anyway.

There was no light. I thought my eyes were open, but the blackness was absolute.

There was a lot of noise. Different noises, loud and confusing. A heavy engine. Rattling noises. Creaks. Rushing noises. I lay in a muzzy state and felt battered by too much sound.

Lay . . . I was lying on some sort of mattress. On my back. Cold, sick and stiff. Aching. Shivering. Physically wretched and mentally bewildered.

I tried to move. Couldn't for some reason lift either hand to my face. They seemed to be stuck to my legs. Very odd.

An interminable time passed. I grew colder, sicker, stiffer, and wide awake.

Tried to sit up. Banged my head on something close above. Lay down again, fought a sudden spurt of panic, and made myself take it step by step.

Hands. Why couldn't I move my hands? Because my wrists seemed to be fastened to my trousers. It didn't make sense, but that was what it felt like.

Space. What of space? I stiffly moved my freezing feet, exploring. Found I had no shoes on. Only socks. On the immediate left, a wall. Close above, a ceiling. On the immediate right, a softer barrier. Possibly cloth.

I shifted my whole body a fraction to the right, and felt with my fingers. Not cloth, but netting. Like a tennis net. Pulled tight. Keeping me in. I pushed my fingers through the mesh, but could feel nothing at all on the far side.

Eyes. If I hadn't gone suddenly blind (and it didn't feel like it), I was lying somewhere where no light penetrated. Brilliant deduction. Most constructive. Ha bloody ha.

Ears. Almost the worst problem. Constant din assaulted them, shutting me close in the narrow black box, preventing me hearing any further than the powerful, nearby, racketing engine. I had a frightening feeling that even if I screamed no one would hear me. I had a sudden even more frightening feeling of *wanting* to scream. To make someone come. To make someone tell me where I was, and why I was there, and what on earth was happening.

I opened my mouth and yelled.

I yelled 'Hey' and 'Come here' and 'Bloody bastard, come and let me out', and thrashed about in useless rage, and all that happened was that my voice and fear bounded back in the confined space and made things worse. Chain reaction. One-way trip to exhaustion.

In the end I stopped shouting and lay still. Swallowed. Ground my teeth. Tried to force my mind into holding on to sense. Disorientation was the road to gibbering.

Concentrate, I told myself. *Think*.

That engine . . .

A big one. Doing a job of work. Situated somewhere close, but not where I was. The other side of a wall. Perhaps behind my head.

If it would only stop, I thought numbly, I would feel less sick, less pulverized, less panicky, less threatened.

The engine went right on hammering, its vibration reaching me through the walls. Not a turbine engine: not smooth enough, and no whine. A piston engine. Heavy duty, like a tractor . . . or a lorry. But I wasn't in a lorry. There was no feeling of movement; and the engine never altered its rate. No slowing or accelerating. No changes of gear. Not a lorry.

A generator. It's a generator, I thought. Making electricity.

I was lying tied up in the dark and on a sort of shelf near an electric generator. Cold, sick and frightened. And where?

As to how I'd got there . . . well, I knew that, up to a

7

point. I remembered the beginning, well enough. I would never forget Thursday, March 17th.

The most shattering questions were those to which I could think of no answer at all.

Why? What for? And *what next?*

CHAPTER TWO

That Thursday morning a client with his life in ruins kept me in the office in Newbury long after I should have left for Cheltenham races, and it seemed churlish to say, 'Yes, Mr Wells, terribly sorry about your agony, but I can't stop to help you now because I want to nip off and enjoy myself.' Mr Wells, staring-eyed and suicidal, simply had to be hauled in from his quicksand.

It took three and a half hours of analysis, sympathy, brandy, discussion of ways and means, and general pep-talk, to restore the slightest hope to his horizon, and I wasn't his doctor, priest, solicitor or other assorted hand-holder, but only the accountant he'd engaged in a frenzy the night before.

Mr Wells had bitten the dust in the hands of a crooked financial adviser. Mr Wells, frantic, desperate, had heard that Roland Britten, although young, had done other salvage jobs. Mr Wells on the telephone had offered double fees, tears, and lifelong gratitude as inducements: and Mr Wells was a confounded nuisance.

For the first and probably the only time in my life I

was that day going to ride in the Cheltenham Gold Cup, the race which ranked next to the Grand National in the lives of British steeplechase riders. No matter that the tipsters gave my mount little chance or the bookies were offering ante-post odds of forty-to-one, the fact remained that for a part-time amateur like myself the offer of a ride in the Gold Cup was as high as one could go.

Thanks to Mr Wells I did not leave the office calmly and early after a quick shuffle through the day's mail. Not until a quarter to one did I begin to unstick his leech-like dependence and get him moving, and only then by promising another long session on the following Monday. Halfway through the door, he froze yet again. Was I sure we had covered every angle? Couldn't I give him the afternoon? Monday, I said firmly. Wasn't there anyone else he could see, then?

'Sorry,' I said. 'My senior partner is away on holiday.'

'Mr King?' he asked, pointing to the neat notice 'King and Britten' painted on the open door.

I nodded, reflecting gloomily that my senior partner, if he hadn't been touring somewhere in Spain, would have been most insistent that I got off to Cheltenham in good time. Trevor King, big, silver-haired, authoritative and worldly, had my priorities right.

We had worked together for six years, ever since he'd enticed me, from the city office where I'd been trained, with the one inducement I couldn't refuse: flexible working hours which allowed time to go racing. He already had five or six clients from the racing world,

Newbury being central for many of the racing stables strung out along the Berkshire Downs, and, needing a replacement for a departing assistant, he'd reckoned that if he engaged me he might acquire a good deal more business in that direction. Not that he'd ever actually said so, because he was not a man to use two words where one would do; but his open satisfaction as his plan had gradually worked made it obvious.

All he had apparently done towards checking my ability as an accountant, as opposed to amateur jockey, was to ask my former employers if they would offer me a substantial raise in salary in order to keep me. They said yes, and did so. Trevor, it seemed, had smiled like a gentle shark, and gone away. His subsequent offer to me had been for a full partnership and lots of racing time; the partnership would cost me ten thousand pounds and I could pay it to him over several years out of my earnings. What did I think?

I'd thought it might turn out just fine; and it had.

In some ways I knew Trevor no better than on that first day. Our real relationship began and ended at the office door, social contact outside being confined to one formal dinner party each year, to which I was invited by letter by his wife. His house was opulent: building and contents circa nineteen twenties, with heavy plate glass cut to fit the top surfaces of polished furniture, and an elaborate bar built into the room he called his 'snug'. Friends tended to be top management types or county councillors, worthy substantial citizens like Trevor himself.

On the professional level, I knew him well. Orthodox establishment outlook, sober and traditional. Patriarchal, but not pompous. Giving the sort of gilt-edged advice that still appeared sound even if in hindsight it turned out not to be.

Something punitive about him, perhaps. He seemed to me sometimes to get a positive pleasure from detailing the extent of a client's tax liabilities, and watching the client droop.

Precise in mind and method, discreetly ambitious, pleased to be a noted local personage, and at his charming best with rich old ladies. His favourite clients were prosperous companies; his least favourite, incompetent individuals with their affairs in a mess.

I finally got rid of the incompetent Mr Wells and took my tensions down to the office car park. It was sixty miles from Newbury to Cheltenham and on the way I chewed my fingernails through two lots of roadworks and an army convoy, knowing also that near the course the crawling racegoing jams would mean half an hour for the last mile. There had been enough said already about the risks of putting up an amateur ('however good' some kind columnist had written) against the top brass of the professionals on the country's best horses in the most important race of the season's most prestigious meeting. 'The best thing Roland Britten can do is to keep Tapestry out of everyone else's way' was the offering of a less kind writer, and although I more or less agreed with him I hadn't meant to do it by not arriving in time. Of all possible unprofessional behaviour, that would be the worst.

Lateness was the last and currently the most acute of a whole list of pressures. I had been riding as an amateur in jump races since my sixteenth birthday, but was now, with thirty-two in sight, finding it increasingly difficult to keep fit. Age and desk work were nibbling away at a stamina I'd always taken for granted: it now needed a lot of effort to do what I'd once done without thought. The hour and a half I spent early every morning riding exercise for a local trainer were no longer enough. Recently, in a couple of tight finishes, I'd felt the strength draining like bathwater from my creaking muscles, and had lost at least one race because of it. I couldn't swear to myself that I was tuned up tight for the Gold Cup.

Work in the office had multiplied to the point where doing it properly was a problem in itself. Half-days off for racing had begun to feel like treachery. Saturdays were fine, but impatient clients viewed Wednesdays at Ascot or Thursdays at Stratford-upon-Avon with irritation. That I worked at home in the evenings to make up for it satisfied Trevor, but no one else. And my case load, as jargon would put it, was swamping me.

Apart from Mr Wells, there had been other jobs I should have done that morning. I should have sent an appeal against a top jockey's tax assessment; I should have signed a certificate for a solicitor; and there had been two summonses for clients to appear before the Tax Commissioners, which needed instant action, even if only evasive.

'I'll apply for postponements,' I told Peter, one of our two assistants. 'Ring both of those clients, and tell them not to worry, I'll start on their cases at once. And check that we've all the papers we need. Ask them to send any that are missing.'

Peter nodded sullenly, unwillingly, implying that I was always giving him too much work. And maybe I was.

Trevor's plans to take on another assistant had been so far halted by an offer which was currently giving both of us headaches. A big London firm wanted to move in on us, merge, amalgamate, and establish a large branch of itself on our patch, with us inside. Materially, we would benefit, as at present the steeply rising cost of overheads like office rent, electricity and secretarial wages was coming straight out of our pockets. We would also be under less stress, as at present when one of us was ill or on holiday, the burden on the other was heavy. But Trevor agonized over the prospect of demotion from absolute boss, and I over the threat of loss of liberty. We had postponed a decision until Trevor's return from Spain in two weeks' time, but at that point bleak realities would have to be faced.

I drummed my fingers on the steering wheel of my Dolomite and waited impatiently for the roadworks' traffic lights to turn green. Looked at my watch for the

hundredth time. 'Come on,' I said aloud. 'Come *on*.'
Binny Tomkins would be absolutely furious.

Binny, Tapestry's trainer, didn't want me on the horse.
'Not in the Gold Cup,' he'd said positively, when the
owner had proposed it. They'd faced each other belligerently outside the weighing room of Newbury racecourse,
where Tapestry had just obliged in the three mile 'chase:
Mrs Moira Longerman, small, blonde and bird-like,
versus sixteen stone of frustrated male.

'... just because he's your *accountant*,' Binny was
saying in exasperation when I rejoined them after
weighing-in. 'It's bloody ridiculous.'

'Well, he won today, didn't he?' she said.

Binny threw his arms wide, breathing heavily. Mrs
Longerman had offered me the Newbury ride on the
spur of the moment when the stable jockey had broken
his ankle in a fall in the previous race. Binny had
accepted me as a temporary arrangement with fair grace,
but Tapestry was the best horse in his yard, and for a
middle-ranker like him a runner in the Gold Cup was an
event. He wanted the best professional jockey he could
get. He did not want Mrs Longerman's accountant who
rode in thirty races in a year, if he was lucky. Mrs
Longerman, however, had murmured something about
removing Tapestry to a more accommodating trainer,
and I had not been unselfish enough to decline the offer,
and Binny had fumed in vain.

Mrs Longerman's previous accountant had for years
let her pay to the Inland Revenue a lot more tax than

she'd needed, and I'd got her a refund of thousands. It wasn't the best grounds for choosing a jockey to ride for you in the Gold Cup, but I understood she was thanking me by giving me something beyond price. I quite passionately did not want to let her down; and that, too, was a pressure.

I was worried about making a reasonable show, but not about falling. When one worried about falling, it was time to stop racing: it would happen to me one day, I supposed, but it hadn't yet. I worried about being unfit, unwanted, and late. Enough to be going on with.

Binny was spluttering like a lit fuse when I finally arrived, panting, in the weighing room.

'Where the hell have you been?' he demanded. 'Do you realize the first race is over already and in another five minutes you'd be fined for not turning up?'

'Sorry.'

I carried my saddle, helmet, and bag of gear through into the changing room, sat down thankfully on the bench, and tried to stop sweating. The usual bustle went on around me; jockeys dressing, undressing, swearing, laughing, accepting me from long acquaintance as a part of the scenery. I did the accounts for thirty-two jockeys and had unofficially filled in tax assessment forms for a dozen more. I was also to date employed as accountant by thirty-one trainers, fifteen stud farms, two Stewards of the Jockey Club, one racecourse, thirteen bookmakers, two horse-transport firms, one blacksmith, five forage merchants, and upwards of forty people who owned racehorses. I probably knew more about the private financial affairs of the racing world than any other single person on the racecourse.

In the parade ring Moira Longerman twittered with happy nerves, her button nose showing kittenishly just above a fluffy upstanding sable collar. Below the collar she snuggled into a coat to match, and on the blonde curls floated a fluffy sable hat. Her middle-aged blue eyes brimmed with excitement, and in the straightforward gaiety of her manner one could see why it was that so many thousands of people spent their hobby money on owning racehorses. Not just for the gambling, nor the display: more likely for the kick from extra adrenalin, and the feeling of being involved. She knew well enough that the fun could turn to disappointment, to tears. The lurking valleys made the mountaintops more precious.

'Doesn't Tapestry look *marvellous*?' she said, her small gloved hands fluttering in the horse's direction as he plodded round the ring under the gaze of the ten-deep banks of intent spectators.

'Great,' I said truthfully.

Binny scowled at the cold sunny sky. He had produced the horse with a gloss seldom achieved by his other runners: impeccably plaited mane and tail, oiled hooves, a new rug, gleamingly polished leather tack, and an intricate geometric pattern brushed into the well-groomed hairs of the hindquarters. Binny was busy telling the world that if his horse failed it would not be from lack of preparation. Binny was going to use me for evermore as his reason for not having won the Gold Cup.

I can't say that it disturbed me very much. Like Moira Longerman, I was feeling the throat-catching once-in-a-lifetime thrill of a profound experience waiting just ahead. Disaster might follow, but whatever happened I would have had my ride in the Gold Cup.

There were eight runners, including Tapestry. We mounted, walked out on to the course, paraded in front of the packed and noisy stands, cantered down to the start. I could feel myself trembling, and knew it was stupid. Only a cool head could produce a worthy result. Tell that to the adrenal glands.

I could pretend, anyway. Stifle the butterfly nerves and act as if races of this calibre came my way six times a season. None of the other seven riders looked anxious or strung up, yet I guessed that some of them must be. Even for the top pros, this was an occasion. I reckoned that their placid expressions were nearly as phoney as mine, and felt better.

We advanced to the tapes in a bouncing line, restraining the eager heads on short reins, and keeping the weight still back in the saddle. Then the starter pressed his lever and let the tapes fly up, and Tapestry took a great bite of air and practically yanked my arms out of their sockets.

Most three and a quarter mile 'chases started moderately, speeded up a mile from home, and maybe finished in a decelerating procession. The Gold Cup field that day set off as if to cover the whole distance in record Derby time, and Moira Longerman told me later that Binny used words she'd never heard before when I failed to keep Tapestry close in touch.

By the time we'd swept over the first two fences, by the stands, I was last by a good six lengths, a gap not much in itself but still an I-told-you-so sort of distance so early in the proceedings. I couldn't in fact make up my mind. Should I go faster? Stick closer to the tails in front? Tapestry had set off at a greater speed already than when he'd won with me at Newbury. If I let him zip along with the others he could be exhausted and tailed off at half-way. If I held him up, we might at least finish the race.

Over the third fence and over the water I saw the gap lengthening and still dithered about tactics. I hadn't expected the others to go off so fast. I didn't know if they hoped to maintain that speed throughout, or whether they would slow and come back to me later. I couldn't decide which was more likely.

But what would Binny say if I guessed wrong and was last the whole way? What wouldn't he say?

What was I doing in this race, out of my class?

Making an utter fool of myself.

Oh God, I thought, why did I try it?

Accountants are held to be cautious by nature but at that point I threw caution to the winds. Almost anything would be better than starting last and staying last.

DICK FRANCIS

Prudence would get me nowhere. I gave Tapestry a kick which he didn't expect and he shot forward like an arrow.

'Steady,' I gasped. 'Steady, dammit.'

Shorten the gap, I thought, but not too fast. Spurt too fast and I'd use the reserves we'd need for the last stretch uphill. If we ever got there. If I didn't fall off. If I didn't let Tapestry meet a fence wrong, or run out, or refuse to jump at all.

Only a mile done, and I'd lived a couple of lifetimes.

I was still last by the end of the first circuit, but no longer a disgrace. Once more round . . . and maybe we'd pass one or two before we'd done. I began at that point to enjoy myself, a background feeling mostly smothered by anxious concentration, but there all the same, and I knew from other days that it would be the enjoyment I remembered most afterwards, not the doubts.

Over the water-jump, still last, the others all in a group just ahead. Open ditch next; Tapestry met it just right and we pegged it back a length in mid-air. Landed nose to tail with the horse in front. Stayed there to the next fence, and again won ground in flight, setting off that time beside the next horse, not behind.

Great. I was no longer last. Just joint last. Whatever I might fear about Tapestry staying to the end, he was surging over the jumps meanwhile with zest and courage.

It was at the next fence, on the far side of the course, that the race came apart. The favourite fell, and the second favourite tripped over him. Tapestry swerved violently as he landed among the rolling bodies and crashed into the horse alongside. The rider of that horse fell off.

It happened so fast. One second, an orderly Gold Cup. Next second, a shambles. Three down, the high hopes of owners, trainers, lads and punters blown to the wind. Tapestry forged his way out like a bull, but when we tackled the hill ahead, we again lay last.

Never try to accelerate uphill, they say, because the horses you pass will pass you again on the way down. Save your strength, don't waste it. I saved Tapestry's strength in last place up the hill and it seemed to me that at the crest the others suddenly swooped away from me, piling on every ounce of everything they had, shooting off while I was still freewheeling.

Come on, I thought urgently, come on, it's now or never. Now, or absolutely never. Get on, Tapestry. Get going. I went down the hill faster than I'd ever ridden in my life.

A fence half-way down. A fractional change of stride. A leap to shame the chamoix.

Another jockey lay on the ground there, curled in a ball to avoid being kicked. Hard luck . . . Too bad . . .

Three horses in front. Two fences to go. I realized abruptly that the three horses in front were all there were. Not far in front, either. My God, I thought, almost laughing, just supposing I can pass one, I'll finish third. Third in the Gold Cup. A dream to last till death.

I urged Tapestry ever faster, and amazingly, he responded. This was the horse whose finishing speed was doubtful, who had to be nursed. This horse, thundering along like a sprinter.

Round the bend . . . only one fence to go . . . I was approaching it faster than the others . . . took off alongside the third horse, landed in front . . . with only the last taxing uphill stretch to the post. I'm third, I thought exultantly. I'm *bloody* third.

Some horses find the Cheltenham finish a painful struggle. Some wander sideways from tiredness, swish their tails and falter when in front, slow to a leaden all-spent pace that barely takes them to the post.

Nothing like that happened to Tapestry, but it did to both of the horses in front. One of them wavered up the straight at a widening angle. The other seemed to be stopping second by second. To my own and everyone else's disbelief, Tapestry scorched past both of them at a flat gallop and won the Gold Cup.

I didn't give a damn that everyone would say (and did say) that if the favourite and second favourite hadn't fallen, I wouldn't have had a chance. I didn't care a fig that it would go down in history as a 'bad' Gold Cup. I lived through such a peak of ecstasy on the lengthy walk round from the winning post to the unsaddling enclosure that nothing after, I thought, could ever match it.

It was impossible . . . and it had happened. Mrs Longerman's accountant had brought her a tax-free capital gain.

A misty hour later, changed into street clothes, with champagne flowing in the weighing room and all the hands I'd ever want slapping me on the shoulder, I was still so wildly happy that I wanted to run up the walls and laugh aloud and turn hand-springs. Speeches, presentations, Moira Longerman's excited tears, Binny's incredulous embarrassment, all had passed in a jumble which I would sort out later. I was high on the sort of glory wave which would put poppies out of business.

Into this ball of a day came a man in a St John's Ambulance uniform, asking for me.

'You Roland Britten?' he said.

I nodded over a glass of bubbles.

'There's a jockey wanting you. In the ambulance. Says he won't go off to hospital before he's talked to you. Proper fussed, he is. So would you come?'

'Who is it?' I asked, putting my drink down.

'Budley. Fell in the last race.'

'Is he badly hurt?'

We walked out of the weighing room and across the crowded stretch of tarmac towards the ambulance which stood waiting just outside the gates. It was five minutes before the time for the last race of the day, and thousands were scurrying about, making for the stands, hurrying to put on the last bet of the meeting. The ambulance man and I walked in the counter-current of those making for the car park before the greater rush began.

'Broken leg,' said the ambulance man.

'What rotten luck.'

23

I couldn't imagine what Bobby Budley wanted me for. There had been nothing wrong with his last annual accounts and we'd had them agreed by the Inspector of Taxes. He shouldn't have had any urgent problems.

We reached the back doors of the white ambulance, and the St John's man opened them.

'He's inside,' he said.

Not one of the big ambulances, I thought, stepping up. More like a white van, with not quite enough headroom to stand upright. They were short of regular ambulances, I supposed, on race days.

Inside there was a stretcher, with a figure on it under a blanket. I went a step towards it, head bent under the low roof.

'Bobby?' I said.

It wasn't Bobby. It was someone I'd never seen before. Young, agile, and in no way hurt. He sprang upwards off the stretcher shedding dark grey blanket like a cloud.

I turned to retreat. Found the ambulance man up beside me, inside the van. Behind him the doors were already shut. His expression was far from gentle and when I tried to push him out of the way he kicked my shin.

I turned again. The stretcher case was ripping open a plastic bag which seemed to contain a hand-sized wad of damp cotton wool. The ambulance man caught hold of one of my arms and the stretcher case the other, and despite fairly desperate heavings and struggles on my part they managed between them to hold the damp cotton wool over my nose and mouth.

It's difficult to fight effectively when you can't stand up straight and every breath you draw is pure ether. The last thing I saw in a greying world was the ambulance man's peaked cap falling off. His light brown hair tumbled out loose into a shaggy mop and turned him from an angel of mercy into a straightforward villain.

I had left racecourses once or twice before on a stretcher, but never fast asleep.

Awake in the noisy dark I could make no sense of it.

Why should they take me? Did it have anything to do with winning the Gold Cup? And if so, what?

It seemed to me that I had grown colder, and still sicker, and that the peripheral noises of creaks and rushing sounds had grown louder. There was also now an uncoordinated feeling of movement: yet I was not in a lorry.

Where, then? In an aeroplane?

The sickness suddenly identified itself into being not the aftermath of ether, as I'd vaguely thought, but a familiar malaise I'd suffered on and off from childhood.

I was seasick.

On a boat.

CHAPTER THREE

I was lying, I realized, on a bunk. The tight net across the open side on my right was to prevent me from falling off. The rushing noises were from the waves washing against the hull. The creaks and rattles were the result of a solid body being pushed by an engine through the resistance of water.

To have made at least some sense of my surroundings was an enormous relief. I could relate myself to space again, and visualize my condition. On the other hand, sorting out the most disorientating part of the mystery left me feeling more acutely the physical discomforts. Cold. Hands tied to legs. Muscles stiff from immobility: and knowing I was on a boat, and knowing boats always made me sick, was definitely making me feel a lot sicker.

Ignorance was a great tranquilliser, I thought. The intensity of a pain depended on the amount of attention one gave it, and one never felt half as bad talking to people in daylight as alone in the dark. If someone would come and talk to me I might feel less cold and less miserable and less quite horribly sick.

No one came for a century or so.

The motion of the boat increased, and my queasiness with it. I could feel my weight rolling slightly from side to side, and had an all too distinct impression that I was also pitching lengthwise, first toe down, then head down, as the bows lifted and fell with the waves.

Out at sea, I thought helplessly. It wouldn't be so rough on a river.

I tried for a while with witticisms like 'Press-ganged, by God', and 'Shanghaied!' and 'Jim lad, Long John Silver's got you', to put a twist of lightness into the situation. Not a deafening success.

In time also I gave up trying to work out why I was there. I gave up feeling apprehensive. I gave up feeling cold and uncomfortable. Finally I was concentrating only on not actually vomiting, and the fact that I'd eaten nothing since breakfast was all that helped.

Breakfast . . .? I had lost all idea of time. I didn't know how long I'd been unconscious, or even how long I'd lain awake in the dark. Unconscious long enough to be shipped from Cheltenham to the coast, and to be carried on board. Awake long enough to long for sleep.

The engine stopped.

The sudden quiet was so marvellous that I only fully realized then how exhausting had been the assault of noise. I actively feared that it would start again. And was this, I wondered, the basis of brainwashing?

There was a new noise, suddenly, from overhead. Dragging sounds, and then metallic sounds, and then, devastatingly, a shaft of daylight.

I shut my dark-adjusted eyes, wincing, and opened them again slowly. Above my head, the shaft had grown to a square. Someone had opened a hatch.

Fresh air blew in like a shower, cold and damp. Without much enthusiasm I glanced around, seeing a small world through a wide-meshed white net.

I was in what one might call the sharp end. In the bows. The bunk where I lay grew narrower at my feet, the side walls of the cabin angling to meet in the centre, like an arrowhead.

The bunk was about two feet wide, and had another bunk above it. I was lying on a cloth-covered mattress; navy blue.

Most of the rest of the cabin was taken up by two large, open-topped, built-in, varnished wooden bins. For stowing sails, I thought. I was in the sail locker of a sailing boat.

Behind my right shoulder a door, now firmly shut, presumably led back to warmth, life, the galley and the saloon.

The matter of my wrists, too, became clear. They were indeed tied to my trousers, one on each side. From what I could see, someone had punched a couple of holes through the material in the region of each side pocket, threaded something which looked like bandage through the holes, and effectively tied each of my wrists to a bunch of cloth.

A good pair of trousers ruined: but then all disasters were relative.

A head appeared above me, framed by the hatch. Indistinctly, seeing him through the net and silhouetted against the grey sky, I got the impression he was fairly young and uncompromisingly tough.

'Are you awake?' he said, peering down.

'Yes,' I said.

'Right.'

He went away, but presently returned, leaning head and shoulders into the hatch.

'If you act sensible, I'll untie you,' he said.

His voice had the bossy strength of one accustomed to dictate, not cajole. A voice which had come up the hard way, gathering aggression on the journey.

'Have you got any dramamine?' I asked.

'No,' he said. 'There's a toilet in the cabin. You can throw up into that. You're going to have to agree you'll act quiet if I come down and untie you. Otherwise I won't. Right?'

'I agree,' I said.

'Right.'

Without more ado he lowered himself easily through the hatch and stood six feet three in his canvas shoes, practically filling all available space. His body moved in effortless balance in the boat's tossing.

'Here,' he said, lifting the lid of what had looked like a

built-in varnished box. 'Here's the head. You open the
stop-cock and pump sea water through with that lever.
Turn the water off when you've done, or you'll have a
flood.' He shut the lid and opened a locker door on the
wall above. 'In here there's a bottle of drinking water and
some paper cups. You'll get your meals when we get
ours.' He fished deep into one of the sail bins, which
otherwise seemed empty. 'Here's a blanket. And a
pillow.' He lifted them out, showed them to me, both
dark blue, dropped them back.

He looked upwards to the generous square of open
sky above him.

'I'll fix you the hatch so you'll have air and light. You
won't be able to get out. And there's nothing to get out
for. We're out of sight of land.'

He stood for a moment, considering, then began to
unfasten the net, which was held simply by chrome hooks
slotted into eyelets on the bunk above.

'You can hook the net up if it gets rough,' he said.

Seen without intervening white meshes, he was not
reassuring. A strong face with vigorous bones. Smallish
eyes, narrow-lipped mouth, open air skin and straight
brown floppy hair. My own sort of age: no natural
kinship, though. He looked down at me without any hint
of sadistic enjoyment, for which I was grateful, but also
without apology or compassion.

'Where am I?' I said. 'Why am I here? Where are we
going? And who are you?'

He said, 'If I untie your hands and you try anything, I'll bash you.'

You must be joking, I thought. Six foot three of healthy muscle against a cold, stiff, seasick five foot ten. No thank you very much.

'What *is* this all about?' I said. Even to my ears, it sounded pretty weak. But then, pretty weak was exactly how I felt.

He didn't answer. He merely bent down, leaned in and over me, and unknotted the bandage from my left wrist. Extracting himself from the small space between the bunks, he repeated the process on the right.

'Stay lying down until I'm out of here,' he said.

'Tell me what's going on.'

He put a foot on the edge of the sail bins, and his hands on the sides of the hatch, and pulled himself halfway up into the outside world.

'I'll tell you,' he said unemotionally, looking down, 'that you're a bloody nuisance to me. I'm having to stow all the sails on deck.'

He gave a heave, a wriggle, and a kick, and hauled himself out.

'Tell me,' I shouted urgently. 'Why am I here?'

He didn't answer. He was fiddling with the hatch. I swung my feet over the side of the bunk and rolled in an exceedingly wobbly fashion to my feet. The pitching of the boat promptly threw me off balance and I ended in a heap on the floor.

31

'Tell me,' I shouted, pulling myself up again and holding on to things. 'Tell me, God dammit.'

The hatch cover slid over and shut out most of the sky. This time, though, it was not clamped down tight, but rested on metal stays, which left a three-inch gap all round: like a lid held three inches above a box.

I put a hand up through the gap and yelled again 'Tell me.'

The only reply I got was the sound of the hatch being made secure against any attempt of mine to dislodge it. Then even those sounds ceased, and I knew he'd gone away; and a minute or two later the engine started again.

The boat rolled and tossed wildly, and the sickness won with a rush. I knelt on the floor with my head over the lavatory bowl and heaved and retched as if trying to rid myself of my stomach itself. I hadn't eaten for so long that all that actually came up was bright yellow bile, but that made nothing any better. The misery of seasickness was that one's body never seemed to realize that there was nothing left to vomit.

I dragged myself onto the bunk and lay there both sweating and shivering, wanting to die.

Blanket and pillow, I thought. In the sail bin.

A terrible effort to get up and get them. I leaned down to pick them up, and my head whirled alarmingly.

Another frightful session over the bowl. Curse the blanket and pillow. But I was so cold.

I got them at the second attempt. Wrapped myself closely in the thick navy wool and put my head thankfully on the navy pillow. There was mercy somewhere, it seemed. I had a bed and a blanket and light and air and a water closet, and a lot of shipboard prisoners before me would have given their souls for all that. It seemed unreasonable to want an explanation as well.

The day passed with increasing awfulness. Anyone who has been comprehensively seasick won't need telling. Head ached and swam, skin sweated, stomach heaved, entire system felt unbelievably ill. If I opened my eyes it was worse.

How long, I thought, will this be going on? Were we crossing the Channel? Surely this relentless churning would soon end. Wherever we were going, it couldn't be far.

At some point he came back and undid the hatch.

'Food,' he said, shouting to be heard against the engine's din.

I didn't answer; couldn't be bothered.

'Food,' he shouted again.

I flapped a weak hand in the air, making go away signals.

I could swear he laughed. Extraordinary how funny seasickness is to those who don't have it. He pushed the hatch into place again and left me to it.

The light faded to dark. I slid in and out of dreams which were a good deal more comforting than reality; and during one of those brief sleeps someone came and fastened the hatch. I didn't care very much. If the boat had sunk, I would have looked upon drowning as a blessed release.

The next time the engine stopped it was only a minor relief compared with the general level of misery. I had supposed it was only in my imagination that the boat was tossing in a storm, but when the engine stopped I rolled clean off the bunk.

Climbing clumsily to my feet, holding on with one hand to the upper bunk, I felt for the door and the light switch beside it. Found the switch, and pressed it. No light. No damned light. Bloody stinking sods, giving me no light.

I fumbled my way back to the lower bunk in the blackness. Tripped over the blanket. Rolled it around me and lay down, feeling most insecure. Felt around for the net: fastened a couple of the hooks, groaning and grunting; not tidily, but enough to do the job.

From the next lot of noises from the outside world, I gathered that someone was putting up sails. On a sailing boat that merely made sense. There were rattlings and flappings and indistinct shouts, about none of which I cared a drip. It seemed vaguely strange someone should be sluicing the decks with buckets of water at such a time, until it dawned on me that the heavy intermittent splashes were made by waves breaking over the bows. The tight-closed hatch made sense. I had never wished for anything more passionately than to get my feet on warm, steady, dry land.

I entirely lost touch of time. Life became merely a matter of total wretchedness, seemingly without end. I would quite have liked a drink of water, but partly couldn't raise the energy to search for it, and partly feared to spill it in the dark, but mostly I didn't bother because every time I lifted my head the whirling bouts of sickness sent me retching to my knees. Water would be no sooner down than up.

He came and undid the hatch: not wide, but enough to let in grey daylight and a flood of fresh air. He did not, it seemed, intend me to die of suffocation.

It was raining hard outside: or maybe it was spray. I saw the bright shine of his yellow oilskins as a shower of heavy drops spattered in through the narrow gap.

His voice came to me, shouting. 'Do you want food?'

I lay apathetically, not answering.

He shouted again. 'Wave your hand if you are all right.'

I reckoned all right was a relative term, but raised a faint flap.

He said something which sounded like 'Gale', and shut the hatch again.

Bloody hell, I thought bitterly. Where were we going that we should run into gales? Out into the Atlantic? And *what for*?

The old jingle about seasickness ran through my head: 'One minute you're afraid you're dying, next minute you're afraid you're not.' For hours through the storm I groaned miserably into the pillow, incredibly ill from nothing but motion.

*

I woke from a sunny dream, the umpteenth awakening into total darkness.

Something different, I thought hazily. Same wild weather outside, the bows crashing against the seas and shipping heavy waves over the deck. Same creaking and slapping of wind-strained rigging. But inside, in me, something quite different.

I breathed deeply from relief. The sickness was going, subsiding slowly like an ebb tide, leaving me acclimatized to an alien environment. I lay for a while in simple contentment, while normality crept back like a forgotten luxury: but then, insistently, other troubles began to surface instead. Thirst, hunger, exhaustion, and an oppressive headache which I eventually put down to dehydration and a dearth of fresh air. A sour taste. An itching stubble of beard. A sweaty feeling of having worn the same clothes for a month. But worse than physical pinpricks, the mental rocks.

Confusion had had its points. Clarity brought no comfort at all. The more I was able to think straight, the less I liked the prospects.

There had to be a reason for any abduction, but the most usual reason made least sense. Ransom ... it couldn't be. There was no one to pay a million for my release: no parents, rich or poor. Hostage ... but hostages were mostly taken at random, not elaborately, from a public place. I had no political significance and no special knowledge: I couldn't be bartered, didn't know any secrets, had no access to Government papers or defence plans or scientific discoveries. No one would care more than a passing pang whether I lived or died, except perhaps Trevor, who would count it a nuisance to have to find a replacement.

I considered as dispassionately as possible the thought of death, but eventually discarded it. If I was there to be murdered, it would already have been done. The cabin had been made ready for a living prisoner, not a prospective corpse. Once out at sea, a weighted heave-ho would have done the trick. So, with luck, I was going to live.

However unrealistic it seemed to me, the only reason I could raise which made any sense at all was that I was there for revenge.

Although the majority of mankind think of auditing accountants as dry-as-dust creatures burrowing dimly into columns of boring figures, the dishonest regard them as deadly enemies.

I had had my share of uncovering frauds. I'd lost a dozen people their jobs and set the Revenue onto others, and seen five embezzlers go to prison, and the spite in some of those eyes had been like acid.

If Connaught Powys, for instance, had arranged this trip, my troubles had hardly started. Four years ago, when I'd last seen him, in court and newly convicted, he'd sworn to get even. He would be out of Leyhill about now. If by getting even he meant the full four years in a sail locker ... well, it couldn't be that. It couldn't. I swallowed, convincing myself that from the solely practical viewpoint, it was impossible.

My throat was dry. From thirst, I told myself firmly: not from fear. Fear would get me nowhere.

I eased myself out of the bunk and onto the small patch of floor, holding on tight to the upper bunk. The black world went on corkscrewing around, but the vertigo had really gone. The fluid in my ears' semi-circular canals had finally got used to sloshing about chaotically: a pity it hadn't done it with less fuss.

I found the catch of the wall locker, opened it, and felt around inside. Paper cups, as promised. Bottle of water, ditto. Big plastic bottle with a screw cap. It was hopeless in the dark to use one of the cups: I wedged myself on the only available seat, which was the lowered lid of the loo, and drank straight from the bottle. Even then, with the violent rolling and pitching, a good deal of it ran down my neck.

I screwed the cap on again carefully and groped my way back to the bunk, taking the bottle with me. Hooked up the net again. Lay on my back with my head propped up on the pillow, holding the water on my chest and whistling 'Oh Susanna' to prove I was alive.

A long time passed during which I drank a good deal and whistled every tune I could think of.

After that I stood up and banged on the cabin door with my fists and the bottle, and shouted at the top of my voice that I was awake and hungry and furious at the whole bloody charade. I used a good deal of energy and the results were an absolute zero.

Back in the bunk I took to swearing instead of whistling. It made a change.

The elements went on giving the boat a bad time. I speculated fruitlessly about where we were, and how big the boat was, and how many people were sailing it, and whether they were any good. I thought about hot sausages and crusty bread and red wine, and for a fairly cheerful hour I thought about winning the Gold Cup.

At about the time that I began to wonder seriously if everyone except me had been washed overboard, the hatch-opening noises returned. He was there, still in his oilskins. I gulped in the refreshing blast of cold air and wondered just how much of a stinking fug was rushing out to meet him.

I unhooked the net and stood up, holding on and swaying. The wind outside shrieked like starlings.

He shouted, 'Do you want food?'

'Yes,' I yelled. 'And more water.' I held the nearly empty bottle up to him, and he reached down for it.

'Right.'

He shut the hatch and went away, but not before I had a terrifying glimpse of the outside world. The boat rolled heavily as usual to one side, to the left, and before it rolled back to the right I saw the sea. A huge uneven wave, towering to obliterate the sky, charcoal grey, shining, swept with gusts of spray. The next heavy crash of water over the hatch made me think happier thoughts of my dry cabin.

He came back, opened the hatch a few inches, and

lowered in a plastic carrier bag on a loop of rope. He shouted down at me.

'Next time I bring you food, you give me back this carrier. Understand?'

'Yes,' I shouted back, untying the rope. 'What time is it?'

'Five o'clock. Afternoon.'

'What day?'

'Sunday.' He pulled the rope up and began to shut the hatch.

'Give me some light,' I yelled.

He shouted something which sounded like 'Batteries' and put me back among the blind. Yes, well . . . one could live perfectly well without sight. I slid back onto the bunk, fastened the net, and investigated the carrier bag.

The water bottle, full; an apple; and a packet of two thick sandwiches, faintly warm. They turned out to be hamburgers in bread, not buns; and very good too. I ate the lot.

Five o'clock on Sunday. Three whole damned days since I'd stepped into the white van.

I wondered if anyone had missed me seriously enough to go to the police. I had disappeared abruptly from the weighing room, but no one would think it sinister. The changing room valet might be surprised that I hadn't collected from him my wallet and keys and watch, which he'd been holding as usual in safe keeping while I raced, and that I hadn't in fact paid him, either; but he would have put my absent-mindedness down to excitement. My car would still, I supposed, be standing in the jockeys' car park, but no one yet would have begun to worry about it.

I lived alone in a cottage three miles outside Newbury: my next-door neighbour would merely think I was away celebrating for the weekend. Our two office assistants, one boy, one girl, would have made indulgent allowances, or caustic allowances perhaps, when I hadn't turned up for work on Friday. The clients I had been supposed to see would have been irritated, but no more.

Trevor was away on his holidays. So no one, I concluded, would be looking for me.

On Monday morning, the bankrupt Mr Wells might make a fuss. But even if people began to realize I had vanished, how would they ever find me? The fact had to be faced that they wouldn't. Rescue was unlikely. Unless I escaped, I would be staying in the sail locker until someone chose to let me out.

Sunday to Monday was a long, cold, wild, depressing night.

CHAPTER FOUR

On Monday, March 21st the hatch opened twice to let in air, food, sprays of water, and brief views of constantly grey skies. On each occasion I demanded information, and got none. The oilskins gave merely an impression that the crew had more than enough to do with sailing the boat in those conditions, and had no time to answer damn fool questions.

I was used to being alone. I lived alone and to a great extent worked alone; solitary by nature, and seldom lonely. An only child, long accustomed to my own company, I tended often to feel oppressed by the constant companionship of a large number of people, and to seek escape as soon as possible. All the same, as the hours dragged on, I found life alone in the sail locker increasingly wearing.

Limbo existence, I thought. Lying in a black capsule, endlessly tossing. How long did it take for the human mind to disintegrate, left alone in uncertainty in the rattling, corkscrewing dark?

A bloody long time, I answered myself rebelliously. If

the purpose of all this incarceration was to reduce me to a crying wreck, then it wasn't going to succeed. Tough thoughts, tough words . . . I reckoned more realistically that it depended on the true facts. I could survive another week of it passably, and two weeks with difficulty. After that . . . unknown territory.

Where could we be going? Across the Atlantic? Or, if the idea really was to break me up, maybe just up and down the Irish Sea? They might reckon that any suitable stretch of rough water would do the trick.

And who were 'they'?

Not him in the oilskins. He looked upon me as a nuisance, not a target for malice. He probably had instructions regarding me, and was carrying them out. How unfunny if his instructions were to take me home once I'd gone mad.

Dammit, I thought. Dammit to bloody hell. He'd have a bloody long job. Bugger him. Bugger and sod him.

There was a great sane comfort to be found in swearing.

At some long time after my second Monday glimpse of the outside, it seemed that the demented motion of the boat was slowly steadying. Standing up out of the bunk was no longer quite such a throw-around affair. Holding on was still necessary, but not holding on for dear life. The bows crashed more gently against the waves. The thuds of water over the hatch diminished in number and weight. There were shouts on deck and a good deal of pulley noise, and I guessed they were resetting the sails.

I found also that for the first time since my first awakening, I was no longer cold.

I was still wearing the clothes I had put on in the far off world of sanity: charcoal business suit, sleeveless waistcoat-shaped pullover underneath, pale blue shirt, underpants, and socks. Somewhere on the floor in the dark was my favourite Italian silk tie, worn to celebrate the Gold Cup. Shoes had vanished altogether. From being inadequate even when reinforced by a blanket, the long-suffering ensemble was suddenly too much.

I took off my jacket and rolled it into a tidy ball. As gent's natty suiting it was already a past number: as an extra pillow it added considerably to life's luxuries. Amazing how deprivation made the smallest extras marvellous.

Time had become a lost faculty. Drifting in and out of sleep with no external references was a queer business. I mostly couldn't tell whether I'd been asleep for minutes or hours. Dreams occurred in a semi-waking state, sometimes in such short snatches that I could have counted them in seconds. Other dreams were deeper and longer, and I knew that they were the product of sounder sleep. None of them seemed to have anything to do with my present predicament, and not one came up with any useful subconscious information as to why I should be there. In my innermost soul, it seemed, I didn't know.

Tuesday morning – it must have been Tuesday

morning – he came without the oilskins. The air which flowed in through the open hatch was as always fresh and clean, but now dry and faintly warm. The sky was pale blue. I could see a patch of white sail and hear the hissing of the hull as it cut through the water.

'Food,' he said, lowering one of the by now familiar plastic carriers.

'Tell me why I'm here,' I said, untying the knot.

He didn't answer. I took the carrier off, and tied on the empty one, and held on to the rope.

'Who are you? What is this boat? Why am I here?' I said.

His face showed no response except faint irritation.

'I'm not here to answer your questions.'

'Then what *are* you here for?' I said.

'None of your business. Let go of the rope.'

I held on to it. 'Please tell me why I'm here,' I said.

He stared down, unmoved. 'If you ask any more questions, and you don't leave go of the rope, you'll get no supper.'

The simplicity of the threat, and the simplicity of the mind that made it, was a bit of a stunner. I let go of the rope, but I made one more try.

'Then please just tell me how long you're going to keep me here.'

He gave me a stubborn scowl as he pulled up the carrier.

'You'll get no supper,' he said, withdrawing his head out of sight, and beginning to shut the hatch.

'Leave the hatch open,' I shouted.

I got no joy from that either. He firmly fastened me back in the dark. I stood swaying with the boat, holding onto the upper bunk, and trying to fight down a sudden overwhelming tide of furious anger. How *dared* they abduct me and imprison me in this tiny place and treat me like a naughty child. How dared they give me no reasons and no horizons. How dared they thrust me into the squalor of my own unwashed, unbrushed, unshaven state. There was a great deal of insulted pride and soaring temper in the fiery outrage with which I literally shook.

I could go berserk and smash up the place, I thought, or calm down again and eat whatever he'd brought in the carrier: and the fact that I'd recognized the choice made it certain I'd choose the latter. The bitter, frustrated fury didn't exactly go away, but at least with a sigh I had it back under control.

The intensity of what I'd felt, and its violent, unexpected onset, both alarmed me. I would have to be careful, I thought. There were so many roads to destruction, and rage, it seemed, was one of them.

If a psychiatrist had been shut up like this, I wondered, would he have had any safety nets that I hadn't? Would his knowledge of what might happen to the mind of someone in this position help him to withstand the symptoms when they occurred? Probably I should have studied psychology, not accountancy. More useful if one were kidnapped. Stood to reason.

The carrier contained two shelled hard-boiled eggs, an apple, and three small foil-wrapped triangles of processed cheese. I saved one of the eggs and two pieces of cheese for later, in case he meant it about no supper.

He did mean it. Uncountable hours passed. I ate the second egg and the rest of the cheese. Drank some water. As the day's total entertainment, hardly a riot.

When the hatch was next opened, it was dark outside, though dark with a luminous greyness quite unlike the black inside the cabin. No carrier of food materialized, and I gathered that the respite was only so that I shouldn't asphyxiate. He had opened the hatch and gone before I got round to risking any more questions.

Gone.

The hatch was wide open. Out on the deck there were voices and a good deal of activity with ropes and sails.

'Let go.'

'You're letting the effing thing fall into the sea . . .'

'Catch that effing sheet . . . Move, can't you . . .'

'You'll have to stow the gennie along the rail . . .'

Mostly his voice, from close by, directing things.

I put one foot on the thigh-high rim of the sail bin, as he had done, and hooked my hands over the side of the hatch, and heaved. My head popped out into the free world and it was about two whole seconds before he noticed.

'Get back,' he said brusquely, punctuating his remark by stamping on my fingers. 'Get down and stay down.' He kicked at my other hand. 'Do you want a bash on the head?' He was holding a heavy chromium winch handle, and he swung it in an unmistakable gesture.

'There's no land in sight,' he said, kicking again. 'So get down.'

I dropped back to the floor, and he shut the hatch. I hugged my stinging fingers and counted it fortunate that no one went sailing in hob-nailed boots.

Two seconds' uninterrupted view of the boat had been worth it, though. I sat on the lid of the loo with my feet on the side of the lower bunk opposite, and thought about the pictures still alive on my retinas. Even in night light, with eyes adjusted to a deeper darkness, I'd been able to see a good deal.

For a start, I'd seen three men.

The one I knew, who seemed to be not only in charge of me but of the whole boat. Two others, both young, hauling in a voluminous sail which hung half over the side, pulling it in with outstretched arms and trying to stop it billowing again once they'd got it on deck.

There might be a fourth one steering: I hadn't been able to see. About ten feet directly aft of the hatch the single mast rose majestically skywards, and with all the cleats and pulleys and ropes clustered around its base it had formed a block to any straight view towards the stern. There might have been a helmsman and three or four crewmen resting below. Or there might have been automatic steering and all hands visible on deck. It seemed a huge boat, though, to be managed by three.

From the roughest of guesses and distant gleams from

chromium winches I would have put it at about a cricket pitch long. Say sixty-five feet. Or say, if you preferred it, nineteen point eight one metres. Give or take an octave.

Not exactly a nippy little dinghy for Sunday afternoons on the Thames. An ocean racer, more like.

I had had a client once who had bought himself a second-hand ocean racer. He'd paid twenty-five thousand for thirty feet of adventure, and beamed every time he thought of it. His voice came back over the years: 'The people who race seriously have to buy new boats every year. There's always something new. If they don't get a better boat they can't possibly win, and the possibility of winning is what it's all about. Now me, all I want is to be able to sail round Britain comfortably at weekends in the summer. So I buy one of the big boys' cast-offs, because they're well-built boats, and just the job.' He had once invited me to Sunday lunch on board. I had enjoyed looking over his pride and joy, but privately had been most relieved when a sudden gale had prevented us leaving the moorings at his yacht club for the promised afternoon's sail.

Highly probable, I thought, that I was now being entertained on some other big boy's cast-off. The great question was, at whose expense?

The improvement in the weather was a mixed blessing, because the engine started again. The din seemed an even worse assault on my nerves than it had at the beginning. I lay on the bunk and tried to shut my ears with the pillow and my fingers, but the roaring vibration easily by-passed such frivolous barriers. I'd either got to get used to it and ignore it, I thought, or go raving, screaming bonkers.

I got used to it.

Wednesday. Was it Wednesday? I got food and air twice. I said nothing to him, and he said nothing to me. The constant noise of the engine made talking difficult. Wednesday was a black desert.

Thursday. I'd been there a week.

When he opened the hatch, I shouted, 'Is it Thursday?'

He looked surprised. Hesitated, then shouted back, 'Yes.' He looked at his watch. 'Quarter to eleven.'

He was wearing a blue cotton tee shirt, and the day outside seemed fine. The light tended to hurt my eyes.

I untied the carrier and fastened on the previous one, which as usual contained an empty water bottle. I looked up at him as he pulled it out, and he stared down at my face. He looked his normal unsmiling self: a hard young man, unfeeling rather than positively brutal.

I didn't consciously ask him, but after a pause, during which he seemed to be inspecting the horizon, he began to fix the hatch as he had done on the first day, so that it was a uniform three inches above the deck, letting in continuous air and light.

The relief at not being locked back in the dark was absolutely shattering. I found I was trembling from head to foot. I swallowed, trying to guard against the possibility that he would change his mind. Trying to tell myself that even if it proved to be only for five minutes, I should be grateful for that.

He finished securing the hatch and went away. I took some shaky deep breaths and gave myself an ineffective lecture about stoical responses, come dark, come shine.

After a while I sat on the lid of the loo and ate the first shipboard meal that I could actually see. Two hard-boiled eggs, some crispbread, three triangles of cheese and an apple. Never much variety in the diet, but at least no one intended me to starve.

He came back about half an hour after he'd gone away.

Hell, I thought. Half an hour. Be grateful for that. I had at least talked myself into facing another dose of darkness without collapsing into rubble.

He didn't, however, shut the hatch. Without altering the way it was fixed, he slid another plastic carrier through the gap. It was not this time tied to a rope, because when he let go of it, it fell to the floor; and before I could raise any remark, he had gone again.

I picked up the carrier, which seemed light and almost empty, and looked inside.

For God's sake, I thought. Laugh. Laugh, but don't bloody snivel. An ounce of kindness was more devastating than a week of misery.

He'd given me a pair of clean socks and a paperback novel.

I spent a good deal of the day trying to look out of the gap. With one foot on the rim of the sail bins, and my hands grasping the hatch opening, I could get my head up to the top well enough, but the view would have been more comprehensive if either the gap had been a couple of inches deeper or my eyes had been located halfway up my forehead. What I did see, mostly by tilting my head and applying one eye at a time, was a lot of ropes, pulleys, and rolled up sails, a lot of green sea, and a dark line of land on the horizon ahead.

None of these things changed all day except that the smudge of land grew slowly thicker, but I never tired of looking.

At closer quarters I also looked at the fittings of the hatch itself, which, I realized after a time, had been modified slightly for my visit. The metal props which held it open were hinged, and folded down inside the cabin when the hatch was closed. Out on deck the hatch cover was mounted on two heavier extending hinges, which allowed it to open outwards completely and lie flat on its back.

Inside the cabin there were two sturdy clips for securing the hatch shut from below, and outside there were two others, for securing the hatch from above.

So far, all as planned by the ship builders. What had been added, though, was extra provision to prevent someone inside the cabin from pushing the hatch wide open after releasing it from the hinged props. Normally, one could have done this. Sail locker hatches were supposed to open easily and wide, so that the sails could be pulled in and out. There was no point in ordinary circumstances in making things difficult. But now, outside, crossing from fore to aft and from port to starboard over the top of the hatch cover, were two lengths of chain, each secured at both ends to cleats which to my eyes looked newly screwed to the deck. The chains held the hatch cover down on the props like guy ropes, taut and forceful. If I could dislodge those chains, I thought, I could get out. If I had anything to dislodge them with. A couple of Everest-sized ifs. I could get my hands out through the three inch gap, but not much arm. Not enough to reach the cleats, let alone undo the chains. As for levers, screwdrivers, hammers and files, all I had were paper cups, a flimsy carrier and a plastic water bottle. Tantalizing, all those hours looking out at unreachable freedom.

In between the long bouts of balancing up by the cciling I sat on the loo lid and read the book, which was an American private-eye thriller with a karate-trained hero who would have chopped his way out of a sail locker in five minutes.

Inspired by him, I had another go at the cabin door. It withstood my efforts like a stolid wall. Obviously I should have studied karate as well as psychiatry. Better luck next time.

The day whizzed past. The light began to fade. Outside the smudge of land had grown into an approaching certainty, and I had no idea what land it was.

He came back, lowered the carrier, and waited while I tied on the empty ones.

'Thank you,' I shouted, as he pulled them up, 'for the book and socks.'

He nodded, and began to close the hatch.

'Please don't,' I shouted.

He paused and looked down. It seemed to be still be-kind-to-prisoners day, because he provided his first explanation.

'We are going into port. Don't waste your breath making a noise when we stop. We'll be anchored. No one will hear you.'

He shut the hatch. I ate sliced tinned ham and a hot baked potato in the noisy stupefying dark, and to cheer myself up thought that now that the journey was ending they surely wouldn't keep me there much longer. Tomorrow, perhaps, I would be out. And after that I might get some answers.

I stifled the gloomy doubts.

*

The engine slowed, the first time it had changed its note. There were footsteps on deck, and shouts, and the anchor went over with a splash. The anchor chain rattled out, sounding as if it were passing practically through the sail locker; behind the panelling, no doubt.

The engine was switched off. There was no sound from anywhere. The creakings and rushing noises had stopped. No perceptible motion any more. I had expected the peace to be a relief, but as time passed it was the opposite. Even aggravating stimuli, it seemed, were better than none at all. I slept in disjointed snatches and lay emptily awake for hours and hours wondering if one really could go mad from too much nothing.

When he next opened the hatch it was full daylight outside. Friday; mid-morning. He lowered the carrier, waited for the exchange, raised the rope, and began to close the hatch.

I made involuntarily a vague imploring gesture with my hands. He paused, looking down.

'I can't let you see where we are,' he said.

It was the nearest he had come to an apology, the nearest to admitting that he might have treated me better, if he didn't have his orders.

'Wait,' I yelled, as he pulled the hatch over.

He paused again: prepared at least to listen.

'Can't you put screens round if you don't want me to see the land?' I said. 'Leave the hatch open . . .'

He considered it. 'I'll see,' he said, 'later.'

It seemed an awfully long time later, but he did come

back, and he did open the hatch. While he was fastening it, I said, 'When are you going to let me out?'

'Don't ask questions.'

'I *must*,' I said explosively. 'I have to know.'

'Do you want me to shut the hatch?'

'No.'

'Then don't ask questions.'

It may have been spineless of me, but I didn't ask any more. He hadn't given me one useful answer in eight days, and if I persevered, all I would get would be no light and no supper and an end to the new era of partial humanity.

When he'd gone I climbed up for a look, and found he had surrounded the hatch area with bulging bolsters of rolled sails. My field of vision had come down to about eighteen inches.

I lay on the top bunk for a change, and tried to imagine what it was about the port, so hopelessly near, that I might recognize. The sky was pale blue, with sun shining through high, hazy cloud. It was warm, like a fine spring day. There were even seagulls.

It evoked in me such a strong picture that I became convinced that if I could only see over the sail bolsters, I would be looking at the harbour and beaches where I'd played as a child. Maybe all that frantic sailing had been nowhere but up and down the English Channel, and we were now safe back home in Ryde, Isle of Wight.

I shook the comforting dream away. All one could

actually tell for sure was that it was not in the Arctic Circle.

There were occasional sounds from outside, but all distant, and nothing of any use. I read the American thriller again, and thought a good deal about escape.

When the day was fading he came back with supper, but this time, after I'd swopped the carriers, he didn't shut the hatch. That evening I watched the light die to dusk and night, and breathed sweet air. Small mercies could be huge mercies, I thought.

Saturday, March 26th. The morning carrier contained fresh bread, fresh cheese, fresh tomatoes: someone had been shopping ashore. It also contained an extra bottle of water and a well-worn piece of soap. I looked at the soap and wondered if it was there from kindness or because I stank; and then with wildly leaping hope wondered if it was there so that I should at least be clean when they turned me loose.

I took off all my clothes and washed from head to foot, using a sock as a sponge. After the week's desultory efforts with salt water from the loo, the lather was a fantastic physical delight. I washed my face and ears and neck and wondered what I looked like with a beard.

After that, dressed in shirt and underpants which were both long overdue for the same treatment, I ate the morning meal.

After that, I tidied the cabin, folding the blanket and my extra clothes and stacking everything neatly.

After that, I still couldn't face for a long time that my soaring hope was unfounded. No one came to let me out.

It was odd how soon the most longed-for luxury became commonplace and not enough. In the dark, I had ached for light. Now that I had light, I took it for granted and ached for room to move.

The cabin was triangular, its three sides each about six feet long. The bunks on the port side, and the loo and sail bins on the starboard side, took up most of the space. The floor area in the centre was roughly two feet wide by the cabin door, but narrowed to a point about four feet in, where the bunks and the forward sail bin met. There was room to take two small paces, or one large. Any attempt at knees-bend-arms-stretch involved unplanned contact with the surrounding woodwork. There was more or less enough space to stand on one's head by the cabin door. I did that a couple of times. It just shows how potty one can get. The second time I bashed my ankle on the edge of the sail bin coming down, and decided to give Yoga a miss. If I'd tried the Lotus position, I'd have been wedged for life.

I felt a continuous urge to scream and shout. I knew that no one would hear me, but the impulse had nothing to do with reason. It stemmed from frustration, fury and induced claustrophobia. I knew that if I gave way to it, and yelled and yelled, I would probably end up sobbing.

The thought that maybe that was precisely what someone wanted to happen to me was an enormous support. I couldn't stop the screaming and shouting from going on inside my head, but at least it didn't get out.

After I'd finally come to terms with the thought that it wasn't Exodus day, I spent a good deal of time contemplating the loo. Not metaphysically: mechanically.

Everything in the cabin was either built-in, or soft. From the beginning I'd been given no possible weapons, no possible implements. All the food had been for eating with my fingers, and came wrapped only in paper or plastic, if at all. No plates. Nothing made of metal, china or glass. The light bulb had not only been unscrewed from its socket, but the glass cover for it, which I guessed should be there, was not.

The pockets of my suit had been emptied. The nail file I usually carried in my breast pocket was no longer there: nor were my pens clipped inside: and my penknife had gone from my trousers.

I sat on the floor, lifted the lid, and at close quarters glared at the loo's mechanics.

Bowl, flushing lever, pump. A good deal of tubing. The stopcock for turning the sea water on and off. Everything made with the strength and durability demanded by the wild motions of the sea, which shook flimsy contraptions to pieces.

The lever was fastened at the back, hinged to the built-in casing of the fitment. At the front, it ended in a wooden handle. Attached at about a third of the way back was the rod which led directly down into the pump, to pull the piston there up and down. The whole lever, from handle to hinge, measured about eighteen inches.

I lusted for that lever like a rapist, but I could see no way, without tools, of getting it off. The hinge and the piston linkage were each fastened with a nut and bolt, and appeared to have been tightened by Atlas. Nut versus thumb and finger was no contest. I had tried on and off for two days.

A spanner. My kingdom for a spanner, I thought.

Failing a spanner, what else?

I tried with my shirt. The cloth saved the pressure on skin and bones, but gave no extra purchase. The nuts sat there like rocks. It was like trying to change a wheel with only fingers and a handkerchief.

Trousers? The cloth itself tended to slip more easily than my shirt. I tried the waistband, and found it a great deal better. Around the inside of the waist was a strip with two narrow rows of rough-surfaced rubber let into it. The real purpose of the strip was to help belt-less trousers stay up by providing a friction grip against a tucked-in shirt. Applying trouser-band to nut gave a good grip and slightly more hope, but despite a lot of heavy effort, no results.

The day ground on. I went on sitting on the floor futilely trying to unscrew nuts which wouldn't unscrew, simply because there was nothing else to do.

*

Tinned ham again for supper. I carefully peeled off all the fat, and ate the lean.

The hatch stayed open.

I said thanks for the soap, and asked no questions.

Sunday. Another Sunday. How *could* anyone keep me locked up so long without explanation? The whole modern world was churning along outside, and there I was cooped up like the man in the iron mask, or as near as dammit.

I applied the strips of ham fat to the nuts, to see if grease would have any effect. I spent most of the day warming the piston-rod nut in my fingers, rubbing fat round its edges, and hauling at it with my trousers.

Nothing happened.

Now and again I stood up and stretched, and climbed up to see if the sail bolsters were still obstructing the view, which they always were. I read bits of the thriller again. I closed the loo lid and sat on it, and looked at the walls. I listened to the seagulls.

My ordinary life seemed far removed. Reality was inside the sail locker. Reality was a mystery. Reality was mind-cracking acres of empty time.

Sunday night drifted in and darkened and slowly became Monday. He came much earlier than usual with my breakfast, and when he had lifted out the exchange carrier, he began to close the hatch.

'Don't,' I yelled.

He paused only briefly, staring down unmoved.

'Necessary,' he said.

I went on yelling for him to open it for a long time after he'd gone away and left me in the dark. Once I'd started making a noise, I found it difficult to stop: all the stifled screams and shouts were trying to burst out through the hole in the dam. If the dam broke up, so would I. I stuffed the pillow into my mouth to make myself shut up, and resisted a desire to bang my head against the door instead.

The engine started. Din and vibration and darkness, all as before. It's too much, I thought. Too much. But there were only two basic alternatives. Stay sane or go crazy. Sanity was definitely getting harder.

Think rational thoughts, I told myself. Repeat verses, do mental arithmetic, remember all the tricks that other solitary prisoners have used to see them through weeks and months and years.

I tore my mind away from such impossible periods and directed it to the present.

The engine ran on fuel. It had used a good deal of fuel on the journey. Therefore if the boat was going far, it would need more.

Engines were always switched off during refuelling. If I made the most colossal racket when we refuelled, just possibly someone might hear. I didn't honestly see how any noise I could make would attract enough attention, but I could try.

The chain rattled back through its hidden chute as the anchor came up, and I presumed the boat was moving, although there was no feeling of motion.

Then someone came and put a radio on top of the hatch, and turned the volume up loud. The music fought a losing battle against the engine for a while, but shortly I felt the boat bump, and almost at once the engine switched off.

I knew we were refuelling. I could hear only loud pop music. And no one on the quayside, whatever I did, could possibly have heard *me*.

After a fairly short while the engine started again. There were a few small thuds outside, felt through the hull, and then nothing. Someone came and collected the radio: I yelled for the hatch to be opened, but might as well not have bothered.

Motion slowly returned to the boat, bringing hopeless recognition with it.

Going out to sea again.

Out to sea, in the noise and the dark. Still not knowing why I was there, or for how long. Growing less fit from lack of exercise and less able to deal with mental pressure. Starting last week's torments all over again.

I sat on the floor with my back against the cabin door, and folded my arms over my knees, and put my head on my arms, and wondered how I could possibly endure it.

Monday I spent in full-blown despair.

On Tuesday, I got out.

CHAPTER FIVE

Monday night the boat was anchored somewhere, but it stopped after I got my supper and started again before Tuesday mid-morning. It rained most of the time, drumming on the hatch. I was glad of the respite from the engine but in general the misery level was a pain.

When he brought the morning food he fixed the hatch open. The extent of my relief was pathetic.

Shortly after, they stopped the engine and put up the sails, and the grey sky outside slowly cleared to blue.

I ate the hard boiled eggs and the apple and thought about the thick slice of bread, upon which, for the first time, he had given me butter. Then I pulled a button off my shirt to use as a scraper, and transferred as much of the butter as I could to the stubborn nuts and bolts on the flushing lever. Then I ate the bread. Then I sat on the floor and one after the other warmed the nuts with my hand in the hope that the butter and ham fat would melt into the screw threads.

After that I ripped a length of the rubberized waistband from my trousers, and fished out of the bottom of one of the sail bins the white net which I had stored there after the storms.

It was activity for activity's sake, more than any real hope. I wound the waistband twice round the piston-rod nut, because it was the nearest, and fitted over that the chromium hook which had attached the net to the upper berth. Then I tugged the net.

After a second of gripping, the hook slid round on the cloth and fell off. I tried again, folding the waistband so that it had an elasticated side against the hook as well as against the nut. That time the hook stayed in place; but so did the nut.

I tugged several times. If I tugged very hard, hook, waistband and all came off. Nothing else happened. I slung the net back into the sail bin in depression.

After that I sat for ages with my hand on the piston-rod nut, until it was as warm as a handful of pennies clutched by a child. Then I wound the strip of waistband round quickly three times, to make the nut larger to grip, and then I tried it with all my remaining muscle power.

The waistband turned in my hand.

Damn it to hell, I thought hopelessly. I pulled it off and wound it on again, trying to grip it more tightly.

It turned again.

It may seem ridiculous, but it was not until it turned more easily the third time that I realized I was turning the nut on the bolt, not the waistband on the nut.

Unbelievable. I sat there looking idiotic, with my

mouth open. Excitement fluttered in my throat like a stifled laugh. If I could get one off, what about the other?

Time hadn't mattered for the first one. I'd had nothing else to do. For the second one, the hinge, I was feverishly impatient.

I warmed the nut, and wound on the waistband, and heaved; and nothing happened.

Heaved again.

A blob.

It had to move, I thought furiously. It simply had to. After several more useless attempts, I went back to basics.

Perhaps after all the tugging session with the hook had had some effect. I scooped out the net and applied it to the hinge nut, and tugged away with enthusiasm, replacing the hook every time it fell off. Then I made myself warm the nut as thoroughly as I had the other one, so that the heat from my hand was conducted right to the inside, where the melted grease and the minute heat-expansion of the metal could do their work. Then I wound on the waistband again and practically tore all the ligaments in my arm and back with a long and mighty heave.

And that time, the waistband turned. That time again I couldn't be sure until the third turn, when the nut started moving more freely, that I'd really done it.

I climbed up on the sail bin and squinted out at the free world. To the left all I could see was sky and a sparkle of sun on the water. I turned my head to the right and nearly fell off my perch. To the right there was a sail, and shining below it, green and rocky and moderately close, there was land.

I thought that if he came along at that moment to shut the hatch I would perversely be grateful.

Only desperation made me do what I did next, because I was sure that if he caught me in mid-escape he'd tie my hands and leave me in the dark on starvation rations.

The risk that I wouldn't get out unseen was appalling. My present conditions were just about bearable; my future afterwards wouldn't be.

Yet if I hadn't meant to risk it, why had I laboured so long on the nuts?

I went back to the loo and unscrewed the nuts completely. I knocked the bolts out, and pulled the whole lever free.

Without it, no one could flush the loo. I thought grimly that it would be an added complication if I found myself back in the cabin with it gone.

There was no sign of anyone on deck, and as usual I couldn't see if the boat was on automatic steering or whether there was anyone at the helm.

Hesitation was only in my mind. Looking back, it seemed as if I did everything very fast.

I pulled the hinged props of the hatch down inside the cabin, which one would do in the normal way if one wanted to shut the hatch oneself from the inside. This had the effect of slackening the guy-rope action of the chains crossed over the top.

Through the much reduced gap, little more than a slit, I poked the lever, aiming at where a link of chain was hooked over the top.

Long hours of inspection had given me the impression that those chains had no other fastening. Putting a link over the hook of the cleat must have seemed safe enough, because they were certain I had no means of dislodging them. I stuck the lever into the chain on the right, wedged it securely, and pushed. With almost miraculous elegance the whole chain slid loosely outwards, and the link fell off the cleat.

Without pausing for anything but mental hip-hoorays I applied the lever again, this time to where the fore and aft chain was fastened on the bow side. Again, with no more fuss, the link slid off.

I was committed. I couldn't get the chains back on again. I had to open the hatch now, and climb out. There was no retreat.

I took the lever with me as a last resort against recapture, putting it out first onto the deck. Then with both hands I released the hatch from the hinged props and pushed it wide. Eased it down gently until it lay flat, fearing to let it crash open and bring them running.

I snaked out onto the deck on my stomach. Rolled to the right, under the jib sail. Reached the railing, grabbed it with both hands, and bunny-hopped fast over the side, going down into the sea straight and feet first, like a pillar.

It wasn't the safest way of disembarking, but I survived it, staying down under the surface until my lungs protested. Surfacing was one of the most anxious moments of my life, but when I cautiously lifted mouth, nose and eyes above the water, there was the boat a hundred yards away, steadily sailing on.

With a great intake of air I sank down again and began to swim underwater towards the shore; gently, so as to make no notice-attracting splash.

The water was chilly, but not as cold as I'd expected. The shore, when I came up again, looked about a mile away, though distances at sea were deceptive.

The boat sailed on peacefully. It must have had a name on it, I supposed, though in the flurry I hadn't seen one. I wondered how long it would be before they found I had gone. Supper time, with luck.

The land ahead looked a most promising haven. To the left it was rocky, with grassy cliffs, but straight ahead lay a much greener part, with houses and hotels, and a strip of sand. Civilization, hot baths, freedom and a razor. I swam towards them steadily, taking rests. A mile was a long way for a moderate swimmer, and I was nothing like as strong as I had been twelve days earlier.

I looked back at the boat. It had gone a good way along the coast: growing smaller.

The big mainsail was sagging down the mast.

God, I thought, my heart lurching, if they're taking down the sails they'll see the open hatch.

Time had run out. They knew I had gone.

I ploughed for the shore until I felt dizzy with the effort. Swam until I had grey dots before the eyes and even greyer dots in the mind.

I wasn't going back into that dark hole. I absolutely couldn't.

When I next looked back all the sails were down and the boat was turning.

The hotels ahead were in a sandy bay. Two big hotels, white, with rows of balconies, and a lot of smaller buildings all around. There were some people on the beach, and four or five standing in the water.

Five hundred yards, perhaps.

It would take me years to swim five hundred yards.

I pushed my absolutely useless muscles into frantic efforts. If I could only reach the other bathers, I would be just one more head.

The boat had not been travelling very fast under sail. They would motor back faster. I feared to look around; to see them close. My imagination heard him shouting and pointing, and steering the boat to intercept me, felt them grabbing me with boathooks and pulling me in. When in the end I did nerve myself for a look, it was bad enough, but still too far to distinguish anyone clearly.

Next time I looked, it was alarming. They were catching up like hares. The nearest point of land was still about three hundred yards away, and it was uneven rock, not easy shelving beach. The sand lay in the centre of the bay: the curving arms were shallow cliffs. I would never reach the sand, I thought.

And yet ... sailing boats had deep keels. They wouldn't be able to motor right up to the beach. Perhaps, after all, I could get there.

I had never felt so tired, so leaden. The hardest steeplechase had never demolished me so completely, even those I'd lost from being unfit. My progress through the water grew slower and slower, when speed was all that mattered. In the end it took me all my time to stay afloat.

There was a current, which I hadn't noticed at first, carrying me to the left, drifting me off my line to the beach. Nothing fierce; but simply sapping. I hadn't enough kick left to overcome it.

Another look back.

Literally terrifying. I could see him on deck, standing in the bows, shading his eyes with his hand. He had come back on a course closer to the shore than when I'd jumped, and it was the shoreline he seemed to be scouring most closely.

I swam on with feeble, futile strokes. I could see that I was not going to reach the sand. The current was taking me inexorably towards the higher, left hand side of the bay, where there were trees to within ten feet of the waterline, and rocks below the trees.

When I'd got to the numb stage of thinking drowning would be preferable to recapture, and doubting if one *could* drown oneself in cold blood, I found suddenly that I could no longer see for miles along the coast. I had at last got within the embracing arms of the bay. When I looked back, I couldn't see the boat.

It didn't stay out of sight long. It crept along in a straight line until it reached the centre of the bay, and there dropped anchor. I watched it in sick glimpses over my shoulder. Saw them unbuckle a black rubber dinghy and lower it over the side. Caught an impression of them lowering an outboard engine, and oars, and of two of them climbing down into the boat.

I heard the outboard splutter into life. Only about thirty feet to go to touch the land. It seemed like thirty miles.

There was a man-made strip of concrete set into the rocks ahead of me at the water's edge. I glanced along the shore towards the beach, and saw that there were others. Aids to bathers. The most heartening aid in the world to the bather approaching at snail's pace with the hounds of hell at his back.

The dinghy pulled away from the anchored boat and pointed its bulky black shape towards the shore.

I reached the strip of concrete. It was a flat step, set only inches above the water.

No grips for hauling oneself out. Just a step. I put one hand flat on it and raised a foot to it, and used jelly muscles to flounder up onto my stomach.

Not enough. Not enough. The dinghy would come while I was lying there.

My heart was pounding. Effort and fear in equal measures. Utter desperation took me to hands and knees and set me crawling up the rocks to find shelter.

Ordinarily it would have been easy. It was a gentle shore, undemanding. A child could have jumped where I laboured. I climbed up about six feet of tumbled rocks and found a shallow gully, half full of water. I rolled into the hollow and lay there panting, hopelessly exhausted, listening to the outboard engine grow steadily louder.

They must have seen me, I thought despairingly. Seen me climbing up out of the sea. Yet if I'd stayed at the water's edge they would have found me just as surely. I lay in defeated misery and wondered how on earth I could live through whatever was coming.

The dinghy approached. I kept my head down. They were going to have to come and find me and carry me, and if I could raise enough breath I'd yell until some of the people on the beach took notice, except that they were far enough away to think it was all a game.

The engine died and I heard his voice, raised but not exactly shouting.

He said, 'Excuse me, but have you seen a friend of ours swim in from the sea? We think he fell overboard.'

A woman's voice answered him, from so close to me that I almost fainted.

'No, I haven't seen anybody.'

He said, 'He takes drugs. He might have been acting funny.'

'Serves him right, then,' she said, sanctimoniously.

'I've been reading. I haven't seen him. Have you come from that boat?'

'That's right. We think he fell overboard about here. We heard a splash, but we thought it was just a fish. Till after.'

'Sorry,' she said. 'Why don't you ask along the beach?'

'Just starting this side,' he said. 'We'll work round.'

There was a noise of oars being fitted into rowlocks, and the splash and squeak as they pulled away. I stayed where I was without moving, hoping she wouldn't have hysterics when she saw me, dreading that she would call them back.

I could hear him, away along the shore, loudly asking the same question of someone else.

Her voice said, 'Don't be frightened. I know you're there.'

I didn't answer her. She'd taken away what was left of my breath.

After a pause she said, 'Do you take drugs?'

'No,' I said. It was little more than a whisper.

'What did you say?'

'No.'

'Hm. Well, you'd better not move. They're methodical. I think I'll go on reading.'

Incredulously, I took her advice, lying half in and half out of the water, feeling heart and lungs subside slowly to a more manageable rhythm.

'They've landed on the beach,' she said.

My heart stirred up again. 'Are they searching?' I said anxiously.

'No. Asking questions, I should think.' She paused. 'Are they criminals?'

'I don't know.'

'But . . . would they take you from here by force? With people watching?'

'Yes. You heard them. If I shouted for help, they'd say I was crazy with drugs. No one would stop them.'

'They're walking round the far side of the bay,' she said. 'Asking people.'

'My name is Roland Britten,' I said. 'I live in Newbury, and I'm an accountant. I was kidnapped twelve days ago, and they've kept me on that boat ever since, and I don't know why. So please, whoever you are, if they do manage to get me back there, will you tell the police? I really do most desperately need help.'

There was a short silence. I thought that I must have overdone it; that she didn't believe me. Yet I'd had to tell her, as a precaution.

She apparently made up her mind. 'Well then,' she said briskly, 'time for you to vanish.'

'Where to?'

'My bedroom,' she said.

She was a great one for punches in the mental solar plexus. In spite of the grimness of things in general, I almost laughed.

'Can you see me?' I said.

'I can see your feet. I saw all of you when you climbed out of the sea and scrambled up here.'

'And how do I get to your bedroom dressed in a wet shirt and underpants and nothing else?'

'Do you want to avoid those men, or don't you?'

There was no answer to that.

'Stay still,' she said sharply, though I had not in fact moved. 'They're looking this way. Someone over there seems to be pointing in this direction.'

'Oh God.'

'Stay still.' There was a longish pause, then she said, 'They are walking back along the beach, towards their boat. If they don't stop there, but come on this way, we will go.'

I waited dumbly, and more or less prayed.

'There's a path above us,' she said. 'I will hand you a towel. Wrap it round you, and climb up to the path.'

'Are they coming?'

'Yes.'

A triangle of brightly striped bathing towel appeared over the rock by my head. There was little I'd ever wanted to do less than stand up out of my secure hiding place. My nerves were all against it.

'Hurry up,' she said. 'Don't look back.'

I stood up, dripping, with my back to the sea. Pulled the towel towards me, wrapped it round like a sarong, and tackled the rocky upgrade to the path. The respite in the gully had given me back a surprising amount of energy: or perhaps it was plain fear. In any case I climbed the second stage a great deal more nimbly than the first.

'I'm behind you,' her voice said. 'Don't look back. Turn right when you reach the path. And don't run.'

'Yes ma'am,' I said under my breath. Never argue with a guardian angel.

The path was fringed on both sides with trees, with a mixture of sand and bare rock underfoot. The sunshine dappled through the branches and at any other time would have looked pretty.

When the path widened she fell into step beside me, between me and the sea.

'Take the branch path to the left,' she said, drawing level. 'And don't walk too fast.'

I glanced at her, curious to see what she looked like. She matched her voice: a no-nonsense middle-aged lady with spectacles and a practical air. Self-confident. Tall: almost six feet. Thin, and far from a beauty.

She was wearing a pale-pink blouse, fawn cotton trousers, and sandshoes, and she carried a capacious canvas beach bag.

Beach. Swimming. In March.

'Where is this place?' I said.

'Cala St Galdana.'

'Where's that?'

'Minorca, of course.'

'*Where*?'

'Don't stop walking. Minorca.'

'Island next to Majorca?'

'Of course.' She paused. 'Didn't you know?'

I shook my head. The branch path reached the top of a shallow gradient and began to descend through more trees on the far side.

She peered to the right as we went over the brow.

'Those men are just coming along the lower path, heading towards where I was sitting. I think it would be a good idea to hurry a little now, don't you?'

'Understatement,' I said.

Hurrying meant stubbing my bare toes on various half-buried stones and feeling the dismal weakness again make rubber of my legs.

'While they are looking for you on the rocks, we will reach my hotel,' she said.

I shuffled along and saved my breath. Glanced over my shoulder. Only empty path. No pursuing furies. So why did I feel that they could see through earth and trees and know exactly where to find me?

'Over that little bridge, and across the road. Over there.' She pointed. 'That's the hotel.'

It was one of the two big white ones. We reached the wide glass doors and went inside. Made it unchallenged across the hall and into the lift. Rose to the fifth floor. She scooped some keys out of her beach bag, and let us into 507.

We had seen almost nobody on the way. Still enough warm sun for holidaymakers to be out on the beach and for the staff to be sleeping.

507 had a sea-view balcony, twin beds, two armchairs,

a yellow carpet, and orange and brown curtains. Regulation hotel room, with almost none of my saviour's belongings in sight.

She walked over to the glass door, which was wide open, and half stepped onto the balcony.

'Do you want to watch?' she said.

I looked cautiously over her shoulder. From that height one could see the whole panorama of the bay. There was the boat, anchored in the centre. There was the dinghy on the sand. The headland where I'd crawled out of the sea was to the right, the path leading to it from the beach showing clearly through the trees like a dappled yellow snake.

Along the path came the two men, my familiar warder in front, making for the sand. They trudged slowly across to the dinghy, still looking continually around, and pushed it into the sea.

They both climbed in. They started the outboard. They steered away from the beach.

I felt utterly drained.

'Do you mind if I sit down?' I said.

CHAPTER SIX

Thanks to telephones, consul, bank, and friends, I flew back to England the following evening, but not before I had collected further unforgettable memories of Miss Hilary Margaret Pinlock.

She asked me my measurements, descended to the local boutiques, and returned with new clothes.

She lent me her bathroom, inspected me cleaned and dressed, and decided to go shopping for a razor. I protested. She went. It was as easy to stop Miss Pinlock as an avalanche.

With some relief I scratched the twelve days' scruffy dark stubble off my face, one glance in the looking glass having persuaded me that I was not going to look better in a beard. The twelve days of indoor life had left me thin and pale, with grey hollows in cheeks and eye sockets which I didn't remember having before. Nothing that a little freedom wouldn't fix.

On her second expedition she had also bought bread, cheese and fruit, explaining that she was there on a package holiday, and that the hotel didn't cater for random visitors.

'I'll go down to dinner at seven as usual,' she said. 'You can eat here.'

Throughout all her remarks and actions ran the positive decision-making of one accustomed to command.

'Are you a children's nurse?' I asked curiously.

'No,' she said, unsmiling. 'A headmistress.'

'Oh.'

The smile came, briefly. 'Of a girls-only comprehensive, in Surrey.'

With a touch of sardonic humour she watched me reassess her in the light of that revelation. Not a do-gooding bossy spinster, but a fulfilled career woman of undoubted power.

'Yes. Well . . .' she shrugged. 'If you give me the numbers, I'll ask the switchboard for your calls.'

'And I need a bedroom,' I said.

'Your friends might return and ask about strangers needing bedrooms,' she said.

It had occurred to me too. 'Yes, but . . .' I said.

She pointed to one of the twin beds. 'You can sleep there. I am here alone. The friend who was coming with me had to cry off at the last minute.'

'But . . .' I stopped.

She waited calmly.

'All right,' I said. 'Thank you.'

When she returned from dinner she brought with her a piece of news and a bottle of wine.

'Your friend from the boat was downstairs in the lobby, asking everyone who speaks English if they saw a crazy young man come ashore today. Everyone said no. He looks extremely worried.'

'Probably thinks I drowned.'

The boat had gone from the bay. He must have reached another mooring and returned to Cala St Galdana by road. I wondered how long and how thoroughly he would persevere in his search: the more he feared whoever he was working for, the less he would give up.

The evening air was chilly. Miss Pinlock shut the glass door against the night sky and expertly opened her bottle of Marqués de Riscal.

'Tell me about your journey,' she said, handing me a glass.

I told her the beginning and the end, and not much of the middle.

'Extraordinary,' she said.

'When I get home I'll have a go at finding out what it was all about . . .'

She looked at me gravely. 'It may not be over.'

She had an uncomfortable habit of putting my worst fears into speech.

We drank the excellent wine and she told me a little of her busy life.

'I enjoy it,' she said positively.

'Yes, I see that.'

There was a pause. She looked carefully at the wine in her glass.

She said, 'Will you go to bed with me?'

I suppose I sat in an ungentlemanly heap with my mouth open. I closed it, conscious of the insult it conveyed.

When I'd got over the first shock, she looked up. Her face was calm and businesslike as before, but also suddenly there was vulnerability and self-consciousness. A blush started on her neck, and spread painfully upwards.

She was between forty-two and forty-six, I guessed. She had dark brown wavy hair, going grey, cut with shape but not much style. A broad, lined forehead, large nose, mouth turning down naturally at the corners, and small chin. Behind her glasses her eyes were brown and looked small, probably the effect of the lenses. Wrinkles grew where wrinkles grow; and there was no glow to her skin. A face of character, but not sexually attractive, at least not to me.

'Why?' I said, which was a pretty stupid question.

She blushed a little deeper and shook her head.

'Look,' I said, 'it isn't as simple as that. I can't ... I mean, one can't just sort of switch that sort of thing on and off, like a tap.'

We sat in awkward silence. She put down her glass, and said, 'I'm sorry. It was a ridiculous thing to say. Please try and forget it.'

'You said it because it was in your mind. So ... well ... you must have meant it.'

She half smiled, ruefully. 'It's been in my mind, now and again, for a long time. You will find it extraordinary, but I have never . . . so to speak, slept with a man.'

'In this permissive age?' I said.

'There you are, you see. You find it hard to believe. But I've never been pretty, even as a child. And also I've always been, well . . . able to do things. Learn. Teach. Organize. Administrate. All the unfeminine things. All my life people have relied on me, because I was capable. I've always had health and energy, and I've enjoyed getting on, being given senior posts, and five years ago, being offered a headship. In most ways my life has been absorbing and gratifyingly successful.'

'But?' I suggested.

She nodded. 'But. I was never interested in boys when I was in my teens, and then I thought them callow, and at university I worked all hours to get a First, and after that I've always taught in girls' schools because frankly it is usually a man who's given the headship in a mixed school, and I've never fancied the role of male-ego-massager in second place. Nothing I've ever been or done has been geared to romance.'

'So why *now*?'

'I hope you won't be angry, but it is mostly curiosity, and the pursuit of knowledge.'

I wasn't angry. Just astounded.

Her blush had subsided as fast as it had risen. She was back on surer ground.

'For some time I've thought I ought to have had the

experience. Of sexual intercourse, that is. It didn't come my way when I was young, but I didn't expect it, you see. I think now that I should have tried to find a man, but then, when I was at college, I was half scared of it, and I didn't have any great urge, and I was engrossed in my work. Afterwards for years it didn't bother me, until I was thirty or so, and of course by that time all the men one meets are married, and in any case, teaching among women, one rarely meets any men, except officials, and so on. I go to many official functions, of course, but people tend not to ask unmarried women to private social occasions.'

'What changed your mind?' I asked, fascinated.

'Oh, having to cope with highly-sexed young girls. The modern lot are so clued up. So brash and outspoken. I like them. But I have to arrange their sex-education lessons, and in my time I've even taught them, from text books. I feel it would be a great deal better if I knew . . . what the sex act felt like. I feel at a disadvantage with many of the older girls, particularly as this last term I had to advise a pregnant fourteen-year-old. Fourteen! She knows more than I do. How can I advise her?'

'Catholic priests don't have this problem,' I commented.

'Catholic priests may be respected for virginity, but school-mistresses are not.' She paused, hesitating, and went on. 'To be honest, I also find myself at a disadvantage with the married members of my staff. Some of them have a tendency to patronize me, even unconsciously. I don't like it. I would be able to cope with it perfectly, though, if I actually knew what they know.'

'Am I,' I said slowly, 'the first man you have asked?'

'Oh yes.' She smiled slightly and drank some wine. 'There are practically no men one *can* ask. Especially if one is a headmistress, and widely known. I certainly wouldn't jeopardize my job.'

'I can see that it would be difficult,' I said, thinking about it.

'So of course holidays are the only possibility,' she said. 'I've been on archaeological cruises to Greece, and all that sort of thing, and I've seen other couples join up, but it never happened to me. And then I've heard that some lonely women throw themselves at ski-instructors and waiters and men who perform for money, but somehow that isn't what I want. I mean, I don't want to despise myself. I want knowledge without guilt or shame.'

'The dream of Eden,' I said.

'What? Oh, yes.'

'What about your friend?' I said, pointing to the second bed.

She smiled twistedly. 'No friend, just an excuse for having come alone.'

'Friends being death to the pursuit of knowledge?'

'Exactly.'

We drank some more wine.

'I've been here since last Saturday,' she said. 'I always

take a complete break straight after the end of term, and then go back refreshed for the new work.'

'A perfect system,' I said absently. 'Why didn't you . . . er . . . throw me back, when the men in the dinghy came after me?'

'If you mean, did I immediately see you as a . . . *possible* . . . then no, of course not. I was fascinated, in a way. I'd never seen anyone in such terror before. I watched you from quite a long way out. Swimming, and looking back. It wasn't until you reached the concrete step, though, and I saw your face clearly, that I realized that you were being *hunted*. It would take a certain mentality to point the hounds at an exhausted quarry gone to ground, and I don't have it.'

'And thank God for that,' I said.

I stood up, and opened the glass door, and went out onto the balcony. The cool night was clear, with bright stars over the ageless Mediterranean. Waves rippled softly round the edges of the bay, and the gentle moonlight shone on the wide, empty expanse where the boat had been anchored.

It was the weirdest of debts. She had saved me from recapture. I certainly owed her my wholeness of mind, if not life itself. If the only payment she wanted was something I didn't much want to give, then that was simply too bad. One extreme favour, I thought sardonically, deserved another.

I went in, and sat down. Drank some wine with a dry mouth.

'We'll try, if you like,' I said.

She sat very still. I had a swift impression that now I'd agreed she was hastily retreating: that the half-fear of her student days was definitely still there.

'You don't have to,' she said.

'No. I want to.' Heaven forgive all liars.

She said, as if speaking to herself, and not to me: 'I'll never have another chance.'

The voice of longing teetering on the brink of the leap in the dark. Her strength of mind, I saw, would carry her through. I admired her. I determined to make Hilary Pinlock's leap something that at least she wouldn't regret: if I could.

'First of all,' I said, 'we'll switch off the lights and sit by the window for a while, and talk about it.'

We sat facing each other in dim reflected moonlight, and I asked her some fairly medical questions, to which she gave straightforward replies.

'What if you get pregnant?' I said.

'I'd solve that later.'

'You want to go ahead?'

She took a deep breath. 'If you do.'

If I *can*, I thought.

'Then I think the best thing to do first would be to get undressed,' I said. 'Do you have a nightdress? And could you lend me a dressing gown?'

I reflected, as I put on her blue candlewick in the privacy of the bathroom, that deep physical tiredness was a rotten basis for the matter in hand. I yawned. I wanted above all to go to sleep.

When I went out she was sitting by the window in a long cotton nightgown which had a frill round the neckline, but was not, of course, transparent.

'Come on,' I said. 'We'll sit on the bed.'

She stood up. The nightgown accentuated her height and thinness, and revealed long narrow feet. I pulled back the bed-clothes, sat on the white sheet, and held my hand out towards her. She came, gripped my hand, and sat beside me.

'Right,' I said. 'Now, if at any point you want to stop, you've only got to say so.'

She nodded.

'Lie down, then,' I said, 'and imagine you are twenty.'

'Why?'

'Because this is not a brain matter. It's about the stimulation of nerve endings. About feeling, not thinking. If you think all the time of who you are, you may find it inhibiting. Age doesn't exist in the dark. If you imagine you are twenty, you will be twenty, and you'll find it liberating.'

'You're a most unusual man.'

'Oh sure,' I said. 'And you're a most unusual woman. So lie down.'

She gave a small unexpected chuckle, and did as I said.

'Take off your glasses,' I said, and she put them without comment on the bedside table. In the dim light her eyes looked larger, as I'd guessed, and her big nose smaller, and her determined mouth softer. I leaned over and kissed her lips, and if it was basically a nephew-to-aunt gesture it brought a smile to her face and a grin to my own.

It was the strangest lovemaking, but it did work. I looked back afterwards to the moment when she first took pleasure in the sensation of my stroking her skin; the ripple of surprise when she felt with her hands the size of an erect man; the passion with which she finally responded; and the stunning release into gasping incredulity.

'Is that,' she said, out of breath, 'is that what every woman feels?'

I knew she had reached a most satisfactory climax. 'I guess so,' I said. 'On good days.'

'Oh my goodness,' she said in a sort of exultation. 'So now I *know*.'

CHAPTER SEVEN

Thursday morning I went back to the office and tried to take up my life where it had left off.

The same smell of typewriters, filing cabinets, reams of paper. Same bustle, adding machines, telephones. Same heaps of too much work. All familiar, all unreal.

Our two assistants, Debbie and Peter, had had a rough time, they said aggrievedly, trying to account to everyone for my unaccountable absence. They had reported my disappearance to the police, who had said I was over twenty-one and had the right to duck out if I wanted to, and that they would look for me only if I'd committed a crime, or was clearly a missing victim. They had thought I had merely gone off on a celebratory binge after winning the Gold Cup.

'We told them you wouldn't have gone away for so long,' Peter said. 'But they didn't show much interest.'

'We wanted them to get in touch with Mr King, through Interpol,' Debbie complained. 'And they laughed at the idea.'

'I expect they would,' I said. 'So Trevor is still on his holiday?'

'He's not due back until Monday,' Peter said, surprised that I should have forgotten something I knew so well.

'Oh yes . . .'

I spent the morning re-organizing the timetable and getting Peter to make new appointments to replace those I'd missed, and the afternoon discovering that as far as the police were concerned, my troubles were still of little interest. I was back home, wasn't I? Unharmed. Without having to pay a ransom? Was there any form of extortion? No. Was I starved? No. Beaten? No. Tied with ropes, straps, shackles? No. Was I sure it wasn't a practical joke? They would look into it, they said: but one of them remarked that *he* wouldn't mind a free fortnight's trip to the Mediterranean, and his colleague laughed. I gathered that if I seriously wanted to get to know, I would have to do the investigating myself.

I did want to know. Not knowing felt dangerously unsafe, like standing behind a bad-tempered horse. If I didn't know why I'd been taken the first time, how was I to stop it happening again?

Thursday evening I collected my Dolomite, which had been moved to the Cheltenham racecourse manager's front drive. ('Where on earth have you been? We traced that it was your car through the police.') Next I drove to the house of the racecourse valet to pick up my wallet and keys and racing saddle. ('Where on earth have you been? I gave the racecourse manager your car keys, I hope that's all right.') Then I drove back to my cottage (having spent the previous night in an airport hotel), and with faint-hearted caution let myself in.

No one was waiting there in the dark, with coshes or ether or one-way tickets to sail lockers. I switched on all the lights and poured myself a stiff Scotch and told myself to calm down and take a better grip.

I telephoned the trainer I regularly rode early morning exercise for ('Where on earth have you been?') and arranged to start again on Monday: and I rang a man who had asked me to ride in a hunter 'chase, to apologize for not turning up. I saw no reason not to answer the questions about where I'd been, so I told them all: abducted and taken on a boat to Minorca, and I didn't know why. I thought at least that someone might come up with a possible explanation, but everyone I told sounded as flummoxed as I felt.

There wasn't much food in the cottage, and the steak in the fridge had grown whiskers. I decided on spaghetti, with chopped up cheese melting on it, but before starting to cook I went upstairs to change new jacket for old sweater, and to make a detour to the bathroom.

I glanced casually out of the bathroom window and spent a frozen instant in pure panic.

There was a man in the garden, looking towards the downstairs rooms of the cottage. The light from the sitting-room window fell brightly on his face.

I hadn't consciously remembered him, but I knew him

at once, in one heart-stopping flash of the inner eye. He was the fake St John's Ambulance man from Cheltenham races.

Behind him, in the road, stood a car, with gleams of light edging its roof and windows. A second man was levering himself out of the passenger's seat, carrying what looked like a plastic bag containing cotton wool. A third figure, dimly seen, was heading through the garden to the back of the house.

They couldn't, I thought: surely they couldn't think they would trick me again. But with three of them, they hardly needed tricks.

The St John's man waved his arm to the man by the car, and pointed, and the two of them took up positions, one on each side of my front door, out of sight of anyone opening it from the inside. The St John's man stretched out an arm and rang my bell.

I unfroze.

Wonderful how terror sharpened the wits. There was only one place I could hide, and that was in my bedroom. The speed with which I'd gone over the side of the boat was nothing compared with my disappearance inside the cottage.

Downstairs in the sitting-room the huge old fireplace had at one side incorporated a bread oven, which the people living there before me had removed, constructing instead a head-high alcove with display shelves. Wanting a safe place in which to keep valuables, they had opened the upper part of the bread oven space into the bedroom above, where it formed a sort of box below the floor of the built-in wardrobe. Not having much in the way of valuables, I stored my two suitcases in there instead.

I opened the wardrobe door, and pulled up the hinged flap of flooring, and hauled out the cases.

The door bell rang again, insistently.

Lowering myself into the space took seconds, and I had the wardrobe door shut and the flap of floor almost in place when they burst in through the front door.

They rampaged through the place, opening and slamming doors, and shouting, and finally gathering all together downstairs.

'He must be bloody here.'

'Britten! Britten, come out, we know you're here.'

'The effing bastard's scarpered.'

I could hear every loud word through the chipboard partition between my hiding place and the sitting-room. I felt horribly vulnerable sitting there, level with the picture over the mantelshelf, practically in the room with them, hidden only by a thin piece of wall.

'He couldn't have seen us coming.'

'He never got out of the back, I'll tell you that for sure.'

'Then where the bleeding hell is he?'

'How about those suitcases of his upstairs?'

'No. He ain't in them. They're too small. And I looked.'

'He must be meaning to bleeding scarper.'

'Yeah.'

'Take another butcher's upstairs. He must be here somewhere.'

They searched the whole house again, crashing about with heavy boots.

One of them opened the wardrobe above me for the second time, and saw nothing but clothes, as before. I sat under their feet and sweated, and felt my pulse shoot up to the hundreds.

'Look under the bed,' he said.

'Can't. The bed's right on the floor.'

'How about the other bedroom, then?'

'I looked. He ain't there.'

'Well, bleeding well look again.'

The wardrobe door closed above me. I wiped the sweat out of my eyes and tried to ease my legs without scraping my shoes on the wall and making a noise. I was half sitting, half lying, in a recess about three feet long by two feet deep, and just wide enough for my shoulders. My knees were bent acutely, with my heels against the backs of my thighs. It was a bad position for every muscle I could think of.

Two of them came into the sitting-room, one after the other.

'What you got there? Here, let me see.'

'None of your bleeding business.'

'It's his wallet. You've got his wallet.'

'Yeah. Well, it was in his bedroom.'

'Well, bleeding well put it back.'

'Not likely, he's got thirty quid in it.'

'You'll effing well do as I say. You know the orders, same as I do. Don't steal nothink, don't break nothink. I told you.'

'You can have half, then.'

'Give it to me. I'll put it back. I don't trust you.' It was the St John's man talking, I thought.

'It's bloody stupid, not nicking what we can get.'

'You want the fuzz on our necks? They didn't bloody look for him last time, and they won't bloody look for him this time, either, but they will if they find his place has been turned over. Use your bloody loaf.'

'We ain't got him yet.'

'Matter of time. He's round here some place. Bound to be.'

'He won't come back if he sees us in here.'

'No, you got a point there. Tell you what, we'll turn the lights off and wait for him, and jump him, like.'

'He left all the lights on, himself. He won't come in if they're off.'

'Best if one of us waits in the kitchen, like, and the other two in the garden. Then when he gets here we can jump him from both sides, right, just as he's coming back through the door.'

'Yeah.'

Into these plans there suddenly came a fresh voice, female and enquiring.

'Mr Britten? Mr Britten, are you there?'

I heard her push the front door open and take the step into the sitting-room.

The voice of my next-door neighbour.

Yes, Mrs Morris, I'm here, I thought. And it would take more than me and a small plump senior citizen to fight off my unwanted guests.

'Who are you?' she said.

'Friends of his. Calling on him, like.'

'He's away,' she said sharply.

'No he's not. He's back. His car's round the side. And he's having a drink, see? Whisky.'

'Then where is he? Mr Britten?' she called.

'Ain't no use, lady. He's out. We're waiting for him, like.'

'I don't think you should be in here.' A brave lady, old Mrs Morris.

'We're friends of his, see.'

'You don't look like his friends,' she said.

'Know his friends, then, do yer?'

A certain nervousness crept into her voice, but the resolution was still there.

'I think you'd better wait outside.'

There was a pause, then the St John's man said, 'Where do you think he could be? We've searched all over for him.'

Let her not know about this hiding place, I prayed. Let her not think of it.

'He might've gone to the pub,' she said. 'Why don't you go down there? To the Fox.'

'Yeah, maybe.'

'Anyway, I think I'll just see you out.'

Intrepid little Mrs Morris. I heard them all go out, and shut the front door behind them. The lock clicked decisively. The cottage was suddenly still.

I lay quiet, listening for their car to start.

Nothing happened.

They were still there, I thought. Outside. Round my house. Waiting.

On the mantelshelf, the clock ticked.

I cautiously pushed up the flap over my head, and sat up, straightening knees, back and neck, with relief.

The light in my bedroom was still on, shining in a crack under the wardrobe door. I left the door shut. If they saw so much as a shadow move they would know for sure I was inside the house.

I reflected that I had had a good deal too much practice at passing uncertain hours in small dark places.

The lock clicked on my front door.

One gets to know the noises of one's own house so well that sight is unnecessary for interpretation. I heard the unmistakable sound of the hinges, and the gritty sound of a shoe on the bare flagstones of the entrance hall. Then there were quiet noises in the sitting-room itself, and low voices, and the squeak of the door to the kitchen. They had come back in a way that would not bring Mrs Morris.

I sat rigidly, wondering whether to slide down into the smaller space and risk them hearing my movements, or stay with head and shoulders above floor level and risk them searching my clothes cupboard yet again. If I coughed or sneezed, or as much as knocked the chip-board with my elbow as I slid down into the safer hiding place, they would hear me. I sat immobile, stretching my own ears and wondering despairingly how long they would stay.

Breathing evenly was difficult, controlling my heart-beat was impossible. Acute anxiety over a period of hours was highly shattering to the nerves.

From time to time I could hear them moving and murmuring, but could no longer distinctly hear their words. I supposed that they too were hiding, waiting out of sight for me to come home. It was almost funny when one thought of it: them hiding behind the furniture and me within the walls.

Unfunny if they found me. More like unfaceable.

I took a deep, shaky breath, one of many.

Someone began to come quietly upstairs. The familiar creaks of the old treads fizzed through my body like electric shocks. The risk of moving had to be taken. I tucked my elbows in and bent my knees, and eased myself back under the floor. The flap came down hard on my hair and I thought wildly that they must have heard it: but no one arrived with triumphant shouts, and the awful suspense just went on and on.

I got pains from being bent up, and I got cramps, but there was nothing I could do about that except sur-render.

One of them spent a good time in my bedroom. I could hear his footfall through the floorboards, and the small thuds of drawers shutting. Guessed he was no longer looking for me, but at what I owned. It didn't make his nearness to me any safer.

The fear seemed endless; but everything ends. I heard them murmuring again in the sitting-room, and shutting the kitchen door. The man upstairs went down again. More murmurings: a chorus. Then silence for a while. Then a step or two in the hall, and the click of the front door closing.

I waited, thinking that only one of them had gone out.

Their car started. Shifted quietly into gear. Drove off.

I still lay without moving, not trusting that it was over, that it wasn't a trick: but the absolute quietness persisted, and in the end I pushed up the flap of the floor and levered myself with much wincing and pins and needles onto my bedroom carpet.

The lights were still on, but the black square of window was grey. The whole night had passed. It was dawn.

I threw a few things into one of the suitcases and left the cottage ten minutes later.

The Yale lock on the front door showed no signs of forcing, and I guessed they must have opened it with a credit card, as I myself had done once when I'd locked myself out. My car stood untouched where I'd left it, and even my half-drunk glass of Scotch was still on the sitting-room table.

Feeling distinctly unsettled I had a wash, shave and breakfast at the Chequers Hotel, and then went to the police.

'Back again?' they said.

They listened, made notes, asked questions.

'Do you know who they were?'

'No.'

'Any evidence of a forced entry?'

'No.'

'Anything stolen?'

'No.'

'Nothing we can do, sir.'

'Look,' I said, 'these people are trying to abduct me. They've succeeded once, and they're trying again. Can't you do a damn thing to help?'

They seemed fairly sympathetic, but the answer was no. They hadn't enough men or money to mount a round-the-clock guard on anyone for an indefinite period without a very good reason.

'Isn't the threat of abduction a very good reason?'

'No. If you believe the threat, you could hire yourself a private bodyguard.'

'Thanks very much,' I said. 'But if anyone reports me missing again, I won't have gone by choice, and you might do me a favour and start looking.'

'If they do, sir, we will.'

*

I went to the office and sat at my desk and watched my hands shake. Whatever I normally had in the way of mental and physical stamina was at a very low ebb.

Peter came in with a cable and his usual expression of not quite grasping the point, and handed me the bad news. CAR BROKEN DOWN RETURNING WEDNESDAY APOLOGIES TREVOR.

'You read this?' I asked Peter.

'Yes.'

'Well, you'd better fetch Mr King's list, for next week, and his appointment book.'

He went on the errand and I sat and looked blankly at the cable. Trevor had sent it from some town I'd never heard of in France, and had given no return address. He wouldn't be worried, wherever he was. He would be sure I could take his extra few days in my stride.

Peter came back with the list and I laced my fingers together to keep them still. What did people take for tranquillizers?

'Get me some coffee,' I said to Peter. His eyebrows rose. 'I know it's only a quarter past nine,' I said, 'but get me some coffee . . . please.'

When he brought the coffee I sent him to fetch Debbie, so that I could share between them the most urgent jobs. Neither of them had a good brain, but they were both persistent, meticulous plodders, invaluable qualities in accountants' assistants. In many offices the assistants were bright and actively studying to become accountants themselves, but Trevor for some reason seemed always to prefer working with the unambitious sort. Peter was twenty-two, Debbie twenty-four. Peter, I thought, was a latent homosexual who hadn't quite realized it. Debbie, mousy-haired, big-busted, and pious, had a boyfriend working in a hardware shop. Peter occasionally made jokes about screws, which shocked her.

They sat opposite my desk with notebooks poised, both of them looking at me with misgiving.

'You really look awfully ill,' Debbie said. 'Worse even than yesterday. Grey, sort of.' There seemed to be more ghoulish relish in her voice than concern.

'Yes, well, never mind that,' I said. 'I've looked at Mr King's list, and there are a few accounts that won't wait until he gets back.' There were two he should have seen to before he went, but no one was perfect. 'Certificate for the solicitors, Mr Crest, and Mr Grant. I'm afraid they are already overdue. Could you bring all the papers for those two in here, Debbie? Later, I mean. Not this instant. Then there are the two summonses to appear before the Commissioners next Thursday. I'll apply for postponements for those, but you'd better bring all the books in here, Debbie, anyway, and I'll try and make a start on them.'

'That's the Axwood stables, is it? And Millrace Stud?'

'Not the stud; that's the week after. Mr King can deal with that. The Axwood stables, yes, and those corn merchants, Coley Young.'

'The Coley Young books aren't here yet,' Peter said.

'Well, for crying out loud, didn't you do what I said two weeks ago, and tell them to send them?' I could hear the scratch in my voice and did my best to stop it. 'OK,' I said slowly. 'Did you ask them to send them?'

'Yes, I did.' Peter tended to look sulky. 'But they haven't come.'

'Ring them again, would you? And what about the Axwood stables?'

'You checked those yourself, if you remember.'

'Did I?' I looked back as if to a previous existence. The two summonses to appear before the Commissioners were not particularly serious. We seldom actually went. The summonses were issued when the Inland Revenue thought a particular set of accounts were long overdue: a sort of goad to action. It meant that Trevor or I asked for a postponement, did the accounts, and sent them in before the revised date. End of drama. The two summonses in question had arrived after Trevor had left for his holidays, which was why he hadn't dealt with them himself.

'You said the petty cash book hadn't arrived,' Peter said.

'Did I? Did you ask them to send it?'

'Yes, I did, but it hasn't come.'

I sighed. 'Ring them again.'

A great many clients saw no urgency at all in getting their accounts done, and requests from us for further information or relevant papers were apt to be ignored for weeks.

'Tell them both they really will have to go before the Commissioners if they don't send those books.'

'But they won't really, will they?' Peter said. Not the brightest of boys, I thought.

'I'll get adjournments anyway,' I said patiently, 'but Trevor will need those books to hand the second he gets back.'

Debbie said, 'Mr Wells rang three times yesterday afternoon.'

'Who is Mr Wells? Oh yes. Mr Wells.'

'He says one of his creditors is applying to have him made bankrupt and he wants to know what you're going to do about it.'

I'd forgotten all the details of Mr Wells' troubles. 'Where are his books?' I asked.

'In one of those boxes,' Debbie said, pointing. A three-high row of large cardboard boxes ran along the wall under the window. Each box had the name of the client on it, in large black letters, and each contained the cash books, invoices, receipts, ledgers, paying-in books, bank statements, petty cash records, stocktakings and general paraphernalia needed for the assessment of taxes. Each of the boxes represented a task I had yet to do.

It took me an average of two working days to draw up the annual accounts for each client. Some audits took longer. I had roughly two hundred clients. The thing was impossible.

Trevor had collared the bigger firms and liked to

spend nearly a week on each. He dealt with seven clients. No wonder Commissioners' summonses fell on us like snow.

Peter and Debbie did most of the routine work, checking bank statements against cheque numbers, and against invoices paid. Someone extra to share that work would only help Trevor and me to a certain extent. Taking a third, fully equal partner would certainly reduce the pressure, but it would also entail dividing the firm's profits into three instead of two, which would mean a noticeable drop in income. Trevor was totally opposed. Amalgamation with the London firm meant Trevor not being boss and me not going racing... a fair sized impasse, all in all.

'Debbie and I didn't get our pay cheques last week,' Peter said. 'Nor did Bess.' Bess was the typist.

'And the water heater in the washroom is running cold,' Debbie added. 'And you did say I could go to the dentist this afternoon at three-thirty.'

'Sorry about all the extra work,' Peter said, not sounding it, 'but I'm afraid it's my Friday for the Institute of Accounting Staff class.'

'Mm,' I said. 'Peter, telephone to Leyhill Prison and ask if Connaught Powys is still there.'

'What?'

'Leyhill Prison. Somewhere in Gloucestershire. Get the number from directory enquiries.'

'But ...'

'Just go and do it,' I said. 'Connaught Powys. Is he still there.'

He went out looking mystified, but then he, like Debbie, dated from after the searchingly difficult court case. Debbie went to fetch the first batch of the papers I needed, and I began on the solicitors' certificates.

Since embezzlement of clients' trust monies had become a flourishing industry, laws had been passed to ensure that auditors checked every six months to see that the cash and securities which were supposed to be in a solicitor's care actually were there. If they weren't, Nemesis swiftly struck the solicitor off the Roll. If they were, the auditor signed the certificate and pocketed his fee.

Peter returned as if he'd come from a dangerous mission, looking noble.

'The prison said he was released six weeks ago, on February 16th.'

'Thanks.'

'I had a good deal of trouble in getting through.'

'Er ... well done,' I said. He still looked as if he thought more praise was due, but he didn't get it.

If Connaught Powys had been out for six weeks, he would have had a whole month to fix me up with a voyage. I tried hard to concentrate on the checking for the certificates but the sail locker kept getting in the way.

Solicitor Grant's affair tallied at about the third shot, but I kept making errors with Denby Crest's. I realized I'd always taken clarity of mind for granted, like walking:

one of those things you don't consciously value until you've lost it. Numbers, from my infancy, had been like a second language, understood without effort. I checked Denby Crest's figures five times and kept getting a fifty thousand pounds' discrepancy, and knowing him, as he occasionally did work for us, it was ridiculous. Denby Crest was no crook, I thought in exasperation. It's my useless muddle-headed thought processes. Somewhere I was transposing a decimal point, making a mountain out of a molehill discrepancy of probably five pounds or fifty pence.

In the end I telephoned his office and asked to speak to him.

'Look, Denby,' I said, 'I'm most awfully sorry, but are you sure we've got all the relevant papers?'

'I expect so,' he said, sounding impatient. 'Why don't you leave it for Trevor? He gets back to England tomorrow, doesn't he?'

I explained about the broken-down car. 'He won't be back in the office until Wednesday or Thursday.'

'Oh.' He sounded disconcerted and there was a perceptible pause. 'All the same,' he said, 'Trevor is used to our ways. Please leave our certificate until he gets back.'

'But it's overdue,' I said.

'Tell Trevor to call me,' he said. 'And now, I'm sorry, but I have a client with me. So if you'll excuse me . . .'

He disconnected. I shuffled his papers together thankfully and thought that if he wanted to risk waiting for Trevor it was certainly all right by me.

At twelve-thirty Peter and Debbie went out to lunch, but I didn't feel hungry. I sat in shirtsleeves before the newly tackled sea of Mr Wells' depressing papers: put my elbows on the desk, and propped my forehead on the knuckles of my right hand, and shut my eyes. Thought a lot of rotten thoughts and wondered about buying myself a one-way ticket to Antarctica.

A voice said, 'Are you ill, asleep or posing for Rodin?'

I looked up, startled.

She was standing in the doorway. Young, fair, slender pretty.

'I'm looking for Trevor,' she said.

One couldn't have everything, I supposed.

CHAPTER EIGHT

'Don't I know you?' I said, puzzled, standing up.

'Sure.' She looked resigned, as if this sort of thing happened often. 'Cast your mind back to long hair, no lipstick, dirty jeans and ponies.'

I looked at the short bouncy bob, the fashionable make-up, the swirling brown skirt topped by a neat waist-length fur-fabric jacket. Someone's daughter, I thought; recently and satisfactorily grown up.

'Whose daughter?' I said.

'My own woman.'

'Reasonable.'

She was enjoying herself, pleased with her impact on men.

'Jossie Finch, actually.'

'Wow,' I said.

'Every grub spreads its wings.'

'To where will you fly?'

'Yes,' she said, 'I've heard you were smooth.'

'Trevor isn't here, I'm afraid.'

'Mm. Still on his hols?'

I nodded.

'Then I was to deliver the same message to you, if you were here instead.'

'Sit down?' I suggested, gesturing to a chair.

'Can't stop. Sorry. Message from Dad. What are you doing about the Commissioners? He said he was absolutely not going before any so-and-so Commissioners next Thursday, or lurid words to that effect.'

'No, he won't have to.'

'He also says he would have sent the petty cash book, or whatever, in with me this morning, but his secretary is sick, and if you ask me she's the sickest thing that ever broke fingernails on a typewriter, and she has not done something or other with petty cash receipts or vouchers, or whatever it is you need. However . . .' she paused, drawing an exaggerated breath. 'Dad says, if you would like to drop in this evening you could go round the yard with him at evening stables, and have a noggin afterwards, and he will personally press into your hot little palms the book your assistant has been driving him mad about.'

'I'd like that,' I said.

'Good. I'll tell him.'

'And will you be there?'

'Ah,' she said, her eyes laughing, 'a little uncertainty is the HP sauce on the chips.'

'And the spice of life to you, too.'

She gave me an excellent smile, spun on her heel so

that the skirt swirled and the hair bounced, and walked out of the office.

Jossie Finch, daughter of William Finch, master of Axwood Stables. I knew her father in the way all long-time amateur riders knew all top trainers; enough to greet and chat to at the races. Since his was one of the racing accounts which pre-dated my arrival in the firm, and which Trevor liked to do himself, I had never before actually visited his yard.

I was interested enough to want to go, in spite of all my troubles. He had approximately ninety horses in his care, both jumpers and flat racers, and winners were taken for granted. Apart from Tapestry, most of the horses I usually rode were of moderate class, owned with more hope than expectation. To see a big stableful of top performers was always a feast. I would be safe from abduction there. And Jossie looked a cherry on the top.

When Peter and Debbie came back I laid into them for going out and leaving the outer door unlocked, and they adopted put-upon expressions and said they thought it was all right, as I was there, which would stop people sneaking in to steal things.

My fault, I thought more reasonably. I should have locked it after them myself. I would have to reshape a lot of habits. It could easily have been the enemy who walked in, not Jossie Finch.

I spent part of the afternoon on Mr Wells, but more of it trying to trace Connaught Powys.

We had his original address on file, left over from the

days when he had rigged the computer and milked his firm of a quarter of a million pounds in five years. The firm's audit was normally Trevor's affair, but one year, when Trevor was away a great deal with an ulcer, I had done it instead, and by some fluke had discovered the fraud. It had been one of those things you don't believe even when it is in front of your eyes. Connaught Powys had been an active director, and had paid his taxes on a comfortable income. The solid, untaxed lolly had disappeared without trace, but Connaught himself hadn't been quick enough.

I tried his old address. A sharp voice on the telephone told me the new occupants knew nothing of the Powys' whereabouts, and wished people would stop bothering them, and regretted the day they'd ever moved into a crook's house.

I tried his solicitors, who froze when they heard who was trying to find him. They could not, they said, divulge his present address without his express permission: which, their tone added, he was as likely to give as Shylock to a church bazaar.

I tried Leyhill Prison. No good.

I tried finally a racing acquaintance called Vivian Iverson who ran a gambling club in London and always seemed to know of corruption scandals before the stories publicly broke.

'My dear Ro,' he said, 'you're fairly non gratis in that quarter, don't you know.'

'I could guess.'

'You put the shivers up embezzlers, my friend. They're leaving the Newbury area in droves.'

'Oh sure. And I pick the Derby winner every year.'

'You may well jest, my dear chap, but the whisper has gone round.' He hesitated. 'Those two little dazzlers, Glitberg and Ownslow, have been seen talking to Powys, who has got rid of his indoor pallor under a sun lamp. The gist, so I'm fairly reliably told, was a hate-Britten chorus.'

'With vengeance intended?'

'No information, my dear chap.'

'Could you find out?'

'I only *listen*, my dear Ro,' he said. 'If I hear the knives are out, I'll tell you.'

'You're a pet,' I said dryly.

He laughed. 'Connaught Powys comes here to play, most Fridays.'

'What time?'

'You do ask a lot, my dear chap. After dinner to dawn.'

'How about making me an instant member?'

He sighed heavily. 'If you are bent on suicide, I'll tell the desk to let you in.'

'See you,' I said. 'And thanks.'

I put down the receiver and stared gloomily into space. Glitberg and Ownslow. Six years apiece, reduced for good behaviour . . . They could have met Connaught Powys in Leyhill, and it would have been no joy to any of them that I had put them all there.

116

Glitberg and Ownslow had served on a local council and robbed the ratepayers blind, and I'd turned them up through some dealings they'd done with one of my clients. My client had escaped with a fine, and had removed his custom from me with violent curses.

I wondered how much time all the embezzlers and bent solicitors and corrupted politicians in Leyhill Prison spent in thinking up new schemes for when they got out. Glitberg and Ownslow must already have been out for about six months.

Debbie had gone to the dentist and Peter to his Institute of Accounting Staff class, and this time I did lock the door behind them.

I felt too wretchedly tired to bother any further with Mr Wells. The shakes of the morning had gone, but even the swift tonic of Jossie Finch couldn't lift the persistent feeling of threat. I spent an hour dozing in the armchair we kept for favoured clients and when it was time, locked the filing cabinets and my desk and every door in the office, and went down to my car.

There was no one hiding behind the front seats. No one lurking round the edges of the car park. Nothing in the boot except the suitcase I'd stowed there that morning. I started up and drove out into the road, assaulted by nothing but my own nerves.

William Finch's yard lay south-west of Newbury: a huge spread of buildings sheltering in a hollow, with a creeper-covered Victorian mansion rising on the hillside above. I arrived at the house just as Finch was coming out of it, and we walked down together to the first cluster of boxes.

'Glad you could come,' he said.

'It's a treat.'

He smiled with easy charm. A tall man, going grey at about fifty, very much in command of himself and everything else. He had a broad face, fine well-shaped mouth, and the eyes of experience. Horses and owners thrived in his care, and years of success had given him a stature he plainly enjoyed.

We went from box to box, spending a couple of minutes in each. Finch told me which horse we were looking at, with some of its breeding and form. He held brief reassurance conversations in each case with the lad holding the horse's head, and with his head lad, who walked round with us. If all was well, he patted the horse's neck and fed him a carrot from a bag which his head lad carried. A practised important routine evening inspection, as carried out by every trainer in the country.

We came to an empty box in a full row. Finch gestured to it with a smile.

'Ivansky. My National runner. He's gone up to Liverpool.'

I almost gaped like an idiot. I'd been out of touch with the normal world so much that I had completely forgotten that the Grand National was due that Saturday.

I cleared my throat. 'He should ... er ... have a fair chance at the weights.' It seemed a fairly safe comment, but he disagreed.

'Ten twelve is far too much on his Haydock form. He's badly in with Wasserman, don't you think?'

I raked back for all the opinions I'd held in the safe and distant life of three weeks ago. Nothing much surfaced.

'I'm sure he'll do well,' I said.

He nodded as if he hadn't noticed the feebleness of the remark, and we went on. The horses were truly an impressive bunch, glowing with good feeding, thorough grooming and well-judged exercise. I ran out of compliments long before he ran out of horses.

'Drink?' he said, as the head lad shut the last door.

'Great.'

We walked up to the house, and he led the way into a sitting-room-cum-office. Chintz-covered sofa and chairs, big desk, table with drinks and glasses, walls covered with framed racing photographs. Normal affluent trainer ambience.

'Gin?' he said.

'Scotch, if you have it.'

He gave me a stiff one and poured gin like water for himself.

'Your health,' he said.

'And yours.'

We drank the ritual first sip, and he gestured to me to sit down.

'I've found that damned cash book for you,' he said, opening a drawer in the desk. 'There you are. Book, and file of petty cash receipts.'

119

'That's fine.'

'And what about these Commissioners?'

'Don't worry, I've applied for a postponement.'

'But will they grant it?'

'Never refused us yet,' I said. 'They'll set a new date about a month ahead, and we'll do your accounts and audit before then.'

He relaxed contentedly over his draught of gin. 'We can expect Trevor here next week, then? Counting hay bales and saddles?' There was humour in his voice at the thoroughness ahead.

'Well,' I said, 'maybe at the end of the week, or the one after. He won't be back until Wednesday or Thursday.' Did 'Returning Wednesday', I wondered, mean *travelling* Wednesday, or turning up for work? 'I'll do a lot of the preliminary paperwork for him, to save time.'

Finch turned to the drinks table and unscrewed the gin. 'I thought he was due back on Monday.'

'His car's broken down somewhere in France.'

'That'll please him.' He drank deeply. 'Still, if you make a start on things, the audit should get done in time.'

'Don't worry about the Commissioners,' I said; but everyone did worry when the peremptory summons dropped through their door. If one neither asked for a postponement nor attended at the due hour, the Commissioners would fix one's year's tax at whatever figure they cared to, and to that assessment there was no appeal. As such assessments were customarily far higher than the amount of tax actually due, one avoided them like black ice.

To my pleasure, the swirly brown skirt and bouncy fair hair made a swooping entrance. She was holding a marmalade cat which was trying to jump out of her arms.

'Damn thing,' she said, 'why won't he be *stroked*.'

'It's a mouser,' said her father, unemotionally.

'You'd think it would be glad of a cuddle.'

The cat freed itself and bolted. Jossie shrugged. 'Hello,' she said to me. 'So you got here.'

'Mm.'

'Well,' she said to her father, 'what did he say?'

'Eh? Oh . . . I haven't asked him yet.'

She gave him a fond exasperated smile and said to me, 'He wants to ask you to ride a horse for him.'

Finch shook his head at her, and I said, 'When?'

'Tomorrow,' Jossie said. 'At Towcester.'

'Er,' I said, 'I'm not really ultra fit.'

'Nonsense. You won the Gold Cup a fortnight ago. You must be.'

'Josephine,' her father said. 'Clam up.' He turned to me. 'I'm flying up to Liverpool in the morning, but I have this horse in at Towcester, and to be blunt he's still entered there only because someone forgot to scratch him by the eleven o'clock deadline this morning . . .'

'The chronically sick secretary,' muttered Jossie.

'So we've either got to run him after all or pay a fine, and I was toying with the idea of sending him up there, if I could get a suitable jockey.'

121

'Most of them having gone to the National,' Jossie added.

'Which horse?' I said.

'Notebook. Novice hurdler. Four-year-old chestnut gelding, in the top yard.'

'The one with the flaxen mane and tail?'

'That's right. He's run a couple of times so far. Shows promise, but still green.'

'Last of twenty-six at Newbury,' Jossie said cheerfully. 'It won't matter a curse if you're not fit.' She paused. 'I've been delegated to saddle it up, so you might do us a favour and come and ride it.'

'Up to you,' Finch said.

The delegated saddler was a powerful attraction, even if Notebook himself was nothing much.

'Yes,' I said weakly. 'OK.'

'Good.' Jossie gave me a flashing smile. 'I'll drive you up there, if you like.'

'I would like,' I said regretfully, 'but I'll be in London tonight. I'll go straight to Towcester from there.'

'I'll meet you outside the weighing room, then. He's in the last race, by the way. He would be.'

Novice hurdles were customarily first or last (or both), on a day's programme: the races a lot of racegoers chose to miss through lunch or leaving early to avoid the crush. The poor-relation races for the mediocre majority, where every so often a new blazing star scorched out of the ruck on its way to fame.

Running horses in novice hurdles meant starting from

home early or getting back late; but there were far more runners in novice hurdles than in any other type of race.

When I left it was Jossie who came back with me through the entrance hall to see me off. As we crossed a vast decrepit Persian rug I glanced at the large dark portraits occupying acres of wall space.

'Those are Nantuckets, of course,' she said, following my gaze. 'They came with the house.'

'Po-faced lot,' I said.

'You did know that Dad doesn't actually own all this?'

'Yes, I actually did know.' I smiled to myself, but she saw it.

She said defensively, 'All right, but you'd be surprised how many people make up to me, thinking that they'll marry the trainer's daughter and step into all this when he retires.'

'So you like to establish the ground rules first?'

'OK, greyhound-brain, I'd forgotten you'd know from Trevor.'

I knew in general that Axwood Stables Ltd belonged to an American family, the Nantuckets, who rarely took much personal interest in the place except as a business asset. It had been bought and brought to greatness in the fifties by a rumbustious tycoon thrown up atypically from prudent banking stock. Old Naylor Nantucket had brought his energies and enterprise to England, had fallen in love with English racing, had built a splendid modern stable yard and filled it with splendid horses. He had engaged the young William Finch to train them for him, and the middle-aged William Finch was still doing it for his heirs, except that nowadays nine tenths of the horses belonged to other owners, and the young Nantuckets, faintly ashamed of Uncle Naylor, never crossed the Atlantic to see their own horses perform.

'Doesn't your father ever get tired of training for absent owners?' I said.

'No. They don't argue. They don't ring him up in the middle of the night. And when they lose, they don't complain. He says training would be a lot easier if *all* owners lived in New York.'

She stood on the doorstep to wave me goodbye, assured and half-mocking, a girl with bright brown eyes, graceful neck, and neat nose and mouth in between.

I booked into the Gloucester Hotel, where I'd never stayed before, and ate a leisurely and much needed dinner in a nearby restaurant. I shouldn't have accepted the ride on Notebook, I thought ruefully; I'd hardly enough strength to cut up a steak.

A strong feeling of walking blindfold towards a precipice dragged at my feet all the way to Vivian Iverson's gambling club. I didn't know which way the precipice lay: ahead, behind, or all round. I only suspected that it was still there, and if I did nothing about finding it, I could walk straight over.

The Vivat Club proved as suave and well-manicured as its owner, and was a matter of interconnecting small rooms, not open expanses like casinos. There were no croupiers in eye-shades with bright dramatic spotlights over the tables, and no ladies tinkling with diamonds in half shadow. There were however two or three discreet chandeliers, a good deal of cigar smoke, and a sort of reverent hush.

Vivian, good as his word, had left a note for me to be let in, and as an extra, treated as a guest. I walked slowly from room to room, balloon glass of brandy in hand, looking for his elegant shape, and not finding it.

There were a good many businessmen in lounge suits earnestly playing chemin-de-fer, and women among them with eyes that flicked concentratedly from side to side with every delivered card. I'd never had an urge towards betting for hours on the turn of a card, but everyone to his own poison.

'Ro, my dear fellow,' Vivian said behind me. 'Come to play?'

'On an accountant's earnings?' I said, turning to him and smiling. 'What are the stakes?'

'Whatever you can afford to lose, my dear fellow.'

'Life, liberty, and a ticket to the Cup Final.'

His eyes didn't smile as thoroughly as his mouth. 'Some people lose honour, fortunes, reputation, and their heads.'

'Does it disturb you?' I asked.

He made a small waving gesture towards the chemin-de-fer. 'I provide a pastime to cater for an impulse. Like bingo.'

He put his hand on my shoulder as if we were long-lost friends and steered me towards a further room. There were heavy gold links in his cuffs, and a silk cord edging to his blue velvet jacket. Dark glossy hair on a well-shaped head, flat stomach, faint smell of fresh talc. About thirty-five, and shrewdly succeeding where others had fallen to bailiffs.

There was a green baize raised-edge gaming table in the further room, but no one was playing cards.

Behind the table, in the club's ubiquitous wooden-armed, studded-leather armchairs, sat three men.

They were all large, smoothly dressed, and unfriendly. I knew them, from way back.

Connaught Powys. Glitberg. Ownslow.

'We hear you're looking for us,' Connaught Powys said.

CHAPTER NINE

I stood still. Vivian closed the door behind me and sat in another armchair on the edge of my left-hand vision. He crossed one leg elegantly over the other and eased the cloth over the knee with a languid hand.

Ownslow watched with disfavour.

'Piss off,' he said.

Vivian's answer was an extra-sophisticated drawl. 'My dear fellow, I may have set him up, but you've no licence to knock him down.'

There were several other empty chairs, pulled back haphazardly from the centre table. I sat unhurriedly in one of them and did my best with Vivian's leg-crossing ritual, hoping that casualness would reduce the atmosphere from bash-up to boardroom. Ownslow's malevolent stare hardly persuaded me that I'd succeeded.

Ownslow and Glitberg had run a flourishing construction racket for years, robbing the ratepayers of literally millions. Like all huge frauds, theirs had been done on paper, with Glitberg in the council's Planning Office, and

127

Ownslow in the Works and Maintenance. They had simply invented a large number of buildings: offices, flats and housing estates. The whole council having approved the buildings in principle, Glitberg, in his official capacity, advertised for tenders from developers. The lowest good-looking tender often came from a firm called National Construction (Wessex) Ltd and the council confidently entrusted the building to them.

National Construction (Wessex) Ltd did not exist except as expensively produced lettterheads. The sanctioned buildings were never built. Huge sums of money were authorized and paid to National Construction (Wessex) Ltd, and regular reports of the buildings' progress came back as Glitberg, from Planning, made regular inspections. After the point when the buildings were passed as ready for occupation the Maintenance department took over. Ownslow's men maintained bonafide buildings, and Ownslow also requisitioned huge sums for the maintenance of the well-documented imaginary lot.

All the paperwork had been punctiliously, even brilliantly, completed. There were full records of rents received from the imaginary buildings, and rates paid by the imaginary tenants; but as all councils took it for granted that council buildings had to be heavily subsidized, the permanent gap between revenue and expenditure was accepted as normal.

Like many big frauds it had been uncovered by accident, and the accident had been my digging a little too deeply into the affairs of one of the smaller operators sharing in the crumbs of the greater rip-off.

The council, when I'd informed them, had refused to believe me. Not, that was, until they toured their area in detail, and found weedy grass where they had paid for, among other things, six storeys of flats for low-income families, a cul-de-sac of maisonettes for single pensioners, and two roadfuls of semi-detached bungalows for the retired and handicapped.

Blind-eye money had obviously been passed to various council members, but bribery in cash was hard to prove. The council had been publicly embarrassed and had not forgiven me. Glitberg and Ownslow, who had seen that the caper could not continue for ever, had been already preparing a quiet departure when the police descended on them in force on a Sunday afternoon. They had not exactly forgiven me either.

In line with all their other attention to detail, neither of them had made the mistake of living above his legal income. The huge sums they had creamed off had been withdrawn from the National Construction (Wessex) Ltd bank account over the years as a stream of cheques and cash which had aroused no suspicion at the bank, and had then apparently vanished into thin air. Of the million-plus which they had each stolen, not a pound had been recovered.

'Whatever you want from us,' Glitberg said, 'you're not going to get.'

'You're a danger to us,' Connaught Powys said.

'And like a wasp, you'll get swatted,' said Ownslow.

I looked at their faces. All three showed the pudgy roundness of self-indulgence, and all three had the sharp, wary eyes of guilt. Separately, Connaught Powys, with his sun-lamp tan and smoothly brushed hair, looked a high-up City gent. Heavy of body, in navy blue pin-stripes. Pale grey silk tie. Overall air of power and opulence, and not a whisper of cell-fug and slopping-out in the mornings.

Ownslow in jail was an easier picture. Fairish hair straggled to his collar from a fringe round a bald dome. Thick neck, bull shoulders, hands like baseball gloves. A hard, tough man whose accent came from worlds away from Connaught Powys.

Glitberg, in glasses, had short bushy grey hair and a fanned-out spread of white side-whiskers, which made him look like a species of ape. If Connaught Powys was power, and Ownslow was muscle, Glitberg was venom.

'Have you already tried?' I said.

'Tried what?' Ownslow said.

'Swatting.'

They stared, all three of them, without expression, at some point in the air between myself and Vivian.

'Someone has,' I said.

Connaught Powys smiled very slightly. 'Whatever we have done, or intend to do, about you,' he said, 'we are not going to be so insane as to admit it in front of a witness.'

'You'll be looking over your shoulder for the rest of your life,' Glitberg said, with satisfaction.

'Don't go near building sites on a dark night,' Ownslow said. 'There's a bit of advice, free, gratis and for nothing.'

'How about a sailing boat on a dark night?' I said. 'An ocean-going sailing boat.'

I wished at once that I hadn't said it. The unfriendliness on all three faces hardened to menace, and the whole room became very still.

Into the silence came Vivian's voice, relaxed and drawling. 'Ro . . . time you and I had a drink together, don't you think?'

He unfolded himself from his chair, and I, feeling fairly weak at the knees, stood up from mine.

Connaught Powys, Glitberg, and Ownslow delivered a collective look of such hatred that even Vivian began to look nervous. His hand fumbled with the door knob, and as he left the room, behind me, he almost tripped over his own feet.

'Whew,' he said in my ear. 'You do play with big rough boys, my dear fellow.' He steered me this time into a luxurious little office; three armchairs, all safely unoccupied. He waved me to one of them and poured brandy into two balloons.

'It's not what they say,' he said, 'as how they say it.'

'And what they don't say.'

He looked at me speculatively over his glass.

'Did you get what you wanted? I mean, was it worth your while, running under their guns?'

I smiled twistedly. 'I think I got an answer.'

'Well then.'

'Yes. But it was to a question I didn't ask.'

'I don't follow you.'

'I'm afraid,' I said slowly, 'that I've made everything a great deal worse.'

I slept soundly at the Gloucester, but more from exhaustion than an easy mind.

From the racing page of the newspaper delivered under my door in the morning I saw that my name was down in the list of runners as the rider of Notebook in the last race at Towcester. I sucked my teeth. I hadn't thought of asking William Finch not to include me in his list for the press, and now the whole world would learn where I would be that afternoon at four-thirty. If, that was, they bothered to turn to an insignificant race at a minor meeting on Grand National day.

'You'll be looking over your shoulder for the rest of your life,' Glitberg had said.

I didn't intend to. Life would be impossible if I feared for demons in every shadow. I wouldn't climb trustingly into any ambulances at Towcester, but I would go and ride there. There was an awfully thin line, it seemed to me, between cowardice and caution.

Jossie, waiting outside the weighing room, sent the heeby-jeebies flying.

'Hello,' she said. 'Notebook is here, looking his usual noble self and about to turn in his standard useless performance.'

'Charming.'

'The trainer's orders to the jockey,' she said, 'are succinct. Stay on, and stay out of trouble. He doesn't want you getting hurt.'

'Nor do I,' I said with feeling.

'He doesn't want anything to spoil the day if Ivansky wins the National.'

'Ah,' I said. 'Does he think he will?'

'He flew off in the air-taxi this morning in the usual agonized euphoria,' she said, with affection. 'Hope zigzagging from conviction to doubt.'

Finch had sent two horses to Towcester, the second of them, Stoolery, being the real reason for Jossie's journey. I helped her saddle it for the two mile handicap 'chase, and cheered with her on the stands when it won. The Grand National itself was transmitted on television all over the racecourse straight afterwards, so that Jossie was already consoled when Ivansky finished fifth.

'Oh well.' She shrugged. 'That's that. Dad will feel flat, the owners will feel flat, the lads will get gloomily drunk, and then they'll all start talking about next year.'

We strolled along without much purpose and arrived at the door to the bar.

'Like a drink?' I asked.

'Might pass the time.'

The bar was crowded with people dissecting the National result, and the elbowing customers jockeying for service were four deep.

'Don't let's bother,' Jossie said.

I agreed. We turned to leave, and a thin hand stretched out from the tight pressed ranks and gripped my wrist hard.

'What do you want?' a voice shouted over the din. 'I've just got served. What do you want? Quick!'

The hand, I saw, belonged to Moira Longerman, and beyond her, scowling as usual, stood Binny Tomkins.

'Jossie?' I said.

'Fruit juice. Grapefruit if poss.'

'Two grapefruit juice,' I said.

The hand let go and disappeared, shortly to reappear with a glass in it. I took it, and also the next issue, and finally Moira Longerman herself, followed by Binny, fought her way out of the throng, holding two glasses high to avoid having the expensive thimblefuls knocked flying.

'How super!' she said. 'I saw you in the distance just now. I've been trying to telephone you for weeks and now I hear some extraordinary story about you being kidnapped.'

I introduced Jossie who was looking disbelievingly at what Moira had said.

'Kidnapped?' Her eyebrows rose comically. 'You?'

'You may well laugh,' I said ruefully.

Moira handed a glass to Binny, who nodded a scant thanks. Graceless man, I thought. Extraordinary to leave any woman to fight her way to get him a drink, let alone the owner of the most important horse in his yard. She was paying, of course.

'My *dear*,' Moira Longerman said to Jossie. 'Right after Ro won the Gold Cup on my darling Tapestry, someone kidnapped him from the racecourse. Isn't that right?' She beamed quizzically up at my face, her blue eyes alight with friendly interest.

'Sure is,' I agreed.

Binny scowled some more.

'How's the horse?' I said.

Binny gave me a hard stare and didn't answer, but Moira Longerman was overflowing with news and enthusiasm.

'I do so want you to ride Tapestry in all his races from now on, Ro, so I hope you will. He's ready for Ascot next Wednesday, Binny says, and I've been trying and trying to get hold of you to see if you'll ride him.'

Binny said sourly, 'I've already engaged another jockey.'

'Then disengage him, Binny dear.' Underneath the friendly birdlike brightness there was the same touch of steel which had got me the Gold Cup ride in the first place. Moira might be half Binny's physical weight but she had twice the mental muscle.

'It might be better to let this other chap ride ...' I began.

'No, no,' she interrupted. 'It's you I want, Ro. I won't have anyone else. I told Binny that, quite definitely, the very moment after you'd won the Cup. Now you're back and safe again it will either be you on my horse or I won't run him.' She glanced defiantly at Binny, impishly at Jossie, and with a determined nod of her blonde curly head, expectantly turned to me. 'Well? What do you say?'

'Er,' I said, which was hardly helpful.

'Oh go on,' Jossie said. 'You'll have to.'

Binny's scowl switched targets. Jossie caught the full blast and showed no discomfiture at all.

'He did win the Gold Cup,' she said. 'You can't say he isn't capable.'

'He does say that, my dear,' beamed Moira Longerman happily. 'Isn't it odd?'

Binny muttered something blackly of which the only audible word was 'amateurs'.

'I think that what Binny really means,' said Moira sweetly and distinctly. 'is that Ro, like most amateurs, always tries very hard to win, and won't listen to propositions to the contrary.'

Binny's face turned a dark red. Jossie practically giggled. Moira looked at me with limpid blue eyes as if not quite aware of what she'd said, and I chewed around helplessly for a sensible answer.

'Like most *jockeys*,' I said finally.

'You're so nice, Ro,' she said. 'You think everyone's honest.'

I tended, like most accountants, to think exactly the opposite, but as it happened I had never much wondered about Binny. To train a horse like Tapestry should have been enough, without trying to rig his results.

Binny himself had decided to misunderstand what Moira had said, and was pretending that he hadn't seen the chasm that was opening at his feet. Moira gave him a mischievous glance and allowed him no illusions about her power to push him in.

'Binny dear,' she said, 'I'll never desert the man who trained a Gold Cup winner for me. Not as long as he keeps turning out my horses beautifully fit, and I choose who rides them.'

Jossie cleared her throat in the following silence and said encouragingly to Binny, 'I expect you had a good bet in the Gold Cup? My father always puts a bit on in the Cup and the National. Too awful if you win, and you haven't. Makes you look such an ass, he says.'

If she had tried to rub salt into his raw wounds, it appeared she couldn't have done a better job. Moira Longerman gave a delighted laugh.

'You naughty girl,' she said, patting Jossie's arm. 'Poor Binny had so little faith, you see, that not only did he not back Tapestry to win, but I've heard he unfortunately laid it to lose. Such a pity. Poor Binny, winning the Gold Cup and ending up out of pocket.'

Binny looked so appalled that I gathered the extent of her information was a nasty shock to him.

'Never mind,' Moira said kindly. 'What's past is past.

And if Ro rides Tapestry next Wednesday, all will be well.'

Binny looked as if everything would be very far from well. I wondered idly if he could possibly have already arranged that Tapestry should lose on Wednesday. On his first outing after a Gold Cup win, any horse would start at short odds. Many a bookmaker would be grateful to know for certain that he wouldn't have to pay out. Binny could already have sold that welcome information, thinking that I wasn't around to upset things. Binny was having a thoroughly bad time.

I reflected that I simply couldn't afford to take Wednesday off. The mountains of undone work made me feel faintly sick.

'Ro?' Moira said persuasively.

'Yes,' I said. 'Nothing I'd like better in the world.'

'Oh goody!' Her eyes sparkled with pleasure. 'I'll see you at Ascot, then. Binny will ring you, of course, if there's a change of plan.'

Binny scowled.

'Tell me all,' Jossie demanded as we walked across to the trainers' stand to watch the next race. 'All this drama about you being kidnapped.'

I told her briefly, without much detail.

'Do you mean they just popped you on a boat and sailed off with you to the Med?'

'That's right.'

138

'What a lark.'

'It was inconvenient,' I said mildly.

'I'll bet.' She paused. 'You said you escaped. How did you do that?'

'Jumped overboard.'

Her mouth twisted with sympathy. I reflected that it was only four days since that frantic swim. It seemed another world.

Jossie was of the real, sensible world, where things were understandable, if not always pleasant. Being with her made me feel a great deal more settled, more normal, and safer.

'How about dinner,' I said, 'on the way home?'

'We've got two cars,' she said.

'Nothing to prevent them both stopping at the same place.'

'How true.'

She was again wearing swirly clothes: a soft rusty red, this time. There was nothing tailored about her, and nothing untidy. An organized girl, amusing and amused.

'There's a fair pub near Oxford,' I said.

'I'll follow you, then.'

I changed in due course for Notebook's race, and weighed out, and gave my lightest saddle to the Axwood travelling head lad, who was waiting for it by the door.

'Carrying overweight, are you?' he said sardonically.

'Four pounds.'

He made an eyes-to-heaven gesture, saying louder than words that trainers should put up professionals in

novice hurdle races, not amateurs who couldn't do ten
stone six. I didn't mention that on Gold Cup day I'd
weighed eight pounds more.

When I went out to the parade ring, he and Jossie
were waiting, while a lad led the noble Notebook round
and round, now wearing my saddle over a number cloth.
Number thirteen. So who was superstitious?

'He bucks a bit,' said the travelling head lad, with
satisfaction.

'When you get home,' Jossie said to him, 'please tell
my father I'm stopping on the way back for dinner with
Roland. So that he doesn't worry about car crashes.'

'Right.'

'Dad fusses,' Jossie said.

The travelling head lad gave me another look which
needed no words, and which speculated on whether I
would get her into bed. I wasn't so sure that I cared all
that much for the travelling head lad.

A good many people had already gone home, and
from the parade ring one could see a steady drift to the
gate. There were few things as disheartening, I thought,
as playing to a vanishing audience. On the other hand, if
one made a frightful mess, the fewer who saw it, the
better.

'They said "jockeys get mounted" half an hour ago,'
Jossie said.

'Two seconds,' I said. 'I was listening.'

The travelling head lad gave me a leg up. Notebook
gave a trial buck.

'Stay out of trouble,' Jossie said.

'It's underneath me,' I said, feeling the noble animal again try to shoot me off.

She grinned unfeelingly. Notebook bounced away, hiccupped sideways down to the start, and then kept everyone waiting while he did a circus act on his hind legs. 'Bucks a bit', I thought bitterly. I'd fall off before the tapes went up, if I wasn't careful.

The race started, and Notebook magnanimously decided to take part, setting off at an uncoordinated gallop which involved a good deal of head-shaking and yawing from side to side. His approach to the first hurdle induced severe loss of confidence in his rider, as he seemed to be trying to jump it sideways, like a crab.

As I hadn't taken the precaution of dropping him out firmly at the back, always supposing I could actually have managed it, as he was as strong as he was wilful, his diagonal crossing of the flight of hurdles harvested a barrage of curses from the other jockeys. 'Sorry' was a useless word in a hurdle race, particularly from an unfit amateur who should have known better than to be led astray by a pretty girl. I yanked Notebook's head straight at the next hurdle with a force which would have had the Cruelty to Animals people swooning. He retaliated by screwing his hindquarters sideways in mid-air and landing on all four feet at once, pointing east-north-east to the rails.

This manoeuvre at least dropped him out into last place, which he tried to put right by running away with me up the stretch in front of the stands. As we fought each other on the way outwards round the mile-and-a-half circuit I understood the full meaning of the trainer's orders to his jockey. 'Stay on, and stay out of trouble.' My God.

I was not in the least surprised that Notebook had finished last of twenty-six at Newbury. He would have been last of a hundred and twenty-six, if his jockey had had any sense. Last place on Notebook was not exactly safe, but if one had to be anywhere on him, last place was wisest. No one, however, had got the message through to the horse.

The circuit at Towcester went out downhill from the stands, flattened into a straight stretch on the far side, and ended with a stamina-sapping uphill pull to the finishing straight and the winning post. Some of the world's slowest finishes had been slogged out there on muddy days at the end of three-mile 'chases. Notebook however set off downhill on firm going at a graceless rush, roller-coastered over the most distant hurdles, and only began to lose interest when he hit the sharply rising ground on the way back.

By that time the nineteen other runners were ahead as of right, as Notebook's stop-go and sideways type of jumping lost at every flight the lengths he made up on the flat.

I suppose I relaxed a little. He met the next hurdle all wrong, ignored my bid to help him, screwed wildly in mid-air, and landed with his nose on the turf and all four feet close together behind it. Not radically different from six other landings, just more extreme.

Being catapulted off at approximately thirty miles an hour is a kaleidoscopic business. Sky, trees, rails and grass somersaulted around my vision in a disjointed jumble, and if I tucked my head in it was from instinct, not thought. The turf smacked me sharply in several places, and Notebook delivered a parting kick on the thigh. The world stopped rolling, and half a ton of horse had not come crashing down on top of me. Life would go on.

I sat up slowly, all breath knocked out, and watched the noble hindquarters charge heedlessly away.

An ambulance man ran towards me, in the familiar black St John's uniform. I felt a flood of panic. A conditioned reflex. He had a kind face: a total stranger.

'All right, mate?' he said.

I nodded weakly.

'You came a proper purler.'

'Mm.' I unclipped my helmet, and pulled it off. Speech was impossible. My chest heaved from lack of air. He put a hand under one of my armpits and helped me as far as my knees, and from there, once I could breathe properly, to my feet.

'Bones OK?'

I nodded.

'Just winded,' he said cheerfully.

'Mm.'

A Land Rover arrived beside us with a jerk, and the vet inside it said that as there were no injured horses needing his attention, he could offer me a lift back to the stands.

'You fell off,' Jossie observed, as I emerged with normal breath and clean bill of health from the doctor in the First Aid room.

I smiled, 'Granted.'

She gave me a sideways glance from the huge eyes.

'I thought all jockeys were frightfully touchy about being told they fell off,' she said. 'All that guff about it's the horse that falls, and the jockey just goes down with the ship.'

'Quite right,' I said.

'But Notebook didn't actually fall, so you fell off.' Her voice was lofty, teasing.

'I don't dispute it.'

'No, aren't you boring.' She smiled. 'They caught Notebook in the next parish, so while you change I'll go along to the stables and see he's OK, and I'll meet you in the car park.'

'Fine.'

I changed into street clothes, fixed with the valet to take my saddles, helmet, and other gear to Ascot for the following Wednesday, and walked the short distance to the car park.

The crowds had gone, and only the stragglers like me were leaving now in twos and threes. The cars still remaining stood singly, haphazardly scattered instead of in orderly rows.

I looked into the back of mine, behind the front seats.

No one there.

I wondered with a shiver what I would have done if there had been. Run a mile, no doubt. I stood leaning on my car waiting for Jossie, and no one looked in the least like trying to carry me off. A quiet spring-like Saturday evening in the Northamptonshire countryside, as friendly as beer.

CHAPTER TEN

She followed me in her pale blue Midget to the pub on the south side of Oxford, and chose a long cold drink with fruit on the top and a kick in the tail.

'Dad has schooled Notebook until he's blue in the face,' she said, pursing her lips to the straw which stuck up like a mast from the log-jam of fruit.

'Some of them never learn,' I said.

She nodded. Polite transaction achieved, I thought: she had obliquely apologized for the horse's frightful behaviour, and I had accepted that her father had done his best to teach him to jump. Some trainers, but not those of William Finch's standing, seemed to think that the best place for a green novice to learn to jump was actually in a race: rather like urging a child up the Eiger without showing him how to climb.

'What made you become an accountant?' she said. 'It's such a dull sort of job.'

'Do you think so?'

She gave me the full benefit of the big eyes. 'You obviously don't,' she said. She tilted her head a little, considering. 'You don't *look* boring and stuffy, and you don't *act* boring and stuffy, so give.'

'Judges are sober, nurses are dedicated, miners are heroes, writers drink.'

'Or in other words, don't expect people to fit the image?'

'As you say,' I said.

She smiled. 'I've known Trevor since I was six.'

A nasty one. Trevor, without any stretch of imagination, could fairly be classed as stuffy and boring.

'Carry on,' she said. 'Why?'

'Security. Steady employment. Good pay. The usual inducements.'

She looked at me levelly. 'You're lying.'

'What makes you think so?'

'People who risk their necks for nothing in jump races are not hell-bent on security, steady employment, and money.'

'Because of me Mum, then,' I said flippantly.

'She bossed you into it?'

'No.' I hesitated, because in fact I never had told anyone why I'd grown up with a fiery zeal as powerful as a vocation. Jossie waited with quizzical expectation.

'She had a rotten accountant,' I said. 'I promised her that when I grew up I would take over. As corny as that.'

'And did you?'

'No. She died.'

'Sob story.'

'Yes, I told you. Pure corn.'

147

She stirred the fruit with her straw, looking less mocking. 'You're afraid I'll laugh at you.'

'Sure of it,' I said.

'Try me, then.'

'Well . . . she was a rotten businesswoman, my Mum. My father got killed in a pointless sort of accident, and she was left having to bring me up alone. She was about thirty. I was nine.' I paused. Jossie was not actually laughing, so I struggled on. 'She rented a house just off the sea-front at Ryde and ran it as a holiday hotel, half a step up from a boarding house. Comfortable, but no drinks licence; that sort of thing. So she could be there when I got home from school, and in the holidays.'

'Brave of her,' Jossie said. 'Go on.'

'You can guess.'

She sucked down to the dregs of her glass and made a bubbling noise through the straw. 'Sure,' she said. 'She was good at cooking and welcoming people and lousy at working out how much to charge.'

'She was also paying tax on money she should have claimed as expenses.'

'And that's bad?'

'Crazy.'

'Well, go on,' she said encouragingly. 'Digging a story out of you is worse than looking for mushrooms.'

'I found her crying sometimes, mostly in the winter when there weren't any guests. It's pretty upsetting for a kid of ten or so to find his mother crying, so you can say I was upset. Protective also, probably. Anyway, at first

I thought it was still because of losing Dad. Then I realized she always cried when she'd been seeing Mr Jones, who was her accountant. I tried to get her to open up on her troubles, but she said I was too young.'

I stopped again. Jossie sighed with exasperation and said, 'Do get *on* with it.'

'I told her to ditch Mr Jones and get someone else. She said I didn't understand, I was too young. I promised her that when I got older I would be an accountant, and I'd put her affairs to rights.' I smiled lopsidedly. 'When I was thirteen she went down to Boots one morning and bought two hundred aspirins. She stirred them into a glass of water, and drank them. I found her lying on her bed when I came home from school. She left me a note.'

'What did it say?'

'It said "Dear Ro, Sorry, Love, Mum." '

'Poor girl.' Jossie blinked. Not laughing.

'She'd made a will,' I said. 'One of those simple things on a form from the stationers. She left me everything, which was actually nothing much except her own personal things. I kept all the account books and bank statements. I got shuttled around uncles and aunts for a few years, but I kept those account books safe, and then I got another accountant to look at them. He told me Mr Jones seemed to have thought he was working for the Inland Revenue, not his client. I told him I wanted to be an accountant, and I got him to show me exactly what Mr Jones had done wrong. So there you are. That's all.'

'Are you still killing Mr Jones to dry your mother's tears?' The teasing note was back, but gentler.

I smiled, 'I enjoy accountancy. I might never have thought of it if it hadn't been for Mr Jones.'

'So God bless villains.'

'He was ultra-righteous. A smug pompous ass. There are still a lot of Mr Joneses around, not pointing out to their clients all the legitimate ways of avoiding tax.'

'Huh?'

'It's silly to pay tax when you don't have to.'

'That's obvious.'

'A lot of people do, though, from ignorance or bad advice.'

I ordered refill drinks and told Jossie it was her turn to unbutton with the family skeletons.

'My Ma?' she said in surprise. 'I thought the whole world knew about my Ma. She canoes up and down the Amazon like a yo-yo, digging up ancient tribes. Sends back dispatches in the shape of earnest papers to obscure magazines. Dad and I haven't seen her for years. We get telegrams in January saying Happy Christmas.'

Revelation dawned. 'Christabel Saffray Finch! Intrepid female explorer, storming about in rain forests?'

'Ma,' Jossie nodded.

'Good heavens.'

'Good grief, more like.'

'Trevor never told me,' I said. 'But then he wouldn't, I suppose.'

Jossie grinned. 'Trevor disapproves. Trevor also

always disapproves of Dad's little consolations. Aunts, I used to call them. Now I call them Lida and Sandy.'

'He's very discreet.' Even on the racecourse, where gossip was a second occupation, I hadn't heard of Lida and Sandy. Or that Christabel Saffray Finch, darling of anthropological documentaries, was William's wife.

'Sandy is his ever-sick secretary,' Jossie said, 'perpetually shuttling between bronchitis, backache and abortion.'

I laughed. 'And Lida?'

Jossie made a face, suddenly vulnerable under all the bright froth.

'Lida's got her hooks into him like a tapeworm. I can't stand her. Let's talk about food; I'm starving.'

We read the menu and ordered, and finished our drinks, and went in to dinner in the centuries-old dining-room: stone walls, uncovered oak beams, red velvet and soft lights.

Jossie ate as if waistlines never expanded, which was refreshing after the finicky picker I'd taken out last.

'Luck of the draw,' she said complacently, smothering a baked-in-the-skin potato with a butter mountain. I reflected that she'd drawn lucky in more ways than metabolism. A quick mind, fascinating face, tall, slender body: there was nothing egalitarian about nature.

Most of the tables around us were filled with softly chattering groups of twos and fours, but over by a far wall a larger party were making the lion's share of the noise.

151

'They keep looking over here,' Jossie said. 'Do you know them?'

'It looks like Sticks Elroy with his back to us.'

'Is it? Celebrating his winner?'

Sticks Elroy, named for the extreme thinness of his legs, had studiously avoided me in the Towcester changing room, and must have been thoroughly disconcerted to find me having dinner in his local pub. He was one of my jockey clients, but for how much longer was problematical. I was not currently his favourite person.

The noise, however, was coming not from him but from the host of the party, a stubborn-looking man with a naturally loud voice.

'Avert your gaze,' I said to Jossie.

The large eyes regarded me over salad and steak.

'An ostrich act?' she said.

I nodded. 'If we bury our heads, maybe the storm won't notice us.'

The storm, however, seemed to be gathering force. Words like 'bastard' rose easily above the prevailing clatter and the uninvolved majority began to look interested.

'Trouble,' Josie said without visible regret, 'is on its feet and heading this way.'

'Damn.'

She grinned. 'Faint heart.'

Trouble arrived with the deliberate movements of the slightly drunk. Late forties, I judged. About five feet

eight, short dark hair, flushed cheeks and aggressive eyes.
He stood four-square and ignored Jossie altogether.

'My son tells me you're that bastard Roland Britten.'
His voice, apart from fortissimo, was faintly slurred.

To ignore him was to invite a punch-up. I laid down
my knife and fork. Leaned back in my chair. Behaved as
if the enquiry was polite.

'Is Sticks Elroy your son?'

'Too right, he bloody is,' he said.

'He had a nice winner today,' I said. 'Well done.'

It stopped him for barely two seconds.

'He doesn't need your bloody "well done".'

I waited mildly, without answering. Elroy senior bent
down, breathed alcohol heavily, and pointed an accusing
finger under my nose.

'You leave my son alone, see? He isn't doing anyone
any harm. He doesn't want any bastard like you snitching
on him to the bloody tax man. Judas, that's what you are.
Going behind his back. Bloody informer, that's what you
are.'

'I haven't informed on him.'

'What's that?' He wagged the finger to and fro, belligerently. 'Costing him hundreds, aren't you, with the
bloody tax man. Bastard like you ought to be locked up.
Serve you bloody well right.'

The head waiter arrived smoothly at Elroy's shoulder.

'Excuse me, sir,' he began.

Elroy turned on him like a bull. 'You trot off. You
majordomo, or whatever you are. You trot off. I'll have

my say, and when I've had my say I'll sit down, see? Not before.'

The head waiter cravenly retired, and Elroy returned to his prime target. Jossie's eyes stared at him with disfavour, which deflected him not at all.

'I hear someone locked you up for ten days or so just now, and you got out. Bloody shame. You deserve to be locked up, you do. Bastard like you. Whoever it was locked you up had the right idea.'

I said nothing. Elroy half turned away, but he had by no means finished. Merely addressing a wider audience.

'You know what this bastard did to my son?' The audience removed its eyes in thoroughly British embarrassment, but they got told the answer whether they liked it or not.

'This boot-licking, creeping bastard went crawling to the tax man and told him my son had some cash he hadn't paid taxes on.'

'I didn't,' I said to Jossie.

He swung round to me again and poked the finger rigidly under my nose. 'Bloody liar. Locking up's too bloody good for bastards like you.'

The manager arrived, with the head waiter hovering behind.

'Mr Elroy,' the manager said courteously. 'A bottle of wine for your party, compliments of the management.' He beckoned a finger to the head waiter, who deftly proffered a bottle of claret.

The manager was young and well-dressed, and

reminded me of Vivian Iverson. His unexpected oil worked marvels on the storm, which abated amid a few extra 'bastards' and went back to its table muttering under its breath.

The people at the other tables watched from the cover of animated conversation, while the head waiter drew the cork for Elroy and poured the free wine. The manager drifted casually back to Jossie and me.

'There will be no charge for your dinner, sir.' He paused delicately. 'Mr Elroy is a valued customer.' He bowed very slightly and drifted on without waiting for an answer.

'How cool of him,' Josie said, near explosion.

'How professional.'

She stared at me. 'Do you often sit still and let people call you a bastard?'

'Once a week and twice on Sundays.'

'Spineless.'

'If I'd stood up and slogged him, our steaks would have gone cold.'

'Mine has, anyway.'

'Have another,' I said. I started to eat again where I had left off, and so, after a moment or two, did Jossie.

'Go on,' she said. 'I'm all agog. Just what was that all about?' She looked round the restaurant. 'You are now the target of whispers, and the consensus looks unfavourable.'

'In general,' I said, spearing lettuce, 'people shouldn't expect their accountants to help them break the law.'

'Sticks?'

'And accountants unfortunately cannot discuss their clients.'

'Are you being serious?'

I sighed. 'A client who wants his accountant to connive at a massive piece of tax-dodging is not going to be madly pleased when the accountant refuses to do it.'

'Mm.' She chewed cheerfully. 'I do see that.'

'And,' I went on, 'an accountant who advises such a client to declare the loot and pay the tax, because otherwise the nasty Revenue men will undoubtedly find out, and the client will have to pay fines on top of tax and will end up very poorly all round, because not only will he get it in the neck for that one offence, but every tax return he makes in the future will be inspected with magnifying glasses and he'll be hounded for evermore over every penny and have inspectors ransacking every cranny of his house at two in the morning . . .' I took a breath ' . . . such an accountant may be unpopular.'

'Unreasonable.'

'And an accountant who refuses to break the law, and says that if his client insists on doing so he will have to take his custom somewhere else, such an accountant may possibly be called a bastard.'

She finished her steak and laid down her knife and fork. 'Does this hypothetical accountant snitch to the tax man?'

I smiled. 'If the client is no longer his client, he doesn't know whether his ex-client is tax-dodging or not. So no, he doesn't snitch.'

'Elroy had it all wrong, then.'

'Er,' I said, 'it was he who set up the scheme from which Sticks drew the cash. That's why he is so furious. And I shouldn't be telling you that.'

'You'll be struck off, or strung up, or whatever.'

'Sky high.' I drank some wine. 'It's quite extraordinary how many people try to get their accountants to help them with tax fiddles. I reckon if someone wants to fiddle, the last person he should tell should be his accountant.'

'Just get on with it, and keep quiet?'

'If they want to take the risk.'

She half laughed. 'What risk? Tax-dodging is a national sport.'

People never understood about taxation, I thought. The ruthlessness with which tax could be collected put Victorian landlords in the shade, and the Revenue people now had frightening extra powers of entry and search.

'It's much safer to steal from your employer than the tax man,' I said.

'You must be joking.'

'Have some profiteroles,' I said.

Jossie eyed the approaching trolley of super-puds and agreed on four small cream-filled buns smothered in chocolate sauce.

'Aren't you having any?' she demanded.

'Think of Tapestry on Wednesday.'

'No wonder jockeys get fat when they finally let themselves eat.' She spooned up the dark brown goo with satisfaction. 'Why is it safer to steal from your employer?'

'He can't sell your belongings to get his money back.'

The big eyes widened.

'Golly!' she said.

'If you run up debts, the courts can send bailiffs to take your furniture. If you steal instead, they can't.'

She paused blankly in mid-mouthful, then went on chewing, and swallowed. 'Carry right on,' she said. 'I'm riveted.'

'Well . . . it's theft which is the national sport, not tax-dodging. Petty theft. Knocking off. Nicking. Most shop-lifting is done by the staff, not the customers. No one really blames a girl who sells tights all day if she tucks a pair into her handbag when she goes home. Pinching from employers is almost regarded as a rightful perk, and if ever a manufacturing firm puts an efficient checker on the staff exits there's practically a riot until he's removed.'

'Because he stops the outward march of spanners and fork-lift trucks?'

I grinned. 'You could feed an army on what disappears from the fridges of hotels.'

'Accountants,' she said, 'shouldn't find it amusing.'

'Especially as they spend their lives looking for fraud.'

'Do you?' she said, surprised. 'Do you really? I thought accountants just did sums.'

'The main purpose of an audit is to turn up fiddles.'

'I thought it was ... well ... to add up the profit or loss.'

'Not really.'

She thought. 'But when Trevor comes to count the hay and saddles and stuff, that's stocktaking.'

I shook my head. 'More like checking on behalf of your father that he hasn't got a stable lad selling the odd bale or bridle on the quiet.'

'Good heavens.' She was truly astounded. 'I'll have to stop thinking of auditors as fuddy-duddies. Change their image to fraud squad policemen.'

'Not that, either.'

'Why not?'

'If an auditor finds that a firm is being swindled by its cashier, for instance, he simply tells the firm. He doesn't arrest the cashier. He leaves it to the firm to decide whether to call in the handcuffs.'

'But surely they always do.'

'Absolutely not. Firms get red faces and tend to lose business if everyone knows their cashier took them for a ride. They sack the cashier and keep quiet, mostly.'

'Are you bored with telling me all this?'

'No,' I said truthfully.

'Then tell me a good fraud.'

I laughed. 'Heard any good frauds lately?'

'Get on with it.'

159

'Um . . .' I thought. 'A lot of the best frauds are complicated juggling with figures. It's the paperwork which deceives the eye, like a three card trick. I paused, then smiled. 'I know a good one, though they weren't my clients, thank God. There was a manager of a broiler-chicken factory farm which sold thousands of chickens every week to a freezing firm. The manager was also quietly selling a hundred a week to a butcher who didn't know the chickens had fallen off the back of a lorry, so to speak. No one could ever tell how many chickens there actually were on the farm, because the turnover was so huge and fast, and baby chicks tend to die. The manager pocketed a neat little untaxed regular income, and like most good frauds it was discovered by accident.'

'What accident?'

'The butcher used to pay the manager by cheque, made out in the manager's name. One day he happened to meet one of the directors of the firm which owned the chicken farm, and to save postage he got out his chequebook, wrote a cheque in the manager's name, and asked the director to give it to him, to pay for that month's delivery of chickens.'

'And the lid blew off.'

'With a bang. They sacked the manager.'

'No prosecution?'

'No. The last I heard, he was selling rose bushes by mail order.'

'And you wondered for whose nursery he was working?'

160

I grinned and nodded. She was quick and funny, and it seemed incredible that I'd met her only the day before.

We drank coffee and talked about horses. She said she had been trying her hand at three-day-eventing, but would be giving it up soon.

'Why?' I asked.

'Lack of talent.'

'What will you do instead?'

'Marry.'

'Oh.' I felt obscurely disappointed. 'Who?'

'I've no idea. Someone will turn up.'

'Just like that?'

'Of course just like that. One finds husbands in the oddest places.'

'What are you doing tomorrow?' I said.

Her eyes gleamed with light and life. 'Visiting a girl friend. What will you do instead?'

'Sums, I expect.'

'But tomorrow's Sunday.'

'And I can have the office to myself all day, without any interruption. I often work on Sundays. Nearly always.'

'Good grief.'

We went out to where the Midget and the Dolomite stood side by side in the car park.

'Thanks for the grub,' Jossie said.

'And for your company.'

'Do you feel all right?'

'Yes,' I said, surprised. 'Why?'

'Just checking,' she said. 'Dad'll ask. It looked such a crunching fall.'

I shook my head. 'A bruise or two.'

'Good. Well, goodnight.'

'Goodnight.' I kissed her cheek.

Her eyes glinted in the dim light from the pub's windows. I kissed her mouth, rather briefly, with closed lips. She gave me the same sort of kiss in return.

'Hm,' she said, standing back. 'That wasn't bad. I do hate wet slobbers.'

She slid expertly into the Midget and started the engine.

'See you in the hay,' she said. 'Counting it.'

She was smiling as she drove away, probably with a mirror expression of my own. I unlocked my car door, and, feeling slightly silly, I looked into the dark area behind the front seats.

No one there.

I sat in the car and started it, debating whether or not to risk going home to the cottage. Friday and Saturday had passed safely enough; but maybe the cats were still watching the mousehole. I decided that another night away would be prudent, and from the pub drove northwards around Oxford again, to the anonymity of the large motel and service station built beside a busy route-connecting roundabout.

The place as usual was bright with lights and bustle: flags flying on tall poles and petrol pumps rattling. I booked in at the reception office, took the key, and drove round to the slightly quieter wing of bedrooms at the rear.

Sleep would be no problem, I thought. The constant rumble of traffic would be soporific. A lullaby.

I yawned, took out my suitcase, locked the car, and fitted the key into the bedroom door.

Something hit me very hard between the shoulders. I fell against the still closed door, and something immediately hit me very hard on the head.

This time, it was brutal. This time, no ether.

I slid in a daze down the door and saw only dark unrecognizable figures bending over to punch and kick. The thuds shuddered through my bones, and another bang on the head slid me deep into peaceful release.

CHAPTER ELEVEN

I awoke in the dark. Black, total darkness.

I couldn't make out why I should be lying on a hard surface in total darkness, aching all over.

A fall, I thought. I had a fall at Towcester. Why couldn't I remember?

I felt cold. Chilled through and through. When I moved, the aches were worse.

I suddenly remembered having dinner with Jossie. Remembered it all clearly, down to kissing her goodnight in the car park.

So then what?

I tried to sit up, but raising my head was as far as I got. The result was whirling nausea and a pile-driving headache. I inched my fingers tentatively through my hair and found a wince-making area of swelling. I let my head down again, gingerly.

There was no sound except the rustle of my clothes. No engine. No creakings or rushings or water noises. I was not lying on a bunk, but on a larger surface, hard and flat.

164

I might not be in a sail locker, but I was certainly still in the dark. In the dark in every sense. Weak frustrated anger mocked me that in four days of freedom I hadn't found out enough to save me from the gloomy present.

Every movement told me what I still couldn't remember. I knew only that the fall off Notebook could not be the source of the soreness all over my body. There would have been a few bruises which would have stiffened up overnight, but nothing like the overall feeling of having been kneaded like dough. I rolled with a grunt on to my stomach and put my head on my folded arms. The only good thing that I could think of was that they hadn't tied my hands.

They. Who were *they?*

When my head stopped hammering, I thought, I would have enough energy to find out where I was and try to get out. Meanwhile it was enough just to lie still and wait for things to get better.

Another thing to be grateful for, I thought. The hard flat surface I was lying on was not swaying about. With luck, I was not on a boat. I wasn't going to be sick. A bruised body was absolutely nothing compared with the agonies of seasickness.

I had no shoes on, just socks. When I squinted at my wrist there was no luminous dial there: no watch. I couldn't be bothered to check all my pockets. I was certain they'd be empty.

After a while I remembered deciding to go to the

motel, and after that, bit by bit, I remembered booking in, and the affray on the doorstep.

They must have followed me all the way from Towcester, I thought. Waited through dinner with Jossie. Followed me to the motel. I hadn't spotted them once. I hadn't even heard their footsteps behind me, against the constant noise of traffic.

My instinctive feeling of being safe with Jossie had been dead right.

Ages passed.

The racket inside my skull gradually subsided. Nothing else happened.

I had a feeling that it was nearly dawn, and time to wake up. It had been ten-thirty when I'd been knocked out. There was no telling how long I'd been unconscious, or lain feebly in my present state, but the body had its own clock, and mine was saying six in the morning.

The dawn feeling stirred me to some sort of action, though if there was dawn outside it was not making its way through to me. Perhaps, I thought uneasily, I was wrong about the time. It was still night outside. I prayed for it to be still night outside.

I had another go at sitting up. One couldn't say that I felt superbly healthy. Concussion took a while to go away, and cold was notoriously bad for bruised muscles. The combination made every movement a nuisance. A familiar sort of pain, because of racing falls in the past. Just worse.

The surface beneath me was dirty: I could feel the gritty dust. It smelled faintly of oil. It was flat and smooth and not wood.

I felt around me in all directions, and on my left connected with a wall. Slithering on one hip, I inched that way and cautiously explored with my fingers.

Another smooth flat surface, at right angles to the floor. I banged it gently with my fist, and got back the noise and vibration of metal.

I thought that if I sat for a while with my back against the wall it would soon get light, and it would be easy then to see where I was. It had to get light, I thought forlornly. It simply had to.

It didn't, of course.

When they'd given me light on the boat, I'd escaped. A mistake to be avoided.

It had to be faced. The darkness was deliberate, and would go on. It was no good, I told myself severely, sitting in a miserable huddle feeling sorry for myself.

I made a further exploration into unmapped territory, and found that my world was a good deal smaller than Columbus's. It seemed prudent to move while still sitting down, on the flat-earth theory that one might fall over the edge; but two feet of shuffling to the right brought me to a corner.

The adjacent wall was also flat, smooth, and metal. I

shifted my spine round on to it, and set off again to the right.

The traverse was short. I came almost at once to another corner. I found that if I sat in the centre of the wall I could reach both side walls at once quite easily with my fingertips. Five feet, approximately, from side to side.

I shuffled round the second corner and pressed on. Three feet down that side, I knew where I was. The flatness of the metal wall was broken there by a big rounded bulge, whose meaning was as clear to my touch as if I'd been seeing it.

It was the semi-circular casing over a wheel; and I was inside a van.

I had a powerful, immediate picture of the fake ambulance I'd climbed into at Cheltenham. A white van, of a standard pattern, with the doors opening outwards at the rear. If I continued past the wheel, I would come to the rear doors.

And I would feel a proper fool, I thought, if all I had to do was open the doors and step out.

I wouldn't have minded feeling a proper fool. The doors were firmly shut, and likely to remain so. There was no handle on the inside.

In the fourth corner I came across what I had this time been given in the way of life support systems, and if my spirits had already been at zero, at that point they went way below.

There was a five-gallon plastic jerrycan full of liquid, and a large carrier bag.

I unscrewed the cap of the jerrycan and sniffed at the contents. No smell. Sloshed some of the liquid out on to my hand, and tasted it.

Water.

I screwed the cap on again, fumbling in the dark.

Five gallons of water.

Oh no, I thought numbly. Oh dear God.

The carrier was packed to the top with flat plastic packets, each about four inches square. There was again no smell. I pulled one of the packets open, and found the contents were thin four-inch squares of sliced processed cheese.

I counted the packets with a sinking heart, taking them one by one from the carrier and stacking them on the floor. There were sixty of them. All, as far as I could tell, exactly the same.

Wretchedly I counted them from the floor back into the carrier, one by one, and there were still sixty. They had given me enough food and water to last for at least four weeks. There were going to be no twice a day visits: no one to talk to at all.

Sod them, I thought violently. If this was revenge, it was worse than anything I'd ever brought on any crook.

Spurred by anger, I stood without caution to explore the top part of the van, and banged my sore head on the roof. It was very nearly altogether too much. I found myself back on my knees, cursing and holding my head, and trying not to weep. A battered feeble figure, sniffing in the dark.

It wouldn't do, I thought. It was necessary to be sternly unemotional. To ignore the aches and pains. To take a good cold grip of things, and make a plan and routine for survival.

When the fresh waves of headache passed, I got on with it.

The presence of food and drink meant, I thought, that survival was expected. That one day, if I didn't manage a second escape, I would be released. Death, again, was not apparently on the agenda. Well, then, why was I getting into such a fuss?

I had read once of a man who had spent weeks down a pothole in silence and darkness to see how a total lack of external reference would affect the human body. He had survived with his mind intact and his body none the worse for wear, and his sense of time had gone remarkably little astray. What he could do, so could I. It was irrelevant, I thought sternly, that the scientist had volunteered for his incarceration, and had had his heartbeat and other vital signs monitored on the surface, and could have got out again any time he felt he'd had enough.

Feeling a good deal steadier for the one-man pep-talk, I got more slowly to my feet, sliding my spine up the side wall, and feeling for the roof with my hands. It was too low for me to stand upright, by four or six inches. With head and knees bent, I felt my way again right round the van.

Both sides were completely blank. The front wall was broken by the shape of a small panel which must have opened through to the driving cab. It seemed to be intended to slide, but was fastened shut as firmly as if it had been welded. There was no handle or bolt on the inside; only smoothed metal.

The rear doors at first seemed to be promising, as I discovered they were not entirely solid, but had windows. One each side, about twelve inches across, the distance from my wrist to my elbow, and half as high.

There was no glass in the windows. I stretched my hand cautiously through the one on the right, and immediately came to a halt. Something hard was jammed against the doors on the outside, holding them shut.

I was concentrating so much on the message from my fingers that I realized that I was crouching there with my eyes shut. Funny, really. I opened them. No light. What good were eyes without light?

Outside each window there was an area of coarse cloth, which felt like heavy canvas. At the outer sides of the window it was possible to push the canvas, to move it three or four inches away from the van. On the inner halves it was held tight against the van by whatever was jamming the doors shut.

I put an arm out of each outer section of window in turn, and felt as much of the outside of the van as I could reach. It was very little, and of no use. The whole of the back of the van was sheeted in canvas.

I slid down again to the floor and tried to visualize

what I'd felt. A van covered in canvas with its rear doors jammed shut. Where could one park such a thing so that it wouldn't be immediately discovered? In a garage? A barn? If I banged on the sides, would anyone hear me?

I banged on the sides of the van, but my fists made little noise, and there was nothing else to bang with. I shouted 'Help' a good many times through the windows, but no one came.

There was air perceptibly leaking in through the missing windows: I could feel it when I pushed the canvas outwards. No fear of asphyxiation.

It irritated me that I could do nothing useful with those windows. They were too small to crawl through, even without the canvas and whatever was holding it against the van. I couldn't get my head through the spaces, let alone my shoulders.

I decided to eat some cheese and think things over. The cheese wasn't bad. The thoughts produced the unwelcome reflection that this time I had no mattress, no blanket, no pillow, and no loo. Also no paperback novel, spare socks, or soap. The sail locker had been a Hilton compared with the van.

On the other hand, in an odd sort of way the time in the sail locker had prepared me better for this dourer cell. Instead of feeling more frightened, more hysterical, more despairing, I felt less. I had already been through all the horrors. Also, during the four days of freedom, I had not gone to the South Pole to avoid capture. I'd feared it and done my best to dodge it, but in returning to my usual life, I'd known it might come.

The reason for the first abduction presumably still existed. I had escaped before the intended time, and in someone's eyes this had been a very bad thing. Bad enough to send the squad to retake me, from the cottage, within a day of my return to England. Bad enough to risk carting me off again when this time there would, I hoped, be a police search.

I was pretty sure I must still be in England. I certainly had no memory of being transported from the motel to wherever I was now, but the impression that I'd been unconscious for only an hour or two was convincingly strong.

Sunday morning. No one would miss me. It would be Monday before Debbie and Peter began to wonder. Tuesday, perhaps, before the police took it seriously, if indeed they did, in spite of their assurance. A day or two more before anyone really started looking: and I had no wife or parents to keep the search alive, if I wasn't to be found soon after that.

Jossie might have done, I thought regretfully, if I'd known her for longer. Jossie with her bright eyes and forthright tongue.

At the very least, at the most hopeful assessment, the future still looked a long, hard, weary grind.

Shortening the perspective dramatically, it was becoming imperative to solve immediately the question of liquid waste disposal. I might be having to live in a tin box, but not, if I could help it, in a filthy stinking tin box.

Necessity concentrated the mind wonderfully, as others before me had observed. I took the cheese slices out of one of the thick plastic packets, and used that, and emptied it in relays out of the rear window, pushing the canvas away from the van as far as I could. Not the most sanitary of arrangements, but better than nothing.

After that little excitement, I sat down again. I was still cold, though not now with the through-and-through chill of injury-shock. I could perhaps have done some warming-up arm-swinging exercises, if it hadn't been for protesting bruises. As things were, with every muscle movement a reminder, I simply sat.

Exploration had kept me busy up to that point, but the next few hours revealed the true extent of my isolation.

There was absolutely no external sound. If I suppressed the faint noise of my own breathing, I could hear literally nothing. No traffic, no hum of aircraft, no wind, no creak, no rustle. Nothing.

There was absolutely no light. Air came steadily in from between the outside of the van and its canvas shroud, but no light came with it. Eyes wide open, or firmly shut, it was all the same.

There was no perceptible change in temperature. It remained just too low for comfort, defying my body's efforts to acclimatize. I had been left trousers, underpants, shirt, sports jacket and socks, though no tie, no belt, no loose belongings of any sort. It was Sunday, April 3rd. It might have been a sunny spring day outside, but wherever I was, it was simply too cold.

People would be reading about the Grand National in their Sunday newspapers, I thought. Lying in bed, warm and comfortable. Getting up and strolling to the pub. Eating hot meals, playing with the kids, deciding not to mow the lawn for another week. Millions of people, living their Sunday.

I served myself a Sunday lunch of cheese slices, and with great care drank some water from the can. It was heavy, being full, and I couldn't afford to tip it over. Enough water went down my neck to make me think of the uses of cheese packets as drinking cups.

After lunch, a snooze, I thought. I made a fairly reasonable pillow by rearranging the cheese packets inside the carrier, and resolutely tried to sleep, but the sum of discomfort kept me awake.

Well, then, I thought, lying on my back and staring at the invisible ceiling, I could sort out what I'd learned during my four free days.

The first of them could be discounted, as I'd spent it in Minorca, organizing my return home. That left two days in the office and one at the races. One night hiding in the cottage, one sleeping soundly in the Gloucester hotel. For all of that period I'd been looking for reasons, which made this present dose of imprisonment a great deal different from the first. Then, I'd been

175

completely bewildered. This time I had at least one or two ideas.

Hours passed.

Nothing got any better.

I sat up for a while, and lay down again, and everything hurt, just the same. I cheered myself up with the thought that the stiff ache of bruises always finally got better, never worse. Suppose, for instance, it had been appendicitis. I'd heard that people going off to Everest or other Backs of Beyond had their perfectly healthy appendix removed, just in case. I wished on the whole that I hadn't thought of appendicitis.

Or toothache.

I had a feeling that it was evening, and then that it was night.

There was no change, except in me. I grew slowly even colder, but as if from the inside out. My eyelids stayed heavily shut. I drifted gradually in and out of sleep, a long drowsy twilight punctuated by short groaning awakenings every time I moved. When I woke with a clear mind, it felt like dawn.

If the cycle held, I thought, I could keep a calendar. One empty cheese packet for every day, stacked in the right-hand front corner of the van. If I put one there at every dawn, I would know the days. One for Sunday: a second for Monday. I extracted two wads of cheese slices and shuffled carefully a couple of feet forward to leave the empties.

I ate and drank what I thought of as breakfast: and I had become, I realized, much more at home in the dark. Physically, I was less clumsy. I found it easier to manage the water can, for instance, and no longer tended to put the cap on the floor and feel frustrated when I couldn't at once find it after I'd drunk. I now put my hand back automatically to where I'd parked the cap in the first place.

Mentally, too, it was less of a burden. On the boat I'd loathed it, and of all the rotten prospects of a second term of imprisonment, it had been being thrown back into the dark which I had shrunk from most. I still hated it, but its former heavy oppression was passing. I found that I no longer feared that the darkness on its own would set me climbing the walls.

I spent the morning thinking about reasons for abduction, and in the afternoon made an abacus out of pieces of cheese arranged in rows, and did a string of mathematical computations. I knew that other solitary captives had kept their minds occupied by repeating verses, but I'd always found it easier to think in numbers and symbols, and I'd not learned enough words by heart for them to be of any present use. Goosey goosey gander had its limitations.

*

Monday night came and went. When I woke I planted another cheese packet in the front right-hand corner, and flexed arms and legs which were no longer too sore to be worth it.

Tuesday morning I spent doing exercises and thinking about reasons for abduction, and Tuesday afternoon I felt my way delicately round the abacus, enlarging its scope as a calculator. Tuesday evening I sat and hugged my knees, and thought disconsolately that it was all very well telling myself to be staunch and resolute, but that staunch and resolute was not really how I felt.

Three days since I'd had dinner with Jossie. Well . . . at least I had her to think about, which I hadn't had on the boat.

The dozing period came round again. I lay down and let it wash over me for hours, and counted it Tuesday night.

Wednesday, for the twentieth time, I felt round the van inch by inch, looking for a possible way out. For the twentieth time, I didn't find one.

There were no bolts to undo. No levers. There was nothing. No way out. I knew it, but I couldn't stop searching.

Wednesday was the day I was supposed to be riding Tapestry at Ascot. Whether because of that, or simply because my body was back approximately to normal, the time passed more slowly than ever.

I whistled and sang, and felt restless, and wished passionately that there was room to stand up straight. The only way to straighten my spine was to lie down flat. I could feel my hard-won calm slipping away round the edges, and it was a considerable effort to give myself something to do with the pieces-of-cheese slide rule.

Wednesday I lost track of whether it was noon or evening, and the idea of days and days more of that existence was demoralizing. Dammit, I thought mordantly. Shut up, shut up with the gloomsville. One day at a time. One day, one hour, one minute at a time.

I ate some cheese and felt sleepy, and that at long last was Wednesday done.

Thursday midday, I heard a noise.

I couldn't believe it.

Some distant clicks, and a grinding noise. I was lying on my back doing bicycling exercises with my legs in the air, and I practically disconnected myself getting to my knees and scrambling over to the rear doors.

I pushed the canvas away from one of the windows, and shouted at the top of my lungs.

'Hey . . . hey . . . Come here.'

There were footsteps; more than one set. Soft footsteps, but in that huge dead silence, quite clear.

I swallowed. Whoever it was, there was no point in keeping quiet.

'Hey,' I shouted again. 'Come here.'

The footsteps stopped.
A man's voice, close to the van, spoke very loudly.
'Are you Roland Britten?'
I said weakly, 'Yes . . . who are you?'
'Police, sir,' he said.

CHAPTER TWELVE

They took a good long while getting me out, because, as
the disembodied voice explained, they would have to
take photographs and notes for use in any future prosecution. Also there was the matter of fingerprints, which
would mean further delay.

'And we can't get you out without moving the van, you
see, sir,' said the voice. 'On account of it's backed hard up
against a brick pillar, and we can't open the rear doors.
On top of that the driving cab doors are both locked, and
the brake's hard on, and there's no key in the ignition. So
if you'll be patient, sir, we'll have you out as soon as we
can.'

He sounded as if he were reassuring a small child who
might scream the place down at any minute, but I found
it easy to be patient, if only he knew.

There were several voices outside after a while, and
from time to time they asked me if I was all right, and I
said yes; and in the end they started the van's engine and
drove it forward a few feet, and pulled off the canvas
cover.

The return of sight was extraordinary. The two small windows appeared as oblongs of grey, and I had difficulty in focusing. A face looked in, roundly healthy, enquiring and concerned, topped by a uniform cap.

'Have you out in a jiffy now, sir,' he said. 'We're having a bit of difficulty with these doors, see, as the handle's been sabotaged.'

'Fine,' I said vaguely. The light was still pretty dim, but to me a luxury like no other on earth. A half-forgotten joy, newly discovered. Like meeting a dead friend. Familiar, lost, precious, and restored.

I sat on the floor and looked around my prison. It was smaller than I'd imagined: cramped and claustrophobic, now that I could see the grey enclosing walls.

The jerrycan of water was of white plastic, with a red cap. The carrier was brown, as I'd imagined it. The little calendar stack of five empty packets lay in its corner, and the hardening pieces of cheese from my counting machine, in another. There was nothing else, except me and dust.

They opened the doors eventually and helped me out, and then took notes and photographs of where I'd been. I stood a pace or two away and looked curiously at my surroundings.

The van was indeed the white one from Cheltenham, or one exactly like it. An old Ford. No tax disc, and no number-plates. The canvas which had covered it was a huge, dirty dark grey tarpaulin, the sort used for sheeting loads on lorries. The van had been wrapped in it like a parcel, and tied with ropes threaded through eyelets in the tarpaulin's edges.

The van, the police and I were all inside a building of about a hundred feet square. All round the walls rose huge lumpy heaps of dust-covered unidentifiable bundles, grey shapes of boxes and things that looked like sandbags. Some of the piles reached the low flat ceiling, which was supported at strategic points by four sturdy brick pillars.

It was against one of these, in the small clear area in the centre, that the van had been jammed.

'What is this place?' I said to the policeman beside me.

'Are you all right, sir?' he said. He shivered slightly. 'It's cold in here.'

'Yes,' I said. 'Where exactly are we?'

'It used to be one of those army surplus stores, selling stuff to the public. Went bust a while back, though, and no one's ever shifted all the muck.'

'Oh. Well . . . whereabouts is it?'

'Down one of those tracks that used to be the railway branch line, before they closed it.'

'Yes,' I said apologetically. 'But what town?'

'Eh?' He looked at me in surprise. 'Newbury, of course, sir.'

The town clocks pointed to five o'clock when the police drove me down to the station. My body's own time had proved remarkably constant, I thought. Much better than on the boat, where noise and tossing and sickness had upset things.

I was given a chair in the office of one of the same policemen as before, who showed no regrets at having earlier thought I was exaggerating.

'How did you find me?' I said.

He tapped his teeth with a pencil, a hard-working Detective Inspector with an air of suspecting the innocent until they were found guilty.

'Scotland Yard had a call,' he said grudgingly. 'We'll want a statement from you, sir, if you don't mind.'

'A cup of tea first,' I suggested.

His gaze wandered over my face and clothes. I must have looked a wreck. He came somewhere near a smile, and sent a young constable on the errand.

The tea tasted marvellous, though I daresay it wasn't. I drank it slowly and told him fairly briefly what had happened.

'So you didn't see their faces at all, this time?'

'No,' I said.

'Pity.'

'Do you think,' I said tentatively, 'that some one could drive me back to the motel, so I can collect my car?'

'No need, sir,' he said. 'It's parked beside your cottage.'

'What?'

He nodded. 'With a lot of your possessions in it. Suit-case. Wallet. Shoes. Keys. All in the boot. Your assistants notified us on Monday that you were missing again. We sent a man along to your cottage. He reported your car was there, but you weren't. We did what you asked, sir. We did look for you. The whole country's been looking for you, come to that. The motel rang us yesterday to say you'd booked in there last Saturday but hadn't used the room, but apart from that there was nothing to go on. No trace at all. We thought you might have been taken off on another boat, to be frank.'

I finished the tea, and thanked him for it.

'Will you run me back to the cottage, then?'

He thought it could be arranged. He came with me out to the entrance hall, to fix it.

A large man with an over-anxious expression came bustling in from the street, swinging the door wide and assessing rapidly the direction from which he would get most satisfaction. My partner at his most bombastic, his deep voice echoing round the hall as he demanded information.

'Hello, Trevor,' I said. 'Take it easy.'

He stopped in mid-commotion, and stared at me as if I were an intrusive stranger. Then he recognized me, and took in my general appearance, and his face went stiff with shock.

'Ro!' He seemed to have trouble with his voice. 'Ro, my dear fellow. My dear fellow. I've just heard . . . My God, Ro . . .'

I sighed. 'Calm down, Trevor. All I need is a razor.'

'But you're so *thin*.' His eyes were appalled. I reflected

that I was probably a good deal thinner than when he'd seen me last, some time in the dim, distant, and safe past.

'Mr King has been bombarding us all day,' said the Detective Inspector with a touch of impatience.

'My dear Ro, you must come back with me. We'll look after you. My *God*, Ro . . .'

I shook my head. 'I'm fine, Trevor. I'm grateful to you, but I'd really rather go home.'

'Alone?' he said anxiously. 'Suppose . . . I mean . . . do you think it's safe?'

'Oh yes,' I nodded. 'Whoever put me in, let me out. It's all over, I think.'

'What's all over?'

'That,' I said soberly, 'is a whole new ball game.'

The cottage embraced me like a balm.

I had a bath, and shaved, and a grey face of gaunt shadows looked at me out of the mirror. No wonder Trevor had been shocked. Just as well, I thought, that he hadn't seen the black and yellow blotches of fading bruises which covered me from head to foot.

I shrugged, and thought the same as before: nothing that a few days' freedom wouldn't fix. I put on jeans and a jersey and went downstairs in search of a large Scotch, and that was the last peaceful moment of the evening.

The telephone rang non-stop. Reporters, to my amazement, arrived at the doorstep. A television camera appeared. When they saw I was astounded, they said hadn't I read the papers.

'What papers?'

They produced them, and spread them out.

The Sporting Life: headline on Tuesday: 'Where is Roland Britten?' followed by an article about my sea trip, as told by me to friends. I had not been seen since Towcester. Friends were worried.

On Wednesday, paragraphs in all the dailies: 'Tapestry's rider again missing' in one of the staider, and 'Fun Jock Twice Removed?' from a tits-and-bums.

Thursday – that day – many front pages carried a broadly smiling picture of me, taken five minutes after the Gold Cup. 'Find Roland Britten' ordered one, and 'Fears for Jockey's Life' gloomed another. I glanced over them in amazement, remembering ironically that I'd been afraid no one would really look for me at all.

The telephone rang beside my hand. I picked up the receiver and said hello.

'Ro? Is that you?' The voice was fresh and unmistakable.

'Jossie!'

'Where the hell have you been?'

'Have dinner with me tomorrow, and I'll tell you.'

'Pick me up at eight,' she said. 'What's all that noise?'

'I'm pressed by Press,' I said. 'Journalists.'

'Good grief.' She laughed. 'Are you all right?'

'Yes, fine.'

'It was on the news, that you'd been found.'

'I don't believe it.'

'Big stuff, buddy boy.' The mockery was loud and clear.

'Did you start it . . . all this publicity?' I said.

'Not me, no. Moira Longerman. Mrs Tapestry. She tried to get you Sunday, and she tried your office on Monday, and they told her you were missing, and they thought you might have been kidnapped again, so she rang up the editor of *The Sporting Life*, who's a friend of hers, to ask him to help.'

'A determined lady,' I said gratefully.

'She didn't run Tapestry yesterday, you know. There's a sob-stuff bit in *The Sporting Life*. "How can I run my horse while Roland is missing" and all that guff. Fair turns your stomach.'

'Fair turned Binny Tomkins's, I'll bet.'

She laughed. 'I can hear the wolves howling for you. See you tomorrow. Don't vanish before eight.'

I put the telephone down, but the wolves had to wait a little longer, as the bell immediately rang again.

Moira Longerman, excited and twittering, coming down the wire like an electric current.

'Thank heavens you're free. Isn't it marvellous? Are you all right? Can you ride Tapestry on Saturday? Do tell me all about the horrible place where they found you . . . and Roland, dear, I don't want you listening to a word Binny Tomkins says about you not being fit to ride after all you've been through.'

188

'Moira,' I said, vainly trying to stop the flow. 'Thank you very much.'

'My dear,' she said, 'it was rather *fun*, getting everyone mobilized. Of course I was truly dreadfully worried that something awful had happened to you, and it was quite clear that somebody had to do *something*, otherwise you might stay kidnapped for *weeks*, and it seemed to me that a jolly good fuss was what was wanted. I thought that if the whole country was looking for you, whoever had taken you might get cold feet and turn you loose, and that's precisely what happened, so I was right and the silly police were all wrong.'

'What silly police?' I said.

'Telling me I might have put you in danger by getting *The Sporting Life* to say you'd vanished again. I ask you! They said if kidnappers get panicky they could kill their victim. Anyway, they were wrong, weren't they?'

'Fortunately,' I agreed.

'So do tell me all about it,' she said. 'Is it true you were shut up in a van? What was it like?'

'Boring,' I said.

'Roland, *really*. Is that all you've got to say?'

'I thought about you all day on Wednesday, imagining you'd be furious when I didn't turn up at Ascot.'

'That's better.' She laughed her tinkly laugh. 'You can make up for it on Saturday. Tapestry's in the Oasthouse Cup at Kempton, though of course he's got top weight there, which was why we wanted to run at Ascot instead. But now we're going to Kempton.'

'I'm afraid . . .' I said, 'that Binny's right. This time, I'm really not fit enough. I'd love to ride him, but . . . well . . . at the moment I couldn't go two rounds with a kitten.'

There was a short silence at the other end.

'Do you mean it?' she demanded doubtfully.

'I hate to say so, but I do.'

The doubt in her voice subsided. 'I'm sure you'll be a hundred per cent after a good night's sleep. After all, you'll have nearly two days to recover, and even Binny admits you're pretty tough as amateurs go . . . so *please*, Roland, *please* ride on Saturday, because the horse is jumping out of his skin, and the opposition is not so strong as it will be in the Whitbread Gold Cup in two weeks' time, and I feel in my bones that he'll win this race but not the other. And I don't want Binny putting up any other jockey, as to be frank I only trust you, which you know. So *please* say you will. I was so *thrilled* when I heard you were free, so that you could ride on Saturday.'

I rubbed my hand across my eyes. I knew I shouldn't agree, and that I was highly unlikely to be fit enough even to walk the course on my feet, let alone control half a ton of thoroughbred muscle on the rampage. Yet to her, if I refused, it would seem like gross ingratitude after her lively campaign to free me, and I too suspected that if Tapestry started favourite with a different jockey of Binny's choice, he wouldn't win. There was also the insidious old desire to race which raised its head in defiance of common sense. Reason told me I'd fall off from weakness at the first fence, and the irresistible temptation of a go at another of the season's top 'chases kidded me not to believe it.

'Well . . .' I said, hesitating.

'Oh, you *will*,' she said delightedly. 'Oh Roland, I'm so *glad*.'

'I shouldn't.'

'If you don't win,' she said gaily, 'I promise I won't blame you.'

I'd blame myself, I thought, and I'd deserve it.

I went to the office at nine the next morning, and Trevor fussed about a great deal too much.

'You need rest, Ro. You should be in bed.'

'I need people and life and things to do.'

He sat in the clients' armchair in my office and looked worried. The sun-tan of his holiday suited him, increasing his air of distinction. His silvery hair was fluffier than usual, and his comfortable stomach looked rounder.

'Did you have a good time,' I said, 'in Spain?'

'What? Oh yes, splendid. Splendid. Until the car broke down, of course. And all the time, while we were enjoying ourselves, you . . .' He stopped and shook his head.

'I'm afraid,' I said wryly, 'that I'm dreadfully behind with the work.'

'For heaven's sake . . .'

'I'll try to catch up,' I said.

'I wish you'd take it easy for a few days.' He looked as

if he meant it, his eyes full of troubled concern. 'It won't do either of us any good if you crack up.'

My lips twitched. That was more like the authentic Trevor.

'I'm made of plasticine,' I said; and despite his protests I stayed where I was and once again tried to sort out the trail of broken appointments.

Mr Wells was in a worse mess than ever, having sent a cheque which had promptly bounced. A prosecution for that was in the offing.

'But you knew the bank wouldn't pay it,' I protested when he telephoned with this latest trouble.

'Yes . . . but I thought they *might*.'

His naïvety was frightening: the same stupid hopefulness which had got him enmeshed in the first place. He blanked out reality and believed in fantasies. I'd known others like him, and I'd never known them change.

'Come on Monday afternoon,' I said resignedly.

'Supposing someone kidnaps you again.'

'They won't,' I said. 'Two-thirty, Monday.'

I went through the week's letters with Debbie and sorted out the most urgent. Their complexity made me wilt.

'We'll answer them on Monday morning,' I said.

Debbie fetched some coffee and said at her most pious that I wasn't fit to be at work.

'Did we get those postponements from the Commissioners for Axwood Stables and Coley Young?' I said.

'Yes, they came on Wednesday.'

'And what about Denby Crest's certificate?'

'Mr King said he'd see about that this morning.'

I rubbed a hand over my face. No use kidding myself. However much I disliked it, I did feel pathetically weak. Agreeing to ride Tapestry had been a selfish folly. The only sensible course was to ring Moira Longerman at once, and cry off: but when it came to race-riding, I'd never been sensible.

'Debbie,' I said, 'please would you go down to the store in the basement, and bring up all the old files on Connaught Powys, and on Glitberg and Ownslow.'

'Who?'

I wrote the names down for her. She glanced at them, nodded, and went away.

Sticks Elroy telephoned, words tumbling out in a rush, incoherent and thick with Oxfordshire accent. A lot more talkative than he'd been at dinner in the pub, when overshadowed by his bull-like dad.

'Stop,' I said. 'I didn't hear a word. Say it slowly.'

'I said I was ever so sorry you got shut up in that van.'

'Well . . . thanks.'

'My old man couldn't have done it, you know.' He sounded anxious, more seeking to convince than convinced.

'Don't you think so?'

'I know he said . . . Look, well, he went on cursing all evening, and I know he's got a van, and all, which is off somewhere getting the gearbox fixed, or something, and I know he was that furious, and he said you should be locked up, but I don't reckon he could have done it, not for real.'

'Did you ask him?' I said curiously.

'Yeah.' He hesitated. 'See . . . we had a bloody big row, him and me.' Another pause. 'He always knocked us about when we were kids. Straps, boots, anything.' A pause. 'I asked him about you . . . he punched me in the face.'

'Mm,' I said. 'What did you decide to do about that cash?'

'Yeah, well, that's what the row was about, see. I reckoned you were right and I didn't want any trouble with the law, and Dad blew his top and said I'd never been grateful for everything he'd done for me. He says if I declare that cash and pay tax on it he'll be in trouble himself, see, and I reckon he was mad enough to do anything.'

I reflected a bit. 'What colour is his van?'

'White, sort of. An old Ford.'

'Um. When did you decide to go to that pub for dinner?'

'Dad drove there straight from the races, for a drink, like, and then he phoned and said they could fit us all in for dinner, and we might as well celebrate my win.'

'Would he be likely,' I said, 'to be able to lay his hands on sixty packets of cheese slices?'

'Whatever are you on about?'

I sighed. 'They were in the van with me.'

'Well, I don't know, do I? I don't live with him any

more. I wouldn't reckon on him going to a supermarket, though. Women's work, see?'

'Yes. If you've decided to declare that cash, there are some legitimate expenses to set off against the profit.'

'Bloody tax,' he said. 'Sucks you dry. I'm not going to bother sweating my guts out on any more schemes. Not bloody worth it.'

He made an appointment for the following week and grumbled his way off the phone.

I sat and stared into space, thinking of Sticks Elroy and his violent father. Heavy taxation was always self-defeating, with the country losing progressively more for every tightening of the screw. Overtime and enterprise weren't worth it. Emigration was. The higher the tax rates, the less there was to tax. It was crazy. If I'd been Chancellor, I'd have made Britain a tax haven, and welcomed back all the rich who had taken their money and left. A fifty per cent tax on millions would be better for the country than a ninety-eight per cent on nothing. As it was, I had to interpret and advise in accordance with what I thought of as bad economics; uphold laws which I thought irrational. If the fury the Elroys felt against the system took the form of abuse of the accountant who forced them to face nasty facts, it wasn't unduly surprising. I did doubt though that even Elroy senior would make his abuse physical. Calling me a bastard was a long way from imprisonment.

Debbie came in with her arms full of files and her face full of fluster.

'There's a lady outside who insists on seeing you. She hasn't got an appointment and Mr King said you were definitely not to be worried today, but she won't go away. Oh!'

The lady in question was walking into the office in Debbie's wake. Tall, thin, assured, and middle-aged.

I stood up, smiling, and shook hands with Hilary Margaret Pinlock.

'It's all right, Debbie,' I said.

'Oh, very well.' She shrugged, put down the files, and went out.

'How are you?' I said. 'Sit down.'

Hilary Margaret Pinlock sat in the clients' chair and crossed her thin legs.

'You,' she said, 'look half-dead.'

'A half-empty bottle is also half-full.'

'And you're an optimist?'

'Usually,' I said.

She was wearing a brownish-grey flecked tweed coat, to which the sunless April day added nothing in the way of life. Behind the spectacles the eyes looked small and bright, and coral-pink lipstick lent warmth to her mouth.

'I've come to tell you something,' she said. 'Quite a lot of things, I suppose.'

'Good or bad?'

'Facts.'

'You're not pregnant?'

She was amused. 'I don't know yet.'

'Would you like some sherry?'

'Yes, please.'

I stood up and produced a bottle and two glasses from a filing cupboard. Poured. Handed her a generous slug of Harvey's Luncheon Dry.

'I came home yesterday,' she said. 'I read about you being kidnapped again, on the aeroplane coming back. They had newspapers. Then I heard on the news that you were found, and safe. I thought I would come and see you myself, instead of taking my information to the police.'

'What information?' I said. 'And I thought you were due back home last Saturday.'

She sipped her sherry sedately.

'Yes, I was. I stayed on, though. Because of you. It cost me a fortune.' She looked at me over her glass. 'I was sorry to read you had been recaptured after all. I had seen . . . your fear of it.'

'Mm,' I said ruefully.

'I found out about that boat for you,' she said.

I almost spilled the sherry.

She smiled. 'About the man, to be more exact. The man in the dinghy, who was chasing you.'

'How?' I said.

'After you'd gone, I hired a car and drove to all the places on Minorca where they said yachts could be moored. The nearest good harbour to Cala St Galdana was Ciudadela, and I should think that's where the boat went after they lost you, but it had gone by the time I started looking.' She drank some sherry. 'I asked some

English people on a yacht there, and they said there had been an English crew on a sixty-footer there the night before, and they'd overheard them talking about wind for a passage to Palma. I asked them to describe the captain, and they said there didn't seem to be a proper captain, only a tall young man who looked furious.' She stopped and considered, and explained further. 'All the yachts at Ciudadela were moored at right angles to the quayside, you see. Stern on. So that they were all close together, side by side, and you walked straight off the back of them on to dry land.'

'Yes,' I said. 'I see.'

'So I just walked along the whole row, asking. There were Spaniards, Germans, French, Swedes ... all sorts. The English people had noticed the other English crew just because they *were* English, if you see what I mean.'

'I do,' I said.

'And also because it had been the biggest yacht that night in the harbour.' She paused. 'So instead of flying home on Saturday, I went to Palma.'

'It's a big place,' I said.

She nodded. 'It took me three days. But I found out that young man's name, and quite a lot about him.'

'Would you like some lunch?' I said.

CHAPTER THIRTEEN

We walked along to La Riviera at the end of the High Street and ordered moussaka. The place was full as usual, and Hilary leaned forward across the table to make herself privately heard. Her strong plain face was full of the interest and vigour she had put into her search on my behalf, and it was typical of her self-confidence that she was concentrating only on the subject in hand and not the impression she was making as a woman. A headmistress, I thought: not a lover.

'His name,' she said, 'is Alastair Yardley. He is one of a whole host of young men who seem to wander around the Mediterranean looking after boats while the owners are home in England, Italy, France, and wherever. They live in the sun, on the water's edge, picking up jobs where they can, and leading an odd sort of drop-out existence which supplies a useful service to boat owners.'

'Sounds attractive.'

'It's bumming around,' she said succinctly.

'I wouldn't mind dropping out, right now,' I said.

'You're made of sterner stuff.'

Plasticine, I thought.

'Go on about Alastair Yardley,' I said.

'I asked around for two days without any success. My description of him seemed to fit half the population, and although I'd seen the boat, of course, I wasn't sure I would know it again, as I haven't an educated eye for that sort of thing. There are two big marinas at Palma, both of them packed with boats. Some boats are moored stern-on, like at Ciudadela, but dozens more were anchored away from the quays. I hired a boatman to take me round the whole harbour in his motorboat, but with no results. I'm sure he thought I was potty. I was pretty discouraged, actually, and was admitting defeat, when he – the boatman, that is – said there was another small harbour less than a day's sail away, and why didn't I look there. So on Wednesday I took a taxi to the port of Andraitx.'

She stopped to eat some moussaka, which had arrived and smelled magnificent.

'Eat,' she said, scooping up a third generous forkful and waving at my still full plate.

'Yes,' I said. It was the first proper meal I'd approached since the dinner with Jossie, and I should have been ravenous. Instead, the diet of processed cheese seemed to have played havoc with my appetite, and I found difficulty in eating much at all. I hadn't been able to face any supper, the evening before, when the journalists had finally gone, and not much breakfast either.

RISK

'Tell me about Andraitx,' I said.

'In a minute,' she said. 'I'm not letting this delicious food get cold.' She ate with enjoyment and disapproved of my unsuccessful efforts to do the same. I had to wait for the next instalment until she had finished the last morsel and lain down her fork.

'That was *good*,' she said. 'A great treat.'

'Andraitx,' I said.

She half laughed. 'All right, then. Andraitx. Small by Palma's standards, but bigger than Ciudadela. The small ports and harbours are the old parts of the islands. The buildings are old . . . there are no new ritzy hotels there, because there are no beaches. Deep water, rocky cliffs, and so on. I found out so much more about the islands this week than if I'd stopped in Cala St Galdana for my week and come home last Saturday. They have such a bloody history of battles and sieges and invasions. A horrible violent history. One may sneer now at the way they've been turned into a tourist paradise, but the brassy modern civilization must be better than the murderous past.'

'Dearest Hilary,' I said. 'Cut the lecture and come to the grit.'

'It was the biggest yacht in Andraitx,' she said. 'I was sure almost at once, and then I saw the young man on the quayside, not far from where I paid off the taxi. He came out of a shop and walked across the big open space that there is there, between the buildings and the water. He was carrying a heavy box of provisions. He dumped it on

201

the edge of the quay, beside that black rubber dinghy which he brought ashore at Cala St Galdana. Then he went off again, up a street leading away from the quay. I didn't exactly follow him, I just watched. He went into a doorway a little way up the street, and soon came out again carrying a bundle wrapped in plastic. He went back to the dinghy, and loaded the box and the bundle and himself, and motored out to the yacht.'

The waiter came to take our plates and ask about puddings and coffee.

'Cheese,' Hilary decided.

'Just coffee,' I said. 'And do go on.'

'Well . . . I went into the shop he'd come out of, and asked about him, but they spoke only Spanish, and I don't. So then I walked up the street to the doorway I'd seen him go into, and that was where I hit the jackpot.'

She stopped to cut cheese from a selection on a board. I wondered how long it would be before I liked the stuff again.

'It was a laundry,' she said. 'All white and airy. And run by an English couple who'd gone to Majorca originally for a holiday and fallen in love with the place. A nice couple. Friendly, happy, busy, and very, very helpful. They knew the young man fairly well, they said, because he always took his washing in when he was in Andraitx. They do the boat people's laundry all the time. They reckon to have a bag of dirty clothes washed and ironed in half a day.'

She ate a biscuit and some cheese, and I waited.

'Alastair Yardley,' she said. 'The laundry people said he is a good sailor. Better than most of his kind. He often takes yachts from one place to another, so that they'll be wherever the owner wants. He can handle big boats, and is known for it. He sails into Andraitx four or five times a year, but three years ago he had a flat there, and used it as his base. The laundry people said they don't really know much about him, except that his father worked in a boat-building yard. He told them once that he'd learned to sail as soon as walk, and his first job was as a paid deck-hand in sea-trials for ocean-racing yachts. Apart from that, he hasn't said much about himself or who he's working for now, and the laundry people don't know because they aren't the prying sort, just chatty.'

'You're marvellous,' I said.

'Hm. I took some photographs of the boat, and I've had them processed at an overnight developers.' She opened her handbag, and drew out a yellow packet, which contained, among holiday scenes, three clear colour photographs of my first prison. Three different views, taken as the boat swung round with the tide.

'You can have them, if you like,' she said.

'I could kiss you.'

Her face lit with amusement. 'If you shuffle through that pack, you'll find a rather bad picture of Alastair Yardley. I didn't get the focus right. I was in a bit of a hurry, and he was walking towards me with his laundry, and I didn't want him to think I was taking a picture of him personally. I had to pretend to be taking a general view of the port, you see, and so I'm afraid it isn't very good.'

She had caught him from the waist up, and, as she said, slightly out of focus, but still recognizable to anyone who knew him. Looking ahead, not at the camera, with a white-wrapped bundle under his arm. Even in fuzzy outline, the uncompromising bones gave his face a powerful toughness, a look of aggressive determination. I thought that I might have liked him, if we'd met another way.

'Will you take the photos to the police?' Hilary asked.

'I don't know.' I considered it. 'Could you lend me the negatives, to have more prints made?'

'Sort them out and take them,' she said.

I did that, and we lingered over our coffee.

'I suppose,' she said, 'that you have thought once or twice about . . . the time we spent together?'

'Yes.'

She looked at me with a smile in the spectacled eyes. 'Do you regret it?'

'Of course not. Do you?'

She shook her head. 'It may be too soon to say, but I think it will have changed my entire life.'

'How could it?' I said.

'I think you have released in me an enormous amount of mental energy. I was being held back by feelings of ignorance and even inferiority. These feelings have entirely gone. I feel full of rocket fuel, ready for blast off.'

'Where to?' I said. 'What's higher than a head-mistress?'

'Nothing measurable. But my school will be better, and there are such things as power and influence, and the ear of policy makers.'

'Miss Pinlock will be a force in the land?'

'We'll have to see,' she said.

I thought back to the time I'd first slept with a girl, when I was eighteen. It had been a relief to find out what everyone had been going on about, but I couldn't remember any accompanying upsurge of power. Perhaps, for me, the knowledge had come too easily, and too young. More likely that I'd never had the Pinlock potential in the first place.

I paid the bill and went out into the street. The April air was cold, as it had been for the past entire week, and Hilary shivered slightly inside her coat.

'The trouble with warm rooms . . . life blasts you when you leave.'

'Speaking allegorically?' I said.

'Of course.'

We began to walk back towards the office, up the High Street, beside the shops. People scurried in and out of the doorways like bees at a hive mouth. The familiar street scene, after the last three weeks, seemed superficial and unreal.

We drew level with a bank: not, as it happened, the one where I kept my own money, nor that which we used as a firm, but one which dealt with the affairs of many of our clients.

'Would you wait a sec?' I said. 'I've had a thought or two this week . . . just want to check something.'

Hilary smiled and nodded cheerfully, and waited without comment while I went on my short errand.

'OK?' I said, rejoining her.

'Fine,' she said. 'Where did they keep you, in that van?'

'In a warehouse.' I looked at my watch. 'Do you want to see it? I want to go back for another look.'

'All right.'

'My car's behind the office.'

We walked on, past a small, pleasant-looking dress shop. I glanced idly into the window, and walked two strides past, and then stopped.

'Hilary . . .'

'Yes?'

'I want to give you a present.'

'Don't be ridiculous,' she said.

She protested her way into the shop and was reduced to silence only by the sight of what I wanted her to wear: the garment I'd seen in the window; a long bold scarlet cloak.

'Try it,' I said.

Shaking her head, she removed the dull tweed coat and let the girl assistant lower the bright swirling cape on to her shoulders. She stood immobile while the girl fastened the buttons and arranged the neat collar. Looked at herself in the glass.

Duck into swan, I thought. She looked imposing and magnificent, a plain woman transfigured, her height making dramatic folds in the drop of clear red wool.

'Rockets,' I said, 'are powered by flame.'

'You can't buy me this.'

'Why not?'

I wrote the girl a cheque, and Hilary for once seemed to be speechless.

'Keep it on,' I said. 'It looks marvellous.'

The girl packed the old coat into a carrier, and we continued our walk to the office. People looked at Miss Pinlock as they passed, as they had not done before.

'It takes courage,' she said, raising her chin.

'First flights always do.'

She thought instantly of the night in Cala St Galdana: I saw it in the movement of her eyes. She smiled to herself, and straightened a fraction to her full height. Nothing wrong with the Pinlock nerve, then or ever.

From the front the warehouse looked small and dilapidated, its paint peeling off like white scabs to leave uneven grey scars underneath. A weatherboard screwed to the wall offered 10,500 square feet to let, but judging from the aged dimness of the sign, the customers had hardly queued.

The building stood on its own at the end of a side road

which now had no destination, owing to the close-down of the branch railway and the subsequent massive re-organization of the landscape into motorways and roundabouts.

There was a small door let into a large one on rollers at the entrance, neither of them locked. The locks, in fact, appeared to have been smashed, but in time gone by. The splintered wood around them had weathered grey with age.

I pushed open the small door for Hilary, and we stepped in. The gloom as the door swung behind us was as blinding as too much light; I propped the door open with a stone, but even then there were enfolding shadows at every turn. It was clear why vandals had stopped at breaking down the doors. Everything inside was so thick with dust that to kick anything was to start a choking cloud.

Sounds were immediately deadened, as if the high, mouldering piles of junk were soaking up every echo before it could go a yard.

I shouted 'Hey' into the small central space, and it seemed to reach no further than my own throat.

'It's cold in here,' Hilary said. 'Colder than outside.'

'Something to do with ventilation bricks, I expect,' I said. 'A draught, bringing in dust and lowering the temperature.'

Our voices had no resonance. We walked the short distance to where the white van stood, with the dark tarpaulin sprawling in a huge heap beside it.

With eyes adjusting to the dim light, we looked inside. The police had taken the water carrier and the bag of cheese, and the van was empty.

It was a small space. Dirty, and hard.

'You spent nearly a week in there,' Hilary said, disbelievingly.

'Five nights and four and a half days,' I said. 'Let's not exaggerate.'

'Let's not,' she said dryly.

We stood looking at the van for a minute or two, and the deadness and chill of the place began to soak into our brains. I shuddered slightly and walked away, out through the door into the living air.

Hilary followed me, and kicked away the door-stop. The peeling door swung shut.

'Did you sleep well, last night?' she said bleakly.

'No.'

'Nightmares?'

I looked up to the grey sky, and breathed deep luxurious breaths.

'Well . . . dreams,' I said.

She swallowed. 'Why did you want to come back here?'

'To see the name of the estate agent who has this place on his books. It's on the board, on the wall. I wasn't noticing things much when the police took me out of here yesterday.'

She gave a small explosive laugh of escaping tension. 'So practical!'

'Whoever put the van in there knew the place existed,' I said. 'I didn't, and I've lived in Newbury for six years.'

'Leave it to the police,' she said seriously. 'After all, they did find you.'

I shook my head. 'Someone rang Scotland Yard to tell them where I was.'

'Leave it to them,' she urged. 'You're out of it now.'

'I don't know. To coin a cliché, there's a great big iceberg blundering around here, and that van's only the tip.'

We got into my car, and I drove her back to the park in town where she'd left her own. She stood beside it, tall in her scarlet cloak, and fished in her handbag for a pen and notebook.

'Here,' she said, writing. 'This is my address and telephone number. You can come at any time. You might need . . .' She paused an instant, ' . . . a safe place.'

'Can I come for advice?' I said.

'For anything.'

I smiled.

'No,' she said. 'Not for that. I want a memory, not a habit.'

'Take your glasses off,' I said.

'To see you better?' She took them off, humouring me quizzically.

'Why don't you wear contact lenses?' I said. 'Without glasses, your eyes are great.'

*

On the way back to the office I stopped to buy food, on the premise that if I didn't stock up with things I liked, I wouldn't get back to normal eating. I also left Hilary's negatives for a rush reprint, so that it was nearly five before I went through the door.

Debbie and Peter had both done their usual Friday afternoon bolt, for which dentists and classes were only sample reasons. The variety they had come up with over the years would have been valuable if applied to their work: but I knew from experience that if I forced them both to stay until five I got nothing productive done after a quarter past four. Bess, infected by them, had already covered her typewriter, and was busy applying thick new make-up on top of the old. Bess, eighteen and curvy, thought of work as a boring interruption of her sex life. She gave me a bright smile, ran her tongue round the fresh glistening lipstick, and swung her hips provocatively on her way to the weekend's sport.

There were voices in Trevor's room. Trevor's loud voice in short sentences, and a client's softer tones in long paragraphs.

I tidied my own desk, and carried the Glitberg, Ownslow and Connaught Powys files into the outer office on my way to the car.

The door to Trevor's room opened suddenly, and Trevor and his client were revealed there, warmly shaking hands.

The client was Denby Crest, solicitor, a short plump man with a stiff moustache and a mouth permanently

twisted in irritation. Even when he smiled at you personally, he gave an impression of annoyance at the state of
things in general. Many of his own clients saw that as
sympathy for their troubles, which was their mistake.

'I'll make it worth your while, Trevor,' he was saying.
'I'm eternally grateful.'

Trevor suddenly saw me standing there and stared at
me blankly.

'I thought you'd gone, Ro,' he said.

'Came back for some files,' I said, glancing down at
them in my arms. 'Good afternoon, Denby.'

'Good afternoon, Roland.'

He gave me a brief nod and made a brisk dive for the
outer door; a brusque departure, even by his standards. I
watched his fast disappearing back and said to Trevor,
'Did you sign his certificate? He said he would wait until
you got back.'

'Yes, I did,' Trevor said. He too showed no inclination
for leisurely chat, and turned away from me towards his
own desk.

'What was I doing wrong?' I said. 'I kept making him
fifty thousand pounds short.'

'Decimal point in the wrong place,' he said shortly.

'Show me,' I said.

'Not now, Ro. It's time to go home.'

I put the files down on Bess's desk and walked into
Trevor's office. It was larger than mine, and much tidier,
with no wall of waiting cardboard boxes. There were

three armchairs for clients, some Stubbs prints on the walls, and a bowl of flowering daffodils on his desk.

'Trevor . . .'

He was busy putting together what I recognized as Denby Crest's papers, and didn't look up. I stood in his room, waiting, until in the end he had to take notice. His face was bland, calm, uninformative, and if there had been any tension there a minute ago, it had now evaporated.

'Trevor,' I said. 'Please show me where I went wrong.'

'Leave it, Ro,' he said pleasantly. 'There's a good chap.'

'If you did sign his certificate, and he really is fifty thousand pounds short, then it concerns me too.'

'You're dead tired, Ro, and you look ill, and this is not a good time to discuss it.' He came round his desk and put his hand gently on my arm. 'My dear chap, you know how horrified and worried I am about what has been happening to you. I am most concerned that you should take things easy and recover your strength.'

It was a long speech for him, and confusing. When he saw me hesitate, he added. 'There's nothing wrong with Denby's affairs. We'll go through them, if you like, on Monday.'

'It had better be now,' I said.

'No.' He was stubbornly positive. 'We have friends coming for the evening, and I promised to be home early. Monday, Ro. It will keep perfectly well until Monday.'

I gave in, partly because I simply didn't want to face

what I guessed to be true, that Trevor had signed the certificate knowing the figures were false. I'd done the sums over and over on my cheese abacus, and the answer came monotonously the same, whichever method I used to work them out.

He shepherded me like an uncle to his door, and watched while I picked up the heap of files from Bess's desk.

'What are those?' he said. 'You really mustn't work this weekend.'

'They're not exactly work. They're back files. I just thought I'd take a look.'

He walked over and peered down at the labels, moving the top file to see what was underneath.

'Why these, for heaven's sake?' he said, frowning, coming across Connaught Powys.

'I don't know . . .' I sighed. 'I just thought they might possibly have some connection with my being abducted.'

He looked at me with compassion. 'My dear Ro, why don't you leave it all to the police?'

'I'm not hindering them.' I picked up the armful of files and smiled. 'I don't think I'm high on their urgency list, though. I wasn't robbed, ransomed, or held hostage, and a spot of unlawful imprisonment on its own probably ranks lower than parking on double yellow lines.'

'But,' he said doubtfully, 'don't you think they will ever discover who, or why?'

'It depends on where they look, I should think.' I shrugged a shoulder, walked to the door, and stopped to look back. He was standing by Bess's desk, clearly troubled. 'Trevor,' I said, 'I don't mind one way or the other whether the police come up with answers. I don't madly want public revenge, and I've had my fill of court-case publicity, as a witness. I certainly don't relish it as a victim. But for my own peace of mind, I would like to know. If I find out, I won't necessarily act on the knowledge. The police would have to. So there's the difference. It might be better – you never know – if it's I who did the digging, not the police.'

He shook his head, perturbed and unconvinced.

'See you Monday,' I said.

CHAPTER FOURTEEN

Jossie met me on the doorstep, fizzing with life.

'Dad says please come in for a drink.' She held the door open for me and looked uncertainly at my face. 'Are you all right? I mean . . . I suppose I didn't realize . . .'

I kissed her mouth. Soft and sweet. It made me hungry.

'A drink would be fine,' I said.

William Finch was already pouring Scotch as we walked into his office-sitting-room. He greeted me with a smile and held out the glass.

'You look as if you could do with it,' he said. 'You've been having a rough time, by all accounts.'

'I've a fellow feeling for footballs.' I took the glass, lifted it in a token toast, and sipped the pale fine spirit.

Jossie said, 'Kicked around?'

I nodded, smiling. 'Somebody,' I said, 'is playing a strategic game.'

Finch looked at me curiously. 'Do you know who?'

'Not exactly. Not yet.'

Jossie stood beside her father, pouring grapefruit juice

out of a small bottle. One could see heredity clearly at work: they both had the same tall, well-proportioned frame, the same high carriage of head on long neck, the same air of bending the world to their ways, instead of being themselves bent. He looked at her fondly, a hint of civilized amusement in his fatherly pride. Even her habitual mockery, it seemed, stemmed from him.

He turned his greying head to me again, and said he expected the police would sort out all the troubles, in time.

'I expect so,' I said neutrally.

'And I hope the villains get shut up in small spaces for years and years,' Jossie said.

'Well,' I said, 'they may.'

Finch buried his nose in a large gin and tonic and surfaced with a return to the subject which interested him most. Kidnappings came a poor second to racing.

'My next ride?' I echoed. 'Tomorrow, as a matter of fact. Tapestry runs in the Oasthouse Cup.'

His astonishment scarcely boosted my non-existent confidence. 'Good heavens,' he said. 'I mean, to be frank, Ro, is it wise?'

'Totally not.'

'Then why?'

'I have awful difficulty in saying no.'

Jossie laughed. 'Spineless,' she said.

The door opened and a dark-haired woman came in, walking beautifully in a long black dress. She seemed to move in a glow of her own; and the joy died out of Jossie like an extinguished fire.

Finch went towards the newcomer with a welcoming smile, took her elbow proprietorially, and steered her in my direction. 'Lida, my dear, this is Roland Britten. Ro, Lida Swann.'

A tapeworm with hooks, Jossie had said. The tapeworm had a broad expanse of unlined forehead, dark blue eyes, and raven hair combed smoothly back. As we shook hands, she pressed my fingers warmly. Her heavy, sweet scent broadcast the same message as full breasts, tiny waist, narrow hips, and challenging smile: the sexual woman in full bloom. Diametrically opposite, I reflected, to my own preference for astringency and humour. Jossie watched our polite social exchanges with a scowl, and I wanted to walk over and hug her.

Why not, I thought. I disengaged myself from the sultry aura of Lida, took the necessary steps, and slid my arm firmly round Jossie's waist.

'We'll be off, then,' I said. 'To feed the starving.'

Jossie's scowl persisted across the hall, into the car, and five miles down the road.

'I hate her,' she said. 'That sexy throaty voice . . . it's all put on.'

'It's gin,' I said.

'What?'

'Too much gin alters the vocal chords.'

'You're having me on.'

'I think I love you,' I said.

'That's a damn silly thing to say.'

'Why?'

'You can't love someone just because she hates her father's girlfriend.'

'A better reason than many.'

She turned her big eyes searchingly my way. I kept my own looking straight ahead, dealing with night on the country road.

'Strong men fall for her like ninepins,' she said.

'But I'm weak.'

'Spineless.' She cheered up a good deal, and finally managed a smile. 'Do you want me to come to Kempton tomorrow and cheer you on?'

'Come and give Moira Longerman a double brandy when I fall off.'

Over dinner she said with some seriousness, 'I suppose it's occurred to you that the last twice you've raced, you've been whipped off into black holes straight after?'

'It has,' I said.

'So are you – uh – at all scared, about tomorrow?'

'I'd be surprised if it happened again.'

'Surprise wouldn't help you much.'

'True.'

'You're absolutely infuriating,' she said explosively. 'If you know why you were abducted, why not tell me?'

'I might be wrong, and I want to ask some questions first.'

'What questions?'

'What are you doing on Sunday?'

'That's not a question.'

'Yes, it is,' I said. 'Would you care for a day on the Isle of Wight?'

With guilty misgivings about riding Tapestry I did my best to eat, and later, after leaving Jossie on her doorstep, to go home and sleep. As my system seemed to be stubbornly resisting my intention that it should return to normal, both enterprises met with only partial success. The Saturday morning face in the shaving mirror would have inspired faith in no one, not even Moira herself.

'You're a bloody fool,' I said aloud, and my reflection agreed.

Coffee, boiled egg and toast to the good, I went down into the town to seek out owners of destitute warehouses. The estate agents, busy with hand-holding couples, told me impatiently that they had already given the information to the police.

'Give it to me, too, then,' I said. 'It's hardly a secret, is it?'

The bearded pale-faced man I'd asked looked harried and went off to consult. He came back with a slip of paper which he handed over as if contact with it had sullied his soul.

'We have ceased to act for these people,' he said earnestly. 'Our board should no longer be affixed to the wall.'

I'd never known anyone actually say the word 'affixed'

before. It wasn't all he could say, either. 'We wish to be considered as disassociated from the whole situation.'

I read the words written on the paper. 'I'm sure you do,' I said. 'Could you tell me when you last heard from these people? And has anyone been enquiring recently about hiring or using the warehouse?'

'Those people,' he said disapprovingly, 'appear to have let the warehouse several years ago to some army surplus suppliers, without informing us or paying fees due to us. We have received no instructions from them, then or since, regarding any further letting or sub-letting.'

'Ta ever so,' I said, and went grinning out to the street.

The words on the paper, which had so fussed the agents in retrospect, were 'National Construction (Wessex) Ltd', or in other words the mythical builders invented by Ownslow and Glitberg.

I picked up the rush reprint enlargements of Hilary's photographs, and walked along to the office. All quiet there, as usual on Saturdays, with undone work still sitting reproachfully in heaps.

Averting my eyes, I telephoned the police.

'Any news?' I said; and they said no there wasn't.

'Did you trace the owner of the van?' I asked. No, they hadn't.

'Did it have an engine number?' I said. Yes, they said, but it was not the original number for that particular vehicle, said vehicle having probably passed through many hands and rebuilding processes on its way to the warehouse.

'And have you asked Mr Glitberg and Mr Ownslow what I was doing in a van inside their warehouse?'

There was silence at the other end.

'Have you?' I repeated.

They wanted to know why I should ask.

'Oh come off it,' I said. 'I've been to the estate agents, same as you.'

Mr Glitberg and Mr Ownslow, it appeared, had been totally mystified as to why their warehouse should have been used in such a way. As far as they were concerned, it was let to an army surplus supply company, and the police should direct their enquiries to them.

'Can you find these army surplus people?' I asked. Not so far, they said. They cleared the police throat and cautiously added that Mr Glitberg and Mr Ownslow had categorically denied that they had imprisoned Mr Britten in a van in their warehouse, or anywhere else, for that matter, as revenge for the said Mr Britten having been instrumental in their custodial sentences for fraud.

'Their actual words?' I asked with interest. Not exactly. I had been given the gist.

I thanked them for the information, and disconnected. I thought they had probably not passed on everything they knew, but then neither had I, which made us quits.

The door of Trevor's private office was locked, as mine had been, but we both had keys for each other's rooms. I knew all the same that he wouldn't have been pleased to see me searching uninvited through the papers in his filing cupboard, but I reckoned that as I'd had access to them anyway while he was on holiday, another peep would be no real invasion. I spent a concentrated hour reading cash books and ledgers; and then with a mind functioning more or less as normal I checked through the Denby Crest figures yet again. I had made no mistake with them, even in a daze. Fifty thousand pounds of clients' trust funds were missing. I stared unseeingly at 'Lady and Gentleman in a Carriage' and thought bleakly about consequences.

There was a photocopier in the outer office, busily operated every weekday by Debbie and Peter. I spent another hour of that quiet Saturday morning methodically printing private copies for my own use. Then I put all the books and papers back where I'd found them, locked Trevor's office, and went down to the store in the basement.

The files I was looking for there were easy to find but were slim and uninformative, containing only copies of audits and not all the invoices, cash books and paying-in books from which the accounts had been drawn.

There was nothing odd in that. Under the Companies Act 1976, and also under the value added tax system, all such papers had to be kept available for three years and could legally be thrown away only after that, but most accountants returned the books to their clients for keeping, as like us they simply didn't have enough storage space for everyone.

I left the files where they were, locked all the office doors, sealed my folder of photocopies into a large envelope, and took it with me in some depression to Kempton Park.

The sight of Jossie in her swirly brown skirt brought the sun out considerably, and we despatched grapefruit juice in amicable understanding.

'Dad's brought the detestable Lida,' she said, 'so I came on my own.'

'Does she live with you?' I asked.

'No, thank God.' The idea alarmed her. 'Five miles away, and that's five thousand miles too close.'

'What does the ever-sick secretary have to say about her?'

'Sandy? It makes her even sicker.' She drank the remains of her juice, smiling over the glass. 'Actually Sandy wouldn't be so bad, if she weren't so wet. And you can cast out any slick theories about daughters being possessive of their footloose fathers, because actually I would have liked it rather a lot if he'd fallen for a peach.'

'Does he know you don't like Lida?'

'Oh sure,' she sighed. 'I told him she was a flesh-eating orchid and he said I didn't understand. End of conversation. The funny thing is,' she added, 'that it's only when I'm with you that I can think of her without spitting.'

'Appendicitis diverts the mind from toothache,' I said.

'What?'

'Thoughts from inside little white vans.'

'Half the time,' she said, 'I think you're crazy.'

She met some friends and went off with them, and I repaired to the weighing room to change into breeches, boots, and Moira Longerman's red and white colours. When I came out, with my jacket on over the bright shirt, Binny Tomkins was waiting. On his countenance, the reverse of warmth and light.

'I want to talk to you,' he said.

'Fine. Why not?'

He scowled. 'Not here. Too many people. Walk down this way.' He pointed to the path taken by the horses on their way from parade ring to track: a broad stretch of grass mostly unpopulated by racegoing crowds.

'What is it?' I said, as we emerged from the throng round the weighing room door, and started in the direction he wanted. 'Is there something wrong with Tapestry?'

He shook his head impatiently, as if the idea were silly.

'I want you to give the horse an easy race.'

I stopped walking. An easy race, in those terms, meant trying not to win.

'No,' I said.

'Come on, there's more . . .' He went on a pace or two, looking back and waiting for me to follow. 'I must talk to you. You must listen.'

There was more than usual scowling bad temper in his manner. Something like plain fear. Shaking my head, I went on with him, across the grass.

'How much would you want?' he said.

I stopped again. 'I'm not doing it,' I said.

'I know, but . . . How about two hundred, tax free?'

'You're stupid, Binny.'

'It's all right for you,' he said furiously. 'But if Tapestry wins today I'll lose everything. My yard, my livelihood – everything.'

'Why?'

He was trembling with tension. 'I owe a lot of money.'

'To bookmakers?' I said.

'Of course to bookmakers.'

'You're a fool,' I said flatly.

'Smug bastard,' he said furiously. 'I'd give anything to have you back inside that van, and not here today.'

I looked at him thoughtfully. 'Tapestry may not win anyway,' I said. 'Nothing's a certainty.'

'I've got to know in advance,' he said incautiously.

'And if you assure your bookmaker Tapestry won't win, he'll let you off the hook?'

'He'll let me off a bit,' he said. 'He won't press for the rest.'

'Until next time,' I said. 'Until you're in deeper still.'

Binny's eyes stared inwards to the hopeless future, and I guessed he would never take the first step back to firm ground, which was in his case to stop gambling altogether.

'There are easier ways for trainers to lose races,' I pointed out, 'than trying to bribe the jockey.'

His scowl reached Neanderthal proportions. 'She pays the lad who does her horse to watch him like a hawk and give her a report on everything that happens. I can't sack him or change him to another horse, because she says if I do she'll send Tapestry to another trainer.'

'I'm amazed she hasn't already,' I said: and she would have done, I thought, if she'd been able to hear that conversation.

'You've only got to ride a bad race,' he said. 'Get boxed in down the far side and swing wide coming into the straight.'

'No,' I said. 'Not on purpose.'

I seemed to be remarkably good at inspiring fury. Binny would happily have seen me fall dead at his feet.

'Look,' I said, 'I'm sorry about the fix you're in. I really am, whether you believe it or not. But I'm not going to try to get you out of it by cheating Moira or the horse or the punters or myself, and that's that.'

'You *bastard*,' he said.

Five minutes later, when I was back in the hub of the racecourse outside the weighing room, a hand touched me on the arm and a drawly voice spoke behind my ear.

'My dear Ro, what are your chances?'

I turned, smiling, to the intelligent face of Vivian Iverson. In the daylight on a racecourse, where I'd first met him, he wore his clothes with the same elegance and flair that he had extended to his Vivat Club. Dark green blazer over grey checked trousers; hair shining black in the April sun. Quiet amusement in the observant eyes.

'In love, war, or the three-thirty?' I said.

'Of remaining at liberty, my dear chap.'

I blinked. 'Um,' I said. 'What would you offer?'

'Five to four against?'

'I hope you're wrong,' I said.

Underneath the banter, he was detectably serious. 'It just so happens that last night in the club I heard our friend Connaught Powys talking on the telephone. To be frank, my dear Ro, after I'd heard your name mentioned, I more or less deliberately *listened*.'

'On an extension?'

'Tut tut,' he said reprovingly. 'Unfortunately not. I don't know who he was talking to. But he said – his exact words – "As far as Britten is concerned you must agree that precaution is better than cure," and a bit later he said "If dogs start sniffing around, the best thing to do is chain them up." '

'Charming,' I said blankly.

'Do you need a bodyguard?'

'Are you offering yourself?'

He shook his head, smiling. 'I could hire you one. Karate. Bulletproof glass. All the mod cons.'

'I think,' I said thoughtfully, 'that I'll just increase the insurance policies.'

'Against kidnapping? No one will take you on.'

'Checks and balances,' I said. 'No one'll push me off a spring-board if it means a rock falling on their own head.'

'Be sure to let them know the rock exists.'

'Your advice,' I said, smiling, 'is worth its weight in ocean-going sailing boats.'

*

228

Moira Longerman twinkled with her bright bird-eyes in the parade ring before Tapestry's race and stroked my arm repeatedly, her small thin hand sliding delicately over the shiny scarlet sleeve.

'Now, Roland, you'll do your best, I know you'll do your best.'

'Yes,' I said guiltily, flexing several flabby muscles and watching Tapestry's highly tuned ones ripple under his coat as he walked round the ring with his lad.

'I saw you talking to Binny just now, Roland.'

'Did you, Moira?' I switched my gaze to her face.

'Yes, I did.' She nodded brightly. 'I was up in the stands, up there in the bar, looking down to the paddock. I saw Binny take you away for a talk.'

She looked at me steadily, shrewdly, asking the vital question in total silence. Her hand went on stroking. She waited intently, expecting an answer.

'I promise you,' I said plainly, 'that if I make a hash of it, it'll be against my will.'

She stopped stroking, patted my arm instead, and smiled. 'That will do nicely, Roland.'

Binny stood ten feet away, unable to make even a show of the civility due from trainer to owner. His face was rigid, his eyes expressionless, and even the usual scowl had frozen into a more general and powerful gloom. I thought I had probably been wrong to think of Binny as a stupid fool. There was something about him at that moment which raised prickles on the skin and images of murder.

The bell rang for jockeys to mount, and it was the lad, not Binny, who gave me a leg-up into the saddle.

'I'm not going to take much more of this,' Moira said pleasantly to the world in general.

Binny ignored her as if he hadn't heard; and maybe he hadn't. He'd also given me no riding instructions, which I didn't mind in the least. He seemed wholly withdrawn and unresponsive, and when Moira waved briefly as I walked away on Tapestry, he did not accompany her across to the stands. Even for him, his behaviour was incredible.

Tapestry himself was in a great mood, tossing his head with excitement and bouncing along in tiny cantering strides as if he had April spring fever in all his veins. I remembered his plunging start in the Gold Cup and realized that this time I'd be lucky if he didn't bolt with me from the post. Far from being last from indecision, this time, in my weakened state, I could be forty lengths in front by the second fence, throwing away all chance of staying power at the end.

Tapestry bounced gently on his toes in the parade past the stands, while the other runners walked. Bounced playfully back at a canter to the start, which in three mile 'chases at Kempton Park was to the left of the stands and in full view of most of the crowd.

There were eleven other jockeys walking around there, making final adjustments to girths and goggles and answering to the starter's roll call. The starter's assistant, tightening the girths of the horse beside me, looked over his shoulder and asked me if mine were all right, or should he tighten those too.

If I hadn't recently been through so many wringers, I would simply have said yes, and he would have pulled the buckles up a notch or two, and I wouldn't have given it another thought. As it was, in my over-cautious state, I had a sudden sharp vision of Binny's dangerous detachment, and remembered the desperation behind his appeal to me to lose. The prickles returned in force.

I slid off Tapestry's back and looped his reins over my arm.

'Just want to check . . .' I said vaguely to the starter's assistant.

He nodded briefly, glancing at his watch. One minute to racetime, his face said, so hurry up.

It was my own saddle. I intimately knew its every flap, buckle, scratch and stain. I checked it thoroughly inch by inch with fingers and eyes, and could see nothing wrong. Girths, stirrups, leathers, buckles; everything as it should be. I pulled the girths tighter myself, and the starter told me to get mounted.

Looking over my shoulder, I thought, for the rest of my life. Seeing demons in shadows. But the feeling of danger wouldn't go away.

'Hurry up, Britten.'

'Yes, sir.'

I stood on the ground, looking at Tapestry tossing his head.

'Britten!'

Reins, I thought. Bridle. Bit Reins. If the bridle broke, I couldn't control the horse and he wouldn't win the race. Many races had been lost, from broken bridles.

It was not too difficult to see, if one looked really closely. The leather reins were stitched on to the rings at each side of the bit, and the stitches on the off-side rein had nearly all been severed.

Three miles and twenty fences at bucketing speed with just two strands of thread holding my right-hand rein.

'*Britten!*'

I gave a jerking tug, and the remaining stitches came apart in my hand. I pulled the rein off the ring and waved the free end in the air.

'Sorry, sir,' I said. 'I need another bridle.'

'What? Oh very well . . .' He used his telephone to call the weighing room to send a replacement out quickly. Tapestry's lad appeared, looking worried, to help change the headpiece, and I pointed out to him, as I gave him Binny's bridle, the parted stitching.

'I don't know how it could have got like that,' he said anxiously. 'I didn't know it was like that, honest. I cleaned it yesterday, and all.'

'Don't worry,' I said. 'It's not your fault.'

'Yes, but . . .'

'Give me a leg-up,' I said, 'and don't worry.'

He continued all the same to look upset. Good lads took it grievously to heart if anything was proved lacking in the way they turned out their horses, and Tapestry's lad was as good as the horse deserved. Binny, I thought not for the first time, was an all-out, one-man disaster area, a blight to himself and everyone around.

'Line up,' shouted the starter, with his hand on the lever. 'We're five minutes late.'

Tapestry did his best to put that right two seconds later with another arm-wrenching departure, but owing to one or two equally impetuous opponents I thankfully got him anchored in mid-field; and there we stayed for all of the first circuit. The pace, once we'd settled down, was nothing like as fast as the Gold Cup, and I had time to worry about the more usual things, like meeting the fences right, and not running out altogether, which was an added hazard at Kempton where the wings leading to the fences were smaller and lower than on other courses, and tended to give tricky horses bad ideas.

During the second circuit my state of unfitness raised its ugly head in no uncertain way, and it would be fair to say that for the last mile Tapestry's jockey did little except cling on. Tapestry truly was, however, a great performer, and in consequence of the cheers and acclaim in the unsaddling enclosure after the Gold Cup, he seemed, like many much-fêted horses, to have become conscious of his own star status. It was the extra dimension of his new pride which took us in a straight faultless run over the last three fences in the straight, and his own will to win which extended his neck and his stride on the run-in. Tapestry won the Oasthouse Cup by four lengths, and it was all the horse's doing, not mine.

Moira kissed her horse with tears running down her

cheeks, and kissed me as well, and everyone else within mouth-shot, indiscriminately. There was nothing uptight or inhibited about the Longerman joy, and the most notable person not there to share it was the horse's trainer. Binny Tomkins was nowhere to be seen.

'Drink,' Moira shrieked at me. 'Owners and trainers bar.'

I nodded, speechless from exertion and back-slapping, and struggled through the throng with my saddle to be weighed in. It was fabulous, I thought dazedly; fantastic, winning another big race. More than I'd ever reckoned possible. A bursting delight like no other on earth. Even knowing how little I'd contributed couldn't dampen the wild inner rejoicing. I'd never be able to give it up, I thought. I'd still be struggling round in the mud and the rain at fifty, chasing the marvellous dream. Addiction wasn't only a matter of needles in the arm.

Moira in the bar was dispensing champagne and bright laughs in copious quantities, and had taken Jossie closely in tow.

'Ro, darling Ro,' Moira said, 'have you seen Binny anywhere?'

'No, I haven't.'

'Wasn't it odd, the bridle breaking like that?' Her innocent-seeming eyes stared up into my own. 'I talked to the lad, you see.'

'These things do happen,' I said.

'You mean, no one can prove anything?'

'Roughly that.'

'But aren't you the teeniest bit angry?'

I smiled from the glowing inner pleasure. 'We won the race. What else matters?'

She shook her head. 'It was a wicked thing to do.'

Desperation, I thought, could spawn deeds the doers wouldn't sanely contemplate. Like cutting loose a rein. Like kidnapping the enemy. Like whatever else lay ahead before we were done. I shut out the shadowy devils and drank to life and the Oasthouse Cup.

Jossie, too, had a go at me when we wandered later out to the car park.

'Is Moira right?' she demanded. 'Did Binny rig it for you to come to grief?'

'I should think so.'

'She says you ought to report it.'

'There's no need.'

'Why not?'

'He's programmed to self-destruct before the end of the season.'

'Do you mean *suicide*?' she said.

'You're too literal. I mean he'll go bust to the bookies with a reverberating bang.'

'You're drunk.'

I shook my head, grinning. 'High. Quite different. Care to join me on my cloud?'

'A puff of wind,' she said, 'and you'd evaporate.'

CHAPTER FIFTEEN

Jossie drove off to some party or other in London, and I, mindful of earlier unscheduled destinations after racing, took myself circumspectly down the road to the nearest public telephone box. No one followed, that I could see.

Hilary Margaret Pinlock answered at the twentieth ring, when I had all but given up, and said breathlessly that she had only that second reached home; she'd been out playing tennis.

'Are you busy this evening?' I said.

'Nothing special.'

'Can I come and see you?'

'Yes.' She hesitated a fraction. 'What do you want? Food? A bed?'

'An ear,' I said. 'And baked beans, perhaps. But no bed.'

'Right,' she said calmly. 'Where are you? Do you need directions?'

She told me clearly how to find her, and I drew up forty minutes later outside a large Edwardian house in a leafy road on the outskirts of a sprawling Surrey town.

Hilary, it transpired, owned the ground floor, a matter of two large, high-ceilinged rooms, modern kitchen, functional bathroom, and a pleasant old-fashioned conservatory with plants, cane armchairs, and steps down to an unkempt garden.

Inside, everything was orderly and organized, and comfortable in an uninspired sort of way. Well-built easy chairs in dim covers, heavy curtains in good velvet but of a deadening colour somewhere between brown and green, patterned carpet in olive and fawn. The home of a vigorous academic mind with no inborn response to refracted light. I wondered just how much she would wear the alien scarlet cloak.

The evening sun still shone into the conservatory, and there we sat, in the cane armchairs, drinking sherry, greenly surrounded by palms and rubber plants and *Monstera deliciosa.*

'I don't mind *watering*,' Hilary said. 'But I detest *gardening*. The people upstairs are supposed to do the garden, but they don't.' She waved disgustedly towards the view of straggly bushes, unpruned roses, weedy paths, and dried coffee-coloured stalks of last year's unmown grass.

'It's better than concrete,' I said.

'I'll use you as a parable for the children,' she said, smiling.

'Hm?'

'When things are bad, you endure what you must, and thank God it's not worse.'

I made a protesting sound in my throat, much taken aback. 'Well,' I said helplessly, 'what else is there to do?'

'Go screaming off to the Social Services.'

'For a gardener?'

'You know darned well what I mean.'

'Endurance is like tax,' I said. 'You're silly to pay more than you have to, but you can't always escape it.'

'And you can whine,' she said, nodding, 'or suffer with good grace.'

She drank her sherry collectedly and invited me to say why I'd come.

'To ask you to keep a parcel safe for me,' I said.

'But of course.'

'And to listen to a fairly long tale, so that . . .' I paused. 'I mean, I want someone to know . . .' I stopped once more.

'In case you disappear again?' she said matter-of-factly.

I was grateful for her calmness.

'Yes,' I said. I told her about meeting Vivian Iverson at the races, and our thoughts on insurance, springboards, and rocks. 'So you see,' I ended, 'you'll be the rock, if you will.'

'You can expect,' she said, 'rock-like behaviour.'

'Well,' I said, 'I've brought a sealed package of photocopied documents. It's in the car.'

'Fetch it,' she said.

I went out to the street and collected the thick envelope from the boot. Habit induced me to look into the back seat floor space, and to scan the harmless street. No one hiding, no one watching, that I could see. No one had followed me from the racecourse, I was sure.

Looking over my shoulder for the rest of my life.

I took the parcel indoors and gave it to Hilary, and also the negatives of her photographs, explaining that I already had the extra prints. She put everything on the table beside her and told me to sit down and get on with the tale.

'I'll tell you a bit about my job,' I said. 'And then you'll understand better.' I stretched out with luxurious weariness in the cane chair and looked at the intent interest on her strong plain face. A pity, I thought, about the glasses.

'An accountant working for a long time in one area, particularly in an area like a country town, tends to get an overall picture of the local life.'

'I follow you,' she said. 'Go on.'

'The transactions of one client tend to turn up in the accounts of others. For instance, a racehorse trainer buys horse food from the forage merchants. I check the invoice through the trainer's accounts, and then, because the forage merchant is also my client, I later check it again through his. I see that the forage merchant has paid a builder for an extension to his house, and later, in the builder's accounts, I see what *he* paid for the bricks and cement. I see that a jockey had paid x pounds on an air-taxi, and later, because the air-taxi firm is also my client, I see the receipt of x pounds from the jockey. I see the movement of money around the neighbourhood . . . the interlocking of interests . . . the pattern of commerce. I learn the names of suppliers, the size of businesses, and the kinds of services people use. My knowledge increases until I have a sort of mental map like a wide landscape, in which all the names are familiar and occur in the proper places.'

'Fascinating,' Hilary said.

'Well,' I said, 'if a totally strange name crops up, and you can't cross-reference it with anything else, you begin to ask questions. At first of yourself, and then of others. Discreetly. And that was how I ran into trouble in the shape of two master criminals called Glitberg and Ownslow.'

'They sound like a music-hall turn.'

'They're as funny as the Black Death.' I drank some sherry ruefully. 'They worked for the council, and the council's accounts and audits were done by a large firm in London, who naturally didn't have any intimate local knowledge. Ownslow and Glitberg had invented a construction firm called National Construction (Wessex) Limited, through which they had syphoned off more than a million pounds each of taxpayers' money. And I had a client, a builders' merchant, who had received several cheques from National Construction (Wessex). I'd never heard of National Construction (Wessex) in any other context, and I asked my client some searching questions, to which his reply was unmistakable panic. Glitberg and

Ownslow were prosecuted and went to jail swearing to
be revenged.'

'On you?'

'On me.'

'Nasty.'

'A few weeks later,' I said, 'much the same thing happened. I turned up some odd payments made by a
director of an electronics firm through the company's
computer. His name was Connaught Powys. He'd taken
his firm for over a quarter of a million, and he too went
to jail swearing to get even. He's out again now, and so
are Glitberg and Ownslow. Since then I've been the basic
cause of the downfall of two more big-time embezzlers,
both of whom descended to the cells swearing severally
to tear my guts out and cut my throat.' I sighed. 'Luckily,
they're both still inside.'

'And I thought accountants led dull lives!'

'Maybe some do.' I drained my sherry. 'There's
another thing that those five embezzlers have in common
besides me, and that is that not a penny of what they
stole has been recovered.'

'Really?' She seemed not to find it greatly significant.
'I expect it's all sitting around in bank deposits, under
different names.'

I shook my head. 'Not unless it is in literally thousands
of tiny weeny deposits, which doesn't seem likely.'

'Why thousands?'

'Banks nowadays have to inform the Tax Inspectors of
the existence of any deposit account for which the annual

interest is £15 or more. That means the Inspectors know of all deposits of over three or four hundred quid.'

'I had no idea,' she said blankly.

'Anyway,' I said, 'I wanted to know if it could be Powys or Glitberg or Ownslow who had kidnapped me for revenge, so I asked them.'

'Good heavens.'

'Yeah. It wasn't a good idea. They wouldn't say yes or no.' I looked back to the night at the Vivat Club. 'They did tell me something else, though . . .' I said, and told Hilary what it was. Her eyes widened behind the glasses and she nodded once or twice.

'I see. Yes,' she said.

'So now,' I said. 'Here we are a few years later, and now I have not only my local area mental map but a broad view of most of the racing world, with uncountable interconnections. I do the accounts for so many racing people, their lives spread out like a carpet, touching, overlapping, each small transaction adding to my understanding of the whole. I'm part of it myself, as a jockey. I feel the fabric around me. I know how much saddles cost, and which saddler does most business, and which owners don't pay their bills, and who bets and who drinks, who saves, who gives to charity, who keeps a mistress. I know how much the woman whose horse I rode today paid to have him photographed for the Christmas cards she sent last year, and how much a bookmaker gave for his Rolls, and thousands and thousands of similar facts. All fitting, all harmless. It's when they don't fit . . . like a jockey suddenly spending more than he's earned, and I find he's running a whole new business and not declaring a penny of it . . . it's when the bits don't fit that I see the monster in the waves. Glimpsed, hidden . . . But definitely there.'

'Like now?' she said, frowning. 'Your iceberg?'

'Mm.' I hesitated. 'Another embezzler.'

'And this one – will he too go to jail swearing to cut your throat?'

I didn't answer at once, and she added dryly, 'Or is he likely to cut your throat before you get him there?'

I gave her half a grin. 'Not with a rock like you, he won't.'

'You be careful, Roland,' she said seriously. 'This doesn't feel to me like a joke.'

She stood up restlessly, towering among the palm fronds, as thin in her way as their stems.

'Come into the kitchen. What do you want to eat? I can do a Spanish omelette, if you like.'

I sat with my elbows on the kitchen table, and while she chopped onions and potatoes and green peppers I told her a good deal more, most of it highly unethical, as an accountant should never disclose the affairs of a client. She listened with increasing dismay, her cooking actions growing slower. Finally she laid down the knife and simply stood.

'Your partner,' she said.

'I don't know how much he's condoned,' I said, 'but on Monday . . . I have to find out.'

'Tell the police,' she said. 'Let them find out.'

'No. I've worked with Trevor for six years. We've always got on well together, and he seems fond of me, in his distant way. I can't shop him, just like that.'

'You'll warn him.'

'Yes,' I said. 'And I'll tell him of the existence of . . . the rock.'

She started cooking again, automatically, her thoughts busy behind her eyes.

'Do you think,' she said, 'that your partner knew about the other embezzlers, and tried to hush them up?'

I shook my head. 'Not Glitberg and Ownslow. Positively not. Not the last two, either. The firms they worked for were both my clients, and Trevor had no contact with them. But Connaught Powys . . .' I sighed. 'I really don't know. Trevor always used to spend about a week at that firm, doing the audit on the spot, as one nearly always does for big concerns, and I went one year only because he had an ulcer. It was Connaught Powys's bad luck that I cottoned on to what he was doing. Trevor might genuinely have missed the warning signs, because he doesn't always work the way I do.'

'How do you mean?'

'Well, a lot of an accountant's work is fairly mechanical. Vouching, for instance. That's checking that cheques written down in the cash book really were issued for the amount stated or, in other words, if the cashier writes down that cheque number 1234 was issued to Joe Bloggs in the sum of eighty pounds to pay for a load of sand, the auditor checks that the bank actually paid eighty pounds to Joe Bloggs on cheque no. 1234. It's routine work and takes a fairly long time on a big account, and it's often, or even usually, done, not by the accountant or auditor himself, but by an assistant. Assistants in our firm tend to come and go, and don't necessarily develop a sense of probability. The present ones wouldn't be likely to query, for instance, whether Joe Bloggs really existed, or sold sand, or sold eighty quid's worth, or delivered only fifty quid's worth, with Joe Bloggs and the cashier conspiring to pocket the thirty pounds profit.'

'Roland!'

I grinned. 'Small fiddles abound. It's the first violins that threaten to cut your throat.'

She broke four eggs into a bowl. 'Do you do all your own . . . er . . . vouching, then?'

'No, not all. It would take too long. But I do all of it for some accounts, and some of it for all accounts. To get the feel of things. To know where I am.'

'To fit into the landscape,' she said.

'Yes.'

'And Trevor doesn't?'

'He does a few himself, but on the whole not. Don't get me wrong. More accountants do as Trevor does, it's absolutely normal practice.'

'You want my advice?' she said.

'Yes, please.'

'Go straight to the police.'

'Thank you. Get on with the omelette.'

She sizzled it in the pan and divided it, succulent and

245

soft in the centre, onto the plates. It tasted like a testi-
monial to her own efficiency, the best I'd ever had. Over
coffee, afterwards, I told her a great deal about Jossie.

She looked into her cup. 'Do you love her?' she said.

'I don't know. It's too soon to say.'

'You sound,' she said dryly, 'bewitched.'

'There have been other girls. But not the same.' I
looked at her downturned face. My mouth twitched. 'In
case you're wondering about Jossie,' I said, 'no, I
haven't.'

She looked up, the spectacles flashing, her eyes suddenly laughing, and a blush starting on her neck. She
uttered an unheadmistressly opinion.

'You're a sod,' she said.

It was an hour's drive home from Hilary's house. No one
followed me, or took the slightest interest, that I could
see.

I rolled quietly down the lane towards the cottage
with the car lights switched off, and made a silent rec-
onnoitre on foot for the last hundred yards.

Everything about my home was dark and peaceful.
The lights of Mrs Morris's sitting-room, next door, shone
dimly through the pattern of her curtains. The night sky
was powdered with stars, and the air was cool.

I waited for a while, listening, and was slowly
reassured. No horrors in the shadows. No shattering

black prisons yawning like mantraps before my feet. No cut-throats with ready steel.

To be afraid, I thought, was no way to live; yet I couldn't help it.

I unlocked the cottage and switched on all the lights; and it was empty, welcoming and sane. I fetched the car from the lane, locked myself into the cottage, pulled shut the curtains, switched on the heaters, and hugged round myself the comforting illusion of being safe in the burrow.

After that I made a pot of coffee, fished out some brandy, and sprawled into an armchair with the ancient records of the misdeeds of Powys, Glitberg and Ownslow.

At one time I'd known every detail in those files with blinding clarity, but the years had blurred my memory. I found notes in my own handwriting about inferences I couldn't remember drawing, and conclusions as startling as acid. I was amazed, actually, at the quality of work I'd done, and it was weird to see it from an objective distance, as with a totally fresh eye. I supposed I could understand the comment there had been then, though at the time what I was doing had seemed a perfectly natural piece of work, done merely as best I could. I smiled to myself in pleased surprise. In that far-off time, I must have been hell to embezzlers. Not like nowadays, when it took me six shots to see Denby Crest.

I came across pages of notes about the workings of computers, details of which I had forgotten as fast as I'd learned them on a crash course in an electronics firm much like Powys's. It had pleased me at the time to be able to dissect and explain just what he'd done, and nothing had made him more furious. It had been vanity on my part, I thought: and I was still vain. Admiring your own work was one of the deadlier intellectual sins.

I sighed. I was never going to be perfect, so why worry.

There was no record anywhere in the Glitberg/ Ownslow file of the buying of the warehouse, but it did seem possible, as I dug deeper in the search for clues, that it actually had been built by Glitberg and Ownslow, and was the sole concrete fabrication of National Construction (Wessex). Anyone who could invent whole streets of dwellings could put up a real warehouse without much trouble.

I wondered why they'd needed it, when everything else had been achieved on paper.

A tangible asset, uncashed, gone to seed, in which I had been dumped. The police had been told I was there, and the estate agent trail had led without difficulty straight to Ownslow and Glitberg.

Why?

I sat and thought about it for a good long time, and then I finished the coffee and brandy and went to bed.

I picked Jossie up at ten in the grey morning, and drove to Portsmouth for the hovercraft ferry to the Isle of Wight.

'The nostalgia kick?' Jossie said. 'Back to the boarding house?'

I nodded. 'The sunny isle of childhood.'

'Oh yeah?' She took me literally and looked up meaningfully at the cloudy sky.

'It heads the British sunshine league,' I said.

'Tell that to Torquay.'

A ten-minute zip in the hovercraft took us across the sea at Spithead, and when we stepped ashore at Ryde, the clouds were behind us, hovering like a grey sheet over the mainland.

'It's unfair,' Jossie said, smiling.

'It's often like that.'

The town was bright with new spring paint, the Regency buildings clean and graceful in the sun. Every year, before the holiday-makers came, there was the big brush-up and every winter, when they'd gone, the comfortable relapse into carpet slippers and salt-caked windows.

'Ryde pier,' I said, 'is two thousand, three hundred and five feet long, and was opened in 1814.'

'I don't want to know that.'

'There are approximately six hundred hotels, motels and boarding houses on this sunny island.'

'Nor that.'

'Nine towns, two castles, a lot of flamingoes and Parkhurst Prison.'

'Nor that, for God's sake.'

'My Uncle Rufus,' I said, 'was chief mucker-out at the local riding school.'

'Good grief.'

'As his assistant mucker-out,' I said, 'I scrambled under horses' bellies from the age of six.'

'That figures.'

'I used to exercise the horses and ponies all winter when the holiday people had gone home. And break in new ones. I can't really remember not being able to ride, but there's no racing here, of course. The first race I ever rode in was the Isle of Wight Foxhounds point-to-point over on the mainland, and I fell off.'

We walked along the Esplanade with the breeze blowing Jossie's long green scarf out like streamers. She waved an arm at the sparkling water and said, 'Why horses? Why not boats, for heaven's sake, when you had them on your doorstep.'

'They made me seasick.'

She laughed. 'Like going to heaven and being allergic to harps.'

I took her to a hotel I knew, where there was a sunny terrace sheltered from the breeze, with a stunning view of the Solent and the shipping tramping by to Southampton. We drank hot chocolate and read the lunch menu, and talked of this and that and nothing much, and the time slid away like a mill-stream.

After roast beef for both of us, and apple pie, ice-cream and cheese for Jossie, we whistled up a taxi. There weren't many operating on a Sunday afternoon in April, but there was no point in being a native if one didn't know where to find the pearls.

The driver knew me, and didn't approve of my having deserted to become a 'mainlander', but as he also knew I knew the roads backwards, we got a straight run over Blackgang Chine to the wild cliffs on the south-west coast, and no roundabout guff to add mileage. We dawdled along there for about an hour, stopping often to stand out of the car, on the windswept grass. Jossie took in great lungfuls of the soul-filling landscape and said whyever did I live in Newbury.

'Racing,' I said.

'So simple.'

'Do you mind if we call on a friend on the way back?' I said. 'Ten minutes or so?'

'Of course not.'

'Wootton Bridge, then,' I said to the driver. 'Frederick's boatyard.'

'They'll be shut. It's Sunday.'

'We'll try, anyway.'

He shrugged heavily, leaving me to the consequences of my own stupidity, and drove back across the island, through Newport and out on the Ryde road to the deep inlet which formed a natural harbour for hundreds of small yachts.

The white-painted façade of the boatyard showed closed doors and no sign of life.

'There you are,' said the driver. 'I told you so.'

I got out of the car and walked over to the door

251

marked 'Office', and knocked on it. Within a few moments it opened, and I grinned back to Jossie and jerked my head for her to join me.

'I got your message,' Johnny Frederick said. 'And Sunday afternoon, I sleep.'

'At your age?'

His age was the same as mine, almost to the day: we'd shared a desk at school and many a snigger in the lavatories. The round-faced, impish boy had grown into a muscular, salt-tanned man with craftsman's hands and a respectable hatred of paperwork. He occasionally telephoned me to find out if his own local accountant was doing things right, and bombarded the poor man with my advice.

'How's your father?' I said.

'Much the same.'

A balk of timber had fallen on Johnny's father's head in days gone by. There had been a lot of unkind jokes about thick as two planks before, three planks after, but the net result had been that an ailing family business had woken up in the hands of a bright new mind. With Johnny's designs and feeling for materials, Frederick Boats were a growing name.

I introduced Jossie, who got a shrewd once-over for aerodynamic lines and a shake from a hand like a piece of calloused teak.

'Pleased to meet you,' he said, which was about the nearest he ever got to social small-talk. He switched his gaze to me. 'You've been in the wars a bit, according to the papers.'

'You might say so.' I grinned. 'What are you building, these days?'

'Come and see.'

He walked across the functional little office and opened the far door, which led straight into the boatyard itself. We went through, and Jossie exclaimed aloud at the unexpected size of the huge shed which sloped away down to the water.

There were several smallish fibreglass hulls supported in building frames, and two large ones, side by side in the centre, with five-foot keels.

'What size are those?' Jossie said.

'Thirty-seven feet overall.'

'They look bigger.'

'They won't on the water. It's the largest size we do, at present.' Johnny walked us round one of them, pointing out subtleties of hull design with pride. 'It handles well in heavy seas. It's stable, and not too difficult to sail, which is what most people want.'

'Not a racer?' I said.

He shook his head. 'Those dinghies are. But the big ocean-racers are specialist jobs. This yard isn't large enough; not geared to that class. And anyway, I like cruisers. A bit of carpet in the saloon and lockers that slide like silk.'

Jossie wandered off down the concrete slope, peering into the half-fitted dinghies and looking contentedly interested. I pulled the envelope of enlarged photographs from my inner pocket and showed them to Johnny. Three views of a sailing boat, one of an out-of-focus man.

'That's the boat I was abducted on. Can you tell anything about it from these photos?'

He peered at them, his head on one side. 'If you leave them with me, maybe. I'll look through the catalogues, and ask the boys over at Cowes. Was there anything special about it, that you remember?'

I explained that I hadn't seen much except the sail locker. 'The boat was pretty new, I think. Or at any rate well maintained. And it sailed from England on Thursday, March 17th, some time in the evening.'

He shuffled the prints to look at the man.

'His name is Alastair Yardley,' I said. 'I've written it on the back. He came from Bristol, and worked from there as a deck-hand on sea-trials for ocean-going yachts. He skippered the boat. He's about our age.'

'Are you in a hurry for all this info?'

'Quicker the better.'

'OK. I'll ring a few guys. Let you know tomorrow, if I come up with anything.'

'That's great.'

He tucked the prints into their envelope and let his gaze wander to Jossie.

'A racing filly,' he said. 'Good lines.'

'Eyes off.'

'I like earthier ones, mate. Big boobs and not too bright.'

'Boring.'

'When I get home, I want a hot tea, and a cuddle when I feel like it, and no backchat about women's lib.'

When I got home, I thought, I wouldn't mind Jossie.

She walked up the concrete with big strides of her long legs, and came to a stop at our side. 'I had a friend whose boyfriend insisted on taking her sailing,' she said. 'She said she didn't terribly mind being wet, or cold, or hungry, or seasick, or frightened. She just didn't like them all at once.'

Johnny's eyes slid my way. 'With this boyfriend she'd be all right. He gets sick in harbour.'

Jossie nodded. 'Feeble.'

'Thanks,' I said.

'Be my guest.'

We went back through the office and into the taxi, and Johnny waved us goodbye.

'Any more chums?' Jossie said.

'Not this trip. If I start on the aunts, we'll be here for ever. Visit one, visit all, or there's a dust-up.'

We drove, however, at Jossie's request, past the guest house where I'd lived with my mother. There was a new glass sun lounge across the whole of the front, and a car park where there had been garden. Tubs of flowers, bright sun-awnings, and a swinging sign saying 'Vacancies'.

'Brave,' Jossie said, clearly moved. 'Don't you think?'

I paid off the taxi there and we walked down to the sea, with seagulls squawking overhead and the white little town sleeping to tea-time on its sunny hillside.

'It's pretty,' Jossie said. 'And I see why you left.'

She seemed as content as I to dawdle away the rest of the day. We crossed again in the hovercraft, and made our way slowly northwards, stopping at a pub at dusk for a drink and rubbery pork pie, and arriving finally outside the sprawling pile of Axwood House more than twelve hours after we'd left.

'That car,' Jossie said, pointing with disfavour at an inoffensive Volvo parked ahead, 'belongs to the detestable Lida.'

The light over the front door shone on her disgruntled face. I smiled, and she transferred the disfavour to me.

'It's all right for you. You aren't threatened with her moving into your home.'

'You could move out,' I said mildly.

'Just like that?'

'To my cottage, perhaps.'

'Good grief!'

'You could inspect it,' I said, 'for cleanliness, dry rot and spiders.'

She gave me her most intolerant stare. 'Butler, cook, and housemaids?'

'Six footmen and a lady's maid.'

'I'll come to tea and cucumber sandwiches. I suppose you do have cucumber sandwiches?'

'Of course.'

'Thin, and without crusts?'

'Naturally.'

I had really surprised her, I saw. She didn't know what to answer. It was quite clear, though, that she was not going to fall swooning into my arms. There was a good deal I would have liked to say, but I didn't know how to. Things about caring, and reassurance, and looking ahead.

'Next Sunday,' she said. 'At half past three. For tea.'

'I'll line up the staff.'

She decided to get out of the car, and I went round to open the door for her. Her eyes looked huge.

'Are you serious?' she said.

'Oh yes. It'll be up to you . . . to decide.'

'After tea?'

I shook my head. 'At any time.'

Her expression slowly softened to unaccustomed gentleness. I kissed her, and then kissed her again with conviction.

'I think I'll go in,' she said waveringly, turning away.

'Jossie . . .'

'What?'

I swallowed. Shook my head. 'Come to tea,' I said helplessly. 'Come to tea.'

CHAPTER SIXTEEN

Monday morning, after another night free of alarms and
excursions, I went back to the office with good intentions
of actually doing some work. Peter was sulking with
Monday morning glooms, Bess had menstrual pains, and
Debbie was tearful from a row with the screw-selling
fiancé: par for office life as I knew it.

Trevor came into my room looking fatherly and
anxious, and seemed reassured to find my appearance
less deathly than on Friday.

'You did rest, then, Ro,' he said relievedly.

'I rode in a race and took a girl to the seaside.'

'Good heavens. At any rate, it seems to have done you
good. Better than spending your time working.'

'Yes . . .' I said. 'Trevor, I did come into the office on
Saturday morning, for a couple of hours.'

His air of worry crept subtly back. He waited for me to
go on with the manner of a patient expecting bad news
from his doctor: and I felt the most tremendous regret in
having to give it to him.

'Denby Crest,' I said.

'Ro . . .' He spread out his hands, palms downwards, in a gesture that spoke of paternal distress at a rebellious son who wouldn't take his senior's word for things.

'I can't help it,' I said. 'I know he's a client, and a friend of yours, but if he's misappropriated fifty thousand pounds and you've condoned it, it concerns us both. It concerns this office, this partnership, and our future. You must see that. We can't just ignore the whole thing and pretend it hasn't happened.'

'Ro, believe me, everything will be all right.'

I shook my head. 'Trevor, you telephone Denby Crest and tell him to come over here today, to discuss what we're going to do.'

'No.'

'Yes,' I said positively. 'I'm not having it, Trevor. I'm half of this firm, and it's not going to do anything illegal.'

'You're uncompromising.' The mixture of sorrow and irritation had intensified. The two emotions, I thought fleetingly, that gave you regrets while you shot the rabbit.

'Get him here at four o'clock,' I said.

'You can't bully him like that.'

'There are worse consequences,' I said. I spoke without emphasis, but he knew quite well that it was a threat.

Irritation won hands down over sorrow. 'Very well, Ro,' he said sourly. 'Very well.'

He went out of my room with none of the sympathetic concern for me with which he had come in, and I felt a lonely sense of loss. I could forgive him anything myself,

I thought in depression, but the law wouldn't. I lived by the law, both by inclination and choice. If my friend broke the law, should I abandon it for his sake: or should I abandon my friend for the sake of the law? In the abstract, there was no difficulty in my mind. In the flesh, I shrank. There was nothing frightfully jolly in being the instrument of distress, ruin, and prosecution. How much easier if the miscreant would confess of his own free will, instead of compelling his friend to denounce him: a sentimental solution, I thought sardonically, which happened only in weepy films. I was afraid that for myself there would be no such easy way out.

Those pessimistic musings were interrupted by a telephone call from Hilary, whose voice, when I answered, sounded full of relief.

'What's the matter?' I said.

'Nothing. I just . . .' She stopped.

'Just what?'

'Just wanted to know you were there, as a matter of fact.'

'Hilary!'

'Sounds stupid, I suppose, now that we both know you *are* there. But I just wanted to be sure. After all, you wouldn't have cast me in the role of rock if you thought you were in no danger at all.'

'Um,' I said, smiling down the telephone. 'Sermons in stones.'

She laughed. 'You just take care of yourself, Ro.'

'Yes, ma'am.'

I put down the receiver, marvelling at her kindness; and almost immediately the bell rang again.

'Roland?'

'Yes, Moira?'

Her sigh came audibly down the wire. 'Thank goodness! I tried all day yesterday to reach you, and there was no reply.'

'I was out all day.'

'Yes, but I didn't know that. I mean, I was imagining all sorts of things, like you being kidnapped again, and all because of me.'

'I'm so sorry.'

'Oh, I don't mind, now that I know you're safe. I've had this terrible picture of you shut up again, and needing someone to rescue you. I've been so worried, because of Binny.'

'What about Binny?'

'I think he's gone really *mad*,' she said. 'Insane. I went over to his stables yesterday morning to see if Tapestry was all right after his race, and he wouldn't let me into the yard. Binny, I mean. All the gates were shut and locked with padlocks and chains. It's insane. He came and stood on the inside of the gate to the yard where Tapestry is, and waved his arms about, and told me to go away. I mean, it's *insane*.'

'It certainly is.'

'I told him he could have caused a terrible accident, tampering with that rein, and he screamed that he hadn't done it, and I couldn't prove it, and anything that happened to you was my fault for insisting that you rode the horse.' She paused for breath. 'He looked so . . . well, so *dangerous*. And I'd never thought of him being dangerous, but just a fool. You'll think I'm silly, but I was quite frightened.'

'I don't think you were silly,' I said truthfully.

'And then it came to me, like a revelation,' she said, 'that it had been Binny who had kidnapped you before, both times, and that he'd done it again, or something even worse . . .'

'Moira . . .'

'Yes, but you didn't *see* him. And then there was no answer to your telephone. I know you'll think I'm silly, but I was so worried.'

'I'm very grateful . . .' I started to say.

'You see, Binny never thought you'd win the Gold Cup,' she said, rushing on. 'And the very second you had, I told him you'd ride Tapestry always from then on, and he was *furious*, absolutely furious. You wouldn't believe. So of course he had you kidnapped at once, so that you'd be out of the way, and I'd *have* to have someone else, and then you escaped, and you were going to ride at Ascot, so he kidnapped you *again*, and he went absolutely berserk when I wouldn't let Tapestry go at Ascot with another jockey. And I made such a fuss in the press that he had to let you out, and so he had to try something else, like cutting the rein, and now I think he's so insane that he doesn't really know what he's doing. I mean, I think he thinks that if he kidnaps you, or kills you even, that I'll *have* to get another jockey for the Whitbread Gold Cup a week next Saturday, and honestly I think he's out of his *senses*, and really awfully dangerous because of that *obsession*, and so you see I really was terribly worried.'

'I do see,' I said. 'And I'm incredibly grateful for your concern.'

'But what are you going to *do*?' she wailed.

'About Binny? Listen, Moira, please listen.'

'Yes,' she said, her voice calming down. 'I'm listening.'

'Do absolutely nothing.'

'But *Roland*,' she protested.

'Listen. I'm sure you are quite right that Binny is in a dangerous mental state, but anything you or I could do would make him worse. Let him cool down. Give him several days. Then send a horsebox with if possible a police escort – and you can get policemen for private jobs like that, you just apply to the local nick, and offer to pay for their time – collect Tapestry, and send him to another trainer.'

'Roland!'

'You can carry loyalty too far,' I said. 'Binny's done marvels with training the horse, I agree, but you owe him nothing. If it weren't for your own strength of mind he'd have manipulated the horse to make money only for himself, as well you know, and your enjoyment would have come nowhere.'

'But about kidnapping you . . .' she began.

'No, Moira,' I said. 'He didn't; it wasn't Binny. I don't doubt he was delighted it was done, but he didn't do it.'

She was astonished. 'He must have.'

'No.'

'But why not?'

'Lots of complicated reasons. But for one thing, he wouldn't have kidnapped me straight after the Gold Cup. He wouldn't have had any need to. If he'd wanted to abduct me to stop me riding Tapestry, he wouldn't have done it until just before the horse's next race, nearly three weeks later.'

'Oh,' she said doubtfully.

'The first abduction was quite elaborate,' I said. 'Binny couldn't possibly have had time to organize it between the Gold Cup and the time I was taken, which was only an hour or so later.'

'Are you sure?'

'Yes, Moira, quite sure. And when he really did try to stop me winning, he did very direct and simple things, not difficult like kidnapping. He offered me a bribe, and cut the rein. Much more in character. He always was a fool, and now he's a dangerous fool, but he isn't a kidnapper.'

'Oh dear,' she said, sounding disappointed. 'And I was so *sure.*'

She cheered up a bit and asked me to ride Tapestry in the Whitbread. I said I'd be delighted, and she deflated my ego by passing on the opinion of a press friend of hers to the effect that Tapestry was one of those horses who liked to be in charge, and an amateur who just sat there doing nothing very much was exactly what suited him best.

Grinning to myself I put down the receiver. The press friend was right; but who cared.

For the rest of the morning I tried to make inroads into the backlog of correspondence, but found it impossible to concentrate. The final fruit of two hours of reading letters and shuffling them around was three heaps marked 'overdue', 'urgent', and 'if you don't get these off today there will be trouble'.

Debbie looked down her pious nose at my inability to apply myself, and primly remarked that I was under-utilizing her capability. Under-utilizing ... Ye Gods! Where did the gobbledegook jargon come from?

'You mean I'm not giving you enough to do.'

'That's what I said.'

At luncheon I stayed alone in the office and stared into space: and my telephone rang again.

Johnny Frederick, full of news.

'Do you mind if I send you a bill for 'phone calls?' he said. 'I must have spent thirty quid. I've been talking all morning.'

'I'll send you a cheque.'

'OK. Well, mate, pin back your lugholes. That boat you were on was built at Lymington, and she sailed from there after dark on March 17th. She was brand spanking new, and she hadn't completed her trials, and she wasn't registered or named. She was built by a top-notch ship-yard called Goldenwave Marine, for a client called Arthur Robinson.'

'Who?'

'Arthur Robinson. That's what he said his name was, anyway. And there was only one slightly unusual thing about Mr Robinson, and that was that he paid for the boat in cash.'

He waited expectantly.

'How much cash?' I said.

'Two hundred thousand pounds.'

'Crikey.'

'Mind you,' Johnny said, 'that's bargain basement stuff for Goldenwave. They do a nice job in mini-liners at upwards of a million, with gold taps, for Arabs.'

'In cash?'

'Near enough, I dare say. Anyway, Arthur Robinson always paid on the nail, in instalments as they came due during the boat-building, but always in your actual folding. Goldenwave Marine wouldn't be interested in knowing whether the cash had had tax paid on it. None of their business.'

'Quite,' I said. 'Go on.'

'That Thursday – March 17th – in the morning, some time, Arthur Robinson rang Goldenwave and said he wanted to take some friends aboard for a party that evening, and would they please see that the water and fuel tanks were topped up, and everything shipshape. Which Goldenwave did.'

'Without question.'

'Of course. You don't argue with two hundred thousand quid. Anyway, the boat was out on a mooring in the deep water passage, so they left her fit for the owner's visit and brought her tender ashore, for him to use when he got there.'

'A black rubber dinghy?'

'I didn't ask. The nightwatchman had been told to expect the party, so he let them in, and helped generally, and saw them off. I got him out of bed this morning to talk to him, and he was none too pleased, but he remembers the evening quite well, because of course the boat sailed off that night and never came back.'

'What did he say?'

'There were two lots of people, he said. One lot came in an old white van, which he didn't think much of for an owner of such a boat. You'd expect a Rolls, he said.' Johnny chuckled. 'The first arrivals, three people, were the crew. They unloaded stores from an estate car and made two trips out to the boat. Then the white van arrived with several more men, and one of those was lying down. They told the nightwatchman he was dead drunk, and that was you, I reckon. Then the first three men and the drunk man went out to the boat, and the other men drove away in the old van and the estate car, and that was that. The nightwatchman thought it a very boring sort of party, and noted the embarkation in his log, and paid no more attention. Next morning, no boat.'

'And no report to the police?'

'The owner had taken his own property, which he'd fully paid for. Goldenwave had expected him to take command of her a week later, anyway, so they made no fuss.'

'You've done absolute marvels,' I said.

'Do you want to hear about Alastair Yardley?'

'There's more?'

'There sure is. He seems to be quite well-known. Several of the bigger shipyards have recommended him to people who want their boats sailed from England, say, to Bermuda, or the Caribbean, and so on, and don't have a regular crew, and also don't want to cross oceans themselves. He signs on his own crew, and pays them himself. He's no crook. Got a good reputation. Tough, though. And he's not cheap. If he agreed to help shanghai you, you can bet Mr Arthur Robinson paid through the nose for the service. But you can ask him yourself, if you like.'

'What do you mean?'

Johnny was justifiably triumphant. 'I struck dead lucky, mate. Mind you, I chased him round six shipyards, but he's in England now to fetch another yacht, and he'll talk to you if you ring him more or less at once.'

'I don't believe it!'

'Here's the number.' He read out the numbers, and I wrote them down. 'Ring him before two o'clock. You can also talk to the chap in charge of Goldenwave, if you like. This is his number. He said he'd help in any way he could.'

'You're fantastic,' I said, stunned to breathlessness by his success.

'We got a real lucky break, mate, because when I took those photographs to Cowes first thing this morning, I asked around everybody, and there was a feller in the third yard I tried who'd worked at Goldenwave last year, and he said it looked like their Golden Sixty Five, so I rang them, and it was the departure date that clinched it.'

'I can't begin to thank you.'

'To tell you the truth, mate, it's been a bit of excitement, and there isn't all that much about, these days. I've enjoyed this morning, and that's a fact.'

'I'll give you a ring. Tell you how things turn out.'

'Great. Can't wait. And see you.'

He disconnected, and with an odd sinking feeling in my stomach I rang the first of the numbers he'd given me. A shipyard. Could I speak to Alastair Yardley? Hang on, said the switchboard. I hung.

'Hullo?'

The familiar voice. Bold, self-assertive, challenging the world.

'It's Roland Britten,' I said.

There was a silence, then he said, 'Yeah,' slowly.

'You said you'd talk to me.'

'Yeah.' He paused. 'Your friend this morning, John Frederick, the boat-builder, he tells me I was sold a pup about you.'

'How do you mean?'

'I was told you were a blackmailer.'

'A *what*?'

'Yeah.' He sighed. 'Well, this guy Arthur Robinson, he said you'd set up his wife in some compromising

269

photographs and were trying to blackmail her, and he wanted you taught a lesson.'

'Oh,' I said blankly. It explained a great deal, I thought.

'Your friend Frederick told me that was all crap. He said I'd been conned. I reckon I was. All the other guys in the yard here know all about you winning that race and going missing. They just told me. Seems it was in all the papers. But I didn't see them, of course.'

'How long,' I said, 'were you supposed to keep me on board?'

'He said to ring him Monday evening, April 4th, and he'd tell me when and where and how to set you loose. But of course, you jumped ship the Tuesday before, and how you got that lever off is a bloody mystery . . . I rang him that night, and he was so bloody angry he couldn't get the words out. So then he said he wouldn't pay me for the job on you, and I said if he didn't he could whistle for his boat, I'd just sail it into some port somewhere and walk away, and he'd have God's own job finding it. So I said he could send me the money to Palma, where I bank, and when I got it I'd do what he wanted, which was to take his boat to Antibes and deliver it to the ship brokers there.'

'Brokers?'

'Yeah. Funny, that. He'd only just bought it. What did he want to sell it for?'

'Well . . .' I said. 'Do you remember his telephone number?'

'No. Threw it away, didn't I, as soon as I was shot of his boat.'

'At Antibes?'

'That's right.'

'Did you meet him?' I asked.

'Yeah. That night at Lymington. He told me not to talk to you, and not to listen, because you'd tell me lies, and not to let you know where we were, and not to leave a mark on you, and to watch out because you were as slippery as an eel.' He paused a second. 'He was right about that, come to think.'

'Do you remember what he looked like?'

'Yeah,' he said, 'what I saw of him; but it was mostly in the dark, out on the quay.' He described Arthur Robinson as I'd expected, and well enough to be conclusive.

'I wasn't intending to go for another week,' he said. 'The weather forecasts were all bad for Biscay, and I'd only been out in her once, in light air, not enough to know how she'd handle in a gale, but he rang Golden-wave that morning and spoke to me, and told me about you, and said gale or no gale he'd make it worth my while if I'd go that evening and take you with me.'

'I hope it was worth it,' I said.

'Yeah,' he said frankly. 'I got paid double.'

I laughed in my throat. 'Er . . .' I said, 'is it possible for a boat just to sail off from England and wander round Mediterranean ports, when it hasn't even got a name? I mean, do you have to pass Customs, and things like that?'

'You can pass Customs if you want to waste a bloody lot of time. Otherwise, unless you tell them, a port doesn't know whether you've come from two miles down the coast, or two thousand. The big ports collect mooring fees, that's all they're interested in. If you drop anchor at somewhere like Formentor, which we did one night with you, no one takes a blind bit of notice. Easy come, easy go, that's what it's like on the sea. Best way to live, I reckon.'

'It sounds marvellous,' I sighed enviously.

'Yeah. Look . . .' he paused a second, 'are you going to set the police on me, or anything? Because I'm off today, on the afternoon tide, and I'm not telling where.'

'No,' I said. 'No police.'

He let his breath out audibly in relief. 'I reckon . . .' He paused. 'Thanks, then. And well, sorry, like.'

I remembered the paperback, and the socks, and the soap and I had no quarrel with him.

From Goldenwave Marine, ten minutes later, I learned a good many background facts about big boats in general and Arthur Robinson in particular.

Goldenwave had four more Golden Sixty Fives on the stocks at the moment, all commissioned by private customers, and Arthur Robinson had been one of a stream. Their Golden Sixty Five had been a successful design, they were pleased and proud to say, and their standard of ship-building was respected the world over.

End of commercial.

I replaced the receiver gratefully. Sat, thinking, chewing bits off my fingernails. Decided, without joy, to take a slightly imprudent course.

Debbie, Peter, Bess and Trevor came back, and the place filled up with tap-tap and bustle. Mr Wells arrived for his appointment twenty minutes before the due time, reminding me of the psychiatrists'-eye-view of patients: if they're early, they're anxious, if they're late, they're aggressive, and if they're on time, they're pathological. I often thought the psychiatrists didn't understand about trains, buses and traffic flow, but in this case there wasn't much doubt about the anxiety. Mr Wells' hair, manner and eyes were all out of control.

'I rang the people you sent the rubber cheque to,' I said. 'They were a bit sticky, but they've agreed not to prosecute if you take care of them after the inevitable Receiving Order.'

'I what?'

'Pay them later,' I said. Jargon . . . I did it myself.

'Oh.'

'The order of paying,' I said, 'will be first the Inland Revenue, who will collect tax in full, and will also charge interest for every day overdue.'

'But I haven't anything to pay them with.'

'Did you sell your car, as we agreed you should?'

He nodded, but wouldn't meet my eyes.

'What have you done with the money?' I said.

'Nothing.'

'Pay it to the Revenue, then, on account.'

He looked away evasively, and I sighed at his folly. 'What have you done with the money?' I repeated.

He wouldn't tell me, and I concluded that he had been following the illegal path of many an imminent bankrupt, selling off his goods and banking the proceeds distantly under a false name, so that when the bailiffs came there wouldn't be much left. I gave him some good advice which I knew he wouldn't take. The suicidal hysterics of his earlier visit had settled into resentment against everyone pressing him, including me. He listened with a mulish stubbornness which I'd seen often enough before, and all he would positively agree to was not to write any more cheques.

By three-thirty I'd had enough of Mr Wells, and he of me.

'You need a good solicitor,' I said. 'He'll tell you the same as me, but maybe you'll listen.'

'It was a solicitor who gave me your name,' he said glumly.

'Who's your solicitor?'

'Fellow called Denby Crest.'

It was a small community, I thought. Touching, overlapping, a patchwork fabric. When the familiar names kept turning up, things were normal.

As it happened, Trevor was in the outer office when I showed Mr Wells to the door. I introduced them, explaining that Denby had sent him to see us. Trevor cast a benign eye, which would have been jaundiced had he known the Wells state of dickiness, and made affable small talk. Mr Wells took in Trevor's substantial air, seniority, and general impression of worldliness, and I practically saw the thought cross his mind that perhaps he had consulted the wrong partner.

And perhaps, I thought cynically, he had.

When he'd gone, Trevor looked at me sombrely.

'Come into my office,' he sighed.

CHAPTER SEVENTEEN

I sat in one of the clients' chairs, with Trevor magisterially behind his desk. His manner was somewhere between unease and cajoling, as if he were not quite sure of his ground.

'Denby said he'd be here by four.'

'Good.'

'But Ro . . . he'll explain. He'll satisfy you, I'm sure. I think I'll leave it to him to explain, and then you'll see . . . that there's nothing for us to worry about.'

He raised an unconvincing smile and rippled his fingertips on his blotter. I looked at the familiar, friendly figure, and wished with all my heart that things were not as they were.

Denby came ten minutes early, which would have gratified the psychiatrists, and he was wound up like a tight spring, as well he might be. His backbone was ramrod stiff inside the short plump frame, the moustache bristling on the forward jutting mouth, the irritated air plainer than ever.

He didn't shake hands with me: merely nodded.

Trevor came round his desk to offer a chair, a politeness I thought excessive.

'Well, Ro,' Denby said crossly. 'I hear you have reservations about my certificate.'

'That's so.'

'What, exactly?'

'Well,' I said. 'To be exact . . . fifty thousand pounds missing from the clients' deposit account.'

'Rubbish.'

I sighed. 'You transferred money belonging to three separate clients from the clients' deposit to the clients' current account,' I said. 'You then drew five cheques from the current account, made out to yourself, in varying sums, over a period of six weeks, three to four months ago. Those cheques add up to fifty thousand pounds exactly.'

'But I've repaid the money. If you'd've looked more carefully you'd have seen the counter credits on the bank statement.' He was irritated. Impatient.

'I couldn't make out where those credits had come from,' I said, 'so I asked the bank to send a duplicate statement. It came this morning.'

Denby sat as if turned to stone.

'The duplicate statement,' I said regretfully, 'shows no record of the money having been repaid. The bank statement you gave us was . . . well . . . a forgery.'

Time ticked by.

Trevor looked unhappy. Denby revised his position.

'I've only *borrowed* the money,' he said. There was

still no regret, and no real fear. 'It's perfectly safe. It will be repaid very shortly. You have my word for it.'

'Um . . .' I said. 'Your word isn't enough.'

'Really, Ro, this is ridiculous. If I say it will be repaid, it will be repaid. Surely you know me well enough for that?'

'If you mean,' I said, 'would I have thought you a thief, then no, I wouldn't.'

'I'm not a thief,' he said angrily. 'I told you, I borrowed the money. A temporary expediency. It's unfortunate that . . . as things turned out . . . I was not able to repay it before the certificate became due. But as I explained to Trevor, it is only a matter of a few weeks, at the most.'

'The clients' money,' I said reasonably, 'is not entrusted to you so that you can use it for a private loan to yourself.'

'We all know that,' Denby said snappily, in a teaching-grandmother-to-suck-eggs manner. My grandmother, I reflected fleetingly, had never sucked an egg in her life.

'You're fifty thousand short,' I said, 'and Trevor's condoned it, and neither of you seems to realize you'll be out of business if it comes to light.'

They both looked at me as if I were a child.

'But there's no need for it to come to light, Ro,' Trevor said. 'Denby will repay the money soon, and all will be well. Like I told you.'

'It isn't ethical,' I said.

'Don't be so pompous, Ro,' Trevor said, at his most fatherly, shaking his head with sorrow.

'Why did you take the money?' I asked Denby. 'What for?'

Denby looked across enquiringly at Trevor, who nodded.

'You'll have to tell him everything, Denby. He's very persistent. Better tell him, then he'll understand, and we can clear the whole thing up.'

Denby complied with bad grace. 'I had a chance,' he said, 'of buying a small block of flats. Brand new. Not finished. Builder in difficulties, wanted a quick sale, that sort of thing. Flats were going cheap, of course. So I bought them. Too good to miss. Done that sort of deal before, of course. Not a fool, you know. Knew what I was doing, and all that.'

'Your own conveyancer?' I said.

'What? Oh yes.' He nodded. 'Well, then, I needed a bit more extra capital to finance the deal. Perfectly safe. Good flats. Nothing wrong with them.'

'But they haven't sold?' I said.

'Takes time. Market's sluggish in the winter. But they're all sold now, subject to contracts. Formalities, mortgages, all that. Takes time.'

'Mm.' I said. 'How many flats in the block, and where is it?'

'Eight flats, small, of course. At Newquay, Cornwall.'

'Have you seen them?' I said.

'Of course.'

'Do you mind if I do?' I said. 'And will you give me the

addresses of all the people who are buying the flats, and tell me how much each is paying?'

Denby bristled. 'Are you saying you don't believe me?'

'I'm an auditor,' I said. 'I don't believe. I check.'

'You can take my word for it.'

I shook my head. 'You sent us a forged bank statement. I can't take your word for anything.'

There was a silence.

'If those flats exist, and if you repay that money this week, I'll keep quiet,' I said. 'I'll want confirmation by letter from the bank. The money must be there by Friday, and the letter here by Saturday. Otherwise, no deal.'

'I can't get the money this week,' Denby said peevishly.

'Borrow it from a loan shark.'

'But that's ridiculous. The interest I would have to pay would wipe out all my profit.'

Serve you right, I thought unfeelingly. I said, 'Unless the clients' money is back in the bank by Friday, the Law Society will have to be told.'

'Ro!' Trevor protested.

'However much you try to wrap it up as "unfortunate" and "expedient",' I said, 'the fact remains that all three of us know that what Denby has done is a criminal offence. I'm not putting my name to it as a partner of this firm. If the money is not repaid by Friday, I'll write a letter explaining that in the light of fresh knowledge we wish to cancel the certificate just issued.'

'But Denby would be struck off!' Trevor said.

They both looked as if the stark realities of life were something that only happened to other people.

'Unfriendly,' Denby said angrily. 'Unnecessarily aggressive, that's what you are, Ro. Righteous. Unbending.'

'All those, I dare say,' I said.

'It's no good, I suppose, suggesting I ... er ... cut you in?'

Trevor made a quick horrified gesture, trying to stop him.

'Denby, Denby,' he said, distressed. 'You'll never bribe him. For God's sake have some sense. If you really want to antagonize Ro, you offer him a bribe.'

Denby scowled at me and got explosively to his feet.

'All right,' he said bitterly. 'I'll get the money by Friday. And don't ever expect any favours from me for the rest of your life.'

He strode furiously out of the office leaving eddies of disturbed air and longer trails of disturbed friendship. Turbulent wake, I thought. Churning and destructive, overturning everything it touched.

'Are you satisfied, Ro?' Trevor said gently, in sorrow.

I sat without answering.

I felt like a man on a high diving board, awaiting the moment of strength. Ahead, the plunge. Behind, the quiet way down. The choice, within me.

I could walk away, I thought. Pretend I didn't know what I knew. Settle for silence, friendship and peace.

Refrain from bringing distress and disgrace and dreary unhappiness.

My friend or the law. To which did I belong? To the law or my own pleasure . . .

O great God almighty.

I swallowed with a dry mouth.

'Trevor,' I said, 'do you know Arthur Robinson?'

There was no fun, no fun at all, in looking into the face of ultimate disaster.

The blood slowly drained from Trevor's skin, leaving his eyes like great dark smudges.

'I'll get you some brandy,' I said.

'Ro . . .'

'Wait.'

I fetched him a tumbler, from his entertaining cupboard, heavy with alcohol, light on soda.

'Drink it,' I said with compassion. 'I'm afraid I've given you a shock.'

'How . . .' His mouth quivered suddenly, and he put the glass to his lips to hide it. He drank slowly, and took the glass a few inches away: a present help in trouble. 'How much . . . do you know?' he said.

'Why I was abducted. Who did it. Who owns the boat. Who sailed her. Where she is now. How much she cost. And where the money comes from.'

'My God . . . My God . . .' His hands shook.

'I want to talk to him,' I said. 'To Arthur Robinson.'

A faint flash of something like hope shone in his eyes.

'Do you know . . . his other name?'

I told him what it was. The spark of light died to a pebble-like dullness. He clattered the glass against his teeth.

'I want you to telephone,' I said. 'Tell him I know. Tell him I want to talk. Tell him, if he has any ideas of doing anything but what I ask, I'll go straight from this office to the police. I want to talk to him tonight.'

'But Ro, knowing you . . .' He sounded despairing. 'You'll go to the police anyway.'

'Tomorrow morning,' I said.

He stared at me for a long, long time. Then with a heavy half-groaning sigh, he stretched out his hand to the telephone.

We went to Trevor's house. Better for talking, he suggested, than the office.

'Your wife?' I said.

'She's staying with her sister, tonight. She often does.'

We drove in two cars, and judging by the daze of his expression Trevor saw nothing consciously of the road for the whole four miles.

His big house sat opulently in the late afternoon sunshine, nineteen-twenties respectability in every brick. Acres of diamond-shaped leaded window panes, black paint, a wide portico with corkscrew pillars, wisteria creeping here and there, lots of gables with beams stuck on for effect.

Trevor unlocked the front door and led the way into dead inside air which smelled of old coffee and furniture polish. Parquet flooring in the roomy hall, and rugs.

'Come into the snug,' he said, walking ahead.

The snug was a longish room which lay between the more formal sitting and dining rooms, looking outwards to the pillared loggia, with the lawn beyond it. To Trevor the snug was psychologically as well as geographically the heart of the house, the place where he most felt a host to his businessmen friends.

There was the bar, built in, where he liked to stand, genially pouring drinks. Several dark red leather armchairs. A small, sturdy dining table, with four leather-seated dining chairs. A large television. Bookshelves. An open brick fireplace, with a leather screen. A palm in a brass pot. More Stubbs prints. Several small chair-side tables. A leaf-patterned carpet. Heavy red velvet curtains. Red lampshades. On winter evenings, with the fire lit, curtains drawn, and lights glowing warmly, snug, in spite of its size, described it.

Trevor switched on the lights, and although it was full daylight, drew the curtains. Then he made straight for the bar.

'Do you want a drink?' he said.

I shook my head. He fixed himself a brandy of twice the size I'd given him in the office.

'I can't believe any of this is happening,' he said.

He took his filled glass and slumped down in one of the red leather armchairs, staring into space. I hitched a hip on to the table, which like so much in that house was protected by a sheet of plate glass. We both waited, neither of us enjoying our thoughts. We waited nearly an hour.

Nothing violent, I told myself numbly, would happen in that genteel house. Violence occurred in back alleys and dark corners. Not in a well-to-do sitting-room on a Monday evening. I felt the flutter of apprehension in every nerve and thought about eyes black with the lust for revenge.

A car drew up outside. A door slammed. There were footsteps outside on the gravel. Footsteps crossing the threshold, coming through the open front door, treading across the parquet, coming to the door of the snug. Stopping there.

'Trevor?' he said.

Trevor looked up dully. He waved a hand towards me, where I sat to one side, masked by the open door.

He pushed the door wider. Stepped into the room.

He held a shotgun; balanced over his forearm, butt under the armpit, twin barrels pointing to the floor.

I took a deep steadying breath, and looked into his firm, familiar face.

Jossie's father. William Finch.

*

'Shooting me,' I said, 'won't solve anything. I've left photostats and all facts with a friend.'

'If I shoot your foot off, you'll ride no more races.'

His voice already vibrated with the smashing hate: and this time I saw it not from across a courtroom thick with policemen, but from ten feet at the wrong end of a gun.

Trevor made jerky calming gestures with his hands.

'William . . . surely you see. Shooting Ro would be disastrous. Irretrievably disastrous.'

'The situation is already irretrievable.' His voice was thick, roughened and deepened by the tension in throat and neck. 'This little creep has seen to that.'

'Well,' I said, and heard the tension in my own voice, 'I didn't make you steal.'

It wasn't the best of remarks. Did nothing to reduce the critical mass: and William Finch was like a nuclear reactor with the rods too far out already. The barrels of the gun swung up into his hands and pointed at my loins.

'William, for God's sake,' Trevor said urgently, climbing ponderously out of his armchair. 'Use your reason. If he says killing him would do no good, you must believe him. He'd never have risked coming here if it wasn't true.'

Finch vibrated with fury through all his elegant height. The conflict between hatred and common sense was plain in the bunching muscles along his jaw and the claw-like curve of his fingers. There was a fearful moment when I was certain that the blood-lust urge to avenge himself would blot out all fear of consequences, and I thought disconnectedly that I wouldn't feel it ... you never felt the worst of wounds in the first few seconds. It was only after, if you lived, that the tide came in. I wouldn't know ... I wouldn't feel it, and I might not even know ...

He swung violently away from me and thrust the shotgun into Trevor's arms.

'Take it. Take it,' he said through his teeth. 'I don't trust myself.'

I could feel the tremors down my legs, and the prickling of sweat over half my body. He hadn't killed me at the very start, when it would have been effective, and it was all very well risking he wouldn't do it now when he'd nothing to gain. It had come a good deal too close.

I leaned my behind weakly against the table, and worked some saliva into my mouth. Tried to set things out in a dry-as-dust manner, as if we were discussing a small point of policy.

'Look ...' It came out half-strangled. I cleared my throat and tried again. 'Tomorrow I will have to telephone to New York, to talk to the Nantucket family. Specifically, to talk to one of the directors on the board of their family empire; the director to whom Trevor sends the annual Axwood audited accounts.'

Trevor took the shotgun and stowed it away out of sight behind the ornate bar. William Finch stood in the centre of the room with unreleased energy quivering through all his frame. I watched his hands clench and

unclench, and his legs move inside his trousers, as if
wanting to stride about.

'What will you tell them, then?' he said fiercely.
'What?'

'That you've been . . . er . . . defrauding the Nantucket
family business during the past financial year.'

For the first time some of the heat went out of him.

'During the past . . .' He stopped.

'I can't tell,' I said, 'about earlier years. I didn't do the
audits. I've never seen the books, and they are not in our
office. They have to be kept for three years, of course, so
I expect you have them.'

There was a lengthy silence.

'I'm afraid,' I said, 'that the Nantucket director will
tell me to go at once to the police. If it was old Naylor
Nantucket who was involved, it might be different. He
might just have hushed everything up, for your sake. But
this new generation, they don't know you. They're hard-
nosed businessmen who disapprove of the stable anyway.
They never come near the place. They do look upon it as
a business proposition, though, and they pay you a good
salary to manage it, and they undoubtedly regard any
profits as being theirs. However mildly I put it, and I'm
not looking forward to it at all, they are going to have to
know that for this financial year their profits have gone
to you.'

My deadpan approach began to have its results.
Trevor poured two drinks and thrust one into William

Finch's hand. He looked at it unseeingly and after a few moments put it down on the bar.

'And Trevor?' he said.

'I'll have to tell the Nantucket director,' I said regretfully, 'that the auditor they appointed has helped to rip them off.'

'Ro,' Trevor said, protesting, I gathered, at the slang expression more than the truth of it.

'Those Axwood books are a work of fiction,' I said to him. 'Cash books, ledgers, invoices . . . all ingenious lies. William would never have got away with such a wholesale fraud without your help. Without, anyway . . .' I said, modifying it slightly, 'without you knowing, and turning a blind eye.'

'And raking off a bloody big cut,' Finch said violently, making sure he took his friend down with him.

Trevor made a gesture of distaste, but it had to be right. Trevor had a hearty appetite for money, and would never have taken such a risk without the gain.

'These books look all right at first sight,' I said. 'They would have satisfied an outside auditor, if the Nantuckets had wanted a check from a London firm, or one in New York. But as for Trevor, and as for me, living here . . .' I shook my head. 'Axwood Stables have paid thousands to forage merchants who didn't receive the money, to saddlers who don't exist, to maintenance men, electricians and plumbers who did no work. The invoices are there, all nicely printed, but the transactions they refer to are thin air. The cash went straight to William Finch.'

Some of the slowly evaporating heat returned fast to Finch's manner, and I thought it wiser not to catalogue aloud all the rest of the list of frauds.

He'd charged the Nantuckets wages for several more lads than he'd employed: a dodge hard to pin down, as the stable-lad population floated from yard to yard.

He'd charged the Nantucket company more than nine thousand pounds for the rent of extra loose boxes and keep for horses by a local farmer, when I knew he had paid only a fraction of that, as the farmer was one of my clients.

He'd charged much more for shares in jockeys' retainers than the jockeys had received; and had invented travelling expenses to the races for horses which according to the form books had never left the yard.

He had pocketed staggering sums from a bloodstock agent in the form of commission on the sales of Nantucket horses to outside owners: fifty thousand or so in the past year, the agent had confirmed casually on the telephone, not knowing that Finch had no right to it.

I imagined Finch had also been sending enlarged bills to all the non-Nantucket owners, getting them to make out their cheques to him personally rather than to the company, and then diverting a slice to himself before paying a reasonable sum into the business.

The Nantuckets were far away, and uninterested. All I guessed they'd wanted had been a profit on the bottom line, and he'd given them just enough to keep them quiet.

As a final irony, he'd charged the Nantuckets six thousand pounds for auditors' fees, and nowhere in our books was there a trace of six thousand pounds from Axwood Stables. Trevor might have had his half, though, on the quiet: it was enough to make you laugh.

A long list of varied frauds. Much harder to detect than one large one. Adding up, though, to an average rake-off for Finch of over two thousand pounds a week. Untaxed.

Year in, year out.

Assisted by his auditor.

Assisted also, it was certain, by the ever-sick secretary, Sandy, though with or without her knowledge I didn't know. If she was ill as often as all that, and away from her post, maybe she didn't know. Or maybe the knowledge made her ill. But as in most big frauds, the paperwork had to be done well, and in the Axwood Stables case, there had been a great deal of it done well.

Ninety to a hundred horses. Well trained, well raced. A big stable with a huge weekly turnover. A top trainer. A trainer, I thought, who didn't own his own stable, who was paid only a salary, and a highly taxed one at that, and who faced having no capital to live on in old age, in a time of inflation. A man in his fifties, an employee, seeing into a future without enough money. An enforced retirement. No house of his own. No power. A man with money at present passing daily through his hands like a river in flood.

All racehorse trainers were entrepreneurs, with

organizing minds. Most were in business on their own account, and had no absent company to defraud. If William Finch had been his own master, I doubted that he would ever have thought of embezzlement. With his abilities, in the normal course of things, he would have had no need.

Need. Ability. Opportunity. I wondered how big a step it had been to dishonesty. To crime.

Probably not very big. A pay-packet for a non-existent stable lad, for a little extra regular cash. The cost of an unordered ton of hay.

Small steps, ingenious swindles, multiplying and swelling, leading to a huge swathing highway.

'Trevor,' I said mildly, 'how long ago did you spot William's . . . irregularities?'

Trevor looked at me sorrowfully, and I half-smiled.

'You saw them . . . some of the first ones . . . in the books,' I said, 'and you told him it wouldn't do.'

'Of course.'

'You suggested,' I said, 'that if he really put his mind to it you would both be a great deal better off.'

Finch reacted strongly with a violent gesture of his whole arm, but Trevor's air of sorrow merely intensified.

'Just like Connaught Powys,' I said. 'I tried hard to believe that you genuinely hadn't seen how he was rigging that computer, but I reckon . . . I have to face it that you were doing it together.'

'Ro . . .' he said sadly.

'Anyway,' I said to Finch, 'you sent the books in for

the annual audit, and after all this time neither you nor Trevor are particularly nervous. Trevor and I have been chronically behind with our work for ages, so I guess he just locked them in his cupboard, to see to as soon as he could. He would know I wouldn't look at your books. I never had, in six years; and I had too many clients of my own. And then, when Trevor was away on his holidays, the unforeseen happened. On Gold Cup day, through your letterbox, and mine, came the summons for you to appear before the Tax Commissioners a fortnight later.'

He stared at me with furious dark eyes, his strong, elegant figure tall and straight like a great stag at bay against an impudent hound. Round the edges of the curtains the daylight was fading to dark. Inside, electric lights shone smoothly on civilized man.

I smiled twistedly. 'I sent you a message. Don't worry, I said, Trevor's on holiday, but I'll apply for a postponement, and make a start on the books myself. I went straight off to ride in the Gold Cup and never gave it another thought. But you, to you, that message meant ruin. Degradation, prosecution, probably prison.'

A quiver ran through him. Muscles moved along his jaw.

'I imagine,' I said, 'that you thought the simplest thing would be to get the books back; but they were locked in Trevor's cupboard, and only he and I have keys. And in any case I would have thought it very suspicious, if, with the Commissioners breathing down our necks, you refused to let me see the books. Especially suspicious if the office had been broken into and those papers stolen. Anything along those lines would have led to investigation, and disaster. So as you couldn't keep the books from *me*, you decided to keep *me* from the books. You had the means to hand. A new boat, nearly ready to sail. You simply arranged for it to go early, and take me with it. If you could keep me away from the office until Trevor returned, all would be well.'

'This is all nonsense,' he said stiffly.

'Don't be silly. It's past denying. Trevor was due back in the office on Monday, April 4th, which would give him three days to apply for a postponement to the Commissioners. A perfectly safe margin. Trevor would then do the Axwood books as usual, and I would be set free, never knowing why I'd been abducted.'

Trevor buried his face in his brandy, which made me thirsty.

'If you've any mineral water, or tonic, Trevor, I'd like some,' I said.

'Give him nothing,' Finch said, the pent-up violence still thick in his voice.

Trevor made fluttery motions with his hands, but after a moment, with apologetic glances at Finch's tightened mouth, he fetched a tumbler and poured into it a bottle of tonic water.

'Ro . . .' he said, giving me the glass. 'My dear chap . . .'

'My dear *shit*,' Finch said.

I drank the fizzy quinine water gratefully.

'I bust things up by getting home a few days early,' I

said. 'I suppose you were frantic. Enough, anyway, to send the kidnapping squads to my cottage to pick me up again. And when they didn't manage it, you sent someone else.' I drank bubbles and tasted gall. 'Next day, you sent your daughter Jossie.'

'She knows nothing, Ro,' Trevor said.

'Shut up,' Finch said. 'She strung him along by the nose.'

'Maybe she did,' I said. 'It was supposed to be only for a day or two. Trevor was due back that Sunday. But I told you, while you were busy filling my time by showing me round your yard, that Trevor's car had broken down in France, and he wouldn't be back until Wednesday or Thursday. And I assured you again that you didn't have to worry, I had already applied for the postponement, and I would start the audit myself. The whole situation was back to square one, and the outlook was as deadly as ever.'

Finch glared, denying nothing.

'You offered me a day at the races with Jossie,' I said. 'And a ride in the novice hurdle. I'm a fool about accepting rides. Never know when to say no. You must have known that Notebook was unable to jump properly. You must have hoped when you flew off to the Grand National, that I'd fall with him and break a leg.'

'Your neck,' he said vindictively, with no vestige of a joke.

Trevor glanced at his face and away again, as if embarrassed by so much raw emotion.

'Your men must have been standing by in case I survived undamaged, which of course I did,' I said. 'They followed us to the pub where I had dinner with Jossie, and then to the motel where I planned to stay. Your second attempt at abduction was more successful, in that I couldn't get out. And when Trevor was safely back, you rang Scotland Yard, and the police set me free. From one point of view all your efforts had produced precisely the desired result, because I had not in fact by then seen one page or one entry of the Axwood books.'

I thought back, and amended that statement. 'I hadn't seen any except the petty cash book, which you gave me yourself. And that, I imagine, was your own private accurate record, and not the one re-written and padded for the sake of the audit. It was left in my car with all my other belongings, and I took it to the office when I went back last Friday. It was still there on Saturday. It was Saturday morning that I got out the Axwood books and studied them, and made the photocopies.'

'But why, Ro?' Trevor asked frustratedly. 'What made you think . . . Why did you think of William?'

'The urgency,' I said. 'The ruthless haste, and the time factors. I believed, you see, when I was on the boat, that I'd been kidnapped for revenge. Any auditor who's been the downfall of embezzlers would think that, if he'd found himself in such a position. Especially if he's been directly threatened, face to face, as I had, by Connaught Powys, and earlier by Ownslow and Glitberg, and later also by others. But when I escaped and came home, there was hardly any interval before I was in danger again. Hunted, really. And caught. So the second time, last week, in the van, I began to think ... that perhaps it wasn't revenge, but *prevention*, and after that, it was a matter of deduction, elimination, boring things, on the whole. But I had hours ...' I swallowed involuntarily, remembering. 'I had hours in which to think of all the possible people, and work it out. So then, on Saturday morning, I went to the office, when I had the place to myself, and checked.'

Finch turned on Trevor, looking for a whipping boy. 'Why the hell did you keep those books where he could see them? Why didn't you lock them in the bloody safe?'

'I've a key to the safe,' I said dryly.

'Christ!' He raised his hands in a violent, exploding, useless gesture. 'Why didn't you take them home?'

'I never take books home,' Trevor said. 'And you told me that Ro was going to the races Saturday, and out with Jossie Sunday, so we'd nothing to worry about. And anyway, neither of us dreamt that he knew ... or guessed.'

Finch swung his desperate face in my direction.

'What's your price?' he said. 'How much?'

I didn't answer. Trevor said protestingly, 'William ...'

'He must want something,' Finch said. 'Why is he telling us all this instead of going straight to the police? Because he wants a deal, that's why.'

'Not money,' I said.

Finch continued to look like a bolt of lightning

trapped in bones and flesh, but he didn't pursue the subject. He knew, as he'd always known, that it wasn't a question of money.

'Where did you get the men who abducted me?' I said.

'You know so much. You can bloody well find out.'

Rent-a-thug, I thought cynically. Someone, somewhere, knew how to hire some bully boys. The police could find out, I thought, if they wanted to. I wouldn't bother.

'The second time,' I said. 'Did you tell them not to leave a mark on me?'

'So what?'

'Did you?' I said.

'I didn't want the police taking any serious interest,' he said. 'No marks. No stealing. Made you a minor case.'

So the fists and boots, I thought, had been a spot of private enterprise. Payment for the general run-around I'd given the troops. Not orders from above. I supposed I was glad, in a sour sort of way.

He'd chosen the warehouse, I guessed, because it couldn't have been easy to find a safer place in a hurry: and because he thought it would divert my attention even more strongly towards Ownslow and Glitberg, and away from any thought of himself.

Trevor said, 'Well . . . What . . . what are we going to do now?' but no one answered, because there were wheels outside on the gravel. Car doors slammed.

'Did you leave the front door open?' Trevor said.

Finch didn't need to answer. He had. Several feet

tramped straight in, crossed the hall, and made unerringly for the snug.

'Here we are then,' said a powerful voice. 'Let's get on
with it.'

The light of triumph shone in Finch's face, and he
smiled with grateful welcome at the newcomers crowding
into the room.

Glitberg. Ownslow. Connaught Powys.

'Got the rat cornered, then?' Powys said.

CHAPTER EIGHTEEN

I had an everlasting picture of the five of them, in that freezing moment. I straightened to my feet, and my heart thumped, and I looked at them one by one.

Connaught Powys in his city suit, as Establishment as a pillar of the government. Coffee-coloured tan on his fleshy face. Smooth hair; pale hands. A large man aiming to throw his weight about, and enjoying it.

Glitberg with his mean eyes and the repulsive four-inch frill of white whiskers, which stood out sideways from his cheeks like a ruff. Little pink lips, and a smirk.

Ownslow the bull, with his bald crown and long straggling blond hair. He'd shut the door of the snug and leaned against it, and folded his arms with massive satisfaction.

William Finch, tall and distinguished, vibrating in the centre of the room in a tangle of fear, and anger, and unpleasant pleasure.

Trevor, silver-haired, worldly, come to dust. Sitting apprehensively in his armchair, facing his future with more sorrow than horror. The only one of them who showed the slightest sign of realizing that it was they who had got themselves into trouble, not I.

Embezzlers were not normally men of violence. They robbed on paper, not with their fists. They might hate and threaten, but actual physical assault wasn't natural to them. I looked bleakly at the five faces and thought again of the nuclear effect of critical mass. Small separate amounts of radio-active matter could release harnessable energy. If small amounts got together into a larger mass, they exploded.

'Why did you come?' Trevor said.

'Finchy rang and told us he'd be here,' Powys said, jerking his head in my direction. 'Never get another opportunity like it, will we? Seeing as you and Finchy will be out of circulation, for a bit.'

Finch shook his head fiercely: but I reckoned there were different sorts of circulation, and it would be a very long time before he was back on a racetrack. I wouldn't have wanted to face the ruin before him: the crash from such a height.

Glitberg said, 'Four years locked in a cell. Four sodding years, because of him.'

'Don't bellyache,' I said. 'Four years in jail for a million pounds is a damned good bargain. You offer it around, you'd get a lot of takers.'

'Prison is dehumanizing,' Powys said. 'They treat you worse than animals.'

'Don't make me cry,' I said. 'You chose the way that led there. And all of you have got what you wanted.

Money, money, money. So run away and play with it.'
Maybe I spoke with too much heat, but nothing was
going to defuse the developing bomb.

Anger that I'd let myself in for such a mess was a stab
in the mind. I simply hadn't thought of Finch summoning
reinforcements. He'd had no need of it: it had been
merely spite. I'd believed I could manage Finch and
Trevor with reasonable safety, and here all of a sudden
was a whole new battle.

'Trevor,' I said, flatly, 'don't forget the photostats I left
with a friend.'

'What friend?' Finch said, gaining belligerence from
his supporters.

'Barclays Bank,' I said.

Finch was furious, but he couldn't prove it wasn't true,
and even he must have seen that any serious attempt at
wringing out a different answer might cost them more
time in the clink.

I had hoped originally to make a bargain with Finch,
but it was no longer possible. I thought merely, at that
point, of getting through whatever was going to happen
with some semblance of grace. A doubtful proposition, it
seemed to me.

'How much does he know?' Ownslow demanded of
Trevor.

'Enough . . .' Trevor said. 'Everything.'

'Bloody hell.'

'How did he find out?' Glitberg demanded.

'Because William took him on his boat,' Trevor said.

'A mistake,' Powys said. 'That was a mistake, Finchy. He came sniffing round us in London, asking about boats. Like I told you.'

'You chain dogs up,' Finch said.

'But not in a floating kennel, Finchy. Not this bastard here with his bloody quick eyes. You should have kept him away from your boat.'

'I don't see that it matters,' Trevor said. 'Like he said, we've all got our money.'

'And what if he tells?' Ownslow demanded.

'Oh, he'll tell,' Trevor said with certainty. 'And of course there will be trouble. Questions and enquiries and a lot of fuss. But in the end, if we're careful, we should keep the cash.'

'Should isn't enough,' Powys said fiercely.

'Nothing's certain,' Trevor said.

'One thing's certain,' Ownslow said. 'This creep's going to get his come-uppance.'

All five of the faces turned my way together, and in each one, even in Trevor's, I read the same intent.

'That's what we came for,' Powys said.

'Four bloody years,' Ownslow said. 'And the sneers my kids suffered.' He pushed off the door and uncrossed his arms.

Glitberg said, 'Judges looking down their bloody noses.'

They all, quite slowly, came nearer.

It was uncanny, and frightening. The forming of a pack.

Behind me there was the table, and behind that, solid wall. They were between me and the windows, and between me and the door.

'Don't leave any marks,' Powys said. 'If he goes to the police it'll be his word against ours, and if he's nothing to show that can't do much.' To me, directly, he said, 'We'll have a bloody good alibi, I'll tell you that.'

The odds looked appalling. I made a sudden thrusting jump to one side, to dodge the menacing advance, out-flank the cohorts, scramble for the door.

I got precisely nowhere. Two strides, no more. Their hands clutched me from every direction, dragging me back, their bodies pushing against me with their collective weight. It was as if my attempt to escape had triggered them off. They were determined, heavy, and grunting. I struggled with flooding fury to disentangle myself, and I might as well have wrestled with an octopus.

They lifted me up bodily and sat me on the end of the table. Three of them held me there with hands like clamps.

Finch pulled open a drawer in the side of the table, and threw out a checked red and white table cloth, which floated across the room and fell on a chair. Under the cloth, several big square napkins. Red and white checks. Tapestry's racing colours. Ridiculous thought at such a moment.

Finch and Connaught Powys each rolled a napkin into a shape like a bandage and knotted it round one of my ankles. They tied my ankles to the legs of the table. They pulled my jacket off. They rolled and tied a red and white napkin round each of my wrists, pulling the knots tight and leaving cheerful bright loose ends like streamers.

They did it fast.

All of the faces were flushed, and the eyes fuzzy, in the fulfilment of lust. Glitberg and Ownslow, one on each side, pushed me down flat on my back. Finch and Connaught Powys pulled my arms over my head and tied the napkins on my wrists to the other two legs of the table. My resistance made them rougher.

The table was, I supposed, about two feet by four. Long enough to reach from my knees to the top of my head. Hard, covered with glass, uncomfortable.

They stood back to admire their handiwork. All breathing heavily from my useless fight. All overweight, out of condition, ripe to drop dead from coronaries at any moment. They went on living.

'Now what?' said Ownslow, considering. He went down on his knees and took off my shoes.

'Nothing,' Trevor said. 'That's enough.'

The pack instinct had died out of him fastest. He turned away, refusing to meet my eyes.

'Enough!' Glitberg said. 'We've done nothing yet.'

Powys eyed me assessingly from head to foot, and maybe he saw just what they had done.

'Yes,' he said slowly. 'That's enough.'

Ownslow said 'Here!' furiously, and Glitberg said,

'Not on your life.' Powys ignored them and turned to Finch.

'He's yours,' he said. 'But if I were you I'd just leave him here.'

'*Leave* him?'

'You've got better things to do than fool around with him. You don't want to leave marks on him, and I'm telling you, the way we've tied him will be enough.'

William Finch thought about it, and nodded, and came half way back to cold sense. He stepped closer until he stood near my ribs. He stared down, eyes full of the familiar hate.

'I hope you're satisfied,' he said.

He spat in my face.

Powys, Glitberg and Ownslow thought it a marvellous idea. They did it in turn, as disgustingly as they could.

Not Trevor. He looked on uncomfortably and made small useless gestures of protest with his hands.

I could hardly see for slime. It felt horrible, and I couldn't get it off.

'All right,' Powys said. 'That's it, then. You push off now, Finchy, and you get packed, Trevor, and then we'll all leave.'

'Here!' Ownslow said again, protestingly.

'Do you want an alibi, or don't you?' Powys said. 'You got to make some effort. Be seen by a few squares. Help the lies along.'

Ownslow gave in with a bad grace, and contented

himself with making sure that none of the table napkins had worked loose. Which they hadn't.

Finch had gone from my diminished sight and also, it appeared, from my life. A car started in the drive, crunched on the gravel, and faded away.

Trevor went out of the room and presently returned carrying a suitcase. In the interval Ownslow sniggered, Glitberg jeered, and Powys tested the amount that I could move my arms. Half an inch, at the most.

'You won't get out of that,' he said. He shook my elbow and watched the results. 'I reckon this'll make us even.' He turned as Trevor came back. 'Are all doors locked?'

'All except the front one,' Trevor said.

'Right. Then let's be off.'

'But what about *him?*' Trevor said. 'We can't just leave him like that.'

'Can't we? Why not?'

'But . . .' Trevor said: and fell silent.

'Someone will find him tomorrow,' Powys said. 'A cleaner, or something. Do you have a cleaner?'

'Yes,' Trevor said doubtfully. 'But she doesn't come in on Tuesdays. My wife will be back though.'

'There you are, then.'

'All right.' He hesitated. 'My wife keeps some money in the kitchen. I'll just fetch it.'

'Right.'

Trevor went on his errand and came back. He stood near me, looking worried.

'Ro . . .'

'Come on,' said Powys impatiently. 'He's ruined you, like he ruined us. You owe him bloody nothing.'

He shepherded them out of the door; Trevor unhappy, Glitberg sneering, Ownslow unassuaged. Powys looked back from the doorway, his own face, what I could see of it, full of smug satisfaction.

'I'll think of you,' he said. 'All night.'

He pulled the door towards him, to shut it, and switched off the light.

Human bodies were not designed to remain for hours in one position. Even in sleep, they regularly shifted. Joints bent and unbent, muscles contracted and relaxed.

No human body was designed to lie as I was lying, with constant strain already running up through legs, stomach, chest, shoulders and arms. Within five minutes, while they were still there, it had become in any normal way intolerable. One would not have stayed in that attitude from choice.

When they had gone, I simply could not visualize the time ahead. My imagination short-circuited. Blanked out. What did one do if one couldn't bear something, and had to?

The worst of the spit slid slowly off my face, but the rest remained, sticky and itching. I blinked my eyes wide open in the dark and thought of being at home in my own quiet bed, as I'd hoped to be that night.

I realized that I was having a surprising amount of difficulty in breathing. One took breathing so much for granted; but the mechanics weren't all that simple. The muscles between the ribs pulled the ribcage out and upwards, allowing air to rush down to the lungs. It wasn't, so to speak, the air going in which expanded the chest, but the expansion of the chest which drew in the air. With the ribcage pulled continuously up, the normal amount of muscle movement was much curtailed.

I still wore a collar and tie. I would choke, I thought.

The other bit that breathed for you was the diaphragm, a nice hefty floor of muscle between the heart-lung cavity and the lower lot of guts. Thank God for diaphragms, I thought. Long may they reign. Mine chugged away, doing its best.

If I passed the night in delirium, I thought, it would be a good idea. If I'd studied Yoga . . . mind out of body. Too late for that. I was always too late. Never prepared.

Stabs of strain afflicted both my shoulders. Needles. Swords.

Think of something else.

Boats. Think of boats. Big expensive boats, built to high standards in top British boat yards, sailing away out of Britain to ship-brokers in Antibes and Antigua.

Huge floating assets in negotiable form. None of the usual bureaucratic trouble about transferring money abroad in huge amounts. No dollar premiums to worry about, or other such hurdles set up by grasping governments. Just put your money in fibreglass and ropes and sails, and float away on it on the tide.

The man at Goldenwave had told me they never lacked for orders. Boats, he said, didn't deteriorate like aeroplanes or cars. Put a quarter of a million into a boat, and it would most likely increase in value, as years went by. Sell the boat, bank the money, and hey presto, all nicely, tidily, and legally done.

There were frightful protests from my arms and legs. I couldn't move them in any way more than an inch: could give them no respite. It really was, I thought, an absolutely bloody revenge.

No use reflecting that it was I who had stirred up Powys and Ownslow and Glitberg. Poke a rattlesnake with a stick, don't be surprised if he bites you. I'd gone to find out if it was they who'd abducted me, and found out instead what they'd done with all the missing money.

Paid for boats. The mention of boats had produced the menace, not the mention of abduction. Boats paid for by the taxpayers, the electronics firm, and the Nantuckets of New York. Gone with the four winds. Exchanged for a pile of nice strong currency, lying somewhere in a foreign bank, waiting for the owners to stroll along and collect.

Trevor linked them all. Maybe the boats had originally been his idea. I hadn't thought of William Finch knowing Connaught Powys: certainly not as well as he clearly did. But through Trevor, along the track from embezzlement to ship building . . . along the way, they had met.

The pains in my arms and legs intensified, and there was a great shaft of soreness up my chest.

I thought: I don't know how to face this. I don't know how. It isn't possible.

Trevor, I thought. Surely Trevor wouldn't have left me like this ... not like this ... if he had realized. Trevor, who had been so distressed at my dishevelled appearance in the police station, who as far as I could see had really cared about my health.

Ye Gods, I thought, I'd go gladly back to the sail locker ... to the van ... to almost anywhere one could think of.

Some of my muscles were trembling. Would the fibres simply collapse? I wondered. Would the muscles just tear apart; the ligaments disconnect from the bones? Oh for God's sake, I told myself, you've got enough to worry about, without that. Think of something cheerful.

I couldn't, off-hand. Even cheerful subjects like Tapestry were no good. I couldn't see me being able to ride in the Whitbread Gold Cup.

Minutes dragged and telescoped, stretching to hours. The various separate pains gradually coalesced into an all pervading fire. Thought became fragmentary, and then, I reckon, more or less stopped.

The unbearable was there, inside, savage and consuming. Unbearable ... there was no such word.

By morning I'd gone a long way into an extreme land I hadn't known existed. A different dimension, where the memory of ordinary pain was a laugh.

An internal place; a heavy core. The external world had retreated. I no longer felt as if I were any particular shape: had no picture of hands or feet, or where they were. Everything was crimson and dark.

I existed as a mass. Unified. A single lump of matter, of a weight and fire like the centre of the earth.

There was nothing else. No thought. Just feeling, and eternity.

A noise dragged me back.

People talking. Voices in the house.

I saw that daylight had returned and was trickling in round the edge of the curtains. I tried to call out, and could not.

Footsteps crossed and recrossed the hall, and at last, at last, someone opened the door, and switched on the light.

Two women came in. I stared at them, and they stared at me: on both sides with disbelief.

They were Hilary Pinlock, and Jossie.

Hilary cut through the red checked table napkins with a small pair of scissors from her handbag.

I tried to sit up and behave with sangfroid, but my stretched muscles wouldn't respond to directions. I ended somehow with my face against her chest and my throat heaving with unstoppable half-stifled groans.

'It's all right, Ro. It's all right, my dear, my dear.'

Her thin arms held me close and tight, rocking me

gently, taking into herself the impossible pain, suffering for me like a mother. Mother, sister, lover, child . . . a woman who crossed the categories and left them blurred.

I had a mouthful of blouse button and was comforted to my soul.

She put an arm round my waist and more or less carried me to the nearest chair. Jossie stood looking on, her face filled with a greater shock than finding me there.

'Do you realize,' she said, 'that Dad's gone?'

I didn't feel like saying much.

'Did you hear?' Jossie said. Her voice was tight, unfriendly. 'Dad's gone. Walked out. Left all the horses. Do you hear? He's cleared half the papers out of the office and burned them in the incinerator, and this lady says it is because my father is an embezzler, and you . . . you are going to give him away to the Nantuckets, and the police.'

The big eyes were hard. 'And Trevor, too. Trevor. I've known him all my life. How could you? And you *knew* . . . you knew on Sunday . . . all day . . . what you were going to do. You took me out, and you knew you were going to ruin all our lives. I think you're hateful.'

Hilary took two strides, gripped her by the shoulders, and positively shook her.

'Stop it, you silly girl. Open your silly eyes. He did all this for you.'

Jossie tore herself free. 'What do you mean?' she demanded.

'He didn't want your father to go to prison. Because he's your father. He's sent others there, but he didn't want it to happen to your father, or to Trevor King. So he warned them, and gave them time to destroy things. Evidence. Paper and records.' She glanced back at me. 'He told me on Saturday what he planned . . . to tell your father how much he knew, and to offer him a bargain. Time, enough time, if he would destroy his tracks and go, in a way which would cause you least pain. Time to go before the police arrived to confiscate his passport. Time to arrange his life as best he could. And they made him pay for the time he gave them. He paid for every second of it . . .' She gestured in frustrated disgust towards the table and the cut pieces of cloth, ' . . . in *agony.*'

'Hilary,' I protested.

There never had been any stopping Hilary Pinlock in full flight. She said fiercely to Jossie, 'He can put up with a lot, but I reckon it's too much to have you reviling him for what he's suffered for your sake. So you just get some sense into your little bird-brain, and beg his pardon.'

I helplessly shook my head. Jossie stood with her mouth open in shattered shock, and then she looked at the table, and discarded the thought.

'Dad would never have done that,' she said.

'There were five of them,' I said wearily. 'People do

things in gangs which they would never have done on their own.'

She looked at me with shadowed eyes. Then she turned abruptly on her heel and walked out of the room.

'She's terribly upset,' Hilary said, making allowances.

'Yes.'

'Are you all right?'

'No.'

She made a face. 'I'll get you something. They must at least have aspirins in this house.'

'Tell me first,' I said, 'how you got here.'

'Oh. I was worried. I rang your cottage all evening. Late into the night. And again this morning, early. I had a feeling . . . I didn't think it would hurt if I came over to check, so I drove to your cottage . . . but of course you weren't there. I saw your neighbour, Mrs Morris, and she said you hadn't been home all night. So then I went to your office. They were in a tizzy because some time between last night and this morning your partner had taken away a great many papers, and neither of you had turned up for work.'

'What time . . .' I said.

'About half past nine, when I went to the office.' She looked at her watch. 'It's a quarter to eleven, now.'

Fourteen hours, I thought numbly. It must have been at least fourteen hours, that I'd been lying there.

'Well, I drove to Finch's house,' she said. 'I had a bit of

trouble finding the way, and when I got there, everything was in a shambles. There was a girl secretary weeping all over the place. People asking what was going on . . . and your girl Jossie in a dumbstruck state. I asked her if she'd seen you. I said I thought you could be in real trouble. I asked her where Trevor King lived. I made her come with me, to show me the way. I tried to tell her what her father had been doing, and how he'd abducted you, but she didn't want to believe it.'

'No.'

'So then we arrived here, and found you.'

'How did you get in?'

'The back door was wide open.'

'Wide . . .?'

I had a sudden picture of Trevor going out to the kitchen, saying it was to fetch some money. To open the door. To give me a tiny chance. Poor Trevor.

'That package I gave you,' I said. 'With all the photostats. When you get home, will you burn it?'

'If that's what you want.'

'Mm.'

Jossie came back and sprawled in a red armchair, all angular legs.

'Sorry,' she said abruptly.

'So am I.'

'You did help him,' she said.

Hilary said, 'Do good to those who despitefully use you.'

I slid my eyes her way. 'That's enough of that.'

'What are you talking about?' Jossie demanded.

Hilary shook her head with a smile and went on an aspirin hunt. Butazolidin, I imagined, would do more good. Things were better now I was sitting in a chair, but a long old way from right.

'He left me a letter,' Jossie said. 'More or less the same as yours.'

'How do you mean?'

'Dear Jossie, Sorry, Love, Dad.'

'Oh.'

'He said he was going to France . . .' She broke off, and stared ahead of her, her face full of misery. 'Life's going to be unutterably bloody, isn't it,' she said, 'for a long time to come?'

'Mm.'

'What am I going to do?' The question was a rhetorical wail, but I answered it.

'I did want to warn you,' I said. 'But I couldn't . . . before I'd talked to your father. I meant it, though, about you coming to live in the cottage. If you thought . . . that you could.'

'Ro . . .' Her voice was little more than a breath.

I sat and ached, and thought in depression about telephoning the Nantuckets, and the chaos I'd have to deal with in the office.

Jossie turned her head towards me and gave me a long inspection.

'You look spineless,' she said. Her voice was halfway back in spirit to the old healthy mockery; shaky, but

317

doing its best. 'And I'll tell you something else.' She paused and swallowed.

'When Dad went, he left *me* behind, but he took the detestable Lida with him.'

There was enough, in that, for the future.

FORFEIT

CHAPTER ONE

The letter from *Tally* came on the day Bert Checkov died. It didn't look like trouble; just an invitation from a glossy to write an article on the Lamplighter Gold Cup. I flicked it across the desk to the Sports Editor and went on opening the mail which always accumulated for me by Fridays. Luke-John Morton grunted and stretched out a languid hand, blinking vacantly while he listened to someone with a lot to say on the telephone.

'Yeah . . . yeah. Blow the roof off,' he said.

Blowing the roof off was the number one policy of *The Sunday Blaze*, bless its cold heart. Why didn't I write for *The Sunday Times*, my wife's mother said, instead of a rag like *The Sunday Blaze*? They hadn't needed me, that was why. She considered this irrelevant, and when she couldn't actively keep it quiet, continued to apologize to every acquaintance for my employment. That the *Blaze* paid twenty-eight per cent more than *The Times*, and that her daughter was expensive, she ignored.

I slit open a cheap brown envelope and found some nut had written to say that only a vicious unscrupulous bum like myself would see any good in the man I had defended last Sunday. The letter was written on lavatory paper and spite oozed from it like marsh gas. Derry Clark read it over my shoulder and laughed.

'Told you you'd stir them up.'

'Anything for an unquiet life,' I agreed.

Derry wrote calm uncontroversial articles each week assessing form and firmly left the crusading rebel stuff to me. My back, as he constantly pointed out, was broader than his.

Eight more of my other correspondents proved to be thinking along the same general lines. All anonymous, naturally. Their problems, I reflected, dumping their work in the waste basket, were even worse than mine.

'How's your wife?' Derry said.

'Fine, thanks.'

He nodded, not looking at me. He'd never got over being embarrassed about Elizabeth. It took some people that way.

Luke-John's conversation guttered to a close. 'Sure ... sure. Phone it through by six at the latest.' He put down the receiver and focused on my letter from *Tally*, his eyes skidding over it with professional speed.

'A study in depth ... how these tarty magazines love that phrase. Do you want to do it?'

'If the fee's good.'

'I thought you were busy ghosting Buster Figg's autobiography.'

'I'm hung up on chapter six. He's sloped off to the Bahamas and left me no material.'

'How far through his horrid little life have you got?' His interest was genuine.

'The end of his apprenticeship and his first win in a classic.'

'Will it sell?'

'I don't know,' I sighed. 'All he's interested in is money, and all he remembers about some races is the starting price. He gambled in thousands. And he insists I put his biggest bets in. He says they can't take away his licence now he's retired.'

Luke-John sniffed, rubbing a heavily freckled hand across the prominent tendons of his scrawny neck, massaging his walnut-sized larynx, dropping the heavy eyelid hoods while he considered the letter from *Tally*. My contract with the *Blaze* was restrictive: books were all right, but I couldn't write articles for any other paper or magazine without Luke-John's permission, which I mostly didn't get.

Derry pushed me out of his chair and sat in it himself. As I spent only Fridays in the office, I didn't rate a desk and usurped my younger colleague's whenever he wasn't looking. Derry's desk held a comprehensive reference library of form books in the top three drawers and a half-bottle of vodka, two hundred purple hearts and a pornographic film catalogue in the bottom one. These were window dressing only. They represented the wicked fellow Derry would like to be, not the lawful, temperate, semi-detached man he was.

I perched on the side of his desk and looked out over the Friday morning clatter, a quarter-acre of type-writers and telephones going at half speed as the week went on towards Sunday. Tuesdays the office was dead: Saturdays it buzzed like flies squirted with DDT. Fridays I felt part of it. Saturdays I went to the races. Sundays and Mondays, officially off. Tuesdays to Thursdays, think up some galvanizing subject to write about, and write it. Fridays, take it in for Luke-John, and then for the editor, to read and vet.

Result, a thousand words a week, an abusive mail-bag, and a hefty cheque which didn't cover my expenses.

Luke-John said, 'Are you or Derry doing the Lamp-lighter?'

Without giving me a second Derry jumped in. 'I am.'

'That all right with you, Ty?' Luke-John asked dubiously.

'Oh sure,' I said. 'It's a complicated handicap. Right up his street.'

Luke-John pursed his thin lips and said with unusual generosity, '*Tally* says they want background stuff, not tips ... I don't see why you shouldn't do it, if you want to.'

He scribbled a large OK, at the bottom of the page and signed his name. 'But of course,' he added, 'if you dig up any dirt, keep it for *us*.'

Generous, be damned, I thought wryly. Luke-John's soul belonged to the *Blaze* and his simple touchstone in all decisions was, 'Could it possibly, directly or indirectly, benefit the paper?' Every member of the sports section had at some time or other been ruthlessly sacrificed on his altar. For cancelled holidays, smashed appointments, lost opportunities, he cared not one jot.

'Sure,' I said mildly. 'And thanks.'

'How's your wife?' he asked.

'Fine, thanks.'

He asked every week without fail. He had his politenesses, when it didn't cost the *Blaze*. Maybe he really cared. Maybe he only cared because when she wasn't 'fine' it affected my work.

I pinched Derry's telephone and dialled the number.

'*Tally* magazine, can I help you?' A girl's voice, very smooth, West Ken, and bored.

'I'd like to talk to Arnold Shankerton.'

'Who's calling?'

'James Tyrone.'

'One moment, please.' Some clicks and a pause. 'You're through.'

An equally smooth, highly sophisticated tenor voice proclaimed itself to be Arnold Shankerton, Features. I thanked him for his letter and said I would like to accept his commission. He said that would be very nice in moderately pleased tones and I gently added, 'If the price is right naturally.'

'Naturally,' he conceded. 'How much do you want?'

Think of a number and double it. 'Two hundred guineas, plus expenses.'

Luke-John's eyebrows rose and Derry said, 'You'll be lucky.'

'Our profit margin is small,' Shankerton pointed out a little plaintively. 'One hundred is our absolute limit.'

'I pay too much tax.'

His sigh came heavily down the wire. 'A hundred and fifty, then. And for that it'll have to be good.'

'I'll do my best.'

'Your best,' he said, 'would scorch the paper. We want the style and the insight but not the scandal. Right?'

'Right,' I agreed without offence. 'How many words?'

'It's the main feature. Say three thousand five hundred, roughly speaking.'

'How about pictures?'

'You can have one of our photographers when you're ready. And within reason, of course.'

'Of course,' I said politely. 'When do you want it by?'

'We go to press on that edition ... let's see ... on November twentieth. So we'd like your stuff on the morning of the seventeenth, at the very latest. But the earlier the better.'

I looked at Derry's calendar. Ten days to the seventeenth.

'All right.'

'And when you've thought out how you'd like to present it, send us an outline.'

'Will do,' I said: but I wouldn't. Outlines were asking for trouble in the shape of editorial alterations. Shankerton could, and would, chop at the finished article to his heart's content, but I was against him getting his scissors into the embryo.

Luke-John skimmed the letter back and Derry picked it up and read it.

'In depth,' he said, sardonically. 'You're used to the deep end. You'll feel quite at home.'

'Yeah,' I agreed absentmindedly. Just what *was* depth, a hundred and fifty guineas worth of it?

I made a snap decision that depth in this case would be the background people, not the stars.

The stars hogged the headlines week by week. The background people had no news valuc. For once, I would switch them over.

Snap decisions had got me into trouble once or twice in the past. All the same, I made this one. It proved to be the most trouble-filled of the lot.

*

Derry, Luke-John, and I knocked off soon after one and walked down the street in fine drizzle to elbow our way into the bar of The Devereux in Devereux Court opposite the Law Courts.

Bert Checkov was there, trying to light his stinking old pipe and burning his fingers on the matches. The shapeless tweed which swathed his bulk was as usual scattered with ash and as usual his toecaps were scuffed and grey. There was more glaze in the washy blue eyes than one-thirty normally found there: an hour too much, at a rough guess. He'd started early.

Luke-John spoke to him and he stared vaguely back. Derry bought us a half-pint each and politely asked Bert to have one, though he'd never liked him.

'Double scotch,' Bert mumbled, and Derry thought of his mortgages and scowled.

'How's things?' I asked, knowing that this too was a mistake. The Checkov grumbles were inexhaustible.

For once, however, the stream was damned. The watery eyes focused on me with an effort and another match sizzled on his skin. He appeared not to notice.

'Gi' you a piesh o' advish,' he said, but the words stopped there. The advice stayed in his head.

'What is it?'

'Piesh o' advish.' He nodded solemnly.

Luke-John raised his eyes to the ceiling in an exasperation that wasn't genuine, for old-time journalists like Bert he had an unlimited regard which no amount of drink could quench.

'Give him the advice, then,' Luke-John suggested. 'He can always do with it.'

The Checkov gaze lurched from me to my boss. The Checkov mouth belched uninhibitedly. Derry's pale face twisted squeamishly, and Checkov saw him. As a gay lunch, hardly a gas. Just any Friday, I thought: but I was wrong. Bert Checkov was less than an hour from death.

Luke-John, Derry, and I sat on stools round the bar counter and ate cold meat and pickled onions, and Bert Checkov stood swaying behind us, breathing pipe smoke and whisky fumes down our necks. Instead of the usually steady rambling flow of grousing to which we were accustomed, we received only a series of grunts, the audible punctuation of the inner Checkov thoughts.

Something on his mind. I wasn't interested enough to find out what. I had enough on my own.

Luke-John gave him a look of compassion and another whisky, and the alcohol washed into the pale blue eyes like a tide, resulting in pin-point pupils and a look of blank stupidity.

'I'll walk him back to his office,' I said abruptly. 'He'll fall under a bus if he goes on his own.'

'Serve him right,' Derry said under his breath, but carefully so that Luke-John shouldn't hear.

We finished lunch with cheese and another half-pint. Checkov lurched sideways and spilt my glass over Derry's knee and the pub carpet. The carpet soaked it

329

up good-temperedly, which was more than could be said for Derry. Luke-John shrugged, resignedly, half laughing, and I finished what was left of my beer with one swallow, and I steered Bert Checkov through the crowd and into the street.

'Not closing time yet,' he said distinctly.

'For you it is, old chum.'

He rolled against the wall, waving the pipe vaguely in his chubby fist. 'Never leave a pub before closing. Never leave a story while it's hot. Never leave a woman on her doorstep. Paragraphs and skirts should be short and pheasants and breasts should be high.'

'Sure,' I said sighing. Some advice.

I took his arm and he came easily enough out on to the Fleet Street pavement. His tottering progress up towards the City end produced several stares but no actual collisions. Linked together we crossed during a lull in the traffic and continued eastwards under the knowing frontages of the *Telegraph* and the black glass *Express*. Fleet Street had seen the lot: no news value in an elderly racing correspondent being helped back from lunch with a skinful.

'A bit of advice,' he said suddenly, stopping in his tracks. 'A bit of advice.'

'Yes?' I said patiently.

He squinted in my general direction.

'We've come past the *Blaze*.'

'Yeah.'

He tried to turn me round to retrace our steps.

'I've business down at Ludgate Circus. I'm going your way today,' I said.

'Zat so?' He nodded vaguely and we shambled on. Ten more paces. He stopped again.

'Piece of advice.'

He was looking straight ahead. I'm certain that he saw nothing at all. No bustling street. Nothing but what was going on inside his head.

I was tired of waiting for the advice which showed no signs of materializing. It had begun to drizzle again. I took his arm to try and get him moving along the last fifty yards to his paper's florid front door. He wouldn't move.

'Famous last words,' he said.

'Whose?'

'Mine. Naturally. Famous last words. Bit of advice.'

'Oh sure,' I sighed. 'We're getting wet.'

'I'm not drunk.'

'No.'

'I could write my column any time. This minute.'

'Sure.'

He lurched off suddenly, and we made it to his door. Three steps and he'd be home and dry.

He stood in the entrance and rocked unsteadily. The pale blue eyes made a great effort towards sobering up, but the odds were against it.

'If anyone asks you,' he said finally, 'don't do it.'

'Don't do what?'

An anxious expression flitted across his pallid fleshy

331

face. There were big pores all over his nose, and his beard was growing out in stiff black millimetres. He pushed one hand into his jacket pocket, and the anxiety turned to relief as he drew it out again with a half-bottle of scotch attached.

''Fraid I'd forgotten it,' he mumbled.

'See you then, Bert.'

'Don't forget,' he said. 'That advice.'

'Right.' I began to turn away.

'Ty?'

I was tired of him. 'What?'

'You wouldn't let it happen to you, I know that . . . but sometimes it's the strong ones get the worst clobbering . . . in the ring, I mean . . . they never know when they've taken enough . . .'

He suddenly leaned forward and grasped my coat. Whisky fumes seeped up my nose and I could feel his hot breath across the damp air.

'You're always broke, with that wife of yours. Luke-John told me. Always bloody stony. So don't do it . . . don't sell your sodding soul . . .'

'Try not to,' I said wearily, but he wasn't listening.

He said, with the desperate intensity of the very drunk, 'They buy you first and blackmail after . . .'

'Who?'

'Don't know . . . Don't sell . . . don't sell your column.'

'No,' I sighed.

'I *mean* it.' He put his face even closer. 'Never sell your column.'

'Bert . . . Have you?'

He closed up. He pried himself off me and went back to rocking. He winked, a vast caricature of a wink.

'Bit of advice,' he said nodding. He swivelled on rubbery ankles and weaved an unsteady path across the lobby to the lifts. Inside he turned round and I saw him standing there under the light clutching the half-bottle and still saying over and over, 'Bit of advice, bit of advice.'

The doors slid heavily across in front of him. Shrugging, puzzled a little, I started on my way back to the *Blaze*. Fifty yards along, I stopped off to see if the people who were servicing my typewriter had finished it. They hadn't. Call back Monday, they said.

When I stepped out into the street again a woman was screaming.

Heads turned. The high-pitched agonized noise pierced the roar of wheels and rose clean above the car horns. With everyone else, I looked to see the cause.

Fifty yards up the pavement a knot of people was rapidly forming and I reflected that in this particular place droves of regular staff reporters would be on the spot in seconds. Nevertheless, I went back. Back to the front door of Bert's paper, and a few steps farther on.

Bert was lying on the pavement. Clearly dead. The

shining fragments of his half-bottle of whisky scattered the paving slabs around him, and the sharp smell of the spilt spirit mixed uneasily with the pervading diesel.

'He fell. He fell.' The screaming woman was on the edge of hysterics and couldn't stop shouting. 'He fell. I saw him. From up there. He fell.'

Luke-John said 'Christ' several times and looked badly shocked. Derry shook out a whole lot of paper clips on to his desk and absentmindedly put them back one by one.

'You're sure he was dead?' he said.

'His office was seven floors up.'

'Yeah.' He shook his head disbelievingly. 'Poor old boy.' Nil nisi bonum. A sharp change of attitude.

Luke-John looked out of the *Blaze* window and down along the street. The smashed remains of Bert Checkov had been decently removed. The pavement had been washed. People tramped unknowingly across the patch where he had died.

'He was drunk,' Luke-John said. 'Worse than usual.'

He and Derry made a desultory start on the afternoon work. I had no need to stay as the editor had OK'd my copy, but I hung around anyway for an hour or two, not ready to go.

They had said in Bert's office that he came back paralytic from lunch and simply fell out of the window. Two girl secretaries saw him. He was taking a drink out of the neck of the bottle of whisky, and he suddenly staggered against the window, which swung open, and he toppled out. The bottom of the window was at hip height. No trouble at all for someone as drunk as Bert.

I remembered the desperation behind the bit of advice he had given me.

And I wondered.

CHAPTER TWO

Three things immediately struck you about the girl who opened the stockbroker Tudor door at Virginia Water. First, her poise. Second, her fashion sense. Third, her colour. She had honey-toast skin, large dark eyes, and a glossy shoulder-length bounce of black hair. A slightly broad nose and a mouth to match enhanced a landscape in which Negro and Caucasian genes had conspired together to do a grand job.

'Good afternoon,' I said. 'I'm James Tyrone. I telephoned . . .'

'Come in,' she nodded. 'Harry and Sarah should be back at any minute.'

'They are still playing golf?'

'Mm.' She turned, smiled slightly, and gestured me into the house. 'Still finishing lunch, I expect.'

It was three thirty-five. Why not?

She led me through the hall (well-polished parquet, careful flowers, studded leather umbrella stand) into a chintz and chrysanthemum sitting-room. Every window in the house was a clutter of diamond-shaped leaded lights which might have had some point when glass could only be made in six-inch squares and had to be joined together to get anywhere. The modern imitation obscured the light and the view and was bound to infuriate window cleaners. Harry and Sarah had opted also for uncovered dark oak beams with machine-made chisel marks. The single picture on the plain cream walls made a wild contrast: a modern impressionistic abstract of some cosmic explosion, with the oils stuck on in lumps.

'Sit down.' She waved a graceful hand at a thickly cushioned sofa. 'Like a drink?'

'No, thank you.'

'Don't journalists drink all day?'

'If you drink and write, the writing isn't so hot.'

'Ah yes,' she said, 'Dylan Thomas said he had to be stone cold for any good to come of it.'

'Different class,' I smiled.

'Same principle.'

'Absolutely.'

She gave me a long inspection, her head an inch tilted to one side and her green dress lying in motionless folds down her slender body. Terrific legs in the latest in stockings ended in shiny green shoes with gold buckles, and the only other accessory on display was a broad-strapped gold watch on her left wrist.

'You'll know me again,' she said.

I nodded. Her body moved subtly inside the green dress.

She said slowly, with more than simple meaning. 'And I'll know you.'

Her voice, face, and manner were quite calm. The brief flash of intense sexual awareness could have been my imagination. Certainly her next remark held no undertone and no invitation.

'Do you *like* horses?'

'Yes, I do,' I said.

'Six months ago I would have said the one place I would never go would be to a race meeting.'

'But you go now?'

'Since Harry won Egocentric in that raffle, life has changed in this little neck of the woods.'

'That,' I said, 'is exactly what I want to write about.'

I was on *Tally* business. Background to the Lamplighter. My choice of untypical racehorse owners, Harry and Sarah Hunterson, came back at that point from their Sunday golf-course lunch, sweeping in with them a breeze compounded of healthy links air, expensive cigar smoke, and half-digested gin.

Harry was big, sixtyish, used to authority, heavily charming, and unshakably Tory. I guessed that he read the *Telegraph* and drove a three-litre Jaguar. With automatic transmission, of course. He gave me a hearty handshake and said he was glad to see his niece had been looking after me.

'Yes, thank you.'

Sarah said, 'Gail dear, you didn't give Mr Tyrone a drink.'

338

'He didn't want one.'

The two women were coolly nice to each other in civilized voices. Sarah must have been about thirty years older, but she had worked hard at keeping nature at bay. Everything about her looked careful, from the soft gold rinse via the russet-coloured dress to the chunky brown golfing shoes. Her well-controlled shape owed much to the drinking man's diet, and only a deep sag under the chin gave the game away. Neither golf nor gin had dug wrinkles anywhere except round her eyes. Her mouth still had fullness and shape. The wrappings were good enough to hold out hopes of a spark-striking mind, but these proved unrealistic. Sarah was all-of-a-piece, with attitudes and opinions as tidy and well-ordered and as imitative as her house.

Harry was easy to interview in the aftermath of the nineteenth hole.

'I bought this raffle ticket at the Golf Club dance, you see. Some chap was there selling them, a friend of a friend, you know, and I gave him a quid. Well, you know how it is at a dance. For charity, he said. I thought a quid was a bit steep for a raffle ticket, even if it was for a horse. Though I didn't want a horse, mind you. Last thing I wanted. And then damn me if I didn't go and win it. Bit of a problem, eh? To suddenly find yourself saddled with a racehorse?' He laughed, expecting a reward for his little joke.

I duly obliged. Sarah and Gail were both wearing the expressions which meant they had heard him say saddled with a racehorse so often that they had to grit their teeth now at each repetition.

'Would you mind,' I said, 'telling me something of your background and history?'

'Life story, eh?' He laughed loudly, looking from Sarah to Gail to collect their approval. His head was heavily handsome though a shade too fleshy round the neck. The bald sunburned crown and the well-disciplined moustache suited him. Thread veins made circular patches of colour on his cheeks. 'Life story,' he repeated. 'Where shall I start?'

'Start from birth,' I said, 'and go on from there.'

Only the very famous who have done it too often, or the extremely introverted, or the sheer bloody-minded, can resist such an invitation. Harry's eyes lit up, and he launched forth with enthusiasm.

Harry had been born in a Surrey suburb in a detached house a size or two smaller than the one he now owned. He had been to a day school and then a minor public school and was turned down by the army because as soon as he left school he had pleurisy. He went to work in the City, in the head office of a finance company, and had risen from junior clerk to director, on the way using occasional snippets of information to make himself modest capital gains via the stockmarket. Nothing shady, nothing rash: but enough so that there should be no drop in his standard of living when he retired.

He married at twenty-four and five years later a

lorry rammed his car and killed his wife, his three-year-old daughter, and his widowed mother. For fifteen years, much in demand at dinner parties, Harry 'looked around'. Then he met Sarah in some Conservative Party committee rooms where they were doing voluntary work addressing pamphlets for a by-election, and they had married three months later. Below the confident fruitiness of successful Harry's voice there was an echo of the motivation of this second marriage. Harry had begun to feel lonely.

As lives went, Harry's had been uneventful. No *Blaze* material in what he had told me, and precious little for *Tally*. Resignedly, I asked him if he intended to keep Egocentric indefinitely.

'Yes, yes, I think so,' he said. 'He has made quite a remarkable difference to us.'

'In what way?'

'It puts them several notches up in lifemanship,' Gail said coolly. 'Gives them something to boast about in pubs.'

We all looked at her. Such was her poise that I found it impossible to tell whether she meant to be catty or teasing, and from his uncertain expression, so did her uncle. There was no ducking it, however, that she had hit to the heart of things, and Sarah smoothly punished her for it.

'Gail dear, would you go and make tea for all of us?'

Gail's every muscle said she would hate to. But she stood up ostentatiously slowly, and went.

'A dear girl,' Sarah said. 'Perhaps sometimes a little trying.' Insincerity took all warmth out of her smile, and she found it necessary to go on, to make an explanation that I guessed she rushed into with every stranger at the first opportunity.

'Harry's sister married a barrister . . . such a clever man, you know . . . but, well . . . *African*.'

'Yes,' I said.

'Of course we're *very* fond of Gail, and as her parents have gone back to his country since it became independent, and as she was born in England and wanted to stay here, well, we . . . well, she lives here with us.'

'Yes,' I said again. 'That must be very nice for her.'

Sad, I thought, that they felt any need to explain. Gail didn't need it.

'She teaches at an art school in Victoria,' Harry added. 'Fashion drawing.'

'Fashion *design*,' Sarah corrected him. 'She's really quite good at it. Her pupils win prizes, and things like that.' There was relief in her voice now that I understood, and she was prepared to be generous. To do her justice, considering the far-back embedded prejudices she clearly suffered from, she had made a successful effort. But a pity the effort showed.

'And you,' I said, 'how about your life? And what do you think of Egocentric?'

She said apologetically that her story wasn't as interesting as Harry's. Her first husband, an optician, had died a year before she met Harry, and all she had done, apart from short excursions into voluntary work, was keep house for the two of them. She was glad Harry had won the horse, she liked going to the races as an owner, she thought it exciting to bet, but ten shillings was her usual, and she and Gail had found it quite fun inventing Harry's racing colours.

'What are they?'

'White with scarlet and turquoise question marks, turquoise sleeves, red cap.'

'They sound fine,' I smiled. 'I'll look out for them.'

Harry said his trainer was planning to fit in one more race for Egocentric before the Lamplighter, and maybe I would see him then. Maybe I would, I said, and Gail brought in the tea.

Harry and Sarah rapidly downed three cups each, simultaneously consulted their watches, and said it was time to be getting along to the Murrows' for drinks.

'I don't think I'll come,' Gail said. 'Tell them thanks, but I have got some work to do. But I'll come and fetch you, if you like, if you think it might be better not to drive home. Give me a ring when you're ready.'

The Murrow drinks on top of the golf club gin were a breathalyser hazard in anyone's book. Harry and Sarah nodded and said they would appreciate it.

'Before you go,' I said, 'could you let me see any newspaper cuttings you have? And any photographs?'

'Certainly, certainly,' Harry agreed. 'Gail will show them to you, won't you, honey? Must dash now, old chap, the Murrows, you know . . . President of the golf club. Nice to have met you. Hope you've got all the gen you need . . . don't hesitate to call if you want to know anything else.'

'Thank you,' I said, but he was gone before I finished. They went upstairs and down, and shut the front door, and drove away. The house settled into quiet behind them.

'They're not exactly alcoholic,' Gail said. 'They just go eagerly from drink to drink.'

Gail's turn to explain. But in her voice, only objectivity: no faintest hint of apology, as there had been in Sarah's.

'They enjoy life,' I said.

Gail's eyebrows rose. 'Do you know,' she said, 'I suppose they do. I've never really thought about it.'

Self-centred, I thought. Cool. Unaffectionate. Everything I disliked in a woman. Everything I needed one to be. Much too tempting.

'Do you want to see those photographs?' she asked.

'Yes, please.'

She fetched an expensive leather folder and we went through them one by one. Nothing in the few clippings that I hadn't learnt already. None of the photographs were arresting enough for *Tally*. I said I'd come back one day soon, with a photographer. Gail put the folder away and I stood up to go.

'It'll be two hours yet before they ring up from the Murrows. Stay and have that drink now?'

I looked at my watch. There was a train every thirty minutes. I supposed I could miss the next. There was Elizabeth. And there was Gail. And it was only an hour.

'Yes,' I said. 'I will.'

She gave me beer and brought one for herself. I sat down again on the sofa and she folded herself gracefully on to a large velvet cushion on the floor.

'You're married, of course?'

'Yes,' I agreed.

'The interesting-looking ones always are.'

'Then why aren't you?'

Her teeth flashed liquid white in an appreciative smile. 'Ah . . . marriage can wait.'

'How long?' I asked.

'I suppose . . . until I find a man I can't bear to part with.'

'You've parted with quite a few?'

'Quite a few.' She nodded and sipped her beer, and looked at me over the rim. 'And you? Are you faithful to your wife?'

I felt myself blink. I said carefully, 'Most of the time.'

'But not always?'

'Not always.'

After a long considering pause she said one short word.

'Good.'

'And is that,' I asked, 'a philosophic comment, or a proposition?'

She laughed. 'I just like to know where I stand.'

'Clear eyed and wide awake . . .?'

'I hate muddle,' she nodded.

'And emotional muddle especially?'

'You're so right.'

She had never loved, I thought. Sex, often. Love, never. Not what I liked, but what I wanted. I battened down the insidious whisper and asked her, like a good journalist, about her job.

'It serves.' She shrugged. 'You get maybe one authentic talent in every hundred students. Mostly their ambition is five times more noticeable than their ideas.'

'Do you design clothes yourself?'

'Not for the rag trade. Some for myself, and for Sarah, and for the school. I prefer to teach. I like being able to turn vaguely artistic ignorance into competent workmanship.'

'And to see your influences all along Oxford Street?'

She nodded, her eyes gleaming with amusement. 'Five of the biggest dress manufacturers now have old students of mine on their design staff. One of them is so individual that I can spot his work every time in the shop windows.'

'You like power,' I said.

'Who doesn't?'

'Heady stuff.'

'All power corrupts?' She was sarcastic.

'Each to his own corruption,' I said mildly. 'What's yours, then?'

She laughed. 'Money, I guess. There's a chronic shortage of the folding stuff in all forms of teaching.'

'So you make do with power.'

'If you can't have everything,' she nodded, 'you make do with *something*.'

I looked down into my beer, unable to stop the contraction I could feel in my face. Her words so completely summed up my perennial position. After eleven years I was less resigned to it than ever.

'What are you thinking about?' she asked.

'Taking you to bed.'

She gasped. I looked up from the flat brown liquid ready for any degree of feminine outrage. I could have mistaken her.

It seemed I hadn't. She was laughing. Pleased.

'That's pretty blunt.'

'Mm.'

I put down the beer and stood up, smiling. 'Time to go,' I said, 'I've a train to catch.'

'After that? You can't go after that.'

'Especially after that.'

For answer she stood up beside me, took hold of my hand, and put my fingers into the gold ring at the top of the zipper down the front of her dress.

'Now go home,' she said.

347

'We've only known each other three hours,' I protested.

'You were aware of me after three minutes.'

I shook my head. 'Three seconds.'

Her teeth gleamed. 'I like strangers.'

I pulled the ring downwards and it was clearly what she wanted.

Harry and Sarah had a large white fluffy rug in front of their fireplace. I imagined it was not the first time Gail had lain on it. She was brisk, graceful, unembarrassed. She stripped off her stockings and shoes, shook off the dress, and stepped out of the diminutive green bra and panties underneath it. Her tawny skin looked warm in the gathering dusk, and her shape took the breath away.

She gave me a marvellous time. A generous lover as well as practised. She knew when to touch lightly, and when to be vigorous. She had strong internal muscles, and she knew how to use them. I took her with passionate gratitude, a fair substitute for love.

When we had finished I lay beside her on the rug and felt the released tension weighing down my limbs in a sort of heavy languorous weakness. The world was a million light-years away and I was in no hurry for it to come closer.

'Wow,' she said, half breathless, half laughing. 'Boy, you sure needed that.'

'Mm.'

'Doesn't your wife let you . . .?'

Elizabeth, I thought. Oh God, Elizabeth. I must sometimes. Just sometimes.

The old weary tide of guilt washed back. The world closed in.

I sat up and stared blindly across the darkening room. It apparently struck Gail that she had been less than tactful, because she got up with a sigh and put her clothes on again, and didn't say another word.

For better or worse, I thought bitterly. For richer, for poorer. In sickness and in health keep thee only unto her as long as you both shall live. I will, I said.

An easy vow, the day I made it. I hadn't kept it. Gail was the fourth girl in eleven years. The first for nearly three.

'You'll miss your train,' she observed prosaically, 'if you sit there much longer.'

I looked at my watch, which was all I had on. Fifteen minutes.

She sighed. 'I'll drive you along to the station.'

We made it with time to spare. I stepped out of the car and politely thanked her for the lift.

'Will I see you again?' she said. Asking for information. Showing no anxiety. Looking out at me through the open window of the estate car outside Virginia Water station she was giving a close imitation of any suburban wife doing the train run. A long cool way from the rough and tumble on the rug. Switch on, switch off. The sort of woman I needed.

349

'I don't know,' I said indecisively. The signal at the
end of the platform went green.

'Goodbye,' she said calmly.

'Do Harry and Sarah,' I asked carefully, 'always play
golf on Sundays?'

She laughed, the yellow station lighting flashing on
teeth and eyes.

'Without fail.'

'Maybe . . .'

'Maybe you'll ring, and maybe you won't.' She
nodded. 'Fair enough. And maybe I'll be in, and maybe
I won't.' She gave me a lengthy look which was half
smile and half amused detachment. She wouldn't weep
if I didn't return. She would accommodate me if I did.
'But don't leave it too long, if you're coming back.'

She wound up the window and drove off without a
wave, without a backward glance.

The green electric worm of a train slid quietly into
the station to take me home. Forty minutes to Waterloo. Underground to King's Cross. Three-quarters of a
mile to walk. Time to enjoy the new ease in my body.
Time to condemn it. Too much of my life was a battlefield in which conscience and desire fought constantly
for the upper hand: and whichever of them won, it left
me the loser.

Elizabeth's mother said with predictable irritation,
'You're late.'

'I'm sorry.'

I watched the jerks of her crossly pulling on her

gloves. Overcoat and hat had already been in place when I walked in.

'You have so little consideration. It'll be nearly eleven when I get back.'

I didn't answer.

'You're selfish. All men are selfish.'

There was no point in agreeing with her, and no point in arguing. A disastrous and short-lived marriage had left hopeless wounds in her mind which she had done her best to pass on to her only child. Elizabeth, when I first met her, had been pathologically scared of men.

'We've had our supper,' my mother-in-law said. 'I've stacked the dishes for Mrs Woodward.'

Nothing could be more certainly relied upon to upset Mrs Woodward than a pile of congealed plates first thing on Monday morning.

'Fine,' I said, smiling falsely.

'Goodbye, Elizabeth,' she called.

'Goodbye, Mother.'

I opened the door for her and got no thanks.

'Next Sunday, then,' she said.

'That'll be nice.'

She smiled acidly, knowing I didn't mean it. But since she worked as a receptionist-hostess in a health farm all week, Sunday was her day for seeing Elizabeth. Most weeks I wished she would leave us alone, but that Sunday it had set me free to go to Virginia

Water. From the following Sunday, and what I might do with it, I wrenched my thoughts away.

When she had gone I walked across to Elizabeth and kissed her on the forehead.

'Hi.'

'Hi yourself,' she said. 'Did you have a good afternoon?'

Straight jab.

'Mm.'

'Good . . . Mother's left the dishes again,' she said.

'Don't worry, I'll do them.'

'What would I do without you!'

We both knew the answer to that. Without me, she would have to spend the rest of her life in a hospital ward, a prisoner with no possibility of escape. She couldn't breathe without the electrically driven pump which hummed at the foot of her high bed. She couldn't cut up her own food or take herself to the bathroom. Elizabeth, my wife, was ninety per cent paralysed from poliomyelitis.

CHAPTER THREE

We lived over a row of lock-up garages in a mews behind Gray's Inn Road. A development company had recently knocked down the old buildings opposite, letting in temporary acres of evening sunshine, and was now at the girder stage of a block of flats. If these made our place too dark and shut in when they were done, I would have to find us somewhere else. Not a welcome prospect. We had moved twice before and it was always difficult.

Since race trains mostly ran from London, and to cut my travelling time down to a minimum, we lived two minutes' walk from the *Blaze*. It had proved much better, in London, to live in a backwater than in a main street: in the small mews community the neighbours all knew about Elizabeth and looked up to her window and waved when they passed, and a lot of them came upstairs for a chat and to bring our shopping.

The district nurse came every morning to do Elizabeth's vapour rubs to prevent bed sores, and I did them in the evenings. Mrs Woodward, a semi-trained but

353

unqualified nurse, came Mondays to Saturdays from nine-thirty to six, and was helpful about staying longer if necessary. One of our main troubles was that Elizabeth could not be left alone in the flat even for five minutes in case there was an electricity failure. If the main current stopped, we could switch her breathing pump over to a battery, and we could also operate it by hand: but someone had to be there to do it quickly. Mrs Woodward was kind, middle-aged, reliable, and quiet, and Elizabeth liked her. She was also very expensive, and since the welfare state turns a fish-faced blind eye on incapacitated wives, I could claim not even so much as a tax allowance for Mrs Woodward's essential services. We had to have her, and she kept us poor: and that was that.

In one of the garages below the flat stood the old Bedford van which was the only sort of transport of any use to us. I had had it adapted years ago with a stretcher-type bed so that it would take Elizabeth, pump, batteries, and all, and although it meant too much upheaval to go out in it every week, it did sometimes give her a change of scenery and some country air. We had tried two holidays by the sea in a caravan, but she had felt uncomfortable and insecure, and both times it had rained, so we didn't bother any more. Day trips were enough, she said. And although she enjoyed them, they exhausted her.

Her respirator was the modern cuirass type: a Spirashell: not the old totally enclosed iron lung. The Spirashell itself slightly resembled the breastplate of a suit of armour. It fitted over the entire front of her chest, was edged with a thick roll of latex, and was fastened by straps round her body. Breathing was really a matter of suction. The pump, which was connected to the Spirashell by a thick flexible hose, alternately made a partial vacuum inside the shell, and then drove air back in again. The vacuum period pulled Elizabeth's chest wall outwards, allowing air to flow downwards into her lungs. The air-in period collapsed her chest and pushed the used breaths out again.

Far more comfortable, and easier for everyone caring for her than a box respirator, the Spirashell had only one drawback. Try how we might, and however many scarves and cardigans we might stuff in round the edges, between the latex roll and her nightdress, it was eternally draughty. As long as the air in the flat was warm it no longer worried her. Summer was all right. But the cold air continually blowing on to her chest not surprisingly distressed her. Cold also reduced to nil the small movements she had retained in her left hand and wrist, and on which she depended for everything. Our heating bills were astronomical.

In the nine and a half years since I had extricated her from hospital we had acquired almost every gadget invented. Wires and pulleys trailed all round the flat. She could read books, draw the curtains, turn on and off the lights, the radio, and television, use the telephone, and type letters. An electric box of tricks called

Possum did most of these tasks. Others worked on a system of levers set off by the feather-light pressure of her left forefinger. Our latest triumph was an electric pulley which raised and rotated her left elbow and forearm, enabling her to eat some things on her own, without always having to be fed. And with a clipped-on electric toothbrush, she could now brush her own teeth.

I slept on a divan across the room from her with a bell beside my ear for when she needed me in the night. There were bells, too, in the kitchen and bath-room, and the tiny room I used for writing in, which with the large sitting-room made up the whole of the flat.

We had been married three years, and we were both twenty-four, when Elizabeth caught polio. We were living in Singapore, where I had a junior job in the Reuter's office, and we flew home for what was intended to be a month's leave.

Elizabeth felt ill on the flight. The light hurt her eyes, and she had a headache like a rod up the back of her neck, and a stabbing pain in her chest. She walked off the aircraft at Heathrow and collapsed half-way across the tarmac, and that was the last time she ever stood on her feet.

Our affection for each other had survived everything that followed. Poverty, temper, tears, desperate frus-trations. We had emerged after several years into our comparative calms of a settled home, a good job, a reasonably well-ordered existence. We were firm close friends.

But not lovers.

We had tried, in the beginning. She could still feel of course, since polio attacks only the motor nerves, and leaves the sensory nerves intact. But she couldn't breath for more than three or four minutes if we took the Spirashell right off, and she couldn't bear any weight or pressure on any part of her wasted body. When I said, after two or three hopeless attempts, that we would leave it for a while she had smiled at me with what I saw to be enormous relief, and we had rarely even mentioned the subject since. Her early upbringing seemed to have easily reconciled her to a sexless existence. Her three years of thawing into a satisfying marriage might never have happened.

On the day after my trip to Virginia Water I set off as soon as Mrs Woodward came and drove the van north-east out of London and into deepest Essex. My quarry this time was a farmer who had bred gold dust in his fields in the shape of Tiddely Pom, ante-post favourite for the Lamplighter Gold Cup.

Weeds luxuriantly edged the pot-holed road which led from a pair of rotting gateless gateposts into Victor Roncey's farmyard. The house itself, an undistin-guished arrangement of mud-coloured bricks, stood in a drift of sodden unswept leaves and stared blankly from symmetrical grubby windows. Colourless paint peeled quietly from the woodwork and no smoke rose from the chimneys.

I knocked on the back door, which stood half open, and called through a small lobby into the house, but there was no reply. A clock ticked with a loud cheap mechanism. A smell of wellington boots richly acquainted with cowpat vigorously assaulted the nose. Someone had dumped a parcel of meat on the edge of the kitchen table from which a thread of watery blood, having by-passed the newspaper wrapping, was making a small pink pool on the floor.

Turning away from the house I wandered across the untidy yard and peered into a couple of outbuildings. One contained a tractor covered with about six years' mud. In another, a heap of dusty-looking coke rubbed shoulders with a jumbled stack of old broken crates and sawn-up branches of trees. A larger shed housed dirt and cobwebs and nothing else.

While I hovered in the centre of the yard wondering how far it was polite to investigate, a large youth in a striped knitted cap with a scarlet pom-pom came round a corner at the far end. He also wore a vast sloppy pale blue sweater, and filthy jeans tucked into heavy-weight gum boots. Fair haired, with a round weather-beaten face, he looked cheerful and uncomplicated.

'Hullo,' he said. 'You want something?' His voice was light and pleasant, with a touch of local accent.

'I'm looking for Mr Roncey.'

'He's round the roads with the horses. Better call back later.'

'How long will he be?'

'An hour, maybe,' he shrugged.

'I'll wait, then, if you don't mind,' I said, gesturing towards my van.

'Suit yourself.'

He took six steps towards the house and then stopped, turned round, and came back.

'Hey, you wouldn't be that chap who phoned?'

'Which chap?'

'James Tyrone?'

'That's right.'

'Well, for crying out loud why didn't you say so? I thought you were a traveller... come on into the house. Do you want some breakfast?'

'Breakfast?'

He grinned. 'Yeah. I know it's nearly eleven. I get up before six. Feel peckish again by now.'

He led the way into the house through the back door, did nothing about the dripping meat, and added to the wellington smell by clumping across the floor to the farthest door, which he opened.

'Ma?' he shouted. 'Ma.'

'She's around somewhere,' he said, shrugging and coming back. 'Never mind. Want some eggs?'

I said no, but when he reached out a half-acre frying pan and filled it with bacon I changed my mind.

'Make the coffee,' he said, pointing.

I found mugs, powdered coffee, sugar, milk, kettle and spoons all standing together on a bench alongside the sink.

'My ma,' he explained grinning, 'is a great one for the time and motion bit.'

He fried six eggs expertly and gave us three each, with a chunk of new white bread on the side.

We sat at the kitchen table, and I'd rarely tasted anything so good. He ate solidly and drank coffee, then pushed his plate away and lit a cigarette.

'I'm Peter,' he said. 'It isn't usually so quiet around here, but the kids are at school and Pat's out with Pa.'

'Pat?'

'My brother. The jockey of the family. Point-to-points, mostly, though. I don't suppose you would know of him?'

'I'm afraid not.'

'I read your column,' he said. 'Most weeks.'

'That's nice.'

He considered me, smoking, while I finished the eggs. 'You don't talk much, for a journalist.'

'I listen,' I said.

He grinned. 'That's a point.'

'Tell me about Tiddely Pom, then.'

'Hell, no. You'll have to get Pa or Pat for that. They're crazy on the horses. I just run the farm.' He watched my face carefully. I guessed for surprise, since in spite of being almost my height he was still very young.

'You're sixteen?' I suggested.

'Yeah.' He sniffed, disgusted. 'Waste of effort, though, really.'

'Why?'

'Why? Because of the bloody motorway, that's why. They've nearly finished that bloody three-lane monster and it passes just over there, the other side of our ten-acre field.' He gestured towards the window with his cigarette. 'Pa's going raving mad wondering if Tiddely Pom'll have a nervous breakdown when those heavy lorries start thundering past. He's been trying to sell the place for two years, but no one will have it, and you can't blame them, can you?' Gloom settled on him temporarily. 'Then, see, you never know when they'll pinch more of our land, they've had fifty acres already, and it doesn't give you much heart to keep the place right, does it?'

'I guess not,' I said.

'They've talked about knocking our house down,' he went on. 'Something about it being in the perfect position for a service station with restaurants and a vast car park and another slip road to Bishops Stortford. The only person who's pleased about the road is my brother Tony, and he wants to be a rally driver. He's eleven. He's a nut.'

There was a scrunch and clatter of hooves outside, coming nearer. Peter and I got to our feet and went out into the yard, and watched three horses plod up the bumpy gravel drive and rein to a halt in front of us. The rider of the leading horse slid off, handed his reins to the second, and came towards us. A trim, wiry man in his forties with thick brown hair and a mustard-coloured moustache.

'Mr Tyrone?'

I nodded. He gave me a brisk hard handshake in harmony with his manner and voice and then stood back to allow me a clear view of the horses.

'That's Tiddely Pom, that bay.' He pointed to the third horse, ridden by a young man very like Peter, though perhaps a size smaller. 'And Pat, my son.'

'A fine-looking horse,' I said insincerely. Most owners expected praise: but Tiddely Pom showed as much high quality to the naked eye as an uncut diamond. A common head, slightly U-necked on a weak shoulder, and herring-gutted into the bargain. He looked just as uncouth at home as he did on a race-course.

'Huh,' snorted Roncey. 'He's not. He's a doer, not a looker. Don't try and butter me up. I don't take to it.'

'Fair enough,' I said mildly. 'Then he's got a common head and neck, a poor shoulder, and doesn't fill the eye behind the saddle either.'

'That's better. So you do know what you're talking about. Walk him round the yard, Pat.'

Pat obliged. Tiddely Pom stumbled around with the floppy gait that once in a while denotes a champion. This horse, bred from a thoroughbred hunter mare by a premium stallion, was a spectacular jumper endowed with a speed to be found nowhere in his pedigree. When an ace of this sort turned up unexpectedly it took the owner almost as long as the public to realize it. The whole racing industry was unconsciously geared against the belief that twenty-two carat stars could come from tiny owner-trained stables. It had taken Tiddely Pom three seasons to become known, where from a big fashionable public stable he would have been newsworthy in his first race.

'When I bred him I was hoping for a point-to-point horse for the boys,' Roncey said. 'So we ran him all one season in point-to-points and apart from one time Pat fell off he didn't get beat. Then last year we thought we would have a go in hunter 'chases as well, and he went and won the Foxhunters' at Cheltenham.'

'I remember that,' I said.

'Yes. So last year we tried him in open handicaps, smallish ones . . .'

'And he won four out of six,' I concluded for him.

'It's your job to know, I suppose. Pat,' he shouted. 'Put him back in his box.' He turned to me again. 'Like to see the others?'

I nodded, and we followed Pat and the other two horses across the yard and round the corner from which Peter had originally appeared.

Behind a ramshackle barn stood a neat row of six well-kept wooden horse boxes with shingle roofs and newly painted black doors. However run down the rest of the farm might be, the stable department was in tip-top shape. No difficulty in seeing where the farmer's heart lay: with his treasure.

'Well now,' Roncey said. 'We've only the one other racehorse, really, and that's Klondyke, that I was riding just now. He ran in hunter 'chases in the spring. Didn't do much good, to be honest.' He walked along to the second box from the far end, led the horse in and tied it up. When he took the saddle off I saw that Klondyke was a better shape than Tiddely Pom, which was saying little enough, but the health in his coat was conspicuous.

'He looks well,' I commented.

'Eats his head off,' said Roncey, dispassionately, 'and he can stand a lot of work, so we give it to him.'

'One-paced,' observed Pat regretfully over my shoulder. 'Can't quicken. Pity. We won just the two point-to-points with him. No more.'

There was the faintest glimmer of satisfaction in the laconic voice, and I glanced at him sideways. He saw me looking and wiped the expression off his face but not before I had seen for certain that he had mixed feelings about the horses' successes. While they progressed to National Hunt racing proper, he didn't. Older amateur riders had been engaged, and then professionals. The father–son relationship had needles in it.

'What do you have in the other boxes?' I asked Roncey, as he shut Klondyke's door.

'My old grey hunter at the end, and two hunter mares here, both in foal. This one, Piglet, she's the dam of Tiddely Pom of course; she's in foal to the same sire again.'

Unlikely, I thought, that lightning would strike twice.

'You'll sell the foal,' I suggested.

He sniffed. 'She's in the farm accounts.'

I grinned to myself. Farmers could train their horses and lose the cost in the general farm accounts, but if they sold one it then came under the heading of income and was taxed accordingly. If Roncey sold either Tiddely Pom or his full brother, nearly half would go to the Revenue.

'Turn the mares out, Joe,' he said to his third rider, a patient-looking old man with skin like bark, and we watched while he set them loose in the nearest field. Peter was standing beside the gate with Pat: bigger, more assured, with far fewer knots in his personality.

'Fine sons,' I said to Roncey.

His mouth tightened. He had no pride in them. He made no reply at all to my fishing compliment, but instead said, 'We'll go into the house and you can ask me anything you want to know. For a magazine, you said?'

I nodded.

'Pat,' he shouted. 'You give these three horses a good strapping and feed them and let Joe get on with the hedging. Peter, you've got work to do. Go and do it.'

Both his boys gave him the blank acquiescing look

which covers seething rebellion. There was a perceptible pause before they moved off with their calm
accepting faces. Lids on a lot of steam. Maybe one day
Roncey would be scalded.

He led the way briskly back across the yard and
into the kitchen. The meat still lay there dripping.
Roncey by-passed it and gestured me to follow him
through the far door into a small dark hall.

'Madge?' he shouted. 'Madge?'

Father had as little success as son. He shrugged in
the same way and led me into a living-room as well
worn and untidy as the rest of the place. Drifts of
clutter, letters, newspapers, clothing, toys, and indis-
criminate bits of junk lay on every flat surface, including the chairs and the floor. There was a vase of dead
and dessiccated chrysanthemums on a window sill, and
some brazen cobwebs networked the ceiling. Cold ash
from the day before filled the grate. A toss-up, I
thought, whether one called the room lived-in or
squalid.

'Sit down if you can find somewhere,' Roncey said.
'Madge lets the boys run wild in the house. Not firm
enough. I won't have it outside, of course.'

'How many do you have?'

'Boys? Five.'

'And a daughter?' I asked.

'No,' he said abruptly. 'Five boys.'

The thought didn't please him. 'Which magazine?'

'*Tally*,' I said. 'They want background stories to the

Lamplighter, and I thought I would give the big stables a miss and shine a bit of the spotlight on someone else for a change.'

'Yes, well,' he said defensively, 'I've been written up before, you know.'

'Of course,' I said soothingly.

'About the Lamplighter, too. I'll show you.' He jumped up and went over to a knee-hole desk, pulled out one of the side drawers bodily, and brought it across to where I sat at one end of the sofa. He put the drawer in the centre, swept a crumpled jersey, two beaten-up dinky cars and a gutted brown paper parcel on to the floor, and seated himself in the space.

The drawer contained a heap of clippings and photographs all thrust in together. No careful sticking into expensive leather folders, like the Huntersons.

My mind leapt to Gail. I saw Roncey talking to me but I was thinking about her body. Her roundnesses. Her fragrant pigmented skin. Roncey was waiting for an answer and I hadn't heard what he'd asked.

'I'm sorry,' I said.

'I asked if you know Bert Checkov.' He was holding a lengthy clipping with a picture alongside and a bold headline, 'Back Tiddely Pom NOW.'

'Yes ... and no,' I said uncertainly.

'How do you mean?' he said brusquely. 'I should have thought you would have known him, being in the same business.'

'I did know him. But he died. Last Friday.'

I took the clipping and read it while Roncey went through the motions of being shocked, with the indifference uppermost in his voice spoiling the effect.

Bert Checkov had gone to town with Tiddely Pom's chances in the Lamplighter. The way he saw it, the handicapper had been suffering from semi-blindness and mental blocks to put Tiddely Pom into the weights at ten stone seven, and all punters who didn't jump on the bandwagon instantly needed to be wet nursed. He thought the ante-post market would open with generous odds, but urged everyone to hurry up with their shirts, before the bookmakers woke up to the bonanza. Bert's pungent phraseology had given Roncey's horse more boost than a four stage rocket.

'I didn't know he'd written this,' I admitted. 'I missed it.'

'He rang me up only last Thursday and this was in the paper on Friday. That must have been the day you said he died. In point of fact I didn't expect it would appear. When he telephoned he was, to my mind, quite drunk.'

'It's possible,' I conceded.

'I wasn't best pleased about it either.'

'The article?'

'I hadn't got my own money on, do you see? And there he went, spoiling the price. When I rang up my bookmaker on Friday he wouldn't give me more than a hundred to eight, and today they've even made him favourite at eight to one, and there's still nearly three weeks to the race. Fair enough he's a good horse, but he's not Arkle. In point of fact I don't understand it.'

'You don't understand why Checkov tipped him?'

He hesitated. 'Not to that extent, then, let's say.'

'But you do hope to win?'

'Hope,' he said. 'Naturally, I hope to win. But it's the biggest race we've ever tried ... I don't *expect* to win, do you see?'

'You've as good a chance as any,' I said. 'Checkov had his column to fill. The public won't read half-hearted stuff, you have to go all out for the positive statement.'

He gave me a small tight smile laced with a sneer for the soft option. A man with no patience or sympathy for anyone else's problems, not even his sons'.

The sitting-room door opened and a large woman in a sunflower dress came in. She had thick fair down on her legs but no stockings, and a pair of puffed ankles bulged over the edges of some battered blue bedroom slippers. Nevertheless she was very light on her feet and she moved slowly, so that her progress seemed to be a weightless drift: no mean feat considering she must have topped twelve stone.

A mass of fine light brown hair hung in an amorphous cloud round her head, from which a pair of dreamy eyes surveyed the world as though half asleep. Her face was soft and rounded, not young, but still in a way immature. Her fantasy life, I guessed uncharitably, was more real to her than the present. She had been far away in the past hour, much farther than upstairs.

'I didn't know you were in,' she said to Roncey.

He stood up several seconds after me. 'Madge, this is James Tyrone. I told you he was coming.'

'Did you?' She transferred her vague gaze to me. 'Carry on, then.'

'Where have you been?' Roncey said. 'Didn't you hear me calling?'

'Calling?' She shook her head. 'I was making the beds, of course.' She stood in the centre of the room, looking doubtfully around at the mess. 'Why didn't you light the fire?'

I glanced involuntarily at the heap of ashes in the grate, but she saw them as no obstacle at all. From a scratched oak box beside the hearth she produced three firelighters and a handful of sticks. These went on top of the ashes, which got only a desultory poke. She struck a match, lit the firelighters, and made a wigwam of coal. The new fire flared up good temperedly on the body of the old while Madge took the hearth brush and swept a few cinders out of sight behind a pile of logs.

Fascinated, I watched her continue with her housework. She drifted across to the dead flowers, opened the window, and threw them out. She emptied the water from the vase after them, then put it back on the window sill and shut the window.

From behind the sofa where Roncey and I sat she

pulled a large brown cardboard box. On the outside was stencilled Kellogg's Cornflakes, 12 × Family Six and on the inside it was half filled with the same sort of jumble which was lying around the room. She wafted methodically around in a large circle taking everything up and throwing it just as it came into the box, a process which took approximately three minutes. She then pushed the box out of sight again behind the sofa and plumped up the seat cushions of two armchairs on her way to the door. The room, tidy and with the brightly blazing fire, looked staggeringly different. The cobwebs were still there but one felt it might be their turn tomorrow. Peter was right. Ma had got the time and motion kick completely buttoned up; and what did it matter if the motive was laziness.

Roncey insisted that I should stay to lunch and filled in the time beforehand with a brisk but endless account of all the horses he had ever owned. Over lunch, cold beef and pickles and cheese and biscuits served at two-thirty on the kitchen table, it was still he who did all the talking. The boys ate steadily in silence and Madge contemplated the middle distance with eyes which saw only the scenes going on in her head.

When I left shortly afterwards Pat asked for a lift into Bishops Stortford and braved his father's frown to climb into the front seat of the van. Roncey shook hands firmly as before and said he hoped to receive a free copy of *Tally*. 'Of course,' I said. But *Tally* were notoriously mean: I would have to send it myself.

He waved me out of the yard and told Pat brusquely to come straight back on the four o'clock bus, and we were barely out through the sagging gateposts before Pat unburdened himself of a chunk of bottled resentment.

'He treats us like children ... Ma's no help, she never listens ...'

'You could leave here,' I pointed out. 'You're what – nineteen?'

'Next month. But I can't leave and he knows it. Not if I want to race. I can't turn professional yet, I'm not well enough known and no one would put me up on their horses. I've got to start as an amateur and make a name for myself, Pa says so. Well, I couldn't be an amateur if I left home and got an ordinary job somewhere, I couldn't afford all the expenses and I wouldn't have any time.'

'A job in a stable ...' I suggested.

'Do me a favour. The rules say you can't earn a salary in any capacity in a racing stable and ride as an amateur, not even if you're a secretary or an assistant or anything. It's bloody unfair. And don't say I could get a job as a lad and do my two and have a professional licence, of course I could. And how many lads ever get as far as jockeys, doing that? None. Absolutely none. You know that.'

I nodded.

'I do a lad's work now, right enough. Six horses, we've got, and I do the bloody lot. Old Joe's the only labour we've got on the whole farm, except us, believe it or not. Pa's always got a dozen jobs lined up for him. And I wouldn't mind the work, and getting practically no pay, I really wouldn't, if Pa would let me ride in anything except point-to-points, but he won't, he says I haven't enough experience, and if you ask me he's making bloody sure I never get enough experience . . . I'm absolutely fed up, I'll tell you straight.'

He brooded over his situation all the way into Bishops Stortford. A genuine grievance, I thought. Victor Roncey was not a father to help his sons get on.

CHAPTER FOUR

They held the inquest on Bert Checkov on that Monday afternoon. Verdict: Misadventure. Dead drunk he was, said the girl typists who saw him fall. Dead drunk.

And after he hit the pavement, just dead.

When I went into the office on Tuesday morning, Luke-John and Derry were discussing whether or not to go to the funeral on the Wednesday.

'Croxley,' Derry said. 'Where's that?'

'Near Watford,' I said. 'On the Metropolitan Line. A straight run into Farringdon Street.'

'What Fleet Street needs,' said Derry gloomily, 'is a tube station a lot nearer than blooming Farringdon. It's three-quarters of a mile if it's an inch.'

'If you're right, Ty, we can manage it easily,' Luke-John said authoritatively. 'We should all go, I think.'

Derry squinted at the small underground map in his diary. 'Croxley. Next to Watford. What do you know?'

I'd had a girl at Watford once. The second one. I'd spent a lot of time on the Metropolitan Line while

374

Elizabeth was under the impression I was extra busy in the *Blaze*. Guilt and deceit were old familiar travelling companions. From Watford, from Virginia Water, from wherever.

'Ty,' Luke-John was saying sharply.

'Huh?'

'The funeral is at two-thirty. An hour, say, to get there . . .?'

'Not me,' I said. 'There's this *Tally* article to be done. It'll take me at least another two days in interviews.'

He shrugged. 'I'd have thought . . .'

'What depths have you plumbed so far?' Derry asked. He was sitting with his feet up on the desk. No work in a Sunday paper on Tuesday.

'The Roncey family,' I said. 'Tiddely Pom.'

Derry sniffed. 'Ante-post favourite.'

'Will he be your tip?' I asked with interest.

'Shouldn't think so. He's won a few races but he hasn't beaten much of any class.'

'Bert tipped him strongly. Wrote a most emphatic piece about catching the odds now before they shorten. He wrote it last Thursday; it must have been straight after the handicap was published in the racing calendar: and it was in his paper on Friday. Roncey showed me the clipping. He said Bert was drunk when he rung up.'

Luke-John sighed. Derry said decisively, 'That does it, then. If Bert tipped him, I'm not going to.'

'Why not?'

'Bert's heavy long-distance tips were nearly always non-starters.'

Luke-John stretched his neck until the tendons stood out like strings, and massaged his nobbly larynx. 'Always the risk of that, of course. It happens to everyone.'

'Do you mean that seriously?' I asked Derry.

'Oh sure. Sorry about your *Tally* article and all that,' he grinned, 'but I'd say just about the time it's published you'll find Tiddely Pom has been taken out of the Lamplighter.'

Derry twiddled unconcernedly with a rubber band and Luke-John shuffled absentmindedly through some papers. Neither of them felt the shiver travelling down my spine.

'Derry,' I said. 'Are you sure?'

'Of what?'

'That Bert always tipped non-starters for big races.'

Derry snapped the band twice in his fingers. 'To be precise, if you want me to be precise, Bert tipped a higher percentage of big-race non-starters than anyone else in the street, and he has been at his best in this direction, or worst, or at any rate his most consistent, during the past year. He'd blow some horse up big, tell everyone to back it at once, and then wham, a day or two before the race it would be scratched.'

'I've never noticed,' said Luke-John forbiddingly, as if it couldn't have happened without.

Derry shrugged. 'Well, it's a fact. Now, if you want

to know something equally useless about that puffed-up Connersley of the *Sunday Hemisphere*, he has a weird habit of always tipping horses which start with his own initial, C. Delusions of grandeur, I imagine.'

'You're having us on,' Luke-John said.

Derry shook his head. 'Uhuh. I don't just sit here with my eyes shut, you know. I read the newspapers.'

'I think,' I said suddenly, 'I will fetch my typewriter.'

'Where is it?'

Over my shoulder on the way back to the door I said, 'Being cleaned.'

This time the typewriter was ready. I collected it and went farther along the street, to Bert's paper. Up in the lift, to Bert's department. Across the busy floor to the sports desk. Full stop beside the assistant sports editor, a constant racegoer, a long-known bar pal.

'Ty! What's the opposition doing here?'

'Bert Checkov,' I said.

We discussed him for a while. The assistant sports editor was hiding something. It showed in half-looks, unfinished gestures, an unsuccessfully smothered embarrassment. He said he was shocked, shattered, terribly distressed by Bert's death. He said everyone on the paper would miss him, the paper would miss him, they all felt his death was a great loss. He was lying.

I didn't pursue it. Could I, I asked tentatively, have a look at Bert's clippings book? I would very much like to reread some of his articles.

The assistant sports editor said kindly that I had little to learn from Bert Checkov or anyone else for that matter, but to go ahead. While he got back to work I sorted out the record racks at the side of the room and eventually found three brown paper clippings books with Bert's work stuck into the pages.

I took my typewriter out of its carrying case and left it lying on an inconspicuous shelf. The three clippings books went into the carrying case, though I had to squeeze to get it shut, and I walked quietly and unchallenged out of the building with my smuggled goods.

Luke-John and Derry goggled at the books of cuttings.

'How on earth did you get them out? And why on earth do you want them?'

'Derry,' I said, 'can now set about proving that Bert always tipped non-starters in big races.'

'You're crazy,' Luke-John said incredulously.

'No,' I said regretfully. 'If I'm right, the *Blaze* is on the edge of the sort of scandal it thrives on. A circulation explosion. And all by courtesy of the sports section.'

Luke-John's interest sharpened instantly from nil to needles.

'Don't waste time then, Derry. If Ty says there's a scandal, there's a scandal.'

Derry gave me a sidelong look. 'Our truffle hound on the scent, eh?' He took his feet off the desk and

378

resignedly got to work checking what Bert had forecast against what had actually happened. More and more form books and racing calendars were brought out, and Derry's written lists slowly grew.

'All right,' he said at last. 'Here it is, just as I said. These books cover the last three years. Up till eighteen months ago he tipped runners and non-runners in about the same proportion as the rest of us poor slobs. Then he went all out suddenly for horses which didn't run when it came to the point. All in big races, which had ante-post betting.' He looked puzzled. 'It can't be just coincidence, I do see that. But I don't see the point.'

'Ty?' said Luke-John.

I shrugged. 'Someone has been working a fiddle.'

'Bert wouldn't.' His voice said it was unthinkable.

'I'd better take these books back before they miss them,' I said, packing them again into the typewriter case.

'Ty!' Luke-John sounded exasperated.

'I'll tell you when I come back,' I said.

There was no denunciation at Bert's office. I returned the books to their shelf and retrieved my typewriter, and thanked the assistant sports editor for his kindness.

'You still here? I thought you'd gone.' He waved a friendly hand. 'Any time.'

'All right,' said Luke-John truculently when I got

back to the *Blaze*. 'I won't believe Bert Checkov was party to any fiddle.'

'He sold his soul,' I said plainly. 'Like he told me not to.'

'Rubbish.'

'He sold his column. He wrote what he was told to write.'

'Not Bert. He was a newspaper man, one of the old school.'

I considered him. His thin face looked obstinate and pugnacious. Loyalty to an old friend was running very strong.

'Well then,' I said slowly, 'Bert wrote what he was forced to write.'

A good deal of the Morton tension subsided and changed course. He wouldn't help to uncover a scandal an old friend was responsible for, but he'd go the whole way to open up one he'd been the victim of.

'Clever beast,' said Derry under his breath.

'Who forced him?' Luke-John said.

'I don't know. Not yet. It might be possible to find out.'

'And *why?*'

'That's much easier. Someone has been making an ante-post book on a certainty. What Bert was doing ... being forced to do ... was persuading the public to part with their money.'

They both looked contemplative. I started again,

explaining more fully. 'Say a villain takes up bookmaking. It can happen, you know.'

Derry grinned. 'Say one villain hits on a jolly scheme for making illegal gains in a foolproof way with very little effort. He only works it on big races which have ante-post betting, because he needs at least three weeks to rake in enough to make it worth the risk. He chooses a suitable horse, and he forces Bert to tip it for all his column's worth. Right? So the public put their money on, and our villain sticks to every penny that comes his way. No need to cover himself against losses. He knows there won't be any. He knows he isn't going to have to pay out on that horse. He knows it's going to be scratched at or after the four-day forfeits. Very nice fiddle.'

After a short silence Derry said, 'How does he know?'

'Ah well,' I said, shrugging. 'That's another thing we'll have to find out.'

'I don't believe it,' Luke-John said sceptically. 'All that just because Bert tipped a few non-starters.'

Derry looked dubiously at the lists he had made. 'There were too many non-starters. There really were.'

'Yes,' I said.

'But you *can't* have worked out all that just from what I said, from just that simple casual remark...'

'No,' I agreed. 'There was something else, of course. It was something Bert himself said, last Friday, when I walked back with him from lunch. He wanted to give me a piece of advice.'

'That's right,' Derry said. 'He never came out with it.'

'Yes he did. He did indeed. With great seriousness. He told me not to sell my soul. Not to sell my column.'

'No,' Luke-John said.

'He said, "First they buy you and then they blackmail you."'

Luke-John said, 'No,' again automatically.

'He was very drunk,' I said. 'Much worse than usual. He called the advice he was giving me his famous last words. He went up in the lift with a half-bottle of whisky, he walked right across his office, he drank from the bottle, and without a pause he fell straight out of the window.'

Luke-John put his freckled fingers on his thin mouth and when he spoke his voice was low, protesting, and thick, 'No ... my *God.*'

After leaving the *Blaze* I collected the van and drove down to a racing stable in Berkshire to interview the girl who looked after the best-known horse in the Lamplighter.

Zig Zag was a household name, a steeplechaser of immense reputation and popularity, automatic headline material: but any day the cracks would begin to show, since he would be turning eleven on January the first.

The Lamplighter, to my mind, would be his last bow as grand old man before the younger brigade shouldered him out. Until Bert Checkov had rammed home the telling difference in weights, Zig Zag, even allotted a punitive twelve stone ten pounds, had been the automatic choice for ante-post favourite.

His girl groom was earnest and devoted to him. In her twenties, unsophisticated, of middling intelligence, Sandy Willis's every sentence was packed with pithy stable language which she used unselfconsciously, and which contrasted touchingly with her essential innocence. She showed me Zig Zag with proprietary pride and could recite, and did, his every race from the day he was foaled. She had looked after him always, she said, ever since he came into the yard as a leggy untried three-year-old. She didn't know what she'd do when he was retired, racing wouldn't be the same without him somehow.

I offered to drive her into Newbury to have tea in a café or an hotel, but she said no, thank you, she wouldn't have time because the evening work started at four. Leaning against the door of Zig Zag's box she told me about her life, hesitantly at first, and then in a rush. Her parents didn't get on, she said. There were always rows at home, so she'd cleared out pretty soon after leaving school, glad to get away, her old man was so mean with the housekeeping and her mum did nothing but screech, nag, nag, at him mostly but at her too and her two kid sisters, right draggy the whole thing was, and she hoped Zig Zag would be racing at Kempton on Boxing Day so she'd have a good excuse not to go home for Christmas. She loved her work, she loved Zig Zag, the racing world was the tops, and no, she wasn't in any hurry to get married, there were always boys around if she wanted them and honestly whoever would swop Zig Zag for a load of draggy housework, especially if it turned out like her mum and dad . . .

She agreed with a giggle to have her photograph taken if Zig Zag could be in the picture too, and said she hoped that *Tally* magazine would send her a free copy.

'Of course,' I assured her, and decided to charge all free copies against expenses.

When I left her I walked down through the yard and called on the trainer, whom I saw almost every time I went racing. A businesslike man in his fifties, with no airs and few illusions.

'Come in, Ty,' he said. 'Did you find Sandy Willis?'

'Thank you, yes. She was very helpful.'

'She's one of my best lads.' He waved me to an armchair and poured some oak-coloured tea out of a silver pot. 'Sugar?' I shook my head. 'Not much in the upstairs department, but her horses are always jumping out of their skins.'

'A spot of transferred mother love,' I agreed. I tasted the tea. My tongue winced at the strength of the tannin.

Norton Fox poured himself another cup and took three deep swallows.

'If I write her up for *Tally*,' I said, 'you won't do the dirty on me and take Zig Zag out of the Lamplighter at the last minute?'

'I don't plan to.'

'Twelve stone ten is a prohibitive weight,' I suggested.

'He's won with twelve thirteen.' He shrugged. 'He'll never come down the handicap.'

'As a matter of interest,' I said, 'what happened to Brevity just before the Champion Hurdle?'

Norton clicked his tongue in annoyance. 'You can rely on it, Zig Zag will *not* be taken out at the last minute. At least, not for no reason, like Brevity.'

'He was favourite, wasn't he?' I knew he was, I'd checked carefully from Derry's list. 'What exactly happened?'

'I've never been so furious about anything.' The eight-month-old grievance was still vivid in his voice. 'I trained that horse to the minute. To the minute. We always had the Champion Hurdle as his main target. He couldn't have been more fit. He was ready to run for his life. And then what? Do you know what? I declared him at the four-day stage, and the owner, the *owner*, mark you, went and telephoned Weatherbys two days later and cancelled the declaration. Took the horse out of the race. I ask you! And on top of that, he hadn't even the courtesy, or the nerve probably, to tell me what he'd done, and the first I knew of it was when Brevity wasn't in the overnight list of runners. Of course I couldn't believe it and rang up Weatherbys in a fury and they told me old Dembley himself had struck his horse out. And I still don't know why. I had the most God almighty row with him about it and all he would say was that he had decided not to run, and that was that. He never once gave me a reason. Not one, after all that planning and all that work. I told him to take his horses away, I was so angry. I mean, how can you train for a man who's going to do that to you? It's impossible.'

'Who trains for him now?' I asked sympathetically.

'No one. He sold all three of his horses, including Brevity. He said he'd had enough of racing, he was finished with it.'

'You wouldn't still have his address?' I asked.

'Look here, Ty, you're not putting all that in your wretched paper.'

'No,' I assured him. 'Just one day I might write an article on owners who've sold out.'

'Well . . . yes, I still have it.' He copied the address from a ledger and handed it to me. 'Don't cause any trouble.'

'Not for you,' I said. Trouble was always Luke-John's aim, and often mine. The only difference was that I was careful my friends shouldn't be on the receiving end. Luke-John had no such difficulties. He counted no one, to that extent, a friend.

Mrs Woodward and Elizabeth were watching the news on television when I got back. Mrs Woodward took a quick look at her watch and made an unsuccessful attempt at hiding her disappointment. I had beaten her to six o'clock by thirty seconds. She charged overtime by the half hour, and was a shade over business-like about it. I never got a free five minutes: five past six and it would have cost me the full half hour. I understood that it wasn't sheer miserliness. She was a widow whose teenage son had a yearning to be a doctor, and as far as I could see it would be mainly Tyrone who put him through medical school.

The time-keeping war was conducted with maximum politeness and without acknowledgement that it existed. I simply synchronized our two clocks and my watch with the BBC time signal every morning, and paid up with a smile when I was late. Mrs Woodward gave me a warmer welcome at ten past six than at ten to, but never arrived a minute after nine-thirty in the mornings. Neither of us had let on to Elizabeth how acutely the clock was watched.

Mrs Woodward was spare and strong, with a little of her native Lancashire in her voice and a lot in her character. She had dark hair going grey, rich brown eyes, and a determined jaw line which had seen her through a jilting fiancé and a work-shy husband. Unfailingly gentle to Elizabeth, she had never yet run out of patience, except with the vacuum cleaner, which occasionally regurgitated where it should have sucked.

In our flat she wore white nylon overalls which she knew raised her status from home-help in the eyes of visitors, and I saw no reason to think any worse of her for it. She took off the overall and hung it up, and I helped her into the dark blue coat she had been wearing every single day for at least three years.

'Night, Mr Tyrone. Night, luv,' she said, as she always said. And as always I thanked her for coming, and said I'd see her in the morning.

'Did you have a good day?' Elizabeth asked, when I kissed her forehead. Her voice sounded tired. The Spirashell tugged her chest up and down in a steady rhythm, and she could only speak easily on the outgoing breaths.

'I went to see a girl about a horse,' I said, smiling, and told her briefly about Sandy Willis and Zig Zag. She liked to know a little of what I'd been doing, but her interest always flagged pretty soon, and after so many years I could tell the exact instant by the microscopic relaxation in her eye muscles. She rarely said she was tired and had had enough of anything because she was afraid I would think her complaining and querulous and find her too much of a burden altogether. I couldn't persuade her to say flatly 'Stop, I'm tired.' She agreed each time I mentioned it that she would, and she never did.

'I've seen three of the people for the *Tally* article,' I said. 'Owner, owner-trainer, and stable girl. I'm afraid after supper I'd better make a start on the writing. Will you be all right watching television?'

'Of course . . .' She gave me the sweet brilliant smile which made every chore for her possible. Occasionally I spotted her manufacturing it artificially, but no amount of reassurance seemed able to convince her that she needn't perform tricks for me, that I wouldn't shove her back into hospital if she lost her temper, that I didn't need her to be angelic, that she was safe with me, and loved, and, in fact very much wanted.

'Like a drink?' I said.

'Love one.'

I poured us both a J and B with Malvern Water, and took hers over and fastened it into a holder I'd rigged up, with the bent drinking straw near to her mouth. Using that she could drink in her own time, and a lot less got spilt on the sheets. I tasted appreciatively the pale fine Scotch, slumping into the big armchair beside her bed, sloughing off the day's travelling with a comfortable feeling of being at home. The pump's steady soft thumping had its usual soporific effect. It sent most of our visitors fast asleep.

We watched a brain-packed quiz game on television and companionably answered most of the questions wrong. After that I went into the kitchen and looked at what Mrs Woodward had put out for supper. Plaice coated with bread crumbs, a bag of frozen chips, one lemon. Stewed apples, custard. Cheddar cheese, square crackers. The Woodward views on food didn't entirely coincide with my own. Stifling thoughts of underdone steak I cooked the chips in oil and the plaice in butter, and left mine to keep hot while I helped Elizabeth. Even with the new pulley gadget some foods were difficult: the plaice broke up too easily and her wrist got tired, and we ended up with me feeding her as usual.

While I washed the dishes I made coffee in mugs, fixed Elizabeth's into the holder, and took mine with my typewriter into the little room which would have been a child's bedroom if we'd ever had a child.

The *Tally* article came along slowly, its price tag reproaching me for every sloppy phrase. The Huntersons, the Ronceys, Sandy Willis. Dissect without hurting, probe but leave whole. Far easier, I thought resignedly, to pick them to bits. Good for *Tally*'s sales too. Bad for the conscience, lousy for the Huntersons, the Ronceys, Sandy Willis. To tell all so that the victim liked it . . . this was what took the time.

After two hours I found myself staring at the wall, thinking only of Gail. With excruciating clearness I went through in my mind every minute of that uninhibited love making, felt in all my limbs and veins an echo of passion. Useless to pretend that once was enough, that the tormenting hunger had been anaesthetized for more than a few days. With despair at my weakness I thought about how it would be on the next Sunday. Gail with no clothes on, graceful and firm.

Gail smiling with my hands on her breasts, Gail fluttering her fingers on the base of my spine.

The bell rang sharply above my head. One ring: not urgent. I stood up slowly, feeling stupid and ashamed. Day-dreaming like Madge Roncey. Just as bad. Probably much worse.

Elizabeth was apologetic. 'Ty, I'm sorry to interrupt you . . .'

How can I do it, I thought. And knew I would.

'My feet are awfully cold.'

I pulled out the hot water bottle, which had no heat left. Her feet were warm enough to the touch, but that meant nothing. Her circulation was so poor that her ankles and feet ached with cold if not constantly warmed from outside.

'You should have said,' I protested.

'Didn't want to disturb you.'

'Any time,' I said fiercely. 'Any time.' And preferably twenty minutes ago. For twenty minutes she'd suffered her cold feet and all I'd done was think of Gail.

I filled her bottle and we went through her evening routine. Rubs with surgical spirit. Washing. Bedpan.

Her muscles had nearly all wasted to nothing so that her bones showed angularly through the skin, and one had to be careful when lifting her limbs, as pressure in some places hurt her. That day Mrs Woodward had painted her toe nails for her instead of only her fingernails as usual.

'Do you like it?' she said. 'It's a new colour, Tawny Pink.'

'Pretty,' I nodded. 'It suits you.'

She smiled contentedly. 'Sue Davis brought it for me. She's a pet, that girl,'

Sue and Ronald Davis lived three doors away: married for six months and it still showed. They had let their euphoria spill over on to us. Sue brought things in to amuse Elizabeth and Ronald used his rugger-bred strength to carry the pump downstairs when we went out in the van.

'It matches my lipstick better than the old colour.'

'Yes, it does,' I agreed.

When we married she had had creamy skin and hair as glossy as new-peeled conkers. She had sun-browned agile limbs, and a pretty figure. The transition to her present and for ever state had been as agonizing for her mentally as it had been physically, and at one point of that shattering progress I was aware she would have killed herself if even that freedom hadn't been denied her.

She still had a good complexion, fine eyebrows, and long-lashed eyes, but the russet lights had turned to grey in both her irises and her hair, as if the colour had drained away with the vitality. Mrs Woodward was luckily expert with shampoo and scissors and I too had long grown accurate with a lipstick, so that Elizabeth always turned a groomed and attractive head to the world and could retain at least some terrifically important feminine assurance.

I settled her for the night, slowing the rate of breathing pump a little and tucking the covers in firmly round her chin to help with the draught. She slept in the same half sitting propped-up position as she spent the days: the Spirashell was too heavy and uncomfortable if she lay down flat, beside not dragging as much air into her lungs.

She smiled when I kissed her cheek. 'Goodnight, Ty.'

'Goodnight, honey.'

'Thanks for everything.'

'Be my guest.'

Lazily I pottered round the flat, tidying up, brushing my teeth, re-reading what I'd written for *Tally* and putting the cover on the typewriter. When I finally made it to bed Elizabeth was asleep, and I lay between the lonely sheets and thought about Bert Checkov and the non-starters like Brevity in the Champion Hurdle, planning in detail the article I would write for the *Blaze* on Sunday.

Sunday.

Inevitably, inexorably, every thought led back to Gail.

CHAPTER FIVE

I telephoned to Charles Dembley, the ex-owner of Brevity, on Wednesday morning, and a girl answered, bright fresh voice, carefree, and inexperienced.

'Golly, did you say Tyrone? *James* Tyrone? Yes, we do have your perfectly frightful paper. At least we used to. At least the gardener does, so I often read it. Well, of course come down and see Daddy, he'll be frightfully pleased.'

Daddy wasn't.

He met me outside his house, on the front step, a smallish man nearing sixty with a grey moustache and heavy pouches under his eyes. His manner was courteous stonewall.

'I am sorry you have had a wasted journey, Mr Tyrone. My daughter Amanda is only fifteen and is apt to rush into things . . . I was out when you telephoned, as I expect she told you. I hope you will forgive her. I have absolutely nothing to say to you. Nothing at all. Good afternoon, Mr Tyrone.'

There was a tiny twitch in one eyelid and the finest

of dews on his forehead. I let my gaze wander across the front of his house (genuine Georgian, not too large, unostentatiously well kept) and brought it gently back to his face.

'What threat did they use?' I asked. 'Amanda?'

He winced strongly and opened his mouth.

'With a fifteen-year-old daughter,' I commented, 'one is dangerously vulnerable.'

He tried to speak but achieved only a croak. After clearing his throat with difficulty he said, 'I don't know what you're talking about.'

'How did they set about it?' I asked. 'By telephone? By letter? Or did you actually see them face to face?'

His expression was a full giveaway, but he wouldn't answer.

I said, 'Mr Dembley, I can write my column about the last-minute unexplained withdrawal of favourites, mentioning you and Amanda by name, or I can leave you out of it.'

'Leave me out,' he said forcefully. 'Leave me out.'

'I will,' I agreed, 'if in return you will tell me what threat was made against you, and in what form.'

His mouth shook with a mixture of fear and disgust. He knew blackmail when he heard it. Only too well.

'I can't trust you.'

'Indeed you can,' I said.

'If I keep silent you will print my name and they will think I told you anyway . . .' He stopped dead.

'Exactly,' I said mildly.

'You're despicable.'

'No,' I said. 'I'd simply like to stop them doing it to anyone else.'

There was a pause. Then he said, 'It *was* Amanda. They said someone would rape her. They said I couldn't guard her twenty-four hours a day for years on end. They said to make her safe all I had to do was call Weatherbys and take Brevity out of the Champion Hurdle. Just one little telephone call, against my daughter's . . . my daughter's health. So I did it. Of course I did. I had to. What did running a horse in the Champion Hurdle matter compared with my daughter?'

What indeed.

'Did you tell the police?'

He shook his head. 'They said . . .'

I nodded. They would.

'I sold all my horses, after,' he said. 'There wasn't any point going on. It could have happened again, any time.'

'Yes.'

He swallowed. 'Is that all?'

'No . . . Did they telephone, or did you see them?'

'It was one man. He came here, driven by a chauffeur. In a Rolls. He was, he seemed to me, an educated man. He had an accent, I'm not sure what it was, perhaps Scandinavian, or Dutch, something like that. Maybe even Greek. He was civilized . . . except for what he said.'

'Looks?'

'Tall . . . about your height. Much heavier, though. Altogether thicker, more flesh. Not a crook's face at all. I couldn't believe what I was hearing him say. It didn't fit the way he looked.'

'But he convinced you,' I commented.

'Yes.' He shuddered. 'He stood there watching me while I telephoned to Weatherbys. And when I'd finished he simply said, "I'm sure you've made a wise decision, Mr Dembley," and he just walked out of the house and the chauffeur drove him away.'

'And you've heard no more from him at all?'

'No more. You will keep your bargain, too, like him?'

My mouth twisted. 'I will.'

He gave me a long look. 'If Amanda comes to any harm through you, I will see it costs you . . . costs you . . .' He stopped.

'If she does,' I said, 'I will pay.'

An empty gesture. Harm couldn't be undone, and paying wouldn't help. I would simply have to be careful.

'That's all,' he said. 'That's all.' He turned on his heel, went back into his house, and shut the front door decisively between us.

For light relief on the way home I stopped in Hampstead to interview the man who had done the handicap for the Lamplighter. Not a well-timed call. His wife had just decamped with an American colonel.

'Damn her eyes,' he said. 'She's left me a bloody note.' He waved it under my nose. 'Stuck up against the clock, just like a ruddy movie.'

'I'm sorry,' I said.

'Come in, come in. What do you say to getting pissed?'

'There's the unfortunate matter of driving home.'

'Take a taxi, Ty, be a pal. Come on.'

I looked at my watch. Four-thirty. Half an hour to home, counting rush hour traffic. I stepped over the threshold and saw from his relieved expression that company was much needed. He already had a bottle out with a half-full glass beside it, and he poured me one the same size.

Major Colly Gibbons, late forties, trim, intelligent, impatient, and positive. Never suffered fools gladly and interrupted rudely when his thoughts leaped ahead, but was much in demand as a handicapper, as he had a clear comprehensive view of racing as a whole, like a master chess player winning ten games at once. He engineered more multiple dead heats than anyone else in the game; the accolade of his profession and a headache to the interpreters of photo finishes.

'A bloody colonel,' he said bitterly. 'Out-ranked, too.'

I laughed. He gave me a startled look and then an unwilling grin.

'I suppose it *is* funny,' he said. 'Silly thing is, he's very like me. Looks, age, character, everything. I even like the guy.'

'She'll probably come back,' I said.

'Why?'

'If she chose a carbon copy of you, she can't hate you all that much.'

'Don't know as I'd have her,' he said aggressively. 'Going off with a bloody colonel, and a Yank at that.'

His pride was bent worse than his heart: none the less painful. He sloshed another stiff whisky into his glass and asked me why, as a matter of interest, I had come. I explained about the *Tally* article, and, seeming to be relieved to have something to talk about besides his wife, he loosened up with his answers more than I would normally have expected. For the first time I understood the wideness of his vision and the grasp and range of his memory. He knew the form book for the past ten years by heart.

After a while I said, 'What can you remember about ante-post favourites which didn't run?'

He gave me a quick glance which would have been better focused three drinks earlier. 'Is this for *Tally*, still?'

'No,' I admitted.

'Didn't think so. Question like that's got the *Blaze* written all over it.'

'I won't quote you.'

'Too right you won't.' He drank deeply, but seemed

no nearer oblivion. 'Put yourself some blinkers on and point in another direction.'

'Read what I say on Sunday,' I said mildly.

'Ty,' he said explosively. 'Best to keep out.'

'Why?'

'Leave it to the authorities.'

'What are they doing about it? What do they know?'

'You know I can't tell you,' he protested. 'Talk to the *Blaze*! I'd lose my job.'

'Mulholland went to jail rather than reveal his sources.'

'All journalists are not Mulholland.'

'Same secretive tendencies.'

'Would you,' he said seriously, 'go to jail?'

'It's never cropped up. But if my sources want to stay unrevealed, they stay unrevealed. If they didn't who would tell me anything?'

He thought it over. 'Something's going on,' he said at last.

'Quite,' I said. 'And what are the authorities doing about it?'

'There's no evidence ... look, Ty, there's nothing you can put your finger on. Just a string of coincidences.'

'Like Bert Checkov's articles?' I suggested.

He was startled. 'All right, then. Yes. I heard it on good authority that he was going to be asked to explain them. But then he fell out of the window ...'

'Tell me about the non-runners,' I said.

He looked gloomily at the note from his wife, which he still clutched in his hand. He took a deep swallow and shrugged heavily. The caution barriers were right down.

'There was this French horse, Polyxenes, which they made favourite for the Derby. Remember? All last winter and spring there was a stream of information about it, coming out of France ... how well he was developed, how nothing could stay with him on the gallops, how he made all the three-year-olds look like knock-kneed yearlings? Every week, something about Polyxenes.'

'I remember,' I said. 'Derry Clark wrote him up for the *Blaze*.'

Colly Gibbons nodded. 'So there we are. By Easter, six to one favourite for the Derby. Right? They leave him in through all the forfeit stages. Right? They declare him at the four-day declarations. Right? Two days later he's taken out of the race. Why? He knocked himself out at exercise and his leg's blown up like a football. Can't run a lame horse. Too bad, everybody who'd backed him. Too bad. All their money down the drain. All right. Now I'll tell you something, Ty. That Polyxenes, I'll never believe he was all that good. What had he ever done? Won two moderate races as a two-year-old at St Cloud. He didn't run this year before the Derby. He didn't run the whole season in the end. They said his leg was still bad. I'll tell you what I think.

He never was good enough to win the Derby, and from the start they never meant him to run.'

'If he were as bad as that they could have run him anyway. He wouldn't have won.'

'Would you risk it, if you were them? The most fantastic outsiders *have* won the Derby. Much more certain not to run at all.'

'Someone must have made thousands,' I said slowly.

'More like hundreds of thousands.'

'If they know it's going on, why don't the racing authorities do something about it?'

'What *can* they do? I told you, no evidence. Polyxenes *was* lame, and he stayed lame. He was seen by dozens of vets. He had a slightly shady owner, but no shadier than some of ours. Nothing, absolutely nothing, could be proved.'

After a pause I said, 'Do you know of any others?'

'God, Ty, you're a glutton. Well . . . yes . . .'

Once started, he left little out. In the next half-hour I listened to the detailed case histories of four more ante-post favourites who hadn't turned up on the day. All could have been bona-fide hard-luck stories. But all, I knew well, had been over-praised by Bert Checkov.

He ran down, in the end, with a faint look of dismay.

'I shouldn't have told you all this.'

'No one will know.'

'You'd get information out of a deaf mute.'

I nodded. 'They can usually read and write.'

'Go to hell,' he said. 'Or rather, don't. You're four behind me, you aren't trying.' He waved the bottle in my general direction and I went over and took it from him. It was empty.

'Got to go home,' I said apologetically.

'What's the hurry?' He stared at the letter in his hand. 'Will your wife give you gip if you're late? Or will she be running off with some bloody Yankee colonel?'

'No,' I said unemotionally. 'She won't.'

He was suddenly very sober. '*Christ*, Ty . . . I forgot.'

He stood up, as steady as a rock. Looked forlornly round his comfortable wifeless sitting-room. Held out his hand.

'She'll come back,' I said uselessly.

He shook his head. 'I don't think so.' He sighed deeply. 'Anyway, I'm glad you came. Needed someone to talk to, you know. Even if I've talked too much . . . better than getting drunk alone. And I'll think of you, this evening. You . . . and your wife.'

I got hung up in a jam at Swiss Cottage and arrived home at eight minutes past seven. An hour and a half's overtime. Mrs Woodward was delighted.

'Isn't she sweet?' Elizabeth said when she had gone. 'She never minds when you are late. She never complains about having to stay. She's so nice and kind.'

'Very,' I said.

As usual I spent most of Thursday at home, writing Sunday's article. Mrs Woodward went out to do the week's shopping and to take and collect the laundry.

Sue Davis came in and made coffee for herself and Elizabeth. Elizabeth's mother telephoned to say she might not come on Sunday, she thought she could be getting a cold.

No one came near Elizabeth with a cold. With people on artificial respiration, colds too often meant pneumonia, and pneumonia too often meant death.

If Elizabeth's mother didn't come on Sunday, I couldn't go to Virginia Water. I spent too much of the morning unproductively trying to persuade myself it would be better if the cold developed, and knowing I'd be wretched if it did.

Luke-John galloped through the article on non-starting favourites, screwed his eyes up tight and leaned back on his chair with his face to the ceiling. Symptoms of extreme emotion. Derry reached over, twitched up the typewritten sheets and read them in his slower intense short-sighted-looking way. When he'd finished he took a deep breath.

'Wowee,' he said. 'Someone's going to love this.'

'Who?' said Luke-John, opening his eyes.

'The chap who's doing it.'

Luke-John looked at him broodingly. 'As long as he can't sue, that's all that matters. Take this down to the lawyers and make sure they don't let it out of their sight.'

Derry departed with a folded carbon copy of the article and Luke-John permitted himself a smile.

'Up to standard, if I may say so.'

'Thanks,' I said.

'Who told you all this?'

'Couple of little birds.'

'Come off it, Ty.'

'Promised,' I said. 'They could get their faces pushed in, one way or another.'

'I'll have to know. The editor will want to know.'

I shook my head. 'Promised.'

'I could scrub the article altogether . . .'

'Tut, Tut,' I said. 'Threats now?'

He rubbed his larynx in exasperation. I looked round the vast busy floor space, each section, like the sports desk, collecting and sorting out its final copy. Most of the feature stuff went down to the compositors on Fridays, some even on Thursdays, to be set up in type. But anything like a scoop stayed under wraps upstairs until after the last editions of the Saturday evening papers had all been set up and gone to press. The compositors were apt to make the odd ten quid by selling a red-hot story to reporters on rival newspapers. If the legal department and the editor both cleared my article, the print shop wouldn't see it until too late to do them any good. The *Blaze* held its scandalous disclosures very close to its chest.

Derry came down from the lawyers without the article.

'They said they'd have to work on it. They'll ring through later.'

The *Blaze* lawyers were of Counsel standard on the

libel laws. They needed to be. All the same they were true *Blaze* men with 'publish and be damned' engraved on their hearts. The *Blaze* accountants allowed for damages in their budget as a matter of course. The *Blaze*'s owner looked upon one or two court cases a year as splendid free advertising, and watched the sales graphs rise. There had however been four actions in the last six months and two more were pending. A mild memo had gone round, saying to cool it just a fraction. Loyal for ever, Luke-John obeyed even where he disapproved.

'I'll take this in to the editor,' he remarked. 'See what he says.'

Derry watched his retreating back with reluctant admiration.

'Say what you like, the sports pages sell this paper to people who otherwise wouldn't touch it with gloves on. Our Luke-John, for all his stingy little ways, must be worth his weight in gumdrops.'

Our Luke-John came back and went into a close huddle with a soccer correspondent. I asked Derry how the funeral had been, on the Wednesday.

'A funeral's a funeral.' He shrugged. 'It was cold. His wife wept a lot. She had a purple nose, blue from cold and red from crying.'

'Charming.'

He grinned. 'Her sister told her to cheer up. Said how lucky it was Bert took out all that extra insurance.'

'He did what?'

'Yeah. I thought you'd like that. I chatted the sister up a bit. Two or three weeks ago Bert trebled his life insurance. Told his wife they'd be better off when he retired. Sort of self-help pension scheme.'

'Well, well,' I said.

'So it had to be an accident,' Derry nodded. 'In front of witnesses. The insurance company might not have paid up if he'd fallen out of the window with no one watching.'

'I wonder if they'll contest it.'

'Don't see how they can, when the inquest said misadventure.'

The editor's secretary came back with my piece. The editor's secretary was an expensive package tied up with barbed wire. No one, reputedly, had got past the prickles to the goodies.

The editor had scrawled 'OK on the lawyer's say so' across the top of the page. Luke-John stretched out a hand for it, nodded in satisfaction, and slid it into the lockable top drawer of his desk, talking all the while to the soccer man. There was no need for me to stay longer. I told Derry I'd be at home most of the day if they wanted me and sketched a goodbye.

I was halfway to the door when Luke-John called after me.

'Ty... I forgot to tell you. A woman phoned, wanted you.'

'Mrs Woodward?'

'Uhuh. Let's see, I made a note ... oh yes, here it

is. A Miss Gail Pominga. Would you ring her back. Something about *Tally* magazine.'

He gave me the slip of paper with the telephone number. I went across to the under-populated news desk and picked up the receiver. My hands were steady. My pulse wasn't.

'The Western School of Art. Can I help you?'

'Miss Pominga . . .'

Miss Pominga was fetched. Her voice came on the line, as cool and uninvolved as at the railway station.

'Are you coming on Sunday?' Crisp. Very much to the point.

'I want to.' Understatement. 'It may not be possible to get away.'

'Well . . . I've been asked out to lunch.'

'Go, then,' I said, feeling disappointment lump in my chest like a boulder.

'Actually, if you are coming I will stay at home.'

Damn Elizabeth's mother, I thought. Damn her and her cold.

'I want to come. I'll come if I possibly can,' I said.

There was a short silence before she said, 'When can you let me know for sure?'

'Not until Sunday, really. Not until I go out to catch the train.'

'Hmm . . .' She hesitated, then said decisively, 'Ring me in any case, whether you can come or whether you can't. I'll fix it so that I can still go to lunch if you aren't coming.'

'That marvellous,' I said, with more feeling than caution.

She laughed. 'Good. Hope to see you, then. Any time after ten. That's when Harry and Sarah go off to golf.'

'It would be eleven-thirty or so.'

She said, 'All right,' and 'Goodbye,' and disconnected. I went home to write up Colly Gibbons for *Tally* and to have lunch with Elizabeth and Mrs Woodward. It was fish again: unspecified variety and not much flavour. I listened to Elizabeth's sporadic conversation and returned her smiles and hoped fiercely not to be there with her forty-eight hours later. I ate automatically, sightlessly. By the end of that meal, treachery tasted of salt.

CHAPTER SIX

Time was running short, *Tally*-wise. With their deadline only two days ahead I went to Heathbury Park races on Saturday to meet Dermot Finnegan, an undistinguished jockey with an undistinguished mount in the Lamplighter.

For a while I couldn't understand a word he said, so impenetrable was his Irish accent. After he had sipped unenthusiastically at a cup of lunch-counter coffee for ten minutes he relaxed enough to tell me he always spoke worse when he was nervous, and after that we got by with him having to repeat some things twice, but not four or five times, as at the beginning.

Once past the language barrier, Dermot unveiled a resigned wit and an accepting contented way of life. Although by most standards his riding success was small, Dermot thought it great. His income, less than a dustman's, seemed to him princely compared with the conditions of his childhood. His father had fed fourteen children on the potatoes he had grown on two and a half exhausted acres. Dermot, being neither the strong eldest nor the spoilt youngest, had usually had to shove for his share and hadn't always got it. At nineteen he tired of the diet and took his under-developed physique across the sea to Newmarket, where an Irish accent, irrespective of previous experience, guaranteed him an immediate job in the labour-hungry racing industry.

He had 'done his two' for a while in a flat-racing stable, but couldn't get a ride in a flat race because he hadn't been apprenticed. Philosophically he moved down the road to a stable which trained jumpers as well, where the 'Governor' gave him a chance in a couple of hurdle races. He still worked in the same stable on a part-time basis, the 'Governor' still put him up as his second string jockey. How many rides? He grinned, showing spaces instead of teeth. Some seasons, maybe thirty. Two years ago, of course, it was only four, thanks to breaking his leg off a brainless divil of a knock-kneed spalpeen.

Dermot Finnegan was twenty-five, looked thirty. Broken-nosed and weatherbeaten, with bright sharp blue eyes. His ambition, he said, was to take a crack at Aintree. Otherwise he was all right with what he had: he wouldn't want to be a classy top jockey, it was far too much responsibility. 'If you only ride the scrubbers round the gaffs at the back end of the season, see, no one expects much. Then they gets a glorious surprise if you do come in.'

He had ridden nineteen winners in all, and he could

remember each of them in sharp detail. No, he didn't think he would do much good in the Lamplighter, not really, as he was only in it because his stable was running there. 'I'll be on the pacemaker, sure. You'll see me right up there over the first, and maybe for a good while longer, but then my old boy will run out of steam and drop out of the back door as sudden as an interrupted burglar, and if I don't have to pull him up it'll be a bloody miracle.'

Later in the afternoon I watched him start out on some prospective ten-year-old dog-meat in a novice chase. Horse and rider disappeared with a flurry of legs into the second open ditch, and when I went to check on his injuries some time after the second race I met Dermot coming out of the ambulance room wearing a bandage and a grin.

'It's only a scratch,' he assured me cheerfully. 'I'll be there for the Lamplighter sure enough.'

Further investigation led to the detail of a fingernail hanging on by a thread. 'Some black divil' had leant an ill-placed hoof on the Finnegan hand.

To complete the *Tally* round-up I spent the last half of the afternoon in the clerk of the course's office, watching him in action.

Heathbury Park, where the Lamplighter was to be held a fortnight later, had become under his direction one of the best organized courses in the country. Like the handicapper, he was ex-forces, in his case RAF, which was unusual in that the racing authorities as a rule leant heavily towards the Army and the Navy for their executives.

Wing Commander Willy Ondroy was a quiet effective shortish man of forty-two who had been invalided out after fracturing his skull in a slight mishap with a Vulcan bomber. He still, he said, suffered from blackouts, usually at the most inconvenient, embarrassing, and even obscene moments.

It wasn't until after racing had finished for the day that he was really ready to talk, and even then he dealt with a string of people calling into his office with statistics, problems, and keys.

The Lamplighter was his own invention, and he was mostly proud of it. He'd argued the Betting Levy Board into putting up most of the hefty stake money, and then drawn up entry conditions exciting enough to bring a gleam to the hardest-headed trainer's eye. Most of the best horses would consequently be coming. They should draw an excellent crowd. The gate receipts would rise again. They'd soon be able to afford to build a warm modern nursery-room, their latest project, to attract young parents to the races by giving them somewhere to park their kids.

Willy Ondroy's enthusiasm was of the enduring, not the bubbling kind. His voice was as gentle as the expression in his amber eyes, and only the small self-mockery in his smile gave any clue to the steel within. His obvious lack of any need to assert his authority in any forceful way was finally explained after I'd dug, or tried to dig, into his history. A glossed over throw-away phrase about a spot of formation flying turned out to be his version of three years as a Red Arrow, flying two feet away from the jet pipe of the aircraft in front. 'We did two hundred displays in one year,' he said apologetically. 'Entertaining at air shows. Like a concert party on Blackpool pier, no difference really.'

He had been lucky to transfer to bombers when he was twenty-six, he said. So many RAF fighter and formation pilots were grounded altogether when their reaction times began to slow. He'd spent eight years on bombers, fifteen seconds knowing he was going to crash, three weeks in a coma, and twenty months find-ing himself a civilian job. Now he lived with his wife and twelve-year-old twins in a house on the edge of the racecourse, and none of them wanted to change.

I caught the last train when it was moving and made a start on Dermot and Willy Ondroy on the way back to London.

Mrs Woodward departed contentedly at a quarter to seven, and I found she had for once left steaks ready in the kitchen. Elizabeth was in good spirits. I mixed us a drink each and relaxed in the armchair, and only after a strict ten minutes of self denial asked her casu-ally if her mother had telephoned.

'No, she hasn't.' She wouldn't have.

'So you don't know if she's coming?'

'I expect she'll ring, if she doesn't.'

'I suppose so,' I said. Damn her eyes, couldn't she at least settle it, one way or another?

Trying to shut my mind to it I worked on the *Tally* article; cooked the supper; went back to *Tally*; stopped to settle Elizabeth for the night; and returned to the typewriter until I'd finished. It was then half past two. A pity, I thought, stretching, that I wrote so slowly, crossed out so much. I put the final version away in a drawer with only the fair copy to be typed the next day. Plenty of time for that even if I spent the rest of it on the primrose path making tracks for Gail.

I despised myself. It was five before I slept.

Elizabeth's mother came. Not a sniffle in sight.

I had spent all morning trying to reconcile myself to her non-appearance at ten-fifteen, her usual time of arrival. As on past occasions, I had turned a calm and everyday face to Elizabeth and found I had consciously to stifle irritation at little tasks for her that normally I did without thought.

At ten-seventeen the door bell rang, and there she was, a well-groomed good-looking woman in her mid-fifties with assisted tortoiseshell hair and a health farm figure. When she showed surprise at my greeting I knew I had been too welcoming. I damped it down a little to more normal levels and saw that she felt more at home with that.

I explained to her, as I had already done to Elizabeth, that I still had people to interview for *Tally*, and by ten-thirty I was walking away down the mews feeling as though a safety valve was blowing fine. The sun was shining too. After a sleepless night, my conscience slept.

Gail met me at Virginia Water, waiting outside in the estate car. 'The train's late,' she said calmly, as I sat in beside her. No warm, loving, kissing hello. Just as well, I supposed.

'They work on the lines on Sunday. There was a delay at Staines.'

She nodded, let in the clutch, and cruised the three-quarters of a mile to her uncle's house. There she led the way into the sitting-room and without asking poured two beers.

'You aren't writing today,' she said, handing me the glass.

'No.'

She gave me a smile that acknowledged the purpose of my visit. More businesslike about sex than most women. Certainly no tease. I kissed her mouth lightly, savouring the knowledge that the deadline of the Huntersons' return was three full hours ahead.

She nodded as if I'd spoken. 'I approve of you,' she said.

'Thanks.'

She smiled, moving away. Her dress that day was of a pale cream colour which looked wonderful against the gilded coffee skin. She was no darker, in fact, than many southern Europeans or heavily sun-tanned English: her mixed origin was distinct only in her face. A well-proportioned, attractive face, gathering distinction from the self-assurance within. Gail, I imagined, had had to come to terms with herself much earlier and more basically than most girls. She had done almost too good a job.

A copy of *The Sunday Blaze* lay on the low table, open at the sports page. Editors or sub-editors write all the headlines, and Luke-John had come up with a beauty. Across the top of my page, big and bold, it said, 'Don't back Tiddely Pom – YET'. Underneath, he'd left in word for word every paragraph I'd written. This didn't necessarily mean he thought each word was worth its space in print, but was quite likely because there weren't too many advertisements that week. Like all newspapers, the *Blaze* lived on advertising: if an advertiser wanted to pay for space, he got it, and out went the deathless prose of the columnists. I'd lost many a worked-on sentence to the late arrival of spiels on Whosit's cough syrup or Wammo's hair tonic. It was nice to see this intact.

I looked up at Gail. She was watching me.

'Do you always read the sports page?' I asked.

She shook her head. 'Curiosity,' she said. 'I wanted to see what you'd written. That article ... it's disturbing.'

'It's meant to be.'

417

'I mean, it leaves the impression that you know a great deal more than you've said, and it's all bad, if not positively criminal.'

'Well,' I said, 'it's always nice to hear one has done exactly what one has intended.'

'What usually happens when you write in this way?'

'Repercussions? They vary from a blast from the racing authorities about minding my own business to abusive letters from nut cases.'

'Do wrongs get righted?'

'Very occasionally.'

'Sir Galahad,' she mocked.

'No. We sell more papers. I apply for a raise.'

She laughed with her head back, the line of her throat leading tautly down into her dress. I put out my hand and touched her shoulder, suddenly wanting no more talk.

She nodded at once, smiling, and said, 'Not on the rug. More comfortable upstairs.'

Her bedroom furnishings were pretty but clearly Sarah's work. Fitted cupboards, a cosy armchair, book shelves, a lot of pale blue carpet, and a single bed.

At her insistence, I occupied it first. Then while I watched, like the time before, she took off her clothes. The simple, undramatized, unselfconscious undressing was more ruthlessly arousing than anything one could ever pay to see. When she had finished she stood still for a moment near the window, a pale bronze naked girl in a shaft of winter sun.

'Shall I close the curtains?'

'Whichever you like.'

She screwed my pulse rate up another notch by stretching up to close them, and then in the mid-day dusk she came to bed.

At three she drove me back to the station, but a train pulled out as we pulled in. We sat in the car for a while, talking, waiting for the next one.

'Do you come home here every night?' I asked.

'Quite often not. Two of the other teachers share a flat, and I sleep on their sofa a night or two every week, after parties, or a theatre, maybe.'

'But you don't want to live in London all the time?'

'D'you think it's odd, that I stay with Harry and Sarah? Quite frankly, it's because of money. Harry won't let me pay for living here. He says he wants me to stay. He's always been generous. If I had to pay for everything myself in London my present standard of living would go down with a reverberating thump.'

'Comfort before independence,' I commented mildly.

She shook her head. 'I have both.' After a considering pause she said, 'Do you live with your wife? I mean, have you separated, or anything?'

'No, we've not separated.'

'Where does she think you are today?'

'Interviewing someone for my *Tally* article.'

She laughed. 'You're a bit of a bastard.'

Nail on the head. I agreed with her.

'Does she know you have ... er ... outside interests? Has she ever found you out?'

I wished she would change the subject. However, I owed her quite a lot, at least some answers, which might be the truth and nothing but the truth, but would certainly not be the whole truth.

'She doesn't know,' I said.

'Would she mind?'

'Probably.'

'But if she won't ... sleep with you ... well, why don't you leave her?'

I didn't answer at once. She went on, 'You haven't any children, have you?' I shook my head. 'Then what's to stop you? Unless, of course, you're like me.'

'How do you mean?'

'Staying where the living is good. Where the money is.'

'Oh ...' I half laughed, and she misunderstood me.

'How can I blame you,' she sighed, 'when I do it myself? So your wife is rich ...'

I thought about what Elizabeth would have been condemned to without me: to hospital ward routine, hospital food, no privacy, no gadgets, no telephone, lights out at nine and lights on at six, no free will at all, for ever and ever.

'I suppose you might say,' I agreed slowly, 'that my wife is rich.'

Back in the flat I felt split in two, with everything familiar feeling suddenly unreal. Half my mind was still down in Surrey. I kissed Elizabeth and thought of Gail. Depression had clamped down like drizzle in the train and wouldn't be shaken off.

'Some man wants to talk to you,' Elizabeth said. 'He telephoned three times. He sounded awfully angry.'

'Who?'

'I couldn't understand much of what he said. He was stuttering.'

'How did he get our number?' I was irritated, bored; I didn't want to have to deal with angry men on the telephone. Moreover our number was ex-directory, precisely so that Elizabeth should not be bothered by this sort of thing.

'I don't know. But he did leave his number for you to ring back, it was the only coherent thing he said.'

Elizabeth's mother handed me a note pad on which she had written down the number.

'Victor Roncey,' I said.

'That's right,' agreed Elizabeth with relief. 'That sounds like it.'

I sighed, wishing that all problems, especially those of my own making, would go away and leave me in peace.

'Maybe I'll call him later,' I said. 'Right now I need a drink.'

'I was just going to make some tea,' said Elizabeth's mother reprovingly, and in silent fury I doubled the quantity I would normally have taken. The bottle was nearly empty. Gloomy Sunday.

Restlessly I took myself off into my writing-room and started the clean unscribbled-on retype for *Tally*, the mechanical task eventually smoothing out the rocky tensions of my guilt-ridden return home. I couldn't afford to like Gail too much, and I did like her. To come to love someone would be too much hell altogether. Better not to visit Gail again. I decided definitely not to. My body shuddered in protest, and I knew I would.

Roncey rang again just after Elizabeth's mother had left.

'What the devil do you mean about this . . . this trash in the paper? Of course my horse is going to run. How dare you . . . how dare you suggest there's anything shady going on?'

Elizabeth had been right: he was stuttering still, at seven in the evening. He took a lot of calming down to the point of admitting that nowhere in the article was it suggested that he personally had anything but good honest upright intentions.

'The only thing is, Mr Roncey, as I said in the article, that some owners have in the past been pressurized into not running their horses. This may even happen to you. All I was doing was giving punters several good reasons why they would be wiser to wait until half an hour before big races to put their money on. Better a short starting price than losing their money in a swindle.'

'I've read it,' he snapped. 'Several times. And no one, believe me, is going to put any pressure on *me*.'

'I very much hope not,' I said. I wondered whether his antipathy to his elder sons extended to the smaller ones; whether he would risk their safety or happiness for the sake of running Tiddely Pom in the Lamplighter. Maybe he would. The stubborn streak ran through his character like iron in granite.

When he had calmed down to somewhere near reason I asked him if he'd mind telling me how he'd got my telephone number.

'I had the devil's own job, if you want to know. All that ex-directory piffle. The enquiries people refused point blank to tell me, even though I said it was urgent. Stupid, I call it, but I wasn't to be put off by that. If you want to know, your colleague on the paper told me. Derrick Clark.'

'I see,' I said resignedly, thinking it unlike Derry to part so easily with my defences. 'Well, thank you. Did the *Tally* photographer find you all right?'

'He came on Friday. I hope you haven't said anything in *Tally* about . . .' His anger was on its way up again.

'No,' I said decisively. 'Nothing like that at all.'

'When can I be sure?' He sounded suspicious.

'That edition of *Tally* is published on the Tuesday before the Lamplighter.'

'I'll ask for an advance copy from the editor. Tomorrow. I'll demand to see what you've written.'

'Do that,' I agreed. Divert the buck to Arnold Shankerton. Splendid.

He rang off still not wholly pacified. I dialled Derry's number and prepared to pass the ill temper along to him.

'*Roncey?*' He said indignantly. 'Of course I didn't give your number to Roncey.' His baby girl was exercising her lungs loudly in the background. 'What did you say?'

'I said, who *did* you give it to?'

'Your wife's uncle.'

'My wife hasn't got any uncles.'

'Oh Christ. Well, he said he was your wife's uncle, and that your wife's aunt had had a stroke, and that he wanted to tell you, but he'd lost your number.'

'Lying crafty bastard,' I said with feeling. 'And he accused me of misrepresenting facts.'

'I'm sorry, Ty.'

'Never mind. Only check with me first, next time, huh? Like we arranged.'

'Yeah. Sure. Sorry.'

'How did he get hold of your number, anyway?'

'It's in the *Directory of the British Turf*, unlike yours. My mistake.'

I put the receiver back in its special cradle near to Elizabeth's head and transferred to the armchair, and we spent the rest of the evening as we usually did, watching the shadows on the goggle box. Elizabeth never tired of it, which was a blessing, though she complained often about the shut-downs in the day time between all the child-orientated programmes. Why couldn't they fill them, she said, with interesting things for captive adults.

Later I made some coffee and did the vapour rubs and other jobs for Elizabeth, all with a surface of tranquil domesticity, going through my part with my thoughts somewhere else, like an actor at the thousandth performance.

On the Monday morning I took my article to the *Tally* offices and left the package at the reception desk, virtuously on the deadline.

After that I caught the race train to Leicester, admitting to myself that although it was technically my day off I did not want to stay in the flat. Also the Huntersons' raffle horse Egocentric was to have its pre-Lamplighter warm-up which gave me an excellent overt reason for the journey.

Raw near-mist was doing its best to cancel the proceedings and only the last two fences were visible. Egocentric finished fourth without enough steam left to blow a whistle, and the jockey told the trainer that

425

the useless bugger had made a right bloody shambles of three fences on the far side and couldn't jump for peanuts. The trainer didn't believe him and engaged a different jockey for the Lamplighter. It was one of those days.

The thin Midland crowd of cloth caps and mufflers strewed the ground with betting slips and newspapers and ate a couple of hundredweight of jellied eels out of little paper cups. I adjourned to the bar with a colleague from the *Sporting Life*, and four people commented on my non-starters with varying degrees of belief. Not much of a day. One, on the whole, to forget.

The journey home changed all that. When I forget it, I'll be dead.

CHAPTER SEVEN

Thanks to having left before the last race I had a chance in the still empty and waiting train of a forward-facing window-seat in a non-smoker. I turned the heating to 'hottest', and opened the newspaper to see what Spyglass had come up with in the late editions.

'Tiddely Pom will run, trainer says. But is your money really safe?'

Amused, I read to the end. He'd cribbed most of my points and rehashed them. Complimentary. Plagiarism is the sincerest form of flattery.

The closed door to the corridor slid open and four bookmaker's clerks lumbered in, stamping their feet with cold and discussing some luckless punter who had lost an argument over a betting slip.

'I told him to come right off it, who did he think he was kidding? We may not be archangels, but we're not the ruddy mugs he takes us for.'

They all wore navy blue overcoats which after a while they shed on the luggage racks. Two of them shared a large packet of stodgy-looking sandwiches

and the other two smoked. They were all in the inter-
mediate thirty-forties, with London-Jewish accents in
which they next discussed their taxi drive to the station
in strictly non Sabbath day terms.

'Evening,' they said to me, acknowledging I existed,
and one of them gestured with his cigarette to the non-
smoking notice on the window and said, 'OK with you,
chum?'

I nodded, hardly taking them in. The train rocked
off southwards, the misty day turned to foggy night,
and five pairs of eyeballs fell gently shut.

The door to the corridor opened with a crash. Reluctantly I opened one eye a fraction, expecting the ticket
collector. Two men filled the opening, looking far from
bureaucratic. Their effect on my four fellow travellers
was a spine-straightening mouth-opening state of
shock. The larger of the newcomers stretched out a
hand and pulled the blinds down on the insides of the
corridor-facing windows. Then he gave the four clerks
a contemptuous comprehensive glance, jerked his head
towards the corridor and said with simplicity, 'Out.'

I still didn't connect any of this as being my business,
not even when the four men meekly took down their
navy blue overcoats and filed out into the train. Only
when the large man pulled out a copy of the *Blaze* and
pointed to my article did I have the faintest prickle on
the spine.

'This is unpopular in certain quarters,' remarked the
larger man. Thick sarcastic Birmingham accent. He

pursed his lips, admiring his own heavy irony. 'Unpopular.'

He wore grubby overalls from shoes to throat, with above that a thick neck, puffy cheeks, a small wet mouth, and slicked-down hair. His companion, also in overalls, was hard and stocky with wide eyes and a flat-topped head.

'You shouldn't do it, you shouldn't really,' the large man said. 'Interfering and that.'

He put his right hand into his pocket and it reappeared with a brass ridge across the knuckles. I glanced at the other man. Same thing.

I came up with a rush, grabbing for the communication cord. Penalty for improper use, twenty-five pounds. The large man moved his arm in a professional short jab and made havoc of my intention.

They had both learned their trade in the ring, that much was clear. Not much else was. They mostly left my head alone, but they knew where and how to hit to hurt on the body, and if I tried to fight off one of them, the other had a go. The most I achieved was a solid kick on the smaller man's ankle which drew from him four letters and a frightening kidney punch. I collapsed on to the seat. They leant over me and broke the Queensberry Rules.

It crossed my mind that they were going to kill me, that maybe they weren't meaning to, but they were killing me. I even tried to tell them so, but if any sound came out, they took no notice. The larger one hauled me bodily to my feet and the small one broke my ribs.

When they let go I crumpled slowly on to the floor and lay with my face against cigarette butts and the screwed-up wrappings of sandwiches. Stayed quite motionless, praying to a God I had no faith in not to let them start again.

The larger one stooped over me.

'Will he cough it?' the smaller one said.

'How can he? We ain't ruptured nothing, have we? Careful, aren't I? Look out the door, time we was off.'

The door slid open and presently shut, but not for a long time was I reassured that they had completely gone. I lay on the floor breathing in coughs and jerky shallow breaths, feeling sick. For some time it seemed in a weird transferred way that I had earned such a beating not for writing a newspaper article but because of Gail; and to have deserved it, to have sinned and deserved it, turned it into some sort of expurgation. Pain flowed through me in a red-hot tide, and only my guilt made it bearable.

Sense returned, as sense does. I set about the slow task of picking myself up and assessing the damage. Maybe they had ruptured nothing: I had only the big man's word for it. At the receiving end it felt as though they had ruptured pretty well everything, including self-respect.

I made it up to the seat, and sat vaguely watching the lights flash past, fuzzy and yellow from fog. Eyes half shut, throat closing with nausea, hands nerveless and weak. No one focus of pain, just too much. Wait, I thought, and it will pass.

I waited a long time.

The lights outside thickened and the train slowed down. London. All change. I would have to move from where I sat. Dismal prospect. Moving would hurt.

The train crept into St Pancras and stopped with a jerk. I stayed where I was, trying to make the effort to stand up and not succeeding, telling myself that if I didn't get up and go I could be shunted into a siding for a cold uncomfortable night, and still not raking up the necessary propulsion.

Again the door slid open with a crash. I glanced up, stifling the beginnings of panic. No man with heavy overalls and knuckleduster. The guard.

Only when I felt the relief wash through me did I realize the extent of my fear, and I was furious with myself for being so craven.

'The end of the line,' the guard was saying.

'Yeah,' I said.

He came into the compartment and peered at me. 'Been celebrating, have you, sir?' He thought I was drunk.

'Sure,' I agreed. 'Celebrating.'

I made the long-delayed effort and stood up. I'd been quite right about it. It hurt.

'Look, mate, do us a favour and don't throw up in here,' said the guard urgently.

I shook my head. Reached the door. Rocked into the corridor. The guard anxiously took my arm and helped me down on to the platform, and as I walked carefully away I heard him behind me say to a bunch of porters, half laughing, 'Did you see that one? Greeny grey and sweating like a pig. Must have been knocking it back solid all afternoon.'

I went home by taxi and took my time up the stairs to the flat. Mrs Woodward for once was in a hurry for me to come, as she was wanting to get home in case the fog thickened. I apologized. 'Quite all right, Mr Tyrone, you know I'm usually glad to stay...' The door closed behind her and I fought down a strong inclination to lie on my bed and groan.

Elizabeth said, 'Ty, you look terribly pale,' when I kissed her. Impossible to hide it from her completely.

'I fell,' I said. 'Tripped. Knocked the breath out of myself, for a minute or two.'

She was instantly concerned; with the special extra anxiety for herself apparent in her eyes.

'Don't worry,' I comforted her. 'No harm done.'

I went into the kitchen and held on to the table. After a minute or two I remembered Elizabeth's pain-killing tablets and took the bottle out of the cupboard. Only two left. There would be. I swallowed one of them, tying a mental knot to remind me to ring the doctor for another prescription. One wasn't quite enough, but better than nothing. I went back into the big room and with a fair stab at normality poured our evening drinks.

By the time I had done the supper and the jobs for Elizabeth and got myself undressed and into bed, the main damage had resolved itself into two or possibly three cracked ribs low down on my left side. The rest slowly subsided into a blanketing ache. Nothing had ruptured, like the man said.

I lay in the dark breathing shallowly and trying not to cough, and at last took time off from simply existing to consider the who and why of such a drastic roughing up, along with the pros and cons of telling Luke-John. He'd make copy of it, put it on the front page, plug it for more than it was worth, write the headlines himself. My feelings would naturally be utterly disregarded as being of no importance compared with selling papers. Luke-John had no pity. If I didn't tell him and he found out later, there would be frost and fury and a permanent atmosphere of distrust. I couldn't afford that. My predecessor had been squeezed off the paper entirely as a direct result of having concealed from Luke-John a red-hot scandal in which he was involved. A rival paper got hold of it and scooped the *Blaze*. Luke-John never forgave, never forgot.

I sighed deeply. A grave mistake. The cracked ribs stabbed back with unnecessary vigour. I spent what could not be called a restful, comfortable, sleep-filled night, and in the morning could hardly move. Elizabeth watched me get up and the raw anxiety twisted her face.

'Ty!'

'Only a bruise or two, honey. I told you, I fell over.'

'You look . . . hurt . . .'

I shook my head. 'I'll get the coffee . . .'

I got the coffee. I also looked with longing at Elizabeth's last pill, which I had no right to take. She still suffered sometimes from terrible cramp, and on these occasions had to have the pills in a hurry. I didn't need any mental knots to remind me to get some more. When Mrs Woodward came, I went.

Doctor Antonio Perelli wrote the prescription without hesitation and handed it across.

'How is she?'

'Fine. Same as usual.'

'It's time I went to see her.'

'She'd love it,' I said truthfully. Perelli's visits acted on her like champagne. I'd met him casually at a party three years earlier, a young Italian doctor in private practice in Welbeck Street. Too handsome, I'd thought at once. Too feminine, with those dark, sparkling, long-lashed eyes. All bedside manner and huge fees, with droves of neurotic women patients paying to have their hands held.

Then just before the party broke up someone told me he specialized in chest complaints, and not to be put off by his youth and beauty, he was brilliant; and by coincidence we found ourselves outside on the pavement together, hailing the same taxi, and going the same way.

At the time I had been worried about Elizabeth. She had to return to hospital for intensive nursing every time she was ill, and with a virtual stamping out of polio, the hospitals geared to care for patients on artificial respiration were becoming fewer and fewer. We had just been told she could not expect to go back any more to the hospital that had always looked after her.

I shared the taxi with Perelli and asked him if he knew of anywhere I could send her quickly if she ever needed it. Instead of answering directly he invited me into his tiny bachelor flat for another drink, and before I left he had acquired another patient. Elizabeth's general health had improved instantly under his care and I paid his moderate fees without a wince.

I thanked him for the prescription and put it in my pocket.

'Ty . . . are the pills for Elizabeth, or for you?'

I looked at him, startled. 'Why?'

'My dear fellow, I have eyes. What I see in your face is . . . severe.'

I smiled wryly. 'All right. I was going to ask you. Could you put a bit of strapping on a couple of ribs?'

He stuck me up firmly and handed me a small medicine glass containing, he said, disprins dissolved in nepenthe, which worked like a vanishing trick: now you feel it, now you don't.

'You haven't told Elizabeth?' he said anxiously.

'Only that I fell and winded myself.'

He relaxed, moving his head in a gesture of approval. 'Good.'

It had been his idea to shield her from worries which ordinary women could cope with in their stride. I had thought him unduly fussy at first, but the strict screening he had urged had worked wonders. She had become far less nervous, much happier, and had even put on some badly needed weight.

'And the police? Have you told the police?'

I shook my head and explained about Luke-John.

'Difficult. Um. Suppose you tell this Luke-John simply that those men threatened you? You'll not be taking your shirt off in the office.' He smiled in the way that made Elizabeth's eyes shine. 'These two men, they will not go about saying they inflicted so much damage.'

'They might,' I frowned, considering. 'It could be a good idea if I turned up in perfect health at the races today and gave them the lie.'

With an assenting gesture he mixed me a small bottle full of disprin and nepenthe. 'Don't eat much,' he said, handing it over. 'And only drink coffee.'

'OK.'

'And do nothing that would get you another beating like this.'

I was silent.

He looked at me with sad understanding. 'That is too much to give up for Elizabeth?'

'I can't just . . . crawl away,' I protested. 'Even for Elizabeth.'

He shook his head. 'It would be best for her. But . . .' He shrugged, and held out his hand in goodbye. 'Stay out of trains, then.'

I stayed out of trains. For ninety-four minutes. Then I caught the race train to Plumpton and travelled down safely with two harmless strangers and a man I knew slightly from the BBC.

Thanks to Tonio's mixture I walked about all day and talked and laughed much the same as usual. Once I coughed. Even that caused only an echo of a stab. For maximum effect I spent a good deal of my time walking about the bookmakers' stalls, inspecting both their prices and their clerks. The fraternity knew something had happened. Their heads swivelled as I passed and they were talking behind my back, nudging each other. When I put ten shillings on a semi-outsider with one of them he said, 'You feeling all right, chum?'

'Why not?' I said in surprise. 'It's a nice enough day.'

He looked perplexed for a second, and then shrugged. I walked on, looking at faces, searching for a familiar one. The trouble was I'd paid the four clerks in the compartment so little attention that I wasn't sure I'd recognize any one of them again, and I wouldn't have done, if he hadn't given himself away. When he saw me looking at him, he jerked, stepped down off his stand, and bolted.

Running was outside my repertoire. I walked quietly up behind him an hour later when he had judged it safe to go back to his job.

'A word in your ear,' I said at his elbow.

He jumped six inches. 'It was nothing to do with me.'

'I know that. Just tell me who the two men were. Those two in overalls.'

'Do me a favour. Do I want to end up in hospital?'

'Twenty quid?' I suggested.

'I dunno about that ... How come you're here today?'

'Why not?'

'When those two've seen to someone ... they stay seen to.'

'Is that so? They seemed pretty harmless.'

'No, straight up,' he said curiously, 'didn't they touch you?'

'No.'

He was puzzled.

'A pony. Twenty-five quid,' I said. 'For their names, or who they work for?'

He hesitated. 'Not here, mate. On the train.'

'Not on the train.' I was positive. 'In the press box. And now.'

He got five minutes off from his grumbling employer and went in front of me up the stairs to the eyrie allotted to newspapers. I gave a shove-off sign to the only press man up there, and he obligingly disappeared.

'Right,' I said. 'Who were they?'

'They're Brummies,' he said cautiously.

'I know that. You could cut their accents.'

'Bruisers,' he ventured.

I stopped myself just in time from telling him I knew that too.

'They're Charlie Boston's boys.' It came out in a nervous rush.

'That's better. Who's Charlie Boston?'

'So who hasn't heard of Charlie Boston? Got some betting shops, hasn't he, in Birmingham and Wolverhampton and such like.'

'And some boys on race trains?'

He looked more puzzled than ever. 'Don't you owe Charlie no money? So what did they want, then? It's usually bad debts they're after.'

'I've never heard of Charlie Boston before, let alone had a bet with him.' I took out my wallet and gave him five fivers. He took them with a practised flick and stowed them away in a pocket like Fort Knox under his left armpit. 'Dirty thieves,' he explained. 'Taking precautions, aren't I?'

He scuttled off down the stairs, and I stayed up in the press box and took another swig at my useful little bottle, reflecting that when Charlie Boston unleashed his boys on me he had been very foolish indeed.

Luke-John reacted predictably with a bridling 'They can't do that to the *Blaze*' attitude.

Wednesday morning. Not much doing in the office. Derry with his feet up on the blotter, Luke-John elbow deep in the dailies' sports pages, the telephone silent, and every desk in the place exhibiting the same feverish inactivity.

Into this calm I dropped the pebble of news that two men, adopting a threatening attitude, had told me not to interfere in the non-starters racket. Luke-John sat up erect like a belligerent bull frog, quivering with satisfaction that the article had produced tangible results. With a claw hand he pounced on the telephone.

'Manchester office? Give me the sports desk ... That you, Andy? Luke Morton. What can you tell me about a bookmaker called Charlie Boston? Has a string of betting shops around Birmingham.'

He listened to a lengthy reply with growing intensity.

'That adds up. Yes. Yes. Fine. Ask around and let me know.'

He put down the receiver and rubbed his larynx. 'Charlie Boston changed his spots about a year ago. Before that he was apparently an ordinary Birmingham bookmaker with about six shops and a reasonable reputation. Now, Andy says he's expanded a lot and become a bully. He says he's been hearing too much about Charlie Boston lately. Seems he hires two ex-boxers to collect unpaid debts from his credit customers, and as a result of all this he's coining it.'

I thought it over. Charlie Boston of Birmingham with his betting shops and bruisers didn't gel at all with the description Dembley had given me of a quiet gentleman in a Rolls with a chauffeur and a Greek, Dutch, or Scandinavian accent. They even seemed an unlikely pair of shoulder to shoulder partners. There might of course be two separate rackets going on, and if so, what happened if they clashed? And by which of them had Bert Checkov been seduced? But if they were all one outfit, I'd settle for the Rolls gent as the brains and Charlie Boston the muscles. Setting his dogs on me had been classic muscle-bound thinking.

Luke-John's telephone rang and he reached out a hand. As he listened his eyes narrowed and he turned his head to look straight at me.

'What do you mean, he was pulped? He certainly was not. He's here in the office at this moment and he went to Plumpton races yesterday. What your paper needs is a little less imagination . . . If you don't believe me, talk to him yourself.' He handed me the receiver, saying with a grimace, 'Connersley. Bloody man.'

'I heard,' said the precise malicious voice on the phone, 'that some Birmingham heavies took you to pieces on the Leicester race train.'

'A rumour,' I said with boredom. 'I heard it myself yesterday at Plumpton.'

'According to my informant you couldn't have gone to Plumpton.'

'Your informant is unreliable. Scrap him.'

A small pause. Then he said, 'I can check if you were there.'

'Check away.' I put the receiver down with a brusque crash and thanked my stars I had reached Luke-John with my version first.

'Are you planning a follow-up on Sunday?' he was asking. Connersley had planted no suspicions: was already forgotten. 'Hammer the point home. Urge the racing authorities to act. Agitate. You know the drill.'

I nodded. I knew the drill. My bruises gave me a protesting nudge. No more, they said urgently. Write a nice mild piece on an entirely different, totally innocuous subject.

'Get some quotes,' Luke-John said.

'OK.'

'Give with some ideas,' he said impatiently. 'I'm doing all your ruddy work.'

I sighed. Shallowly and carefully. 'How about us making sure Tiddely Pom starts in the Lamplighter? Maybe I'll go fix it with the Ronceys . . .'

Luke-John interrupted, his eyes sharp. 'The *Blaze* will see to it that Tiddely Pom runs. Ty, that's genius.

Start your piece with that. The *Blaze* will see to it . . . Splendid. Splendid.'

Oh God, I thought. I'm the world's greatest bloody fool. Stay out of race trains, Tonio Perelli had said. Nothing about lying down on the tracks.

CHAPTER EIGHT

Nothing had changed at the Ronceys'. Dead leaves, cobwebs, still in place. No dripping meat on the kitchen table: two unplucked pheasants sagged with limp necks there instead. The sink overflowed with unwashed dishes and the wellington smell had intensified.

I arrived unannounced at two-thirty and found Roncey himself out in the yard watching Pat and the old man saw up a large hunk of dead tree. He received me with an unenthusiastic glare but eventually took me through into the sitting-room with a parting backwards instruction to his son to clean out the tackroom when he'd finished the logs.

Madge was lying on the sofa, asleep. Still no stockings, still the blue slippers, still the yellow dress, very dirty now down the front. Roncey gave her a glance of complete indifference and gestured me to one of the armchairs.

'I don't need help from the *Blaze*,' he said, as he'd said outside in the yard. 'Why should I?'

444

'It depends on how much you want Tiddely Pom to run in the Lamplighter.'

'Of course he's going to run.' Roncey looked aggressive and determined. 'I told you. Anyone who tries to tell me otherwise has another think coming.'

'In that case,' I said mildly, 'one of two things will happen. Either the men operating the racket will abandon the idea of preventing Tiddely Pom from running, as a result of all the publicity they've been getting. Or they will go ahead and stop him. If they've any sense they'll abandon the idea. But I don't see how one can count on them having any sense.'

'They won't stop him.' Pugnacious jaw, stubborn eyes.

'You can be sure they will, one way or another, if they want to.'

'I don't believe you.'

'But would you object to taking precautions, just in case? The *Blaze* will foot the bills.'

He stared at me long and hard. 'This is not just a publicity stunt to cover your sensation-hunting paper with glory?'

'Dual purpose,' I said. 'Half for you and betting public. Half for us. But only one object: to get Tiddely Pom safely off in the Lamplighter.'

He thought it over.

'What sort of precautions?' he said at last.

I sighed inwardly with mixed feelings, a broken-ribbed skier at the top of a steep and bumpy slope, with only myself to thank.

'There are three main ones,' I said. 'The simplest is a letter to Weatherbys, stating your positive intention to run in the Lamplighter, and asking them to check carefully with you if they should receive any instructions to strike out the horse either before or after the four-day declaration stage next Tuesday. You do realize, don't you, that I or anyone else could send a telegram or a telex striking out the horse, and you would have a bit of a job getting him put back again?'

His mouth dropped open. '*Anyone?*'

'Anyone signing your name. Of course. Weatherbys receive hundreds of cancellations a week. They don't check to make sure the trainer really means it. Why should they?'

'Good God,' he said, stunned. 'I'll write at once. In fact I'll ring them up.' He began to stand up.

'There won't be that much urgency,' I said. 'Much more likely a cancellation would be sent in at the last moment, in order to allow as much time as possible for ante-post bets to be made.'

'Oh ... quite.' A thought struck him as he sat down again. 'If the *Blaze* declares it is going to make Tiddely Pom safe and then he *doesn't* run for some reason, you are going to look very silly.'

I nodded. 'A risk. Still ... We'll do our best. But we do need your whole-hearted cooperation, not just your qualified permission.'

He made up his mind. 'You have it. What next?'

'Tiddely Pom will have to go to another stable.'

That rocked him. 'Oh no.'

'He's much too vulnerable here.'

He swallowed. 'Where, then?'

'To one of the top trainers. He will still be expertly prepared for the race. He can have the diet he's used to. We'll give you a report on him every day.'

He opened and shut his mouth several times, speechless.

'Thirdly,' I said, 'your wife and at least your three youngest sons must go away for a holiday.'

'They can't,' he protested automatically.

'They must. If one of the children were kidnapped, would you set his life against running Tiddely Pom?'

'It isn't possible,' he said weakly.

'Just the threat might be enough.'

Madge got up and opened her eyes. They were far from dreamy. 'Where and when do we go?' she said.

'Tomorrow. You will know where after you get there.'

She smiled with a vivid delight. Fantasy had come to life. Roncey himself was not enchanted.

'I don't like it,' he said frowning.

'Ideally, you should all go. The whole lot of you,' I said.

Roncey shook his head. 'There are the other horses, and the farm. I can't leave them And I need Pat here, and Peter.'

447

I agreed to that, having gained the essentials. 'Don't tell the children they are going,' I said to Madge. 'Just keep them home from school in the morning, and someone will call for you at about nine. You'll need only country clothes. And you'll be away until after the race on Saturday week. Also, please do not on any account write any letters straight to here, or let the children send any. If you want to write, send the letters to us at the *Blaze*, and we will see that Mr Roncey gets them.'

'But Vic can write to us?' Madge said.

'Of course . . . but also via the *Blaze*. Because he won't know where you are.'

They both protested, but in the end saw the sense of it. What he didn't know, he couldn't give away, even by accident.

'It won't only be people working the racket who might be looking for them,' I explained apologetically. 'But one or two of our rival newspapers will be hunting for them, so as to be able to black the *Blaze*'s eye. And they are quite skilled at finding people who want to stay hidden.'

I left the Ronceys looking blankly at each other and drove the van back to London. It seemed a very long way, and too many aches redeveloped on the journey. I'd finished Tonio's mixture just before going into the office in the morning and was back on Elizabeth's pills, which were not as good. By the time I got home I was tired, thirsty, hurting, and apprehensive.

Dealt with the first three: armchair and whisky. Contemplated the apprehension, and didn't know which would be worse, another encounter with the Boston boys or a complete failure with Tiddely Pom. It would likely be one or the other. Could even be both.

'What's the matter, Ty?' Elizabeth looked and sounded worried.

'Nothing.' I smiled at her. 'Nothing at all, honey.'

The anxious lines relaxed in her face as she smiled back. The pump hummed and thudded, pulling air into her lungs. My poor, poor Elizabeth. I stretched my hand over and touched her cheek in affection, and she turned her head and kissed my fingers.

'You're a fantastic man, Ty,' she said. She said something like it at least twice a week. I twitched my nose and made the usual sort of answer, 'You're not so bad yourself.' The disaster that a virus had made of our lives never got any better. Never would. For her it was total and absolute; for me there were exits, like Gail. When I took them, the guilt I felt was not just the ordinary guilt of an unfaithful husband, but that of a deserter. Elizabeth couldn't leave the battlefield; but when it got too much for me, I just slid out and left her.

At nine o'clock the next morning Derry Clark collected Madge and the three Roncey boys in his own Austin and drove them down to Portsmouth and straight on to the Isle of Wight car ferry.

At noon I arrived at the farm with a car and Rice

trailer borrowed from the city editor, whose daughter went in for show jumping. Roncey showed great reluctance at parting with Tiddely Pom, and loaded the second stall of the trailer with sacks of feed and bales of hay, adding to these the horse's saddle and bridle, and also three dozen eggs and a crate of beer. He had written out the diet and training regime in four-page detail scattered with emphatic underlinings. I assured him six times that I would see the new trainer followed the instructions to the last full stop.

Pat helped with the loading with a twisted smile, not unhappy that his father was losing control of the horse. He gave me a quick look full of ironic meaning when he saw me watching him, and said under his breath as he humped past with some hay, 'Now he knows what it feels like.'

I left Victor Roncey standing disconsolately in the centre of his untidy farmyard watching his one treasure depart, and drove carefully away along the Essex lanes, heading west to Berkshire. About five miles down the road I stopped near a telephone box and rang up the Western School of Art.

Gail said, 'Surprise, surprise.'

'Yes,' I agreed. 'How about Sunday?'

'Um.' She hesitated. 'How about tomorrow?'

'Won't you be teaching?'

'I meant,' she explained, 'tomorrow night.'

'Tomorrow . . . *all* night?'

'Can you manage it?'

I took so deep a breath that my sore ribs jumped. It depended on whether Mrs Woodward could stay, as she sometimes did.

'Ty?' she said. 'Are you still there?'

'Thinking.'

'What about?'

'What to tell my wife.'

'You slay me,' she said. 'Is it yes or no?'

'Yes,' I said with a sigh. 'Where?'

'A hotel, I should think.'

'All right,' I agreed. I asked her what time she finished work, and arranged a meeting point at King's Cross railway station.

When I called the flat, Elizabeth answered.

'Ty? Where are you?'

'On the road. There's nothing wrong. It's just that I forgot to ask Mrs Woodward before I left if she could stay with you tomorrow night . . . so that I could go up to Newcastle ready for the races on Saturday.' Louse, I thought. Mean, stinking louse. Lying, deceiving louse. I listened miserably to the sounds of Elizabeth asking Mrs Woodward and found no relief at all in her answer.

'She says yes, Ty, she could manage that perfectly. You'll be home again on Saturday?'

'Yes, honey. Late, though.'

'Of course.'

'See you this evening.'

"Bye, Ty,' she said with a smile in her voice. 'See you.'

I drove all the way to Norton Fox's stable wishing I hadn't done it. Knowing that I wouldn't change it. Round and round the mulberry bush and a thumping headache by Berkshire.

Norton Fox looked curiously into the trailer parked in the private front drive of his house.

'So that's the great Tiddely Pom. Can't say I think much of him from this angle.'

'Nor from any other,' I agreed. 'It's good of you to have him.'

'Happy to oblige. I'm putting him in the box next to Zig Zag, and Sandy Willis can look after both of them.'

'You won't tell her what he is?' I asked anxiously.

'Of course not.' He looked resigned to my stupidity. 'I've recently bought a chaser over in Kent . . . I've just postponed collecting it a while, but Sandy and all the other lads think Tiddely Pom is him.'

'Great.'

'I'll just get my head lad to drive the trailer into the yard and unload. You said on the phone that you wanted to stay out of sight . . . come inside for a cuppa.'

Too late, after I'd nodded, I remembered the near black tea of my former visit. The same again. Norton remarked that his housekeeper had been economizing, he never could get her to make it strong enough.

'Did the *Tally* photographer get here all right?' I

asked as he came in from the yard, filled his cup, and sat down opposite me.

He nodded. 'Took dozens of pics of Sandy Willis and thrilled her to bits.' He offered me a slice of dry-looking fruit cake and when I said no, ate a large chunk himself, undeterred. 'That article of yours last Sunday,' he said past the currants, 'that must have been a bombshell in certain quarters.'

I said, 'Mm, I hope so.'

'Brevity . . . that Champion Hurdler of mine . . . that was definitely one of the non-starters you were talking about, wasn't it? Even though you didn't mention it explicitly by name?'

'Yes, it was.'

'Ty, did you find out *why* Dembley struck his horse out, and then sold out of racing altogether?'

'I can't tell you why, Norton,' I said.

He considered this answer with his head on one side and then nodded as if satisfied. 'Tell me one day, then.'

I smiled briefly. 'When and if the racket is extinct.'

'You go on the way you are, and it will be. If you go on exposing it publicly, the ante-post market will be so untrustworthy that we'll find ourselves doing as the Americans do, only betting on a race on the day of the race, and never before. They don't have any off-the-course betting at all, over there, do they?'

'Not legally.'

He drank in big gulps down to the tea leaves. 'Might

shoot our attendances up if punters had to go to the races to have a bet.'

'Which would shoot up the prize money too ... did you see that their champion jockey earned well over three million dollars last year? Enough to make Gordon Richards weep.'

I put down the half-finished tea and stood up. 'Must be getting back, Norton. Thank you again for your help.'

'Anything to prevent another Brevity.'

'Send the accounts to the *Blaze*.'

He nodded. 'And ring the sports desk every day to give a report, and don't speak to anyone except you or Derry Clark or a man called Luke-John Morton. Right?'

'Absolutely right,' I agreed. 'Oh ... and here are Victor Roncey's notes. Eggs and beer in Tiddely Pom's food every night.'

'I've one owner,' Norton said, 'who sends his horse champagne.'

I drove the trailer back to the city editor's house, swapped it for my van, and went home. Ten to seven on the clock. Mrs Woodward was having a grand week for overtime and had cooked chicken à la king for our supper, leaving it ready and hot. I thanked her. 'Not at all, Mr Tyrone, a pleasure I'm sure. Ta ta, luv, see you tomorrow, I'll bring my things for stopping the night.'

I kissed Elizabeth, poured the drinks, ate the

chicken, watched a TV programme, and let a little of
the day's tension trickle away. After supper there was
my Sunday article to write. Enthusiasm for the project:
way below zero. I went into the writing-room determined to put together a calm played-down sequel to
the previous week, with a sober let's-not-rush-our-
fences approach. Somewhere along the line most of
these good intentions vanished. Neither Charlie Boston
nor the foreign gent in the Rolls was going to like the
result.

Before setting off to the office in the morning I
packed an overnight bag, with Elizabeth reminding me
to take my alarm clock and a clean shirt.

'I hate it when you go away,' she said. 'I know
you don't go often, probably not nearly as much as you
ought to. I know you try not to get the faraway
meetings . . . Derry nearly always does them, and I feel
so guilty because his wife has those tiny children to
look after all alone . . .'

'Stop worrying,' I said, smiling. 'Derry likes to go.'
I had almost convinced myself that I really was taking
the afternoon train to Newcastle. Gail was hours away,
unreal. I kissed Elizabeth's cheek three times and
dearly regretted leaving her. Yet I left.

Luke-John and Derry were both out of the office when
I arrived. Luke-John's secretary handed me a large
envelope which she said had come for me by hand just

after I left on Wednesday. I opened it. The galley-proofs of my *Tally* article: please would I read and OK immediately.

'*Tally* telephoned for you twice yesterday,' Luke-John's secretary said. 'They go to press today. They wanted you urgently.'

I read the article. Arnold Shankerton had changed it about here and there and had stamped his own slightly pedantic views of grammar all over it. I sighed. I didn't like the changes, but a hundred and fifty guineas plus expenses softened the impact.

Arnold Shankerton said in his perfectly modulated tenor, with a mixture of annoyance and apology, 'I'm afraid we've had to go ahead and print, as we hadn't heard from you.'

'My fault. I've only just picked up your letter.'

'I see. Well, after I'd worked on it a little I think it reads very well, don't you? We're quite pleased with it. We think it will be a success with our readers. They like that sort of intimate human touch.'

'I'm glad,' I said politely. 'Will you send me a copy?'

'I'll make a note of it,' he said suavely. I thought I would probably have to buy one on a bookstall. 'Let me have your expenses. Small, I hope?'

'Sure,' I agreed. 'Tiny.'

Luke-John and Derry came back as I disconnected and Luke-John, without bothering to say good morning, stretched out a hand for my Sunday offering. I took it out of my pocket and he unfolded it and read it.

'Hmph,' he said. 'I expected a bit more bite.'

Derry took one of the carbon copies from me and read it.

'Any more bite and he'd have chewed up the whole page,' he said, disagreeing.

'Couldn't you emphasize a bit more that only the *Blaze* knows where Tiddely Pom is?' Luke-John said. 'You've only implied it.'

'If you think so.'

'Yes, I do think so. As the *Blaze* is footing the bills we want all the credit we can get.'

'Suppose someone finds him ... Tiddely Pom?' I asked mildly. 'Then we'd look right nanas, hiding him, boasting about it, and then having him found.'

'No one will find him. The only people who know where he is are us three and Norton Fox. To be more precise, only you and Fox know *exactly* where he is. Only you and Fox know which in that yard full of sixty horses is Tiddely Pom. Neither of you is going to tell anyone else. So how is anyone going to find him? No, no, Ty. You make that article absolutely definite. The *Blaze* is keeping the horse safe, and only the *Blaze* knows where he is.'

'Charlie Boston may not like it,' Derry observed to no one in particular.

'Charlie Boston can stuff it,' Luke-John said impatiently.

'I meant,' Derry explained, 'that he might just send

his thug-uglies to take Ty apart for so obviously ignoring their keep-off-the-grass.'

My pal. Luke-John considered the possibility for two full seconds before shaking his head. 'They wouldn't dare.'

'And even if they did,' I said, 'it would make a good story and you could sell more papers.'

'Exactly.' Luke-John started nodding and then looked at me suspiciously. 'That was a joke?'

'A feeble one.' I sighed, past smiling.

'Change the intro, then, Ty. Make it one hundred per cent specific.' He picked up a pencil and put a line through the first paragraph. Read the next, rubbed his larynx thoughtfully, let that one stand. Axed the next. Turned the page.

Derry watched sympathetically as the pencil marks grew. It happened to him, too, often enough. Luke-John scribbled his way through to the end and then returned to the beginning, pointing out each alteration that he wanted made. He was turning my moderately hard-hitting original into a bulldozing battering ram.

'You'll get me slaughtered,' I said, and meant it.

I worked on the rewrite most of the morning, fighting a rearguard action all the way. What Luke-John finally passed was a compromise between his view and mine, which still left me so far out on a limb as to be balancing on twigs. Luke-John took it in to the editor, stayed there while he read it, and brought it triumphantly back.

'He liked it. Thinks it's great stuff. He liked Derry's piece yesterday too, summing up the handicap. He told me the sports desk is a big asset to the paper.'

'Good,' Derry said cheerfully. 'When do we get our next raise?'

'Time for a jar at The Devereux,' Luke-John suggested, looking at his watch. 'Coming today, Ty?'

'Norton Fox hasn't rung through yet.'

'Call him then.'

I telephoned to Fox. Tiddely Pom was fine, ate his feed the previous evening, had settled in well, had done a mile at a working canter that morning, and no one had looked at him twice. I thanked him and relayed the news to Roncey, who sounded both agitated and depressed.

'I don't like it,' he said several times.

'Do you want to risk having him at home?'

He hesitated, then said, 'I suppose not. No. But I don't like it. Don't forget to ring tomorrow evening. I'll be at Kempton races all afternoon.'

'The sports editor will ring,' I assured him. 'And don't worry.'

He put the receiver down saying an explosive 'Huh.' Luke-John and Derry were already on the way to the door and I joined them to go to lunch.

'Only a fortnight since Bert Checkov died,' observed Derry, sitting on a bar stool. 'Only ten days since we spotted the non-starters. Funny.'

Hilarious. And eight more days to go to the

Lamplighter. This Monday, I decided, I would stay safely tucked away at home.

'Don't forget,' I said to Derry. 'Don't tell anyone my phone number.'

'What brought that on all of a sudden?'

'I was thinking about Charlie Boston. My address isn't in the phone book...'

'Neither Derry nor I will give your address to anyone,' Luke-John said impatiently. 'Come off it, Ty, anyone would think you were frightened.'

'Anyone would be so right,' I agreed, and they both laughed heartily into their pints.

Derry was predictably pleased that I wanted to go to Newcastle instead of Kempton, leaving the London meeting for once for him.

'Is it all right?' he said, embarrassed. 'With your wife, I mean?'

I told him what Elizabeth had said, but as usual anything to do with her made him uncomfortable. Luke-John said dutifully, 'How is she?' and I said 'Fine.'

I kicked around the office all the afternoon, arranging a travel warrant to Newcastle, putting in a chit for expenses for Heathbury Park, Leicester, and Plumpton, and collecting the cash from Accounts. Luke-John was busy with a football columnist and the golfing correspondent, and Derry took time off from working out his tips for every meeting in the following week to tell me about taking the Roncey kids to the Isle of Wight.

'Noisy little devils,' he said disapprovingly. 'Their mother has no control over them at all. She seemed to be in a dream most of the time. Anyway, none of them actually fell off the ferry, which was a miracle considering Tony, that was the eldest one, was trying to lean over far enough to see the paddles go round. I told him they were under the water. Made no difference.'

I made sympathetic noises, trying not to laugh out of pity for my ribs. 'They were happy enough, then?'

'Are you kidding? No school and a holiday at the sea? Tony said he was going to bathe, November or no November. His mother showed no signs of stopping him. Anyway, they settled into the boarding house all right though I should think we shall get a whacking bill for damage, and they thought it tremendous fun to change their names to Robinson, no trouble there. They thought Robinson was a smashing choice, they would all pretend they were cast away on a desert island . . . Well, I tell you, Ty, by the time I left them I was utterly exhausted.'

'Never mind. You can look forward to bringing them back.'

'Not me,' he said fervently. 'Your turn for that.'

*

At four I picked up my suitcase and departed for King's Cross. The Newcastle train left at five. I watched it go.

At five forty-eight she came up from the Underground, wearing a beautifully cut darkish-blue coat and carrying a creamy-white suitcase. Several heads turned to look at her, and a nearby man who had been waiting almost as long as I had watched her steadfastly until she reached the corner where I stood.

'Hullo,' she said. 'Sorry I'm late.'

'Think nothing of it.'

'I gather,' she said with satisfaction, 'that you fixed your wife.'

CHAPTER NINE

She moved against me in the warm dark and put her mouth on the thin skin somewhere just south of my neck. I tightened my arms round her, and buried my nose in her clean, sweet-scented hair.

'There's always something new,' she said sleepily. 'Broken ribs are quite a gimmick.'

'I didn't feel them.'

'Oh yes you did.'

I stroked my hands slowly over her smooth skin and didn't bother to answer. I felt relaxed and wholly content. She had been kind to my ribs, gentle to my bruises. They had even in an obscure way given her pleasure.

'How did it happen?'

'What?'

'The black-and-blue bit.'

'I lost an argument.'

She rubbed her nose on my chest. 'Must have been quite a debate.'

I smiled in the dark. The whole world was inside

the sheets, inside the small private cocoon wrapping two bodies in intimate primeval understanding.

'Ty?'

'Mm?'

'Can't we stay together all weekend?'

I said through her hair, 'I have to phone in a report from Newcastle. Can't avoid it.'

'Damn the *Blaze*.'

'There's Sunday, though.'

'Hurrah for the Golf Club.'

We lay quiet for a long while. I felt heavy with sleep and fought to stay awake. There were so few hours like this. None to waste.

For Gail time was not so precious. Her limbs slackened and her head slid down on to my arm, her easy breath fanning softly against my chest. I thought of Elizabeth lying closely curled against me like that when we were first married, and for once it was without guilt, only with regret.

Gail woke of her own accord a few hours later and pulled my wrist round to look at the luminous hands on my watch.

'Are you awake?' she said. 'It's ten to six.'

'Do you like it in the morning?'

'With you, Ty, any time.' Her voice smiled in the darkness. 'Any old time you care to mention.'

I wasn't that good. I said, 'Why?'

'Because you're normal, maybe. Nice bread and

butter love.' She played the piano down my stomach. 'Some men want the weirdest things . . .'

'Let's not talk about them.'

'OK,' she said. 'Let's not.'

I caught the Newcastle express at eight o'clock with ten seconds in hand. It was a raw cold morning with steam hissing up from under the train. Hollow clanking noises and unintelligible station announcements filled the ears, and bleary-eyed shiving passengers hurried greyly through the British Standard dawn.

I took my shivering bleary-eyed self into the dining car and tried some strong black coffee, but nothing was going to shift the dragging depression which had settled in inexorably as soon as I left Gail. I imagined her as I had left her, lying warm and luxuriously lazy in the soft bed and saying Sunday was tomorrow. We could start again where we'd left off. Sunday was certainly tomorrow, but there was Saturday to get through first. From where I sat it looked like a very long day.

Four and a half hours to Newcastle. I slept most of the way, and spent the rest remembering the evening and night which were gone. We had found a room in a small private hotel near the station and I had signed the register Mr and Mrs Tyrone. No one there had shown any special interest in us; they had presently shown us to a clean uninspiring room and given us the key, had asked if we wanted early tca, and said they were sorry they didn't do dinner, there were several good restaurants round about. I paid them in advance, explaining that I had an early train to catch. They smiled, thanked me, withdrew, asked no questions, made no comment. Impossible to know what they guessed.

We talked for a while and then went out to a pub for a drink and from there to an Indian restaurant where we took a long time eating little, and an even longer time drinking coffee. Gail wore her usual air of businesslike poise and remained striking-looking even when surrounded by people of her own skin colour. I, with my pale face, was in a minority.

Gail commented on it. 'London must be the best place in the world for people like me.'

'For anyone.'

She shook her head. 'Especially for people of mixed race. In so many countries I'd be on the outside looking in. I'd never get the sort of job I have.'

'It never seems to worry you, being of mixed race,' I said.

'I accept it. In fact I wouldn't choose now to be wholly white or wholly black, if I could alter it. I am used to being me. And with people like you, of course, it is easy, because you are unaffected by me.'

'I wouldn't say that, exactly,' I said, grinning.

'Damn it, you know what I mean. You don't mind me being brown.'

'You're brown and you're beautiful. A shattering combination.'

'You're not being serious,' she complained.

'And you're glossy to the bone.'

Her lips curved in amusement. 'If you mean I've a hard core instead of a soft centre, then I expect you're right.'

'And one day you'll part from me without a twinge.'

'Will we part?' No anxiety, no involvement.

'What do you think?'

'I think you wouldn't leave your wife to live with me.'

Direct, no muddle, no fluffy wrappings.

'Would you?' she asked, when I didn't quickly answer.

'I'll never leave her.'

'That's what I thought. I like to get things straight. Then I can enjoy what I have, and not expect more.'

'Hedging your bets.'

'What do you mean?' she asked.

'Insuring against disappointment.'

'When people desperately want what they can never have, they *suffer*. Real grinding misery. That's not for me.'

'You will be luckier than most,' I said slowly, 'if you can avoid it altogether.'

'I'll have a damned good try.'

One day uncontrollable emotion would smash up all that organized level-headedness. Not while I was around, if I could help it. I prized it too much. Needed her to stay like that. Only while she demanded so little could I go on seeing her, and since she clearly knew it, we had a good chance of staying clearly on the tightrope for as long as we wanted.

With the coffee we talked, as before, about money. Gail complained that she never had enough.

'Who has?' I said sympathetically.

'Your wife, for one.' There was a faint asperity in her voice, which made me stifle my immediate impulse to deny it.

'Sorry,' she said almost at once. 'Shouldn't have said that. What your wife has is quite irrelevant. It's what I haven't got that we're talking about. Such as a car of my own, a sports car, and not having to borrow Harry's all the time. And a flat of my own, a sunny one over-looking the park. Never having to budget every penny. Buying lavish presents for people if I feel like it. Flying to Paris often for a few days, and having a holiday in Japan ...'

'Marry a millionaire,' I suggested.

'I intend to.'

We both laughed, but I thought she probably meant it. The man she finally didn't part with would have to have troubles with his surtax. I wondered what she would do if she knew I could only afford that dinner and the hotel bill because *Tally*'s fee would be plugging for a while the worst holes in the Tyrone economy. What would she do if she knew that I had a penniless paralysed wife, not a rich one. On both counts, wave a rapid goodbye, probably. For as long as I could, I wasn't going to give her the opportunity.

I missed the first Newcastle race altogether and only reached the press stand halfway through the second. Delicate probes among colleagues revealed that nothing dramatic had happened in the hurdle race I had spent urging the taxi driver to rise above twenty. Luke-John would never know.

After the fourth race I telephoned through a report, and another after the fifth, in which one of the top northern jockeys broke his leg. Derry came on the line and asked me to go and find out from the trainer who would be riding his horse in the Lamplighter instead, and I did his errand thanking my stars I had had the sense actually to go to Newcastle, and hadn't been tempted to watch the racing on television and phone through an 'on-the-spot' account from an armchair three hundred miles away, as one correspondent of my acquaintance had been known to do.

Just before the last race someone touched my arm. I turned. Colly Gibbons, the handicapper, looking harassed and annoyed.

'Ty. Do me a favour.'

'What?'

'You came by train? First class?'

I nodded. The *Blaze* wasn't mean about comfort.

'Then swap return tickets with me.' He held out a slim booklet which proved to be an air ticket, Newcastle to Heathrow.

'There's some damn meeting been arranged here which I shall have to go to after this race,' he explained. 'And I won't be able to catch the plane. I've only just found out . . . it's most annoying. There's a later train . . . I particularly want to get to London tonight.'

'Done,' I said. 'Suits me fine.'

He smiled, still frowning simultaneously. 'Thanks. And here are the keys to my car. It's in the multi-storey park opposite the Europa building.' He told me its number and position. 'Drive yourself home.'

'I'll drive to your house and leave the car there,' I said. 'Easier than bringing it over tomorrow.'

'If you're sure . . .' I nodded, giving him my train ticket.

'A friend who lives up here was going to run me back to the airport,' he said. 'I'll get him to take you instead.'

'Have you heard from your wife?' I asked.

'That's just it . . . she wrote to say we'd have a trial reconciliation and she'd be coming home today. If I stay away all night she'll never believe I had a good reason . . . She'll be gone again.'

'Miss the meeting,' I suggested.

'It's too important, especially now I've got your help. I suppose you couldn't explain to her, if she's there, that I'm on my way?'

'Of course,' I said.

So the friend whisked me off to the airport and I flew to Heathrow, collected the car, drove to

Hampstead, explained to Mrs Gibbons, who promised to wait, and arrived home two and a half hours early. Elizabeth was pleased, even if Mrs Woodward wasn't.

Sunday morning. Elizabeth's mother didn't come.

Ten-fifteen, ten-thirty. Nothing. At eleven someone telephoned from the health farm and said they were so sorry, my mother-in-law was in bed with a virus infection, nothing serious, don't worry, she would ring her daughter as soon as she was a little better.

I told Elizabeth. 'Oh well,' she said philosophically, 'we'll have a nice cosy day on our own.'

I smiled at her and kept the shocking disappointment out of my face.

'Do you think Sue Davies would pop along for a moment while I get some whisky?' I asked.

'She'd get it for us.'

'I'd like to stretch my legs . . .'

She smiled understandingly and rang Sue, who came at twelve with flour down the sides of her jeans. I hurried round corners to the nearest phone box and gave the Huntersons' number. The bell rang there again and again, but no one answered. Without much hope I got the number of Virginia Water station and rang there: no, they said, there was no young woman waiting outside in an estate car. They hadn't seen one all morning. I asked for the Huntersons' number again. Again, no reply.

Feeling flat I walked back to our local pub and

bought the whisky, and tried yet again on the telephone too publicly installed in the passage there.

No answer. No Gail.

I went home.

Sue Davis had read out to Elizabeth my piece in the *Blaze*.

'Straight between the eyeballs,' she observed cheerfully. 'I must say, Ty, no one would connect the punch you pack in that paper with the you we know.'

'What's wrong with the him you know?' asked Elizabeth with real anxiety under the surface gaiety. She hated people to think me weak for staying at home with her. She never told anyone how much nursing she needed from me: always pretended Mrs Woodward did everything. She seemed to think that what I did for her would appear unmanly to others; she wanted in public a masculine never-touch-the-dishes husband, and since it made her happy I played that role except when we were alone.

'Nothing's wrong with him,' Sue protested. She looked me over carefully. 'Nothing at all.'

'What did you mean, then?' Elizabeth was smiling still, but she wanted an answer.

'Oh . . . only that this Ty is so quiet, and that one . . .' she pointed to the paper, 'bursts the eardrums.' She put her head on one side, summing me up, then turned to Elizabeth with the best of motives and said: 'This one is so gentle . . . that one is tough.'

'Gentle nothing,' I said, seeing the distress under

472

Elizabeth's laugh. 'When you aren't here, Sue, I throw her round the room and black her eyes regularly on Fridays.' Elizabeth relaxed, liking that. 'Stay for a drink,' I suggested to Sue, 'now that I've fetched it.'

She went, however, back to her half-baked Yorkshire pudding, and I avoided discussing what she had said by going out to the kitchen and rustling up some omelettes for lunch. Elizabeth particularly liked them, and could eat hers with the new feeding gadget, up to a point. I helped her when her wrist tired, and made some coffee and fixed her mug in its holder.

'Do you really know where the horse is?' she asked.

'Tiddely Pom? Yes, of course.'

'Where is it?'

'Dark and deadly secret, honey,' I said. 'I can't tell anyone, even you.'

'Oh, go on,' she urged. 'You know I won't tell either.'

'I'll tell you next Sunday.'

Her nose wrinkled. 'Thanks for nothing.' The pump heaved away, giving her breath. 'You don't think anyone would try to ... well ... *make* you tell. Where he is, I mean.' More worry, more anxiety. She couldn't help it. She was always on the edge of a precipice, always on the distant look-out for anything which would knock her over.

'Of course not, honey. How could they?'

'I don't know,' she said; but her eyes were full of horrors.

'Stop fussing,' I said with a smile. 'If anyone threatened me with anything really nasty, I'd say quick enough where he is. No horse is worth getting in too deep for.' Echoes of Dembley. The matrix which nurtured the germ. No one would sacrifice themselves or their families for the sake of running a horse.

Elizabeth detected the truth in my voice and was satisfied. She switched on the television and watched some fearful old movie which bored me to death. Three o'clock came and went. Even if I'd gone to Virginia Water, I would have been on the way back again. And I'd had Friday night. Rare, unexpected Friday night. Trouble was, the appetite grew on what it fed on, as someone else once said. The next Sunday was at the wrong end of a telescope.

Drinks, supper, jobs for Elizabeth, bed. No one else called, no one telephoned. It crossed my mind once or twice as I lazed in the armchair in our customary closed-in little world, that perhaps the challenge implicit in my column had stirred up, somewhere, a hive of bees.

Buzz buzz, busy little bees. Buzz around the *Blaze*. And don't sting me.

I spent all Monday in and around the flat. Washed the van, wrote letters, bought some socks, kept off race trains from Leicester.

Derry telephoned twice to tell me (*a*) that Tiddely Pom was flourishing, and (*b*) the Roncey children had sent him a stick of peppermint rock.

'Big deal,' I said.

'Not bad kids.'

'You'll enjoy fetching them.'

He blew a raspberry and hung up.

Tuesday morning I walked to the office. One of those brownish late November days, with saturated air and a sour scowl of fog to come. Lights shone out brightly at 11 a.m. People hurried along Fleet Street with pinched, mean eyes working out whose neck to scrunch on the next rung of the ladder, and someone bought a blind man's matches with a poker chip.

Luke-John and Derry wore moods to match.

'What's the matter?' I asked mildly.

'Nothing's happened,' Derry said.

'So?'

'So where's our reaction?' Luke-John enquired angrily. 'Not a letter. No one's phoned, even. Unless,' he brightened, 'unless Charlie Boston's boys have called on you with a few more threats?'

'They have not.'

Relapse into gloom for the sports desk. I alone wasn't sorry the article had fallen with a dull thud. If it had. I thought it was too soon to be sure. I said so.

'Hope you're right, Ty,' Luke-John said sceptically. 'Hope it hasn't all been a coincidence . . . Bert Checkov and the non-starters . . . hope the *Blaze* hasn't wasted its time and money for nothing on Tiddely Pom . . .'

'Charlie Boston's boys were not a coincidence.'

'I suppose not.' Luke-John sounded as though he

thought I might have misunderstood what the Boston boys had said.

'Did your friend in Manchester find out any more about Charlie B?' I asked.

Luke-John shrugged. 'Only that there was some talk about his chain of betting shops being taken over by a bigger concern. But it doesn't seem to have happened. He is still there, anyway, running the show.'

'Which bigger concern?'

'Don't know.'

To pass the time we dialled four of the biggest London bookmaking businesses which had chains of betting shops all over the country. None of them admitted any immediate interest in buying out Charlie Boston. But one man was hesitant, and when I pressed him, he said, 'We did put out a feeler, about a year ago. We understood there was a foreign buyer also interested. But Boston decided to remain independent and turned down both offers.'

'Thanks,' I said, and Luke-John commented that that took us a long way, didn't it. He turned his attention crossly to a pile of letters which had flooded in contradicting one of the football writers, and Derry began to assess the form for the big race on Boxing Day. All over the vast office space the Tuesday picking of teeth and scratching of scabs proceeded without haste, the slow week still lumbering. Tuesday was gossip day. Wednesday, planning. Thursday, writing. Friday, editing. Saturday, printing. Sunday, *Blaze* away. And on

Mondays the worked-on columns lit real fires or wrapped fish and chips. No immortality for a journalist.

Tuesday was also *Tally* day. Neither at home nor at the office had a copy come for me by post. I went downstairs to the next-door magazine stand, bought one, and went back inside the *Blaze*.

The pictures were off-beat and rather good, the whole article well presented. One had to admit that Shankerton knew his stuff. I forgave him his liberties with my syntax.

I picked up Derry's telephone and got through to the *Tally* despatch department. As expected, they didn't send free copies to the subjects of any articles: not their policy. Would they send them? Oh sure, give us the addresses, we'll let you have the bill. I gave them the six addresses, Huntersons, Ronceys, Sandy Willis, Colly Gibbons, Dermot Finnegan, Willie Ondroy.

Derry picked up the magazine and plodded through the article, reading at one third Luke-John's wide-angled speed.

'Deep, deep,' he said ironically, putting it down. 'One hundred and fifty fathoms.'

'Sixty will go in tax.'

'A hard life,' Derry sighed. 'But if you hadn't picked on Roncey, we would never have cottoned on to this non-starter racket.'

Nor would I have had any cracked ribs. With them, though, the worst was over. Only coughing, sneezing, laughing, and taking running jumps were sharply undesirable. I had stopped eating Elizabeth's pills. In another week, the cracks would have knitted.

'Be seeing you,' I said to Derry. Luke-John waved a freckled farewell hand. Carrying *Tally* I went down in the lift and turned out of the front door up towards the Strand, bound for a delicatessen shop which sold Austrian apple cake which Elizabeth liked.

Bought the cake. Came out into the street. Heard a voice in my ear. Felt a sharp prick through my coat abeam the first lumbar vertebra.

'It's a knife, Mr Tyrone.'

I stood quite still. People could be stabbed to death in busy streets and no one noticed until the body cluttered up the fairway. Killers vanished into crowds with depressing regularity.

'What do you want?' I said.

'Just stay where you are.'

Standing on the Fleet Street pavement, holding a magazine and a box of apple cake. Just stay where you are. For how long?

'For how long?' I said.

He didn't answer. But he was still there, because his knife was. We stood where we were for all of two minutes. Then a black Rolls rolled to a silent halt at the kerb directly opposite where I stood. The door to the back seat swung open.

'Get in,' said the voice behind me.

I got in. There was a chauffeur driving, all black

uniform and a stolid acne-scarred neck. The man with the knife climbed in after me and settled by my side. I glanced at him, I knew I'd seen him somewhere before, didn't know where. I put *Tally* and the apple cake carefully on the floor. Sat back. Went for a ride.

CHAPTER TEN

We turned north into the Aldwych and up Drury Lane to St Giles Circus. I made no move towards escape, although we stopped several times at traffic lights. My companion watched me warily, and I worked on where I had seen him before and still came up with nothing. Up Tottenham Court Road. Left, right, left again. Straight into Regent's Park and round the semi-circle. Stopped smoothly at the turnstile entrance to the Zoo.

'Inside,' said my companion, nodding.

We stepped out of the car, and the chauffeur quietly drove off.

'You can pay,' I remarked.

He gave me a quick glance, tried to juggle the money out of his pocket one-handed, and found he couldn't manage it if he were to be of any use with his knife.

'No,' he said. 'You pay. For us both.'

I paid, almost smiling. He was nowhere near as dangerous as he wanted to be thought.

We checked through the turnstiles. 'Where now?' I said.

'Straight ahead. I'll tell you.'

The Zoo was nearly empty. On that oily Tuesday November lunch time, not even the usual bus loads from schools. Birds shrieked mournfully above the aviary and a notice board said the vultures would be fed at three.

A man in a dark overcoat and black homburg hat was sitting on a seat looking towards the lions' outdoor compounds. The cages were empty. The sun-loving lions were inside under the sun lamps.

'Over there,' said my companion, nodding.

We walked across. The man in the black homburg watched us come. Every line of his clothes and posture spoke of money, authority, and high social status, and his manner of irritating superiority would have done credit to the Foreign Office. As Dembley had said, his subject matter was at variance with his appearance.

'Did you have any trouble?' he asked.

'None at all,' said the knife man smugly.

A bleak expression crept into pale grey eyes as cold as the stratosphere. 'I am not pleased to hear it.'

The accent in his voice was definite but difficult. A thickening of some consonants, a clipping of some vowels.

'Go away, now,' he said to the knife man. 'And wait.'

My nondescript abductor in his nondescript raincoat nodded briefly and walked away, and I nearly remembered where I'd seen him. Recollection floated up, but not far enough.

'You chose to come,' the man in the homburg said flatly.

'Yes and no.'

He stood up. My height, but thicker. Yellowish skin, smooth except for a maze of wrinkles round his eyes. What I could see of his hair was nearly blond, and I put his age down roughly as five or six years older than myself.

'It is cold outside. We will go in.'

I walked with him round inside the Big Cats' House, where the strong feral smell seemed an appropriate background to the proceedings. I could guess what he wanted. Not to kill: that could have been done in Fleet Street or anywhere on the way. To extort. The only question was how.

'You show too little surprise,' he said.

'We were waiting for some ... reaction. Expecting it.'

'I see.' He was silent, working it out. A bored-looking tiger blinked at us lazily, claws sheathed inside rounded pads, tail swinging a fraction from side to side. I sneered at him. He turned and walked three paces and three paces back, round and round, going nowhere.

'Was last week's reaction not enough for you?'

'Very useful,' I commented. 'Led us straight to Charlie Boston. So kind of you to ask. That makes you a sidekick of his.'

He gave me a blazingly frosty glare. 'I *employ* Boston.'

I looked down, not answering. If his pride were as easily stung as that he might give me more answers than I gave him.

'When I heard about it I disapproved of what they did on the train. Now, I am not so sure.' His voice was quiet again, the voice of culture, diplomacy, tact.

'You didn't order it, then?'

'I did not.'

I ran my hand along the thick metal bar which kept visitors four feet away from the animals' cages. The tiger looked tame, too gentle to kill. Too indifferent to maul, to maim, to scrape to the bone.

'You know what we want,' said the polite tiger by my side. 'We want to know where you have hidden the horse.'

'Why?' I said.

He merely blinked at me.

I sighed. 'What good will it do you? Do you still seriously intend to try to prevent it from running? You would be much wiser to forget the whole thing and quietly fold your tent and steal away.'

'You will leave that decision entirely to me.' Again, the pride stuck out a mile. I didn't like it. Few enemies were as ruthless as those who feared a loss of face. I began to consider before how wide an acquaintance-ship the face had to be preserved. The wider, the worse for me.

'Where is it?'

'Tiddely Pom?' I said.

'Tiddely Pom.' He repeated the name with fastidious disgust. 'Yes.'

'Quite safe.'

'Mr Tyrone, stop playing games. You can't hide for ever from Charlie Boston.'

I was silent. The tiger yawned, showing a full set of fangs. Nasty.

'They could do more damage next time,' he said.

I looked at him curiously, wondering if he seriously thought I would crumble under so vague a threat. He stared straight back and was unmoved when I didn't answer. My heart sank slightly. More to come.

'I suspected,' he said conversationally, 'when I heard that you were seen at Plumpton races the day following Boston's ill-judged attack, that physical pressure would run us into too much difficulty in your case. I see that this assessment was correct. I directed that a different lever should be found. We have, of course, found it. And you will tell us where the horse is hidden.'

He took out the black crocodile wallet and removed from it a small sheet of paper, folded once. He gave it to me. I looked. He saw the deep shock in my face and he smiled in satisfaction.

It was a photo-copy of the bill of the hotel where I had stayed with Gail. Mr and Mrs Tyrone, one double room.

'So you see, Mr Tyrone, that if you wish to keep

this interesting item of news from your wife, you must give us the address we ask.'

My mind tumbled over and over like a dry-cleaning machine and not a useful thought came out.

'So quiet, Mr Tyrone? You really don't like that, do you? So you will tell us. You would not want your wife to divorce you, I am sure. And you have taken such pains to deceive her that we are certain you know she would throw you out if she discovered this . . .' He pointed to the bill. 'How would she like to know that your mistress is coloured? We have other dates, too. Last Sunday week, and the Sunday before that. Your wife will be told it all. Wealthy women will not stand for this sort of thing, you know.'

I wondered numbly how much Gail had sold me for.

'Come along, Mr Tyrone. The address.'

'I need time,' I said dully.

'That's right,' he said calmly. 'It takes time to sink in properly, doesn't it? Of course you can have time. Six hours. You will telephone us at precisely seven o'clock this evening.' He gave me a plain white card with numbers on it. 'Six hours is all, Mr Tyrone. After that, the information will be on its way to your wife, and you will not be able to stop it. Do you clearly understand?'

'Yes,' I said. The tiger sat down and shut its eyes. Sympathetic.

'I thought you would.' He moved away from me

towards the door. 'Seven o'clock precisely. Good day, Mr Tyrone.'

With erect easy assurance he walked straight out of the Cat House, turned a corner, and was gone. My feet seemed to have become disconnected from my body. I was going through the disjointed floating feeling of irretrievable disaster. A disbelieving part of my mind said that if I stayed quite still the nutcracker situation would go away.

It didn't, of course. But after a while I began to think normally instead of in emotional shock waves; began to look for a hole in the net. I walked slowly away from the tiger, out into the unwholesome air and down towards the gate, all my attention turned inward. Out of the corner of my eye I half caught sight of my abductor in his raincoat standing up a side path looking into an apparently empty wire-netted compound, and when I'd gone out of the turnstile on to the road it hit me with a thump where I'd seen him before. So significant a thump that I came to a rocking halt. Much had urgently to be understood.

I had seen him at King's Cross station while I waited for Gail. He had been standing near me: had watched her all the way from the Underground until she had reached me. Looking for a lever. Finding it.

To be watching me at King's Cross, he must have followed me from the *Blaze*.

Today, he had picked me up outside the *Blaze*.

I walked slowly, thinking about it. From King's

Cross in the morning I had gone on the train to Newcastle, but I hadn't come back on my return ticket. Colly Gibbons had. I'd taken that unexpected roundabout route home, and somewhere, maybe back at Newcastle races, I'd shaken off my tail.

Someone also must either have followed Gail, or have gone straight into the hotel to see her after I had left. I baulked at thinking she would sell me out with my imprint still on our shared sheets. But maybe she would. It depended on how much they had offered her, I supposed. Five hundred would have tempted her mercenary heart too far.

No one but Gail could have got a receipt from the hotel. No one but Gail knew of the two Sunday afternoons. No one but Gail thought my wife was rich. I coldly faced the conclusion that I had meant little to her. Very little indeed. My true deserts. I had sought her out because she could dispense sex without involvement. She had been consistent. She owed me nothing at all.

I reached the corner and instinctively turned my plodding steps towards home. Not for twenty paces did I realize that this was a desperate mistake.

Gail didn't know where I lived. She couldn't have told them. They didn't know the true facts about Elizabeth: they thought she was a rich woman who would divorce me. *They picked me up this morning outside the* Blaze . . . At the same weary pace I turned right at the next crossing.

If the man in the black homburg didn't know where I lived, the Raincoat would be following to find out. Round the next corner I stopped and looked back through the thick branches of a may bush, and there he was, hurrying. I went on slowly as before, heading round imperceptibly towards Fleet Street.

The Homburg Hat had been bluffing. He couldn't tell Elizabeth about Gail, because he didn't know where to find her. Ex-directory telephone. My address in none of the reference books. By sheer luck I twice hadn't led them straight to my own front door.

All the same, it couldn't go on for ever. Even if I fooled them until after the Lamplighter, one day, somehow, they would tell her what I'd done.

First they buy you, then they blackmail, Bert Checkov had said. Buy Gail, blackmail me. All of a piece. I thought about blackmail for three long miles back to the *Blaze*.

Luke-John and Derry were surprised to see me back. They made no comment on a change in my appearance. I supposed the inner turmoil didn't show.

'Have any of the crime reporters a decent pull with the police?' I asked.

Derry said, 'Jimmy Sienna might have. What do you want?'

'To trace a car number.'

'Someone bashed that ancient van of yours?' Luke-John asked uninterestedly.

'Hit and run,' I agreed with distant accuracy.

'We can always try,' Derry said with typical helpfulness. 'Give me the number, and I'll go and ask him.'

I wrote down for him the registration of Homburg Hat's Silver Wraith.

'A London number,' Derry remarked. 'That might make it easier.' He took off across the room to the crime desk and consulted a mountainous young man with red hair.

I strolled over to the deserted news desk and with a veneer of unconcern over a thumping heart dialled the number Homburg Hat had told me to ring at seven. It was three-eighteen. More than two hours gone out of six.

A woman answered, sounding surprised.

'Are you sure you have the right number?' she said.

I read it out to her.

'Yes, that's right. How funny.'

'Why is it funny?'

'Well, this is a public phone box. I had just shut the door and was going to make a call when the phone started ringing . . . Are you *sure* you have the right number?'

'I can't have,' I said. 'Where is this phone box, exactly?'

'It's one of a row in Piccadilly underground station.'

I thanked her and rang off. Not much help.

489

Derry came back and said Jimmy Sienna was doing what he could, good job it was Tuesday, he was bored and wanted something to pass the time with.

I remembered that I had left my copy of *Tally* and Elizabeth's cake on the floor of the Rolls. Debated whether or not to get replacements. Decided there was no harm in it, and went out and bought them. I didn't see Raincoat, but that didn't mean he wasn't there or that they hadn't swapped him for someone I wouldn't know.

Derry said Jimmy Sienna's police friend was checking the registration number but would use his discretion as to whether it was suitable to pass on to the *Blaze*. I sat on the side of Derry's desk and bit my nails.

Outside, the fog which had been threatening all day slowly cleared right away. It would. I thought about unobserved exits under the bright Fleet Street lights.

At five, Luke-John said he was going home, and Derry apologetically followed. I transferred myself to Jimmy Sienna's desk and bit my nails there instead. When he too was lumbering to his feet to leave, his telephone finally rang. He listened, thanked, scribbled.

'There you are,' he said to me. 'And good luck with the insurance. You'll need it.'

I read what he'd written. The Silver Wraith's number had been allocated to an organization called 'Hire Cars Lucullus'.

*

I left the *Blaze* via the roof. *Tally*, apple cake, and mending ribs complicated the journey, but after circumnavigating ventilation shafts and dividing walls I walked sedately in through the fire door of the next-door newspaper, a popular daily in the full flood of going to press.

No one asked me what I was doing. I went down in the lift to the basement and out to the huge garage at the rear where rows of yellow vans stood ready to take the wet ink bundles off to the trains. I knew one of the drivers slightly, and asked him for a lift.

'Sure, if you want Paddington.'

'I do.' I wanted anywhere he was going.

'Hop in, then.'

I hopped in, and after he was loaded he drove briskly out of the garage, one indistinguishable van among a procession. I stayed with him to Paddington, thanked him, and backtracked home on the underground, as certain as I could be that no one had followed.

I beat Mrs Woodward to six by two minutes but had no heart for the game.

From six-thirty to seven I sat in the armchair holding a glass of whisky and looking at Elizabeth, trying to make up a beleaguered mind.

'Something worrying you, Ty,' she said, with her ultra-sensitive feeling for trouble.

'No, honey.'

The hands galloped round the clock. At seven o'clock precisely I sat absolutely still and did nothing at all. At five past I found I had clenched my teeth so hard that I was grinding them. I imagined the telephone box in Piccadilly Circus, with Homburg Hat or Raincoat or the chauffeur waiting inside it. Tiddely Pom was nothing compared with Elizabeth's peace of mind, and yet I didn't pick up the receiver. From seven onwards the clock hands crawled.

At half past Elizabeth said again, with detectable fear, 'Ty, there *is* something wrong. You never look so ... so bleak.'

I made a great effort to smile at her as usual, but she wasn't convinced. I looked down at my hands and said with hopeless pain, 'Honey, how much would it hurt you if I went ... and slept with a girl?'

There was no answer. After an unbearable interval I dragged my head up to look at her. Tears were running down her cheeks. She was swallowing, trying to speak.

From long, long habit I pulled a tissue out of the box and wiped her eyes, which she couldn't do for herself.

'I'm sorry,' I said uselessly. 'I'm sorry ...'

'Ty ...' She never had enough breath for weeping. Her mouth strained open in her need for more air.

'Honey, don't cry. Don't cry. Forget I said it. You

know I love you, I'd never leave you, Elizabeth, honey, dear Elizabeth, don't cry . . .'

I wiped her eyes again and cursed the whim which had sent me down to the Huntersons for *Tally*. I could have managed without Gail. Without anyone. I had managed without for most of eleven years.

'Ty.' The tears stopped. Her face looked less strained. 'Ty.' She gulped, fighting for more breath. 'I can't bear to think about it.'

I stood beside her, holding the tissue, wishing she didn't have to.

'We never talk about sex,' she said. The Spirashell heaved up her chest, let it drop, rhythmically. 'I don't want it any more . . . you know that . . . but sometimes I remember . . . how you taught me to like it . . .' Two more tears welled up. I wiped them away. She said, 'I haven't ever asked you . . . about girls . . . I couldn't, somehow.'

'No,' I said slowly.

'I've wondered sometimes . . . if you ever have, I mean . . . but I didn't really want to know . . . I know I would be too jealous . . . I decided I'd never ask you . . . because I would want you to say yes . . . and yet I know that's selfish . . . I've always been told men are different, they need women more . . . is it true?'

'Elizabeth,' I said helplessly.

'I didn't expect you ever to say anything . . . after all these years . . . yes, I would be hurt, if I knew . . . I couldn't help it . . . Why did you ask me? I wish you hadn't.'

'I would never have said anything,' I said with regret, 'but someone is trying to blackmail me.'

'Then . . . you *have* . . .?'

'I'm afraid so.'

'Oh.' She shut her eyes. 'I see.'

I waited, hating myself. The tears were over. She never cried for long. She physically couldn't. If she progressed into one of her rare bursts of rebellious anger she would utterly exhaust herself. Most wives could scream or throw things. Elizabeth's furies were the worse for being impotent. It must have been touch and go, because when she spoke her voice was low, thick, and deadly quiet.

'I suppose you couldn't afford to be blackmailed.'

'No one can.'

'I know it's unreasonable of me to wish you hadn't told me. To wish you hadn't done it at all. Any man who stays with a paralysed wife ought to have *something* . . . So many of them pack up and leave altogether . . . I know you say you never will and I do mostly believe it, but I must be such an unbearable burden to you . . .'

'That,' I said truthfully, 'is just not true.'

'It must be. Don't tell me . . . about the girl.'

'If I don't, the blackmailer will.'

'All right . . . get it over quickly . . .'

I got it over quickly. Briefly. No details. Hated

myself for having to tell her, and knew that if I hadn't, Homburg Hat wouldn't have stopped his leverage with the whereabouts of Tiddely Pom. Blackmailers never did. Don't sell your soul, Bert Checkov said. Don't sell your column. Sacrifice your wife's peace instead.

'Will you see her again?' she asked.

'No.'

'Or . . . anyone else?'

'No.'

'I expect you will,' she said. 'Only if you do . . . don't tell me . . . Unless of course someone tries to blackmail you again . . .'

I winced at the bitterness in her voice. Reason might tell her that total lifelong celibacy was a lot to demand, but emotion had practically nothing to do with reason, and the tearing emotions of any ordinary wife on finding her husband unfaithful hadn't atrophied along with her muscles. I hadn't expected much else. She would have to have been a saint or a cynic to have laughed it off without a pang, and she was neither of those things, just a normal human being trapped in an abnormal situation. I wondered how suspicious she would be in future of my most innocent absences; how much she would suffer when I was away. Reassurance, always tricky, was going to be doubly difficult.

She was very quiet and depressed all evening. She wouldn't have any supper, wouldn't eat the apple cake. When I washed her and did the rubs and the other intimate jobs I could almost feel her thinking about the other body my hands had touched. Hands, and much else. She looked sick and strained, and for almost the first time since her illness, embarrassed. If she could have done without me that evening, she would have.

I said, meaning it, 'I'm sorry, honey.'

'Yes.' She shut her eyes. 'Life's just bloody, isn't it.'

CHAPTER ELEVEN

The uncomfortable coolness between Elizabeth and myself persisted in the morning. I couldn't go on begging for a forgiveness she didn't feel. At ten I said I was going out, and saw her make the first heart-rending effort not to ask where.

'Hire Cars Lucullus' hung out in a small plushy office in Stratton Street, off Piccadilly. Royal blue Wilton carpet, executive-type acre of polished desk, tasteful prints of vintage cars on dove grey walls. Along one side, a wide gold-upholstered bench for wide gold-upholstered clients. Behind the desk, a deferential young man with Uriah Heep eyes.

For him I adopted a languid voice and my best imitation of the homburg hat manners. I had, I explained, left some property in one of his firm's cars, and I hoped he could help me get it back.

We established gradually that no, I had not hired one of their cars, and no, I did not know the name of the man who had, he had merely been so kind as to give me a lift. Yesterday.

Ah. Then had I any idea which car . . .?

A Rolls-Royce, a Silver Wraith.

They had four of those. He briefly checked a ledger, though I suspected he didn't need to. All four had been out on hire yesterday. Could I describe the man who had given me a lift? 'Certainly. Tallish, blondish, wearing a black homburg. Not English. Possibly South African.'

'Ah. Yes.' He had no need to consult the ledger this time. He put his spread fingertips carefully down on the desk. 'I regret, sir, I cannot give you his name.'

'But surely you keep records?'

'This gentleman puts great store on privacy. We have been instructed not to give his name and address to anyone.'

'Isn't that a bit odd?' I said, raising eyebrows.

He considered judicially. 'He is a regular customer. We would, of course, give him any service he asked for, without question.'

'I suppose it wouldn't be possible to . . . um . . . purchase the information?'

He tried to work some shock into his deference. It was barely skin deep.

'Was your lost property very valuable?' he asked.

Tally and apple cake. 'Very,' I said.

'Then I am sure our client will return it to us. If you

would let us have your own name and address, perhaps we could let you know?'

I said the first name I thought of, which nearly came out as Kempton Park. 'Kempton Jones. 31 Cornwall Street.'

He wrote it down carefully on a scratch pad. When he had finished, I waited. We both waited.

After a decent interval he said, 'Of course, if it is really important, you could ask in the garage . . . they would let you know as soon as the car comes in, whether your property is still in it.'

'And the garage is where?' The only listed number and address of the Lucullus Cars had been the office in Stratton Street.

He studied his fingertips. I produced my wallet and resignedly sorted out two fivers. The twenty-five for the bookmaker's clerk's information about Charlie Boston's boys I had put down to expenses and the *Blaze* had paid. This time I could be on my own. Ten pounds represented six weeks' whisky, a month's electricity, three and a half days of Mrs Woodward, one and a half weeks' rent.

He took it greedily, nodded, gave me a hypocritical obsequious smile, and said, 'Radmor Mews, Lancaster Gate.'

'Thanks.'

'You do understand, sir, that it's more than my job is worth to give you our client's name?'

'I understand,' I said. 'Principles are pretty things.'

Principles were luckily not so strongly held in Radnor Mews. The foreman sized me up and another tenner changed hands. Better value for money this time.

'The chauffeur comes here to collect the car, see? We never deliver it or supply a driver. Unusual, that. Still, the client is always right, as long as he pays for it, I always say. This foreigner, see, he likes to travel in style when he comes over here. 'Course, most of our trade is like that. Americans mostly. They hire a car and a driver for a week, two weeks, maybe three. We drive them all over, see, Stratford, Broadway, the Cotswold run most often, and Scotland a good deal too. Never have all the cars in here at once, there'd hardly be room, see, four Silver Wraiths for a start, and then two Austin Princesses, and three Bentleys and a couple of large Wolseleys.'

I brought him back gently to the Silver Wraith in question.

'I'm telling you, aren't I?' he protested. 'This foreign chap, he takes a car, always a Rolls mind you, though of course not always the same one, whenever he's over here. Started coming just over a year ago, I'd say. Been back several times, usually just for three or four days. Longer this time, I'd say. Let's see, the chauffeur came for a car last week. I could look it up ... Wednesday. Yes, that's right. What they do, see, is the chauffeur flies over first, picks up the car and then drives out to

Heathrow to fetch his gent off the next flight. Neat, that. Shows money, that does.'

'Do you know where they fly from?'

'From? Which country? Not exactly. Mind, I think it varies. I know once it was Germany. But usually farther than that, from somewhere hot. The chauffeur isn't exactly chatty, but he's always complaining how cold it is here.'

'What is the client's name?' I asked patiently.

'Oh sure, hang on a minute. We always put the booking in the chauffeur's name, see, it's easier, being Ross. His gent's name is something chronic. I'll have to look back.'

He went into his little boarded cubicle of an office and looked back. It took him nearly twenty minutes, by which time he was growing restive. I waited, making it plain I would wait all day. For ten pounds he could keep on looking. He was almost as relieved as I was when he found it.

'Here it is, look.' He showed me a page in a ledger, pointing to a name with a black-rimmed fingernail. 'That one.'

There was a pronunciation problem, as he'd said.

Vjoersterod.

'Ross is easier,' the foreman repeated. 'We always put Ross.'

'Much easier,' I agreed. 'Do you know where I could find them, or where they keep the car while they're in England?'

He sniffed immediately, shutting the ledger with his finger in the page.

'Can't say as I do, really. Always a pretty fair mileage on the clock, though. Goes a fair way in the three or four days, see? But then that's regular with our cars, most times. Mind you, I wouldn't say that this Ross and his gent go up to Scotland, not as far as that.'

'Birmingham?' I suggested.

'Easily. Could be, easily. Always comes back immaculate, I'll say that for Ross. Always clean as a whistle. Why don't you ask in the front office, if you want to find them?'

'They said they couldn't help me.'

'That smarmy crumb,' he said disgustedly, 'I'll bet he knows, though. Give him his due, he's good at that job, but he'd sell his grandmother if the price was right.'

I started to walk in the general direction of Fleet Street, thinking. Vjoersterod had to be the real name of Homburg Hat. Too weird to be an alias. Also, the first time he had hired a Silver Wraith from Hire Cars Lucullus he would have had to produce cast iron references and a passport at least. The smarmy crumb was no fool. He wouldn't let five thousand pounds' worth of machinery be driven away without being certain he would get it back.

Vjoersterod. South African of Afrikaner stock.

Nothing like Fleet Street if one wanted information. The only trouble was, the man who might have heard of Vjoersterod worked on the racing page of a deadly rival to the *Blaze*. I turned into the first telephone box and rang his office. Sure, he agreed cautiously, he would meet me in the Devereux for a pint and a sandwich. He coped manfully with stifling any too open speculation about what I wanted. I smiled, and crossed the road to catch a bus. A case of who pumped who. He would be trying to find out what story I was working on, and Luke-John would be slightly displeased if he were successful and scooped the *Blaze*.

Luke-John and Derry were both among the crowd in the Devereux. Not so, Mike de Jong. I drank a half-pint while Luke-John asked me what I planned to write for Sunday.

'An account of the Lamplighter, I suppose.'

'Derry can do that.'

I lowered my glass, shrugging. 'If you like.'

'Then you,' said Luke-John, 'can do another follow-up to the Tiddely Pom business. Whether he wins or loses, I mean. Give us a puff for getting him to the starting gate.'

'He isn't there yet,' I pointed out.

Luke-John sniffed impatiently. 'There hasn't been a vestige of trouble. No reaction at all. We've frightened them off, that's what happened.'

I shook my head, wishing we had. Asked about the reports on Tiddely Pom and the Roncey children.

'All OK,' said Derry cheerfully. 'Everything going smoothly.'

Mike de Jong appared in the doorway, a quick, dark, intense man with double strength glasses and a fringe of black beard outlining his jaw. Caution rolled over him like a sea mist when he saw who I was with, and most of the purposefulness drained out of his stride. It took too much manoeuvring to get Luke-John and Derry go to into the further bar to eat without me, and Luke-John left looking back over his shoulder with smouldering suspicion, wanting to know why.

Mike joined me, his sharp face alight with appreciation.

'Keeping secrets from the boss, eh?'

'Sometimes he's butter-fingered with other people's TNT.'

Mike laughed. The cogs whirred round in his high-speed brain. 'So what you want is private? Not for the *Blaze*?'

I dodged a direct answer. 'What I want is very simple. Just anything you may have heard about a fellow countryman of yours.'

'Who?' His accent was a carbon copy, clipped and flat.

'A man called Vjoersterod.'

There was a tiny pause while the name sank in, and then he choked on his beer. Recovered, and pretended someone had jogged his elbow. Made a playing-for-time fuss about brushing six scattered drops off his trouser leg. Finally he ran out of alibis and looked back at my face.

'Vjoersterod?' His pronunciation was subtly different from mine. The real thing.

'That's right,' I agreed.

'Yes . . . well, Ty . . . why do you ask me about him?'

'Just curiosity.'

He was silent for thirty seconds. Then he said carefully again, 'Why are you asking about him?' Who pumped who.

'Oh, come on,' I said in exasperation. 'What's the big mystery? All I want is a bit of gen on a harmless chap who goes racing occasionally . . .'

'*Harmless.* You must be mad.'

'Why?' I sounded innocently puzzled.

'Because he's . . .' He hesitated, decided I wasn't on to a story, and turned thoroughly helpful. 'Look here, Ty, I'll give you a tip, free, gratis, and for nothing. Just steer clear of anything to do with that man. He's poison.'

'In what way?'

'He's a bookmaker, back home. Very big business, with branches in all the big cities and a whole group of them round Johannesburg. Respectable enough on the surface. Thousands of perfectly ordinary people bet with him. But there have been some dreadful rumours . . .'

'About what?'

'Oh . . . blackmail, extortion, general high-powered thuggery. Believe me, he is not good news.'

'Then why don't the police ...?' I suggested tentatively.

'Why don't they? Don't be so naïve, Ty. They can't find anyone to give evidence against him, of course.'

I sighed. 'He seemed so charming.'

Mike's mouth fell open and his expression became acutely anxious.

'You've *met* him?'

'Yeah.'

'Here ... in England?'

'Well, yes, of course.'

'Ty ... for God's sake ... keep away from him.'

'I will,' I said with feeling. 'Thanks a lot, Mike. I'm truly grateful.'

'I'd hate anyone I liked to tangle with Vjoersterod,' he said, the genuine friendship standing out clear in his eyes, unexpectedly affecting. Then with a born newspaper man's instinct for the main chance, a look of intense curiosity took over.

'What did he want to talk about with you?' he asked.

'I really don't know,' I said, sounding puzzled.

'Is he going to get in touch with you again?'

'I don't know that, either.'

'Hm ... give me a ring if he does, and I'll tell you something else.'

'Tell me now.' I tried hard to make it casual.

He considered, shrugged, and friendship won again over journalism. 'All right. It's nothing much. Just that

I too saw him here in England; must have been nine or ten months ago, back in the spring.' He paused.

'In that case,' I said, 'why ever were you so horrified when I said I'd met him?'

'Because when I saw him he was in the buffet on a race train, talking to another press man. Bert Checkov.'

With an enormous effort, I kept my mildly puzzled face intact.

Mike went on without a blink. 'I warned Bert about him later, just like I have you. In here, actually. Bert was pretty drunk. He was always pretty drunk after that.'

'What did he say?' I asked.

'He said I was three months too late.'

Mike didn't know any more. Bert had clammed up after that one indiscretion and had refused to elaborate or explain. When he fell out of the window, Mike had wondered. Violent and often unexplained deaths among people who had had dealings with Vjoersterod were not unknown, he said. When I said I had met Vjoersterod, it had shocked him. He was afraid for me. Afraid I could follow Bert down on to the pavement.

I put his mind at rest. After what he'd told me, I would be forewarned, I said.

'I wonder why he got his hooks into Bert...' Mike said, his eyes on the middle distance, all the cogs whirring.

'I've no idea,' I said, sighing, and distracted his attention on to another half-pint and a large ham sandwich. Luke-John's thin freckled face looked over his shoulder, and he turned to him with a typical bounce, as if all his body were made of springs.

'So how's the Gospel Maker? What's cooking on the *Blaze*?'

Luke-John gave him a thin smile. He didn't care for his Fleet street nickname; nor for puns in general. Nor, it seemed, for Mike de Jong's puns in particular. Mike received the message clearly, sketched me a farewell, and drifted over to another group.

'What did he want?' Luke-John asked sharply.

'Nothing,' I said mildly. 'Just saying hullo.'

Luke-John gave me a disillusioned look, but I knew very well that if I told him at that stage about Vjoersterod he would dig until he stumbled on the blackmail, dig again quite ruthlessly to find out how I could have been blackmailed, and then proceed to mastermind all subsequent enquiries with a stunning absence of discretion. Vjoersterod would hear his steam-roller approach clean across the country. Luke-John was a brilliant sports editor. As a field marshal his casualty list would have been appalling.

He and Derry drank around to closing time at three, by which time the crowd had reduced to Sunday writers only. I declined their invitation to go back with them to the doldrums of the office, and on reflection telephoned to the only member of the racing authorities I knew well enough for the purpose.

Eric Youll at thirty-seven was the youngest and newest of the three stewards of the National Hunt Committee, the ruling body of steeplechasing. In two years, by natural progression he would be Senior Steward. After that, reduced to the ranks until re-elected for another three-year term. As a steward he made sense because until recently he had himself ridden as an amateur, and knew at first hand all the problems and mechanics of racing. I had written him up in the *Blaze* a few times and we had been friendly acquaintances for years. Whether he either could or would help me now was nonetheless open to doubt.

I had a good deal of trouble getting through to him, as he was a junior sprig in one of the grander merchant banks. Secretaries with bored voices urged me to make an appointment.

'Right now,' I said, 'will do very well.'

After the initial shock the last voice conceded that right now Mr Youll could just fit me in. When I got there, Mr Youll was busily engaged in drinking a cup of tea and reading the *Sporting Life*. He put them both down without haste, stood up, and shook hands.

'This is unexpected,' he said. 'Come to borrow a million?'

'Tomorrow, maybe.'

He smiled, told his secretary on the intercom to bring me some tea, offered me a cigarette, and leaned

back in his chair, his manner throughout one of indecision and uncertainty. He was wary of me and of the
purpose of my visit. I saw that uneasy expression
almost every day of my life: the screen my racing
friends erected when they weren't sure what I was
after, the barrier that kept their secrets from publi-
cation. I didn't mind that sort of withdrawal. Understood it. Sympathized. And never printed anything
private, if I could help it. There was a very fine edge to
be walked when one's friends were one's raw material.

'Off the record,' I assured him. 'Take three deep
breaths and relax.'

He grinned and tension visibly left his body. 'How
can I help you then?'

I waited until the tea had come and been drunk,
and the latest racing news chewed over. Then, without
making much of it, I asked him if he'd ever heard of
a bookmaker called Vjoersterod.

His attention pin-pointed itself with a jerk.

'Is that what you've come to ask?'

'For openers.'

He drummed his fingers on the desk. 'Someone
showed me your column last week and the week
before . . . Stay out of it, Ty.'

'If you racing bigwigs know what's going on and
who is doing it, why don't you stop him?'

'How?'

The single bald word hung in the air, cooling. It told

me a lot about the extent of their knowledge. They should have known how.

'Frankly,' I said at last, 'that's your job, not mine. You could of course ban all ante-post betting, which would knock the fiddle stone dead.'

'That would be highly unpopular with the Great British Public. Anyway your articles have hit the ante-post market badly enough as it is. One of the big firms was complaining to me bitterly about you a couple of hours ago. Their Lamplighter bets are down by more than twenty per cent.'

'Then why don't they do something about Charlie Boston?'

He blinked. 'Who?'

I took a quiet breath. 'Well, now ... just what do the stewards know about Vjoersterod?'

'Who is Charlie Boston?'

'You first,' I said.

'Don't you trust me?' He looked hurt.

'No,' I said flatly. 'You first.'

He sighed resignedly and told me that all the stewards knew about Vjoersterod was hearsay, and scanty at that. None of them had ever actually seen him, and wouldn't know him if they did. A member of the German horse racing authorities had sent them a private warning that Vjoersterod was suspected of stage managing a series of non-starting ante-post favourites in big races in Germany, and that they had heard rumours he was now beginning to operate in England.

Pursuit had almost cornered him in Germany. He was now moving on. The British stewards had noted the alarming proportion of non-starters in the past months and were sure the German authorities were right, but although they had tried to find out the facts from various owners and trainers, they had been met with only a brick wall of silence everywhere.

'It's a year since Vjoersterod came here first,' I remarked. 'A year ago he bought out Charlie Boston's string of betting shops round Birmingham and started raking in the dough. He also found a way to force Bert Checkov to write articles which persuaded ante-post punters to believe they were on to a good thing. Vjoersterod chose a horse, Checkov wrote it up, Vjoersterod stopped it running, and bingo, the deed was done.'

His face was a mixture of astonishment and satisfaction. 'Ty, are you sure of your facts?'

'Of course I am. If you ask me, both the bookmakers and the authorities have been dead slow on the trail.'

'And how long exactly have you been on it?'

I grinned, conceding the point. I said, 'I met Vjoersterod yesterday. I referred to Charlie Boston being his partner and he told me he owned Charlie Boston. Vjoersterod wanted to know where Tiddely Pom was.'

He stared. 'Would you . . . um . . . well, if necessary, testify to that?'

'Certainly. But it would be only my word against his. No corroboration.'

'Better than anything we've had before.'

'There might be a quicker way to get results, though.'

'How?' he asked again.

'Find a way to shut Charlie Boston's shops, and you block off Vjoersterod's intakes. Without which there is no point in him waiting around to stop any favourites. If you can't get him convicted in the courts, you might at least freeze him out, back to South Africa.'

There was another long pause during which he thought complicated thoughts. I waited, guessing what was in his mind. Eventually, he said it.

'How much do you want for your help?'

'An exclusive for the *Blaze*.'

'As if I couldn't guess . . .'

'It will do,' I conceded, 'if the *Blaze* can truthfully claim to have made the ante-post market safe for punters to play in. No details. Just a few hints that but for the libel laws, all would and could be revealed.'

'Why ever do you waste your time with that dreadful rag?' he exclaimed in exasperation.

'Good pay,' I said. 'It's a good paper to work for. And it suits me.'

'I'll promise you one thing,' he said, smiling. 'If through you personally we get rid of Vjoersterod, I'll take it regularly.'

From Eric Youll's bank, I went home. If the youngest steward did his stuff, Vjoersterod's goose was on its way to the oven and would soon be cooked. He might of course one day read the *Blaze* and send someone to carve up the chef. It didn't trouble me much. I didn't believe it would happen.

Elizabeth had had Mrs Woodward put her favourite rose pink, white-embroidered sheets on the bed. I looked at her searchingly. Her hair had been done with particular care. Her makeup was flawless.

'You look pretty,' I said tentatively.

Her expression was a mixture of relief and misery. I understood with a sudden rocking wince what had led her to such scenery painting: the increased fear that if she were bitchy I would leave her. No matter if I'd earned and deserved the rough side of her tongue; I had to be placated at all costs, to be held by the best she could do to appear attractive, to be obliquely invited, cajoled, entreated to stay.

'Did you have a good day?' Her voice sounded high and near to cracking point.

'Quite good . . . how about a drink?'

She shook her head, but I poured her one all the same, and fixed it in the clip.

'I've asked Mrs Woodward to find someone to come and sit with me in the evenings,' she said. 'So that you can go out more.'

'I don't want to go out more,' I protested.

'You must do.'

514

'Well, I don't.' I sat down in the armchair and took a hefty mouthful of nearly neat whisky. At best, I thought, in an unbearable situation alcohol offered postponement. At worst, aggravation. And anyway it was too damned expensive, nowadays, to get drunk.

Elizabeth didn't answer. When I looked at her, I saw she was quietly crying again. The tears rolled down past her ears and into her hair. I took a tissue out of the box and dried them. Had she but known it, they were harder for me to bear than any amount of fury.

'I'm getting old,' she said. 'And you still look so young. You look . . . strong . . . and dark . . . and young.'

'And you look pale and pretty and about fifteen. So stop fretting.'

'How old is . . . that girl?'

'You said you didn't want to hear about her.'

'I suppose I don't really.'

'Forget her,' I said. 'She is of no importance. She means nothing to me. Nothing at all.' I sounded convincing, even to myself. I wished it were true. In spite of the scope of her betrayal, in a weak inner recess I ached to be able to sleep with her again. I sat with the whisky glass in my hand and thought about her on the white rug and in her own bed and in the hotel, and suffered dismally from the prospect of the arid future.

After a while I pushed myself wearily to my feet and went to fix the supper. Fish again. Mean little bits of frozen plaice. I cooked and ate them with aversion and fed Elizabeth when her wrist tired on the gadget.

All evening she kept up the pathetic attempt to be nice to me, thanking me exaggeratedly for every tiny service, apologizing for needing me to do things for her which we had both for years taken for granted, trying hard to keep the anxiety, the embarrassment, and the unhappiness out of her eyes and voice, and nowhere near succeeding. She couldn't have punished me more if she had tried.

Late that evening Tiddely Pom developed violent colic.

Norton Fox couldn't get hold of Luke-John or Derry, who had both long gone home. The *Blaze* never divulged home addresses, however urgent the enquiry. Norton didn't know my telephone number either; didn't know anyone who did.

In a state of strong anxiety, and on his vet's advice, he rang up Victor Roncey and told him where his horse was, and what they were doing to save its life.

CHAPTER TWELVE

I heard about it in the morning. Roncey telephoned at ten-thirty, when I was sitting in the writing-room looking vacantly at the walls and trying to drum up some preliminary gems for my column on Sunday. Mrs Woodward had gone out to the launderette, and Elizabeth called me to the telephone with two rings on the bell over my head: two rings for come at once but not an emergency. Three rings for 999. Four for panic.

Roncey had calmed down from the four-ring stage he had clearly been in the night before. He was calling, he said, from Norton Fox's house, where he had driven at once after being given the news. I sorted out that he had arrived at 2 a.m. to find that the vet had got Tiddely Pom over the worst, with the stoppage in the horse's gut untangling into normal function. Norton Fox had given Roncey a bed for the rest of the night, and he had just come in from seeing Tiddely Pom walk and trot out at morning exercise. The horse was showing surprisingly few ill effects from his rocky experience, and it was quite likely he would be fit enough to run in the Lamplighter on Saturday.

I listened to his long, brisk detailed saga with uncomfortable alarm. There were still two whole days before the race. Now that Roncey knew where he was, Tiddley Pom's safety was halved. When he had come to the end of the tale I asked him whether anyone had tried to find out from him at home where his horse had gone.

'Of course they did,' he said. 'Exactly as you said. Several other newspapers wanted to know. Most of them telephoned. Three or four actually turned up at the farm, and I know they asked Peter and Pat as well as me. Some of their questions were decidedly tricky. I thought at the time you'd been quite right, we might have let it slip if we'd known ourselves.'

'When did these people come to the farm? What did they look like?'

'They didn't look like anything special. Just nondescript. One of them was from the *Evening Peal*, I remember. All the enquiries were on Sunday and Monday, just after your article came out.'

'No one turned up in a Rolls?' I asked.

He laughed shortly. 'They did not.'

'Were any of your visitors tallish, thickish, blondish, with a faintly yellow skin and a slightly foreign accent?'

'None that I saw were like that. One or two saw only the boys, because they called while I was in Chelmsford. You could ask them, if you like.'

'Maybe I will,' I agreed. 'No one tried any threats?'

'No, I told your sports editor that. No one has tried any pressure of any sort. To my mind, all your elaborate precautions have been a waste of time. And now that I know where Tiddely Pom is, you may as well tell me where my family is too . . .'

'I'll think about it,' I said. 'Would you ask Norton Fox if I could have a word with him?'

He fetched Norton, who apologized for bursting open the secrecy, but said he didn't like the responsibility of keeping quiet when the horse was so ill.

'Of course not. It can't be helped,' I said. 'As long as it goes no further than Roncey himself it may not be too bad, though I'd prefer . . .'

'His sons knew, of course,' Norton interrupted. 'Though I don't suppose that matters.'

'*What?*' I said.

'Roncey told one of his sons where he was. He telephoned to him just now. He explained to me that he couldn't remember your telephone number, but he'd got it written down somewhere at home, from having rung you up before sometime. So he rang his son . . . Pat, I think he said . . . and his son found it for him. I think he, the son, asked Roncey where he was calling from, because Roncey said that as everyone had stopped enquiring about where the horse was he didn't see any harm in his son knowing, so he told him.'

'Damn it,' I said. 'The man's a fool.'

'He might be right.'

'And he might be wrong,' I said bitterly. 'Look, Norton, I suppose there was no question of Tiddely Pom's colic being a misjudged case of poisoning?'

'For God's sake, Ty ... no. It was straightforward colic. How on earth could he have been poisoned? For a start, no one knew then who he was.'

'And now?' I asked. 'How many of your lads know now that he is Tiddely Pom?'

There was a brief, supercharged silence.

'All of them,' I said flatly.

'Some of them knew Roncey by sight,' he explained. 'And they'd all read the *Blaze*. So they put two and two together.'

One of them would soon realize he could earn a fiver by ringing up a rival newspaper. Tiddely Pom's whereabouts would be as secret as the Albert Memorial. Tiddely Pom, at that moment, was a certain non-starter for the Lamplighter Gold Cup.

Even if Victor Roncey thought that the opposition had backed out of the project, I was certain they hadn't. In a man like Vjoersterod, pride would always conquer discretion. He wouldn't command the same respect in international criminal circles if he turned out and ran just because of a few words in the *Blaze*. He wouldn't, therefore, do it.

*

520

At the four-day declaration stage, on the Tuesday, Roncey had confirmed with Weatherbys that his horse would be a definite runner. If he now withdrew him, as he could reasonably do because of the colic, he would forfeit his entry fee, a matter of fifty pounds. If he left his horse at Norton's still intending to run, he would forfeit a great deal more.

Because I was certain that if Tiddely Pom stayed where he was, he would be lame, blind, doped, or dead by Saturday morning.

Norton listened in silence while I outlined these facts of life.

'Ty, don't you think you are possibly exaggerating . . .?'

'Well,' I said with a mildness I didn't feel, 'how many times will you need to have Brevity – or any other of your horses – taken out of the Champion Hurdle at the last moment without any explanation, before you see any need to do something constructive in opposition?'

There was a short pause. 'Yes,' he said. 'You have a point.'

'If you will lend me your horsebox, I'll take Tiddely Pom off somewhere else.'

'Where?'

'Somewhere safe,' I said non-committally. 'How about it?'

'Oh, all right,' he sighed. 'Anything for a quiet life.'

'I'll come as soon as I can.'

'I'll repel boarders until you do.' The flippancy in his voice told me how little he believed in any threat to the horse. I felt a great urge to leave them to it, to let Roncey stew in his own indiscretion, to let Vjoersterod interfere with the horse and stop it running, just to prove I was right. Very childish urge indeed. It didn't last long, because in my way I was as stubborn as Vjoersterod. I wasn't going to turn and run from him either, if I could help it.

When I put the telephone receiver back in its special cradle, Elizabeth was looking worried and with a more normal form of anxiety.

'That Tiddely Pom,' I said lightly, 'is more trouble than a bus load of eleven-year-old boys. As I expect you gathered, I'll have to go and shift him off somewhere else.'

'Couldn't someone else do it?'

I shook my head. 'Better be me.'

Mrs Woodward was still out. I filled in the time until her return by ringing up Luke-John and giving him the news that the best laid plan had gone astray.

'Where are you taking the horse, then?'

'I'll let you know when I get there.'

'Are you sure it's necessary . . .?' he began.

'Are you,' I interrupted, 'sure the *Blaze* can afford to take any risk, after boasting about keeping the horse safe?'

'Hm.' He sighed. 'Get on with it, then.'

When Mrs Woodward came back I took the van

and drove to Berkshire. With me went Elizabeth's best effort at a fond wifely farewell. She had even offered her mouth for a kiss, which she did very rarely, as mouth to mouth kissing interfered with her frail breathing arrangements and gave her a feeling of suffocation. She liked to be kissed on the cheek or forehead, and never too often.

I spent most of the journey worrying about whether I should not after all have allowed myself to be blackmailed: whether any stand against pressure was a luxury when compared with the damage I'd done to Elizabeth's weak hold on happiness. After all the shielding, which had improved her physical condition, I'd laid into her with a bulldozer. Selfishly. Just to save myself from a particularly odious form of tyranny. If she lost weight or fretted to breakdown point it would be directly my fault; and either or both seemed possible.

A hundred and fifty guineas, plus expenses, less tax. A study in depth. *Tally* had offered me the deeps. And in I'd jumped.

On the outskirts of London I stopped to make a long and involved telephone call, arranging a destination and care for Tiddely Pom. Norton Fox and Victor Roncey were eating lunch when I arrived at the stables, and I found it impossible to instil into either of them enough of a feeling for urgency to get them to leave their casseroled beef.

'Sit down and have some,' Norton said airily.

'I want to be on my way.'

They didn't approve of my impatience and proceeded to gooseberry crumble and biscuits and cheese. It was two o'clock before they agreed to amble out into the yard and see to the shifting of Tiddely Pom.

Norton had at least had his horsebox made ready. It stood in the centre of the yard with the ramp down. As public an exit as possible. I sighed resignedly. The horsebox driver didn't like handing over to a stranger and gave me some anxious instructions about the idiosyncratic gear change.

Sandy Willis led Tiddely Pom across the yard, up the ramp, and into the centre stall of the three-stall box. The horse looked worse than ever, no doubt because of the colic. I couldn't see him ever winning any Lamplighter Gold Cup. Making sure he ran in it seemed a gloomy waste of time. Just as well, I reflected, that it wasn't to Tiddely Pom himself that I was committed, but to the principle that if Roncey wanted to run Tiddely Pom, he should. Along the lines of 'I disagree that your horse has the slightest chance, but I'll defend to the death your right to prove it.'

Sandy Willis finished tying the horse into his stall and took over where the box driver left off. Her instructions on how Tiddely Pom was to be managed were detailed and anxious. In her few days with the horse she had already identified herself with its wellbeing. As Norton had said, she was one of the best of his lads. I wished I could take her too, but it was useless expecting Norton to let her go, when she also looked after Zig Zag.

She said, 'He will be having proper care, won't he?'

'The best,' I assured her.

'Tell them not to forget his eggs and beer.'

'Right.'

'And he hates having his ears messed about with.'

'Right.'

She gave me a long searching look, a half smile, and a reluctant farewell. Victor Roncey strode briskly across to me and unburdened himself along similar lines.

'I want to insist that you tell me where you are taking him.'

'He will be safe.'

'Where?'

'Mr Roncey, if you know where, he is only half as safe. We've been through all this before . . .'

He pondered, his glance darting about restlessly, his eyes not meeting mine. 'Oh, very well,' he said finally, with impatience. 'But it will be up to you to make sure he gets to Heathbury Park in good time on Saturday.'

'The *Blaze* will arrange that,' I agreed. 'The Lamplighter is at three. Tiddely Pom will reach the racecourse stables by noon, without fail.'

'I'll be there,' he said. 'Waiting.'

I nodded. Norton joined us, and the two of them discussed this arrangement while I shut up the ramp with the help of the hovering box driver.

'What time do you get Zig Zag to Heathbury?' I asked Norton, pausing before I climbed into the cab.

'Midday,' he said. 'It's only thirty-two miles . . . He'll be setting off at about eleven.'

I climbed into the driving seat and looked out of the window. The two men looked back, Roncey worried, Norton not. To Norton I said, 'I'll see you this evening, when I bring the horsebox back.' To Roncey, 'Don't worry, he'll be quite safe. I'll see you on Saturday. Ring the *Blaze*, as before, if you'd like to be reassured tonight and tomorrow.'

I shut the window, sorted out the eccentric gears, and drove Tiddely Pom gently out of the yard and up the lane to the village. An hour later than I intended, I thought in disgust. Another hour for Mrs Woodward. My mind shied away from the picture of Elizabeth waiting for me to come back. Nothing would be better. Nothing would be better for a long time to come. I felt the first stirrings of resentment against Elizabeth and at least had the sense to realize that my mind was playing me a common psychological trick. The guilty couldn't stand the destruction of their self-esteem involved in having to admit they were wrong, and wriggled out of their shame by transferring it into resentment against the people who had made them feel it. I resented Elizabeth because I had wronged her. Of all ridiculous injustices. And of all ridiculous injustices, one of the most universal.

I manoeuvred the heavy horsebox carefully through

the small village and set off northeastwards on the road over the Downs, retracing the way I had come from London. Wide rolling hills with no trees except a few low bushes leaning sideways away from the prevailing wind. No houses. A string of pylons. Black furrows in a mile of plough. A bleak early December sky, a high sheet of steel-grey cloud. Cold, dull, mood-matching landscape.

There was very little traffic on the unfenced road, which served only Norton's village and two others beyond. A blue-grey Cortina appeared on the brow of the next hill, coming towards me, travelling fast. I pulled over to give him room, and he rocked past at a stupid speed for the space available.

My attention was so involved with Elizabeth that it was several seconds before the calamity got through. With a shattering jolt the casually noticed face of the Cortina's driver kicked my memory to life. It belonged to one of Charlie Boston's boys from the train. The big one. With the brass knuckles.

December couldn't stop the prickly sweat which broke out on my skin. I put my foot on the accelerator and felt Tiddely Pom's weight lurch behind me from the sudden spurt. All I could hope for was that the big man had been too occupied judging the width of his car to look up and see me.

He had, of course, had a passenger.

I looked in the driving mirror. The Cortina had gone out of sight over the hill. Charlie Boston's boys hurrying towards Norton Fox's village was no mild coincidence, but Tiddley Pom's whereabouts must have been transmitted with very little delay for them to be here already, especially if they had had to come from Birmingham. Just who, I wondered grimly, had told who where Tiddely Pom was to be found. Not that it mattered at that moment. All that mattered was to get him lost again.

I checked with the driving mirror. No Cortina. The horsebox was pushing sixty-five on a road wiser for forty. Tiddely Pom's hooves clattered inside his stall. He didn't like the swaying. He would have to put up with it until I got him clear of the Downs road, which was far too empty and far too visible from too many miles around.

When I next looked in the mirror there was a pale speck on the horizon two hills behind. It might not be them, I thought. I looked again. It was them. I swore bitterly. The speedometer needle crept to sixty-eight. That was the lot. My foot was down on the floorboards and they were gaining. Easily.

There was no town close enough to get lost in, and once on my tail they could stay there all day, waiting to find out where I took Tiddley Pom. Even in a car it would have been difficult to lose them: in a lumbering horsebox, impossible. Urgent appraisal of a depressing situation came up with only a hope that Charlie Boston's boys would again be propelled by more aggression than sense.

They were. They came up fast behind me, leaning on the horn. Maybe they thought I hadn't had time to see *them* as they went past me the other way, and wouldn't know who wanted to pass.

If they wanted to pass, they didn't want to follow. I shut my teeth. If they wanted to pass, it was now, it was here, that they meant to make certain that Tiddely Pom didn't run in the Lamplighter. What they intended to do about me was a matter which sent my mending ribs into a tizzy. I swallowed. I didn't want another hammering like the last time, and this time they might not be so careful about what they did or didn't rupture.

I held the horsebox in the centre of the road so that there wasn't room enough for their Cortina to get by. They still went on blowing the horn. Tiddely Pom kicked his stall. I took my foot some way off the accelerator and slowed the proceedings down to a more manageable forty-five. They would guess I knew who they were. I didn't see that it gave them any advantage.

A hay lorry appeared round a hill ahead with its load over-hanging the centre of the road. Instinctively I slowed still further, and began to pull over. The Cortina's nose showed sharply in the wing mirror, already up by my rear axle. I swung the horsebox back into the centre of the road, which raised flashing headlights from the driver of the advancing hay lorry. When I was far too close to a radiator to radiator confrontation he started blowing his horn furiously as well. I swung back to my side of the road when he was almost stationary from standing rigidly on his brakes, and glimpsed a furious face and a shaking fist as I swerved past. Inches to spare. Inches were enough.

The Cortina tried to get past in the short second before the horsebox was re-established on the crown of the road. There was a bump, this time, as I cut across its bows. It dropped back ten feet, and stayed there. It would only stay there, I thought despairingly, until Charlie Boston's boys had got what they came for.

Less than a mile ahead lay my likely Waterloo, in the shape of a crossroads. A halt sign. It was I who would have to halt. Either that or risk hitting a car speeding legitimately along the major road, risk killing some innocent motorist, or his wife, or his child . . . Yet if I stopped, the Cortina with its faster acceleration would pass me when I moved off again, whether I turned right, as I had intended to, or left, back to London, or went straight on, to heaven knew where.

There wouldn't be anyone at the crossroads to give me any help. No police car sitting there waiting for custom. No AA man having a smoke. No life-saving bystander of any sort. No troop of United States cavalry to gallop up in the nick of time.

I changed down into second to climb a steepish hill and forgot Norton's box driver's instructions. For a frightening moment the gears refused to mesh and the horsebox's weight dragged it almost to a standstill.

Then the cogs slid together, and with a regrettable jolt we started off again. Behind me, Charlie Boston's boys still wasted their energy and wore out their battery by almost non-stop blasts on their horn.

The horsebox trundled to the top of the hill, and there already, four hundred yards down the other side, was the crossroads.

I stamped on the accelerator. The horsebox leaped forward. Charlie Boston's boys had time to take in the scene below, and to realize that I must be meaning not to halt at the sign. In the wing mirror, I watched him accelerate to keep up, closing enough to stick to me whatever I did at the crossroads.

Two hundred yards before I got there, I stood on the brake pedal as if the road ended in an abyss ten yards ahead. The reaction was more than I'd bargained for. The horsebox shuddered and rocked and began to spin. Its rear slewed across the road, hit the verge, rocked again. I feared the whole high-topped structure would overturn. Instead, there was a thudding, crunching, anchoring crash as the Cortina bounced on and off at the rear.

The horsebox screeched and slid to a juddering stop. Upright. Facing the right way.

I hauled on the hand brake and was out of the cab on to the road before the glass from the Cortina had stopped tinkling on to the tarmac.

The grey-blue car had gone over on to its side and was showing its guts to the wind. It lay a good twenty yards behind the horsebox, and from the dented look of the roof it had rolled completely over before stopping. I walked back towards it, wishing I had a weapon of some sort, and fighting an inclination just to drive off and leave without looking to see what had happened to the occupants.

There was only one of them in the car. The big one; the driver. Very much alive, murderously angry, and in considerable pain from having his right ankle trapped and broken among the pedals. I turned my back on him and ignored his all too audible demands for assistance. Revenge, I assessed, would overcome all else if I once got within reach of his hands.

The second Boston boy had been flung out by the crash. I found him on the grass verge, unconscious and lying on his face. With anxiety I felt for his pulse, but he too was alive. With extreme relief I went back to the horsebox, opened the side door, and climbed in to take a look at Tiddely Pom. He calmly swivelled a disapproving eye in my direction and began to evacuate his bowels.

'Nothing much wrong with you, mate,' I said aloud. My voice came out squeaky with tension. I wiped my hand round my neck, tried to grin, felt both like copying Tiddely Pom's present action and being sick.

The horse really did not seem any the worse for his highly unorthodox journey. I took several deep breaths, patted his rump, and jumped down again into the road. Inspection of the damage at the back of the horsebox revealed a smashed rear light and a dent in the sturdy off rear wing no larger than a soup plate. I hoped that Luke-John would agree to the *Blaze* paying for the repairs. Charlie Boston wouldn't want to.

His unconscious boy was beginning to stir. I watched him sit up, put his hands on his head, begin to remember what had happened. I listened to his big colleague still shouting furiously from inside the car. Then with deliberate non-haste I climbed back into the cab of the horsebox, started the engine, and drove carefully away.

I had never intended to go far. I took Tiddely Pom to the safest place I could think of: the racecourse stables at Heathbury Park. There he would be surrounded by a high wall and guarded by a security patrol at night. Everyone entering racecourse stables had to show a pass: even owners were not allowed in unless accompanied by their trainer.

Willy Ondroy, consulted on the telephone, had agreed to take in Tiddely Pom, and to keep his identity a secret. The stables would in any case be open from midday and the guards would be on duty from then on: any time after that, he said, Tiddely Pom would be just one of a number of horses arriving for the following day's racing. Horses which came from more than a hundred miles away normally travelled the day before their race and stayed overnight in the racecourse stables. A distant stable running one horse on Friday and another on Saturday would send them both down on Thursday and leave them both at the racecourse stables for two nights, or possibly even three. Tiddely Pom's two nights' stay would be unremarkable and inconspicuous. The only oddity about him was that he had no lad to look after him, an awkward detail to which Willy Ondroy had promised to find a solution.

He was looking out for me and came across the grass outside the stable block to forestall me from climbing down from the cab. Instead, he opened the door on the passenger side, and joined me.

'Too many of these lads know you by sight,' he said, waving an arm to where two other horseboxes were unloading. 'If they see you, they will know you would not have brought any other horse but Tiddely Pom. And as I understand it, you don't want to land us with the security headache of a bunch of crooks trying to injure him. Right?'

'Right,' I agreed thankfully.

'Drive down this road, then. First left. In through the white gate posts, fork left, park outside the rear door of my house. Right?'

'Right,' I said again, and followed his instructions, thankful for his quick grasp of essentials and his jet formation pilot's clarity of decision.

'I've had a word with the racecourse manager,' he said. 'The stables and security are his pigeon really. Had to enlist his aid. Hope you don't mind. He's a very sound fellow, very sound indeed. He's fixing up a lad to look after Tiddely Pom. Without telling him what the horse is, naturally.'

'That's good,' I said with relief.

I stopped the horsebox and we both disembarked. The horse, Willy Ondroy said, could safely stay where he was until the racecourse manager came over for him. Meanwhile, would I care for some tea? He looked at his watch. Three-fifty. He hesitated. Or a whisky, he added.

'Why a whisky?' I asked.

'I don't know. I suppose you look as though you need it.'

'You may be right,' I said, dredging up a smile. He looked at me assessingly, but how could I tell him that I'd just risked killing two men to bring Tiddely Pom safe and unfollowed to his door. That I had been extremely lucky to get away with merely stopping them. That only by dishing out such violence had I avoided a second beating of proportions I couldn't contemplate. It wasn't really surprising that I looked as if I needed a whisky. I did. It tasted fine.

CHAPTER THIRTEEN

Norton Fox was less than pleased when I got back.

He heard me rumble into the yard and came out of his house to meet me. It was by then full dark, but there were several external lights, and more light flooded out of open stable doors as the lads bustled around with the evening chores. I parked, climbed stiffly down from the cab, and looked at my watch. Five-fifty. I'd spent two hours on a roundabout return journey to fool the box driver over the distance I'd taken Tiddely Pom. Heathbury Park and back was probably the driver's most beaten track; he would know the mileage to a hundred yards, recognize it instantly he saw it on the clock, know for a certainty where the horse was, and make my entire afternoon a waste of time.

'You're in trouble, Ty,' Norton said, reaching me and frowning. 'What in God's name were you thinking of? First the man delivering my hay gets here in a towering rage and says my horsebox drove straight at him with some maniac at the wheel and that there'd be an accident if he was any judge, and the next thing is we hear there has been an accident over by Long Barrow crossroads involving a horsebox and I've had the police here making enquiries . . .'

'Yes.' I agreed. 'I'm very sorry, Norton. Your horsebox has a dent in it, and a broken rear light. I'll apologize to the hay lorry driver. And I guess I'll have to talk to the police.'

Dangerous driving. Putting it mildly. Very difficult to prove it was a case of self-preservation.

Norton looked near to explosion. 'What on earth were you *doing*?'

'Playing cowboys and Indians,' I said tiredly. 'The Indians bit the dust.'

He was not amused. His secretary came out to tell him he was wanted on the telephone, and I waited by the horsebox until he came back, gloomily trying to remember the distinction between careless, reckless, and dangerous, and the various penalties attached. Failing to stop. Failing to report an accident. How much for those?

Norton came back less angry than he went. 'That was the police,' he said abruptly. 'They still want to see you. However, it seems the two men involved in the crash have vanished from the casualty department in the hospital and the police have discovered that the Cortina was stolen. They are less inclined to think that the accident was your fault, in spite of what the hay lorry driver told them.'

'The men in the Cortina were after Tiddely Pom,' I said flatly. 'And they damn nearly got him. Maybe you could tell Victor Roncey that there is some point to our precautions, after all.'

'He's gone home,' he said blankly. I began to walk across the dark stable yard to where I'd left my van, and he followed me, giving me directions about how to find the police station.

I stopped him. 'I'm not going there. The police can come to me. Preferably on Monday. You tell them that.'

'Why on Monday?' He looked bewildered. 'Why not now?'

'Because,' I spelled it out, 'I can tell them roughly where to find those men in the Cortina and explain what they were up to. But I don't want the police issuing any warrants before Monday, otherwise the whole affair will be *sub judice* and I won't be able to get a squeak into the *Blaze*. After all this trouble, we've earned our story for Sunday.'

'You take my breath away,' he said sounding as if I had. 'And the police won't like it.'

'For God's sake, don't tell them,' I said in exasperation. 'That was for your ears only. If and when they ask you where I am, simply say I will be getting in touch with them, and that you don't know where I live, and that they could reach me through the *Blaze*, if they want me.'

'Very well,' he agreed doubtfully. 'If you're sure. But

it sounds to me as though you're landing yourself in serious trouble. I wouldn't have thought Tiddely Pom was worth it.'

'Tiddely Pom, Brevity, Polyxenes, and all the rest ... individually none of them was worth the trouble. That's precisely why the racket goes on.'

His disapproving frown lightened into a half-smile. 'You'll be telling me next that the *Blaze* is more interested in justice than sensationalism.'

'It says so. Often,' I agreed sardonically.

'Huh,' said Norton. 'You can't believe everything you read in the papers.'

I drove home slowly, tired and depressed. Other times, trouble had been a yeast lightening the daily bread. A positive plus factor. Something I needed. But other times, trouble hadn't bitterly invaded my marriage or earned me such a savage physical attack.

This time, although I was fairly confident that Tiddely Pom would start in his race, the successful uncovering and extermination of a racing scandal was bringing me none of the usual upsurging satisfaction. This time, dust and ashes. This time, present grief and a grey future.

I stopped on the way and rang the *Blaze*. Luke-John had left for the day. I got him at home.

'Tiddely Pom is in the racecourse stables at Heathbury,' I said. 'Guarded by an ex-policeman and a large Alsatian. The clerk of the course and the racecourse manager both know who he is, but no one else does. OK?'

'Very, I should think.' He sounded moderately pleased, but no more. 'We can take it as certain now that Tiddely Pom will start in the Lamplighter. It's made a good story, Ty, but I'm afraid we exaggerated the danger.'

I disillusioned him. 'Charlie Boston's boys were three miles from Norton Fox's stable by two-thirty this afternoon.'

'Christ,' he said. 'So it's really true . . .'

'You've looked at it so far as a stunt for the *Blaze*.'

'Well . . .'

'Well, so it is,' I agreed. 'Anyway, Charlie Boston's boys had a slight accident with their car, and they are now back to square one as they don't know where I took Tiddely Pom.'

'What sort of accident?'

'They ran into the back of the horsebox. Careless of them. I put the brakes on rather hard, and they were following a little too close.'

A shocked silence. Then he said, 'Were they killed?'

'No. Hardly bent.' I gave him an outline of the afternoon's events. Luke-John's reaction was typical and expected, and the enthusiasm was alive again in his voice.

'Keep away from the police until Sunday.'

'Sure thing.'

'This is great, Ty.'

'Yeah,' I said.

'Knock out a preliminary version tonight and bring it in with you in the morning,' he said. 'Then we can discuss it tomorrow, and you can phone me in the final touches from Heathbury after the Lamplighter on Saturday.'

'All right.'

'Oh, and give Roncey a ring, would you, and tell him the horse is only safe thanks to the *Blaze*.'

'Yes,' I said. 'Maybe I will.'

I put down the receiver and felt like leaving Roncey severely alone. I was tired and I wanted to go home. And when I got home, I thought drearily, there would be no let off, only another dose of self hate and remorse.

Roncey answered the telephone at the first ring and needed no telling. Norton Fox had already been through.

'Tiddely Pom is safe and well looked after,' I assured him.

'I owe you an apology,' he said abruptly.

'Be my guest,' I said.

'Look here, there's something worrying me. Worrying me badly.' He paused, swallowing a great deal of pride. 'Do you . . . I mean, have you any idea . . . how those men appeared so quickly on the scene?'

'The same idea as you,' I agreed. 'Your son, Pat.'

'I'll break his neck,' he said, with real and unfatherly viciousness.

'If you've any sense, you'll let him ride your horses in all their races, not just the unimportant ones.'

'What are you talking about?'

'About Pat's outsize sense of grievance. You put up anyone except him, and he resents it.'

'He's not good enough,' he protested.

'And how will he ever be, if you don't give him the experience? Nothing teaches a jockey faster than riding a good horse in a good race.'

'He might lose,' he said pugnaciously.

'He might win. When did you ever give him the chance?'

'But to give away the secret of Tiddely Pom's whereabouts . . . what would he expect to gain?'

'He was getting his own back, that's all.'

'*All!*'

'There's no harm done.'

'I hate him.'

'Then send him to another stable. Give him an allowance to live on and let him see if he's going to ride well enough to turn professional. That's what he wants. If you stamp on people's ambitions too hard, it's not frantically astonishing if they bite back.'

'It's a son's duty to work for his father. Especially a farmer's son.'

I sighed. He was half a century out of date and no amount of telling from me was going to change him. I said I'd see him on Sunday, and disconnected.

Like his father, I took no pleasure at all in Pat

Roncey's vengeful disloyalty. Understand, maybe. Admire, far from it.

One of the men who came to enquire at Roncey's farm must have sensed Pat's obvious disgruntlement and have given him a telephone number to ring if he ever found out where Tiddely Pom had gone, and wanted to revenge himself on his father. One might give Pat the benefit of enough doubt to suppose that he'd thought he was only telling a rival newspaperman to the *Blaze*; but even so he must have known that a rival newspaper would spread the information to every corner of the country. To the ears which waited to hear. Exactly the same in the end. But because of the speed with which Charlie Boston's boys had reached Norton Fox's village, it must have been Raincoat or the chauffeur, or even Vjoersterod himself who had talked to Pat at the farm.

It had to be Pat. Norton Fox's stable lads might have passed the word on to newspapers, but they couldn't have told Vjoersterod or Charlie Boston because they didn't know they wanted to know, and probably didn't even know they existed.

I drove on, back to London. Parked the van in the garage downstairs. Locked up. Walked slowly and unenthusiastically up to the flat.

'Hi,' said Elizabeth brightly.

'Hi yourself.' I kissed her cheek.

It must have looked, to Mrs Woodward, a normal

greeting. Only the pain we could read in each other's eyes said it wasn't.

Mrs Woodward put on her dark blue coat and checked the time again to make sure it was ten to, not ten after. She'd had three hours extra, but she wanted more. I wondered fleetingly if I could charge her overtime to the *Blaze*.

'We've had our meal,' Mrs Woodward said. 'I've left yours ready to warm up. Just pop it in the oven, Mr Tyrone.'

'Thanks.'

''Night, then, luv,' she called to Elizabeth.

''Night.'

I opened the door for her and she nodded briskly, smiled, and said she'd be there on the dot in the morning. I thanked her appreciatively. She would indeed be there on the dot. Kind, reliable, necessary Mrs Woodward. I hoped the *Tally* cheque wouldn't be too long coming.

Beyond that first greeting Elizabeth and I could find little to say to each other. The most ordinary enquiries and remarks seemed horribly brittle, like a thin sheet of glass over a pit.

It was a relief to both of us when the door bell rang.

'Mrs Woodward must have forgotten something,' I said. It was barely ten minutes since she had left.

'I expect so,' Elizabeth agreed.

I opened the door without a speck of intuition. It swung inward with a rush, weighted and pushed by a heavy man in black. He stabbed a solid leather gloved fist into my diaphragm and when my head came forward chopped down with something hard on the back of my neck.

On my knees, coughing for breath, I watched Vjoersterod appear in the doorway, take in the scene, and walk past me into the room. A black-booted foot kicked the door shut behind him. There was a soft whistling swish in the air and another terrible thump high up between my shoulder blades. Elizabeth cried out. I staggered to my feet and tried to move in her direction. The heavy man in black, Ross, the chauffeur, slid his arm under mine and twisted and locked my shoulder.

'Sit down, Mr Tyrone,' Vjoersterod said calmly. 'Sit there.' He pointed to the tapestry-covered stool Mrs Woodward liked to knit on as there were no arms or back to get in the way of her busy elbows.

'Ty,' Elizabeth's voice rose high with fear. 'What's happening?'

I didn't answer. I felt stupid and sunk. I sat down on the stool when Ross released my arm and tried to work some control into the way I looked at Vjoersterod.

He was standing near Elizabeth's head, watching me with swelling satisfaction.

'So now we know just where we are, Mr Tyrone. Did you really have the conceit to think you could defy me and get away with it? No one does, Mr Tyrone. No one ever does.'

I didn't answer. Ross stood beside me, a pace to the rear. In his right hand he gently swung the thing he had hit me with, a short elongated pear-shaped truncheon. Its weight and crushing power made a joke of Charlie Boston's boys' knuckledusters. I refrained from rubbing the aching places below my neck.

'Mr Tyrone,' Vjoersterod said conversationally, 'where is Tiddely Pom?'

When I still didn't answer immediately he half turned, looked down, and carefully put the toe of his shoe under the switch of the electric point. From there the cable led directly to Elizabeth's breathing pump. Elizabeth turned her head to follow my eyes and saw what he was doing.

'No,' she said. It was high-pitched, terrified. Vjoersterod smiled.

'Tiddely Pom?' he said to me.

'He's in the racecourse stables at Heathbury Park.'

'Ah.' He took his foot away, put it down on the floor. 'You see how simple it is? It's always a matter of finding the right lever. Of applying the right pressure. No horse, I find, is ever worth a really serious danger to a loved one.'

I said nothing. He was right.

'Check it,' Ross said from behind me.

Vjoersterod's eyes narrowed. 'He couldn't risk a lie.'

'He wouldn't be blackmailed. He was out to get

you, and no messing. Check it.' There was advice in
Ross's manner, not authority. More than a chauffeur.
Less than an equal.

Vjoersterod shrugged but stretched out a hand and
picked up the receiver. Telephone enquiries. Heathbury Park racecourse. The clerk of the course's house?
That would do very well.

Willie Ondroy himself answered. Vjoersterod said,
'Mr Tyrone asked me to call you to check if Tiddely
Pom had settled in well . . .'

He listened to the reply impassively, his pale yellow
face immobile. It accounted for the fact, I thought
inconsequentially, that his skin was unlined. He never
smiled; seldom frowned. The only wrinkles were
around his eyes, which I suppose he screwed up against
his native sun.

'Thank you so much,' he said. His best Foreign
Office voice, courteous and charming.

'Ask him which box the horse is in,' Ross said. 'The
number.'

Vjoersterod asked. Willy Ondroy told him.

'Sixty-eight. Thank you. Goodnight.'

He put the receiver carefully back in its cradle and
let a small silence lengthen. I hoped that since he had
got what he came for he would decently go away again.
Not a very big hope to start with, and one which never
got off the ground.

He said, studying his fingernails, 'It is satisfactory, Mr Tyrone, that you do at last see the need to

cooperate with me.' Another pause. 'However, in your case, I would be foolish to think that this state of affairs would last very long if I did nothing to convince you that it must.'

I looked at Elizabeth. She didn't seem to have followed Vjoersterod's rather involved syntax. Her head lay in a relaxed way on the pillow and her eyes were shut. She was relieved that I had told where the horse was: she thought that everything was now all right.

Vjoersterod followed my glance and my thought. He nodded. 'We have many polio victims on respirators in my country. I understand about them. About the importance of electricity. The importance of constant attendance. The razor edge between life and death. I understand it well.'

I said nothing. He said, 'Many men desert wives like this. Since you do not, you would care if harm came to her. Am I right? You have, in fact, just this minute proved it, have you not? You wasted so little time in telling me correctly what I wanted to know.'

I made no comment. He waited a fraction, then went smoothly on. What he said, as Dembley had found out, was macabrely at variance with the way he said it.

'I have an international reputation to maintain. I simply cannot afford to have pipsqueak journalists interfering with my enterprises and trying to hold me up to ridicule. I intend to make it clear to you once and for all, to impress upon you indelibly, that I am not a man to be crossed.'

Ross moved a pace at my side. My skin crawled. I made as good a job as I could of matching Vjoersterod's immobility of expression.

Vjoersterod had more to say. As far as I was concerned, he could go on all night. The alternative hardly beckoned.

'Charlie Boston reports to me that you have put both his men out of action. He too cannot afford such affronts to his reputation. Since all you learned from his warning attentions on the train was to strike back, we will see if my chauffeur can do any better.'

I tucked one foot under the stool, pivoted on it, and on the way to my feet struck at Ross with both hands, one to the stomach, one to the groin. He bent over, taken by surprise, and I wrenched the small truncheon out of his hand, raised it to clip him on the head.

'Ty . . .' Elizabeth's voice rose in an agonized wail. I swung round with the truncheon in my hand and met Vjoersterod's fiercely implacable gaze.

'Drop it.'

He had his toe under the switch. Three yards between us.

I hesitated, boiling with fury, wanting above anything to hit him, knock him out, get rid of him out of my life and most particularly out of the next hour of it. I couldn't risk it. One tiny jerk could cut off the current. I couldn't risk not being able to reach the switch again in time, not with Vjoersterod in front of it and Ross behind me. Under the weight of the Spirashell she would suffocate almost immediately. If I resisted any more I could kill her. He might really do it. Let her die. Leave me to explain her death and maybe even be accused of slaughtering her myself. The unwanted wife bit . . . He didn't know I knew his name or anything about him. He would think he could kill Elizabeth with reasonable safety. I simply couldn't risk it.

I put my arm down slowly and dropped the truncheon on the carpet. Ross, breathing heavily, bent and picked it up.

'Sit down, Mr Tyrone,' Vjoersterod said. 'And stay sitting down. Don't get up again. Do I make myself clear?'

He still had his toe under the switch. I sat down, seething inside, rigid outside, and totally apprehensive. Twice in a fortnight was definitely too much.

Vjoersterod nodded to Ross, who hit me solidly with the truncheon on the back of the shoulder. It sounded horrible. Felt worse.

Elizabeth cried out. Vjoersterod looked at her without pity and told Ross to switch on the television. They both waited while the set warmed up. Ross adjusted the volume to medium loud and changed the channel from a news magazine to song and dance. No neighbours, unfortunately, would call to complain about the noise. The only ones who lived near enough were out working in a nightclub.

Ross had another go with the truncheon. Instinctively I started to stand up . . . to retaliate, to escape, heaven knows.

'Sit down,' Vjoersterod said.

I looked at his toe. I sat down. Ross swung his arm and that time I fell forward off the stool on to my knees.

'Sit,' Vjoersterod said. Stiffly I returned to where he said.

'Don't,' Elizabeth said to him in a wavering voice. 'Please don't.'

I looked at her, met her eyes. She was terrified. Scared to death. And something else. Beseeching. Begging me. With a flash of blinding understanding I realized she was afraid I wouldn't take any more, that I wouldn't think she was worth it, that I would somehow stop them hurting me even if it meant switching off her pump. Vjoersterod knew I wouldn't. It was ironic, I thought mordantly, that Vjoersterod knew me better than my own wife.

It didn't last a great deal longer. It had anyway reached the stage where I no longer felt each blow separately but rather as a crushing addition to an intolerable whole. It seemed as though I had the whole weight of the world across my shoulders. Atlas wasn't even in the race.

I didn't see Vjocrsterod tell Ross to stop. I had the heels of my hands against my mouth and my fingertips in my hair. Some nit on the television was advising

DICK FRANCIS

everyone to keep their sunny side up. Ross cut him off abruptly in mid note.

'Oh God,' Elizabeth said. 'Oh God.'

Vjoersterod's smooth voice dryly comforted her. 'My dear Mrs Tyrone, I assure you that my chauffeur knows how to be a great deal more unpleasant than that. He has, I hope you realize, left your husband his dignity.'

'Dignity,' Elizabeth said faintly.

'Quite so. My chauffeur used to work in the prison service in the country I come from. He knows about humiliation. It would not have been suitable, however, to apply certain of his techniques to your husband.'

'Russia?' she asked. 'Do you come from Russia?'

He didn't answer her. He spoke to me.

'Mr Tyrone, should you try to cross me again, I would allow my chauffeur to do anything he liked. Anything at all. Do you understand?'

I was silent. He repeated peremptorily, 'Do you understand?'

I nodded my head.

'Good. That's a start. But only a start. You will also do something more positive. You will work for me. You will write for me in your newspaper. Whatever I tell you to write, you will write.'

I detached my hands slowly from my face and rested my wrists on my knees.

'I can't,' I said dully.

'I think you will find that you can. In fact you will.

552

You must. And neither will you contemplate resigning from your paper.' He touched the electric switch with his brown polished toe cap. 'You cannot guard your wife adequately every minute for the rest of her life.'

'Very well,' I said slowly. 'I will write what you say.'

'Ah.'

Poor old Bert Checkov, I thought drearily. Seven floors down to the pavement. Only I couldn't insure myself for enough to compensate Elizabeth for having to live for ever in a hospital.

'You can start this week,' Vjoersterod said. 'You can say on Sunday that what you have written for the last two weeks turns out to have no foundation in fact. You will restore the situation to what it was before you started interfering.'

'Very well.'

I put my right hand tentatively over my left shoulder. Vjoersterod watched me and nodded.

'You'll remember that,' he said judiciously. 'Perhaps you will feel better if I assure you that many who have crossed me are now dead. You are more useful to me alive. As long as you write what I say, your wife will be safe, and my chauffeur will not need to attend to you.'

His chauffeur, did he but know it, had proved to be a pale shadow of the Boston boys. For all my fears, it now seemed to me that the knuckledusters had been worse. The chauffeur's work was a bore, a present burden, yet not as crippling as before. No broken ribs.

No all-over weakness. This time I would be able to move.

Elizabeth was close to tears. 'How can you,' she said. 'How can you be so . . . beastly.'

Vjoersterod remained unruffled. 'I am surprised you care so much for your husband after his behaviour with that coloured girl.'

She bit her lip and rolled her head away from him on the pillow. He stared at me calmly. 'So you told her.'

There was no point in saying anything. If I'd told him where Tiddely Pom had been on Tuesday, when he first tried to make me, I would have saved myself a lot of pain and trouble. I would have saved Elizabeth from knowing about Gail. I would have spared her all this fear. Some of Bert Checkov's famous last words floated up from the past . . . 'It's the ones who don't know when to give in who get the worst clobbering . . . in the ring, I mean . . .'

I swallowed. The ache from my shoulders was spreading down my back. I was dead tired of sitting on that stool. Mrs Woodward could keep it, I thought scrappily. I wouldn't want it in the flat any more.

Vjoersterod said to Ross, 'Pour him a drink.'

Ross went over to where the whisky bottle stood on its tray with two glasses and the Malvern Water. The bottle was nearly half full. He unscrewed the cap, picked up one of the tumblers, and emptied into it all the whisky. It was filled to the brim.

Vjoersterod nodded. 'Drink it.'

Ross gave me the glass. I stared at it.

'Go on,' Vjoersterod said. 'Drink it.'

I took a breath to protest. He moved his toe towards the switch. I put the glass to my lips and took a mouthful. Jump through hoops when the man said.

'All of it,' he said. 'Quickly.'

I had eaten nothing for more than twenty-four hours. In spite of a natural tolerance, a tumbler full of alcohol on an empty stomach was not my idea of fun. I had no choice. Loathing Vjoersterod, I drank it all.

'He seems to have learned his lesson,' Ross said.

CHAPTER FOURTEEN

They stood in silence for nearly fifteen minutes, watching me. Then Vjoersterod said, 'Stand up.'

I stood.

'Turn round in a circle.'

I turned. Lurched. Staggered. Swayed on my feet.

Vjoersterod nodded in satisfaction. 'That's all, Mr Tyrone. All for today. I expect to be pleased by what you write in the paper on Sunday. I had better be pleased.'

I nodded. A mistake. My head swam violently. I overbalanced slightly. The whisky was being absorbed into my bloodstream at a disastrous rate.

Vjoersterod and Ross let themselves out unhurriedly and without another word. As soon as the door closed behind them I turned and made tracks for the kitchen. Behind me Elizabeth's voice called in a question, but I had no time to waste and explain. I pulled the tin of salt from the shelf, poured two inches of it into a tumbler and splashed in an equal amount of water.

Stirred it with my fingers. No time for a spoon. Seconds counted. Drank the mixture. It tasted like the Seven Seas rolled into one. Scorched my throat. An effort to get more than one mouthful down. I was gagging over the stuff before it did its work and came up again, bringing with it whatever of the whisky hadn't gone straight through my stomach wall.

I leaned over the sink, retching and wretched. I had lurched for Vjoersterod more than was strictly necessary, but the alcohol had in fact taken as strong and fast a hold as I had feared it would. I could feel its effects rising in my brain, disorganizing coordination, distorting thought. No possible antidote except time.

Time. Fifteen minutes, maybe, since I had taken the stuff. In ten minutes more, perhaps twenty, I would be thoroughly drunk.

I didn't know whether Vjoersterod had made me drink for any special purpose or just from bloody-mindedness. I did know that it was a horrible complication to what I had planned to do.

I rinsed my mouth out with clean water and straightened up. Groaned as the heavy yoke of bruises across my shoulders reminded me I had other troubles beside drink. Went back to Elizabeth concentrating on not knocking into the walls and doors, and picked up the telephone.

A blank. Couldn't remember the number.
Think.
Out it came. Willy Onroy answered.

'Willie,' I said. 'Move that horse out of box sixty-eight. That was the opposition you were talking to earlier. Put on all the guards you can, and move the horse to another box. Stake out sixty-eight and see if you can catch any would-be nobblers in the act.'

'Ty! Will do.'

'Can't stop, Willy. Sorry about this.'

'Don't worry. We'll see no one reaches him. I think, like you, that it's essential that he should be kept safe until the race.'

'They may be determined . . .'

'So am I.'

I put the receiver back in its cradle with his reassurance shoring me up, and met Elizabeth's horrified gaze.

'Ty,' she said faintly, 'what are you doing?'

I sat down for a moment on the arm of the chair. I felt terrible. Battered, sick and drunk.

I said, 'Listen, honey. Listen well. I can't say it twice. I can't put things back to where they were before I wrote the articles.'

'You told him you would,' she interrupted in bewilderment.

'I know I did. I had to. But I can't. I've told the stewards about him. I can't go back on that. In fact I won't. He's utter poison, and he's got to be stopped.'

'Let someone else do it.'

'That's the classic path to oppression.'

'But why you?' A protesting wail, but a serious question.

'I don't know . . . someone has to.'

'But you gave in to him . . . you let him . . .' She looked at me with wide, appalled eyes, struck by sudden realization. 'He'll come back.'

'Yes. When he finds out that Tiddely Pom has changed boxes and the whole stable is bristling with guards, he'll guess I warned them, and he'll come back. So I'm moving you out of here. Away. At once.'

'You don't mean now?'

'I do indeed.'

'But Ty . . . all that whisky . . . Wouldn't it be better to leave it until the morning?'

I shook my head. The room began spinning. I held on to the chair and waited for it to stop. In the morning I would be sore and ill, much worse than at that moment; and the morning might anyway be too late. Heathbury and back would take less than three hours in a Rolls.

'Ring up Sue Davis and see if Ron can come along to help. I'm going downstairs to get the van out, OK?'

'I don't want to go.'

I understood her reluctance. She had so little grasp on life that even a long-planned daytime move left her worried and insecure. This sudden bustle into the night seemed the dangerous course to her, and staying in a familiar warm home the safe one. Whereas they were the other way round.

'We must,' I said. 'We absolutely must.'

I stood up carefully and concentrated on walking a

straight path to the door. Made it with considerable success. Down the stairs. Opened the garage doors, started the van, and backed it out into the mews. A new set of batteries for Elizabeth's pump were in the garage. I lifted them into the van and put them in place. Waves of giddiness swept through me every time I bent my head down. I began to lose hope that I could retain any control of my brain at all. Too much whisky sloshing about in it. Too much altogether.

I went upstairs again. Elizabeth had the receiver to her ear and her eyes were worried.

'There isn't any reply. Sue and Ron must be out.'

I swore inwardly. Even at the best of times it was difficult to manage the transfer to the van on my own. This was far from the best of times.

I took the receiver out of the cradle, disconnected the Davises' vainly ringing number, and dialled that of Antonio Perelli. To my bottomless relief, he answered.

'Tonio, will you call the nursing home and tell them I'm bringing Elizabeth over.'

'Do you mean now, tonight?'

'Almost at once, yes.'

'Bronchial infection?' He sounded brisk, preparing to be reassuring, acknowledging the urgency.

'No. She's well. It's a different sort of danger. I'll tell you later. Look . . . could you possibly down tools and come over here and help me with her?'

'I can't just now, Ty. Not if she isn't ill.'

'But life and death, all the same,' I said with desperate flippancy.

'I really can't, Ty. I'm expecting another patient.'

'Oh. Well, just ring the nursing home, huh?'

'Sure,' he said. 'And . . . er . . . bring Elizabeth here on the way. Would you do that? It isn't much of a detour. I'd like just to be sure she's in good shape. I'll leave my patient for a few minutes, and just say hello to her in the van. All right?'

'All right,' I said. 'Thanks, Tonio.'

'I'm sorry . . .'

'Don't give it a thought,' I said. 'Be seeing you.'

The room whirled when I put the receiver down. I held on to the bedhead to steady myself, and looked at my watch. Couldn't focus on the dial. The figures were just a blur. I made myself see. Concentrated hard. The numbers and the hands came back sharp and clear. Ten thirty-seven. As if it mattered.

Three more trips to make up and down the stairs. Correction: five. Better start, or I'd never finish. I took the pillows and blankets off my bed, folded them as I would need them in the van, and took them down. When I'd made up the stretcher bed ready for Elizabeth, I felt an overpowering urge to lie down on it myself and go to sleep. Dragged myself back to the stairs instead.

Ridiculous, I thought. Ridiculous to try to do anything in the state I was in. Best to unscramble the eggs and go to bed. Wait till morning. Go to sleep. Sleep.

If I went to sleep I would sleep for hours. Sleep away our margin of safety. Put it into the red time-expired section. Cost us too much.

I shook myself out of it. If I walked carefully, I could stop the world spinning round me. If I thought slowly, I could still think. There was a block now somewhere between my brain and my tongue, but if the words themselves came out slurred and wrong, I still knew with moderate clarity what I had intended them to be.

'Honey,' I said to Elizabeth. 'I'm going to take the pump down first. Then you and the Shira . . . Spira.'

'You're drunk,' she said miserably.

'Not surprising,' I agreed. 'Now listen, love. You'll have to breathe on your own. Four minutes. You know you can do it eash . . . easily.' She did four minutes every day, while Mrs Woodward gave her a bed bath.

'Ty, if you drop the pump . . .'

'I won't,' I said, 'I won't . . . drop . . . the pump.'

The pump was the only one we had. There was no replacement. Always we lived in the shadow of the threat that one day its simple mechanism would break down. Spares were almost impossible to find, because respirators were an uneconomic item to the manufacturers, and they had discontinued making them. If the pump needed servicing, Mrs Woodward and I worked the bellows by hand while it was being done in the flat. Tiring for an hour. Impossible for a lifetime. If I dropped the pump and punctured the bellows, Elizabeth's future could be precisely measured.

Four minutes.

'We'd better,' I said, considering, 'pack some things for you first. Clean nightdress, f'rinstance.'

'How long . . . how long will we be going for?' She was trying hard to keep the fear out of her voice, to treat our flight on a rational, sensible basis. I admired her, understood her effort, liked her for it, loved her, had to make and keep her safe . . . and I'd never do it, I thought astringently, if I let my mind dribble on in that silly way.

How long? I didn't know how long. Until Vjoersterod had been jailed or deported. Even then, it would be safer to find another flat.

'A few days,' I said.

I fetched a suitcase and tried to concentrate on what she needed. She began to tell me, item by item, realizing I couldn't think.

'Washing things. Hair brush. Make-up. Bedsocks. Hot water bottle. Cardigans. Pills . . .' She looked with longing at the Possum machine and all the gadgets.

'I'll come soon . . . come back soon for those,' I promised. With company, just in case.

'You'll need some things yourself,' she said.

'Hm?' I squinted at her. 'Yeah . . .'

I fetched toothbrush, comb, electric razor. I would sleep in the van, dressed, on the stretcher bed. Better take a clean shirt. And a sweater. Beyond that, I couldn't be bothered. Shoved them into a grip. Packing done.

'Could you leave a note for Mrs Woodward?' she asked. 'She'll be so worried if we aren't here in the morning.'

A note for Mrs Woodward. Found some paper. Ball point pen in my pocket. Note for Mrs Woodward. 'Gone away for few days. Will write to you.' Didn't think she would be much less worried when she read that, but didn't know what else to put. The writing straggled upwards, as drunk as I felt.

'All set,' I said.

The packing had postponed the moment we were both afraid of. I looked at the pump. Its works were encased in a metal cabinet of about the size of a bed-side table, with a handle at each side for carrying. Like any large heavy box, it was easy enough for two to manage, but difficult for one. I'd done it often enough before, but not with a whirling head and throbbing bruises. I made a practice shot at picking it up, just to find out.

I found out.

Elizabeth said weakly, 'Ty . . . you can't do it.'

'Oh yes . . . I can.'

'Not after . . . I mean, it's hurting you.'

'The best thing about being drunk,' I said carefully, 'is that what you feel you don't feel, and even if you feel it you don't care.'

'What did you say?'

'Live now, hurt later.'

I pulled back her sheets and my fingers fumbled on the buckle which unfastened the Spirashell. That wouldn't do, I thought clearly. If I fumbled the buckle I'd never have a chance of doing the transfer in four minutes. I paused, fighting the chaos in my head. Sometimes in my youth I'd played a game against alcohol, treating it like an opponent, drinking too much of it and then daring it to defeat me. I knew from experience that if one concentrated hard enough it was possible to carry out quite adequately the familiar jobs one did when sober. This time it was no game. This time, for real.

I started again on the buckle, sharpening every faculty into that one simple task. It came undone easily. I lifted the Spirashell off her chest and laid it over her knees, where it hissed and sucked at the blankets.

Switched off the electricity. Unplugged the lead. Wound it on to the lugs provided. Disconnected the flexible tube which led to the Spirashell.

Committed now. I tugged the pump across the floor, pulling it on its rocky old castors. Opened the door. Crossed the small landing. The stairs stretched downwards. I put my hand on the wall to steady myself and turned round to go down backwards.

Step by step. One foot down. Lift the pump down one step. Balance it. One foot down. Lift the pump. Balance . . .

Normally, if Ron or Sue or Mrs Woodward were

not there to help, I simply carried it straight down. This time, if I did that, I would fall. I leaned against the wall. One foot down. Lift the pump down. Balance it . . . It overhung the steps. Only its back two castors were on the ground, the others out in space . . . If it fell forward, it would knock me down the stairs with it . . .

Hurry. Four minutes. Halfway down it seemed to me with an uprush of panic that the four minutes had already gone by. That I would be still on the stairs when Elizabeth died. That I would never, never get it to the bottom unless I fell down there in a tangled heap.

Step by deliberate step, concentrating acutely on every movement, I reached the ground below. Lugged the pump across the small hall, lifted it over the threshold on to the street. Rolled it to the van.

The worst bit. The floor of the van was a foot off the ground. I climbed in, stretched down, grasped the handles, and tugged. I felt as if I'd been torn apart, like the old Chinese torture of the two trees. The pump came up, in through the door, on to the floor of the van. The world whirled violently round my head. I tripped over the end of the stretcher and fell backwards still holding the pump by one handle. It rocked over, crashed on its side, broke the glass over the gauge which showed the pressures and respirations per minute.

Gasping, feeling I was clamped into a hopeless

nightmare, I bent over the pump and lifted it upright. Shoved it into its place. Fastened the straps which held it. Pushed the little wedges under its wheels. Plugged in the leads to and from the batteries. Couldn't believe I had managed it all, and wasted several seconds checking through again.

If it didn't work . . . If some of the broken glass was inside . . . If it rubbed a hole in its bellows . . . I couldn't think straight, didn't know what to do about it, hoped it would be all right.

Up the stairs. Easy without the pump. Stumbled over half the steps, reached the landing on my knees.

Elizabeth was very frightened, her eyes wide and dark, looking at death because I was drunk. When she had to do her own breathing she had no energy or air left for talking, but this time she managed one appalled, desperate word.

'Hurry.'

I remembered not to nod. Picked her up, one arm under her knees, one arm round her shoulders, pulling her towards me so that she could rest her head against my shoulder. Like one carries a baby.

She was feather light, but not light enough. She looked at my face and did my moaning for me.

'Hush,' I said. 'Just breathe.'

I went down the stairs leaning against the wall, one step at a time, refusing to fall. Old man alcohol was losing the game.

The step up into the van was awful. More trees. I

laid her carefully on the stretcher, putting her limp limbs straight.

Only the Spirashell now. Went back for it, up the stairs. Like going up a down escalator, never ending, moving where it should have been still. Picked up the Spirashell. The easiest burden. Very nearly came to grief down the stairs through tripping over the long concertina connecting tube. Stumbled into the van and thrust it much too heavily on to Elizabeth's knees.

She was beginning to labour, the tendons in her neck standing out like strings under her effort to get air.

I couldn't get the tube to screw into its connection in the pump. Cursed, sweated, almost wept. Took a deep breath, choked down the panic, tried again. The tricky two-way nut caught and slipped into a crossed thread, caught properly at last, fastened down firmly. I pressed the battery switch on the pump. The moment of truth.

The bellows nonchalantly swelled and thudded. Elizabeth gave the smallest sound of inexpressible relief. I lifted the Spirashell gently on to her chest, slipped the strap underneath her, and couldn't do up the buckle because my fingers were finally trembling too much to control. I just knelt there holding the ends tight so that the Spirashell was close enough for its vacuum to work. It pulled her chest safely up and down, up and down, filling her lungs with air. Some of the agonized apprehension drained out of her face, and some fragile colour came back.

Sixteen life-giving breaths later I tried again with the buckle. Fixed it after two more attempts. Sat back on the floor of the van, rested my elbows on my bent knees, and my head on my hands. Shut my eyes. Everything spun in a roaring black whirl. At least, I thought despairingly, at least I had to be nearly as drunk as I was going to get. Which, thanks to having got some of the stuff up, might not now be paralytic.

Elizabeth said with effortful calm, 'Ty, you aren't fit to drive.'

'Never know what you can do till you try.'

'Wait a little while. Wait till you're better.'

'Won't be better for hours.' My tongue slipped on the words, fuzzy and thick. It sounded terrible. I opened my eyes, focused carefully on the floor in front of me. The swimming gyrations in my head gradually slowed down to manageable proportions. Thought about the things I still had to do.

'Got to get the shoot . . . suitcases.'

'Wait, Ty. Wait a while.'

She didn't understand that waiting would do no good. If I didn't keep moving I would go to sleep. Even while I thought it I could feel the insidious languour tempting me to do just that. Sleep. Sleep deadly sleep.

I climbed out of the van, stood holding on to it, waiting for some sort of balance to come back.

'Won't be long,' I said. Couldn't afford to be long. She couldn't be left alone. In case.

Coordination had again deteriorated. The stairs proved worse than ever. I kept lifting my feet up far higher than was necessary, and half missing the step when I put them down. Stumbled upwards, banging into the walls. In the flat, propped up the note for Mrs Woodward so she couldn't miss it. Tucked Elizabeth's hot water bottle under my arm, carried the suitcases to the door, switched off the light, let myself out. Started down the stairs and dropped the lot. It solved the problem of carrying them, anyway. To prevent myself following them I finished the journey sitting down, lowering myself from step to step.

I picked up the hot water bottle and took it out to Elizabeth.

'I thought . . . Did you fall?' She was acutely anxious.

'Dropped the cases.' I felt an insane urge to giggle. 'S'all right.' Dropped the cases, but not the pump, not Elizabeth. Old man alcohol could stuff it.

I fetched the bags and put them on the floor of the van. Shut the doors. Swayed round to the front and climbed into the driving seat. Sat there trying very hard to be sober. A losing battle, but not yet lost.

I looked at Elizabeth. Her head was relaxed on the pillows, her eyes shut. She'd reached the stage, I supposed, when constant fear was too much of a burden and it was almost a relief to give up hope and surrender to disaster. She'd surrendered for nothing, if I could help it.

Eyes front. Method needed. Do things by numbers, slowly. Switched off the light inside the van. Suddenly very dark. Switched it on again. Not a good start. Start again.

Switched on the side lights. Much better. Switch on ignition. Check fuel. Pretty low after the run to Berkshire, but enough for five miles. Pull out the choke. Start engine. Turn out light inside van.

Without conscious thought I found the gear and let out the clutch. The van rolled forward up the mews.

Simple.

Stopped at the entrance, very carefully indeed. No one walking down the pavement, stepping out in front of me. Turned my head left and right, looking for traffic. All the lights in the road swayed and dipped. I couldn't see anything coming. Took my foot off the clutch. Turned out into the road. Gently accelerated. All clear so far.

Part of my mind was stone cold. In that area, I was sharply aware that to drive too slowly was as obvious a giveaway as meandering all over the road. To drive too fast meant no margin for a sudden stop. My reaction times were a laugh. Hitting someone wouldn't be.

As long as I kept my head still and my eyes front, it wasn't impossible. I concentrated fiercely on seeing pedestrian crossings, stationary cars, traffic lights. Seeing them in time to do something about them. I seemed to be looking down a small cone of clarity: everything in my peripheral vision was a shimmering blue.

I stopped without a jerk at some red lights. Fine. Marvellous. They changed to green. A sudden hollow void in my stomach. I couldn't remember the way. Knew it well, really. The man in the car behind began flashing his headlights. Thought of the old joke... What's the definition of a split second? The interval between the lights going green and the man behind hooting or flashing. Couldn't afford to sit there doing nothing. Let in the clutch and went straight on, realizing that if I strayed off course and got lost I would be sunk. The small print on my maps was for other times. Couldn't ask anyone the way, they might turn me over to the police. Breathalysers, and all that. I'd turn the crystals black.

Ten yards over the crossing I remembered the way to Welbeck Street. I hadn't gone wrong. A vote of thanks to the unconscious mind. Hip hip hooray. For God's sake mind that taxi... U-turns in front of drunken drivers ought to be banned...

Too much traffic altogether. Cars swimming out of side roads like shiny half-seen fish with yellow eyes. Cars with orange rear direction blinkers as blinding as the sun. Buses charging across to the kerb and pulling up in six feet at the stops. People running where they shouldn't cross, saving the seconds and risking the years.

Fight them all. Defeat the inefficiency of crashing. Stamp on the enemy in the blood, beat the drug confusing the brain . . . Stop the world spinning, hold tight to a straight and steady twenty miles an hour through an imaginary earthquake. Keep death off the roads. Arrive alive. Fasten your safety belts. London welcomes careful drivers . . .

I wouldn't like to do it again. Apart from the sheer physical exertion involved in keeping control of my arms and legs there was also a surging recklessness trying to conquer every care I took. An inner voice saying, 'Spin the wheel largely, go on, you can straighten out fine round the bend' and an answering flicker saying faintly, 'Careful, careful, careful, careful . . .'

Caution won. Mainly, I imagine, through distaste at what would happen to me if I were caught. Only pulling up safely at the other end could possibly justify what was to all intents a crime. I knew that, and clung to it.

Welbeck Street had receded since I went there last.

CHAPTER FIFTEEN

Tonio must have been looking out for us, because he opened the front door and came out on the pavement before I had climbed out of the van. True, I had been a long time climbing out of the van. The waves of defeated intoxication had swept in as soon as I'd put on the brakes. Not defeated after all. Just postponed.

I finally made it on the road. Put one foot in front of the other round the front of the van, and leaned against the nearside wing.

Tonio peered at me with absolute incredulity.

'You're drunk.'

'You're so right.'

'Elizabeth . . .' he said anxiously.

I nodded my head towards the van and wished I hadn't. Hung on to the wing mirror. Still liable for drunk in charge, even on his pavement.

'Ty,' he said, 'for God's sake, man. Pull yourself together.'

'You try,' I said. 'I can't.'

He gave me a withering look and went round to the

back of the van to open the doors. I heard him inside,
talking to Elizabeth. Tried hard not to slither down the
wing and fold up into the gutter. Remotely watched a
man in a raincoat get out of a taxi away down the
street and cross into a telephone box. The taxi waited
for him. Knew I couldn't drive any farther, would have
to persuade Tonio to do it, or get someone else. No
use thinking any more that one could remain sober
by will power. One couldn't. Old bloody man alcohol
sneaked up on you just when you thought you had him
licked.

Tonio reappeared at my elbow.

'Get in the passenger seat,' he said. 'And give me
the keys, so that you can't be held to be in charge. I'll
drive you to the nursing home. But I'm afraid you'll
have to wait ten minutes or so, because I still have
that patient with me and there's a prescription to
write . . . Are you taking in a word I say?'

'The lot.'

'Get in, then.' He opened the door for me, and put
his hand on my arm when I rocked. 'If Elizabeth needs
me, blow the horn.'

'Right.'

I sat in the seat, slid down, and put my head back.
Sleep began to creep in round the edges.

'You all right?' I said to Elizabeth.

Her head was behind me. I heard her murmur
quietly, 'Yes.'

The pump hummed rhythmically, aiding and

abetting the whisky. The sense of urgency drifted away. Tonio would drive us . . . Elizabeth was safe. My eyelids gave up the struggle. I sank into a pit, whirling and disorientated. Not an unpleasant feeling if one didn't fight it.

Tonio opened the door and shook me awake.

'Drink this,' he said. A mug of coffee, black and sweet. 'I'll be with you in a minute.'

He went back into the house, propping the door open with a heavy wrought-iron facsimile of the Tower of Pisa. The coffee was too hot. With exaggerated care I put the mug down on the floor. Straightened up wishing the load of ache across my shoulders would let up and go away, but was much too full of the world's oldest anaesthetic to feel it very clearly.

I had been as drunk as that only once before, and it wasn't the night they told me Elizabeth would die, but four days later when they said she would live. I'd downed uncountable double whiskies and I'd eaten almost nothing for a week. It was odd to remember the delirious happiness of that night because of course it hadn't after all been the end of an agony but only the beginning of the years of pain and struggle and waste . . .

I found myself staring vacantly at the off-side wing mirror. If I conshen . . . well, concentrated . . . very hard, I thought bemusedly, I would be able to see what it reflected. A pointless game. It simply irritated me that I couldn't see clearly if I wanted to. Looked obstinately at the mirror and waited for the slowed-down focusing process to come right. Finally, with a ridiculous smile of triumph, I saw what it saw down the street. Nothing much. Nothing worth the trouble. Only a silly old taxi parked by the kerb. Only a silly man in a raincoat getting into it.

Raincoat.

Raincoat.

The alarm bells rang fuzzily in my sluggish head. I opened the door and fumbled my way on to the pavement, kicking the coffee over in the process. Leaned against the side of the van and looked down towards the taxi. It was still parked. By the telephone box. Where the man in the raincoat had been ringing someone up.

They say sudden overwhelming disaster sobers you, but it isn't true. I reeled across the pavement and up the step to Tonio's door. Forget all about blowing the car horn. Banged the solid knocker on his door, and called him loudly. He appeared at the top of the stairs, which led to his consulting-room on the first floor and his flat above that.

'Shut up, Ty,' he said. 'I won't be long.'

'Shome ... someone's followed us,' I said. 'It's dangerous.' He wouldn't understand, I thought confusedly. He wouldn't know what I was talking about. I didn't know where to start explaining.

Elizabeth, however, must have told him enough.

'Oh. All right, I'll be down in one minute.' His head

577

withdrew round the bend in the stairs and I swivelled unsteadily to take another look down the street. Taxi still there in the same place. Light out, not for hire. Just waiting. Waiting to follow us again if we moved. Waiting to tell Vjoersterod where we'd gone.

I shook with futile rage. Vjoersterod hadn't after all been satisfied that Ross's truncheon and the threats against Elizabeth had been enough to ensure a permanent state of docility. He'd left Raincoat outside to watch. Just in case. I hadn't spotted him. Had been much too drunk to spot anything. But there he was. Right on our tail.

I'll fix him, I thought furiously. I'll fix him properly.

Tonio started to come down the stairs, escorting a thin, bent, elderly man whose breath rasped audibly through his open mouth. Slowly they made it to the bottom. Tonio held his arm as they came past me, and helped him over the threshold and down the step to the pavement. An almost equally elderly woman emerged from the Rover parked directly behind my van. Tonio handed him over, helped him into the car, came back to me.

'He likes to come at night,' he explained. 'Not so many fumes from the traffic, and easier parking.'

'Lord Fore . . . Fore something,' I said.

'Forlingham,' Tonio nodded. 'Do you know him?'

'Used to go racing. Poor old thing.' I looked wuzzily up the street. 'See that taxi?'

'Yes.'

'Following us.'

'Oh.'

'So you take 'Lizabeth on to the nursing home. I'll stop the taxi.' A giggle got as far as the first ridiculous note. 'What's worse than raining cats and dogs? I'll tell you . . . hailing taxis.'

'You're drunk,' Tonio said. 'Wait while I change my coat.' He was wearing formal consultant's dress and looked young and glamorous enough to be a pop singer. 'Can we wait?'

I swung out a generous arm in a wide gesture. 'The taxi,' I said owlishly, 'is waiting for *us*.'

He went to change his coat. I could hear Elizabeth's pump thudding safely away; wondered if I ought to go and reassure her; thought that in my state I probably couldn't. The Forlinghams started up and drove away. The taxi went on waiting.

At first I thought what I saw next was on the pink elephant level. Not really there. Couldn't be there. But this time, no hallucination. Edging smoothly round the corner, pulling gently into the kerb, stopping behind the taxi, one Silver Wraith, property of Hire Cars Lucullus.

Raincoat emerged from the taxi and reported to the Rolls. Two minutes later he returned to the taxi, climbed in, and was driven away.

Tonio ran lightly down the stairs and came to a halt beside me in a black sweater instead of a coat.

'Let's get going,' he said.

579

I put my hand clumsily on his arm.

'Shee . . . I mean, see that Rolls down there, where the taxi was.'

'Yes.'

'In that,' I said carefully, 'is the man who . . . oh God, why can't I think . . . who said he would . . . kill . . .'Lizabeth if I didn't do what he wanted . . . well . . . he might . . . he might not . . . but can't rish . . . risk it. Take her . . . Take her. I'll stop . . . him following you.'

'How?' Tonio said unemotionally.

I looked at the Tower of Pisa holding the door open.

'With that.'

'It's heavy,' he objected, assessing my physical state.

'Oh for God's sake stop arguing.' I said weakly. 'I want her to go where they can't find her. Please . . . please get going . . . go on, Tonio. And drive away slowly.'

He hesitated, but finally showed signs of moving. 'Don't forget,' he said seriously, 'that you are no use to Elizabeth dead.'

''Spose not.'

'Give me your coat,' he said suddenly. 'Then they'll think it's still you in the van.'

I took off my coat obediently, and he put it on. He was shorter than me. It hung on him. Same dark head, though. They might mistake us from a distance.

Tonio gave a rip-roaring impression of my drunken

walk, reeling right round the back of the van on his way to the driving seat. I laughed. I was that drunk.

He started the van and drove slowly away. I watched him give one artistic weave across the road and back. Highly intelligent fellow, Tonio Perelli.

Down the road, the Silver Wraith began to move. Got to stop him, I thought fuzzily. Got to stop him smashing up our lives, smashing up other people's lives. Someone, somewhere, had to stop him. In Welbeck Street, with a doorstop. Couldn't think clearly beyond that one fact. Had to stop him.

I bent down and picked up the Leaning Tower by its top two storeys. As Tonio had said, it was heavy. Bruised-muscle-tearingly heavy. Tomorrow its effects would be awful. Fair enough. Tomorrow would be much more awful if I put it down again ... or if I missed.

The Rolls came towards me as slowly as Tonio had driven away. If I'd been sober I'd have had all the time in the world. As it was, I misjudged the pace and all but let him go cruising by.

Down one step. Don't trip. Across the pavement. Hurry. Swung the wrought-iron Tower round with both hands as if I was throwing the hammer and forgot to leave go. Its weight and momentum pulled me after it; but although at the last moment Ross saw me and tried to swerve, the heavy metal base crashed exactly where I wanted it. Drunks' luck. Dead centre of the windscreen.

Scrunch went the laminated glass in a radiating star. Silver cracks streaked across Ross's vision. The huge car swerved violently out into the centre of the road and then in towards the kerb as Ross stamped on the brakes. A screech of tyres, a scraping jolt. The Rolls stopped abruptly at a sharp angle to the pavement with its rear end inviting attention from the police. No police appeared to pay attention. A great pity. I wouldn't have minded being scooped in for being drunk and disorderly and disturbing the peace . . .

I had rebounded off the smooth side of the big car and fallen in a heap in the road. The Rolls had stopped, and that was that. Job done. No clear thought of self-preservation spearheaded its way through the mist in my head. I didn't remember that Tonio's solid front door stood open only a few yards away. Jelly had taken over from bone in my legs. Welbeck Street had started revolving around me and was taking its time over straightening out.

It was Ross who picked me up. Ross with his truncheon. I was past caring much what he did with it: and what he intended, I don't know, because this time I was saved by the bell in the shape of a party of people in evening dress who came out into the street from a neighbouring house. They had cheerful, gay voices full of a happy evening, and they exclaimed in instant sympathy over the plight of the Rolls.

'I say, do you need any help . . .?'

'Shall we call anyone . . . the police, or anything?'

'Can we give you a lift . . .?'

'Or call a garage?'

'No, thank you,' said Vjoersterod in his most charming voice. 'So kind of you . . . but we can manage.'

Ross picked me to my feet and held on grimly to my arm. Vjoersterod was saying, 'We've been having a little trouble with my nephew. I'm afraid he's very drunk . . . still, once we get him home everything will be all right.'

They murmured sympathetically. Began to move away.

'S'not true,' I shouted. 'They'll prob'ly kill me.' My voice sounded slurred and much too melodramatic. They paused, gave Vjoersterod a group of sympathetic, half-embarrassed smiles, and moved off up the street.

'Hey,' I called. 'Take me with you.'

Useless. They didn't even look back.

'What now?' Ross said to Vjoersterod.

'We can't leave him here. These people would remember.'

'In the car?'

While Vjoersterod nodded he shoved me towards the Rolls, levering with his grasp on my right arm. I swung at him with the left, and missed completely. I could see two of him, which made it difficult. Between them they more or less swung me into the back of the car and I sprawled there face down, half on and half off the seat, absolutely furious that I still could not climb out of that crippling alcoholic stupor. There was a ringing in my head like the noise of the livid green corridors of gas at the dentist's. But no stepped-up awakening to daylight and the taste of blood. Just a continuing extraordinary sensation of being conscious and unconscious, not alternately, but both at once.

Ross knocked out a few of the worst-cracked pieces of the windscreen and started the car.

Vjoersterod, sitting beside him, leaned over the back of his seat and said casually, 'Where to, Mr Tyrone? Which way to your wife?'

'Round and round the mulberry bush,' I mumbled indistinctly. 'And goodnight to you too.'

He let go with four-letter words which were much more in keeping with his character than his usual elevated chat.

'It's no good,' Ross said disgustedly. 'He won't tell us unless we take him to pieces and even then . . . if we did get it out of him . . . what good would it do? He'll never write for you. Never.'

'Why not?' said Vjoersterod obstinately.

'Well, look at it this way. We threatened to kill his wife. Does he knuckle under? Yes, as long as we're there. The moment our backs are turned, first thing he does is to move her out. We follow, find her, he shifts her off again . . . That could go on and on. All we can do more is actually kill her, and if we do that we've no hold on him anyway. So he'll never write for you, whatever we do.'

Full marks, I said to myself fatuously. Masterly summing up of the situation. Top of the class.

'You didn't hit him hard enough,' Vjoersterod said accusingly, sliding out of the argument.

'I did.'

'You can't have.'

'If you remember,' Ross said patiently, 'Charlie Boston's boys made no impression either. They either do or don't respond to the treatment. This one doesn't. Same with the threats. Same with the drink. Usually one method is enough. This time we use all three, just to make sure. And where do we get? We get nowhere at all. Just like Gunther Braunthal last year.'

Vjoersterod grunted. I wondered remotely what had become of Gunther Braunthal. Decided I didn't really want to know.

'I can't afford for him to get away with it,' Vjoersterod said.

'No,' Ross agreed.

'I don't like disposals in England,' Vjoersterod went on in irritation. 'Too much risk. Too many people everywhere.'

'Leave it to me,' Ross said calmly.

I struggled up into a sitting position, propping myself up on my hands. Looked out of the side window. Lights flashing past, all one big whirl. We weren't going very fast, on account of the broken windscreen, but the December night air swept into the car in gusts, freezing me in my cotton shirt. In a minute, when my head cleared a fraction, I would open the door and roll out. We weren't going very fast . . . If I waited for a bit of main street, with people . . . couldn't wait too long. Didn't want Ross attending to my disposal.

Vjoersterod's head turned round my way. 'You've only yourself to thank, Mr Tyrone. You shouldn't have crossed me. You should have done what I said. I gave you your chance. You've been very stupid, Mr Tyrone. Very stupid indeed. And now, of course, you'll be paying for it.'

'Huh?' I said.

'He's still drunk,' Ross said. 'He doesn't understand.'

'I'm not so sure. Look what he's done in the past hour. He's got a head like a bullet.'

My eyes suddenly focused on something outside. Something I knew, that everyone knew. The Aviary in Regent's Park, pointed angular wire opposite the main entrance to the Zoo. Been there before with Vjoersterod. He must be staying somewhere near there. I thought. Must be taking me to where he lived. It didn't matter that it was near the Zoo. What did matter was that this was also the way to the nursing home where Tonio had taken Elizabeth. It was less than a mile ahead.

I thought for one wild horror-stricken moment that I must have told Vjoersterod where to go; then remembered and knew I hadn't. But he was much too close. Much too close. Supposing his way home took him actually past the nursing home, and he saw the van ... saw them unloading Elizabeth even ... He might change his mind and kill her and leave me alive ... which would be unbearable, totally and literally unbearable.

Distract his attention.

I said with as much clarity as my tongue would allow: 'Vjoersterod and Ross. Vjoersterod and Ross.'

'*What?*' said Vjoersterod.

The shock to Ross resulted in a swerve across the road and a jolt on the brakes.

'Go back to South Africa before the bogies get you.'

Vjoersterod had twisted round and was staring at me. Ross had his eyes too much on the mirror and not enough on the road. All the same, he started his indicator flashing for the right turn which led over the bridge across Regent's Canal and then out of the Park. Which led straight past the nursing home, half a mile ahead.

'I told the stewards,' I said desperately. 'I told the stewards ... all about you. Last Wednesday. I told my paper ... it'll be there on Sunday. So you'll remember me too, you'll remember ...'

Ross turned the wheel erratically, sweeping wide to the turn. I brought my hands round with a wholly uncoordinated swing and clamped them hard over his eyes. He took both of his own hands off the wheel to try to detach them and the car rocked straight halfway through the turn and headed across the road at a tangent, taking the shortest distance to the bank of the canal.

Vjoersterod shouted frantically and pulled with all his strength at my arm, but my desperation was at least the equal of his. I hauled Ross's head back towards me harder still, and it was their own doing that I was too drunk to care where or how the car crashed.

'Brake,' Vjoersterod screamed. 'Brake, you stupid fool.'

Ross put his foot down. He couldn't see what he was doing. He put his foot down hard on the accelerator.

The Rolls leaped across the pavement and on to the grass. The bank sloped gently and then steeply down to the canal, with saplings and young trees growing here and there. The Rolls scrunched sideways into one trunk and ricocheted into a sapling which it mowed down like corn.

Vjoersterod grabbed the wheel, but the heavy car was now pointed downhill and going too fast for any change of steering. The wheel twisted and lurched out of his hand under the jolt of the front wheel hitting another tree and slewing sideways. Branches cracked around the car and scraped and stabbed at the glossy coachwork. Vjoersterod fumbled on the glove shelf and found the truncheon, and twisted round in his seat and began hitting my arm in panic-stricken fury.

I let go of Ross. It was far too late for him both to assess the situation and do anything useful about it. He was just beginning to reach for the hand brake when the Rolls crashed down over the last sapling and fell into the canal.

The car slewed convulsively on impact, throwing me around like a rag doll in the back and tumbling Vjoersterod and Ross together in the front. Black water immediately poured through the broken windscreen and began filling the car with lethal speed.

How to get out ... I fumbled for a door handle in the sudden dark, couldn't find one, and didn't know what I had my feet on, didn't know which way up I was. Didn't know if the car was on its back or its nose ... Didn't know anything except that it was sinking.

Vjoersterod began screaming as the water rose up his body. His arm was still flailing about and knocking into me. I felt the truncheon still in his hand. Snatched it from him and hit it hard against where I thought the rear window must be. Connected only with material. Felt around wildly with my hand, found glass above my head, and hit at that.

It cracked. Laminated and tough. Cursed Rolls-Royce for their standards. Hit again. Couldn't get a decent swing. Tried again. Crunched a hole. Water came through it. Not a torrent, but too much. The window was under the surface. Not far under. Tried again. Bash, bash. Made a bigger hole but still not enough ... and water fell through it and over me and from the front of the car the icy level was rising past my waist.

Great to die when you're dead drunk, I thought. And when I die don't bury me at all, just pickle my bones in alcohol . . . Crashed the truncheon against the hole. Missed. My arm went right through it. Felt it up there in the air, out of the water. Stupid. Silly. Drowning in less than an inch of Regent's Canal.

Pulled my arm back and tried again. Absolutely no good. Too much water, too much whisky. One outside, one in. No push in my battered muscles and not much compression in my mind. Floating off on the river of death . . . sorry, Elizabeth.

Suddenly there were lights shining down over me. Hallucinations, I thought. Hallelujah hallucinations. Death was a blinding white light and a crashing noise in the head and a shower of water and glass and voices calling and arms grasping and pulling and raising one up . . . up . . . into a free cold wind . . .

'Is there anyone else in the car?' a voice said. A loud urgent voice, speaking to me. The voice of earth. Telling me I was alive. Telling me to wake up and do something. I couldn't adjust. Blinked at him stupidly.

'Tell us,' he said. 'Is there anyone else in the car?' He shook my shoulder. It hurt. Brought me back a little. He said again, 'Is there anyone else?'

I nodded weakly. 'Two.'

'Christ,' he muttered. 'What a hope.'

I was sitting on the grass on the canal bank, shivering. Someone put a coat around my shoulders. There were a lot of people and more coming, black figures against the reflection on the dark water, figures lit on one side only by the headlights of the car which had come down the path ploughed by the Rolls. It was parked there on the edge, with its lights on the place where the Rolls had gone. You could see the silver rim of the rear window shimmering just below the surface, close to the bank. You could see the water sliding shallowly through the gaping hole my rescuers had pulled me through. You could see nothing inside the car except darkness and water.

A youngish man had stripped to his underpants and was proposing to go through the rear window to try to rescue the others. People tried to dissuade him, but he went. I watched in a daze, scarcely feeling. His head came back through the window into the air, and several hands bent over to help him.

They pulled Vjoersterod out and laid him on the bank.

'Artificial respiration,' one said. 'Kiss of life.'

Kiss Vjoersterod . . . if they wanted to, they were welcome.

The diver went back for Ross. He had to go down twice. A very brave man. The Rolls could have toppled over on to its side at any moment and trapped him inside. People, I thought groggily, were amazing.

They put Ross beside Vjoersterod, and kissed him too. Neither of them responded.

Cold was seeping into every cell of my body. From the ground I sat on it rose, from the wind it pierced, from my wet clothes it clung clammily to my skin. Bruises stiffen fast in those conditions. Everything started hurting at once, climbing from piano to fortissimo. The noises in my head were deafening. A fine time for the drink to begin dying out on me, I thought. Just when I needed it most.

I lay back on the grass, and someone put something soft under my head. Their voices sprayed over me, questioning and solicitous.

'How did it happen?'

'We've sent for an ambulance . . .'

'What he needs is some good hot tea . . .'

'We're so sorry about your friends . . .'

'Can you tell us your name?'

I didn't answer them. Didn't have enough strength. Could let it all go, now. Didn't have to struggle any more. Old man alcohol could have what was left.

I shut my eyes. The world receded rapidly.

'He's out cold,' a tiny faraway voice said.

It wasn't true at that moment. But a second later, it was.

CHAPTER SIXTEEN

I was in a dim long room with a lot of bodies laid out in white. I, too, was in white, being painfully crushed in a cement sandwich. My head, sticking out of it, pulsed and thumped like a steam hammer.

The components of this nightmare gradually sorted themselves out into depressing reality. Respectively, a hospital ward, a savage load of bruises, and an emperor-sized hangover.

I dragged my arm up and squinted at my watch. Four-fifty. Even that small movement had out-of-proportion repercussions. I put my hand down gently on top of the sheets and tried to duck out by going to sleep again.

Didn't manage it. Too many problems. Too many people would want too many explanations. I'd have to edit the truth here and there, juggle the facts a little. Needed a clear head for it, not a throbbing dehydrated morass.

I tried to sort out into order exactly what had happened the evening before, and wondered profitlessly what I would have done if I hadn't been drunk. Thought numbly about Vjoersterod and Ross being pulled from the wreck. If they were dead, which I was sure they were, I had certainly killed them. The worst thing about that was that I didn't care.

If I shut my eyes the world still revolved and the ringing noise in my head grew more persistent. I thought wearily that people who poisoned themselves with alcohol for pleasure had to be crazy.

At six they woke up all the patients, who shook my tender brain with shattering decibels of coughing, spitting, and brushing of teeth. Breakfast was steamed haddock and weak tea. I asked for water and something for a headache, and thought sympathetically about the man who said he didn't like Alka-seltzers because they were so noisy.

The hospital was equipped with telephone trolleys, but for all my urging I couldn't get hold of one until nine-thirty. I fed it with coins salvaged from my now drying trousers and rang Tonio. Caught him luckily in his consulting room having insisted his receptionist tell him I was calling.

'Ty! *Deo gratias* . . . where the hell have you been?'

'Swimming,' I said. 'I'll tell you later. Is Elizabeth OK?'

'She's fine. But she was extremely anxious when you didn't turn up again last night . . . Where are you now? Why haven't you been to find out for yourself how she is?'

'I'm in University College Hospital. At least, I'm here for another few hours. I got scooped in here last night, but there's not much damage.'

'How's the head?'

'Lousy.'

He laughed. Charming fellow.

I rang the nursing home and talked to Elizabeth. There was no doubt she was relieved to hear from me, though from the unusual languor in her voice it was clear they had given her some sort of tranquillizer. She was almost too calm. She didn't ask me what happened when Tonio had driven her away; she didn't want to know where I was at that moment.

'Would you mind staying in the nursing home for a couple of days?' I asked. 'Just till I get things straight.'

'Sure,' she said. 'Couple of days. Fine.'

'See you soon, honey.'

'Sure,' she said again, vaguely. 'Fine.'

After a while I disconnected and got through instead to Luke-John. His brisk voice vibrated loudly through the receiver and sent javelins through my head. I told him I hadn't written my Sunday column yet because I'd been involved in a car crash the night before, and held the receiver six inches away while he replied.

'The car crash was yesterday afternoon.'

'This was another one.'

'For God's sake, do you make a habit of it?'

'I'll write my piece this evening and come in with

it in the morning before I go to Heathbury for the Lamplighter. Will that do?'

'It'll have to, I suppose,' he grumbled. 'You weren't hurt in the second crash, were you?' He sounded as if an affirmative answer would be highly unpopular.

'Only bruised,' I said, and got a noncommittal unsympathetic grunt.

'Make that piece good,' he said. 'Blow the roof off.'

I put down the receiver before he could blow the roof off my head. It went on thrumming mercilessly. Ross's target area also alternately burned and ached and made lying in bed draggingly uncomfortable. The grim morning continued. People came and asked me who I was. And who were the two men with me, who had both drowned in the car? Did I know their address?

No, I didn't.

And how had the accident happened?

'The chauffeur had a blackout,' I said.

A police sergeant came with a notebook and wrote down the uninformative truth I told him about the accident. I didn't know Mr Vjoersterod well: he was just an acquaintance. He had insisted on taking me in his car to the nursing home where my wife was at present a patient. The chauffeur had had a blackout and the car had run off the road. It had all happened very quickly. I couldn't remember clearly, because I was afraid I had had a little too much to drink. Mr Vjoersterod had handed me something to smash our way out of the car with, and I had done my best. It was very sad about Mr Vjoersterod and the chauffeur. The man who had fetched them out ought to have a medal. The sergeant said I would be needed for the inquest and went away.

The doctor who came to examine me at midday sympathized with my various discomforts and said it was extraordinary sometimes how much bruising one could sustain through being thrown about in a somersaulting car. I gravely agreed with him and suggested I went home as soon as possible.

'Why not?' he said. 'If you feel like it.'

I felt like oblivion. I creaked into my rough-dried crumpled shirt and trousers and left my face unshaven, my hair unbrushed and my tie untied, because lifting my arms up for those jobs was too much trouble. Tottered downstairs and got the porter to ring for a taxi, which took me the short distance to Welbeck Street and decanted me on Tonio's doorstep. Someone had picked up the Leaning Tower and put it back in place. There wasn't a mark on it. More than could be said for the Rolls. More than could be said for me.

Tonio gave me one penetrating look, an armchair, and a medicine glass of disprin and nepenthe.

'What's this made of?' I asked, when I'd drunk it.

'Nepenthe? A mixture of opium and sherry wine. Very useful stuff. How often do you intend to turn up here in dire need of it?'

'No more,' I said. 'It's finished.'

He wanted to know what had happened after he had driven Elizabeth away, and I told him, save for the one detail of my having blacked out the chauffeur myself. He was no fool, however. He gave me a twisted smile of comprehension and remarked that I had behaved like a drunken idiot.

After that he fetched my jacket from his bedroom and insisted on driving me and the van back to the flat on the basis that Elizabeth needed me safe and sound, not wrapped round one of the lamp posts I had miraculously missed the night before. I didn't argue. Hadn't the energy. He put the van in the garage for me and walked away up the mews to look for a taxi, and I slowly went up the stairs to the flat feeling like a wet dishcloth attempting the Matterhorn.

The flat was stifling hot. I had left all the heaters on the night before and Mrs Woodward hadn't turned them off. There was a note from her on the table. 'Is everything all right? Have put milk in fridge. Am very anxious. Mrs W.'

I looked at my bed. Nothing on it but sheets. Remembered all the blankets and pillows were still downstairs on the stretcher in the van. Going down for them was impossible. Pinched Elizabeth's. Spread one pink blanket roughly on the divan, lay down on it still dressed, pulled another over me, put my head down gingerly on the soft, cool pillow.

Bliss.

The world still spun. And otherwise, far too little to

put out flags for. My head still manufactured its own sound track. And in spite of the nepenthe the rest of me still felt fresh from a cement mixer. But now there was luxuriously nothing more to do except drift over the edge of a precipice into a deep black heavenly sleep . . .

The telephone bell rang sharply, sawing the dream in half. It was Mrs Woodward, Lancashire accent very strong under stress, sounding touchingly relieved that no unbearable disaster had happened to Elizabeth.

'It's me that's not well,' I said. 'My wife's spending a couple of days in the nursing home. If you'll ring again I'll let you know when she'll be back . . .'

I put the receiver down in its cradle and started across to my bed. Took two steps, yawned, and wondered if I should tell Victor Roncey to go fetch Madge and the boys. Wondered if I should tell Willy Ondroy to slacken the ultra-tight security. Decided to leave things as they were. Only twenty-four hours to the race. Might as well be safe. Even with Vjoer-sterod dead, there was always Charlie Boston.

Not that Tiddely Pom would win. After all the trouble to get him there his chances were slender, because the bout of colic would have taken too much out of him. Charlie Boston would make his profit, just as if they'd nobbled him as planned.

I retraced the two steps back to the telephone and after a chat with Enquiries put through a personal call to Birmingham.

'Mr Boston?'

'Yes.'

'This is James Tyrone.'

There was a goggling silence at the other end punctuated only by some heavy breathing.

I asked, 'What price are you offering on Tiddely Pom?'

No answer except a noise halfway between a grunt and a growl.

'The horse will run,' I commented.

'That's all you know,' he said. A rough, bad-tempered voice. A rough, bad-tempered man.

'Don't rely on Ross or Vjoersterod,' I said patiently. 'You won't be hearing from them again. The poor dear fellows are both dead.'

I put down the receiver without waiting for the Boston reactions. Felt strong enough to take off my jacket. Made it back to bed and found the friendly precipice still there, waiting. Didn't keep it waiting any longer.

A long while later I woke up thirsty and with a tongue which felt woolly and grass-green. The nepenthe had worn off. My shoulders were heavy, stiffly sore, and insistent. A bore. All pain was a bore. It was dark. I consulted my luminous watch. Four o'clock, give or take a minute. I'd slept twelve hours.

I yawned. Found my brain no longer felt as if it

was sitting on a bruise and remembered with a wide-awakening shock that I hadn't written my column for the *Blaze*. I switched on the light and took a swig of Tonio's mixture, and after it had worked went to fetch a notebook and pencil and a cup of coffee. Propped up the pillows, climbed back between the blankets, and blew the roof off for Luke-John.

'The lawyers will have a fit,' he said.

'As I've pointed out, the man who ran the racket died this week, and the libel laws only cover the living. The dead can't sue. And no one can sue for them. Also you can't accuse or try the dead. Not in this world, anyway. So nothing they've done can be *sub judice*. Right?'

'Don't quote *Blaze* dictums to me, laddie. I was living by them before you were weaned.' He picked up my typed sheets as if they would burn him.

'Petrified owners can come out of their caves,' he read aloud. 'The reign of intimidation is over and the scandal of the non-starting favourites can be fully exposed.'

Derry lifted his head to listen, gave me a grin, and said, 'Our troubleshooter loosing the big guns again?'

'Life gets tedious otherwise,' I said.

'Only for some.'

Luke-John eyed me appraisingly. 'You look more as if you'd been the target. I suppose all this haggard-eyed stuff is the result of a day spent crashing about in cars.' He flicked his thumb against my article. 'Did you invent this unnamed villain, or did he really exist? And if so who was he?'

If I didn't tell, Mike de Jong in his rival newspaper might put two and two together and come up with a filling-in-the-gaps story that Luke-John would never forgive me for. And there was no longer an urgent reason for secrecy.

I said, 'He was a South African called Vjoersterod, and he died the night before last in the second of those car crashes.'

Their mouths literally fell open.

'Dyna . . . *mite*,' Derry said.

I told them most of what had happened. I left Gail and Ross's trucheon out altogether but put in the threat to Elizabeth. Left out the drunken driving and the hands over Ross's eyes. Made it bald and factual. Left out the sweat.

Luke-John thought through the problem and then read my article again.

'When you know what you've omitted, what you've included seems pale. But I think this is enough. It'll do the trick, tell everyone the pressure's off and that they can safely bet ante-post again, thanks entirely to investigations conducted by the *Blaze*.'

'That's after all what we wanted.'

'Buy the avenging *Blaze*,' said Derry only half-sardonically. 'Racket-smashing a speciality.'

Luke-John gave him a sour look for a joke in bad taste, as usual taking the *Blaze*'s role with unrelieved seriousness. I asked him if he would ring up a powerful bookmaking friend of his and ask him the present state of the Lamplighter market, and with raised eyebrows but no other comment he got through. He asked the question, listened with sharpening attention to the answer, and scribbled down some figures. When he had finished he gave a soundless whistle and massaged his larynx.

'He says Charlie Boston has been trying to lay off about fifty thousand on Tiddely Pom since yesterday afternoon. Everyone smells a sewer full of rats because of your articles and the *Blaze*'s undertaking to keep the horse safe and they're in a tizzy whether to take the bets or not. Only one or two of the biggest firms have done so.'

I said, 'If Boston can't lay off and Tiddely Pom wins, he's sunk without trace, but if Tiddely Pom loses he'll pocket all Vjoersterod's share of the loot as well as his own and be better off than if we'd done nothing at all. If he manages to lay off and Tiddely Pom wins, he'll be smiling, and if he lays off and Tiddely Pom loses he'll have thrown away everything the crimes were committed for.'

'A delicate problem,' said Derry judicially. 'Or what you might call the antlers of a dilemma.'

'Could he know about the colic?' Luke-John asked.

We decided after picking it over that as he was

trying to lay off he probably couldn't. Luke-John rang back to his bookmaker friend and advised him to take as much of the Boston money as he could.

'And after that,' he said gloomily, as he put down the receiver, 'every other bloody horse will fall, and Tiddely Pom will win.'

Derry and I went down to Heathbury Park together on the race train. The racecourse and the sponsors of the Lamplighter had been smiled on by the day. Clear, sunny, still, frosty: a perfect December morning. Derry said that fine weather was sure to bring out a big crowd, and that he thought Zig Zag would win. He said he thought I looked ill. I said he should have seen me yesterday. We completed the journey in our usual relationship of tolerant acceptance and I wondered inconsequentially why it had never solidified into friendship.

He was right on the first count. Heathbury Park was bursting at the seams. I went first to Willy Ondroy's office beside the weighing-room and found a scattered queue of people wanting a word with him, but he caught my eye across the throng and waved a beckoning hand.

'Hey,' he said, swinging round in his chair to talk to me behind his shoulder. 'Your wretched horse has caused me more bother ... that Victor Roncey, he's a bloody pain in the neck.'

'What's he been doing?'

'He arrived at ten this morning all set to blow his top if the horse arrived a minute after twelve and when he found he was there already he blew his top anyway and said he should have been told.'

'Not the easiest of characters,' I agreed.

'Anyway, that's only the half of it. The gateman rang me at about eight this morning to say there was a man persistently trying to get in. He'd offered him a bribe and then increased it and had tried to slip in unnoticed while he, the gateman, was having an argument with one of the stable lads. So I nipped over from my house for a reccy, and there was this short stout individual walking along the back of the stable block looking for an unguarded way in. I marched him round to the front and the gateman said that was the same merchant, so I asked him who he was and what he wanted. He wouldn't answer. Said he hadn't committed any crime. I let him go. Nothing else to do.'

'Pity.'

'Wait a minute. My racecourse manager came towards us as the man walked away, and the first thing he said to me was, "What's Charlie Boston doing here?" '

'What?'

'Ah. I thought he might mean something to you. But he was extraordinarily clumsy, if he was after Tiddely Pom.'

'No brains and no brawn,' I agreed.

He looked at me accusingly. 'If Charlie Boston was the sum total of the threat to Tiddely Pom, haven't you been overdoing the melodrama a bit?'

I said dryly, 'Read the next thrilling instalment in the *Blaze*.'

He laughed and turned back decisively to his impatient queue. I wandered out into the paddock, thinking of Charlie Boston and his futile attempt to reach the horse. Charlie Boston who thought with his muscles. With other people's muscles, come to that. Having his boys on the sick list and Vjoersterod and Ross on the dead, he was as naked and vulnerable as an opened oyster.

He might also be desperate. If he was trying to lay off fifty thousand pounds, he had stood to lose at least ten times that – upwards of half a million – if Tiddely Pom won. A nosedive of epic proportions. A prospect to induce panic and recklessness in ever-increasing intensity as the time of the race drew near.

I decided that Roncey should share the care of his horse's safety, and began looking out for him in the throng. I walked round the corner with my eyes scanning sideways and nearly bumped into someone standing at the Results-at-other-Meetings notice board. The apology was halfway to my tongue before I realized who it was.

Gail.

I saw the pleasure which came first into her eyes, and the uncertainty afterwards. Very likely I was showing her exactly the same feeling. Very likely she, like me, felt a thudding shock at meeting. Yet if I'd considered it at all, it was perfectly reasonable that she should come to see her uncle's horse run in the Lamplighter.

'Ty?' she said tentatively, with a ton less than her usual poise.

'Surprise, surprise.' It sounded more flippant than I felt.

'I thought I might see you,' she said. Her smooth black hair shone in the sun and the light lay along the bronze lines of her face, touching them with gold. The mouth I had kissed was a rosy pink. The body I had liked naked was covered with a turquoise coat. A week today, I thought numbly. A week today I left her in bed.

'Are Harry and Sarah here?' I said. Social chat. Hide the wound which hadn't even begun to form a scar tissue. I'd no right to be wounded in the first place. My own fault. Couldn't complain.

'They're in the bar,' she said. 'Where else?'

'Would you like a drink?'

She shook her head. 'I want to . . . to explain. I see that you know . . . I have to explain.'

'No need. A cup of coffee, perhaps?'

'Just listen.'

I could feel the rigidity in all my muscles and realized it extended even into my mouth and jaw. With a conscious effort I loosened them and relaxed.

'All right.'

'Did she ... I mean, is she going to divorce you?'

'No.'

'Ohhhh.' It was a long sigh. 'Then I'm sorry if I got you into trouble with her. But why did she have you followed if she didn't want to divorce you?'

I stared at her. The wound half healed in an instant.

'What's the matter?' she said.

I took a deep breath. 'Tell me what happened after I left you. Tell me about the man who followed me.'

'He came up and spoke to me in the street just outside the hotel.'

'What did he look like?'

'He puzzled me a bit. I mean, he seemed too ... I don't know ... civilized, I suppose is the word, to be a private detective. His clothes were made for him, for instance. He had an accent of some sort and a yellowish skin. Tall. About forty, I should think.'

'What did he say?'

'He said your wife wanted a divorce and he was working on it. He asked me for ... concrete evidence.'

'A bill from the hotel?'

She nodded, not meeting my eyes. 'I agreed to go in again and ask for one.'

'Why, Gail?'

She didn't answer.

'Did he pay you for it?'

'God, Ty,' she said explosively. 'Why not? I needed

the money. I'd only met you three times and you were just as bad as me, living with your wife just because she was rich.'

'Yes,' I said. 'Well, how much?'

'He offered me fifty pounds and when I got used to the idea that he was ready to pay I told him to think again, with all your wife's money she could afford more than that for her freedom.'

'And then what?'

'He said ... if I could give him full and substantial facts, he could raise the payment considerably.' After a pause, in a mixture of defiance and shame, she added, 'He agreed to a thousand pounds, in the end.'

I gave a gasp which was half a laugh.

'Didn't your wife tell you?' she asked.

I shook my head. 'He surely didn't have that much money on him? Did he give you a cheque?'

'No. He met me later, outside the art school, and gave me a brown carrier bag ... Beautiful new notes, in bundles. I gave him the bill I'd got, and told him ... everything I could.'

'I know,' I said.

'Why did he pay so much, if she doesn't want a divorce?' When I didn't answer at once she went on, 'It wasn't really only the money ... I thought if she wanted to divorce you, why the hell should I stop her. You said you wouldn't leave her, but if she sort of left *you*, then you would be free, and maybe we could have more than a few Sundays ...'

609

I thought that one day I might appreciate the irony of it.

I said, 'It wasn't my wife who paid you that money. It was the man himself. He wasn't collecting evidence for a divorce, but evidence to blackmail me with.'

'Ohh.' It was a moan. 'Oh no, Ty. Oh God, I'm so sorry.' Her eyes widened suddenly. 'You must have thought . . . I suppose you thought . . . that I sold you out for *that*.'

'I'm afraid so,' I apologized. 'I should have known better.'

'That makes us quits, then.' All her poise came back at one bound. She said, with some concern but less emotional disturbance, 'How much did he take you for?'

'He didn't want money. He wanted me to write my column in the *Blaze* every week according to his instructions.'

'How extraordinary. Well, that's easy enough.'

'Would you design dresses to dictation by threat?'

'Oh.'

'Exactly. Oh. So I told my wife about you myself. I had to.'

'What . . . what did she say?'

'She was upset,' I said briefly. 'I said I wouldn't be seeing you again. There'll be no divorce.'

She slowly shrugged her shoulders. 'So that's that.'

I looked away from her, trying not to mind so appallingly much that that was that. Tomorrow was Sunday.

Tomorrow was Sunday and I could be on my own, and there was nothing on earth that I wanted so much as to see her again in her smooth warm skin and hold her close and tight in the half dark . . .

She said thoughtfully, 'I suppose if that man was a blackmailer it explains why I thought he was so nasty.'

'Nasty? He was usually fantastically polite.'

'He spoke to me as if I'd crawled out of the cracks. I wouldn't have put up with it . . . except for the money.'

'Poor Gail,' I said sympathetically. 'He was South African.'

She took in the implication and her eyes were furious. 'That explains it. A beastly Afrikaner. I wish I'd never agreed.'

'Don't be silly,' I interrupted. 'Be glad you cost him so much.'

She calmed down and laughed. 'I've never even been to Africa. I didn't recognize his accent or give it a thought. Stupid, isn't it?'

A man in a check tweed suit came and asked us to move as he wanted to read the notices on the board behind us. We walked three or four steps away, and paused again.

'I suppose I'll see you sometimes at the races,' she said.

'I suppose so.'

She looked closely at my face and said, 'If you really feel like that, why . . . *why* don't you leave her?'

'I can't.'

'But we could . . . you want to be with me. I know you do. Money isn't everything.'

I smiled twistedly. I did after all mean something to her, if she could ever say that.

'I'll see you sometimes,' I repeated emptily. 'At the races.'

CHAPTER SEVENTEEN

I caught Victor Roncey coming out of the luncheon room and told him that the danger to Tiddely Pom was by no means over.

'He's here, isn't he?' he said squashingly.

'He's here thanks to us,' I reminded him. 'And there are still two hours to the race.'

'What do you expect me to do? Hold his hand?'

'It wouldn't hurt,' I said flatly.

There was the usual struggle between aggressive independence and reasonable agreement. He said grudgingly, 'Peter can sit outside his box over in the stables.'

'Where is Peter now?'

He waved a hand behind him. 'Finishing lunch.'

'You'll have to take him in yourself, if he hasn't got a stable lad's pass.'

He grumbled and agreed, and went back to fetch his son. I walked over to the stables with them and checked with the man on the gate who said he'd had the usual number of people trying to get in, but not the man he'd turned away in the morning. Wing Commander Ondroy had told him to sling that man in the storeroom and lock him in, if he came sniffing round again.

I smiled appreciatively and went in with Roncey to look at the horse. He stood patiently in his box, propped on one hip, resting a rear leg. When we opened the door he turned his head lazily and directed on us an unexcited eye. A picture of a racehorse not on his toes, not strung up by the occasion, not looking ready to win Lamplighter Gold Cups.

'Is he always like this before a race?' I said. 'He looks doped.'

Roncey gave me a horrified glance and hurried to his horse's head. He looked in his mouth and eyes, felt his neck and legs, and kicked open and studied a small pile of droppings. Finally he shook his head.

'No dope that I can see. No signs of it.'

'He never has nerves,' Peter observed. 'He isn't bred for it.'

He looked bred for a milk cart. I refrained from saying so. I walked back into the paddock with Roncey and got him to agree to saddle up his horse in the stables, not in the saddling boxes, if the stewards would allow it.

The stewards, who included Eric Youll, didn't hesitate. They said only that Tiddely Pom would have to walk the three stipulated times round the parade ring for the public to see him before the jockey mounted, but were willing for him to walk six feet in from the rails and be led and guarded by Peter and myself.

'All a waste of time,' Roncey muttered. 'No one will try anything here.'

'Don't you believe it,' I said. 'You'd try anything if you stood to lose half a million you hadn't got.'

I watched the first two races from the press box and spent the time in between aimlessly wandering about in the crowd trying to convince myself that I wasn't really looking for another glimpse of Gail.

I didn't see her. I did see Dermot Finnegan. The little Irish jockey walked in front of me and gave me a huge gap-toothed grin. I took in, as I was supposed to, that he was dressed in colours, ready to ride in a race. The front of his jacket was carefully unbuttoned. I added up the purple star on the pink and white horizontal stripes and he laughed when he saw my astonishment.

'Be Jasus, and I'm almost as staggered as yourself,' he said. 'But there it is, I've got my big chance on the Guvnor's first string and if I make a mess of it may God have mercy on my soul because I won't.'

'You won't make a mess of it.'

'We'll see,' he said cheerfully. 'That was a grand job you made of me in *Tally*, now. Thank you for that. I took that when it came and showed it to the Guvnor but he'd already seen it, he told me. And you know I wouldn't be certain that it wasn't the magazine that put him in mind of putting me up on Rockville, when the other two fellows got hurt on Thursday. So thank you for that, too.'

When I told Derry about it in the press box during the second race he merely shrugged. 'Of course he's riding Rockville. Don't you read the papers?'

'Not yesterday.'

'Oh. Well yes, he's got as much as he can chew this time. Rockville's a difficult customer, even with the best of jockeys and our Dermot isn't that.' He was busy polishing the lenses of his race glasses. 'Luke-John's bookmaker friend must have accepted a good deal of Boston's fifty thousand, because the price on Tiddely Pom has come crashing down like an express lift from 100 to 8 to only 4 to 1. That's a stupid price for a horse like Tiddely Pom, but there you are.'

I did a small sum. If Boston had taken bets at 10 or 12 to 1 and had only been able to lay them off at 4 to 1, that left him a large gap of 6 or 8 to 1. If Tiddely Pom won, that would be the rate at which he would have to pay: which added up still to more than a quarter of a million pounds and meant that he would have to sell off the string of betting shops to pay his debts. Dumb Charlie Boston, trying to play with the big boys and getting squeezed like a toothpaste tube.

There was no sign of him in the paddock. Roncey saddled his horse in the stables and brought him straight into the parade ring very shortly before the time for the jockeys to mount. Peter led him round and I walked along by his quarters; but no one leaned over the rails to squirt him with acid. No one tried anything at all.

'Told you so,' Roncey muttered. 'All this fuss.' He put up his jockey, slapped Tiddely Pom's rump, and hurried off to get a good position on the trainer's stand. Peter led the horse out on to the course and let him go, and Tiddely Pom cantered off unconcernedly with the long lolloping stride so at variance with his looks. I sighed with relief and went up to join Derry in the press box to watch the race.

'Tiddely Pom's favourite,' he said. 'Then Zig Zag, then Rockville. Zig Zag should have it in his pocket.' He put his race glasses to his eyes and studied the horses milling round at the start. I hadn't taken my own glasses as I'd found the carrying strap pressed too heavily on tender spots. I felt lost without them, like a snail without antennae. The start for the Lamplighter was a quarter of a mile down the course from the stands. I concentrated on sorting out the colours with only force four success.

Derry exclaimed suddenly, 'What the devil . . .'

'Tiddely Pom,' I said fearfully. Not now. Not at the very post. I should have foreseen . . . should have stationed someone down there . . . But it was so public. So many people walked down there to watch the start. Anyone who tried to harm a horse there would have a hundred witnesses.

'There's someone hanging on to his reins. No, he's been pulled off. Great God . . .' Derry started laughing

617

incredulously. 'I can't believe it. I simply can't believe it.'

'What's happening?' I said urgently. All I could see was a row of peacefully lining up horses, which miraculously included Tiddely Pom, and some sort of commotion going on in the crowd on the far side of the rails.

'It's Madge . . . Madge Roncey. It must be. No one else looks like that . . . She's rolling about on the grass with a fat little man . . . struggling. She pulled him away from Tiddely Pom . . . Arms and legs are flying all over the place . . .' He stopped, laughing too much. 'The boys are with her . . . they're all piling on to the poor little man in a sort of rugger scrum . . .'

'It's a pound to a penny the poor little man is Charlie Boston,' I said grimly. 'And if it's Madge and not the *Blaze* who's saved the day, we'll never hear the end of it from Victor Roncey.'

'Damn Victor Roncey,' Derry said. 'They're off.'

The line of horses bounded forward, heading for the first jump. Seventeen runners, three and a half miles, and a gold trophy and a fat cheque to the winner.

One of them crumpled up over the first. Not Tiddely Pom, whose scarlet and white chevrons bobbed in a bunch at the rear. Not Zig Zag, already positioned in the fourth place, from where he usually won. Not Egocentric, leading the field up past the stands to give the Huntersons their moment of glory. Not Rockville, with Dermot Finnegan fighting for his career in a battle not to let the horse run away with him.

They jumped the water jump in front of the stands. A gasp from the crowd as one of them splashed his hind legs right into it. The jockey in orange and green was dislodged and rolled.

'That horse always makes a balls of the water,' Derry said dispassionately. 'They should keep it for hurdles.' No tremor of excitement in his voice or hands. It had cost him nothing to get Tiddely Pom on to the track. It had cost me too much.

They swept round the top bend and started out round the circuit. Twice round the course to go. I watched Tiddely Pom all the way, expecting him to fall, expecting him to drop out at the back and be pulled up, expecting him to be too weak from colic to finish the trip.

They came round the bottom bend and up over the three fences in the straight towards the stands. Egocentric was still in front. Zig Zag still fourth. Dermot Finnegan had Rockville in decent control somewhere in the middle, and Tiddely Pom was still there and not quite last.

Over the water. Zig Zag stumbled, recovered, raced on. Not fourth any more, though. Sixth or seventh. Tiddely Pom scampered over it with none of the grace of Egocentric but twice the speed. Moved up two places.

Out they went again into the country. Derry remarked calmly, 'Tiddely Pom has dropped his bit.'

'Damn,' I said. The jockey was working with his arms, urging the horse on. Hopeless. And half the race still to run.

I shut my eyes. Felt the fatigue and illness come swamping back. Wanted to lie down somewhere soft and sleep for a week and escape from all the problems and torments and disillusionments of weary life. A week alone, to heal in. A week to give a chance for some energy for living to come creeping back. I needed a week at least. If I were lucky, I'd have a day.

'There's a faller at that fence.' The race commentator's amplified voice jerked my eyes open. 'A faller among the leaders. I think it was Egocentric... yes, Egocentric is down...'

Poor Huntersons. Poor Harry, poor Sarah.

Gail.

I didn't want to think about her. Couldn't bear to, and couldn't help it.

'He's still going,' Derry said. 'Tiddely Pom.'

The red and white chevrons were too far away to be clear. 'He's made up a bit,' Derry said. 'He's taken a hold again.'

They jumped the last fence on the far side and began the sweeping bend round into the straight, very strung out now, with great gaps between little bunches. One or two staggered fifty yards in the rear. There was a roar from the crowd and the commentator's voice rose above it . . . 'And here is Zig Zag coming to the front . . . opening up a commanding lead . . .'

'Zig Zag's slipped them,' Derry said calmly. 'Caught all the others napping.'

'Tiddely Pom . . .?' I asked.

'He's well back. Still plodding on, though. Most we could expect.'

Zig Zag jumped the first fence in the straight five seconds clear of the rest of the field.

'Nothing will catch him,' Derry said. I forgave him the satisfaction in his voice. He had tipped Zig Zag in his column. It was nice to be right. 'Tiddely Pom's in the second bunch. Can you see him? Even if he hasn't won, he's not disgraced.'

Zig Zag jumped the second last fence well ahead, chased after an interval by four horses more or less abreast. After these came Tiddely Pom, and behind him the other half-dozen still standing. If we had to settle for that, at least the ante-post punters had had some sort of run for their money.

It was clear twenty yards from the last fence that Zig Zag was meeting it wrong. The jockey hesitated fatally between pushing him on to lengthen his stride and take off sooner or shortening the reins to get him to put in an extra one before he jumped. In the end he did neither. Simply left it to the horse to sort himself out. Some horses like to do that. Some horses like to be told what to do. Zig Zag went into the fence like a rudderless ship, took off too late and too close, hit the fence hard with his forelegs, slewed round in mid air, crashed down in a tangle of hooves, and treated his rider to a well-deserved thump on the turf.

'Stupid *bastard*,' Derry said, infuriatedly lowering his glasses. 'An apprentice could have done better.'

I was watching Tiddely Pom. The four horses ahead of him jumped the last fence. One of them swerved to avoid Zig Zag and his supine jockey and bumped heavily into the horse next to him. Both of them were thoroughly unbalanced and the jockey of one fell off. When Tiddely Pom came away from the fence to tackle the straight he was lying third.

The crowd roared. 'He's got a chance,' Derry yelled. 'Even now.'

He couldn't quicken. The low lolloping stride went on at the same steady pace and all the jockey's urging was having no constructive effect. But one of the two in front of him was tiring and rolling about under pressure. Tiddely Pom crept up on him yard by yard but the winning post was coming nearer and there was still one more in front . . .

I looked at the leader, taking him in for the first time. A jockey in pink and white stripes, riding like a demon on a streak of brown, straining, hard-trained muscle. Dermot Finnegan on Rockville, with all his future in his hands.

While I watched he swept conclusively past the post, and even from the stands one could see that Irish grin bursting out like the sun.

Three lengths behind, Tiddely Pom's racing heart defeated the colic and put him second. A genuine horse, I thought thankfully. Worth all the trouble. Or at least, worth some of it.

'All we need now,' said Derry, 'is an objection.'

He wrapped the strap round his race glasses, put them in their case, and hurriedly made for the stairs. I followed him more slowly down and edged gingerly through the crowd milling round the unsaddling enclosure until I reached the clump of other press men waiting to pick up something to print. There was a cheer as Rockville was led through into the winner's place. Another cheer for Tiddely Pom. I didn't join in. Had nothing to contribute but a dead feeling of anti-climax.

All over. Tiddely Pom hadn't won. What did I expect?

The crowd parted suddenly like the Red Sea and through the gap struggled a large, untidy earth mother surrounded by planets. Madge Roncey and her sons.

She walked purposefully across the comparatively empty unsaddling enclosure and greeted her husband with a gentle pat on the arm. He was astounded to see her and stood stock still with his mouth open and Tiddely Pom's girth buckles half undone. I went across to join them.

'Hullo,' Madge said. 'Wasn't that splendid?' The far-away look in her eyes had come a few kilometres nearer since fact had begun to catch up on fantasy. She wore a scarlet coat a shade too small. Her hair floated in its usual amorphous mass. She had stockings on. Laddered.

'Splendid,' I agreed.

Roncey gave me a sharp look. 'Still fussing?'

I said to Madge, 'What happened down at the start?'

She laughed. 'There was a fat little man there going absolutely berserk and screaming that he would stop Tiddely Pom if it was the last thing he did.'

Roncey swung round and stared at her. 'He started hanging on to Tiddely Pom's reins,' she went on, 'and he wouldn't let go when the starter told him to. It was absolutely crazy. He was trying to kick Tiddely Pom's legs. So I just ducked under the rails and walked across and told him it was our horse and would he please stop it, and he was frightfully rude . . .' A speculative look came into her eye. 'He used some words I didn't know.'

'For God's sake,' said Roncey irritably. 'Get on with it.'

She went on without resentment, 'He still wouldn't let go so I put my arms round him and lifted him up and carried him off and he was so surprised he dropped the reins, and then he struggled to get free and I let him fall down on the ground and rolled him under the rails, and then the boys and I sat on him.'

I said, trying to keep a straight face, 'Did he say anything after that?'

'Well, he hadn't much breath,' she admitted judiciously. 'But he did say something about killing you, as a matter of fact. He didn't seem to like you very much. He said you'd smashed everything and stopped him getting to Tiddely Pom, and as a matter of fact he was so hysterical he was jolly nearly in tears.'

'Where is he now?' I asked.

'I don't know exactly. When I let him get up, he ran away.'

Roncey gave me a mean look. 'So it took my wife to save my horse, not the *Blaze*.'

'Oh no, dear,' she said placidly. 'If Mr Tyrone hadn't been looking after him, the little man would have been able to reach him sooner, and if I hadn't come back from the Isle of Wight because I thought it would be quite safe if no one knew, and we all wanted to see the race, if I hadn't been there at the starting gate, someone else would have taken the little man away. Lots of people were going to. It was just that I got to him first.' She gave me a sweet smile. 'I haven't had so much fun for years.'

The day fragmented after that into a lot of people saying things to me that I didn't really hear. Pieces still stick out: Dermot Finnegan being presented with a small replica of the Lamplighter Gold Cup and looking as if he'd been handed the Holy Grail. Willy Ondroy telling me that Charlie Boston had been slung off the racecourse, and Eric Youll outlining the stewards' plan for warning him off permanently, which would mean the withdrawal of his betting licence and the closing of all his shops.

Derry telling me he had been through to Luke-John, whose bookmaker friend had taken all of Charlie Boston's fifty thousand and was profoundly thankful Tiddely Pom hadn't won.

Colly Gibbons asking me to go for a drink. I declined. I was off drink. He had his wife with him, and not an American colonel in sight.

Pat Roncey staring at me sullenly, hands in pockets. I asked if he'd passed on my own telephone number along with the whereabouts of Tiddely Pom. Belligerently he tried to justify himself: the man had been even more keen to know where I lived than where the horse was. What man? The tall yellowish man with some sort of accent. From the *New Statesman*, he'd said. Didn't Pat know that the *New Statesman* was the one paper with no racing page? Pat did not.

Sandy Willis walking past leading Zig Zag, giving me a worried smile. Was the horse all right, I asked. She thought so, poor old boy. She muttered a few unfeminine comments on the jockey who had thrown the race away. She said she'd grown quite fond of Tiddely Pom, she was glad he'd done well. She'd won a bit on him, as he'd come in second. Got to get on, she said, Zig Zag needed sponging down.

The Huntersons standing glumly beside Egocentric while their trainer told them their raffle horse had broken down badly and wouldn't run again for a year, if ever.

That message got through to me razor sharp and clear. No Egocentric racing, no Huntersons at the races. No Gail at the races. Not even that.

I'd had enough. My body hurt. I understood the full meaning of the phrase sick at heart. I'd been through too many mangles, and I wasn't sure it was worth it. Vjoersterod was dead, Bert Checkov was dead, the non-starter racket was dead ... until someone else tried it, until the next wide boy came along with his threats and his heavies. Someone else could bust it next time. Not me. I'd had far, far more than enough.

I wandered slowly out on to the course and stood beside the water jump, looking down into the water. Couldn't go home until the race train went, after the last race. Couldn't go home until I'd phoned in to Luke-John for a final check on what my column would look like the next day. Nothing to go home to, anyway, except an empty flat and the prospect of an empty future.

Footsteps swished towards me through the grass. I didn't look up. Didn't want to talk.

'Ty,' she said.

I did look then. There was a difference in her face. She was softer; less cool, less poised. Still extraordinarily beautiful. I badly wanted what I couldn't have.

'Ty, why didn't you tell me about your wife?'

I shook my head. Didn't answer.

She said, 'I was in the bar with Harry and Sarah, and someone introduced us to a Major Gibbons and his wife, because he had been in your *Tally* article too, like Harry and Sarah. They were talking about you . . . Major Gibbons said it was such a tragedy about your wife . . . I said, what tragedy . . . and he told us . . .'

She paused. I took a deep difficult breath: said nothing.

'I said it must be some help that she was rich, and he said what do you mean rich, as far as I know she hasn't a bean because Ty is always hard-up with looking after her, and he'd be reasonably well off if he put her in hospital and let the country pay for her keep instead of struggling to do it himself . . .'

She turned half away from me and looked out across the course. 'Why didn't you tell me?'

I swallowed and loosened my mouth. 'I don't like . . . I didn't want . . . consolation prizes.'

After a while she said, 'I see.' It sounded as if she actually did.

There was a crack in her cool voice. She said, 'If it was me you'd married, and I'd got polio . . . I can see that you must stay with her. I see how much she needs you. If it had been me . . . and you left me . . .' She gave a small laugh which was half a sob. 'Life sure kicks you in the teeth. I find a man I don't want to part with . . . a man I'd live on crumbs with . . . and I can't have him . . . even a little while, now and then.'

CHAPTER EIGHTEEN

I spent Sunday alone in the flat, mostly asleep. Part of the time I pottered around tidying things up, trying to put my mind and life into order along with my house. Didn't have much success.

On Monday morning I went to fetch Elizabeth. She came home in an ambulance, with two fit uniformed men to carry her and the pump upstairs. They laid her on the bed I had made up freshly for her, checked that the pump was working properly, helped replace the Spirashell on her chest, accepted cups of coffee, agreed that the weather was raw and cold but what could you expect in December, and eventually went away.

I unpacked Elizabeth's case and made some scrambled eggs for lunch, and fed her when her wrist packed up, and fixed another mug of coffee into the holder.

She smiled and thanked me. She looked tired, but very calm. There was a deep difference in her, but for some time I couldn't work out what it was. When I finally identified it, I was surprised. She wasn't anxious any more. The long-established, deep-rooted insecurity no longer looked out of her eyes.

'Leave the dishes, Ty,' she said. 'I want to talk to you.'

I sat in the armchair. She watched me. 'It still hurts . . . what that man did.'

'A bit,' I agreed.

'Tonio told me they were both killed that night . . . trying to find me again.'

'He did, did he?'

She nodded. 'He came to see me yesterday. We had a long talk. A long, long talk. He told me a lot of things . . .'

'Honey,' I said, 'I . . .'

'Shut up, Ty. I want to tell you . . . what he said.'

'Don't tire yourself.'

'I won't. I am tired, but it feels different from usual. I feel just ordinary tired, not . . . not *worried* tired. Tonio did that. And you. I mean, he made me understand what I saw on Thursday, that you would let yourself be smashed up . . . that you would drive when you were drunk and risk going to prison . . . that you would do anything, however dangerous . . . to keep me safe . . . He said, if I'd seen that with my own eyes, why did I doubt . . . why did I ever doubt that you would stay with me . . . It was such a relief . . . I felt as if the whole world were lighter . . . I know you've always told me . . . but now I do believe it, through and through.'

'I'm glad,' I said truthfully. 'I'm very glad.'

She said, 'I talked to Tonio about . . . that girl.'

'Honey . . .'

'Hush,' she said. 'I told him about the blackmail. We talked for ages . . . He was so understanding. He said of course I would be upset, anyone would, but that I shouldn't worry too much . . . He said you were a normal, healthy man and if I had any sense I would see that the time to start worrying would be if you *didn't* want to sleep with someone.' She smiled. 'He said if I could face it, we would both be happier if I didn't mind if sometimes . . . He said you would always come home.'

'Tonio said a great deal.'

She nodded. 'It made such sense. I haven't been fair to you.'

'Elizabeth,' I protested.

'No. I really haven't. I was so afraid of losing you, I couldn't see how much I was asking of you. But I understand now that the more I can let you go, the easier you will find it to live with me . . . and the more you will want to.'

'Tonio said that?'

'Yes, he did.'

'He's very fond of you,' I said.

She grinned. 'He said so. He also said some pretty ear-burning things about you, if you want to know.' She told me some of them, her mouth curving up at the corners and the new security gleaming in her eyes.

631

'Exaggeration,' I said modestly.

She laughed. A breathy giggle. Happy.

I got up and kissed her on the forehead and on the cheek. She was the girl I'd married. I loved her very much.

On Tuesday morning, when Mrs Woodward came back, I went out along the mews, round the corner and into the telephone box, and dialled the number of the Western School of Art.

REFLEX

My thanks to the Photographers
Bernard Parkin and David Hastings
and especially RON MASSEY
who made me the puzzles.

CHAPTER ONE

Winded and coughing, I lay on one elbow and spat out a mouthful of grass and mud. The horse I'd been riding raised its weight off my ankle, scrambled untidily to its feet and departed at an unfeeling gallop. I waited for things to settle: chest heaving, bones still rattling from the bang, sense of balance recovering from a thirty-mile-an-hour somersault and a few tumbling rolls. No harm done. Nothing broken. Just another fall.

Time and place: sixteenth fence, three-mile steeple-chase, Sandown Park racecourse, Friday, November, in thin, cold, persistent rain. At the return of breath and energy I stood wearily up and thought with intensity that this was a damn silly way for a grown man to be spending his life.

The thought itself was a jolt. Not one I'd ever thought before. Riding horses at high speed over various jumps was the only way I knew of making a living, and it was a job one couldn't do if one's heart wasn't in it. The chilling flicker of disillusion nudged like the first twinge of toothache, unexpected, unwelcome, an uneasy hint of possible trouble.

I repressed it without much alarm. Reassured myself that I loved the life, of course I did, the way I always had. Believed quite easily that nothing was wrong except the weather, the fall, the lost race . . . minor, everyday stuff, business as usual.

Squelching uphill to the stands in paper-thin racing boots unsuitable for hiking, I thought only and firmly about the horse I'd started out on, sorting out what I might and might not say to its trainer. Discarded 'How do you expect it to jump if you don't school it properly?' in favour of 'The experience will do him good.' Thought better of 'useless, panicky, hard-mouthed, underfed dog', and decided on 'might try him in blinkers'. The trainer, anyway, would blame me for the fall and tell the owner I'd misjudged the pace. He was that sort of trainer. Every crash was a pilot error.

I thanked heaven in a mild way that I didn't ride often for that stable, and had been engaged on that day only because Steve Millace, its usual jockey, had gone to his father's funeral. Spare rides, even with disaster staring up from the form books, were not lightly to be turned down. Not if you needed the money, which I did. And not if, like me, you needed your name up on the number boards as often as possible, to show you were useful and wanted and *there*.

The only good thing, I supposed, about my descent at the fence was that Steve Millace's father hadn't been there to record it. George Millace, pitiless photographer of moments all jockeys preferred to ignore, was safe in his box and approximately at that moment being lowered underground to his long sleep. And good riddance, I thought uncharitably. Goodbye to the snide sneering pleasure George got from delivering to owners the irrefutable evidence of their jockeys' failings. Goodbye to the motorised camera catching at three and a half frames per second one's balance in the wrong place, one's arms in the air, one's face in the mud.

Where other sports photographers played fair and shot you winning from time to time, George trafficked exclusively in ignominy and humiliation. George was a natural-born dragger-down. Newspapers might mourn the passing of his snigger-raising pictures, but there had been little sorrow in the changing room the day Steve told us his father had driven into a tree.

Out of liking for Steve himself, no one had said much. He had listened to the silence, though, and he knew. He had been anxiously defending his father for years; and he knew.

Trudging back in the rain it seemed odd to me still that we wouldn't actually be seeing George Millace again. His image, too familiar for too long, rose sharply in the mind: bright clever eyes, long nose, drooping moustache, twisted mouth sourly smiling. A terrific photographer, one had to admit, with an exceptional talent for anticipation and timing, his lens always pointing in the right direction at the right moment. A comic, too, in his way, showing me less than a week ago a black and white glossy of me taking a dive, nose to ground, bottom up, with a caption written on the back, 'Philip Nore, arse high to a grasshopper.' One would have laughed but for the genuine ill-will which had prompted his humour. One might always have at least tolerated his debunking approach but for the cruelty sliding out of his eyes. He had been a mental thrower of banana skins, lying in wait to scoff at the hurt; and he would be missed with thankfulness.

When I finally reached the shelter of the verandah outside the weighing room, the trainer and owner were waiting there with the expected accusing expressions.

'Misjudged things pretty badly, didn't you?' said the trainer aggressively.

'He took off a stride too soon.'

'Your job to put him right.'

No point in saying that no jockey on earth could get every horse to jump perfectly always, and particularly not a badly schooled rogue. I simply nodded, and smiled a shade ruefully at the owner.

'Might try him in blinkers,' I said.

'*I'll* decide about that,' said the trainer sharply.

'Not hurt, are you?' asked the owner timidly.

I shook my head. The trainer brusquely stamped on this humane jockey-orientated enquiry and wheeled his money-source away from the danger that I might say something truthful about why the horse wouldn't jump when asked. I watched them go without rancour and turned towards the weighing room door.

'I say,' said a young man, stepping in front of me, 'are you Philip Nore?'

'That's right.'

'Well . . . could I have a word with you?'

He was about twenty-five, tall as a stork and earnest, with office-coloured skin. Charcoal flannel suit, striped tie, no binoculars, and no air of belonging where he stood, in the business-only section of the racecourse.

'Sure,' I said. 'If you'll wait while I check with the doctor and get into something dry.'

'Doctor?' He looked alarmed.

'Oh . . . routine. After a fall. I shan't be long.'

When I went out again, warmed and in street clothes, he was still waiting; and he was more or less alone on the verandah, as nearly everyone else had gone to watch the last race, already in progress.

'I . . . er . . . my name is Jeremy Folk.' He produced a card from inside the charcoal jacket and held it out to me. I took it, and read: *Folk, Langley, Son and Folk.*

Solicitors. Address in St Albans, Hertfordshire.

'That last Folk,' said Jeremy, pointing diffidently, 'is me.'

'Congratulations,' I said.

He gave me an anxious half smile and cleared his throat.

'I've been sent . . . er . . . I've come to ask you to . . .

er . . .' He stopped, looking helpless and not in the least like a solicitor.

'To what?' I said encouragingly.

'They said you wouldn't like . . . but well . . . I've been sent to ask you . . . er . . .'

'Do get on with it,' I said.

'To come and see your grandmother.' The words came out in a nervous rush, and he seemed relieved to be rid of them.

'No,' I said.

He scanned my face and seemed to take heart from its calmness.

'She's dying,' he said. 'And she wants to see you.'

Death all around, I thought. George Millace and my mother's mother. Negative grief in both cases.

'Did you hear?' he said.

'I heard.'

'Now, then? I mean, today?'

'No,' I said. 'I'm not going.'

'But you must.' He looked troubled. 'I mean . . . she's old . . . and she's dying . . . and she wants you . . .'

'Too bad.'

'And if I don't persuade you, my uncle . . . that's Son . . .' He pointed to the card again, getting flustered. 'Er. Folk is my grandfather and Langley is my great-uncle, and . . . er . . . they sent me . . .' He swallowed. 'They think I'm frightfully useless, to be honest.'

'And that's blackmail,' I said.

A faint glint in his eyes told me that he wasn't basically as silly as he made out.

'I don't want to see her,' I said.

'But she is dying.'

'Have you yourself seen her . . . dying?'

'Er . . . no . . .'

'I'll bet she isn't. If she wants to see me, she would say she was dying just to fetch me, because she'd guess nothing else would.'

He looked shocked. 'She's seventy-eight, after all.'

I looked gloomily out at the non-stop rain. I had never met my grandmother and I didn't want to, dying or dead. I didn't approve of death-bed repentances, last minute insurances at the gates of hell. It was too damned late.

'The answer,' I said, 'is still no.'

He shrugged dispiritedly and seemed to give up. Walked a few steps out into the rain, bareheaded, vulnerable, with no umbrella. Turned round after ten paces and came tentatively back again.

'Look . . . she really needs you, my uncle says.' He was as earnest, as intense, as a missionary. 'You can't just let her die.'

'Where is she?' I said.

He brightened. 'In a nursing home.' He fished in another pocket. 'I've got the address. But I'll lead you there, straight away, if you'll come. It's in St Albans. You live in Lambourn, don't you? So it isn't terribly far out of your way, is it? I mean, not a hundred miles, or anything like that.'

'A good fifty, though.'

'Well . . . I mean . . . you always do drive around an awful lot.'

I sighed. The options were rotten. A choice between meek capitulation or a stony rejection. Both unpalatable. That she had dished out to me the stony rejection from my birth gave me no excuse, I supposed, for doing it to her at her death. Also I could hardly go on smugly despising her, as I had done for years, if I followed her example. Irritating, that.

The winter afternoon was already fading, with electric lights growing brighter by the minute, shining fuzzily through the rain. I thought of my empty cottage; of nothing much to fill the evening, of two eggs, a piece of cheese and black coffee for supper, of wanting to eat more and not doing so. If I went, I thought, it would at least take my mind off food, and anything which helped with the perennial fight against weight couldn't be wholly bad. Not even meeting my grandmother.

'All right,' I said, resignedly, 'lead on.'

The old woman sat upright in bed staring at me, and if she was dying it wasn't going to be on that evening, for sure. The life force was strong in the dark eyes and there was no mortal weakness in her voice.

'Philip,' she said, making it a statement and looking me up and down.

'Yes.'

'Hah.'

The explosive sound contained both triumph and contempt and was everything I would have expected. Her ramrod will had devastated my childhood and done worse damage to her own daughter, and there was to be, I was relieved to see, no maudlin plea for forgiveness. Rejection, even if in a moderated form, was still in operation.

'I knew you'd come running,' she said, 'when you heard about the money.' As a cold sneer it was pretty unbeatable.

'What money?'

'The hundred thousand pounds, of course.'

'No one,' I said, 'has mentioned any money.'

'Don't lie. Why else would you come?'

'They said you were dying.'

She gave me a startled and malevolent flash of the eyes and a baring of teeth which had nothing to do with smiling. 'So I am. So are we all.'

'Yeah,' I said, 'and all at the same rate. One day at a time.'

She was no one's idea of a sweet little pink-cheeked grannie. A strong stubborn face with disapproval lines cut deep around the mouth. Iron grey hair still vigorous, clean and well shaped. Blotchy freckles of age showing brown on an otherwise pale skin, and dark ridged veins on the backs of the hands. A thin woman, almost gaunt; and tall, as far as I could judge.

The large room where she lay was furnished more as a sitting room with a bed in it than as a hospital, which was all of a piece with what I'd seen of the place on the way in. A country house put to new use: hotel with nurses. Carpets everywhere, long chintz curtains, armchairs for visitors, vases of flowers. Gracious dying, I thought.

'I instructed Mr Folk,' she said, 'to make you the offer.'

I reflected. 'Young Mr Folk? About twenty-five? Jeremy?'

'Of course not.' She was impatient. 'Mr Folk, my solicitor. I told him to get you here. And he did. Here you are.'

'He sent his grandson.'

I turned away from her and sat unasked in an arm-chair. Why, I wondered, had Jeremy not mentioned a hundred thousand pounds? It was the sort of trifle, after all, that one didn't easily forget.

My grandmother stared at me steadily with no sign of affection, and I stared as steadily back. I disliked her certainty that she could buy me. I was repelled by her contempt, and mistrusted her intentions.

'I will leave you a hundred thousand pounds in my will, upon certain conditions,' she said.

'No, you won't,' I said.

'I beg your pardon?' Icy voice, stony look.

'I said no. No money. No conditions.'

'You haven't heard my proposition.'

I said nothing. I felt in fact the first stirrings of curiosity, but I was definitely not going to let her see it. Since she seemed in no hurry, the silence lengthened. More stocktaking on her part, perhaps. Simple patience, on mine. One thing my haphazard upbringing had given me was an almost limitless capacity for waiting. Waiting for people to come, who didn't; and for promises to be fulfilled, that weren't.

Finally she said, 'You're taller than I expected. And tougher.'

I waited some more.

'Where is your mother?' she said.

My mother, her daughter. 'Scattered on the winds,' I said.

'What do you mean?'

'I think she's dead.'

'*Think!*' She looked more annoyed than anxious. 'Don't you *know*?'

'She didn't exactly write to me to say she'd died; no.'

'Your flippancy is disgraceful.'

'Your behaviour since before my birth,' I said, 'gives you no right to say so.'

She blinked. Her mouth opened, and stayed open for fully five seconds. Then it shut tight with rigid muscles showing along the jaw, and she stared at me darkly in a daunting mixture of fury and ferocity. I saw, in that expression, what my poor young mother had had to face, and felt a great uprush of sympathy for the feck-less butterfly who'd borne me.

There had been a day, when I was quite small, that I had been dressed in new clothes and told to be exceptionally good as I was going with my mother to see my grandmother. My mother had collected me from where I was living and we had travelled by car to a large house, where I was left alone in the hall, to wait. Behind a white painted closed door there had been a lot of shouting. Then my mother had come out, crying, and had grabbed me by the hand, and pulled me after her to the car.

'Come on, Philip. We'll never ask her for anything, ever again. She wouldn't even see you. Don't you ever forget, Philip, that your grandmother's a hateful *beast*.'

I hadn't forgotten. I'd thought of it rarely, but I still clearly remembered sitting in the chair in the hall, my feet not touching the ground, waiting stiffly in my new clothes, listening to the shouting.

I had never actually lived with my mother, except for a traumatic week or two now and then. We had had no house, no address, no permanent base. Herself always on the move, she had solved the problem of what to do with me by simply dumping me for varying periods with a long succession of mostly astonished married friends, who had been, in retrospect, remarkably tolerant.

'Do look after Philip for me for a few days, darling,' she would say, giving me a push towards yet another

strange lady. 'Life is so unutterably *cluttered* just now
and I'm at my wits' end to know what to do with
him, you know how it is, so, darling Deborah ... (or
Miranda, or Chloe, or Samantha, or anyone else under
the sun) ... do be an absolute *sweetie*, and I'll pick him
up on Saturday, I promise.' And mostly she would have
soundly kissed darling Deborah or Miranda or Chloe
or Samantha and gone off with a wave in a cloud of
Joy.

Saturdays came and my mother didn't, but she
always turned up in the end, full of flutter and laughter
and gushing thanks, retrieving her parcel, so to speak,
from the left luggage office. I could remain uncollected
for days or for weeks or for months: I never knew
which in advance, and nor, I suspect, did my hosts.
Mostly, I think, she paid something towards my keep,
but it was all done with a giggle.

She was, even to my eyes, deliciously pretty, to the
extent that people hugged her and indulged her and lit
up when she was around. Only later, when they were
left literally holding the baby, did the doubts creep in.
I became a bewildered silent child forever tiptoeing
nervously around so as not to give offence, perennially
frightened that someone, one day, would abandon me
altogether out in the street.

Looking back, I knew I owed a great deal to Samantha, Deborah, Chloe, *et al.* I never went hungry,
was never ill-treated, nor was ever, in the end, totally
rejected. Occasionally people took me in twice or three

times, sometimes with welcome, mostly with resignation. When I was three or four someone in long hair and bangles and an ethnic smock taught me to read and write, but I never stayed anywhere long enough to be formally sent to school. It was an extraordinary, disorientating and rootless existence from which I emerged at twelve, when I was dumped in my first long-stay home, able to do almost any job around the house and unable to love.

She left me with two photographers, Duncan and Charlie, standing in their big bare-floored studio that had a darkroom, a bathroom, a gas ring and a bed behind a curtain.

'Darlings, look after him until Saturday, there's a sweet pair of lambs . . .' And although birthday cards arrived, and presents at Christmas, I didn't see her again for three years. Then when Duncan departed she swooped in one day and took me away from Charlie, and drove me down to a racehorse trainer and his wife in Hampshire, telling those bemused friends, 'It's only until Saturday, darlings, and he's fifteen and strong, he'll muck out the horses for you, and things like that . . .'

Cards and presents arrived for two years or so, always without an address to reply to. On my eighteenth birthday there was no card, and no present the following Christmas, and I'd never heard from her again.

She must have died, I had come to understand, from

drugs. There was a great deal, as I grew older, that I'd sorted out and understood.

The old woman glared across the room, as unforgiving and destructive as ever, and still angry at what I'd said.

'You won't get far with me if you talk like that,' she said.

'I don't want to get far.' I stood up. 'This visit is pointless. If you wanted to find your daughter you should have looked twenty years ago. And as for me . . . I wouldn't find her for you, even if I could.'

'I don't want you to find Caroline. I dare say you're right, that she's dead.' The idea clearly caused her no grief. 'I want you to find your sister.'

'My . . . *what*?'

The hostile dark eyes assessed me shrewdly. 'You didn't know you had a sister? Well, you have. I'll leave you a hundred thousand pounds in my will if you find her and bring her here to me. And don't think,' she went on caustically, before I had time to utter, 'that you can produce any little imposter and expect me to believe it. I'm old but I'm far from a fool. You would have to prove to Mr Folk's satisfaction that the girl was my grandchild. And Mr Folk would not be easy to convince.'

I scarcely heard the acid words, but felt only a curiously intense thrust of shock. There had been only one of me. One single fruit of the butterfly. I felt an unreasonable but stinging jealousy that she had had another. She had been mine alone, and now I had to share her: to revise and share her memory. I thought in confusion that it was ridiculous to be experiencing at thirty the displacement emotions of two.

'Well?' my grandmother said sharply.

'No,' I said.

'It's a lot of money,' she snapped.

'If you've got it.'

She was again outraged. 'You're insolent!'

'Oh, sure. Well, if that's all, I'll be going.' I turned and went towards the door.

'Wait,' she said urgently. 'Don't you even want to see her picture? There's a photograph of your sister over there on the chest.'

I glanced over my shoulder and saw her nodding towards a chest of drawers across the room. She must have seen the hesitation that slowed my hand on the doorknob because she said with more confidence, 'Just look at her, then. Why don't you look?'

Without positively wanting to but impelled by un-deniable curiosity I walked over to the chest and looked. There was a snapshot lying there, an ordinary postcard-sized family-album print. I picked it up and tilted it towards the light.

A little girl, three or four years old, on a pony.

The child, with shoulder-length brown hair, wore a red and white striped T-shirt and a pair of jeans. The pony was an unremarkable Welsh grey, with clean-looking tack. Photographed in what was evidently a stable yard, they both looked contented and well fed, but the photographer had been standing too far away to bring out much detail in the child's face. Enlargement would help to some extent.

I turned the print over, but there was nothing on the back of it to indicate where it had come from, or who had held the camera.

Vaguely disappointed, I put it down again on the chest and saw, with a wince of nostalgia, an envelope lying there addressed in my mother's handwriting. Addressed to my grandmother, Mrs Lavinia Nore, at the old house in Northamptonshire where I'd had to wait in the hall.

In the envelope, a letter.

'What are you doing?' said my grandmother in alarm.

'Reading a letter from my mother.'

'But I . . . That letter shouldn't be out. Put it down at once. I thought it was in the drawer.'

I ignored her. The loopy, extravagant, extrovert writing came as freshly to me off the paper as if she'd been there in the room, gushing and half laughing, calling out as always for help.

That letter, dated only October 2nd, was no joke.

Dear Mother,

 I know I said I would never ask you for anything ever again but I'm having one more try because
I still hope, silly me, that one day you might change

your mind. I am sending you a photograph of my daughter Amanda, your granddaughter. She is very sweet and darling and she's three now, and she needs a proper home and to go to school and everything, and I know you wouldn't want a child around but if you'd just give her an allowance or even do one of those covenant things for her, she could live with some perfectly angelic people who love her and want to keep her but simply can't afford everything for another child as they've three of their own already. If you could pay something regularly into their bank account you wouldn't even notice it and it would mean your granddaughter was brought up in a happy home and I am so desperate to get that for her that I'm writing to you now.

She hasn't the same father as Philip, so you couldn't hate her for the same reasons, and if you'd see her you'd love her, but even if you won't see her, please, Mother, look after her. I'll hope to hear from you soon. Please, please, Mother, answer this letter.

Your daughter,
Caroline,

Staying at Pine Woods Lodge,
Mindle Bridge, Sussex.

I looked up and across at the hard old woman.
'When did she write this?'

'Years ago.'

'And you didn't reply,' I said flatly.

'No.'

I supposed it was no good getting angry over so old a tragedy. I looked at the envelope to try to see the date of the letter from the postmark, but it was smudged and indecipherable. How long, I wondered, had she waited at Pine Woods Lodge, hoping and caring and desperate. Desperation, of course, when it concerned my mother, was always a relative term. Desperation was a laugh and an outstretched hand – and the Lord (or Deborah or Samantha or Chloe) would provide. Desperation wouldn't be grim and gritty: but it must have been pretty deep to make her ask her own mother for help.

I put the letter, the envelope and the photograph in my jacket pocket. It seemed disgusting to me that the old woman had kept them all these years when she had ignored their plea, and I felt in an obscure way that they belonged to me, and not her.

'So you'll do it,' she said.

'No.'

'But you're taking the photograph.'

'Yes.'

'Well, then.'

'If you want ... Amanda ... found, you should hire a private detective.'

'I did,' she said impatiently. 'Naturally. Three detect-ives. They were all useless.'

655

'If three failed, she can't be found,' I said. 'There's no way I could succeed.'

'More incentive,' she said triumphantly. 'You'll try your damnedest, for that sort of money.'

'You're wrong.' I stared bitterly at her across the room and from her pillow-piled bed she stared unsmilingly back. 'If I took any money from you I'd vomit.'

I walked over to the door and this time opened it without hesitation.

To my departing back, she said, 'Amanda shall have my money . . . if you find her.'

CHAPTER TWO

When I went back to Sandown Park the following day the letter and photograph were still in my pocket but the emotions they had engendered had subsided. The unknown half-sister could be contemplated without infantile rage, and yet another chunk of the past had fallen into place.

It was the present, in the shape of Steve Millace, which claimed everyone's attention. He came steaming into the changing room half an hour before the first race with drizzle on his hair and righteous fury in his eyes.

His mother's house, he said, had been burgled while they were all out at his father's funeral.

We sat in rows on the benches, half changed into riding clothes, listening with shock. I looked at the scene – jockeys in all stages of undress, in underpants, bare-chested, in silks and pulling on nylon tights and boots, and all of them suddenly still, as if in suspended animation, listening with open mouths and eyes turned towards Steve.

Almost automatically I reached for my Nikon, twiddled the controls, and took a couple of photographs: and they were all so accustomed to me doing that sort of thing that no one took any notice.

'It was awful,' Steve said. 'Bloody disgusting. She'd made some cakes and things, Mum had, for the aunts and everyone, for when we got back from the cremation, and they were all thrown around the place, squashed flat, jam and such, onto the walls, and stamped into the carpet. And there was more mess everywhere, in the kitchen . . . bathroom . . . It looked as if a herd of mad children had rampaged round the whole house making it as filthy as they could. But it wasn't children . . . children wouldn't have stolen all that was taken, the police said.'

'Your mother have a load of jewels, did she?' said someone, teasing.

One or two laughed and the first tension was broken, but the sympathy for Steve was genuine enough, and he went on talking about it to anyone who cared to listen: and I did listen, not only because his peg at Sandown was next to mine, which gave me little choice, but also because we always got on well together in a day-to-day, superficial way.

'They stripped Dad's darkroom,' he said. 'Just ripped everything out. And it was senseless . . . like I told the police . . . because they didn't just take things you could sell, like the enlarger and the developing stuff, but all his work, all those pictures taken over all those years, they're all gone. It's such a bloody shame. There's Mum with all that mess, and Dad dead, and now she hasn't even got what he spent his life doing. Just *nothing*. And they took her fur jacket and even the scent Dad gave her for her birthday, that she hadn't opened, and she's just sitting there crying . . .'

He stopped suddenly and swallowed, as if it was all too much for him too. At twenty-three, although he no longer lived with them, he was still very much his parents' child, attached to them with a difficult loyalty most people admired. George Millace himself might have been widely disliked, but he had never been belittled by his son.

Small-boned, slight in build, Steve had bright dark eyes and ears that stuck out widely, giving him an overall slightly comic look: but in character he was more intense than humorous, and was apt, even without so much cause as on that day, to keep on returning obsessively to things which upset him.

'The police said that burglars do it for spite,' Steve said ' . . . mess up people's houses and steal their photographs. They told Mum it's always happening. They said to be thankful there wasn't urine and shit over everything, which there often was, and she was lucky she didn't have the chairs and settee slashed and all the furniture scratched.' He went on compulsively talking to all comers, but I finished changing and went out to ride in the first race, and more or less forgot the Millace burglary for the rest of the afternoon.

It was a day I had been looking forward to, and trying not to, for nearly a month. The day that Daylight was to run in the Sandown Handicap Pattern 'Chase. A big race, a good horse, moderate opposition, and a great chance of winning. Such combinations came my way rarely enough to be prized, but I never liked to believe in them until I was actually on my way down to the post. Daylight, I'd been told, had arrived at the course safe and sound, and for me there was just the first race, a novice hurdle, to come back unscathed from, and then, perhaps, I would win the big Pattern 'Chase and half a dozen people would fall over themselves to offer me the favourite for the Gold Cup.

Two races a day was about my usual mark, and if I ended a season in the top twenty on the jockeys' list, I was happy. For years I'd been able to kid myself that the modesty of my success was due to being taller and heavier than was best for the job. Even with constant semi-starvation I weighed ten stone seven stripped, and was cut off, consequently, from the countless horses running at ten stone or less. Most seasons I rode in about two hundred races with forty or so winners, and I knew that I was considered 'strong', 'reliable', 'good over fences', and 'not first class in a close finish'.

Most people think, when they're young, that they're going to the top of their chosen world, and that the climb up is only a formality. Without that faith, I suppose, they might never start. Somewhere on the way they lift their eyes to the summit and know they aren't going to reach it; and happiness then is looking down and enjoying the view they've got, not envying the one they haven't. At around twenty-six I'd come to terms with the view I'd reached, and with knowing I wasn't going any further: and oddly, far from depressing me, the realization had been a relief. I'd never been graspingly ambitious, but only willing to do anything as well as I could. If I couldn't do better, well, I couldn't, and that was that. All the same, I'd no positive objection to having Gold Cup winners thrust upon me, so to speak.

On that afternoon at Sandown I completed the novice hurdle in an uneventful way ('useful but uninspired'), finishing fifth out of eighteen runners. Not too bad. Just the best that I and the horse could do on the day, same as usual.

I changed into Daylight's colours and in due course walked out to the parade ring, feeling nothing but pleasure for the coming race. Daylight's trainer, for whom I rode regularly, was waiting there, and also Daylight's owner.

Daylight's owner waved away my cheerful opener about it being splendid the drizzle had stopped and said without preamble, 'You'll lose this one today, Philip.'

I smiled. 'Not if I can help it.'

'Indeed you will,' he said sharply. 'Lose it. My money's on the other way.'

I don't suppose I kept much of the dismay and anger out of my face. He had done this sort of thing before, but not for about three years, and he knew I didn't like it.

Victor Briggs, Daylight's owner, was a sturdily built man in his forties, about whose job and background I knew almost nothing. Unsociable, secretive, he came to the races with a closed unsmiling face, and never talked to me much. He always wore a heavy navy-blue overcoat, a black broad-brimmed hat, and thick black leather gloves. He had been, in the past, an aggressive gambler, and in riding for him I had had the choice of doing what he said or losing my job with the stable. Harold Osborne, the trainer, had said to me plainly, soon after I'd joined him, that if I wouldn't do what Victor Briggs wanted, I was out.

I had lost races for Victor Briggs that I might have won. It was a fact of life. I needed to eat and to pay off the mortgage on the cottage. For that I needed a good big stable to ride for, and if I had walked out of the one that was giving me a chance I might easily not have found another. There weren't so very many of them, and apart from Victor Briggs the Osborne set-up was just right. So, like many another rider in a like fix, I had done what I was told, and kept quiet.

Back at the beginning Victor Briggs had offered me a fair-sized cash present for losing. I'd said I didn't want it: I would lose if I had to, but I wouldn't be paid. He said I was a pompous young fool, but after I'd refused his offer a second time he'd kept his bribes in his pocket and his opinion of me to himself.

'Why don't you take it?' Harold Osborne had said. 'Don't forget you're passing up the 10 per cent you'd get for winning. Mr Briggs is making it up to you, that's all.'

I'd shaken my head, and he hadn't persevered. I thought that probably I was indeed a fool, but somewhere along the line it seemed that Samantha or Chloe or the others had given me this unwelcome uncomfortable conviction that one should pay for one's sins. As for three years or more I'd been let off the dilemma it was all the more infuriating to be faced with it again.

'I can't lose,' I protested. 'Daylight's the best of the bunch. Far and away. You know he is.'

'Just do it,' Victor Briggs said. 'And lower your voice, unless you want the Stewards to hear you.'

I looked at Harold Osborne. He was busy watching the horses plod around the ring and pretending not to listen to what Victor Briggs was saying.

'Harold,' I said.

He gave me a brief unemotional glance. 'Victor's right. The money's on the other way. You'll cost us a packet if you win, so don't.'

'Us?'

He nodded. 'Us. That's right. Fall off, if you have to. Come in second, if you like. But not first. Understood?'

I nodded. I understood. Back in the old pincers, three years on.

I cantered Daylight down to the start with reality winning out over rebellion, as before. If I hadn't been able to afford to lose the job at twenty-three, still less could I at thirty. I was known as Osborne's jockey. I'd been with him seven years. If he chucked me out, all I'd get would be other stables' odds and ends; ride second string to other jockeys; be on a one-way track to oblivion. He wouldn't say to the Press that he'd got rid of me because I wouldn't any longer lose to order. He would tell them (regretfully, of course) that he was looking for someone younger . . . had to do what was best for the owners . . . terribly sad, but an end came to every jockey's career . . . naturally sorry, and all that, but time marches on, don't you know?

God damn it, I thought. I didn't want to lose that race. I hated to be dishonest . . . and the 10 per cent I would lose this time was big enough to make me even angrier. Why the bloody hell had Briggs gone back to this caper, after this long time? I'd thought that he'd stopped it because I'd got just far enough as a jockey for him to think it likely I would refuse. A jockey who got high enough on the winners' list was safe from that sort of pressure, because if his own stable was silly enough to give him the kick, another would welcome him in. And maybe he thought I'd gone past that stage now that I was older, and was back again in the danger area: and he was right.

We circled around while the starter called the roll, and I looked apprehensively at the four horses ranged against Daylight. There wasn't a good one among them. Nothing that on paper could defeat my own powerful gelding; which was why people were at that moment staking four pounds on Daylight to win one.

Four to one on . . .

Far from risking his own money at those odds, Victor Briggs in some subterranean way had taken bets from other people, and would have to pay out if his horse won. And so, it seemed, would Harold also: and however I might feel I did owe Harold some allegiance.

After seven years of a working relationship that had a firmer base than many a trainer-jockey alliance, I had come to regard him if not with close personal warmth at least with active friendship. He was a man of rages and charms, of black moods and boisterous highs, of tyrannical decisions and generous gifts. His voice could out-shout and out-curse any other on the Berkshire Downs, and stable lads with delicate sensibilities left his employ in droves. On the first day that I rode work for him his blistering opinion of my riding could be heard fortissimo from Wantage to Swindon, and, in his house immediately afterwards, at ten in the morning, he had opened a bottle of champagne, and we had drunk to our forthcoming collaboration.

He had trusted me always and entirely, and had defended me against criticism where many a trainer would not. Every jockey, he had said robustly, had bad patches; and he had employed me steadily through mine. He assumed that I would be, for my part, totally committed to himself and his stable, and for the past three years that had been easy.

The starter called the horses into line, and I wheeled Daylight round to point his nose in the right direction.

No starting stalls. They were never used for jump racing. A gate of elastic tapes instead.

In cold angry misery I decided that the race, from Daylight's point of view, would have to be over as near the start as possible. With thousands of pairs of binoculars trained my way, with television eyes and patrol cameras and perceptive pressmen acutely focussed, losing would be hard enough anyway, and practically suicidal if I left it until it was clear that Daylight would win. Then, if I just fell off in the last half mile for not much reason, there would be an enquiry and I might lose my licence; and it would be no comfort to know that I deserved to.

The starter put his hand on the lever and the tapes flew up, and I kicked Daylight forward into his business. None of the other jockeys wanted to make the running, and we set off in consequence at a slow pace, which compounded my troubles. Daylight, with all the time in the world, wouldn't stumble at any fence. A fluent jumper always, he hardly ever fell. Some horses couldn't be put right on the approach to a fence: Daylight couldn't be put wrong. All he accepted were the smallest indications from his jockey, and he would do the rest himself. I had ridden him many times. Won six races on him. Knew him well.

Cheat the horse. Cheat the public.

Cheat.

Damn it, I thought. *Damn and damn and damn.*

I did it at the third fence, on the decline from the top of the hill, round the sharpish bend, going away from the stands. It was the best from the credibility angle as it was the least visible to the massed watchers, and it had a sharp downhill slope on the approach side: a fence that claimed many a victim during the year.

Daylight, confused by getting the wrong signals from me, and perhaps feeling some of my turmoil and fury in the telepathic way that horses do, began to waver in the stride before take-off, putting in a small jerky extra stride where none was needed.

God, boy, I thought, I'm bloody sorry, but down you go, if I can make you: and I kicked him at the wrong moment and twitched hard on the bit in his mouth while he was in mid-air, and shifted my weight forward in front of his shoulder.

He landed awkwardly and stumbled slightly, dipping his head down to recover his balance. It wasn't really enough . . . but it would have to do. I whisked my right foot out of the stirrup and over his back, so that I was entirely on his left side, out of the saddle, clinging onto his neck.

It's almost impossible to stay on, from that position. I clung to him for about three bucking strides and then slid down his chest, irrevocably losing my grip and bouncing onto the grass under his feet. A flurry of thuds from his hooves, and a roll or two, and the noise and the galloping horses were gone.

I sat on the quiet ground and unbuckled my helmet, and felt absolutely wretched.

'Bad luck,' they said briefly in the weighing room. 'Rotten luck', and got on with the rest of the day. I wondered if any of them guessed, but maybe they didn't. No one nudged or winked or looked sardonic. It was my own embarrassed sense of shame which kept me staring mostly at the floor.

'Cheer up,' Steve Millace said, buttoning some orange and blue colours. 'It's not the end of the world.' He picked up his whip and his helmet. 'Always another day.'

'Yeah.'

He went off to ride and I changed gloomily back into street clothes. So much, I thought, for the sense of excitement in which I'd arrived. So much for winning, for half a dozen mythical trainers climbing over themselves to secure my services for the Gold Cup. So much for a nice boost to the finances, which were wilting a bit after buying a new car. On all fronts, depression.

I went out to watch the race.

Steve Millace, with more courage than sense, drove his horse at leg-tangling pace into the second last fence and crashed on landing. It was the sort of hard fast fall which cracked bones, and one could see straight away that Steve was in trouble. He struggled up as far as his knees, and then sat on his heels with his head bent forward and his arms wrapped round his body, as if he was hugging himself. Arm, shoulder, ribs . . . something had gone.

His horse, unhurt, got up and galloped away, and I stood for a while watching while two first aid men gingerly helped Steve into an ambulance. A bad day for him, too, I thought, on top of all his family troubles. What on earth made us do it? Whatever drove us to persist, disregarding injury and risk and disappointment? What lured us continually to speed, when we could earn as much sitting in an office?

I walked back to the weighing room feeling the bits of me that Daylight had trodden on beginning to stiffen with bruises. I'd be crimson and black the next day, which was nothing but usual. The biffs and bangs of the trade had never bothered me much and nothing I'd so far broken had made me frightened about the next lot. I normally had, in fact, a great feeling of physical well-being, of living in a strong and supple body, of existing as an efficient coordinated athletic whole. Nothing obtrusive. It was there. It was health.

Disillusion, I thought, would be the killer. If the job no longer seemed worth it, if people like Victor Briggs soured it beyond acceptance, at that point one would give up. But not yet. It was still the life I wanted; still the life I was far from ready to leave.

Steve came into the changing room in boots, breeches, undervest, clavicle rings, bandage and sling, with his head inclined stiffly to one side.

'Collar bone,' he said crossly. 'Bloody nuisance.' Discomfort was making his thin face gaunt, digging hollows in his cheeks and round his eyes, but what he clearly felt most was annoyance.

His valet helped him to change and dress, touching him with the gentleness of long practice, and pulling off his boots smoothly so as not to jar the shoulder. A crowd of other jockeys around us jostled and sang and made jokes, drank tea and ate fruit cake, slid out of colours and pulled on trousers, laughed and cursed and hurried. Knocking-off time, the end of the working week, back again Monday.

'I suppose,' Steve said to me, 'you couldn't possibly drive me home?' He sounded tentative, as if not sure if our friendship stretched that far.

'Yes, I should think so,' I said.

'To my mother's house? Near Ascot.'

'OK.'

'I'll get someone to fetch my car tomorrow,' he said. 'Sodding nuisance.'

I took a photograph of him and his valet, who was pulling off the second boot.

'What do you ever do with all them snaps?' the valet said.

'Put them in a drawer.'

He gave a heaven-help-us jerk of the head. 'Waste of time.'

Steve glanced at the Nikon. 'Dad said once he'd

670

seen some of your pics. You would put him out of business one of these days, he said.'

'He was laughing at me.'

'Yeah. Maybe. I don't know.' He inched one arm into his shirt and let the valet fasten the buttons over the other. 'Ouch,' he said, wincing.

George Millace had seen some pictures I'd had in my car, catching me looking through them as I sat in the car park at the end of a sunny spring day, waiting for the friend I'd given a lift to, to come out of the racecourse.

'Proper little Cartier Bresson,' George had said, faintly smiling. 'Let's have a look.' He'd put his arm through the open window and grasped the stack, and short of a tug-o'-war I couldn't have prevented him. 'Well, well,' he said, going through them methodically. 'Horses on the Downs, coming out of a mist. Romantic muck.' He handed them back. 'Keep it up, kid. One of these days you might take a photograph.'

He'd gone off across the car park, the heavy camera bag hanging from his shoulder, with him hitching it from time to time to ease its weight: the only photographer I knew with whom I didn't feel at home.

Duncan and Charlie, in the three years I'd lived with them, had patiently taught me all I could learn. No matter that when I was first dumped on them I was only twelve: Charlie had said from the start that as I was there I could sweep the floors and clean up in the darkroom, and I'd been glad to. The rest had come gradually and thoroughly, and I'd finished by regularly doing all of Duncan's printing, and the routine half of Charlie's. 'Our lab assistant' Charlie called me. He mixes our chemicals,' he would say. 'A dab hand with a hypodermic. Mind now, Philip, only one point four millilitres of benzol alcohol.' And I'd suck the tiny amounts accurately into the syringe and add them to the developer, and feel as if I were perhaps of some use in the world after all.

The valet helped Steve into his jacket and gave him his watch and wallet, and we went at Steve's tender pace out to my car.

'I promised to give Mum a hand with clearing up that mess, when I got back. What a bloody hope.'

'She's probably got neighbours.' I eased him into the modern Ford and went round to the driving seat. Started up in the closing dusk, switched on the lights and drove off in the direction of Ascot.

'I can't get used to the idea of Dad not being there,' Steve said.

'What happened?' I asked. 'I mean, you said he drove into a tree . . .'

'Yes.' He sighed. 'He went to sleep. At least, that's what everyone reckons. There weren't any other cars, nothing like that. There was a bend, or something, and he didn't go round it. Just drove straight ahead. He must have had his foot on the accelerator . . . The front of the car was smashed right in.' He shivered. 'He was on his way home from Doncaster. Mum's always warned him about driving on the motorway at night when he's had a long day, but this wasn't the motorway . . . he was much nearer home.'

He sounded tired and depressed, which no doubt he was, and in brief sideways glances I could see that for all my care the car's motion was hurting his shoulder.

'He'd stopped for half an hour at a friend's house,' Steve said. 'And they'd had a couple of whiskies. It was all so stupid. Just going to sleep . . .'

We drove for a long way in silence, he with his problems, and I with mine.

'Only last Saturday,' Steve said. 'Only a week ago.'

Alive one minute, dead the next . . . the same as everybody.

'Turn left here,' Steve said.

We turned left and right and left a few times and came finally to a road bordered on one side by a hedge and on the other by neat detached houses in shadowy gardens.

In the middle distance along there things were happening. There were lights and people. An ambulance with its doors open, its blue turret flashing on top. A police car. Policemen. People coming and going from one of the houses, hurrying. Every window uncurtained, spilling out light.

'My *God*,' Steve said. 'That's *their* house. Mum's and Dad's.'

I pulled up outside, and he sat unmoving, staring, stricken.

'It's Mum,' he said. 'It must be. It's Mum.'

There was something near cracking point in his voice. His face was twisted with terrible anxiety and his eyes in the reflected light looked wide and very young.

'Stay here,' I said practically. 'I'll go and see.'

CHAPTER THREE

His mum lay on the sofa in the sitting room, quivering and coughing and bleeding. Someone had attacked his mum pretty nastily, splitting her nose and mouth and eyelid and leaving her with bright raw patches on cheek and jaw. Her clothes were torn here and there, her shoes were off, and her hair stuck out in straggly wisps.

I had seen Steve's mother at the races from time to time: a pleasant well-dressed woman nearing fifty, secure and happy in her life, plainly proud of her husband and son. As the grief-stricken, burgled, beaten-up person on the sofa, she was unrecognizable.

There was a policeman sitting on a stool beside her, and a policewoman, standing, holding a bloodstained cloth. Two ambulance men hovered in the background, with a stretcher propped upright against one wall. A neighbourly looking woman stood around looking grave and worried. The room itself was a shambles, with papers and smashed furniture littering the floor. On the wall, the signs of jam and cakes, as Steve had said.

When I walked in the policeman turned his head. 'Are you the doctor?'

'No . . .' I explained who I was.

'Steve!' his mother said. Her mouth trembled, and her hands. 'Steve's hurt.' She could hardly speak, yet the fear for her son came across like a fresh torment, overshadowing anything she'd yet suffered.

'It's not bad, I promise you,' I said hastily. 'He's here, outside. It's just his collar bone. I'll get him straight away.'

I went outside and told him, and helped him out of the car. He was hunched and stiff, but seemed not to feel it.

'Why?' he said, uselessly, going up the path. 'Why did it happen? What for?'

The policeman indoors was asking the same question, and others as well.

'You were just saying, when your son came home, that there were two of them, with stockings over their faces. Is that right?'

She nodded slightly. 'Young,' she said. The word came out distorted through her cut, swollen lips. She saw Steve and held her hand out to him, to hold his own hand tight. He himself, at the sight of her, grew still paler and even more gaunt.

'White youths or black?' the policeman said.

'White.'

'What were they wearing?'

'Jeans.'

'Gloves?'

She closed her eyes. The cut one looked puffed and angry. She whispered, 'Yes.'

'Mrs Millace, please try to answer,' the policeman said. 'What did they want?'

'Safe,' she said, mumbling.

'What?'

'Safe. We haven't got a safe. I told them.' A pair of tears rolled down her cheeks. 'Where's the safe, they said. They hit me.'

'There isn't a safe here,' Steve said furiously. 'I'd like to kill them.'

'Yes, sir,' the policeman said. 'Just keep quiet, sir, if you wouldn't mind.'

'One . . . smashed things,' Mrs Millace said. 'The other just hit me.'

'Bloody *animals*,' Steve said.

'Did they say what they wanted?' the policeman asked.

'Safe.'

'Yes, but is that all? Did they say they wanted money? Jewellery? Silver? Gold coins? What exactly did they say they wanted, Mrs Millace?'

She frowned slightly, as if thinking. Then forming the words with difficulty, she said, 'All they said was "where is the safe?" '

'I suppose you do know,' I said to the policeman, 'that this house was also burgled yesterday?'

'Yes, I do, sir. I was here yesterday myself.' He

looked at me assessingly for a few seconds and turned back to Steve's mother.

'Did these two young men in stocking masks say anything about being here yesterday? Try to remember, Mrs Millace.'

'I don't . . . think so.'

'Take your time,' he said. 'Try to remember.'

She was silent for a long interval, and two more tears appeared. Poor lady, I thought. Too much pain, too much grief, too much outrage: and a good deal of courage.

At last she said, 'They were . . . like bulls. They shouted. They were rough. Rough voices. They . . . shoved me. Pushed. I opened the front door. They shoved in. Pushed me . . . in here. Started . . . smashing things. Making this mess. Shouting . . . Where is the safe. Tell us, where is the safe . . . Hit me.' She paused. 'I don't think . . . they said anything . . . about yesterday.'

'I'd like to *kill* them,' Steve said.

'Third time,' mumbled his mother.

'What was that, Mrs Millace?' the policeman said.

'Third time burgled. Happened . . . two years ago.'

'You can't just let her lie here,' Steve said violently. 'Asking all these questions . . . Haven't you got a doctor?'

'It's all right, Steve dear,' the neighbourly woman said, moving forward as if to give comfort. 'I've rung Dr Williams. He said he would come at once.' Caring and bothered, she was nonetheless enjoying the

678

drama, and I could envisage her looking forward to telling it all to the locals. 'I was over here helping your mother earlier, Steve dear,' she said rushing on, 'but of course I went home – next door, as you know, dear – to get tea for my family, and then I heard all this shouting and it seemed all wrong, dear, so I was just coming back to see, and calling out to your mother to ask if she was all right, and those two dreadful young men just burst out of the house, dear, just *burst* out, so of course I came in here . . . and well . . . your poor mother . . . so I rang for the police and for the ambulance, and Dr Williams . . . and everybody.' She looked as if she would like at least a pat on the back for all this presence of mind, but Steve was beyond such responses.

The policeman was equally unappreciative. He said to her, 'And you still can't remember any more about the car they drove off in?'

Defensively she said, 'It was dark.'

'A lightish-coloured car, medium sized. Is that all?'

'I don't notice cars much.'

No one suggested that this was a car she should have noticed. Everyone thought it.

I cleared my throat and said diffidently to the policeman, 'I don't know if it would be of any use, and of course you may want your own man or something, but I've a camera in my car, if you could do with any photographs of all this.'

He raised his eyebrows and considered and said yes:

so I fetched both cameras and took two sets of pictures, in colour and in black and white, with close-ups of the damaged face and wide-angle shots of the room. Steve's mother bore the flashlight without complaint, and none of it took very long.

'Professional, are you, sir?' the policeman said.

I shook my head. 'Just had a lot of practice.'

He told me where to send the photographs when they were printed, and the doctor arrived.

'Don't go yet,' Steve said to me, and I looked at the desperation in his overstretched face, and stayed with him through all the ensuing bustle, sitting on the stairs out in the hall.

'I don't know what to do,' he said, joining me there. 'I can't drive like this, and I'll have to go and see that she's all right. They're taking her to hospital for the night. I suppose I can get a taxi...'

He didn't actually ask it, but the question was there. I stifled a small sigh and offered my services, and he thanked me as if I'd thrown him a lifebelt.

I found myself finally staying the night, because when we got back from the hospital he looked so exhausted that one simply couldn't drive away and leave him. I made us a couple of omelettes as by that time, ten o'clock, we were both starving, neither of us having eaten since breakfast; and after that I picked up some of the mess.

He sat on the edge of the sofa looking white and strained and not mentioning that his fracture was hurting quite a bit. Perhaps he hardly felt it, though one could see the pain in his face. Whenever he spoke it was of his mother.

'I'll kill them,' he said. 'Those *bastards*.'

More guts than sense, I thought; same as usual. By the sound of things, if nine-stone-seven Steve met up with the two young bulls, it would be those bastards who'd do the killing.

I started at the far end of the room, picking up a lot of magazines, newspapers, and old letters, and also the base and lid of a flat ten-by-eight-inch box which had once held photographic printing paper. An old friend.

'What shall I do with all this?' I asked Steve.

'Oh, just pile it anywhere,' he said vaguely. 'Some of it came out of that rack over there by the television.'

A wooden-slatted magazine rack, empty, lay on its side on the carpet.

'And that's Dad's rubbish box, that battered old orange thing. He kept it in that rack with the papers. Never threw it away. Just left it there, year after year. Funny really.' He yawned. 'Don't bother too much. Mum's neighbour will do it.'

I picked up a small batch of oddments; a transparent piece of film about three inches wide by eight long, several strips of 35 mm colour negatives, developed but blank, and an otherwise pleasant picture of Mrs Millace spoilt by splashes of chemical down the hair and neck.

'Those were in Dad's rubbish box, I think,' Steve said, yawning again. 'You might as well throw them away.'

I put them in the wastepaper basket, and added to them a nearly black black-and-white print which had been torn in half, and some more colour negatives covered in magenta blotches.

'He kept them to remind himself of his worst mistakes,' Steve said. 'It doesn't seem *possible* that he isn't coming back.'

There was another very dark print in a paper folder, showing a shadowy man sitting at a table. 'Do you want this?' I asked.

He shook his head. 'Dad's junk.'

I put some feminine magazines and a series on woodwork back in the magazine rack, and piled the letters on the table. The bulk of the mess left on the floor seemed to be broken china ornaments, the remnants of a spindly-legged sewing box which had been thoroughly smashed, and a small bureau, tipped on its side, with cascades of writing paper falling out of the drawers. None of the damage seemed to have had any purpose beyond noise and speed and frightening power, all of a piece with the pushing, shoving and shouting that Mrs Millace had described. A rampage designed to confuse and bewilder: and when they got no results from attacking her possessions, they'd started on her face.

I stood the bureau up again and shovelled most of

the stuff back into it, and collected together a heap
of scattered tapestry patterns and dozens of skeins of
wool. One began at last to see clear stretches of carpet.

'*Bastards,*' Steve said. 'I hate them. I'll kill them.'

'Why would they think your mother had a safe?'

'God knows. Perhaps they just go round ripping
off new widows, screaming "safe" at them on the off-
chance. I mean, if she'd had one, she'd have told them
where it was, wouldn't she? After losing Dad like that.
And yesterday's burglary, while we were at the funeral.
Such dreadful shocks. She'd have told them. I know
she would.'

I nodded.

'She can't take any more,' he said. There were tears
in his voice, and his eyes were dark with the efforts of
trying not to cry. It was he, I thought, who was closest
to the edge. His mother would be tucked up with sympathy and sedation.

'Time for bed,' I said abruptly. 'Come on. I'll help
you undress. She'll be better tomorrow.'

I woke early after an uneasy night and lay watching
the dingy November dawn creep through the window.
There was a good deal about life that I didn't want to
get up and face; a situation common, no doubt, to the
bulk of mankind. Wouldn't it be marvellous, I thought
dimly, to be pleased with oneself, to look forward to
the day ahead, to not have to think about mean-minded

dying grandmothers and one's own depressing dishonesty. Normally fairly happy-go-lucky, a taking-things-as-they-come sort of person, I disliked being backed into uncomfortable corners from which escape meant action.

Things had happened to me, had arrived, all my life. I'd never gone out looking. I had learned whatever had come my way, whatever was there. Like photography, because of Duncan and Charlie. And like riding, because of my mother dumping me in a racing stable: and if she'd left me with a farmer I would no doubt be making hay.

Survival for so many years had been a matter of accepting what I was given, of making myself useful, of being quiet and agreeable and no trouble, of repression and introversion and self-control, that I was now, as a man, fundamentally unwilling to make a fuss or fight.

I had taught myself for so long not to want things that weren't offered to me that I now found very little to want. I had made no major decisions. What I had, had simply come.

Harold Osborne had offered me the cottage, along with the job of stable jockey. I'd accepted. The bank had offered a mortgage. I'd accepted. The local garage had suggested a certain car. I'd bought it.

I understood why I was as I was. I knew why I just drifted along, going where the tide took me. I knew why I was passive, but I felt absolutely no desire to change things, to stamp about and insist on being the master of my own fate.

I didn't want to look for my half-sister, and I didn't want to lose my job with Harold. I could simply drift along as usual doing nothing very positive ... and yet for some obscure reason that instinctive course was seeming increasingly *wet*.

Irritated, I put my clothes on and went downstairs, peering in at Steve on the way and finding him sound asleep.

Someone had perfunctorily swept the kitchen floor since the funeral-day burglary, pushing into a heap a lot of broken crockery and spilled groceries. The coffee and sugar had turned out the evening before to be down there in the dust, but there was milk along with the eggs in the refrigerator, and I drank some of that. Then, to pass the time, I wandered round the downstairs rooms, just looking.

The room which had been George Millace's darkroom would have been far and away the most interesting, had there been anything there: but it was in there that the original burglary had been the most thorough. All that was left was a wide bench down one side, two large deep sinks down the other, and rows of empty shelves across the end. Countless grubby outlines and smudges on the walls showed where the loads of equipment had stood, and stains on the floor marked where he'd stored his chemicals.

He had, I knew, done a lot of his own colour

developing and printing, which most professional photographers did not. The development of colour slides and negatives was difficult and exacting, and it was safer, for consistent results, to entrust the process to commercial large-scale labs. Duncan and Charlie had sent all their colour developing out: it was only the printing from negatives, much easier, which they had done themselves.

George Millace had been a craftsman of the first order. Pity about his unkind nature.

From the looks of things he had had two enlargers, one big and one smaller, enlargers being machines which held the negatives in what was basically a box up a stick, so that a bright light could shine through the negative onto a baseboard beneath.

The head of the enlarger, holding the light and the negative, could be wound up and down the stick. The higher one wound the head above the baseboard, the larger one saw the picture. The lower the head, the smaller the picture. An enlarger was in fact a projector, and the baseboard was the screen.

To take a print from a negative one wound the enlarger head up or down to get the size required, then sharpened the focus, then in darkness put a piece of photographic paper on the baseboard, then shone the light through the negative onto the photographic paper for a few seconds, then put the photographic paper through developer, fixer, washer and stabilizer, and hey presto, if one hadn't stuck thumb marks all over it, one

ended up with a clear print, enlarged to the size
one wanted.

Besides the enlargers, George would have had an
electric box of tricks for regulating the length of
exposures, and a mass of developing equipment, and a
drier for drying the finished prints. He would have had
dozens of sheets of various types of photographic paper
in different sizes, and light-tight dispensers to store
them in. He would have had rows of files holding all
his past work in reference order, and safe-lights and
measuring jugs and paper-trimmers and filters.

The whole lot, every scrap, had gone.

Like most serious photographers he had kept his
unexposed films in the refrigerator. They too had gone,
Steve had said, and were presumably at the root of the
vandalism in the kitchen.

I went aimlessly into the sitting room and switched
on the lights, wondering how soon I could decently
wake Steve and say I was going. The half-tidied room
looked cold and dreary, a miserable sight for poor Mrs
Millace when she got home. From habit and from
having nothing else to do I slowly carried on from
where I'd stopped the night before, picking up broken
scraps of vases and ornaments and retrieving reels of
cotton and bits of sewing from under the chairs.

Half under the sofa itself lay a large black light-proof
envelope, an unremarkable object in a photographer's
house. I looked inside, but all it seemed to contain
was a piece of clear thickish plastic about eight inches

square, straight cut on three sides but wavy along the fourth. More rubbish. I put it back in the envelope and threw it in the wastepaper basket.

George Millace's rubbish box lay open and empty on the table. For no reason in particular, and certainly impelled by nothing more than photographic curiosity, I picked up the wastepaper basket and emptied it again on the carpet. Then I put all of George's worst mistakes back in the box where he'd kept them, and returned the broken bits of glass and china to the waste basket.

Why, I wondered, looking at the spoiled prints and pieces of film, had George ever bothered to keep them. Photographers, like doctors, tended to be quick to bury their mistakes, and didn't usually leave them hanging around in magazine racks as permanent mementoes of disasters. I had always been fond of puzzles. I thought it would be quite interesting to find out why such an expert as George should have found these particular things interesting.

Steve came downstairs in his pyjamas looking frail and hugging his injured arm, wanly contemplating the day.

'Good Lord,' he said. 'You've tidied the lot.'

'Might as well.'

'Thanks, then.' He saw the rubbish box on the table, with all its contents back inside. 'He used to keep that lot in the freezer,' he said. 'Mum told me there was a terrible fuss one day when the freezer broke down and all the peas and stuff unfroze. Dad didn't care a damn about the chickens and things and all the pies she'd made which had spoiled. All he went on and on about, she said, was that some ice-cream had melted all over his rubbish.' Steve's tired face lit into a remembering smile. 'It must have been quite a scene. She thought it was terribly funny, and when she laughed he got crosser and crosser . . .' He broke off, the smile dying. 'I can't believe he isn't coming back.'

'Did your father often keep things in the freezer?'

'Oh sure. Of course. Masses of stuff. You know what photographers are like. Always having fits about colour dyes not being permanent. He was always raving on about his work deteriorating after twenty years. He said the only way to posterity was through the deep freeze, and even that wasn't certain.'

'Well . . .' I said. 'Did the burglars also empty the freezer?'

'Good Lord.' He looked startled. 'I don't know. I never thought of that. But why should they want his films?'

'They stole the ones that were in the darkroom.'

'But the policeman said that that was just spite. What they really wanted was the equipment, which they could sell.'

'Um,' I said. 'Your father took a lot of pictures which people didn't like.'

'Yes, but only as a joke.' He was defending George, the same as ever.

'We might look in the freezer,' I suggested.

'Yes. All right. It's out at the back, in a sort of shed.'

He picked a key out of the pocket of an apron hanging in the kitchen and led the way through the back door into a small covered yard, where there were dustbins and stacks of logs and a lot of parsley growing in a tub.

'In there,' Steve said, giving me the key and nodding to a green painted door set into a bordering wall; and I went in and found a huge chest freezer standing between a motor lawn mower and about six pairs of gum boots.

I lifted the lid. Inside, filling one end and nestling next to joints of lamb and boxes of beefburgers, was a stack of three large grey metal cash boxes, each one closely wrapped in transparent polythene sheeting. Taped to the top one was a terse message:

DO NOT STORE ICE CREAM NEAR THESE BOXES

I laughed.

Steve looked at the boxes and the message and said, 'There you are. Mum said he went berserk when it all melted, but in the end nothing of his was really damaged. The food was all spoilt, but his best transparencies were OK. It was after that that he started storing them in these boxes.'

I shut the lid, and we locked the shed and went back into the house.

'You don't really think,' Steve said doubtfully, 'that the burglars were after Dad's pictures? I mean, they stole all sorts of things. Mum's rings, and his cuff-links, and her fur coat, and everything.'

'Yes . . . so they did.'

'Do you think I should mention to the police that all that stuff's in the freezer? I'm sure Mum's forgotten it's there. We never gave it a thought.'

'You could talk it over with her,' I said. 'See what she says.'

'Yes, that's best.' He looked a shade more cheerful. 'One good thing, she may have lost all the indexes and the dates and places saying where all the pictures were taken, but she has at least still got some of his best work. It hasn't all gone. Not all of it.'

I helped him to get dressed and left soon afterwards, as he said he felt better, and looked it; and I took with me George Millace's box of disasters, which Steve had said to throw in the dustbin.

'But you don't mind if I take it?' I said.

'Of course not. I know you like messing about with films, the same as he does . . . same as he did. He liked that old rubbish. Don't know why. Take it, if you want, by all means.'

He came out into the drive and watched me stow the box in the boot, alongside my two camera bags.

'You never go anywhere without a camera, do you?' he said. 'Just like Dad.'

'I suppose not.'

'Dad said he felt naked without one.'

'It gets to be part of you.' I shut the boot and locked

691

it from long habit. 'It's your shield. Keeps you a step away from the world. Makes you an observer. Gives you an excuse not to feel.'

He looked extremely surprised that I should think such things, and so was I surprised, not that I'd thought them, but that I should have said them to him. I smiled to take the serious truth away and leave only an impression of satire, and Steve, photographer's son, looked relieved.

I drove the hour from Ascot to Lambourn at a Sunday morning pace and found a large dark car standing outside my front door.

The cottage was one of a terrace of seven built in the Edwardian era for the not-so-rich and currently inhabited, apart from me, by a schoolteacher, a horsebox driver, a curate, a vet's assistant, sundry wives and children, and two hostels-ful of stable lads. I was the only person living alone. It seemed almost indecent, among such a crowd, to have so much space to myself.

My house was in the centre: two up, two down, with a modern kitchen stuck on at the back. A white painted brick front, nothing fancy, facing straight out onto the road, with no room for garden. A black door, needing paint. New aluminium window frames replacing the original wood, which had rotted away. An old thing patched up. Not impressive, but home.

I drove slowly past the visiting car and turned into

the muddy drive at the end of the row, continuing round to the back and parking under the corrugated plastic roof of the carport next to the kitchen. As I went I caught a glimpse of a man getting hastily out of the car, and knew he had seen me; and for my part thought only that he had no business to be pursuing me on a Sunday.

I went through the house from the back and opened the front door. Jeremy Folk stood there, tall, thin, physically awkward, using earnest diffidence as a lever, as before.

'Don't solicitors sleep on Sundays?' I said.

'Well, I say, I'm awfully sorry . . .'

'Yeah,' I said. 'Come on in, then. How long have you been waiting?'

'Nothing to . . . ah . . . worry about.'

He stepped through the door with a hint of expectancy and took the immediate disappointment with a blink. I had rearranged the interior of the cottage so that what had once been the front parlour was now divided into an entrance hall and dark-room, and in the hall section there was only a filing cabinet and the window which looked out to the street. White walls, white floor tiles; uninformative.

'This way,' I said amused, and led him past the dark-room to what had once been the back kitchen but was now mostly bathroom and in part a continuation of the hall. Beyond lay the new kitchen, and to the left, the narrow stairs.

'Which do you want,' I said. 'Coffee or talk?'

'Er . . . talk.'

'Up here, then.'

I went up the stairs, and he followed. I used one of the two original bedrooms as the sitting room, because it was the largest room in the house and had the best view of the Downs; and the smaller room next to it was where I slept.

In the sitting room, white walls, brown carpet, blue curtains, track lighting, bookshelves, sofa, low table and floor cushions. My guest looked around with small flickering glances, making assessments.

'Well?' I said neutrally.

'Er . . . that's a nice picture.' He walked over to take a closer look at the only thing hanging on the wall, a view of pale yellow sunshine falling through some leafless silver birches onto snow. 'It's . . . er . . . a print?'

'It's a photograph,' I said.

'Oh! Is it really? It looks like a painting.' He turned away and said, 'Where would you live if you had a hundred thousand pounds?'

'I told her I didn't want it.' I looked at the angular helpless way he was standing there, dressed that day not in working charcoal flannel but in a tweed jacket with decorative leather patches on the elbows. The brain under the silly ass act couldn't be totally disguised, and I wondered vaguely whether he had developed that surface because he was embarrassed by his own acuteness.

'Sit down,' I said, gesturing to the sofa, and he folded his long legs as if I'd given him a gift. I sat on a bean-bag floor cushion and said, 'Why didn't you mention the money when I saw you at Sandown?'

He seemed almost to wriggle. 'I just...ah... thought I'd try you first on blood-stronger-than-water, don't you know?'

'And if that failed, you'd try greed?'

'Sort of.'

'So that you would know what you were dealing with?'

He blinked.

'Look,' I sighed. 'I do understand thoughts of one syllable, so why don't you just ... drop the waffle?'

His body relaxed for the first time into approximate naturalness and he gave me a small smile that was mostly in the eyes.

'It gets to be a habit,' he said.

'So I gathered.'

He cast a fresh look around the room, and I said, 'All right, say what you see.'

He did so, without squirming and without apology. 'You like to be alone. You're emotionally cold. You don't need props. And unless you took that photograph, you've no vanity.'

'I took it.'

'Tut tut.'

'Yes,' I said. 'So what did you come for?'

'Well, obviously, to persuade you to do what you don't want to.'

'To try to find the half-sister I didn't know I had?'

He nodded.

'Why?'

After a very short pause into which I could imagine him packing a lot of pros and cons he said, 'Mrs Nore is insisting on leaving a fortune to someone who can't be found. It is . . . unsatisfactory.'

'Why is she insisting?'

'I don't know. She instructs my grandfather. She doesn't take his advice. He's old and he's fed up with her, and so is my uncle, and they've shoved the whole mess onto me.'

'Three detectives couldn't find Amanda.'

'They didn't know where to look.'

'Nor do I,' I said.

He considered me. 'You'd know.'

'No.'

'Do you know who your father is?' he said.

CHAPTER FOUR

I sat with my head turned towards the window, looking out at the bare calm life of the Downs. A measurable silence passed. The Downs would be there for ever.

I said, 'I don't want to get tangled up in a family I don't feel I belong to. I don't like their threads falling over me like a web. That old woman can't claw me back just because she feels like it, after all these years.'

Jeremy Folk didn't answer directly, and when he stood up some of the habitual gaucheness had come back into his movements, though not yet into his voice.

'I brought the reports we received from the three firms of detectives,' he said. 'I'll leave them with you.'

'No, don't.'

'It's useless,' he said. He looked again around the room. 'I see quite plainly that you don't want to be involved. But I'm afraid I'm going to plague you until you are.'

'Do your own dirty work.'

He smiled. 'The dirty work was done about thirty

years ago, wasn't it? Before either of us was born. This is just the muck floating back on the tide.'

'Thanks a bunch.'

He pulled a long bulging envelope out of the inside pocket of his country tweed and put it carefully down on the table. 'They're not very long reports. You could just read them, couldn't you?'

He didn't expect an answer, or get one. He just moved vaguely towards the door to indicate that he was ready to leave, and I went downstairs with him and saw him out to his car.

'By the way,' he said, pausing awkwardly halfway into the driving seat, 'Mrs Nore really is dying. She has cancer of the spine. Secondaries, they say. Nothing to be done. She'll live maybe six weeks, or maybe six months. They can't tell. So ... er ... no time to waste, don't you know?'

I spent the bulk of the day contentedly in the dark-room, developing and printing the black-and-white shots of Mrs Millace and her troubles. They came out clear and sharp so that one could actually read the papers on the floor, and I wondered casually just where the borderline fell between positive vanity and simple pleasure in a job efficiently done. Perhaps it had been vanity to mount and hang the silver birches ... but apart from the content the large size of the print had been a technical problem, and it had all come out right . . . and what did a sculptor do, throw a sack over his best statue?

Jeremy Folk's envelope stayed upstairs on the table where he'd put it; unopened, contents unread. I ate some tomatoes and some muesli when I grew hungry, and cleared up the darkroom, and at six o'clock locked my doors and walked up the road to see Harold Osborne.

Sundays at six o'clock he expected me for a drink, and each Sunday from six to seven we talked over what had happened in the past week and discussed plans for the week ahead. For all his unpredictable up-and-down moods Harold was a man of method and he hated anything to interrupt these sessions, which he referred to as our military briefings. His wife during that hour answered the telephone and took messages for him to ring back as requested, and they had once had a blazing row with me there because she had burst in to say their dog had been run over and killed.

'You could have told me in twenty minutes,' he yelled. 'Now how the hell am I going to concentrate on Philip's orders for the Schweppes?'

'But the dog,' she wailed.

'Damn the dog.' He'd ranted at her for several minutes and then he'd gone out into the road and wept over the body of his mangled friend. Harold, I supposed, was everything I wasn't: moody, emotional, flamboyant, bursting with peaks of feeling, full of rage and love and guile and gusto. Only in our basic belief in getting things right were we alike, and that tacit agreement stuck us together in underlying peace. He might scream at me violently, but he didn't expect me to mind, and because I knew him well, I didn't. Other jockeys and trainers and several pressmen had said to me often in varying degrees of exasperation or humour, 'I don't know how you put up with it,' and the answer was always the true one ... 'Easily.'

On that particular Sunday the sacrosanct hour had been interrupted before it could begin, because Harold had a visitor. I walked through his house from the stable entrance and went into the comfortable cluttered sitting room-office, and there in one of the armchairs was Victor Briggs.

'Philip!' Harold said, welcoming and smiling. 'Pour yourself a drink. We're just going to run through the videotape of yesterday. Sit down. Are you ready? I'll switch on.'

Victor Briggs gave me several nods of approval and a handshake. No gloves, I thought. Cold pale dry hands with nothing aggressive in the grasp. Without the broadrimmed hat he had thick glossy straight black hair which was receding slightly above the eyebrows to leave a centre peak: and without the heavy navy overcoat, a plain dark suit. Indoors he still wore the close-guarded expression as if afraid his thoughts might show, but there was overall a distinct air of satisfaction. Not a smile, just an atmosphere.

I opened a can of Coca-Cola and poured some into a glass.

'Don't you drink?' Victor Briggs asked.

'Champagne,' Harold said. 'That's what he drinks, don't you, Philip?' He was in great good humour, his voice and presence amplifying the warm russet colours of the room, resonant as brass.

Harold's reddish-brown hair sprang in wiry curls all over his head, as untamable as his nature. He was fifty-two at that time and looked ten years younger, a big burly six feet of active muscle commanded by a strong but ambiguous face, his features more rounded than hawkish.

He switched on the video machine and sat back in his armchair to watch Daylight's débâcle in the Sandown Pattern 'Chase, as pleased as if he'd won the Grand National. A good job no Stewards were peering in, I thought. There was no mistaking the trainer's joy in his horse's failure.

The recording showed me on Daylight going down to the start, and lining up, and setting off: odds-on favourite at four to one on, said the commentator; only got to jump round to win. Immaculate leaps over the first two fences. Strong and steady up past the stands. Daylight just in the lead, dictating the pace, but all five runners closely bunched. Round the top bend, glued to the rails ... faster downhill. The approach to the third fence ... everything looking all right ... and then the screw in the air and the stumbling landing, and the figure in red and blue silks going over the horse's neck and down under the feet. A groaning roar from the crowd, and the commentator's unemotional voice. 'Daylight's down at that fence, and now in the lead is Little Moth . . .'

The rest of the race rolled on into a plodding undistinguished finish, and then came a re-run of Daylight's departure, with afterthought remarks from the commentator. 'You can see the horse try to put in an extra stride, throwing Philip Nore forward . . . the horse's head ducks on landing, giving his jockey no chance . . . poor Philip Nore clinging on . . . but hopeless . . . horse and jockey both unhurt.'

Harold stood up and switched the machine off. 'Artistic,' he said, beaming down. 'I've run through it twenty times. It's impossible to tell.'

'No one suspected,' Victor Briggs said. 'One of the Stewards said to me "what rotten bad luck".' There was a laugh somewhere inside Victor Briggs, a laugh not quite breaking the surface but quivering in the chest. He picked up a large envelope which had lain beside his gin and tonic, and held it out to me. 'Here's my thank you, Philip.'

I said matter-of-factly, 'It's kind of you, Mr Briggs. But nothing's changed. I don't like to be paid for losing . . . I can't help it.'

Victor Briggs put the envelope down again without comment, and it wasn't he who was immediately angry, but Harold.

'Philip,' he said loudly, towering above me. 'Don't be such a bloody prig. There's a great deal of money in that envelope. Victor's being very generous. Take it and thank him, and shut up.'

'I'd . . . rather not.'

'I don't care what you'd bloody rather. You're not so squeamish when it comes to committing the crime, are you, it's just the thirty pieces of silver you turn your pious nose up at. You make me sick. And you'll take that bloody money if I have to ram it down your throat.'

'Well, you will,' I said.

'I will what?'

'Have to ram it down my throat.'

Victor Briggs actually laughed, though when I glanced at him his mouth was tight shut as if the sound had escaped without his approval.

'And,' I said slowly, 'I don't want to do it any more.'

'You'll do what you're bloody told,' Harold said.

Victor Briggs rose purposefully to his feet, and the two of them, suddenly silent, stood looking down at me.

It seemed that a long time passed, and then Harold said in a quiet voice which held a great deal more threat than his shouting. 'You'll do what you're told, Philip.'

I stood up in my turn. My mouth had gone dry, but I made my voice sound as neutral, as calm, as unprovoking as possible.

'Please . . . don't ask me for a repeat of yesterday.'

Victor Briggs narrowed his eyes. 'Did the horse hurt you? He trod on you . . . you can see it on the video.'

I shook my head. 'It's not that. It's the losing. You know I hate it. I just . . . don't want you to ask me . . . again.'

More silence.

'Look,' I said. 'There are degrees. Of course I'll give a horse an easy ride if he isn't a hundred per cent fit and a hard race would ruin him for next time out. Of course I'll do that, it only makes sense. But no more like Daylight yesterday. I know I used to . . . but yesterday was the last.'

Harold said coldly, 'You'd better go now Philip. I'll talk to you in the morning,' and I nodded, and left, and there were none of the warm handshakes which had greeted my arrival.

What would they do? I wondered. I walked in the windy dark down the road from Harold's house to mine as I had on hundreds of Sundays, and wondered if it would be for the last time. If he wanted to he could put other jockeys up on his horses from that day onwards. He was under no obligation to give me rides. I was classed as self-employed, because I was paid per race by the owners, and not per week by the trainer; and there was no such thing as 'unfair dismissal' inquiries for the self-employed.

I suppose it was too much to hope that they would let me get away with it. Yet for three years they had run the Briggs horses honestly, so why not in future?

And if they insisted on fraud, couldn't they get some other poor young slob just starting his career, and put the squeezers on him when they wanted a race lost? Foolish wishes, all of them. I'd put my job down at their feet like a football and at that moment they were probably kicking it out of the ground.

It was ironic. I hadn't known I was going to say what I had. It had just forced its own way out, like water through a new spring.

All those races I'd thrown away in the past, not liking it, but doing it . . . Why was it so different now? Why was the revulsion so strong now that I didn't think I *could* do a Daylight again, even if to refuse meant virtually the end of being a jockey?

When had I changed . . . and how could it have happened without my noticing? I didn't know. I just had a sense of having already travelled too far to turn back. Too far down a road where I didn't want to go.

I went upstairs and read the three detectives' reports on Amanda because it was better, on the whole, than thinking about Briggs and Harold.

Two of the reports had come from fairly large firms and one from a one-man outfit, and all three had spent a lot of ingenuity padding out very few results. Justifying their charges, no doubt. Copiously explaining what they had all spent so long not finding out: and all three, not surprisingly, had not found out approximately the same things.

None of them, for a start, could find any trace of her birth having been registered. They all expressed doubt and disbelief over this discovery, but to me it was no surprise at all. I had discovered that I myself was unregistered when I tried to get a passport, and the fuss had gone on for months.

I knew my name, my mother's name, my birth date, and that I'd been born in London. Officially, however, I didn't exist. 'But here I am,' I'd protested, and I'd been told, 'Ah yes, but you don't have a piece of paper to prove it, do you?' There had been affidavits by the ton and miles of red tape, and I'd missed the race I'd been offered in France by the time I got permission to go there.

The detectives had all scoured Somerset House for records of Amanda Nore, aged between ten and twenty-five, possibly born in Sussex. In spite of the fairly unusual name, they had all completely failed.

I sucked my teeth, thinking that I could do better than that about her age.

She couldn't have been born before I went to live with Duncan and Charlie, because I'd seen my mother fairly often before that, about five or six times a year, and often for a week at a time, and I would have known if she'd had a child. The people she left me with used to talk about her when they thought I wasn't listening, and I gradually understood what I remembered them saying, though sometimes not for years afterwards: but none of them, ever, had hinted that she was pregnant.

That meant that I was at least twelve when Amanda was born; and consequently she couldn't at present be older than eighteen.

At the other end of things she couldn't possibly be as young as ten. My mother, I was sure, had died sometime between Christmas and my eighteenth birthday. She might have been desperate enough at that time to write to her own mother and send her the photograph. Amanda in the photograph had been three . . . so Amanda, if she was still alive, would be at least fifteen.

Sixteen or seventeen, most likely. Born during the three years when I hadn't seen my mother at all, when I'd lived with Duncan and Charlie.

I went back to the reports . . .

All three detectives had been given the last known address of Caroline Nore, Amanda's mother: Pine Woods Lodge, Mindle Bridge, Sussex. All three had trekked there 'to make enquiries'.

Pine Woods Lodge, they rather plaintively reported, was not as the name might suggest a small private hotel complete with guest register going back umpteen years, forwarding addresses attached. Pine Woods Lodge was an old Georgian mansion gone to ruin and due to be demolished. There were trees growing in what had been the ballroom. Large sections had no roof.

It was owned by a family which had largely died out

twenty-five years earlier, leaving distant heirs who had no wish and no money to keep the place up. They had let the house at first to various organizations (list attached, supplied by Estate Agents) but of latter years it had been inhabited by squatters and vagrants. The dilapidation was now so advanced that even such as they had moved out, and the five acres the house was built on were to come up for auction within three months; but as whoever bought the land was going to have to demolish the mansion, it was not expected to fetch much of a price.

I read through the list of tenants, none of whom had stayed long. A nursing home. A sisterhood of nuns. An artists' commune. A boys' youth club adventure project. A television film company. A musicians' cooperative. Colleagues of Supreme Grace. The Confidential Mail Order Corporation.

One of the detectives, persevering, had investigated the tenants as far as he could, and had added unflattering comments.

Nursing home	– euthanasia for all. Closed by council.
Nuns	– disbanded through bitchiness.
Artists	– left disgusting murals.
Boys	– broke everything still whole.
T.V.	– needed a ruin to film.

Musicians	– fused all the electricity.
Colleagues	– religious nutters.
Mail order	– perverts' delights.

There were no dates attached to the tenancies, but presumably if the Estate Agents could still furnish the list, they would have kept some other details. If I was right about when my mother had written her desperate letter, I should at least be able to find out which bunch of kooks she had been staying with.

If I wanted to, of course.

Sighing, I read on.

Copies of the photograph of Amanda Nore had been extensively displayed in public places (newsagents' shop windows) in the vicinity of the small town of Mindle Bridge, but no one had come forward to identify either the child or the stable yard or the pony.

Advertisements had been inserted (accounts attached) in various periodicals and one national Sunday newspaper (for six weeks) stating that if Amanda Nore wished to hear something to her advantage she should write to Folk, Langley, Son and Folk, solicitors, of St Albans, Herts.

One of the detectives, the one who had persisted with the tenants, had also enterprisingly questioned the Pony Club, but to no avail. They had never had a member called Amanda Nore. He had furthermore written to the British Show Jumping Association, with the same result.

709

A canvass of schools in a wide area round Mindle Bridge had produced no one called Amanda Nore on the registers, past or present.

She had not come into council care in Sussex. She was on no official list of any sort. No doctor or dentist had heard of her. She had not been confirmed, married, buried or cremated within the county.

The reports came to the same conclusions: that she had been, or was being, brought up elsewhere (possibly under a different name), and was no longer interested in riding.

I shuffled the typed sheets together and returned them to the envelope. They had tried, one had to admit. They had also indicated their willingness to continue to search through each county in the land, if the considerable expenditure should be authorized: but they couldn't in any way guarantee success.

Their collective fee must already have been fearful. The authorization, anyway, seemed not to have been forthcoming. I wondered sardonically if the old woman had thought of me to look for Amanda because it would cost so much less. A promise, a bribe . . . no foal, no fee.

I couldn't understand her late interest in her long ignored grandchildren. She'd had a son of her own, a boy my mother had called 'my hateful little brother'. He would have been about ten when I was born, which made him now about forty, presumably with children of his own.

Uncle. Cousins. Half-sister. Grandmother.

I didn't want them. I didn't want to know them or be drawn into their lives. I was in no way whatever going to look for Amanda.

I stood up with decision and went down to the kitchen to do something about cheese and eggs: and to stave off the thought of Harold a bit longer I fetched George Millace's box of trash in from the car and opened it on the kitchen table, taking out the items and looking at them one by one.

On a closer inspection it still didn't seem to make much sense that he should have kept those particular odds and ends. They didn't have the appearance of interesting or unique mistakes. Sorting my way through them I concluded with disappointment that it had been a waste of time after all to bring them home.

I picked up the folder which contained the dark print of a shadowy man sitting at a table and thought vaguely that it was odd to have bothered to put such an over-exposed mess into a mount.

Shrugging, I slid the dark print out onto my hand ... and it was then that I found George's private pot of gold.

CHAPTER FIVE

It was not, at first sight, very exciting.

Sellotaped onto the back of the print there was an envelope made of the special sort of sulphur-free paper used by careful professionals for the long-term storage of developed film. Inside the envelope, a negative.

It was the negative from which the print had been made, but whereas the print was mostly black and elsewhere very dark greys, the negative itself was clear and sharp with many details and highlights.

I looked at the print and at the negative, side by side.

I had no quickening of the pulse. No suspicions, no theories, merely curiosity. As I also had the means and the time, I went back into the darkroom and made four five-by-four inch prints, each at a different exposure, from one second to eight seconds.

Not even the longest exposure looked exactly like George's dark print, so I started again with the most suitable exposure, six seconds, and left the photograph in the developer too long, until the sharp outlines first went dark and then mostly disappeared, leaving a grey man sitting at a table against blackness. At that point I lifted the paper from the tray of developer and transferred it to the one containing fixer; and what I had then was another print almost exactly like George's.

Leaving a print too long in the developing fluid had to be one of the commonest mistakes on earth. If George's attention had been distracted and he'd left a print too long in developer, he'd simply have cursed and thrown the ruin away. Why, then, had he kept it? And mounted it. And stuck the clear sharp negative onto the back?

It wasn't until I switched on a bright light and looked more closely at the best of the four original exposures I'd made that I understood why: and I stood utterly still in the darkroom, taking in the implications in disbelief.

With something approaching a whistle I finally moved. I switched off the white light, and, when my eyes had accustomed themselves again to the red safe-light, I made another print, four times as large, and on higher contrast grade of paper, to get as clear a result as I could possibly manage.

I switched on the white light again and fed the finished print through the drier, and then I looked at what I'd got.

What I'd got was a picture of two people talking together who had sworn on oath in a court of law that they had never met.

There wasn't the slightest possibility of a mistake.

The shadowy man was now revealed as a customer sitting at a table outside a café somewhere in France. The man himself was a Frenchman with a moustache who had merely happened to be sitting there, a plate and a glass by his hand. The café had a name: Le Lapin d'Argent. There were advertisements for beer and lottery tickets in its half-curtained window, and a waiter in an apron standing in the doorway. A woman some way inside was sitting at a cash desk in front of a mirror, looking out to the street. The detail was sharp throughout, with remarkable depth of focus. George Millace at his usual expert best.

Sitting together at a table outside the café window were two men, both of them facing the camera but with their heads turned towards each other, unmistakably deep in conversation. A wine glass stood in front of each of them, half full, with a bottle to one side. There were coffee cups also, and an ashtray with a half-smoked cigar balanced on the edge. All the signs of a lengthy meeting.

Both men had been involved in an affair which had shaken the racing world like a thunderclap eighteen months earlier. Elgin Yaxley, the one on the left of the photograph, had owned five expensive steeplechasers which had been trained in Lambourn. At the end of the 'chasing season all five had been sent to a local farmer for a few weeks' summer break out at grass; and then, out in the fields, they had all been shot dead with a rifle. Terence O'Tree, the man on the right in the photograph, had shot them.

Some smart police work (aided by two young boys out at dawn when their parents thought them safe in bed) had tracked down and identified O'Tree, and brought him to court.

All five horses had been heavily insured. The insurance company, screeching with disbelief, had tried their damnedest to prove that Yaxley himself had hired O'Tree to do the killing, but both men had consistently denied it, and no link between them had been found.

O'Tree, saying he'd shot the horses just because he'd felt like it ... 'for a bit o' target practice, like, your honour, and how was I to know they was valuable racehorses' ... had been sent to jail for nine months with a recommendation that he should see a psychiatrist.

Elgin Yaxley, indignantly proclaiming his virtue and threatening to sue the insurance company for defamation of character if they didn't instantly pay up, had wrung out of them the whole insured amount and had then faded out of the racing scene.

The insurance company, I thought, would surely have paid George Millace a great deal for his photograph, if they had known it existed. Probably 10 per cent of what they would not have had to pay Yaxley. I couldn't remember the exact sums, but I knew the total insured value of the five horses had been getting on for a hundred and fifty thousand pounds. It had been, in fact, the very size of the pay-out which had infuriated the insurers into suspecting fraud.

So why hadn't George asked for a reward... and why had he so carefully hidden the negative... and why had his house been burgled three times? For all that I'd never liked George Millace, it was the obvious answer to those questions that I disliked even more.

In the morning I walked up to the stables and rode out at early exercise as usual. Harold behaved in his normal blustery fashion, raising his voice over the scouring note of the November wind. The lads scowled and sulked as the vocal lash landed, and one or two, I reckoned, would be gone by the week's end. When lads left any stable nowadays they tended simply not to turn up one morning, nor ever again. They would sidle off to some other stable and the first news their old masters would have would be requests for references from the new. Notice, for many of the modern breed of lads, was something they never gave. Notice led to arguments and aggro, and who wanted that, man, when ducking out was so much easier? The lad population washed in and out of British stables like a swirling endless river, with long-stayers being an exception rather than the rule.

'Breakfast,' Harold bellowed at me at one point. 'Be there.'

I nodded. I usually went home for breakfast even

if I were riding out second lot, which I did only on non-racing days, and not always even then. Breakfast, in Harold's wife's view, consisted of a huge fry-up accompanied by mountains of toast served on the big kitchen table with generosity and warmth. It always smelled and looked delicious, and I always fell.

'Another sausage, Philip?' Harold's wife said, lavishly shovelling straight from the pan. 'And some hot fried potatoes?'

'You're destroying him, woman,' Harold said, reaching for the butter.

Harold's wife smiled at me in her special way. She thought I was too thin; and she thought I needed a wife. She told me so, often. I disagreed with her on both counts, but I dare say she was right.

'Last night,' Harold said. 'We didn't discuss the week's plans.'

'No.'

'There's Pamphlet at Kempton on Wednesday,' he said. 'In the two mile hurdle; and Tishoo and Sharpener on Thursday . . .'

He talked about the races for some time, munching vigorously all the while, so that I got my riding instructions out of the side of his mouth accompanied by crumbs.

'Understood?' he said finally.

'Yes.'

It appeared that after all I had not been given the instant sack, and for that I was relieved and grateful, but it was clear all the same that the precipice wasn't all that far away.

Harold glanced across the big kitchen to where his wife was stacking things in the dishwasher and said, 'Victor doesn't like your attitude.'

I didn't answer.

Harold said, 'The first thing one demands from a jockey is loyalty.'

That was rubbish. The first thing one demanded from a jockey was value for money.

'My Füehrer, right or wrong?' I said.

'Owners won't stand for jockeys passing moral judgements on them.'

'Owners shouldn't defraud the public, then.'

'Have you finished eating?' he demanded.

I sighed regretfully. 'Yes.'

'Then come into the office.'

He led the way into the russet-coloured room which was filled with chill bluish Monday morning light and had no fire yet in the grate.

'Shut the door,' he said.

I shut it.

'You'll have to choose, Philip,' he said. He stood by the fireplace with one foot on the hearth, a big man in riding clothes, smelling of horses and fresh air and fried eggs.

I waited non-committally.

'Victor will eventually want another race lost. Not at once, I grant you, because it would be too obvious.

But in the end, yes. He says if you really mean you won't do it, we'll have to get someone else.'

'For those races only?'

'Don't be stupid. You're not stupid. You're too bloody smart for your own good.'

I shook my head. 'Why does he want to start this caper again? He's won a lot of prize money playing it straight these last three years.'

Harold shrugged. 'I don't know. What does it matter? He told me on Saturday when we got to Sandown that he'd laid his horse and that I was on to a big share of the profit. We've all done it before . . . why not again? Just what has got into you, Philip, that you're swooning over a little fiddle like a bloody virgin?'

I didn't know the answer. He swept on anyway before I'd thought of a reply. 'Well, you just work it out, boy. Whose are the best horses in the yard? Victor's. Who buys good new horses to replace the old? Victor. Who pays his training bills on the nose, bills for usually five horses? Victor. Who owns more horses in this yard than anyone else? Victor. And which owner can I least afford to lose, particularly as he has been with me for more than ten years and has provided me with a large proportion of the winners I've trained in the past, and is likely to provide most of those I train in the future? Just who, do you think, my business most depends on?'

I stared at him. I supposed that I hadn't realized

until then that he was in perhaps the same position as myself. Do what Victor wanted, or else.

'I don't want to lose you, Philip,' he said. 'You're a prickly bastard, but we've got on all right all these years. You won't go on for ever, though. You've been racing . . . what . . . ten years?'

I nodded.

'Three or four more, then. At the most, five. Pretty soon you won't bounce back from those falls the way you do now. And at any time a bad one might put you out of action for good. So look at it straight, Philip. Who do I need most in the long term, you or Victor?'

In a sort of melancholy we walked into the yard, where Harold shouted, but half-heartedly, at a couple of dawdling lads.

'Let me know,' he said, turning towards me.

'All right.'

'I want you to stay.'

I was surprised, but also pleased.

'Thanks,' I said.

He gave me a clumsy buffet on the shoulder, the nearest he'd ever come to the slightest show of affection. More than all the threatening and screaming on earth it made me want to agree to do what he asked; a reaction, I acknowledged flickeringly, as old as the hills. It was often kindness that finally broke the prisoner's spirit, not torture. One's defences were always defiantly angled outward to withstand aggression: it was kindness which crept round behind and stabbed you in the back, so that your will evaporated into tears and gratitude. Defences against kindness were much harder to build. And not the defences I would ever have thought I needed against Harold.

I sought instinctively to change the subject, and came up with the nearest thought to hand, which was George Millace and his photograph.

'Um,' I said, as we stood a shade awkwardly. 'Do you remember those five horses of Elgin Yaxley's, that were shot?'

'What?' He looked bewildered. 'What's that got to do with Victor?'

'Nothing at all,' I said. 'I was just thinking about them, yesterday.'

Irritation immediately cancelled out the passing moment of emotion, which was probably a relief to us both.

'For God's sake,' he said sharply. 'I'm serious. Your career's at stake. You can do what you damn well like. You can bloody well go to hell. It's up to you.'

I nodded.

He turned away abruptly and took two purposeful steps. Then he stopped, looked back, and said, 'If you're so bloody interested in Elgin Yaxley's horses, why don't you ask Kenny?' He pointed to one of the lads, who was filling two buckets by the tap. 'He looked after them.'

He turned his back again and firmly strode away, outrage and anger thumping down with every foot.

I walked irresolutely over to Kenny, not sure what questions I wanted to ask, or even if I wanted to ask questions at all.

Kenny was one of those people whose defences were the other way round: impervious to kindness, open to fright. Kenny was a natural near-delinquent who had been treated with so much understanding by social workers that he could shrug off pleasant approaches with contempt.

He watched me come with an expression wilfully blank to the point of insolence, his habitual expression. Skin reddened by the wind; eyes slightly watering; spots.

'Mr Osborne said you used to work for Bart Underfield,' I said.

'So what?'

The water splashed over the top of the first bucket. He bent to remove it, and kicked the second one forward under the tap.

'And looked after some of Elgin Yaxley's horses?'

'So what?'

'So were you sorry when they were shot?'

He shrugged. 'Suppose so.'

'What did Mr Underfield say about it?'

'Huh?' His gaze rested squarely on my face. 'He didn't say nothing.'

'Wasn't he angry?'

'Not as I noticed.'

'He must have been,' I said.

Kenny shrugged again.

'At the very least,' I said. 'He was five horses short, and no trainer with his size stable can afford that.'

'He didn't say nothing.' The second bucket was nearly full, and Kenny turned off the tap. 'He didn't seem to care much about losing them. Something cheesed him off a bit later, though.'

'What did?'

Kenny looked uninterested and picked up the buckets. 'Don't know. He was right grumpy. Some of the owners got fed up and left.'

'So did you,' I said.

'Yeah.' He started walking across the yard with water sloshing gently at each step. I went with him, warily keeping a dry distance. 'What's the point of staying when a place is going down the drain?'

'Were Yaxley's horses in good shape when they went off to the farm?' I asked.

'Sure.' He looked slightly puzzled. 'Why are you asking?'

'No real reason. Someone mentioned those horses . . . and Mr Osborne said you looked after them. I was just interested.'

'Oh.' He nodded. 'They had the vet in court, you know, to say the horses were fine the day before they died. He went to the farm to give one of them some anti-tetanus jabs, and he said he looked them all over, and they were OK.'

'Did you go to the trial?'

'No. Read it in the *Sporting Life*.' He reached the row of boxes and put the buckets down outside one of the doors. 'That all, then?'

'Yes. Thanks, Kenny.'

'Tell you something . . .' He looked almost surprised at his own sudden helpfulness.

'What?'

'That Mr Yaxley,' he said. 'You'd've thought he'd been pleased getting all that lolly, even if he had lost his horses, but he came into Underfield's yard one day in a right proper rage. Come to think of it, it was after that that Underfield went sour. And Yaxley, of course, he buggered off out of racing and we never saw no more of him. Not while I was there, we didn't.'

I walked thoughtfully home, and when I got there the telephone was ringing.

'Jeremy Folk,' a familiar voice said.

'Oh, not again,' I protested.

'Did you read those reports?'

'Yes, I did. And I'm not going looking for her.'

'Be a good fellow,' he said.

'No.' I paused. 'To get you off my back, I'll help you a bit. But you must do the looking.'

'Well . . .' He sighed. 'What sort of help?'

I told him my conclusions about Amanda's age, and also suggested he should get the dates of the various tenancies of Pine Woods Lodge from the estate agents.

'My mother was probably there thirteen years ago,' I said. 'And now it's all yours.'

'But I *say* . . .' he almost wailed. 'You simply can't stop there.'

'I simply can.'

'I'll get back to you.'

'Just leave me alone,' I said.

I drove into Swindon to take the colour film to the processors, and on the way thought about the life and times of Bart Underfield.

I knew him in the way one got to know everyone in racing if one lived long enough in Lambourn. We met occasionally in the village shops and in other people's houses, as well as at the races. We exchanged 'Good mornings' and 'Hard lucks' and a variety of vague nods. I had never ridden for him because he had never asked me; and he'd never asked me, I thought, because he didn't like me.

He was a small busy man full of importance, given to telling people confidentially what other more successful trainers had done wrong. 'Of course Walwyn shouldn't have run such-and-such at Ascot,' he would say. 'The distance was all wrong, one could see it a mile off.'

Strangers thought him very knowledgeable. Lambourn thought him an ass.

No one had suggested, however, that he was such an ass as to deliver his five best horses to the slaughter. Everyone had undoubtedly felt sorry for him, particularly as Elgin Yaxley had not spent the insurance money on buying new and equal animals, but had merely departed altogether, leaving Bart a great deal worse off.

Those horses, I reflected, had undoubtedly been good, and must always have earned more than their keep, and could have been sold for high prices. They had been insured above their market value, certainly, but not by impossible margins if one took into account the prizes they couldn't win if they were dead. It was the fact that there seemed to be little profit in killing them that had finally baffled the suspicious insurers into paying up.

That . . . and no trace of a link between Elgin Yaxley and Terence O'Tree.

In Swindon the processors, who knew me well, said I was lucky, they were just going to feed a batch through, and if I cared to hang about I could have my negatives back in a couple of hours. I did some oddments of shopping and in due course picked up the developed films, and went home.

In the afternoon I printed the coloured versions of Mrs Millace, and sent them off with the black-and-white lot to the police; and in the evening I tried –

and failed – to stop thinking in uncomfortable circles about Amanda and Victor Briggs and George Millace.

By far the worst was Victor Briggs and Harold's ultimatum. The jockey life suited me fine in every way, physically, mentally, financially. I'd put off for years the thought that one day I would have to do something else: the 'one day' had always been in the mists of the future, not staring me brutally in the face.

The only thing I knew anything about besides horses was photography, but there were thousands of photographers all over the place ... everyone took photographs, every family had a camera, the whole western world was awash with photographers ... and to make a living at it one had to be exceptionally good.

One also had to work exceptionally hard. The photographers I knew on the racecourse were always running about: scurrying from the start to the last fence and from there up to the unsaddling enclosures before the winner got there, and then down the course again for the next race, and six times, at least, every afternoon, five or six days a week. Some of their pictures they rushed off to news agencies who might offer them to newspapers, and some they sent to magazines, and some they flogged to the owners of the horses, and some to sponsors handing over cups.

If you were a racing photographer the pictures didn't come to you, you had to go out looking. And when you'd got them, the customers didn't flock to your door, you had to go out selling. It was all a lot different from

Duncan and Charlie, who had mostly done still-life things like pots and pans and clocks and garden furniture for advertisements.

There were very few full-time successful racing photographers. Fewer than ten, probably. Of those perhaps four were outstanding; and one of those four had been George Millace.

If I tried to join their ranks the others wouldn't hinder me, but they wouldn't help me either. I'd be out there on my own, stand or fall.

I wouldn't mind the running about, I thought: it was the selling part that daunted. Even if I considered my pictures good enough, I couldn't push.

And what else?

Setting up as a trainer was out. I hadn't the capital, and training racehorses was no sort of life for someone who liked stretches of silent time and being alone. Trainers talked to people from dawn to bedtime and lived in a whirl.

What I wanted, and instinctively knew that I would always need, was to continue to be self-employed. A regular wage packet looked like chains. An illogical feeling, but overwhelming. Whatever I did, I would have to do it on my own.

The habit of never making decisions would have to be broken. I could drift, I saw, into jobs which had none of the terrific satisfactions of being a jockey. I had been lucky so far, but if I wanted to find contentment in the next chapter I would have for once to be positive.

Damn Victor Briggs, I thought violently.

Inciting jockeys to throw races was a warning-off offence, but even if I could manage to get Victor Briggs warned-off the person who would most suffer would be Harold. And I'd lose my job anyway, as Harold would hardly keep me on after that, even if we didn't both lose our licences altogether because of the races I'd thrown in the past. I couldn't prove Victor Briggs's villainy without having to admit Harold's and my own.

Cheat or retire. A stark choice . . . absolutely bloody.

Nothing changed much on the Tuesday, but when I went to Kempton on Wednesday to ride Pamphlet the weighing room was electric with two pieces of gossip.

Ivor den Relgan had been made a Member of the Jockey Club, and Steve Millace's mother's house had burned down.

CHAPTER SIX

'Ivor den Relgan!' I heard the name on every side, repeated in varying tones of astonishment and disbelief. 'A Member of the Jockey Club! Incredible!'

The Jockey Club, that exclusive and gentlemanly body, had apparently that morning voted into its fastidious ranks a man they had been holding at arm's length for years, a rich self-important man from no one knew where, who had spread his money about in racing and done a certain amount of good in a way that affronted the recipients.

He was supposed to be of Dutch extraction. Extraction, that is, from some unspecified ex-Dutch colony. He spoke with an accent that sounded like a mixture of South African, Australian and American, a conglomerate mid-globe amalgam of vowels and consonants which could have been attractive but came out as patronizing. He, the voice seemed to say, was a great deal more sophisticated than the stuffy British upper crust. He sought not favours from the entrenched powers, but admiration. It was they, he implied, who would prosper if they took his advice. He offered it to them free, frequently, in letters to the *Sporting Life*.

Until that morning the Jockey Club had indeed observably taken his advice on several occasions while steadfastly refusing to acknowledge he had given it. I wondered fleetingly what had brought them to such a turnaround; what had caused them suddenly to embrace the anathema.

Steve Millace was in the changing room, waiting by my peg.

The strain in him that was visible from the doorway was at close quarters overpowering. White-faced, vibrating, he stood with his arm in a black webbing sling and looked at me from sunken desperate eyes.

'Have you heard?' he said.

I nodded.

'It happened on Monday night. Well, yesterday morning, I suppose . . . about three o'clock. By the time anyone noticed the whole place had gone.'

'Your mother wasn't there?'

'They'd kept her in hospital. She's still there. It's too much for her. I mean . . .' He was trembling ' . . . too much.'

I made some sincerely sympathetic noises.

'Tell me what to do,' he said; and I thought, he's elected me as some sort of elder brother, an unofficial advice bureau.

'Didn't you say something about aunts?' I asked. 'At the funeral?'

He shook his head impatiently. 'They're Dad's sisters. Older sisters. They've never liked Mum.'

'All the same . . .'

'They're *cats*,' he said, exploding. 'I rang them . . . they said what a shame.' He mimicked their voices venomously. ' "Tell poor dear Marie she can get quite a nice little bungalow near the seaside with the insurance money." They make me sick.'

I began taking off my street clothes to change into colours, aware that to Steve the day's work was irrelevant.

'Philip,' he said imploringly. 'You saw her. All bashed about . . . and without Dad . . . and now the whole house . . . Please . . . *please* . . . help me.'

'All right,' I said resignedly. What else could one say? 'When I've finished riding, we'll work something out.'

He sat down on the bench as if his legs wouldn't hold him and just stayed there staring into space while I finished changing and went to weigh out.

Harold was by the scales as usual, waiting to take my saddle when I'd been weighed. Since Monday he'd made no reference to the life-altering decision he'd handed me, and perhaps he took my silence not for spirit-tearing indecision but tacit acceptance of a return to things past. At any rate it was with a totally normal manner that he said, as I put the saddle over his arm, 'Did you hear who's been elected to the Jockey Club?'

'Yeah.'

'They'll take Genghis Khan next.'

He walked out with the saddle to go and put it on Pamphlet, and in due course I joined him in the parade ring, where the horse walked nonchalantly round and his pop star owner bit his nails with concentration.

Harold had gleaned some more news. 'I hear that it was the Great White Chief who insisted on den Relgan joining the Club.'

'Lord White?' I was surprised.

'Old Driven Snow himself.'

Pamphlet's youngish owner flicked his fingers and said, 'Hey, man, how's about a little sweet music on this baby?'

'A tenner each way,' Harold suggested, having learnt the pop star's language. The pop star was using the horse for publicity and would only let it run when its race would be televized: and he was, as usual, wholly aware of the positions of the cameras, so that if they should chance to point his way he would not be carelessly obscured behind Harold or me. I admired his expertise in this respect, and indeed his whole performance, because off-stage, so to speak, he was apt to relapse into middle-class suburban. The jazzed-up working-class image was all a fake.

He had come to the races that day with dark blue hair. The onset of a mild apoplexy could be observed in the parade ring all about us, but Harold behaved as if he hadn't noticed, on the basis that owners who paid their bills could be as eccentric as they liked.

733

'Philip, darling,' said the pop star, 'bring this baby back for Daddy.'

He must have learned it out of old movies, I thought. Surely not even pop musicians talked like that any more. He reverted to biting his nails and I got up on Pamphlet and rode out to see what I could do about the tenner each way.

I was not popularly supposed to be much good over hurdles, but maybe Pamphlet had winning on his mind that day as much as I did. He soared round the whole thing with bursting *joie de vivre*, even to the extent of passing the favourite on the run-in, and we came back to bear hugs from the blue hair (for the benefit of television) and an offer to me of a spare ride in the fifth race, from a worried-looking small-time trainer. Stable jockey hurt ... would I mind? I wouldn't mind, I'd be delighted. Fine, the valet has the colours, see you in the parade ring. Great.

Steve was still brooding by my peg.

'Was the shed burnt?' I asked.

'What?'

'The shed. The deep freeze. Your Dad's photos.'

'Oh, well, yes it was ... but Dad's stuff wasn't in there.'

I stripped off the pop star's orange and pink colours and went in search of the calmer green and brown of the spare ride.

'Where was it, then?' I said, returning.

'I told Mum what you said about people maybe not

liking Dad's pictures of them, and she reckoned that you thought all the burglaries were really aimed at the photos, not at her fur and all that, and that if so she didn't want to leave those transparencies where they could still be stolen, so on Monday she got me to move them next door, to her neighbours. And that's where they are now, in a sort of outhouse.'

I buttoned the green and brown shirt, thinking it over.

'Do you want me to visit her in the hospital?' I said.

Almost on my direct route home. No great shakes. He fell on it, though, with embarrassing fervour. He had come to the races, he said, with the pub-keeper from the Sussex village where he lived in digs near the stable he rode for, and if I would visit his mother he could go home with the pub-keeper, because otherwise he had no transport, because of his collarbone. I hadn't exactly meant I would see Mrs Millace alone, but on reflection I didn't mind.

Having shifted his burden Steve cheered up a bit and asked if I would telephone him when I got home.

'Yes,' I said absently. 'Did your father often go to France?'

'France?'

'Ever heard of it?' I said.

'Oh . . .' He was in no mood to be teased. 'Of course he did. Longchamps, Auteuil, St Cloud. Everywhere.'

'And round the world?' I said, packing lead into my weight cloth.

'Huh?' He was decidedly puzzled. 'What do you mean?'

'What did he spend his money on?'

'Lenses, mostly. Telephotos as long as your arm. Anything new.'

I took my saddle and weight-cloth over to the trial scales and added another flat pound of lead. Steve got up and followed me.

'What do you mean, what did he spend his money on?'

I said, 'Nothing. Nothing at all. Just wondered what he liked doing, away from the races.'

'He just took pictures. All the time, everywhere. He wasn't interested in anything else.'

In time I went out to ride the green-and-brown horse and it was one of those days, which happened so seldom, when absolutely everything went right. In unqualified euphoria I dismounted once again in the winners' enclosure, and thought that I couldn't possibly give up the life; I couldn't *possibly*. Not when winning put you higher than heroin.

My mother had likely died of heroin.

Steve's mother lay alone in a glass-walled side-ward, isolated but indecently exposed to the curious glances of any stranger walking past. There were curtains which might have shielded her from public gaze, but they were not pulled across. I hated the system which denied privacy to people in hospital: who on earth, if they were ill or injured, wanted their indignities gawped at?

Marie Millace lay on her back with two flat pillows under her head and a sheet and a thin blue blanket covering her. Her eyes were shut. Her brown hair, greasy and in disarray, straggled on the pillow. Her face was dreadful.

The raw patches of Saturday night were now covered by extensive dark scabs. The cut eyelid, stitched, was monstrously swollen and black. The nose was crimson under some shaping plaster of Paris, which had been stuck onto forehead and cheeks with white sticky tape. Her mouth, open and also swollen, looked purple. All the rest showed deep signs of bruising: crimson, grey, black and yellow. Fresh, the injuries had looked merely nasty: it was in the healing process that their true extent showed.

I'd seen people in that state before, and worse than that, damaged by horses' galloping hooves; but this, done out of malice to an inoffensive lady in her own home, was differently disturbing. I felt not sympathy but anger: Steve's 'I'll kill the bastards' anger.

She heard me come in, and opened her less battered eye a fraction as I approached. What I could see of an expression looked merely blank, as if I was the last person she would have expected.

'Steve asked me to come,' I said. 'He couldn't get here because of his shoulder. He can't drive . . . not for a day or two.'

The eye closed.

I fetched a chair from against the wall and put it by the bed, to sit beside her. The eye opened again; and then her hand, which had been lying on the blanket, slowly stretched out towards me. I took it, and she gripped me hard, holding on fiercely, seeking, it seemed, support and comfort and reassurance. The spirit of need ebbed after a while, and she let go of my hand and put her own weakly back on the blanket.

'Did Steve tell you,' she said, 'about the house?'

'Yes, he did. I'm so sorry.' It sounded feeble. Anything sounded feeble in the face of such knocks as she'd taken.

'Have you seen it?' she said.

'No. Steve told me about it at the races. At Kempton, this afternoon.'

Her speech was slurred and difficult to understand, as she moved her tongue as if it were stiff inside the swollen lips.

'My nose is broken,' she said, fluttering her fingers on the blanket.

'Yes,' I said. 'I broke mine once. They put a plaster on me, too, just like yours. You'll be as good as new in a week.'

Her silent response couldn't be interpreted as anything but dissent.

'You'll be surprised,' I said.

There was the sort of pause that occurs at hospital bedsides. Perhaps it was there that the ward system scored, I thought: when you'd run out of platitudes you could always discuss the gruesome symptoms in the next bed.

'George said you took photographs, like him,' she said.

'Not like him,' I said. 'George was the best.'

No dissent at all, this time. Discernibly the intentions of a smile.

'Steve told me you'd had George's boxes of transparencies moved out before the fire,' I said. 'That was lucky.'

Her smile, however, disappeared, and was slowly replaced by distress.

'The police came today,' she said. A sort of shudder shook her, and her breathing grew more troubled. She could get no air through her nose so the change was audible and rasped in her throat.

'They came here?' I asked.

'Yes. They said ... Oh God ...' Her chest heaved and she coughed.

I put my hand flatly over hers on the blanket and said urgently. 'Don't get upset. You'll make everything hurt worse. Just take three slow deep breaths. Four or five, if you need them. Don't talk until you can make it cold.'

She lay silent for a while until the heavy breathing slackened. I watched the tightened muscles relax under the blanket, and eventually she said, 'You're much older than Steve.'

'Eight years,' I agreed, letting go of her hand.

'No. Much... much older.' There was a pause. 'Could you give me some water?'

There was a glass on the locker beside her bed. Water in the glass, angled tube for drinking. I steered the tube to her mouth, and she sucked up a couple of inches.

'Thanks.' Another pause, then she tried again, this time much more calmly. 'The police said... The police said it was arson.'

'Did they?'

'You're not... surprised?'

'After two burglaries, no.'

'Paraffin,' she said. 'Five-gallon drum. Police found it in the hall.'

'Was it your paraffin?'

'No.'

Another pause.

'The police asked... if George had any enemies.' She moved her head restlessly. 'I said of course not... and they asked... if he had anything someone would want... enough... enough... oh...'

'Mrs Millace,' I said matter-of-factly. 'Did they ask if George had any photographs worth burglary and burning?'

'George wouldn't...' she said intensely.

George had, I thought.

'Look,' I said slowly, 'You might not want me to... you might not trust me... but if you like I could look through those transparencies for you, and I could tell you if I thought there were any which could possibly come into the category we're talking about.'

After a while she said only, 'Tonight?'

'Yes, certainly. Then if they're OK you can tell the police they exist . . . if you want to.'

'George isn't a blackmailer,' she said. Coming from the swollen mouth the words sounded extraordinary, distorted but passionately meant. She was not saying 'I don't want to believe George could blackmail anyone,' but 'George didn't.' Yet she hadn't been sure enough to give the transparencies to the police. Sure but not sure. Emotionally sure. Rationally unsure. In a nonsensical way, that made sense.

She hadn't much left except that instinctive faith. It was beyond me entirely to tell her it was misplaced.

I collected the three metal boxes from the neighbour, who had been told, it appeared, that they contained just odds and ends the burglars had missed, and I was given by her a conducted tour of the burned mess next door.

Even in the dark one could see that there was nothing to salvage. Five gallons of paraffin had made no mistake. The house was a shell, roofless, windowless, acrid and creaking: and it was to this savage destruction of her nest that Marie would have to return.

I drove home with George's life's work and spent

the rest of the evening and half of the night projecting his slides onto the flat white wall of my sitting room.

His talent had been stupendous. Seeing his pictures there together, one after the other, and not scattered in books and newspapers and magazines across a canvas of years, I was struck continually by the speed of his vision. He had caught life over and over and over again at the moment when a painter would have composed it: nothing left out, nothing disruptive let in. An absolute master.

The best of his racing pictures were there, some in colour, some in black and white, but there were also several stunning series on unexpected subjects like card players and alcoholics and giraffes and sculptors in action and hot Sundays in New York. These series stretched back almost to George's youth, the date and place being written on each mount in tiny fine-nibbed letters.

There were dozens of portraits of people: some posed in a studio, mostly not. Again and again he had caught the fleeting expression which exposed the soul, and even if he had originally taken twenty shots to keep but one, the ones he had kept were collectively breathtaking.

Pictures of France. Paris, St Tropez, cycle racing, fish docks. No pictures of people sitting outside cafés, talking to whom they shouldn't.

When I'd got to the end of the third box I sat for a

while thinking of what George hadn't photographed, or hadn't in any case kept.

No war. No riots. No horrors. No mangled bodies or starving children or executions or bombed-apart cars.

What had yelled from my wall for hours had been a satirical baring of the essence under the external; and perhaps George had felt the external satire of violence left him nothing to say.

I was rather deeply aware that I was never going to see the world in quite the same way again: that George's piercing view of things would intrude when I least expected it and nudge me in the ribs. But George had had no compassion. The pictures were brilliant. Objective, exciting, imaginative and revealing; but none of them kind.

None of them either, in any way that I could see, could have been used as a basis for blackmail.

I telephoned Marie Millace in the morning, and told her so. The relief in her voice when she answered betrayed the existence of her doubts, and she heard it herself and immediately began a cover-up.

'I mean,' she said, 'of course I knew George wouldn't . . .'

'Of course,' I said. 'What shall I do with the pictures?'

'Oh dear, I don't know. No one will try to steal them

now though, will they?' The mumbling voice was even less distinct over the wire. 'What do you think?'

'Well,' I said. 'You can't exactly advertise that although George's pictures still exist no one needs to feel threatened. So I do think they may still be at risk.'

'But that means . . . that means . . .'

'I'm terribly sorry. I know it means that I agree with the police. That George did have something which someone desperately wanted destroyed. But please don't worry. Please don't. Whatever it was has probably gone with the house . . . and it's all over.' And God forgive me, I thought.

'Oh dear . . . George didn't . . . I know he didn't . . .'

I could hear the distress rising again in the noise of her breathing.

'Listen,' I said quickly. 'About those transparencies. Are you listening?'

'Yes.'

'I think the best thing for now would be to put them into a cold store somewhere. Then when you feel better, you could get an agent to put on an exhibition of George's work. The collection is marvellous, it really is. An exhibition would celebrate his talent, and make you a bit of money . . . and also reassure anyone who might be worrying that there was nothing to . . . er . . . worry about.'

There was a silence, but I knew she was still there, because of the breathing.

'George wouldn't use an agent,' she said at last. 'How could I find one?'

'I know one or two. I could give you their names.'

'Oh . . .' She sounded weak and there was another long pause. Then she said, 'I know . . . I'm asking such a lot . . . but could you . . . put those transparencies into store? I'd ask Steve . . . but you seem to know . . . what to do.'

I said that I would, and when we had disconnected I wrapped the three boxes in their polythene sheets and took them along to the local butcher, who already kept a box of my own in his walk-in freezer room. He cheerfully agreed to the extra lodgers, suggested a reasonable rental, and gave me a receipt.

Back home I looked at the negative and the print of Elgin Yaxley talking to Terence O'Tree, and wondered what on earth I should do with them.

If George had extorted from Elgin Yaxley all the profits from the shot-horse affair – and it looked as if he must have done, because of Bart Underfield's gloominess and Yaxley's own disappearance from racing – then it had to be Elgin Yaxley who was now desperate to find the photograph before anyone else did.

If Elgin Yaxley had arranged the burglaries, the beating-up and the burning, should retribution not follow? If I gave the photograph to the police, with explanations, Elgin Yaxley would be in line for prosecution for most crimes on the statutes, not least perjury

745

and defrauding an insurance company of a hundred and fifty thousand.

If I gave the photograph to the police I was telling the world that George Millace had been a blackmailer.

Which would Marie Millace prefer, I thought: never to know who had attacked her, or to know for sure that George had been a villain . . . and to have everyone else know it too.

There was no doubt about the answer.

I had no qualms about legal justice. I put the negative back where I'd found it, in its envelope stuck onto the back of the dark print in its paper mount. I put the mount back into the box of rubbish which still lay on the kitchen dresser, and I put the clear big print I'd made into a folder in the filing cabinet in the hall.

No one knew I had them. No one would come looking. No one would burgle or burn my house, or beat me up. Nothing at all would happen from now on.

I locked my doors and went to the races to ride Tishoo and Sharpener and to agonize over that other thorny problem, Victor Briggs.

CHAPTER SEVEN

Ivor den Relgan was again the big news, and what was more, he was there.

I saw him immediately I arrived, as he was standing just outside the weighing room door talking to two pressmen. I was a face among many to him, but to me, as to everyone else whose business was racing, he was as recognizable as a poppy in corn.

He wore, as he often did, an expensively soft camel-coloured coat, buttoned and belted, and he stood bare-headed with greying hair neatly brushed, a stocky, slightly pugnacious-looking man with an air of expecting people to notice his presence. A lot of people considered it a plus to be in his favour, but for some reason I found his self-confidence repellent, and his strong gravitational pull was something I instinctively resisted.

I would have been more than happy never to have come into his focus, but as I was passing them one of the pressmen shot out a hand and fastened it on my arm.

'Philip,' he said, 'you can tell us. You're always on the business end of a camera.'

'Tell you what?' I said, hovering in mid-stride, and intending to walk on.

'How do you photograph a wild horse?'

'Point and click,' I said pleasantly.

'No, Philip,' he said, exasperated. 'You know Mr den Relgan, don't you?'

I inclined my head slightly and said, 'By sight.'

'Mr den Relgan, this is Philip Nore. Jockey, of course.' The pressman was unaccustomedly obsequious: I'd noticed den Relgan often had that effect. 'Mr den Relgan wants photographs of all his horses, but one of them rears up all the time when he sees a camera. How would you get him to stand still?'

'I know one photographer,' I said, 'who got a wild horse to stand still by playing a tape of a hunt in full cry. The horse just stood and listened. The pictures were great.'

Den Relgan smiled superciliously as if he didn't want to hear good ideas that weren't his own, and I nodded with about as much fervour and went on into the weighing room thinking that the Jockey Club must have been mad. The existing members of the Jockey Club were for the most part forward-looking people who put good will and energy into running a huge industry fairly. That they were also self-electing meant in practice that the members were almost all aristocrats or upper class, but the ideal of service bred into them worked pretty well for the good of racing. The old autocratic change-resistant bunch had died out, and there were fewer bitter jokes nowadays about bone-heads at the top. All the more surprising that they should have beckoned to a semi-phoney like den Relgan.

Harold was inside in the weighing room talking to Lord White, which gave me a frisson like seeing a traffic warden standing next to one's wrongly parked car: but it appeared that Lord White, powerful Steward of the Jockey Club, was not enquiring into the outcome of the Sandown Pattern 'Chase, nor into any other committed sins. He was telling Harold that there was a special trophy for Sharpener's race, and, should he happen to win it, both Harold and I, besides the owner, would be required to put in an appearance and receive our gifts.

'It wasn't advertised as a sponsored race,' Harold said, surprised.

'No . . . but Mr den Relgan has generously made this gesture. And incidentally it will be his daughter who does the actual presentations.' He looked directly at me. 'Nore, isn't it?'

'Yes, sir.'

'You heard all that? Good. Fine.' He nodded, turned, and left us, crossing to speak to another trainer with a runner in the same race.

'How many trophies does it take,' Harold said under his breath, 'to buy your way into the Jockey Club?' And in a normal voice he added, 'Victor's here.'

I said anxiously, 'But Sharpener will do his best.'

Harold looked amused. 'Yes, he will. This time. Win that pot if you can. It would really give Victor a buzz, taking Ivor den Relgan's cup. They can't stand each other.'

'I didn't know they knew . . .'

'Everyone knows everyone,' Harold said, shrugging. 'I think they belong to the same gaming club.' He lost interest and went out of the weighing room, and I stood for a few aimless moments watching Lord White make his way towards yet another trainer to pass on the instructions.

Lord White, in his fifties, was a well-built good-looking man with thick light-grey hair progressively turning the colour of his name. He had disconcertingly bright blue eyes and a manner that disarmed anyone advancing on him with a grievance; and it was he, although not Senior Steward, who was the true leader of the Jockey Club, elected not by votes but by the natural force born in him.

An upright man, widely respected, whose nickname Driven Snow (spoken only behind his back) had been coined, I thought, only partly through admiration and mostly to poke fun at the presence of so much notice-able virtue.

I went off to the changing room and on into the business of the day, and was guiltily relieved to find Steve Millace had not made the journey. No beseeching eyes and general helplessness to inveigle me into yet another round of fetching and carrying and visiting the sick. I changed into Tishoo's colours and thought only about the race he was due to start in, which was for novices over hurdles.

In the event there were no great problems but no repeat either of the previous day's joys. Tishoo galloped willingly enough into fourth place at the finish, which pleased his woman owner, and I carried my saddle to the scales to be weighed in, and so back to my changing-room peg to put on Victor Briggs's colours for Sharpener. Just another day's work. Each day unique in itself, but in essence the same. On two thousand days, or thereabouts, I had gone into changing rooms and put on colours and passed the scales and ridden the races. Two thousand days of hope and effort and sweat and just the unjust rewards. More than a job: part of my fabric.

I put on a jacket over Victor Brigg's colours, because there were two other races to be run before Sharpener's, and went outside for a while to see what was happening in general: and what was happening in particular was Lady White with a scowl on her thin aristocratic face.

Lady White didn't know me especially, but I, along with most other jump jockeys, had shaken her hand as she stood elegantly at Lord White's side at two parties they had given to the racing world. The parties had been large everyone-invited affairs three or four years apart, held at Cheltenham racecourse during the March meeting; and they had been Lord White's own idea, paid for by him, and given, one understood, because of his belief that everyone in jump racing belonged at heart to a brotherhood of friends, and should meet as such to enjoy themselves. Old Driven Snow at his priceless best, and like everyone else I'd gone to the parties and enjoyed them.

Lady White was hugging her mink around her and almost glaring forth from under a wide-brimmed brown hat. Her intensity was such that I followed her gaze and found it fixed on her paragon of a husband, who was himself talking to a girl.

Lord White was not simply talking to the girl but revelling in it, radiating flirtatious fun from his sparkling eyes to his gesturing fingertips. I looked sardonically back from this picture telling the old old story and found Lady White's attention still balefully fixed on it, and I thought in amusement 'Oh dear', as one does. The pure white lord, that evening, would be in for an unaristocratic ticking off.

Ivor den Relgan was still holding court to a clutch of journalists, among whom were two racing writers and three gossip columnists from the larger daily papers. Ivor den Relgan was definitely a gossip man's man.

Bart Underfield was loudly telling an elderly married couple that Osborne should know better than to run Sharpener in a three mile 'chase when any fool knew that the horse couldn't go further than two. The elderly couple nodded, impressed.

I gradually became aware that a man standing near me was also, like Lady White, intently watching Lord White and the girl. The man near me was physically unremarkable; an ordinary average man, no longer young, not quite middle-aged, with dark thinning hair and black-framed glasses. Grey trousers, olive green jacket, suede, not tweed, well-cut. When he realized that I was looking at him he gave me a quick annoyed glance and moved away: and I thought no more about him for another hour.

Victor Briggs, when I joined him in the parade ring before Sharpener's race, was heavily pleasant and made no reference to the issue hanging between us. Harold had boosted himself into a state of confidence and was standing with his long legs apart, his hat tipped back on his head, and his binoculars swinging rhythmically from one hand.

'A formality,' he was saying. 'Sharpener's never been better, eh, Philip? Gave you a good feel on the Downs, didn't he? Worked like a train.' His robust voice floated easily over several nearby owner-trainer-jockey groups who were all suffering from their own pre-race tensions and could have done without Harold's.

'Jumping out of his skin,' Harold said, booming. 'Never been better. He'll run the legs off 'em, today, eh, Victor?'

The only good thing one could say about Harold's

bursts of over-confidence was that if in the event they proved to be misplaced he would not relapse into acrimony and gloom. Failures were apt to be expansively forgiven with 'it was the weight that beat him, of course' and were seldom held to be the jockey's fault, even when they were.

Sharpener himself reacted to Harold's optimism in a thoroughly positive way, and encouraged also perhaps by my confidence left over from the two winners the day before, ran a faultless race with energy and courage, so that for the third time at that meeting my mount returned to applause.

Harold was metaphorically by this time two feet off the ground, and even Victor allowed his mouth a small smile.

Ivor den Relgan manfully shaped up to the fact that his fancy trophy had been won by a man he disliked, and Lord White fluttered around the girl he'd been talking to, clearing a passage for her through the throng.

When I'd weighed in and handed my saddle to my valet, and combed my hair and gone out to the prize-giving, the scene had sorted itself out into a square table with a blue cloth bearing one large silver object and two smaller ones surrounded by Lord White, the girl, Ivor den Relgan, Victor and Harold.

Lord White said through a hand microphone to the small watching crowd that Miss Dana den Relgan would present the trophies so kindly given by her father: and it cannot have been only in my mind that the cynical speculation arose. Was it the Dad that Lord White wanted in the Jockey Club, or Dad's daughter? Perish the thought. Lord White with a girlfriend? Impossible.

At close quarters it was clear that he was attracted beyond sober good sense. He touched her continually under the guise of arranging everyone suitably for the presentations, and he was vivacious where normally staid. It all remained just within the acceptable limits of roguishly avuncular behaviour, but discreet it was not.

Dana den Relgan was enough, I supposed, to excite any man she cared to respond to: and to Lord White she was responding with sweetness. Slender and graceful and not very tall, she had a lot of blonde-flecked hair curling casually onto her shoulders. There was also a curving mouth, very wide-apart eyes and excellent skin, and a quality of being not all dolly-bird in the brain. Her manner was observably more restrained than Lord White's, as if she didn't dislike his attentions but thought them too obvious, and she presented the trophies to Victor and Harold and myself without much conversation attached.

To me she said merely, 'Well done,' and gave me the small silver object (which turned out to be a saddle-shaped paperweight) with the bright surface smile of someone who isn't really looking at you and is going to forget you again within five minutes. Her voice, from what I heard of it, held the same modified American accent as her father's, but in her it lacked the patronizing quality and was, to me at least, attractive. A pretty girl, but not mine. Life was full of them.

While Victor and Harold and I compared trophies the average-looking man in spectacles reappeared, walking quietly up to Dana den Relgan's shoulder and speaking softly into her ear. She turned away from the presentation table and began slowly to move off with him, nodding and smiling a little, and listening to what he was saying.

This apparently harmless proceeding had the most extraordinary effect upon den Relgan, who stopped looking fatuously pleased with himself in one five-hundredth of a second and flung himself into action. He almost ran after his daughter, gripped the inoffensive-looking man by the shoulder and threw him away from her with such force that he staggered and went down on one knee.

'I've told you to keep away from her,' den Relgan said, looking as if kicking a man when he was down was something he had no reservations about; and Lord White muttered, 'I say' and 'Oh dear' and looked uncomfortable.

'Who is that man?' I asked of no one in particular, and it was Victor Briggs, surprisingly, who answered.

'Film director. Fellow called Lance Kinship.'

'And why the fuss?'

Victor Briggs knew the answer, but it took a fair

amount of internal calculation before he decided to part with it. 'Cocaine,' he said finally. 'White powder, for sniffing straight up the nose. Very fashionable. All these stupid little girls . . . their noses will collapse when the bone dissolves, and then where will they be?'

Both Harold and I looked at him with astonishment, as it was the longest speech I'd ever heard him make, and certainly the only one containing any private opinion.

'Lance Kinship supplies it,' he said. 'He gets asked to the parties for what he takes along.'

Lance Kinship was up on his feet and brushing dirt off his trousers; setting his glasses firmly on his nose and looking murderous.

'If I want to talk to Dana, I'll talk to her,' he said.

'Not while I'm there, you won't.'

Den Relgan's Jockey Club manners were in tatters and the bedrock under the camouflage was plainly on view. A bully, I thought; a bad enemy, even if his cause was just.

Lance Kinship seemed unintimidated. 'Little girls don't always have their daddies with them,' he said nastily; and den Relgan hit him; a hard sharp efficient crunch on the nose.

Noses bleed easily, and there was a good deal of blood. Lance Kinship tried to wipe it away with his hands and succeeded only in smearing it all over his face. It poured down on his mouth and chin, and fell in big splashing drops on his olive suede jacket.

Lord White, hating the whole thing, stretched out an arm towards Kinship and held out a huge white handkerchief as if in tongs. Kinship grabbed it without thanks and soaked it scarlet as he tried to staunch the flow.

'First aid room, don't you think?' Lord White said, looking round. 'Er . . . Nore,' he said, his gaze alighting. 'You know where the first aid room is, don't you? Take this gentleman there, would you? Awfully good of you . . .' He waved me towards the errand, but when I put a hand out towards the olive green sleeve, to guide Kinship in the direction of cold compresses and succour, he jerked away from me.

'Bleed, then,' I said.

Unfriendly eyes behind the black frames glared out at me, but he was too busy mopping to speak.

'I'll show you,' I said. 'Follow if you want.'

I set off past the parade ring towards the green-painted hut where the motherly ladies would be waiting to patch up the damaged, and not only did Kinship follow, but den Relgan also. I heard his voice as clearly as Kinship did, and there was no doubt about the message.

'If you come near Dana again, I'll break your neck.'

Kinship again didn't answer.

Den Relgan said, 'Did you hear, you vicious little ponce?'

We had gone far enough for there to be plenty of people blocking us from the view of the group outside the weighing room. I heard a scuffle behind me and looked over my shoulder in time to see Kinship aim a hard karate kick at den Relgan's crutch and land deftly on target. Kinship turned back to me and gave me another unfriendly stare over the reddening handkerchief, which he had held uninterruptedly to his nose.

Den Relgan was making choking noises and clutching himself. The whole fracas was hardly what one expected as the outcome of a decorous racecourse presentation on a Thursday afternoon.

'In there,' I said to Kinship, jerking my head, and he gave me a final reptilian glance as the first aid room opened its doors. Den Relgan said 'Aaah . . .' and walked round in a small circle half doubled over, one hand pressed hard under the lower front of his camel-hair coat.

A pity George Millace had gone to his fathers, I thought. He of all people would have relished the ding-dong, and he, unlike everyone else, would have been here with his lens sharply focussed, pointing the right way and taking inexorable notes at three point five frames a second. Den Relgan could thank George's couple of Scotches and a tree in the wrong place that he wouldn't find his tangle with Kinship illustrating in the daily papers the edifying news of his elevation to the Jockey Club.

Harold and Victor Briggs were still where I'd left them, but Lord White and Dana den Relgan had gone.

'His lordship took her off to calm her nerves,' Harold

said dryly. 'The old goat's practically dancing round her, silly fool.'

'She's pretty,' I said.

'Wars have been fought for pretty girls,' said Victor Briggs.

I looked at him with renewed astonishment and received in return the usual stonewall closed-in expression. Victor might have unexpected hidden depths, but that was just what they still were, hidden.

When I went out of the weighing room later to set off for home I was apologetically intercepted by the tall loitering figure of Jeremy Folk.

'I don't believe it,' I said.

'I did ... er ... warn you.'

'So you did.'

'Could I ... um ... have a word with you?'

'What do you want?'

'Ah yes ... well ...'

'The answer's no,' I said.

'But you don't know what I'm going to ask.'

'I can see that it's something I don't want to do.'

'Um,' he said. 'Your grandmother asks you to visit her.'

'Absolutely not,' I said.

There was a pause. People around us were going home, calling goodnights. It was four o'clock. Goodnights started early in the racing world.

'I went to see her,' Jeremy said. 'I told her you wouldn't look for your sister for money. I told her she would have to give you something else.'

I was puzzled. 'Give me what?'

Jeremy looked vaguely around from his great height and said, 'You could find her, couldn't you, if you really tried?'

'I don't think so.'

'But you might.'

I didn't answer, and his attention came gently back to my face.

'Your grandmother agreed,' he said, 'that she had a flaming row with Caroline ... your mother ... and chucked her out when she was pregnant.'

'My mother,' I said, 'was seventeen.'

'Um. That's right.' He smiled. 'Funny, isn't it, to think of one's mother being so *young*.'

Poor defenceless little butterfly ... 'Yes,' I said.

'Your grandmother says ... has agreed ... that if you will look for Amanda she will tell you why she threw Caroline out. And also she will tell you who your father is.'

'My God!'

I took two compulsive steps away from him, and stopped, and turned, and stared at him.

'Is that what you said to her?' I demanded. 'Tell him who his father is, and he'll do what you want?'

'You don't know who your father is,' he said reasonably. 'But you'd want to know, wouldn't you?'

'No,' I said.

'I don't believe you.'

We practically glared at each other.

'You have to want to know,' he said. 'It's human nature.'

I swallowed. 'Did she tell you who he is?'

He shook his head. 'No. She didn't. She's apparently never told anyone. No one at all. If you don't go and find out, you'll never know.'

'You're a real bastard, Jeremy,' I said.

He wriggled his body with an embarrassment he didn't actually feel. The light in his eyes, which would have done a check-mating chess-player justice, was a far more accurate indicator of how he operated.

I said bitterly, 'I thought solicitors were supposed to sit behind desks and pontificate, not go tearing about manipulating old ladies.'

'This particular old lady is a . . . a challenge.'

I had an idea he had changed his sentence in mid-stride, but I said only, 'Why doesn't she leave her money to her son?'

'I don't know. She won't give reasons. She told my grandfather simply that she wanted to cancel her old will, which left everything to her son, and make a new one in favour of Amanda. The son will contest it, of course. We've told her that, but it makes no difference. She's . . . er . . . stubborn.'

'Have you met her son?'

'No,' he said. 'Have you?'

I shook my head. Jeremy took another long vague look around the racecourse and said, 'Why don't we get cracking on this together? We'd turn Amanda up in no time, wouldn't we? Then you could go back into your shell and forget the whole thing, if you want.'

'You couldn't forget . . . who your father was.'

His gaze sharpened instantly. 'Are you on, then?'

He would persevere, I thought, with or without my help. He would bother me whenever he wanted, catch me at the races any day he cared to read the programmes in the newspapers, and never let up, because he wanted, as he'd told me at the beginning, to prove to his grandfather and uncle that when he set his mind to sorting something out, it got sorted.

As for me . . . the mists round my birth were there for the parting. The cataclysm which had echoed like a storm receding over the horizon through my earliest memories could at last be explained and understood. I could know what the shouting had been about behind the white painted door, while I waited in the hall in my new clothes.

I might in the event detest the man who'd fathered me. I might be horrified. I might wish I hadn't been told anything about him. But Jeremy was right. Given the chance . . . one had to know.

'Well?' he said.

'All right.'

'Find her together?'

'Yes.'

He was visibly pleased. 'That's great.'

I wasn't so sure; but it was settled.

'Can you go this evening?' he said. 'I'll telephone and tell her you're coming.' He plunged lankily towards the public telephone box and disappeared inside with his eyes switched anxiously my way, watching all through his call to make sure I didn't go back on my decision and scram.

The call, however, gave him no joy.

'Blast,' he said, rejoining me. 'I spoke to a nurse. Mrs Nore had a bad day and they've given her an injection. She's asleep. No visitors. Ring tomorrow.'

I felt a distinct sense of relief, which he noticed.

'It's all very well for you,' I said. 'But how would you like to be on the verge of finding out that you owe your existence to a quickie in the bushes with the milkman?'

'Is that what you think?'

'Something like that. It has to be, doesn't it?'

'All the same . . .' he said doubtfully.

'All the same,' I agreed resignedly, 'one wants to know.'

I set off towards the car park thinking that Jeremy's errand was concluded, but it appeared not. He came in my wake, but slowly, so that I looked back and waited.

'About Mrs Nore's son,' he said. 'Her son James.'

'What about him?'

'I just thought you might visit him. Find out why he's been disinherited.'

'You just thought . . .'

'As we're working together,' he said hastily.

'You could go yourself,' I suggested.

'Er, no,' he said. 'As Mrs Nore's solicitor, I'd be asking questions I shouldn't.'

'And I can just see this James bird answering mine.'

He pulled a card out of his charcoal pocket. 'I brought his address,' he said, holding it out. 'And you've promised to help.'

'A pact is a pact,' I said, and took the card. 'But you're still a bastard.'

CHAPTER EIGHT

James Nore lived in London, and since I was more than
halfway there I drove straight from the races to the
house on Camden Hill. I hoped all the way there that
he would be out, but when I'd found the street and the
number and pressed the right bell, the door was opened
by a man of about forty who agreed that James Nore
was his name.

He was astounded, as well he might be, to find an
unknown nephew standing unannounced on his mat,
but with only a slight hesitation he invited me in,
leading the way into a sitting room crammed with
Victorian bric-à-brac and vibrant with colour.

'I thought Caroline had aborted you,' he said badly.
'Mother said the child had been got rid of.'

He was nothing like my memories of his sister. He
was plump, soft-muscled and small-mouthed, and had
a mournful droop to his eyes. None of her giggly lightness or grace of movement or hectic speed could ever
have lived in his flaccid body. I felt ill at ease with him
on sight, disliking my errand more by the minute.

766

He listened with his small lips pouted while I explained about looking for Amanda, and he showed more and more annoyance.

'The old bag's been saying for months that she's going to cut me off,' he said furiously. 'Ever since she came here.' He glanced round the room, but nothing there seemed to me likely to alienate a mother. 'Everything was all right as long as I went to Northamptonshire now and then. Then she came *here*. Uninvited. The old bag.'

'She's ill now,' I said.

'Of course she is.' He flung out his arms in an exaggerated gesture. 'I suggest visiting. She says no. Won't see me. Pig-headed old crone.'

A brass clock on the mantelshelf sweetly chimed the half hour, and I took note that everything there was of fine quality and carefully dusted. James Nore's bric-a-brac wasn't just junk but antiques.

'I'd be a fool to help you find this wretched second by-blow of Caroline's, wouldn't I?' he said. 'If no one can find her the whole estate reverts to me anyway, will or no will. But I'd have to wait years for it. Years and years. Mother's just being spiteful.'

'Why?' I said mildly.

'She loved Noël Coward,' he said resentfully, meaning, by the sound of it, if she loved Noël Coward she should have loved *him*.

'The abstract,' I said, enlightened, 'isn't always the same as the particular.'

767

'I didn't want her to come here. It would have saved all this fuss if she hadn't.' He shrugged. 'Are you going now? There's no point in your staying.'

He began to walk towards the door, but before he reached it it was opened by a man wearing a plastic cooking apron and limply carrying a wooden spoon. He was much younger than James, naturally camp, and unmistakable.

'Oh, hello, dear,' he said, seeing me. 'Are you staying for supper?'

'He's just going,' James said sharply. 'He's not ... er ...'

They both stood back to leave me room to pass, and as I went out into the hall I said to the man in the apron, 'Did you meet Mrs Nore when she came here?'

'Sure did, dear,' he said ruefully, and then caught sight of James shaking his head vigorously at him and meaning shut up. I smiled halfheartedly at a point in the air near their heads, and went to the front door.

'I wish you bad luck,' James said. 'That beastly Caroline, spawning all over the place. I never did like her.'

'Do you remember her?'

'Always laughing at me and tripping me up. I was glad when she went.'

I nodded, and opened the door.

'Wait,' he said suddenly.

He came towards me along the hall, and I could see he had had an idea that pleased him.

'Mother would never leave *you* anything, of course,' he began.

'Why not?' I said.

He frowned. 'There was a terrible drama, wasn't there, when Caroline got pregnant? Frightful scenes. Lots of screaming. I remember it . . . but no one would ever explain. All I do know is that everything changed because of you. Caroline went and Mother turned into a bitter old bag and I had beastly miserable years in that big house with her, before I left. She hated you . . . the thought of you. Do you know what she called you? "Caroline's disgusting foetus", that's what. Caroline's disgusting foetus.'

He peered at me expectantly, but in truth I felt nothing. The old woman's hatred hadn't troubled me for years.

'I'll give you some of the money, though,' he said, 'if you can prove that Amanda is dead.'

On Saturday morning Jeremy Folk telephoned.

'Will you be at home tomorrow?' he said.

'Yes, but . . .'

'Good. I'll pop over.' He put down his receiver without giving me a chance to say I didn't want him. It was an advance, I supposed, that he'd announced his visit and not simply turned up.

Also on Saturday I ran into Bart Underfield in the

post office and in place of our usual unenthusiastic 'good mornings' I asked him a question.

'Where is Elgin Yaxley these days, Bart?'

'Hong Kong,' he said. 'Why?'

'For a holiday?' I said.

'Of course not. He lives there.'

'But he's over here now, isn't he?'

'No, he isn't. He'd have told me.'

'But he must be,' I said insistently.

Bart said irritably, 'Why must he be? He isn't. He's working for a bloodstock agency and they don't give him much time off. And what's it to do with you?'

'I just thought . . . I saw him.'

'You couldn't have. When?'

'Oh . . . last week. A week ago yesterday.'

'Well, you're wrong,' Bart said triumphantly. 'That was the day of George Millace's funeral, and Elgin sent me a cable . . .' He hesitated and his eyes flickered, but he went on, ' . . . and the cable came from Hong Kong.'

'A cable of regrets, was it?'

'George Millace,' Bart said with venom, 'was a shit.'

'You didn't go to the funeral yourself, then?'

'Are you crazy? I'd have spat on his coffin.'

'Catch you bending with his camera, did he, Bart?'

He narrowed his eyes and didn't answer.

'Oh well,' I said, shrugging, 'I dare say a good many people will be relieved now he's gone.'

'More like down on their knees giving thanks.'

'Do you ever hear anything nowadays about that

chap who shot Elgin's horses? What's his name ...
Terence O'Tree?'

'He's still in jail,' Bart said.

'But,' I said, counting with my fingers, 'March, April,
May ... he should be out by now.'

'He lost his remission,' Bart said. 'He hit a warder.'

'How do you know?' I asked curiously.

'I ... er ... heard.' He had suddenly had too much
of this conversation, and began to move off, backing
away.

'And did you hear also that George Millace's house
had burned down?' I said.

He nodded. 'Of course. Heard it at the races.'

'And that it was arson?'

He stopped in mid-stride. 'Arson?' he said, looking
surprised. 'Why would anyone want ...? Oh!' He
abruptly at that point understood why; and I thought
that he couldn't possibly have achieved that revela-
tionary expression by art.

He hadn't known.

Elgin Yaxley was in Hong Kong and Terence O'Tree
was in jail, and neither they nor Bart Underfield had
burgled, or bashed, or burned.

The easy explanations were all wrong.

I had jumped, I thought penitently, to conclusions.

It was only because I'd disliked George Millace that
I'd been so ready to believe ill of him. He had taken

that incriminating photograph, but there was really nothing to prove that he'd used it, except that Elgin Yaxley had taken a paid job in Hong Kong instead of ploughing his insurance money back into racehorses. Any man had a right to do that. It didn't make him a villain.

Yet he had been a villain. He had sworn he'd never met Terence O'Tree; and he had. And it had to have been before the trial in February at least, since O'Tree had been in jail ever since. Not during the winter months just before the trial either, because it had been sitting-in-the-street weather; and there had been ... I had unconsciously noticed and now remembered ... there had been a newspaper lying on the table in front of the Frenchman, on which one might possibly see a date.

I walked slowly and thoughtfully home, and projected my big new print hugely onto the sitting room wall through an epidiascope.

The Frenchman's newspaper lay too flat on the table. Neither the date nor any useful headlines could be seen.

Regretfully I studied the rest of the picture for anything at all which might date it; and in the depths, beside Madame at her cash desk inside the café, there was a calendar hanging on a hook. The letters and numbers on it could be discerned by the general shape even if not with pin-sharp clarity, and they announced that it was Avril of the previous year.

Elgin Yaxley's horses had been sent out to grass late that April, and they had been shot on the fourth of May.

I switched off the projector and drove to Windsor races puzzling over the inconsistencies and feeling that I had gone round a corner in a maze confidently expecting to have reached the centre, only to find myself in a dead end surrounded by ten-foot hedges.

It was a moderate day's racing at Windsor, all the star names having gone to the more important meeting at Cheltenham, and because of the weak opposition one of Harold's slowest old 'chasers finally had his day. Half of the rest of the equally old runners obligingly fell, and my geriatric pal with his head down in exhaustion loped in first after three and a half miles of slog.

He stood with his chest heaving in the unsaddling enclosure as I, scarcely less tired, lugged at the girth buckles and pulled off my saddle, but the surprised delight of his faithful elderly lady owner made it all well worth the effort.

'I knew he'd do it one day,' she said enthusiastically. 'I knew he would. Isn't he a great old boy?'

'Great,' I agreed.

'It's his last season, you know. I'll have to retire him.' She patted his neck and spoke to his head. 'We're all getting on a bit, old boy, aren't we? Can't go on for ever, more's the pity. Everything ends, doesn't it, old boy? But today it's been great.'

I went in and sat on the scales and her words came

with me: everything ends, but today it's been great. Ten years had been great, but everything ends.

Most of my mind still rebelled against the thought of ending, particularly an ending dictated by Victor Briggs; but somewhere the frail seedling of acceptance was stretching its first leaf in the dark. Life changes, everything ends. I myself was changing. I didn't want it, but it was happening. My long contented float was slowly drifting to shore.

Outside the weighing room one wouldn't have guessed it. I had uncharacteristically won four races that week. I was the jockey in form. I had brought a no-hoper home. I was offered five rides for the following week by trainers other than Harold. The success-breeds-success syndrome was coming up trumps. Everything on a high note, with smiles all around. Seven days away from Daylight, and seven leagues in mood.

I enjoyed the congratulations and thrust away the doubt, and if anyone had asked me in that moment about retiring I'd have said 'Oh yes . . . in five years' time.'

They didn't ask me. They didn't expect me to retire. Retire was a word in my mind, not in theirs.

Jeremy Folk arrived the following morning, as he'd said he would, angling his stork-like figure apologetically through my front door and following me along to the kitchen.

'Champagne?' I said, picking a bottle out of the refrigerator.

'It's ... er ... only ten o'clock,' he said.

'Four winners,' I said, 'need celebrating. Would you rather have coffee?'

'Er ... actually ... no.'

He took his first sip all the same as if the wickedness of it would overwhelm him, and I thought that for all his wily ways he was a conformist at heart.

He had made an effort to be casual in his clothes: wool checked shirt, woolly tie, neat pale blue sweater. Whatever he thought of my unbuttoned collar, unbuttoned cuffs and unshaven jaw, he didn't say. He let his gaze do its usual inventorial travel-around from a great height and as usual return to my face when he'd shaped his question.

'Did you see ... ah ... James Nore?'

'Yes, I did.'

I gestured to him to sit on the leather-covered corner bench round the kitchen table, and joined him, with the bottle in reach.

'He's cohabiting happily on Camden Hill.'

'Oh,' Jeremy said. 'Ah.'

I smiled. 'Mrs Nore visited his house unexpectedly one day. She hadn't been there before. She met James's friend, and she realized, I suppose for the first time, that her son was 100 per cent homosexual.'

'Oh,' Jeremy said, understanding much.

I nodded. 'No descendants.'

'So she thought of Amanda.' He sighed and drank some pale gold fizz. 'Are you sure he's homosexual. I mean . . . did he say so?'

'As good as. But anyway, I'm used to homosexuals. I lived with two of them for a while. You get to know, somehow.'

He looked slightly shocked and covered it with a relapse into the silly ass waffle.

'Did you? I mean . . . are you . . .? Er . . . I mean . . . living alone . . .? I shouldn't ask. Sorry.'

'If I take someone to bed, she's female,' I said mildly. 'I just don't like permanence.'

He buried his nose and his embarrassment in his glass, and I thought of Duncan and Charlie who had hugged and kissed and loved each other all around me for three years. Charlie had been older than Duncan; a mature man in his forties, solid and industrious and kind. Charlie, to me, had been father, uncle, guardian, all in one. Duncan had been chatty and quarrelsome and very good company, and neither of them had tried to teach me their way.

Duncan had slowly grown less chatty, more quarrelsome and less good company, and one day he fell in love with someone else and walked out. Charlie's grief had been white-faced and desperately deep. He had put his arm round my shoulders and hugged me, and wept; and I'd wept for Charlie's unhappiness.

My mother had arrived within a week, blowing in like a whirlwind. Huge eyes, hollow cheeks, fluffy silk scarves.

'But you must see, Charlie darling,' she said, 'that I can't leave Philip with you now that Duncan's gone. Look at him, darling, he's hardly ugly, the way he's grown up. Darling Charlie, you must see that he can't stay here. Not any more.' She'd looked across at me, bright and more brittle than I remembered, and less beautiful. 'Go and pack, Philip darling. We're going down to the country.'

Charlie had come into the little box-like room he and Duncan had built for me in one corner of the studio, and I'd told him I didn't want to leave him.

'Your mother's right, boy,' he said. 'It's time you were off. We must do what she says.'

He'd helped me pack and given me one of his cameras as a goodbye present, and from the old life I'd been flung straight into the new in the space of a day. That evening I learned how to muck out a horse box, and the next morning I started to ride.

After a week I'd written to Charlie to say I was missing him, and he replied encouragingly that I'd soon get over it: and get over it I did, while Charlie himself pined miserably for Duncan and swallowed two hundred sleeping pills. Charlie made a will a week before the pills leaving all his possessions to me, including all his other cameras and darkroom equipment. He also left a letter saying he was sorry and wishing me luck.

'Look after your mother,' he wrote. 'I think she's sick. Keep on taking photographs, you already have the eye. You'll be all right, boy. So long now. Charlie.'

I drank some champagne and said to Jeremy, 'Did you get the list of the Pine Woods Lodge tenancies from the estate agents?'

'Oh gosh, yes,' he said, relieved to be back on firm ground. 'I've got it here somewhere.' He patted several pockets but stuck two fingers unerringly and only into the one where he'd stored the slip of paper he wanted: and I wondered how much energy he wasted each day in camouflage movements.

'Here we are . . .' He spread the sheet of paper out, and pointed. 'If your mother was there thirteen years ago, the people she was with would have been the boy scouts, the television company, or the musicians. But the television people didn't live there, the agents say. They just worked there during the day. The musicians did live there, though. They were . . . er . . . experimental musicians, whatever that means.'

'More soul than success.'

He gave me a quick bright glance. 'A man in the estate agents' says he remembers they ruined the electric wiring and were supposed to be high all the time on drugs. Does any of that sound . . . er . . . like your mother?'

I pondered.

'Boy scouts don't sound like her a bit,' I said. 'We can leave them out. Drugs sounds like her, but musicians don't. Especially unsuccessful musicians. She never left me with anyone unsuccessful . . . or anyone musical, come to that.' I thought some more. 'I suppose if she was really drug-dependent by that time, she mightn't have cared. But she liked comfort.' I paused again. 'I think I'd try the television company first. They could at least tell us what programme they were making then, and who worked on it. They're bound to have kept the credits somewhere.'

Jeremy's face showed a jumble of emotions varying, I thought, from incredulity to bewilderment.

'Er . . .' he said, 'I mean . . .'

'Look,' I interrupted. 'Just ask the questions. If I don't like them I won't answer.'

'You're so frantically direct,' he complained. 'All right, then. What do you mean about your mother leaving you with people, and what do you mean about your mother and drugs?'

I outlined the dumping procedure and what I owed to the Deborahs, Samanthas and Chloes. Jeremy's shattered expression alone would have told me that this was not every child's experience of life.

'Drugs,' I said, 'are more difficult. I didn't understand about the drugs until I grew up, and I only saw her once after I was twelve . . . the day she took me away from the homosexuals and put me in the racing stable. But certainly she was taking drugs for as long as I remember. She kept me with her for a week, sometimes, and there would be a smell, an acrid distinctive smell. I smelled it again years later . . . I must have been past twenty . . . and it was marihuana. Cannabis. I smoked it when I was little. One of my mother's friends gave it to me when she was out, and she was furious. She did try, you know, in her way, to see I grew up properly. Another time a man she was with gave me some acid. She was absolutely livid.'

'Acid,' Jeremy said. 'Do you mean LSD?'

'Yeah. I could see all the blood running through my arteries and veins, just as if the skin was transparent. I could see the bones, like X-rays. It's extraordinary. You realize the limitations of our everyday senses. I could hear sounds as if they were three-dimensional. A clock ticking. Amazing. My mother came into the room and found me wanting to fly out of the window. I could see the blood going round in her, too.' I remembered it all vividly, though I'd been about five. 'I didn't know why she was so angry. The man was laughing, and she slapped him.' I paused. 'She did keep me away from drugs. She died from heroin, I think, but she kept me free of even the sight of it.'

'Why do you think she died of heroin?'

I poured refills of champagne.

'Something the racing people said. Margaret and Bill. Soon after I got there I went into the sitting room one day when they were arguing. I didn't realise at first that it was about me, but they stopped abruptly when they saw me, so then I did. Bill had been saying "his place is with his mother", and Margaret interrupted, "She's a heroin . . ." and then she saw me and stopped. It's ironic, but I was so pleased they should think my mother a heroine. I felt warmly towards them.' I smiled lop-sidedly. 'It wasn't for years that I realized what Margaret had really been going to say was "she's a heroin addict". I asked her later and she told me that she and Bill had known that my mother was taking heroin, but they didn't know, any more than I did, where to find her. They guessed, as I did, that she'd died, and of course, long before I did, they guessed why. They didn't tell me, to save me pain. Kind people. Very kind.'

Jeremy shook his head. 'I'm so sorry,' he said.

'Don't be. It was all long ago. I never grieved for my mother. I think perhaps now that I should have done, but I didn't.'

I had grieved for Charlie, though. For a short intense time when I was fifteen, and vaguely, sporadically, ever since. I used Charlie's legacy almost every day, literally in the case of photographic equipment and figuratively in the knowledge he'd given me. Any photograph I took was thanks to Charlie.

'I'll try the television people,' Jeremy said.

'OK.'

'And you'll see your grandmother?'

I said without enthusiasm, 'I suppose so.'

Jeremy half smiled. 'Where else can we look? For

Amanda, I mean. If your mother dumped you all over the place like that, she must have done the same for Amanda. Haven't you thought of that?'

'Yes, I have.'

'Well, then?'

I was silent. All those people. All so long in the past. Chloe, Deborah, Samantha . . . all shadows without faces. I wouldn't know any of them if they walked into the room.

'What are you thinking?' Jeremy demanded.

'No one I was left with had a pony. I would have remembered a pony. I was never left where Amanda was in the photograph.'

'Oh, I see.'

'And I don't think,' I said, 'that the same friends would be pressed into looking after a second child. I very rarely went back to the same place myself. My mother at least spread the load.'

Jeremy sighed. 'It's all so irregular.'

I said slowly, unwillingly, 'I might find one place I stayed. Perhaps I could try. But even then . . . there might be different people in the house after all this time, and anyway they're unlikely to know anything about Amanda . . .'

Jeremy pounced on it. 'It's a chance.'

'Very distant.'

'Well worth trying.'

I drank some champagne and looked thoughtfully across the kitchen to where George Millace's box of rubbish lay on the dresser: and a hovering intention suddenly crystallized. Well worth trying. Why not?

'I've lost you,' Jeremy said.

'Yes.' I looked at him. 'You're welcome to stay, but I want to spend the day on a different sort of puzzle. Nothing to do with Amanda. A sort of treasure hunt . . . but there may be no treasure. I just want to find out.'

'I don't . . .' he said vaguely: and I got up and fetched the box and put it on the table.

'Tell me what you think of that lot,' I said.

He opened the box and poked through the contents, lifting things out and putting them back. From expectancy his face changed to disappointment, and he said, 'They're just . . . nothing.'

'Mm.' I stretched over and picked out the piece of clear-looking film which was about two and a half inches across by seven inches long. 'Look at that against the light.'

He took the piece of film and held it up. 'It's got smudges on it,' he said. 'Very faint. You can hardly see them.'

'They're pictures,' I said. 'Three pictures on one-twenty roll film.'

'Well . . . you can't see them.'

'No,' I agreed. 'But if I'm careful . . . and lucky . . . we might.'

He was puzzled. 'How?'

'With intensifying chemicals.'

'But what's the point? Why bother?'

I sucked my teeth. 'I found something of great interest in that box. All those things were kept by a great photographer who was also an odd sort of man. I just think that maybe some more of those bits aren't the rubbish they look.'

'But ... which ones?'

'That's the question. Which ones ... if any.'

Jeremy took a gulp of champagne. 'Let's stick to Amanda.'

'You stick to Amanda. I'm better at photographs.'

He watched with interest, however, while I rummaged in one of the cupboards in the darkroom.

'This all looks frightfully workmanlike,' he said, doing the eye-travel round the enlargers and print processor. 'I'd no idea you did this sort of thing.'

I explained briefly about Charlie and finally found what I was looking for, a tucked away bottle that I'd acquired on an American holiday three years earlier. It said Negative Intensifier on the label, followed by instructions. Most helpful. Many manufacturers printed their instructions on separate flimsy sheets of paper, which got wet or lost. I carried the bottle across to the sink, where there was a water filter fixed under the tap.

'What's that?' Jeremy asked, pointing at its round bulbous shape.

'You have to use ultra-clean soft water for photographic processing. And no iron pipes, otherwise you get a lot of little black dots on the prints.'

'It's all mad,' he said.

'It's precise.'

In a plastic measure I mixed water and intensifier into the strength of solution that the instructions said, and poured it into the developing tray.

'I've never done this before,' I said to Jeremy. 'It may not work. Do you want to watch, or would you rather stay with the bubbly in the kitchen?'

'I'm . . . ah . . . absolutely riveted, as a matter of fact. What exactly are you going to do?'

'I'm going to contact-print this clear strip of film with the ultra-faint smudges onto some ordinary black-and-white paper and see what it looks like. And then I'm going to put the negative into this intensifying liquid, and after that I'm going to make another black-and-white print to see if there's any difference. And after that . . . well, we'll have to see.'

He watched while I worked in dim red light, peering into the developing tray with his nose right down to the liquid.

'Can't see anything happening,' he said.

'It's a bit trial-and-error,' I agreed. I tried printing the clear film four times at different exposures, but all we got on the prints was a fairly uniform black, or a uniform grey, or a uniform white.

'There's nothing there,' Jeremy said. 'It's useless.'

'Wait until we try the intensifier.'

With more hope than expectation I slid the clear film into the intensifying liquid and sloshed it about in there for a good deal longer than the required minimum time. Then I washed it and looked at it against the light: and the ultra-faint smudges were still ultra-faint.

'No good?' Jeremy asked, disappointed.

'I don't know. I don't really know what should happen. And maybe that intensifier is too old. Some photographic chemicals lose their power with age. Shelf life, and so on.'

I printed the negative again at the same variety of exposures as before, and as before we got a uniform black and a uniform dark grey, but this time on the light grey print there were patchy marks, and on the nearly white print, swirly shapes.

'Huh,' Jeremy said. 'Well, that's that.'

We retreated to the kitchen for thought and revivers.

'Too bad,' he said. 'Never mind, it was impossible to start with.'

I sipped a few bubbles and popped them round my teeth.

'I think,' I said reflectively, 'that we might get further if I print that negative not onto paper, but onto another film.'

'Print it onto a film? Do you mean the stuff you load into cameras? I didn't know it was possible.'

'Oh yes. You can print onto anything which has a photographic emulsion. And you can coat practically anything with photographic emulsion. I mean, it doesn't have to be paper, though that's the way everyone thinks of it, because of seeing snapshots in family albums, and all that. But you could coat canvas with emulsion, and print on that. Or glass. Or wood. On the back of your hand, I dare say, if you'd like to stand around in darkness for a while.'

'Good gracious.'

'Black-and-white, of course,' I said. 'Not colour.'

I popped a few more bubbles.

'Let's have another go, then,' I said.

'You really do love this sort of thing, don't you?' Jeremy said.

'Love it? Do you mean photography . . . or puzzles?'

'Both.'

'Well . . . I suppose so.'

I got up and went back to the darkroom, and he again followed to watch. In the dim red light I took a new roll of high-contrast Kodak 2556 film, pulling it off its spool into a long strip and cutting it into five pieces. Onto each separate piece I printed the almost-clear negative, exposing it under the white light of the enlarger for various exposure times: one second the shortest, up to ten seconds the longest. Each piece of high-contrast film after exposure went into the tray of developer, with Jeremy sloshing the liquid about and bending down to see the results.

The results, after taking each piece of film out of the developer at what looked like the best moment, and transferring it to the fixing tray, and finally washing it, were five new positives. From those positives I repeated the whole process, ending with negatives. Seen in bright light, all of the new negatives were much denser than the one I'd started with. On two of them there was a decipherable image . . . and the smudges had come alive.

'What are you smiling at?' Jeremy demanded.

'Take a look,' I said.

He held the negative strip I gave him up to the light and said, 'I can see that you've got much clearer smudges. But they're still smudges, all the same.'

'No they're not. They're three pictures of a girl and a man.'

'How can you tell?'

'You get used to reading negatives, after a while.'

'And you look smug,' Jeremy complained.

'To be honest,' I said, 'I'm dead pleased with myself. Let's finish the champagne and then do the next bit.'

'What next bit?' he said, as we again drank in the kitchen.

'Positive prints from the new negatives. Black-and-white pictures. All revealed.'

'What's so funny?'

'The girl's nude, more or less.'

He nearly spilt his drink. 'Are you sure?'

'You can see her breasts.' I laughed at him. 'They're the clearest parts of the negatives, actually.'

'What . . . I mean . . . about her face?'

'We'll see better soon. Are you hungry?'

'Good heavens. It's one o'clock.'

We ate ham and tomatoes and brown toast, and

finished the bubbles: and then returned to the darkroom.

Printing onto paper from such faint negatives was still a critical business as again one had first to judge the exposures right and then stop the developing print at exactly the best instant and switch it to the fixer, or all that came out was a flat light or a dark grey sheet with no depth and no highlights. It took me several tries with each of the two best new strips to get truly visible results, but I finished with three pictures which were moderately clear, and more than clear enough to reveal what George had photographed. I looked at them with the bright lights on, and with a magnifying glass; and there was no chance of a mistake.

'What's the matter?' Jeremy said. 'They're wonderful. Unbelievable. Why aren't you blowing your trumpets and patting yourself on the back?'

I put the finished articles into the print drier, and silently cleared up the developing trays.

'What is it?' Jeremy asked. 'What's the matter?'

'They're bloody dynamite,' I said.

CHAPTER NINE

I took Jeremy and the new pictures upstairs and switched on the epidiascope, which hummed slightly in its idiosyncratic way as it warmed up.

'What's that?' Jeremy said, looking at the machine.

'You must have seen one,' I said, surprised. 'It's pretty old, I know. I inherited it from Charlie. But all the same, they must still be around. You put things in here on this baseboard and their image is projected large and bright onto a screen – or in my case, a wall. You can project anything. Pages of books, illustrations, photographs, letters, dead leaves. All done by mirrors.'

The photograph of Elgin Yaxley and Terence O'Tree still lay in position, and at the flick of a switch came into sharp focus as before, calendar and dates and all.

I drew the curtains against the fading afternoon light and let the picture shine bright in the dark room. After a minute I unclamped it and took it out, and put in instead the best strip I'd made downstairs, adjusting the lens, and enlarging each third separately, showing each of the three pictures on its own.

Even in their unavoidably imperfect state, even in shades of white to dark grey, they pulsated off the wall. The first one showed the top half of a girl as far down as the waist, and also the head and shoulders of a man. They were facing each other, the girl's head higher than the man's. Neither of them wore clothes. The man had his hands under the girl's breasts, lifting them up, with his mouth against the nipple furthest away from the camera.

'Good heavens,' Jeremy said faintly.

'Mm,' I said. 'Do you want to see the others?'

'They didn't look so bad in snapshot size.'

I projected the second picture, which was of much the same pose, except that the camera had been at a different angle, showing less of the girl's front and nearly all of the man's face.

'It's just pornography,' Jeremy said.

'No, it isn't.'

I unclamped the second picture and showed the third, which was different entirely. Events had moved on. The girl, whose own face this time was clearly visible, seemed to be lying on her back. The picture now stretched down to her knees, which were apart. Over her lay the man, his head turned to one side, showing his profile. His hand cupped the one visible breast, and there wasn't much doubt about the activity they were engaged in.

There was nothing to indicate where the pictures had been taken. No distinguishable background. The faint smudges on the transparent film had turned into people, but behind them there was nothing but grey.

I switched off the epidiascope and put on the room lights.

'Why do you say it isn't pornography?' Jeremy said. 'What else is it?'

'I've met them,' I said. 'I know who they are.'

He stared.

'As you're a lawyer,' I said. 'You can tell me. What do you do if you find out after a man's death that he may have been a blackmailer while he was alive?'

'Are you serious?'

'Absolutely.'

'Well . . . ah . . . he can't be prosecuted, exactly.'

'So one does nothing?'

He frowned. 'Are you . . . um . . . going to tell me what you're on about?'

'Yes, I think so.'

I told him about George Millace. About the burglaries, the attack on Marie Millace, and the burning of their house. I told him about Elgin Yaxley and Terence O'Tree and the five shot horses: and I told him about the lovers.

'George very carefully kept those oddments in that box,' I said. 'I've deciphered two of them. What if some of the others are riddles? What if they all are?'

'And all . . . the basis for blackmail?'

'Heaven knows.'

'Heaven knows . . . and you want to find out.'

I slowly nodded. 'It's not so much the blackmail angle, but the photographic puzzles. If George made them, I'd like to solve them. Just to see if I can. You were quite right. I do enjoy that sort of thing.'

Jeremy stared at the floor. He shivered as if he were cold. He said abruptly, 'I think you should destroy the whole lot.'

'That's instinct, not reason.'

'You have the same instinct. You said ... dynamite.'

'Well ... someone burgled and burnt George Millace's house. When I found the first picture I thought it must have been Elgin Yaxley who'd done it, but he was in Hong Kong, and it doesn't seem likely ... And now one would think the lovers did it ... but it might not be them either.'

Jeremy stood up and moved restlessly around the room in angular uncoordinated jerks.

'I don't like the feel of it,' he said. 'It could be dangerous.'

'To me?'

'Of course to you.'

'No one knows what I've got,' I said. 'Except, of course, you.'

His movements grew even more disturbed, his elbows bending and flapping almost as if he were imitating a bird. Agitation in his mind, I thought: real agitation, not camouflage.

'I suppose ...' he said. 'Um ... ah ...'

'Ask the question.'

He shot me a glance. 'Oh yes . . . Well . . . Was there any doubt . . . about the way George Millace died?'

'Dear . . . God,' I said. I felt as if he'd punched the air out of my lungs. 'I don't think so.'

'What happened exactly?'

'He was driving home from Doncaster, and he went to sleep and ran into a tree.'

'Is that all? Precisely all?'

'Um . . .' I thought back. 'His son said his father stopped at a friend's house for a drink. Then he drove on towards home. Then he hit a tree.'

Jeremy jerked around a little more and said, 'How did anyone know he had stopped at the friend's house? And how does anyone know he went to sleep?'

'These are true lawyers' questions,' I said. 'I don't know the answer to the first, and as to the second, of course nobody knows; it's just what everyone supposes. Going to sleep in the dark towards the end of a long drive isn't all that uncommon. Deadly. Tragic. But always happening.'

'Did they do an autopsy?' he said.

'I don't know. Do they usually?'

He shrugged. 'Sometimes. They'd have tested his blood for the alcohol level. They might have checked for heart attack or stroke, if he wasn't too badly damaged. If there were no suspicious circumstances, that would be all.'

'His son would have told me – have told everyone

on the racecourse – if there had been any odd questions asked. I'm sure there weren't any.'

'Those burglaries must have made the police think a bit, though,' he said frowning.

I said weakly, 'The first serious burglary occurred actually during the funeral.'

'Cremation?'

I nodded. 'Cremation.' I pondered. 'The police might have wondered . . . in fact they did hint very broadly to Marie Millace, and upset her considerably . . . about George possessing photographs other people might not want found. But they don't *know* he had them.'

'Like we do.'

'As you say.'

'Give it up,' he said abruptly. 'Burn those pictures. Stick to looking for Amanda.'

'You're a lawyer. I'm surprised you want to suppress incriminating evidence.'

'You can damn well stop laughing,' he said. 'You could end up like George Millace. Splat on a tree.'

Jeremy left at six, and I walked along to the military briefing with Harold. He had six runners planned for me during the week, and with those and the five spare rides I'd been offered at Windsor I looked like having an exceptionally busy time.

'Don't come crashing down on one of those hyenas

you've accepted,' Harold said. 'What you take them for when you've got all my horses to ride I don't know.'

'Money,' I said.

'Huh.'

He never liked me taking outside rides, although as I was self-employed he couldn't stop me. He never admitted that some of the biggest races I'd won had been for other stables. In those cases, he would point out, if pressed, I had been riding those stables' second strings, which had confounded the trainer's assessments and won when they weren't expected.

'Next Saturday at Ascot I'm running two of Victor's,' he said. 'Chainmail . . . and Daylight.'

I glanced at him quickly, but he didn't meet my eyes.

'He didn't have a proper race at Sandown, of course,' he said. 'He's still at his peak.'

'He'll have a harder job at Ascot. Much stronger opponents.'

He nodded, and after a pause he said casually, 'Chainmail might be the best bet. Depends what's left in at the four day stage, of course. And there's the overnights . . . We'll see better what the prospects are on Friday.'

There was a silence.

'Prospects for winning?' I said at last. 'Or for losing?'

'Philip . . .'

'I'm not going to,' I said.

'But . . .'

'You tell me, Harold,' I said. 'Tell me early Saturday

morning, if you've any feeling for me at all. I'll get acute stomach ache. Bilious. The trots. Won't be able to go racing.'

'But there's Daylight.'

I compressed my mouth and stifled the tremble of anger.

'We had four winners last week,' I said tightly. 'Isn't that enough for you?'

'But Victor . . .'

I said, 'I'll ride my bloody guts out for Victor as long as we're trying to win. You tell him that. Tell him just that.' I stood up, unable to sit calmly. 'And don't you forget, Harold, that Chainmail's still only four, and pretty wayward, for all that he's fast. He pulls like a train and tries to duck out at the hurdles, and he's not above sinking his teeth into any horse that bumps him. He's the devil of a hard ride, but he's brave and I like him . . . and I'm not going to help you ruin him. And you *will* damn well ruin him if you muck him about. You'll turn him sour. You'll make him a real rogue. Apart from dishonest, it's stupid.'

'Have you finished?'

'I guess so.'

'Then I agree with you about Chainmail. I'll say it all to Victor. But in the end it's Victor's horse.'

I stood without speaking. Anything I said, I thought, could prove too decisive. While I was still riding for the stable, there was hope.

'Do you want a drink?' Harold said; and I said

yes, coke; and the fraught moment passed. We talked normally about the chances and plans for the other three runners, and only when I was leaving did Harold make any reference to the awaiting chasm.

'If necessary,' he said heavily, 'I'll give you time to get sick.'

At Fontwell races the next day I rode one horse for Harold, which fell three from home, and two for other people, resulting in a second place and a third, and faint congratulatory noises but no avalanches of further work. An average sort of day; better than some. The fall had been slow and easy: a bruise but no damage.

No hot gossip in the weighing room.

No unseemly fighting between newly elected Jockey Club members and cocaine-pushing film directors. No elderly Lords drooling over delectable dollies. Not even any worried broken-collarboned jockeys agonizing over battered mothers.

No heavy-blue-overcoated owners putting pressure on their going-straight jockeys.

A quiet day at the office.

Tuesday, with no racing engagements, I rode out both lots with Harold's string and schooled some of the horses over training jumps. It was a raw damp morning, the sort to endure, not enjoy, and even Harold seemed to take no pleasure in the work. The mood of the Downs, I thought, walking my mount back through Lambourn, infected the whole village. On days like this the inhabitants scarcely said good morning.

From twelve o'clock onwards the day was my own.

Eating some muesli I contemplated George Millace's box of riddles, but felt too restless for another long spell in the dark-room.

Thought of my promised visit to my grandmother, and hastily sought a good reason for postponing it.

Decided to placate the accusing image of Jeremy Folk by seeing if I could find the house in my childhood. A nice vague expedition with no expectation of success. A drift-around day; undemanding.

I set off accordingly to London and cruised up and down a whole lot of little streets between Chiswick and Hammersmith. All of them looked familiar to me in a way: rows of tidy terraces of mostly three storeys and a basement, bow-fronted townhouses for middle-income people, misleadingly narrow frontages stretching far back to small enclosed gardens. I had lived in several houses like that at some time or another, and I couldn't remember even the name of a road.

The years, too, had brought a host of changes. Whole streets had obviously disappeared with the building of bigger roads. Little remaining blocks of houses stood in lonely islands, marooned. Cinemas had closed. Asian shops had moved in. The buses looked the same.

Bus routes.

The buses triggered the memory. The house I was looking for had been three or four from the end of the road, and just round the corner there had been a bus-stop. I had been on the buses often, catching them at that stop.

Going to where?

Going to the river, for walks.

The knowledge drifted quietly back across twenty-plus years. We'd gone down to the river in the afternoons, to look at the houseboats and the seagulls and the mud when the tide was out; and we'd looked across to the gardens at Kew.

I drove down to Kew Bridge and reversed, and started from there, following buses.

A slow business, because I stopped when the bus did. Unproductive also, because none of the stops anywhere seemed to be near the corners of roads. I gave it up after an hour and simply cruised around, resigned to not finding anything I recognized. Probably I'd got even the district wrong. Probably I should be looking in Hampstead, where I knew I'd been also.

It was a pub that finally orientated me. The Willing Horse. An old pub. Dark brown paint. Frosted glass in the windows with tracery patterns round the edges. I parked the car round the corner and walked back to the chocolate doors, and simply stood there, waiting.

After a while I seemed to know which way to go.

Turn left, walk three hundred yards, cross the road, first turning on the right.

I turned into a street of bow-fronted terrace houses, three storeys high, narrow and neat and typical. Cars lined both sides of the street, with many front gardens converted to parking places. There were a few bare-branched trees growing from earth-patches near the edge of the pavement, and hedges and shrubs by the houses. Three steps up to a small flat area outside each front door.

I crossed that road and walked slowly up it, but the impetus had gone. Nothing told me whether I was in the right place, or which house to try. I walked more slowly, indecisively, wondering what to do next.

Four houses from the end I went up the short footpath, and up the steps, and rang the doorbell.

A woman with a cigarette opened the door.

'Excuse me,' I said. 'Does Samantha live here?'

'Who?'

'Samantha?'

'No.' She looked me up and down with the utmost suspicion, and closed the door.

I tried six more houses. Two no answers, one 'clear off', one 'no dear, I'm Popsy, like to come in?', one 'we don't want no brushes', and one 'is that a cat?'

At the eighth an old lady told me I was up to no good, she'd watched me go from house to house, and if I didn't stop it she would call the police.

'I'm looking for someone called Samantha,' I said. 'She used to live here.'

'I'm watching you,' she said. 'If you try to climb in through any windows, I'll call the police.'

I walked away from her grim little face and she came right out into the street to watch me.

It wasn't much good, I thought. I wouldn't find Samantha. She might be out, she might have moved, she might never have lived in the street in the first place. Under the old woman's baleful gaze I tried another house where no one answered, and another where a girl of about twenty opened the door.

'Excuse me,' I said. 'Does anyone called Samantha live here?' I'd said it so often it now sounded ridiculous. This is the last one, I thought. I may as well give it up and go home.

'Who?'

'Samantha?'

'Samantha what? Samantha who?'

'I'm afraid I don't know.'

She pursed her lips, not quite liking it.

'Wait a moment,' she said. 'I'll go and see.' She shut the door and went away. I walked down the steps to the front garden where a small red car stood on some tarmac. Hovered, waiting to see if the girl returned, aware of the old woman beadily watching from along the road.

The door behind me opened as I turned. There were two people there, the girl and an older woman. When

I took a step towards them the woman made a sharp movement of the arm, to keep me away. Raising her voice she said, 'What do you want?'

'Well . . . I'm looking for someone called Samantha.'

'So I hear. What for?'

'Are you,' I said slowly, 'Samantha?'

She looked me up and down with the suspicion I was by now used to. A comfortably sized lady, grey-brown wavy hair to her shoulders.

'What do you want?' she said again, unsmiling.

I said, 'Would the name Nore mean anything to you? Philip Nore, or Caroline Nore?'

To the girl the names meant nothing, but in the woman there was a fast sharpening of attention.

'What exactly do you want?' she demanded.

'I'm . . . Philip Nore.'

The guarded expression turned to incredulity. Not exactly to pleasure, but certainly to acknowledgement.

'You'd better come in,' she said. 'I'm Samantha Bergen.'

I went up the steps and through the front door, and didn't have, as I'd half-expected, the feeling of coming home.

'Downstairs,' she said, leading the way and looking over her shoulder, and I followed her through the hall and down the stairs which in all those London houses led to the kitchen and the door out to the garden. The girl followed after me, looking mystified and still wary.

'Sorry not to have been more welcoming,' Samantha

said, 'but you know what it is these days. So many burglaries. You have to be careful. And strange young men coming to the door asking for Samantha . . .'

'Yes,' I said.

She went through a doorway into a large room which looked more like a country kitchen than most kitchens in the country. A row of pine-covered fitments on the right. A big table, with chairs. A red-tiled floor. French windows to the garden. A big basket-chair hanging on a chain from the ceiling. Beams. Inglenook with gas fire. Bits of gleaming copper.

Without thinking I walked across the red floor and sat in the hanging basket chair, beside the inglenook, tucking my feet up under me, out of sight.

Samantha Bergen stood there looking astounded.

'You are!' she said. 'You are Philip. Little Philip. He always used to sit there like that, with his feet up. I'd forgotten. But seeing you do it . . . Good gracious heavens.'

'I'm sorry,' I said, half stammering and standing up again, steadying the swinging chair. 'I just . . . did it.'

'My dear man,' she said. 'It's all right. It's extraordinary to see you, that's all.' She turned to the girl but said still to me, 'This is my daughter, Clare. She wasn't born when you stayed here.' And to her daughter she said, 'I looked after a friend's child now and then. Heavens . . . it must be twenty-two years since the last time. I don't suppose I ever told you.'

The girl shook her head but looked less mystified

and a good deal more friendly. They were both of them attractive in an unforced sort of way, both of them wearing jeans and sloppy jerseys and unpainted Tuesday afternoon faces. The girl was slimmer and had darker and shorter hair, but they both had large grey eyes, straight noses, and unaggressive chins. Both were self-assured; and both undefinably intelligent.

The work I had interrupted lay spread out on the table. Galley proofs and drawings and photographs, the makings of a book. When I glanced at it Clare said, 'Mother's cookery book,' and Samantha said, 'Clare is a publisher's assistant,' and they invited me to sit down again.

We sat round the table, and I told them about looking for Amanda, and the off-chance which had brought me to their door.

Samantha regretfully shook her head. 'An off-chance is all it was,' she said. 'I never saw Caroline after she took you away the last time. I didn't even know she had a daughter. She never brought her here.'

'Tell me about her,' I said. 'What was she like?'

'Caroline? So pretty you wanted to hug her. Full of light and fun. She could get anyone to do anything. But . . .' she stopped.

'But what?' I said. 'And please do be frank. She's been dead for twelve years, and you won't hurt my feelings.'

'Well . . . she took drugs.' Samantha looked at me anxiously, and seemed relieved when I nodded.

'Cocaine. LSD. Cannabis. Almost anything. Poppers and uppers and downers. She tried the lot. She told me she didn't want you around when she and her friends were all high. She begged me to look after you for a few days . . . it always turned into a few weeks . . . and you were such a quiet little mouse . . . you were quite good company, actually. I never minded, when she brought you.'

'How often?' I said slowly.

'How often did she bring you? Oh . . . half a dozen times. You were about four the first time . . . and about eight at the end, I suppose. I told her I couldn't take you again, as Clare was imminent.'

'I've always been grateful to you,' I said.

'Have you?' She seemed pleased. 'I wouldn't have thought you'd remember . . . but I suppose you must have done, as you're here.'

'Did you know anyone called Chloe or Deborah or Miranda?' I said.

'Deborah Baederbeck? Went to live in Brussels?'

'I don't know.'

Samantha shook her head dubiously. 'She wouldn't know anything about your Amanda. She must have been in Brussels for . . . oh . . . twenty-five years.'

Clare made some tea and I asked Samantha if my mother had ever told her anything about my father.

'No, nothing,' she said positively. 'An absolutely taboo subject, I gathered. She was supposed to have an abortion, and didn't. Left it too late. Just like Caroline,

806

absolutely irresponsible.' She made a comical face. 'I suppose you wouldn't be here if she'd done what she'd promised her old dragon of a mother.'

'She made up for it by not registering my birth.'

'Oh God.' She chuckled with appreciation. 'I must say that's typical Caroline. We went to the same school. I'd known her for years. We'd not long left when she got landed with you.'

'Did she take drugs then? At school?'

'Heavens, no.' She frowned, thinking. 'Afterwards. We all did. I don't mean she and I together. But our generation . . . we all tried it, I should think, some time or other, when we were young. Pot mostly.'

Clare looked surprised, as if mothers didn't do that sort of thing.

I said, 'Did you know the friends she got high with?'

Samantha shook her head. 'Never met any of them. Caroline called them friends in the plural, but I always thought of it as one friend, a man.'

'No,' I said. 'Sometimes there were more. People lying on floor cushions half asleep, with the room full of haze. All enormously peaceful.'

They were the people with words like 'skins' and 'grass' and 'joints', which never seemed to mean what my childish brain expected; and it was one of those who had given me a cigarette and urged me to suck in the smoke. Suck it into your lungs, he'd said, and then hold your breath while you count ten. I'd coughed all the smoke out before I'd counted two, and he'd laughed and told me to try again. Three or four small drags, I'd had.

The result, which I'd dreamed of occasionally afterwards rather than actively remembered, was a great feeling of tranquillity. Relaxed limbs, quiet breathing, slight lightness of head. My mother had come home and slapped me, which put paid to all that. The friend who'd initiated me never reappeared. I hadn't met hash again until I was twenty, when I'd been given a present of some greeny-yellow Lebanese resin to sprinkle like an OXO cube onto tobacco.

I'd smoked some, and given some away, and never bothered again. The results, to me, weren't worth the trouble and expense. They would have been, a doctor friend had told me, if I'd had asthma. Cannabis was terrific for asthmatics, he'd said, sadly. Pity they couldn't smoke it on the National Health.

We drank the tea Clare had made, and Samantha asked what I did in the way of a job.

'I'm a jockey.'

They were incredulous. 'You're too tall,' Samantha said, and Clare said, 'People just aren't jockeys.'

'People are,' I said. 'I am. And steeplechase jockeys don't have to be small. Six-footers have been known.'

'Extraordinary thing to be,' Clare said. 'Pretty pointless, isn't it?'

'Clare!' Samantha said, protesting.

'If you mean,' I said equably, 'that being a jockey contributes nothing useful to society, I'm not so sure.'

'Proceed,' Clare said.

'Recreation gives health. I provide recreation.'

'And betting?' she demanded. 'Is that healthy?'

'Sublimation of risk-taking. Stake your money, not your life. If everyone actually set out to climb Everest, just think of the rescue parties.'

She started to smile and converted it into a chewing motion with her lips. 'But you yourself . . . take the risks.'

'I don't bet.'

'Clare will tie you in knots,' her mother said. 'Don't listen to her.'

Clare, however, shook her head. 'I would think your little Philip is as easy to tie in knots as a stream of water.'

Samantha gave her a surprised glance and asked me where I lived.

'In Lambourn. It's a village in Berkshire. Out on the Downs.'

Clare frowned and looked at me with sharpened concentration.

'Lambourn . . . isn't that the village where there are a lot of racing stables, rather like Newmarket?'

'That's right.'

'Hm.' She thought for a minute. 'I think I'll just ring up my boss. He's doing a book on British villages and village life. He was saying this morning the book's still a bit thin – asked me if I had any ideas. He has a writer chap doing it. Going to villages, staying a week and writing a chapter. He's just done one on a village that produces its own operas ... Look, do you mind if I give him a call?'

'Of course not.'

She was on her feet and going across to a telephone extension on the kitchen worktop before I'd even answered. Samantha gave her a fond motherly look, and I thought how odd it was to find Samantha in her late forties, when I'd always imagined her perpetually young. From under the unrecognizable exterior, though, the warmth, the directness, the steady values and the basic goodness came across to me as something long known: and I was reassured to find that those half-buried impressions had been right.

'Clare will bully you into things,' she said. 'She bullied me into doing this cookery book. She's got more energy than a power station. She told me when she was about six that she was going to be a publisher, and she's well on her way. She's already second-in-command to the man she's talking to. She'll be running the whole firm before they know where they are.' She sighed with pleased resignation, vividly illuminating the trials and pride of mothering a prodigy.

The prodigy herself, who looked normal enough, finished talking on the telephone and came back to the table nodding.

'He's interested. He says we'll both go down and

look the place over, and then if it's OK he'll send the writer, and a photographer.'

I said diffidently, 'I've taken pictures of Lambourn . . . If you'd like to . . .'

She interrupted with a shake of the head. 'We'd need professional work. Sorry and all that. But my boss says if you don't mind we'll call at your digs or whatever, if you'd be willing to help us with directions and general info.'

'Yes . . . I'd be willing.'

'That's great.' She gave me a sudden smile that was more like a pat on the back than a declaration of friendship. She knows she's bright, I thought. She's used to being brighter than most. She's not as good as Jeremy Folk at concealing that she knows it.

'Can we come on Friday?' she said.

CHAPTER TEN

Lance Kinship was wandering around at the head of a retinue of cameramen, sound recordists and general dogsbodies when I arrived at Newbury racecourse on the following day, Wednesday. We heard in the changing room that he was taking stock shots for a film with the blessing of the management and that jockeys were asked to cooperate. Not, it was said, to the point of grinning into the camera lens at every opportunity, but just to not treading on the crew if one found them underfoot.

I slung my Nikon round my neck inside my raincoat and unobtrusively took a few pictures of the men taking pictures.

Technically speaking, cameras were not welcome at race meetings except in the hands of recognized photographers, but most racecourses didn't fidget unduly about the general public taking snaps anywhere except in the Members' enclosure. Most racecourse managers, because I'd been doing it for so long, looked tolerantly upon my own efforts and let me get on with

it. Only at Royal Ascot was the crack-down on amateurs complete: the one meeting where people had to
park their shooters at the entrance, like gunslingers
riding into a bullet-free town.

Lance Kinship looked as if he had tried hard not to
look like a film director. In place of his olive suede
jacket, now presumably having its bloodstains removed
at the cleaners, he wore a brownish tweed suit topped
by a brown trilby set at a conservative angle and
accompanied by checked shirt, quiet tie, and race-
glasses. He looked, I thought, as if he'd cast himself as
an uppercrust extra in his own film.

He was telling his crew what to do with pomposity
in his voice and with indecisive gestures. It was only in
the tenseness with which they listened to him, their
eyes sliding his way every time he spoke, that one saw
any authority. I took a couple of shots of that reaction;
the eyes all looking towards him from averted heads. I
reckoned that when printed, those pictures might quite
clearly show men obeying someone they didn't like.

At one point, round by the saddling boxes, where
the crew were filming the trainers fitting on the saddles
before the first race, Lance Kinship turned his head in
the instant I pressed the button, and stared straight
into my lens.

He strode across to me, looking annoyed.

'What are you doing?' he said, though it must have
been obvious.

'I was just interested,' I said inoffensively.

He looked at my boots, my white breeches and the red and yellow shirt which I wore under the raincoat.

'A jockey,' he said, as to himself. He peered through his black framed spectacles at my camera. 'A Nikon.' He raised his eyes to my face and frowned with half-recognition.

'How's the nose?' I said politely.

He grunted, finally placing me.

'Don't get into shot,' he said. 'You're not typical. I don't want Nikon-toting jocks lousing up the footage. Right?'

'I'll be careful,' I said.

He seemed on the point of telling me to go away altogether, but he glanced from side to side and took note that a few race-goers were listening, and decided against it. With a brief disapproving nod he went back to his crew, and presently they moved off and began taking shots of the saddled horses walking into the parade ring.

The chief cameraman carried his big movie camera on his shoulder and mostly operated it from there. An assistant walked one step behind, carrying a tripod. One sound recorder carried the charcoal sausage-shaped boom and a second fiddled endlessly with knobs on an electric box. A young man with frizzy hair operated a clapper board, and a girl took copious notes. They trailed round all afternoon getting in everyone's way and apologizing like mad so that no one much minded.

They were down at the start when I lined up on a scatty novice 'chaser for Harold, and thankfully absent from the eighth fence, where the novice 'chaser put his fore-feet into the open ditch on the take-off side and crossed the birch almost upside down. Somewhere during this wild somersault I fell out of the saddle, but by the mercy of heaven when the half-ton of horse crashed to the ground I was not underneath it.

He lay prostrate for a few moments, winded and panting, giving me plenty of time to grasp hold of the reins and save his lad the frustrating job of catching him loose. Some horses I loved: and some I didn't. This was a clumsy stubborn delinquent with a hard mouth, just starting what was likely to be a long career of bad jumping. I'd schooled him at home several times and knew him too well. If he met a fence right, he was safe enough, but if he met it wrong he ignored signals to change his stride; and every horse met a fence wrong now and then, however skilful his rider. I reckoned every time he completed a race, I'd be lucky.

Resignedly I waited until he was on his feet and prancing about a bit, then remounted him and trotted him back to the stands, and made encouraging remarks to the downcast owner and honest ones to Harold.

'Tell him to cut his losses and buy a better horse.'

'He can't afford it.'

'He's wasting the training fees.'

'I dare say,' Harold said, 'but we're not telling him, are we?'

I grinned at him. 'No, I guess not.'

I took my saddle into the weighing room and Harold went off to join the owner in a consolatory drink. Harold needed the training fees. I needed the riding fees. The owner was buying a dream and kidding himself. It happened every day, all the time, in racing. It was only occasionally that the dream came superbly, soul-fillingly true, and when that happened you saw points of light like stars in the owner's eyes. Thank God for the owners, I thought. Without them racing wouldn't exist.

When I was changing back into street clothes someone came and told me there was a man outside asking for the jockey with the camera.

I went to see, and found Lance Kinship trudging up and down and looking impatient.

'Oh there you are,' he said, as if I'd seriously kept him waiting. 'What's your name?'

'Philip Nore.'

'Well, Phil, what do you say? You took some photographs today. If they're any good I'll buy them from you. How's that?'

'Well . . .' I was nonplussed. 'Yes, if you like.'

'Good. Where's your camera? Get it then, get it. The crew is over by the winning post. Take some photographs of them shooting the finish of the next race. Right? Right?'

'Yes,' I said dazedly.

'Come on then. Come on.'

I fetched the camera from the changing room and found him still waiting for me but definitely in a hurry. I would have to get over there and assess the best angles, he explained, and I'd only have one chance because the crew would be moving out to the car park presently to film the racegoers going home.

He had apparently tried to get the regular racing photographers to do the present job, but they had said they were too busy.

'I thought of you. Worth trying, I thought. With the camera, you at least have to be able to focus. Right?'

We were walking fast. He broke now and then into a sort of trotting stride, and his breathing gradually grew shorter. His mental energy, however, was unflagging.

'We need these pics for publicity. Right?'

'I see,' I said.

His words and manner were so much at variance with his appearance that the whole expedition seemed to me powerfully unreal. Urgent film producers (who might or might not provide cocaine for sniffing at parties) were surely not accustomed to look the country gentleman, nor tweeded country gentlemen to speak with slovenly vowels and glottal-stop consonants. The 'right?' he was so fond of was pronounced without its final 't'.

I would have thought, if he wanted publicity pictures, that he would have brought a photographer of his own; and I asked him.

'Sure,' he said. 'I had one lined up. Then he died. Didn't get around to it again. Then today, saw you. Reminded me. Asked the news photographers. No dice. Thought of you, right? Asked them about you. They said you were good, you could do it. You may be lousy. If your pics are no good, I don't buy, right?'

He panted across the course to the winning post on the far side, and I asked him which photographer had died.

'Fellow called Millace. Know him?'

'I knew him,' I said.

'He said he'd do it. Died in a crash. Here we are. You get on with it. Take what you want. Got colour film in there, have you?'

I nodded and he nodded, and he turned away to give instructions to the crew. They again listened to him with the slightly averted heads, and I wandered away. Lance Kinship was not immediately likeable, but I again had a strong feeling that his crew felt positive discontent. He wouldn't buy photographs showing that response, I thought dryly, so I waited until the crew were not looking at him, and shot them absorbed in their work.

Lance Kinship's breathing returned to normal and he himself merged again into the racing background as if he'd been born there. An actor at heart, I thought: but unlike an actor he was dressing a part in real life, which seemed odd.

'What film are you making?' I asked.

'Stock shots,' he said uninformatively. 'Background.'

I left it, and walked round the crew looking for useful angles for pictures. The horses came out onto the course and cantered down to the start, and the frizzy-haired boy with the clapper board, who happened to be close to me, said with sudden and unexpected fierceness, 'You'd think he was God Almighty. You'd think this was an epic, the way he frigs about. We're making commercials. Half a second on screen, flash off. Huh!'

I half smiled. 'What's the product?'

'Some sort of brandy.'

Lance Kinship came towards me and told me it was important that he should be included in my photographs, and that I should take them from where he would be prominently in shot.

The frizzy-haired boy surreptitiously raised his eyebrows into comical peaks, and I assured Lance Kinship with a trembling straight face that I would do my absolute best.

I did by good luck get one or two reasonable pictures, but no doubt George Millace with his inner eye and his motor-drive camera would have outstripped me by miles. Lance Kinship gave me a card with his address on and told me again that he would buy the pictures if he liked them, right?

He didn't say for how much, and I didn't like to ask.

I would never be a salesman.

Taking photographs for a living, I thought ruefully, would find me starving within a week.

Reaching home I switched on the lights and drew the curtains, and sat by the kitchen table going again through George Millace's rubbish box, thinking of his talents and his cruel mind, and wondering just how much profit he had made from his deadly photographs.

It was true that if he'd left any more pictures in that box I wanted to decipher them. The urge to solve the puzzles was overpowering. But if I learned any more secrets, what would I do with them . . . and what ought I to do with those I already had?

In a fairly typical manner I decided to do pretty well nothing. To let events take their course. To see what happened.

Meanwhile there were those tantalizing bits that looked so pointless. . . .

I lifted out the black plastic light-proof envelope which was of about the same size as the box and lying at the bottom of it, under everything else. I looked again at its contents, as I had in Steve Millace's house, and saw again the page-sized piece of clear plastic, and also, which hadn't registered before, two sheets of paper of about the same size.

I looked at them briefly and closed them again into their light-proof holder, because it had suddenly occurred to me that George might not have stored them like that unless it was necessary. That plastic and that paper might bear latent images . . . which I might already have destroyed by exposing them to light.

The piece of plastic and the sheets of paper didn't actually look to me like photographic materials at all. They looked like a piece of plastic and two sheets of typing paper.

If they bore latent images, I didn't know how to develop them. If they didn't, why had George kept them in a light-proof envelope?

I sat staring vaguely at the silent black plastic and thinking about developers. To bring out the image on any particular type of film or any type of paper one had to use the right type of developer, the matched mixture of chemicals made for the task. All of which meant that unless I knew the make and type of the plastic and of the two sheets of paper I couldn't get any further.

A little pensively I pushed the black envelope aside and took up the strips of blank negatives, which at least didn't have the built-in difficulty of being still sensitive to light. They had already been developed. They just looked as if when they had been developed there had been no latent images on them to bring out.

They were thirty-five millimetre colour film negatives, and there were a lot of them, some simply blank and others blank with uneven magenta blotches here and there. The negatives were in strips, mostly six to a strip. I laid them all out end to end and made the first interesting discovery.

All the plain blank negatives had come from one film, and those with magenta blotches from another. The frame numbers along the top of each strip ran consecutively from one to thirty-six in each case. Two films of thirty-six exposures each.

I knew what make of film they were, because each manufacturer placed the frame numbers differently, but I didn't suppose that that was important. What might be important, however, was the very nature of colour negatives.

While slide films – transparencies – appeared to the eye in their true lifelike colours, negative film appeared in the reciprocal colours: and to get back to the true colours one had of course to make a print from the negative.

The primary colours of light were blue, green, and red. The reciprocal colours, in which they appeared on a negative, were yellow, magenta and cyan. Negatives therefore would have looked like mixtures of yellow, deep pink (magenta) and greeny-blue (cyan), except that to get good whites and highlights all manufacturers gave their negatives an overall pale orange cast. Colour negatives therefore always looked a pale clear orange at the edges.

The overall orange colour also had the effect of masking the yellow sections so that they didn't show to the eye as yellow bits of negative, but as orange.

George Millace's negatives looked a pale clear transparent orange throughout.

Just suppose, I thought, that under the orange there was an image in yellow, which at the moment didn't show.

If I printed those negatives, the yellow would become blue.

An invisible yellow negative image could turn into a totally visible printed image in blue.

Worth trying, I thought. I went into the darkroom and mixed the developing chemicals, and set up the colour print processor. It meant waiting half an hour for the built-in thermostatic heaters to raise the various chemical baths to the correct temperatures, but after that the prints were conveyed automatically inside the closed processor from one bath to another on rollers, each sheet of photographic paper taking seven minutes to travel from entry to exit.

I found out almost at once, by making contact prints, that under the orange masking there was indeed blue: but not blue images. Just blue.

There were so many variables in colour printing that searching for an image on blank negatives was like walking blindfold through a forest, and although in the end I printed every negative separately and tried every way I knew, I was only partially successful.

I ended, in fact, with thirty-six solid blue oblongs, enlarged to four inches by five and printed four to a sheet, and thirty-six more with greenish blotches here and there.

The only thing one could say, I thought, as I let them wash thoroughly in running water, was that George wouldn't have taken seventy-two pictures of a blue oblong for nothing.

I dried some of the prints and looked at them closely, and it did seem to me that there were faint darker marks on some of them. Nothing one could plainly see, but something.

When it dawned on me far too late what George had done I was too tired to start all over again. I cleaned up the processor and everything else, and went to bed.

Jeremy Folk telephoned early the next morning and asked if I'd been to see my grandmother.

Give me time, I said, and he said I'd had time, and did I remember I had promised?

'Well . . . I'll go,' I said. 'Saturday, after Ascot.'

'What have you been doing?' he asked plaintively. 'You could have gone any day this week. Don't forget she really is dying.'

'I've been working,' I said. 'And printing.'

'From that box?' he said suspiciously.

'Uh huh.'

'Don't do it,' he said, and then, 'What have you got?'

'Blue prints. Blue pictures.'

'What?'

'Blue as in blue. Pure deep blue. Forty-seven B.'

'*What* did you say? Are you sober?'

'I am awake and yawning,' I said. 'So listen. George Millace screwed a deep blue filter onto his camera and pointed it at a black and white picture, and he photographed the black and white picture through the blue filter onto colour negative film. Forty-seven B is the most intense blue filter you can buy, and I bet that's what he used.'

'You're talking Chinese.'

'I'm talking Millace. Crafty double Millace. Second cousin to double Dutch.'

'You really are drunk.'

'Don't be silly. As soon as I work out how to unscramble the blue, and do it, the next riveting Millace instalment will fall into our hands.'

'I seriously think you should burn the lot.'

'Not a chance.'

'You think of it as a game. It isn't a game.'

'No.'

'For God's sake be careful.'

I said I would. One says things like that so easily.

I went to Wincanton races in Somerset and rode twice for Harold and three times for other people. The day was dry with a sharp wind that brought tears to the eyes, tears which the standard of racing did nothing to dispel, since all the good horses had cried off and gone to Newbury or Ascot instead, leaving chances for the blundering majority. I fumbled and booted my way around five times in safety, and in the novice 'chase, owing to most of the field having fallen over each other at the first open ditch, found myself finishing in front, all alone.

My mount's thin little trainer greeted my return with a huge grin, tear-filled eyes and a blue dripping nose.

'By gum, lad, well done. By gum, it's bloody cold. Get thee in and weighed. Don't stand about. By gum, then, that was a bit of all right, wasn't it, all them others falling?'

'You'd schooled yours a treat,' I said, pulling off the saddle. 'He jumped great.'

His mouth nearly split its sides with pleasure. 'By gum, lad, he'd jump Aintree, the way he went today. Get thee in. Get thee in.'

I went in and weighed, and changed and weighed out, and raced, and returned, and changed and weighed . . .

There had been a time, when it was all new, that my heart had pumped madly every time I walked from the changing room to the parade ring, every time I cantered to the start. After ten years my heart pumped above normal only for the big ones, the Grand National and so on, and then only if my horse had a reasonable chance. The once fiendish excitement had turned to routine.

Bad weather, long journeys, disappointment and injuries had at first been shrugged off as 'part of the job'. After ten years I saw that they *were* the job. The peaks, the winners, those were the bonuses. Extras.

The tools of my trade were a liking for speed and a liking for horses, and the power to combine those two feelings. Also strong bones, an ability to bounce, and a tendency to mend quickly when I didn't.

None of these tools, except probably the liking for horses, would be of the slightest use to me as a photographer.

I walked irritably out to my car at the end of that afternoon. I didn't want to be a photographer. I wanted to remain a jockey. I wanted to stay where I was, in the known: not to step irrevocably into the future. I wanted things to go on as they were, and not to change.

Early the following morning Clare Bergen appeared on my doorstep accompanied by a dark young man whose fingertips in a handshake almost tingled with energy. Publishers, I had vaguely supposed, were portly father-figures. Another out-of-date illusion gone bust.

Clare herself had come in a bright woolly hat, bright scarf, Afghan sheepskin jacket, yellow satin ski-pants and huge fleece-lined boots. Ah well, I thought, she would only frighten half of the horses. The nervous half.

I drove them up onto the Downs in the Land Rover

borrowed from Harold for the occasion, and we watched a few strings work. Then I drove them round the village, pointing out which trainers lived where. Then I took them back to the cottage for coffee and cogitation.

The publisher said he would like to poke round a little on foot, and walked off. Clare drank her second steaming cup and said how on earth did we bear it with a wind like that sawing everyone in half.

'It always seems to be windy here,' I agreed, thinking about it.

'All those naked hills.'

'Good for horses.'

'I don't think I've ever actually touched a horse.' She looked faintly surprised. 'Most of the people I know despise horse people.'

'Everyone likes to feel superior,' I said, uninsulted. 'Particularly when they aren't.'

'Ouch,' she said. 'That's a damned fast riposte.'

I smiled. 'You'd be surprised the sort of hate that gets aimed at horses. Anything from sneers to hysteria.'

'And you don't mind?'

'What those people feel is their problem, not mine.'

She looked at me straightly with the wide grey eyes. 'What hurts you?' she said.

'People saying I jumped overboard when I went down with the ship.'

'Er . . . what?'

'People saying I fell off when it was the horse which fell, and took me with it.'

'And there's a distinction?'

'Most important.'

'You're having me on,' she said.

'A bit.' I took her empty cup and put it in the dish-water. 'So what hurts you?'

She blinked, but after a pause she answered, 'Being held to be a fool.'

'That,' I said, 'is a piercingly truthful reply.'

She looked away from me as if embarrassed, and said she liked the cottage and the kitchen and could she borrow the bathroom. She emerged from there shortly minus the woolly hat and plus some fresh lip-stick and asked if the rest of the house was on a par.

'You want to see it?' I said.

'Love to.'

I showed her the sitting room, the bedroom, and finally the darkroom. 'And that's all,' I said.

She turned slowly from the darkroom to where I stood behind her in the hall.

'You said you took photographs.'

'Yes, I do.'

'But I thought you meant . . .' She frowned. 'Mother said I was short with you when you offered . . . but I'd no idea . . .'

'It doesn't matter,' I said. 'It's quite all right.'

'Well . . . can I see them?'

'If you like. They're in that filing cabinet over there.'

I pulled open one of the drawers and sorted through the folders. 'Here you are, Lambourn village.'

'What are all those others?' she said.

'Just pictures.'

'What of?'

'Fifteen years.'

She looked at me sharply as if I wasn't making sense, so I added, 'Since I owned my own camera.'

'Oh.' She looked along the tags on the folders, reading, aloud. 'America, France, Children, Harold's Place, Jockey's Life ... What's Jockey's Life?'

'Just everyday living, if you're a jockey.'

'Can I look?'

'Sure.'

She eased the well-filled holder out of the drawer and peered inside. Then she carried it away towards the kitchen and I followed with the pictures of Lambourn.

She laid the folder she carried on the kitchen table, and opened it, and went through the bulky contents picture by picture, steadily and frowning.

No comments.

'Can I see Lambourn?' she said.

I gave her Lambourn, and she looked through those also in silence.

'I know they're not marvellous,' I said mildly. 'You don't have to rack your brains for something kind to say.'

She looked up at me fiercely. 'You're lying. You know damned well they're good.'

She closed the Lambourn file and drummed her fingers on it. 'I can't see why we can't use these,' she said. 'But it's not my decision, of course.'

She fished into her large brown handbag and came up with cigarettes and a lighter. She put a cigarette to her mouth and lit it, and I noticed with surprise that her fingers were trembling. What on earth, I wondered, could have made her nervous. Something had disturbed her deeply, because all the glittery extrovert surface had vanished, and what I saw was a dark-haired young woman concentrating acutely on the thoughts in her head.

She took several deep inhaling breaths of smoke, and looked unseeingly at her fingers, which went on trembling.

'What's the matter?' I said at last.

'Nothing.' She gave me a quick glance and looked away, and said, 'I've been looking for something like you.'

'Something?' I echoed, puzzled.

'Mm.' She tapped off some ash. 'Mother told you, didn't she, that I wanted to be a publisher?'

'Yes, she did.'

'Most people smile, because I'm still young. But I've worked in publishing for five years . . . and I know what I'm doing.'

'I don't doubt it.'

'No . . . but I need . . . I want . . . I need to make a book that will establish my own personal reputation in publishing. I need to be known as the person who produced such-and-such a book. A very successful book. Then my whole future in publishing will be assured. Do you understand?'

'Yes.'

'So I've been looking for that book for a year or two now. Looking and despairing, because what I want is exceptional. And now . . .' she took a deep breath, 'now I've found it.'

'But,' I said, puzzled, 'Lambourn's not news, and anyway I thought it was your boss's book . . .'

'Not that, you fool,' she said. 'This.' She put her hand on the Jockey's Life folder. 'The pictures in here. They don't need a text. They tell the story on their own.' She drew on the cigarette. 'Arranged in the right order . . . presented as a way of living . . . as an autobiography, a social comment, an insight into human nature . . . as well as how an industry works . . . it'll make a spectacular change from flowers and fish.'

'The flowers sold about two million copies, didn't they?'

'You don't believe me, do you?' she demanded. 'You simply don't see . . .' She broke off and frowned. 'You haven't had any of these photographs published before, have you? In papers or magazines, or anywhere?'

I shook my head. 'Nowhere. I've never tried.'

'You're amazing. You have this talent, and you don't use it.'

'But . . . everyone takes photographs.'

'Sure they do. But not everyone takes a long series of photographs which illustrate a whole way of life.' She tapped off the ash. 'It's all there, isn't it? The hard work, the dedication, the bad weather, the humdrum, the triumphs, the pain... I've only looked through these pictures once, and in no sort of order, and I know what your life's like. I know it *intimately*. Because that's how you've photographed it. I know your life from inside. I see what you've seen. I see the enthusiasm in those owners. I see their variety. I see what you owe to the stable-lads. I see the worry of trainers, it's everywhere. I see the laughter in jockeys, and the stoicism. I see what you've felt. I see what you've understood about people. I see people in a way I hadn't before, because of what you've seen.'

'I didn't know,' I said slowly, 'that those pictures were quite so revealing.'

'Look at this last one,' she said, pulling it out. 'This picture of a man in an overall pulling the boot off this boy with the broken shoulder... you don't need any words to say the man is doing it as gently as he can, or that it hurts... you can see it all, in every line of their bodies and faces.' She replaced the picture in the folder and said seriously, 'It's going to take me some time to set things up the way I want. Will you give me your assurance that you won't go straight off and sell these pictures to someone else?'

'Of course,' I said.

'And don't mention any of this to my boss when he comes back. I want this to be my book, not his.'

I half smiled. 'All right.'

'You may have no ambition,' she said sharply, 'but I have.'

'Yes.'

'And my ambition won't do you any harm either,' she said. 'If the book's a seller . . . and it will be . . . you'll get royalties.' She paused. 'You can have an advance, anyway, as soon as the contracts are signed.'

'Contracts . . .'

'Contracts, naturally,' she said. 'And keep these pictures safe, will you? I'll come back for them soon, on my own.'

She thrust the folder into my hands and I replaced it in the filing cabinet, so that when her energetic young boss returned it was only the views of Lambourn that he saw. He said without too much excitement that they would do well enough, and shortly afterwards he and Clare bore them away.

When they'd gone I thought that Clare's certainty about her book would evaporate. She would remember that most of the people she knew despised horse people. She would work out that a book of pictures taken by a jockey about his life would have a very limited appeal, and she would write apologetically, or briskly, and say that after all, on reflection . . .

I shrugged. I had no expectations. When the letter came, that would be that.

CHAPTER ELEVEN

I went into Swindon to collect the films I'd left there for processing on my way to Wincanton the previous morning, and spent the rest of that Friday printing the shots of Lance Kinship and his crew.

Apart from those showing clearly the crew's unease in his company, which I didn't intend in any case to show him, I thought that quite likely he might approve. I'd been fortunate in the way the crew had arranged themselves often into natural patterns, and there was Kinship himself looking frantically upper-class in his racing tweeds directing them with a conductor's gestures, and in one sequence the horses behind them were all coming head on satisfactorily towards the winning post.

There were also several close-ups of Kinship with the crew in blurred focus behind him, and a couple of slightly surrealistic views which I'd taken from directly behind the cameraman, in which the camera itself looked large with Kinship's sharply focussed figure standing in a stray shaft of sunlight in the middle field.

The total effect, looking through them all, was a record of a substantial operator in command of his job, and that, I presumed, was what he'd wanted. No matter that the product had been two seconds in a commercial, the production itself looked an epic.

In the evening I captioned the dried prints with typed strips of thin paper sellotaped onto the backs, and feeling faintly foolish added the words *Copyright Philip Nore*, in the way I'd seen Charlie do, all those long years ago. Charlie seemed almost to be leaning over my shoulder, reminding me to keep control of my work.

Work.

The very word filled me with disquiet. It was the first time I'd actively thought of my photographs in those terms.

No, I thought, I'm a jockey.

When I woke early on Saturday morning I waited for Harold to telephone and tell me to get sick, and it wouldn't have been much trouble as I already felt sick with waiting.

He called at a quarter to ten.

'Are you well?' he said.

'Christ.'

'You'd better be,' he said. 'Victor rang just now. I didn't wait to hear what he meant to say. I told him straight away that Chainmail's future depended on his being handled right in all his races.'

'What happened?'

'Victor said an easy race wouldn't hurt him, so I told him what you said. Word for word. And I told him you'd said you would ride your bloody guts out for him as long as we're trying to win.' Harold's voice boomed down the wire with cheerfulness. 'And do you know what Victor said? He said tell that pious bastard that that's just what I'll expect.'

'Do you mean . . .?'

'I mean,' Harold bellowed, 'he's changed his mind. You can win on Chainmail if you can. In fact you'd better.'

'But Chainmail isn't . . .'

'Dammit, do you want to ride the horse or don't you?'

'I do.'

'Right, then. See you at Ascot.' He slammed the receiver down, informing me that he didn't think I'd been properly grateful for his efforts with Victor: but if he had promised Victor that Chainmail would win – and it seemed only too likely that he had – I would be in a worse fix than ever.

At Ascot I sought out Harold's head travelling lad, who had as usual come with the horses, and asked how Chainmail was feeling that day.

'Bucking and kicking fit to murder.'

'And Daylight?'

'Placid as an old cow.'

'Where have the lads put their money?'

He gave me a sharp sideways look. 'A bit on both of them. Why, shouldn't they?'

'Sure,' I said casually. 'They should. But you know how it is . . . sometimes the lads know more about a horse's chances than the trainer does.'

He grinned. 'I'll say. But today . . .' He shrugged. 'A bit on both. Not the week's wages, mind. Just some beer money, like.'

'Thanks.' I nodded and went off to the weighing room with at least no added anxieties. The lads wouldn't be staking even beer money without what they considered to be good reason. The legs, stomachs and spirits of both horses could be held to be normal. One didn't ask more.

I saw Victor Briggs standing in a group of one on the area of grass outside the weighing room door. Always the same clothes: the broad-brimmed hat, the thick navy overcoat, the black leather gloves. Always the same expression: the wiped-clean slate. He saw me, and no doubt he also saw the falter in my stride as I wondered whether I could possibly walk right past him without speaking.

I couldn't.

'Good morning, Mr Briggs.'

'Morning.' His voice was curt, but no more. He didn't seem to want me to stop for conversation, so after a slight hesitation I went on towards the weighing room. As I passed him he said grittily, 'I'll see your guts.'

I stopped and turned my head. His face was still expressionless. His eyes looked cold and hard. I stopped myself from swallowing, and said merely 'All right', and went on again, wishing I'd never made that stupidly flamboyant promise.

Inside the changing room someone was telling a funny story about two statues, and Steve Millace was flexing his mending arm and complaining that the doctor wouldn't pass him fit to ride, and someone else was voicing the first rumours of a major racing upheaval. I took off my street clothes and listened to all three at once.

'So these two naked statues, the man and the woman, they had been standing looking at each other in this park for a hundred years . . .'

'I told him I'd got all the movement back. It's not fair . . .'

'Is it true the Jockey Club are forming a new committee . . .'

'So an angel comes to visit them, and says that as they've stood there patiently through such ages of summers and winters, they will be rewarded by half an hour of human life to do what they have been wanting to do most . . .'

'Look, I can swing my arm round in a circle. What do you think?'

'A committee for appointing paid Stewards, or something.'

'So these two statues come to life, and look at each other and laugh a bit, and say "Shall we?" and "Yes, let's", and then they nip off behind some bushes, and there's a lot of rustling . . .'

'I could hold any horse. I told him so, but the sod wouldn't listen.'

' . . . like paying the Senior Steward a salary.'

'After a quarter of an hour they come out from behind the bushes all hot and flustered and happy and the angel says they've only used half the time, why don't they start all over again . . .'

'How long do collar-bones usually take, anyway?'

'I heard Lord White has agreed to the scheme . . .'

'So the statues giggle a bit and the man statue says to the girl statue, "OK, let's do it again, only this time we'll do it the other way round. I'll hold down the effing pigeon, and you shit on it." '

Amid the burst of laughter I heard the rumour man say ' . . . and Ivor den Relgan is to be chairman.'

I turned to him. 'What did you say?'

'I don't know if it's true . . . one of the gossip writers told me Ivor den Relgan's been appointed to set up a committee to appoint paid Stewards.'

I frowned. 'That gives den Relgan an awful lot of power all of a sudden, doesn't it?'

He shrugged. 'Don't know.'

He might not, but others did. During the afternoon

one could almost see the onward march of the rumour as uneasy surprise spread from one Jockey Club face to the next. The only group seeming unaffected by the general reaction were the ill-assorted bunch of people attracting the glances of everyone else.

Lord White. Lady White. Ivor den Relgan. Dana den Relgan.

They stood outside the weighing room in weak November sunshine, the women both dressed in mink. Lady White, always thin, looked gaunt and plain and unhappy. Dana den Relgan glowed with health, laughed with bright teeth, twinkled her eyes at Lord White, and cast patronizing glances at his Lady.

Lord White basked in the light of Dana's smile, shedding years like snakeskins. Ivor den Relgan smirked at the world in general and smoked a cigar with proprietorial gestures, as if Ascot racecourse were his own. He wore again the belted camel overcoat and the swept back greyish hair, and commanded attention as his natural right.

Harold appeared at my elbow, following my gaze.

'Ghengis Khan,' he said, 'is setting out to rule the world.'

'This committee?'

'Wouldn't you say,' Harold asked acidly, 'that asking someone like den Relgan to chair a committee of his own choosing is a paint job?'

'Cosmetic . . . or camouflage?'

'Both. What they're really doing is saying to den

Relgan "OK you choose anyone you like as Stewards, and we'll pay them." It's incredible.'

'Yes, it is.'

'Old Driven Snow,' Harold said, 'is so besotted with that girl that he'll give her father *anything*.'

'Was it all Lord White's idea?'

Harold grimaced wolfishly. 'Be your age, Philip. Just who has been trying for years to muscle into the Jockey Club? And just who has a knock-out of a daughter who is now old enough to play up to old Driven Snow? Ivor den Relgan has at last got his lever into the door to power in racing, and once he's inside the citadel and making decisions the old guard will have a hopeless job trying to get him out.'

'You really care,' I said wonderingly.

'Of course I bloody do. This is a great sport, and at the moment, free. Who the hell wants the top management of racing to be carved up and manipulated and sold and *tainted* like some other sports we could mention. The health of racing is guaranteed by having unpaid aristocrats working for the love of it. Sure, they make stupid fuck-ups occasionally, but we get them put right. If den Relgan appoints paid Stewards, for whom do you think those Stewards will be working? For us? For racing? Or for the interests of Ivor den bloody Relgan?'

I listened to his passion and his conviction and felt the tremor of his extreme dismay.

'Surely,' I said, 'the Jockey Club won't let it happen.'

'It is happening. The ones at the top are all so used to being led by Lord White that they've agreed to his proposal for this committee without thinking it through. They take it for granted he's virtuous and well-meaning and dead honest. And so he is. But he's also infatuated. And that's damn bloody dangerous.'

We watched the group of four. Lord White made continual small gestures which involved laying his hand on Dana's arm, or across her shoulders, or against her cheek. Her father watched with an indulgent smile and a noticeable air of satisfaction: and poor Lady White seemed to shrink even further and more greyly into her mink. When she eventually walked away, not one of the others seemed to notice her go.

'Someone,' Harold said grimly, 'has got to do something to stop all this. And before it goes too far.'

He saw Victor Briggs standing as usual alone in the distance and strode off to join him, and I watched Lord White and Dana flirt together like two joyful humming birds, and thought that today she was responding to him with much less discretion than she had at Kempton.

I turned away, troubled, and found Lance Kinship coming slowly towards me, his gaze flicking rapidly from me to the den Relgans and back again. It struck me that he wanted to talk to me without den Relgan noticing he was there, and with an inward smile I went to meet him.

'I've got your pictures in the car,' I said. 'I brought them in case you were here.'

'Have you? Good, good. I want to talk to that girl.'
He flicked another quick glance. 'Can you get near
her? Give her a message? Without that man hearing.
Without either of them hearing. Can you?'

'I might try,' I said.

'Right. Good. You tell her, then, that I'll meet her
after the third race in one of the private boxes.' He
told me the number. 'You tell her to come up there.
Right?'

'I'll try,' I said again.

'Good. I'll watch you. From over there.' He pointed.
'When you've given her the message, you come and
tell me. Right?'

I nodded, and with another quick peek at Dana he
scuttled away. His clothes that day were much as they
had been at Newbury, except that he'd ruined the
overall true-blue impression with some pale green
socks. A pathetic man, I thought. Making himself out
to be what he wasn't. Neither a significant film producer
nor bred in the purple. They ask him to parties, Victor
Briggs had said, because of what he brings. A sad
ineffectual man buying his way into the big time with
little packets of white powder.

I looked from him to den Relgan, who was using
Dana, instead, for much the same purpose. Nothing
sad or pathetic, though, about Ivor den Relgan. A bully
boy on the march, power hungry and complacent, a
trampler of little men.

I went up to him, and in an ingratiating voice, which

after years of buttering-up owners I could regrettably do quite convincingly, thanked him again for the gifts he had scattered at Kempton.

'The silver saddle . . . thought I must tell you,' I said. 'Great to have around, just to look at.'

'So glad,' he said, his gaze passing over me without interest. 'My daughter selected it.'

'Splendid taste,' Lord White said fondly, and I said directly to Dana, 'Thank you very much.'

'So glad,' she murmured also with an almost identical lack of interest.

'Please do tell me,' I said, 'whether it is unique, or whether it is one of many.'

I moved a step or two so that to answer she had to turn away from the two men, and almost before she had finished replying that it was the only one she'd seen, but she couldn't be certain . . . I said to her quietly, 'Lance Kinship is here, wanting to see you.'

'Oh.' She glanced quickly to the two men, returned Lord White's automatic smile with a dazzling one of her own, and softly said to me, 'Where?'

'After the third race in a private box.' I gave her the number.

'So glad you liked the saddle,' she said clearly, turning back towards Lord White. 'Isn't it fun,' she said to him, 'to give pleasure?'

'My dear girl,' he said roguishly, 'you give pleasure just by being yourself.'

Enough to bring angels to tears, I thought.

I wandered away and by a roundabout route arrived at Lance Kinship's side.

'She's got the message,' I said, and he said 'Good,' and we arranged for me to give him his pictures outside the weighing room during the running of the last race.

Daylight's race was third on the card, and Chainmail's the fourth. When I went out for the third I was stopped on my way from weighing room to parade ring by a pleasant-mannered woman who I realized with delayed shock was Marie Millace.

Marie Millace with scarcely a trace showing of the devastation of her face. Mrs Millace on her feet, dressed in brown, pale and ill-looking, but healed.

'You said there wouldn't be a mark,' she said, 'and there isn't.'

'You look great.'

'Can I talk to you?'

I looked to where all the other jockeys I'd started out with were already filing into the parade ring. 'Well . . . how about later? How about . . . um . . . after the fourth race. After I've changed. In the warm somewhere.'

She mentioned a particular bar, and we agreed on it, and I went on to the ring where Harold and Victor Briggs waited. Neither of them said anything to me, nor I to them. Everything of importance had already been said and for the unimportant there was no appetite. Harold gave me a leg up onto Daylight, and I nodded to him and Victor and got a grade-one blank Briggs stare in return.

There was no certainty that day that Daylight would win. With much stronger opponents, he wasn't even favourite, let alone odds-on.

I cantered down to the starting gate thinking about courage, which was not normally a word I found much in my mind. The process of getting a horse to go fast over jumps seemed to me merely natural, and something I very much liked doing. One knew theoretically that there would be falls and injuries, but the risk of them seldom affected the way I rode. I had no constant preoccupation with my own safety.

On the other hand I'd never been reckless, as some were, as Steve Millace was, and perhaps my aim had been a little too much to bring myself and the horse back together, and not enough to throw my heart over a fence and let the horse catch up if he could.

It was the latter style of riding that Victor Briggs would expect on that day. My own fault, I thought. And moreover I'd have to do it twice.

On Daylight it turned out to be fairly easy, as his jumping style held good even though I could sense his surprise at the change of mental gears in his rider. The telepathic quality of horses, that remarkable extra sense, picked up instantaneously the strength of my intention, and although I knew horses did tune in in that way, it freshly amazed me. One got used to a certain response from horses, because it was to oneself they were responding. When one's own cast of mind changed radically, so did the horse's response.

Daylight and I therefore turned in what was for us a thoroughly uncharacteristic performance, leaving more to luck than judgement. He was accustomed to measure his distance from a fence and alter his stride accordingly; but infected by my urgency he began not to do that but simply to take-off when he was vaguely within striking distance of getting over. We hit the tops of three fences hard, which was unheard of for him, and when we came to the last and met it right we raced over it as if it had been but a shadow on the ground.

Hard as we tried, we didn't win the race. Although we persevered to the end, a stronger, faster, fitter, (whatever) horse beat us into second place by three lengths.

In the unsaddling enclosure I unbuckled the girths while Daylight panted and rocketed around in a highly excitable state which was a world away from his 'placid cow' image; and Victor Briggs watched without giving a thought surface life.

'Sorry,' I said to Harold, as he walked in with me to the scales.

He grunted, and said merely, 'I'll wait for your saddle.'

I nodded, went into the changing room for a change of lead weights in the weight cloth, and returned to the scales to check out for Chainmail.

'Don't kill yourself,' Harold said, taking my saddle.

'It won't prove anything except that you're a bloody fool.'

I smiled at him. 'People die crossing the road.'

'What you're doing is no accident.'

He walked off with the saddle and I noticed that he had not in fact instructed me to return to a more sober style for his second runner. Perhaps he too, I reflected, wanted Victor to run his horses straight, and if this was the only way to achieve that, well . . . so be it.

With Chainmail things were different to the extent that the four-year-old hurdler was unstable to begin with, and what I was doing to him was much like urging a juvenile delinquent to go mugging. The rage within him, which made him fight against his jockey and duck out at the jumps and bite other horses, needed to be controlled by a calm mind and steady handling: or so I'd always thought.

On that day he didn't get it. He got a rider prepared to overlook every aggressive act except that of ducking out, and when he tried that at the third hurdle he got such a fierce slash from my whip that I could almost feel him thinking resentfully, 'Hey, that's not like you'; and it wasn't.

He fought and scrambled and surged and flew. I went with him to his ultimate speed, to total disregard of good sense. I did without any reservation ride my bloody guts out for Victor Briggs.

It wasn't enough. Chainmail finished third in a field of fourteen. Undisgraced. Better, probably, than one would realistically have expected. Beaten only by a length and a neck. But still third.

Victor Briggs unsmilingly watched me pull the saddle off his second stamping, tossing, hepped-up horse. I wrapped the girths round the saddle and paused for a moment face to face with him. He said nothing at all, and nor did I. We looked with equal blankness into each other's eyes for a space of seconds, and then I went on, past him, away to the scales.

When I had changed and come out again, he was nowhere in sight. I had needed two winners to save my job, and got none. Recklessness wasn't enough. He wanted winners. If he couldn't have certain winners, he'd want certain losers. Like before. Like three years ago. Like when I and my soul were young.

With a deep feeling of weariness I went to meet Marie Millace in the appointed bar.

CHAPTER TWELVE

She was sitting in an armchair deep in conversation with another woman, whom I found to my surprise to be Lady White.

'I'll come back later,' I said, preparing to retreat.

'No, no,' Lady White said, standing up. 'I know Marie wants to talk to you.' She smiled with all her own troubles showing in lines of anxiety, her eyes screwed up as if in permanent pain. 'She tells me you've been so helpful.'

'Nothing,' I said, shaking my head.

'Not what she says.'

The two women smiled and kissed cheeks, and said goodbye, and Lady White with a nod and another vague smile for me made her way out of the bar. I watched her go; a thin defeated lady trying to behave as if the whole racing world were not aware of her discomfiture, and not altogether succeeding.

'We were at school together,' Marie Millace said. 'We shared a bedroom, in our last year there. I'm very fond of her.'

'You know about . . . er . . .?'

'About Dana den Relgan? Yes.' She nodded. 'Would you like a drink?'

'Let me get you one.'

I fetched a gin and tonic for her and some coke for me, and sat in the armchair Lady White had left.

The bar itself, an attractive place of bamboo furniture and green and white colours, was seldom crowded and often, as on that day, almost empty. Tucked away up on the stands far away from the parade ring and the bookmakers, it was a better place for talking than for following the horses, and as such was also warm where most of the stands were not. Semi-invalids tended to spend a lot of time there, with nephews and nieces scurrying backwards and forwards with Tote tickets.

Marie Millace said, 'Wendy . . . Wendy White . . . was asking me if I thought her husband's affair with Dana den Relgan would just blow over. But I don't know. I couldn't tell her. How could I tell her? I said I was sure it would . . .' She paused, and when I didn't answer, said, 'Do you think it will?'

'Not for a while, I wouldn't think.'

She gloomily swilled the ice around in her drink. 'Wendy says he's been away with her. He took her to some friends overnight. He told Wendy he was going to shoot, which she finds boring. She hasn't gone with him to shooting parties for years. But he took Dana den Relgan with him this week, and Wendy says when the party went out with the guns, her husband and Dana den Relgan stayed in the house ... I suppose I shouldn't be telling you all this. She heard it from someone who was there. You're not to repeat what I've just said. You won't, will you?'

'Of course not.'

'It's so awful for Wendy,' Marie Millace said. 'She thought it was all over long ago.'

'All over? I thought it had just started.'

She sighed. 'Wendy says her husband fell like a ton of bricks for this Dana creature months ago, but then the wretched girl faded off the scene and didn't go racing at all, and Wendy thought that he'd stopped seeing her. And now she's back in full view and it's obvious to everyone. Wendy says that her husband is more overpoweringly in love than ever, and also *proud* of it. I'm sorry for Wendy. It's all so horrid.' She looked genuinely sympathetic, and yet her own troubles, by any standard, were much worse.

'Do you know Dana den Relgan yourself?' I asked.

'No, not at all. George knew her, I think. Or at least he knew her by sight. He knew everyone. He said when we were in St Tropez last summer that he thought he'd seen her there one afternoon, but I don't know if he meant it, he was laughing when he said it.'

I drank some coke and asked her conversationally if she and George had enjoyed St Tropez, and if they had been there often. Yes they had loved it, and no, only once. George as usual had spent most of the time glued to his camera, but he and Marie had lain on their balcony looking out to sea every afternoon and had tanned marvellously . . .

'Anyway,' she said, 'that's not what I wanted to talk to you about. I wanted to thank you for your kindness and ask you about that exhibition you suggested . . . and about how I might make some money out of those photographs. Because . . . and I know it's a sordid subject . . . I'm going to need . . . er . . .'

'Everyone needs,' I said comfortingly. 'But didn't George leave things like insurance policies?'

'Yes. Some. And I'll have the money for the house, though not its full value, unfortunately. But it won't be enough to live on, not with inflation and everything.'

'Didn't George,' I asked delicately, 'have any . . . well . . . savings . . . in any separate bank accounts?'

Her friendly expression began to change to suspicion. 'Are you asking me the same sort of things as the police?'

'Marie . . . Think of the burglaries, and your face, and the arson.'

'He wasn't,' she said explosively. 'George wouldn't . . . I told you before. Don't you believe me?'

I sighed and didn't answer, and asked her if she knew which friend George had stopped for a drink with, on his way back from Doncaster.

'Of course I know. He wasn't a friend. Barely an acquaintance. A man called Lance Kinship. George rang me from Doncaster in the morning, as he often did when he stayed away overnight, and he mentioned he'd be half an hour or so late as he was calling at this man's house, as it was on his way home. This Lance Kinship wanted George to take some pictures of him working. He's a film director, or something. George said he was a pernicious self-deluding little egotist, but if he flattered him he'd pay well. That was almost the last thing he said to me.' She took a deep breath and tried to control the tears which stood suddenly in her eyes. 'I'm so sorry...' She sniffed and straightened her face with an effort, fishing in her pocket for a handkerchief.

'It's natural to cry,' I said. It was only three weeks, after all, since George had died.

'Yes, but...' she tried to smile. 'Not at the races.' She wiped the edge of the handkerchief along under her lower eyelids and sniffed again. 'The very last thing he said,' she said, trying too hard, 'was to ask me to buy some Ajax window cleaner. It's stupid, isn't it? I mean, except for saying "See you," the last thing George ever said to me was "get some liquid Ajax, will you?" and I don't even know...' She gulped. The tears were winning. 'I don't even know what he wanted it for.'

'Marie...' I held my hand out towards her and she gripped it as fiercely as at the hospital.

'They say you always remember the last thing that someone you love says to you...' Her lips quivered hopelessly.

'Don't think about it now,' I said.

'No.'

She wiped her eyes again and held onto my hand, but presently the turmoil subsided and she loosened her grip and gave a small laugh of embarrassment: and I asked her if there had been an autopsy.

'Oh ... alcohol, do you mean? Yes, they tested his blood. They said it was below the limit ... he'd only had two small whiskies with that Kinship. The police asked him ... Lance Kinship ... after I told them about George planning to stop there. He wrote to me, you know, saying he was sorry. But it wasn't his fault. I'd told George over and over to be careful. He often got dozy when he'd been driving a long way.'

I told her how it had happened that it had been I who took the photographs of Lance Kinship that George had been going to do, and she was more interested than I had expected.

'George always said you'd wake up one day and pinch his market.' She produced a wavery smile to make it the joke it had undoubtedly been. 'I wish he knew. I wish ... oh dear, oh dear.'

We just sat for a while until the fresh tears subsided, and she apologized again for them, and again I said one would expect them.

I asked for her address so that I could put her in touch with an agent for George's work, and she said she was staying with some friends who lived near Steve. She didn't know, she said forlornly, where she would be going from there. Because of the arson she had no clothes except the few new ones she was wearing. No furniture. Nothing to make a home of. Worse . . . much worse . . . she had no photograph of George.

By the time I left Marie Millace the fifth race had been run. I went straight out to the car to fetch Lance Kinship's pictures, and returned towards the weighing room to find Jeremy Folk standing outside the door on one leg.

'You'll fall over,' I said.

'Oh . . . er . . .' He put the foot down gingerly as if to stand on two legs made him more positively there. 'I thought . . . er . . .'

'You thought if you weren't here I might not do what you want.'

'Er . . . yes.'

'You may well be right.'

'I came here by train,' he said contentedly. 'So can you take me with you to St Albans?'

'I guess I'll have to.'

Lance Kinship, seeing me there, came over to collect his prints. I introduced him and Jeremy to each other out of habit, and added for Jeremy's sake that it was at Lance Kinship's house that George Millace had taken his last drink.

Lance Kinship, untucking the flap of the stiffened

envelope, gave each of us a sharp glance followed by a sorrowful shake of the head.

'A great fellow, George,' he said. 'Too bad.'

He pulled the pictures out of the envelope and looked through them with his eyebrows rising even higher above his spectacle frames.

'Well, well,' he said. 'I like them. How much do you want?'

I mentioned a figure which I thought exorbitant but he merely nodded, pulled out a stuffed wallet, and paid me there and then in cash.

'Reprints?' he said.

'Certainly. They'd be less.'

'Get me two sets,' he said. 'Right?'

As before, the last 't' of right stuck somewhere in his throat.

'Complete sets?' I said surprised. 'All of them?'

'Sure. All of them. Very nice, they are. Want to see?'

He flicked them invitingly at Jeremy, who said he'd like to see them very much: and he too inspected them with his eyebrows rising.

'You must be,' he said to Kinship, 'a director of great note.'

Kinship positively beamed and tucked his pictures back into the envelope. 'Two more sets,' he said. 'Right?'

'Right.'

He nodded and walked away, and before he'd gone

ten paces he was pulling the pictures out again to show them to someone else.

'He'll get you a lot of work if you don't look out,' Jeremy said, watching.

I didn't know whether or not I wanted to believe him, and in any case my attention was caught by something much more extraordinary. I stood very still, and stared.

'Do you see,' I said to Jeremy, 'those two men over there, talking?'

'Of course I see them.'

'One of them is Bart Underfield, who trains in Lambourn. And the other is one of the men in that photograph of the French café. That's Elgin Yaxley . . . come home from Hong Kong.'

Three weeks after George's death, two weeks after the burning of his house; and Elgin Yaxley back on the scene.

I had jumped to conclusions before, but surely this time it was reasonable to suppose that Elgin Yaxley believed the incriminating photograph had safely gone up in smoke.

Reasonable to suppose, watching him standing there expansively smiling and full of confidence, that he felt freed and secure.

When a blackmailer and all his possessions were cremated, his victims rejoiced.

Jeremy said, 'It can't be coincidence.'

'No.'

'He looks pretty smug.'

'He's a creep.'

Jeremy glanced at me. 'You've still got that photo?'

'I sure have.'

We stood for a while looking on while Elgin Yaxley clapped Bart Underfield on the back and smiled like a crocodile and Bart Underfield looked happier than he had since soon after the trial.

'What will you do with it?'

'Just wait, I suppose,' I said, 'to see what happens.'

'I think I was wrong,' Jeremy said thoughtfully, 'to say you should burn all those things in the box.'

'Mm,' I smiled faintly. 'Tomorrow I'll have a go at the blue oblongs.'

'So you've worked out how?'

'Well, I hope so. Have to see.'

'How, then?'

He looked genuinely interested, his eyes switching from their customary scanning of the neighbourhood to a steady ten seconds in my direction.

'Um . . . do you want a lecture on the nature of light, or just the proposed order of events?'

'No lecture.'

'OK. Then I think if I enlarge the orange negatives through blue light onto high contrast black and white paper I might get a picture.'

He blinked. 'In black and white?'

'With luck.'

'How do you get blue light?'

'That's rather where the lecture comes in,' I said. 'Do you want to watch the last race?'

We had a slight return of angular elbow movements and of standing on one leg and of hesitated waffle, all on account, I guessed, of squaring the solicitorial conscience with the condoning of gambling.

I had done him an injustice, however. When we were watching on the stands for the race to start he said, 'I did...ah...in point of fact...er...watch you ride...this afternoon.'

'Did you?'

'I thought...it, ah, might be instructive.'

'And how did it grab you?'

'To be honest,' he said, 'rather you than me.'

He told me, as we drove towards St Albans, about his researches into the television company.

'I got them to show me the credits, as you suggested, and I asked if they could put me in touch with anyone who worked on the play at Pine Woods Lodge. It was only a single play, by the way. The unit was there for only about six weeks.'

'Not very promising,' I said.

'No. Anyway, they told me where to find the director. Still working in television. Very dour and depressing man, all grunts and heavy moustache. He was sitting on the side of a road in Streatham watching some electricians holding a union meeting before they went on strike and refused to light the scene he wanted to shoot in a church porch. His mood, in a word, was vile.'

'I can imagine.'

'I'm afraid,' Jeremy said regretfully, 'that he wasn't much help. Thirteen years ago? How the hell did I expect him to remember one crummy six weeks thirteen years ago? How the hell did I expect him to remember some crummy girl with a crummy brat? And much more to that effect. The only positive thing he said was that if he'd been directing there would have been no crummy hangers on anywhere near Pine Woods Lodge. He couldn't stand outsiders hanging about when he was working, and would I, too, please get the hell out.'

'Pity.'

'After that I tracked down one of the main actors in the play, who is temporarily working in an art gallery, and got much the same answer. Thirteen years? Girl with small child? Not a chance.'

I sighed. 'I had great hopes of the television lot.'

'I could carry on,' Jeremy said. 'They aren't difficult to find. I just rang up a few agents, to get the actor.'

'It's up to you, really.'

'I think I might.'

'How long were the musicians there?' I said.

Jeremy fished out a by now rather worn-looking piece of paper, and consulted.

'Three months, give or take a week.'

'And after them?'

'The religious fanatics.' He grimaced. 'I don't suppose your mother was religious?'

'Heathen.'

'It's all so long ago.'

'Mm.' I said, 'Why don't we try something else? Why not publish Amanda's photograph in the *Horse and Hound*, and ask specifically for an identification of the stable? Those buildings are probably still standing, and looking just the same.'

'Wouldn't a big enough picture cost a lot?'

'Not compared with private detectives,' I reflected. 'I think *Horse and Hound* charges for space, not for what you put in it. Photographs cost no more than words. So I could make a good sharp black and white print of Amanda ... and we could at least see.'

He sighed. 'OK, then. But I can see the final expenses of this search costing more than the inheritance.'

I glanced at him. 'Just how rich is she ... my grand-mother?'

'She may be broke, for all I know. She's incredibly secretive. I dare say her accountant has some idea, but he makes a clam look sloppy.'

We reached St Albans and detoured around to the nursing home; and while Jeremy read old copies of *The*

Lady in the waiting room I talked upstairs with the dying old woman.

Sitting up, supported by pillows, she watched me walk into her room. The strong harsh face was still full of stubborn life, the eyes as unrelentingly fierce. She said not something gentle like 'Hallo' or 'Good evening,' but merely 'Have you found her?'

'No.'

She compressed her mouth. 'Are you trying?'

'Yes and no.'

'What does that mean?'

'It means I've used some of my spare time looking for her but not my whole life.'

She stared at me with narrowed eyes, and presently I sat in the visitors' armchair and continued to stare back.

'I went to see your son,' I said.

Her face melted for a passing moment into an unguarded and revealing mixture of rage and disgust, and with a sense of surprise I saw the passion of her disappointment. I had already understood that a non-marrying non-child-producing son had essentially robbed her not of daughter-in-law and grand-children as such, to whom on known form she might anyway have behaved tyrannically, but of continuation itself: but I certainly hadn't realized that her search for Amanda sprang from obsession and not pique.

'Your genes to go on,' I said slowly. 'Is that what you want?'

'Death is pointless otherwise.'

I thought that life itself was pretty pointless, but I didn't say so. One woke up alive, and did what one could, and died. Perhaps she was in fact right . . . that the point of life was for genes to go on. Genes surviving, through generations of bodies.

'Whether you like it or not,' I said, 'your genes may go on through me.'

The idea still displeased her. The muscles tightened along her jaw, and it was in a hard unfriendly voice that at length she said, 'That young solicitor thinks I should tell you who your father was.'

I stood up at once, unable to stay calm. Although I had come to find out, I now didn't want to. I wanted to escape. To leave the room. Not to hear. I felt nervous in a way I hadn't done for years, and my mouth was sticky and dry.

'Don't you want to know?' she demanded.

'No.'

'Are you afraid?' She was scornful. Sneering.

I simply stood there, not answering, wanting to know and not wanting, afraid and not afraid: in an absolute muddle.

'I have hated your father since before you were born,' she said bitterly. 'I can hardly bear even now to look at you, because you're like him . . . like he was at your age. Thin . . . and physical . . . and with the same eyes.'

I swallowed, and waited, and felt numb.

'I loved him,' she said, spitting the words out as if they themselves offended her. 'I doted on him. He was thirty and I was forty-four. I'd been a widow for five years... I was lonely. Then he came. He lived with me... and we were going to marry. I adored him. I was stupid.'

She stopped. There really was no need to go on. I knew all the rest. All the hatred she had felt for me all those years was finally explained. So simply explained... and understood... and forgiven. Against all expectations what I suddenly felt for my grandmother was pity.

I took a deep breath. I said, 'Is he still alive?'

'I don't know. I haven't spoken to him or heard of him since.'

'And what... was his name?'

She stared at me straightly, nothing in her own persistent hatred being changed a scrap. 'I'm not going to tell you. I don't want you seeking him out. He ruined my life. He bedded my seventeen-year-old daughter under my own roof and he was after my money. That's the sort of man your father was. The only favour I'll do you is not to tell you his name. So be satisfied.'

I nodded. I made a vague gesture with one hand and said awkwardly, 'I'm sorry.'

Her scowl if anything deepened.

'Now find Amanda for me,' she said. 'That solicitor said you would, if I told you. So go away and do it.' She closed her eyes and looked immediately more ill,

866

more vulnerable. 'I don't like you,' she said. 'So go away.'

'Well?' Jeremy said, downstairs.

'She told me.'

'The milkman?'

'Near enough.' I relayed to him the gist of it, and his reaction was the same as mine.

'Poor old woman.'

'I could do with a drink,' I said.

CHAPTER THIRTEEN

In printing colour photographs one's aim was usually to produce a result that looked natural, and this was nowhere near as easy as it sounded. Apart from trifles like sharp focus and the best length and brightness of exposure, there was the matter of colour itself, which came out differently on each make of film, and on each type of photographic printing paper, and even on paper from two boxes of the same type from the same manufacturer: the reason for this being that the four ultra-thin layers of emulsion laid onto colour printing paper varied slightly from batch to batch. In the same way that it was almost impossible to dye two pieces of cloth in different dye baths and produce an identical result, so it was with light-sensitive emulsions.

To even this out and persuade all colours to look natural one used colour filters – pieces of coloured glass inserted between the bright light on the enlarger and the negative. Get the mixture of filters right, and in the finished print blue eyes came out blue and cherry lips, cherry.

In my enlarger, as on the majority worldwide, the three filters were the same colours as the colours of negatives: yellow, magenta, and cyan. Using all three filters together produced grey, so one only ever used two at once, and those two, as far as my sort of photographs were concerned, were always yellow and magenta. Used in delicate balance they could produce skin colours that were neither too yellow nor too pink for human faces, and it was to a natural-looking skin colour that one normally geared one's prints.

However, if one put a square of magenta-coloured glass on a square of yellow-coloured glass, and shone a light through both together, one saw the result as red.

Shine a light through yellow and cyan, and you got green. And through magenta and cyan . . . a pure royal blue.

I had been confused when Charlie had first shown me, because mixing coloured light produced dramatically different results from mixing coloured paints. Even the primary colours were different. Forget paint, Charlie had said. This is light. You can't make blue by mixing other coloured paints, but you can with light.

'Cyan?' I'd said. 'Like cyanide?'

'Cyanide turns you blue,' he said. 'Cyan is a Greek word for blue. Kyanos. Don't forget. Cyan is greeny blue, and not surprisingly you get it by mixing blue light with green.'

'You do?' I'd said doubtfully, and he had shown me

the six colours of light, and mixed them for me before my eyes until I got their relationship fixed in my head forever, until they were as basic in my brain as the shape of letters.

In the beginning were red, green, and blue . . .

I went into my darkroom on that fateful Sunday morning and adjusted the filters in the head of the enlarger so that the light which shone through the negatives would be that unheard-of combination for normal printing: full cyan and full magenta filtration, producing a deep clear blue.

I was going to print George's blank colour negatives onto black and white paper, which would certainly rid me of the blue of the oblongs: but all I might get instead were grey oblongs.

Black and white printing paper was sensitive only to blue light (which was why one could print in black and white in red safe-light). I thought that if I printed the black-looking negatives through heavy pure blue filtration I might get a greater contrast between the yellow dye image on the negative and the orange mask covering it. Make the image, in fact, emerge from its surroundings.

I had a feeling that whatever was hidden by the mask would not itself be sharply black and white anyway . . . because if it had been it would have been visible through and in spite of the blue. What I was looking for would in itself be some sort of grey.

I set out the trays of developer and stop bath and

fixer, and put all of the first thirty-six un-blotched negatives into a contact-printing frame. In this the negative
was held directly against the printing paper when the
light was passed through it, so that the print, when
finished, was exactly the same size as the negative. The
frame merely held all the negatives conveniently so
that all thirty-six could be printed at once onto one
eight-by-ten inch sheet of paper.

Getting the exposure time right was the biggest difficulty, chiefly because the heavy blue filtration meant
that the light getting to the negatives was far dimmer
than I was used to. I wasted about six shots in tests,
getting useless results from grey to black, all the little
oblongs still stubbornly looking as if there was nothing
on them to see, whatever I did.

Finally in irritation I cut down the exposure time to
far below what it was reasonable to think right, and
came up with a print that was almost entirely white. I
stood in the dim red light watching the white sheet lie
in the developer with practically nothing happening
except that the frame numbers of the negatives very
palely appeared, followed by faint lines showing where
the edges of the negatives had been.

Sighing with frustration I left it in the developer
until nothing else emerged and then, feeling depressed,
dipped it in the stop bath and then fixed it and washed
it, and switched on the bright lights.

Five of the oblongs were not entirely white. Five of

the little oblongs, scattered at random through the thirty-six, bore very pale grey geometric shapes.

I had found them.

I could feel myself smiling with ridiculous joy. George had left a puzzle, and I had almost solved it. If I was going to take his place, it was right that I should.

If I . . . My God, I thought. Where did thoughts come from? I had no intention of taking his place. No conscious intention. That thought had come straight from the subconscious, unbidden, unwanted.

I shivered slightly and felt vaguely alarmed, and without any smile at all wrote down the frame numbers of the five grey-patterned prints. Then I wandered round the house for a while doing mindless jobs like tidying the bedroom and shaking out the bean bags and stacking a few things in the dishwasher. Made a cup of coffee and sat down in the kitchen to drink it. Considered walking down to the village to fetch a Sunday paper, and instead went compulsively back to the darkroom.

It made all the difference knowing which negatives to look at, and roughly what to look for.

I took the first one numerically, which happened to be number seven, and enlarged it to the full size of the ten-by-eight inch paper. A couple more bad guesses at exposure time left me with unclear dark grey prints, but in the end I came up with one which developed into mid-grey on white; and I took it out of the developer as soon as it had reached its peak of contrast, and stopped it and fixed it and washed it, and carried it out to the daylight in the kitchen.

Although the print was still wet one could see exactly what it was. One could read it without difficulty. A typewritten letter starting 'Dear Mr Morton' and ending 'Yours sincerely, George Millace.'

A letter typed onto white paper with an old greyish ribbon, so that the typing itself looked pale grey. Pale grey, but distinct.

The letter said:

Dear Mr Morton,

I am sure you will be interested in the enclosed two photographs. As you will see, the first one is a picture of your horse Amber Globe running poorly in your colours in the two-thirty race at Southwell on Monday, May 12th.

As you will also see, the second picture is of your horse Amber Globe winning the four o'clock race at Fontwell on Wednesday, August 27th.

If you look closely at the photographs you will see that they are not of the same horse. Alike, but not identical.

I am sure that the Jockey Club would be interested in this difference. I will ring you shortly, however, with an alternative suggestion.

Yours sincerely,
George Millace.

I read it through about six times, not because I didn't take it in the first time, but simply as an interval for assimilation and thought.

There were some practical observations to be made, which were that the letter bore no heading and no date and no handwritten signature. There was an assumption to be drawn that the other four pale grey geometric patterns would also turn out to be letters; and that what I had found was George's idiosyncratic filing system.

Beyond those flat thoughts lay a sort of chaos: a feeling of looking into a pit. If I enlarged and read the other letters I could find that I knew things which would make 'waiting to see what happens' impossible. I might feel, as in the case of the grey-smudge lovers I already did feel, that doing nothing was weak and wrong. If I learned all George's secrets I would have to accept the moral burden of deciding what to do about them . . . and of doing it.

To postpone the decision I went upstairs to the sitting room and looked through the form books to find out in which year Amber Globe had won at Fontwell on August 12th; and it had been four years previously.

I looked up Amber Globe's career from start to finish, and what it amounted to on average was three or four poorer showings followed by an easy win at high odds, this pattern being repeated twice a season for four years. Amber Globe's last win had been the one on August 12th, and from then on he had run in no more races at all.

A supplementary search showed that the trainer of Amber Globe did not appear in the list of trainers for any subsequent years, and had probably gone out of business. There was no way of checking from those particular books whether 'Dear Mr Morton' had subsequently owned or run any more horses, although such facts would be stored in central official racing records.

Dear Mr Morton and his trainer had been running two horses under the name of Amber Globe, switching in the good one for the big gambles, letting the poor one lengthen the odds. I wondered if George had noticed the pattern and gone deliberately to take his photographs; or whether he had taken the photographs merely in the course of work, and then had noticed the difference in the horses. There was no way of knowing or even guessing, as I hadn't found the two photographs in question.

I looked out of the window at the Downs for a while, and wandered round a bit fingering things and doing nothing much, waiting for the arrival of a comfortable certainty that knowledge did not involve responsibility.

I waited in vain. I knew that it did. The knowledge was downstairs, and I would have to acquire it. I had come too far to want to stop.

Unsettled, fearful, but with a feeling of inevitability, I went down to the darkroom and printed the other four negatives one by one, and read the resulting letters in the kitchen.

With all five in the drier I sat for ages staring into space, thinking disjointed thoughts.

George had been busy.

The sly malice of George's mind spoke out as clearly as if I could hear his voice.

George's ominous letters must have induced fear and despondency in colossal proportions.

The second of them said:

Dear Bonnington Ford,

I am sure you will be interested in the enclosed series of photographs, which, as you will see, are a record of your entertaining in your training stables on Sunday afternoons a person who has been 'warned off'. I don't suppose I need to remind you that the racing authorities would object strongly to this continuous association, even to the extent of reviewing your licence to train.

I could of course send copies of these photographs to the Jockey Club. I will ring you shortly, however, with an alternative suggestion.

Yours sincerely,
George Millace.

Bonnington Ford was a third-rate trainer who by general consensus was as honest and trustworthy as a pickpocket at Aintree, and he trained in a hollow in the Downs at a spot where any passing motorist could glance down into his yard. It would have been no trouble at all for George Millace, if he had wanted to, to sit in his car at that spot and take telephoto pictures at his leisure.

Again I hadn't found the photographs in question, so there was nothing I could do about that particular letter, even if I had wanted to. George hadn't even mentioned the name of the disqualified person. I was let off any worrying choice.

The last three letters were a different matter, one in which the dilemma sharply raised its head: where did duty lie, and from how much could one opt out.

Of these three letters the first said:

Dear Elgin Yaxley,

I am sure you will be interested in the enclosed photograph. As you will see, it clearly contradicts a statement you recently made on oath at a certain trial.

I am sure that the Jockey Club would be interested to see it, and also the police, the judge, and the insurance company. I could send all of them copies simultaneously.

I will ring you shortly, however, with an alternative suggestion.

Yours sincerely,
George Millace.

The one next to it on the film roll would have driven the nails right in. It said:

Dear Elgin Yaxley,

I am happily able to tell you that since I wrote to you yesterday there have been further developments.

Yesterday I also visited the farmer upon whose farm you boarded your unfortunate steeplechasers, and I showed him in confidence a copy of the photograph, which I sent to you. I suggested that there might be a full further enquiry, during which his own share in the tragedy might be investigated.

He felt able to respond to my promise of silence with the pleasing information that your five good horses were not after all dead. The five horses which died had been bought especially and cheaply by him (your farmer friend) from a local auction, and it was these which were shot by Terence O'Tree at the appointed time and place. Terence O'Tree was not told of the substitution.

Your farmer friend also confirmed that when the veterinary surgeon had given your good horses their anti-tetanus jabs and had left after seeing them in good health, you yourself arrived at the farm in a horsebox to supervise their removal.

Your friend understood you would be shipping them out to the Far East, where you already had a buyer.

I enclose a photograph of his signed statement to this effect.

I will ring you shortly with a suggestion.

> Yours sincerely,
> George Millace.

The last of the five prints was different from the others in that its letter was handwritten, not typed: but as it had been apparently written in pencil, it was still of the same pale grey. It said:

Dear Elgin Yaxley,

    I bought the five horses that T. O'Tree shot. You fetched your own horses away in a horsebox, to export them to the East. I am satisfied with what you paid me for this service.

> Yours faithfully,
> David Parker.

I thought of Elgin Yaxley as I had seen him the previous day at Ascot, smirking complacently and believing himself safe.

I thought of right and wrong, and justice. Thought of Elgin Yaxley as the victim of George Millace, and of the insurance company as the victim of Elgin Yaxley. Thought of Terence O'Tree who had gone to jail, and David Parker, who hadn't.

I couldn't decide what to do.

*

After a while I got up stiffly and went back to the darkroom. I put all of the magenta-splashed set of negatives into the contact-printing frame, and made a nearly white print: and this time there were not five little oblongs with grey blocks on, but fifteen.

With a hollow feeling of horror I switched off all the lights, locked the doors, and walked up the road to my briefing with Harold.

'Pay attention,' Harold said sharply.

'Er . . . yes.'

'What's the matter?'

'Nothing.'

'I'm talking about Coral Key at Kempton on Wednesday, and you're not listening.'

I dragged my attention back to the matter in hand.

'Coral Key,' I said. 'For Victor Briggs.'

'That's right.'

'Has he said anything . . . about yesterday?'

Harold shook his head. 'We had a drink after the race, but if Victor doesn't want to talk you can't get a word out of him, and all he uttered were grunts. But until he tells me you're off his horses you're still on them.'

He gave me a glass and a can of coke, and poured a large whisky for himself.

'I haven't much for you this week,' he said. 'Nothing Monday or Tuesday. Pebble was going to run at

Leicester but there's some heat in his leg... There's just Coral Key on Wednesday, Diamond Buyer and the mare Friday, and two on Saturday, as long as it doesn't rain. Have you any outside rides lined up?'

'A novice 'chaser at Kempton on Thursday.'

'I hope it can bloody jump.'

I went back to the quiet cottage and made prints from the fifteen magenta-splashed negatives, getting plain white and grey results as before, as the blotchy shapes were filtered out along with the blue.

To my relief they were not fifteen threatening letters: only the first two of them finished with the promise of alternative suggestions.

I had expected one on the subject of the lovers, and it was there. It was the second one which left me breathless and weakly laughing in the kitchen: and certainly it put me in a better frame of mind for any revelations to come.

The last thirteen prints, however, turned out to be George's own notes of where and when he had taken his incriminating pictures, and on what film, and at which exposures, and on what dates he had sent the frightening letters. I guessed he had kept his records in this form because it had turned out to be easy for him, and had seemed safer than leaving such damaging material lying legibly around on paper.

As a back-up to the photographs and letters they

were fascinating: but they all failed to say what the 'alternative suggestions' had been. There was no record of what monies George had extorted, nor of any bank, safe deposit, or hiding place where he could have stashed the proceeds. Even to himself, George on this subject had been reticent.

I went late to bed and couldn't sleep, and in the morning made some telephone calls.

One to the editor of *Horse and Hound*, whom I knew, begging him to include Amanda's picture in that week's issue, emphasizing that time was short. He said dubiously that he would print it if I got it to his office that morning, but after that it would be too late.

'I'll be there,' I said. 'Two columns wide, photograph seven centimetres deep, with some wording top and bottom. Say eleven centimetres altogether. On a nice right-hand page near the front where no one can miss it.'

'Philip!' he protested, but then sighed audibly, and I knew he would do it. 'That camera of yours... if you've got any racing pics I might use, bring them along. I'll have a look anyway. No promises, mind, but a look. It's people I want, not horses. Portraits. Got any?'

'Well... yes.'

'Good. Soon as possible, then. See you.'

I telephoned Marie Millace for Lord White's home number, and then I telephoned Old Driven Snow at his home in the Cotswolds.

'You want to see me?' he said. 'What about?'

'About George Millace, sir.'

'Photographer? Died recently?'

'Yes, sir. His wife is a friend of Lady White.'

'Yes, yes,' he said, impatiently. 'I could see you at Kempton, if you like.'

I asked if I could call on him at his home instead, and although he wasn't overpoweringly keen he agreed to my taking half an hour of his time at five o'clock the next day. With slightly sweating palms I replaced the receiver and said 'Phew' and thought that all I had to do to back out was to ring him again and cancel.

After that I telephoned to Samantha, which was a great deal easier, and asked if I could take her and Clare out to dinner. Her warm voice sounded pleased.

'Tonight?' she said.

'Yes.'

'I can't go. But I'm sure Clare can. She'd like it.'

'Would she?'

'Yes, you silly man. What time?'

I said I would pick her up at about eight, and Samantha said fine and how was the search for Amanda going, and I found myself talking to her as if I'd known her all my life. As indeed, in a way, I had.

I drove to London to the *Horse and Hound* offices and fixed with the editor to print Amanda's picture captioned *'Where is this stable? Ten pounds reward for the first person – and particularly for the first child – who can telephone Philip Nore to tell him.'*

'Child?' said the editor, raising his eyebrows and adding my telephone number. 'Do they read this paper?'

'Their mothers do.'

'Subtle stuff.'

He said, looking through the folder I'd brought of racing faces, that they were starting a series on racing personalities, and he wanted new pictures that hadn't already appeared all over the place, and he could use some of mine, if I liked.

'Er . . . yes.'

'Usual rates,' he said casually, and I said fine: and only after a pause did I ask him what the usual rates were. Even to ask, it seemed to me, was a step nearer to caring as much for the income as for the photographs themselves. Usual rates were a commitment. Usual rates meant joining the club. I found it disturbing. I accepted them, all the same.

Samantha was out when I went to fetch Clare.

'Come in for a drink first,' Clare said, opening the door wide. 'It's such a lousy evening.'

I stepped in out of the wind and cold rain of late November and we went not downstairs to the kitchen but into the long, gently lit ground-floor sitting room, which stretched from the front to the back of the house. I looked around, seeing its comfort, but feeling no familiarity.

'Do you remember this room?' Clare said.

I shook my head.

'Where's the bathroom?' she said.

I answered immediately, 'Up the stairs, turn right, blue ba . . .'

She laughed. 'Straight from the subconscious.'

'It's so odd.'

There was a television set in one corner with a programme of talking heads, and Clare walked over and switched it off.

'Don't, if you're in the middle of watching,' I said.

'It was just another anti-drug lecture. All these pontificating so-called experts. How about that drink? What would you like? There is some wine . . .' She held up a bottle of white Burgundy, opened, so we settled on that.

'Some smug little presenter was saying,' she said, pouring into the glasses, 'that one in five women take tranquillizers, but only one in ten men. Implying that poor little women are so much less able to deal with life, the feeble little dears.' She handed me a glass. 'Makes you laugh.'

'Does it?'

She grinned. 'I suppose it never occurs to the doctors who write out the prescriptions that the poor feeble little women sprinkle those tranquillizers all over their husbands' dinner when he comes home from work.'

I laughed.

'They do,' she said. 'The ones with great hulking

bastards who knock them about, and the ones who don't like too much sex ... they mix the nice tasteless powder into the brute's meat and two veg, and lead a quiet life.'

'It's a great theory.'

'Fact,' she said.

We sat in a couple of pale velvet armchairs sipping the cool wine, she, in a scarlet silk shirt and black trousers, making a bright statement against the soft colouring of the room. A girl given to positive statements. A girl of decision and certainty and mental energy. Not at all like the gentle undemanding girls I occasionally took home.

'I saw you racing on Saturday,' she said. 'On television.'

'I didn't think you were interested.'

'Of course I am, since I saw your photos.' She drank a mouthful. 'You do take some frightful risks.'

'Not always like Saturday.' She asked why not, and rather to my surprise, I told her.

'But my goodness,' she said indignantly, 'that's not fair.'

'Life's not fair. Too bad.'

'What a gloomy philosophy.'

'Not really. Take what comes, but hope for the best.'

She shook her head. 'Go out looking for the best.' She drank and said, 'What happens if you're really smashed up by one of those falls?'

'You curse.'

'No, you fool. To your life, I mean.'

'Mend as fast as possible and get back in the saddle. While you're out of it, some other jockey is pinching your rides.'

'Charming,' she said. 'And what if it's too bad to mend?'

'You've got a problem. No rides, no income. You start looking at "sits vac".'

'And what happens if you're killed?'

'Nothing much,' I said.

'You don't take it seriously,' she complained.

'Of course not.'

She studied my face. 'I'm not used to people who casually risk their lives most days of the week.'

I smiled at her. 'The risk is less than you'd think. But if you're really unlucky, there's always the Injured Jockeys Fund.'

'What's that?'

'The racing industry's private charity. It looks after the widows and orphans of dead jockeys and gives succour to badly damaged live ones, and makes sure no one pops off in old age for want of a lump of coal.'

'Can't be bad.'

We went out a little later and ate in a small restaurant determinedly decorated as a French peasant kitchen with scrubbed board tables, rushes on the floor, and dripping candles stuck in wine bottles. The food turned out to be as bogus as the surroundings, never having seen the light of anyone's *pot au feu*. Clare however seemed not to mind and we ate microwaved veal in a blanket white sauce, trying not to remember the blanquettes in France, where she too had been frequently, though for holidays, not racing.

'You race in France?'

'After Christmas, if it freezes here, there's always the chance of some rides at Cagnes sur Mer . . . down on the south coast.'

'It sounds marvellous.'

'It's still winter. And still work. But yes, not bad.'

She returned to the subject of photographs, and said she would like to come down to Lambourn again to go through the Jockey's Life file.

'Don't worry if you want to change your mind,' I said.

'Of course I don't.' She looked at me in seeming alarm. 'You haven't sold any to anyone else, have you? You did say you wouldn't.'

'Not those.'

'What, then?'

I told her about *Horse and Hound*, and about Lance Kinship, and how odd I found it that all of a sudden people seemed to be wanting to buy my work.

'I would think,' she said judiciously, 'that the word has gone round.' She finished her veal and sat back, her face serious with thought. 'What you need is an agent.'

I explained about having to find one for Marie Millace anyway, but she brushed that aside.

'Not *any* agent,' she said. 'I mean me.'

She looked at my stunned expression and smiled. 'Well?' she said. 'What does any agent do? He knows the markets and sells the goods. Your goods will sell . . . obviously. So I'll learn pretty damn quick what the markets are, that I don't know already. The sports side of it, I mean. And what if I got you commissions for illustrations for other books . . . on any subject . . . would you do them?'

'Yes, but . . .'

'No buts,' she said. 'There's no point in taking super pics if no one sees them.'

'But there are thousands of photographers.'

'Why are you so defeatist?' she said. 'There's always room for one more.'

The candlelight shone on the intent expression and lay in apricot shadows under cheekbone and chin. Her grey eyes looked steadily at a future I still shied away from. I wondered what she'd say if I said I wanted to kiss her, when her thoughts were clearly more practical.

'I could try,' she said persuasively. 'I'd like to try. Will you let me? If I'm no good, I'll admit it.'

She'll bully you into things, Samantha had said.

Take what comes, and hope for the best.

I stuck to my old philosophy and said, 'All right', and she said 'Great' as if she meant it: and later, when I delivered her to her doorstep and kissed her, she didn't object to that either.

CHAPTER FOURTEEN

Four times on Tuesday morning I lifted the telephone to cancel my appointment with Lord White. Once I got as far as hearing the bell ring at the other end.

Four times I put the receiver down and decided I would have to go. I would have liked to have gone with more certainty that I was doing right; but anyway, I went.

Lord White's house in Gloucestershire turned out to be a weathered stone pile with more grandeur than gardeners. Noble windows raised their eyebrows above drifts of unswept leaves. A stubble of fawn stalks indicated lawn. A mat of dead weeds glued the gravel together. I rang the front doorbell and wondered about the economics of barony.

The third Baron White received me in a small sitting room which gave onto a view of straggly rose bushes and an unclipped hedge. Inside, everything was of venerable antiquity, dusted and gleaming. Holes in the chintz chair covers had been patched. Less money than was needed, I diagnosed briefly, but still enough to keep at bay a three-bedroomed semi.

Lord White shook hands and offered me a chair in a mixture of puzzlement and civility, waiting for me to say why I had come: and although I'd spent the whole journey inventing possible openings, I found it an agony to begin.

'Sir . . .' I said. 'I'm sorry . . . very sorry, sir . . . but I'm afraid what I've come about may be a great shock to you.'

He frowned slightly. 'About George Millace?' he said. 'You said it was something about George Millace.'

'Yes . . . about some photographs he took.'

I stopped. Too late, I wished fervently that I hadn't come. I should after all have adhered to the lifetime habit of non-involvement, of wait and see. I should never have set out to use George's wicked arsenal. But I had. I was there. I had made the decision and acted on it. What I was there for . . . had to be done.

My errand was to give pain. Purposely to hurt. To go against all the instincts of compassion I owed to Samantha and Charlie and Margaret and Bill. To serve as a wrecker, with a brutal celluloid axe.

'Get on with it, Nore,' Lord White said comfortably, unsuspecting.

With foreboding I opened the large envelope I carried. I pulled out the first of the three pictures of the lovers, and put it into his outstretched hand: and for all that I thought he was behaving foolishly over Dana den Relgan, I felt deeply sorry for him.

His first reaction was of extreme anger. How dared I, he said, standing up and quivering, how dared I bring him anything so filthy and *disgusting*.

With the greatest difficulty, I thought; but he wouldn't have appreciated it. I took the second and third photographs out of the envelope and rested them picture-side-down on the arm of my chair.

'As you will see,' I said, and my voice was hoarse, 'the others are if anything worse.'

I reckoned it took him a lot of courage to pick up the other two pictures. He looked at them in desperate silence, and slowly sank down again in his chair.

His face told of his anguish. Of his disbelief. Of his horror.

The man making love to Dana was Ivor den Relgan.

'They say,' Lord White said, 'that they can fake pictures of anything.' His voice shook. 'Cameras do lie.'

'Not this one,' I said regretfully.

'It can't be true.'

I took from the envelope a print of the letter George Millace had written, and gave it to him. He had difficulty in bringing himself to read it, so physically shaking was his distress.

The letter, which I knew by heart, read:

Dear Ivor den Relgan,

I am sure you will be interested in the enclosed photographs, which I was happily able to take a few days ago in St Tropez.

As you will see, they show you in a compromising position with the young lady who is known as your daughter. (It is surely unwise to do this sort of thing on hotel balconies without making sure that one cannot be seen by telephoto lenses?)

There seem to be two possibilities here.

One. Dana den Relgan IS your daughter, in which case this is incest.

Two. Dana den Relgan is NOT your daughter, in which case why are you pretending she is? Can it have anything to do with the ensnaring of a certain member of the Jockey Club? Are you hoping for entry to the Club, and other favours?

I could of course send these photographs to the Lord in question. I will ring you shortly, however, with an alternative suggestion.

Yours sincerely,
George Millace.

Lord White became much older before my eyes, the glow that loving had given him shrinking greyly back into deepening wrinkles. I looked away. Looked at my hands, my feet, the spindly rose bushes outside. Anywhere but at that devastated man.

After a very long time he said, 'Where did you get these?'

'George Millace's son gave me a box with some things of his father's in, after his father died. These photos were in it.'

He suffered through another silence, and said, 'Why did you bring them to me? For the sake of causing me ... mortification?'

I swallowed and said as flatly as possible, 'You won't really have noticed, sir, but people are worried about how much power has been given recently to Ivor den Relgan.'

He shuddered slightly at the name but raised the blue eyes to give me a long unfriendly inspection.

'And you have taken it upon yourself to try to stop it?'

'Sir ... yes.'

He looked grim, and as if seeking refuge in anger he said authoritatively, 'It's none of your business, Nore.'

I didn't answer at once. I'd had enough trouble in persuading myself that it *was* my business to last a lifetime. But in the end, diffidently, I said, 'Sir, if you are certain in your own mind that Ivor den Relgan's sudden rise to unheard-of power is nothing whatever to do with your affection for Dana den Relgan, then I do most abjectly beg your pardon.'

He merely stared.

I tried again. 'If you truly believe that racing would

benefit by Ivor den Relgan appointing paid Stewards, I apologize.'

'Please leave,' he said rigidly.

'Yes, sir.'

I stood up and walked over to the door, but when I reached it I heard his voice from behind me.

'Wait. Nore . . . I must think.'

I turned, hovering. 'Sir,' I said, 'you're so respected . . . and liked . . . by everyone. It's been no fun to watch what's been happening.'

'Will you please come back and sit down?' His voice was still stern, still full of accusation and judgement. Still full of defence.

I returned to the armchair, and he went and stood by the window with his back to me, looking out at the dead roses.

His thoughts took time. So would mine have done, in the same situation. The result of them was a deep change in his voice in both pitch and content, for when he finally spoke again he sounded not shattered nor furious, but normal. He spoke, however, without turning round.

'How many people,' he said, 'have seen these pictures?'

'I don't know how many George Millace showed them to,' I said. 'As for me, they've been seen only by one friend. He was with me when I found them. But he doesn't know the den Relgans. He doesn't often go racing.'

'So you didn't consult with anyone before you came here?'

'No, sir.'

Another long pause. I was good, anyway, at waiting. The house around us was very quiet: holding its breath, I thought fancifully, as I in a way, held mine.

'Do you intend,' he said quietly, 'to make jokes about this on the racecourse?'

'No.' I was horrified. 'I do not.'

'And would you . . .' he paused, but went on, 'would you expect any reward, in service . . . or cash . . . for this silence?'

I stood up as if he had actually hit me, not delivered his thrust from six paces with his back turned.

'I would not,' I said. 'I'm not George Millace. I think . . . I think I'll go now.' And go I did, out of the room, out of the house, out of his weedy domain, impelled by a severe hurt to the vanity.

On Wednesday nothing much happened; less, in fact, than expected, as I was met when I went to ride out first lot with the news that Coral Key wouldn't be running that day at Kempton after all.

'Bloody animal got cast in its box during the night,' Harold said. 'I woke and heard him banging. God knows how long he'd been down; he was halfway exhausted. It won't please Victor.'

With the riding fee down the drain it wasn't worthwhile spending money on petrol to go spectating at the races, so I stayed at home and did Lance Kinship's reprints.

Thursday I set off to Kempton with only one ride, thinking it was a very thin week on the earning front; but almost as soon as I'd stepped through the gate I was grabbed by a fierce little man who said his guv'nor was looking for me, and if I wanted his spare rides I should shift my arse.

I shifted, and got the rides just before the trainer in question thought I wouldn't get there in time and gave them to someone else.

'Very annoying,' he said, puffing as if breathless, though I gathered he had been standing still waiting for me for fifteen minutes. 'My fellow said yesterday he'd no ill effects from a fall he'd had. And then this morning, cool as you please, he rings to say he's got 'flu.'

'Well . . . er . . .' I swallowed a laugh. 'I don't suppose he can help it.'

'Damned inconsiderate.'

His horse turned out to have better lungs than their master, but were otherwise no great shakes. I got one of them round into third place in a field of six, and came down on the other two fences from home; a bit of a crash but nothing broken in either him or me.

The third horse, the one I'd gone originally to ride, wasn't much better: a clumsy underschooled baby of a horse with guts about equal to his skill. I took him round carefully in the novice 'chase to try to teach him his job, and got no thanks from the trainer who said I hadn't gone fast enough to keep warm.

'There were six or seven behind us,' I said mildly.

'And six or seven in front.'

I nodded. 'He needs time.' And patience, and weeks and months of jumping practice. He probably wouldn't get either, and I probably wouldn't be offered the mount again. The trainer would go for speed regardless, and the horse would crash at the open ditch, and it would serve the trainer right. Pity the poor horse.

The relief of the afternoon, as far as I was concerned, was the absence of Lord White.

The surprise of the afternoon was the presence of Clare.

She was waiting outside the weighing room when I'd changed back into street clothes and was leaving for home.

'Hullo,' she said.

'Clare!'

'Just thought I'd come and take a look at the real thing.' Her eyes smiled. 'Is today typical?'

I looked at the grey windy sky and the thin Thursday crowd, and thought of my three nondescript races.

'Pretty much,' I said. 'How did you get here?'

'By race-train. Very educational. And I've been walking around all afternoon all a-goggle. I never knew people actually *ate* jellied eels.'

I laughed. 'I've never looked one in the face. Er . . .

what would you like? A drink? A cup of tea? A trip to Lambourn?'

She thought it over briefly. 'Lambourn,' she said. 'I can get a train back from there, can't I?'

I drove her to Berkshire with an unaccustomed feeling of contentment. It felt right to have her sitting there in the car. Natural. Probably, I thought, rationalizing, because she was Samantha's daughter.

The cottage was dark and cold, but soon warmed. I went round switching on lights and heat and the kettle for tea; and the telephone rang. I answered it in the kitchen, which was where it happened to be plugged in, and had my ear-drum half-shattered by a piercing voice which shrieked, 'Am I first?'

'Um,' I said, wincing and holding the receiver away from my ear. 'Are you first what?'

'First!' A very young voice. A child. Female. 'I've been ringing every five minutes for *hours*. Honestly. So am I first? Do say I'm first.'

Realization dawned. 'Yes,' I said. 'You're the very first. Have you been reading *Horse and Hound*? It isn't published until tomorrow...'

'It gets to my auntie's bookshop on Thursdays.' She sounded as if anyone in their right mind would know things like that. 'I collect it for Mummy on my way home from school. And she saw the picture, and told me to ring you. So can I have the ten pounds? Can I really?'

'If you know where the stable is, yes, of course.'

'Mummy knows. She'll tell you. You'd better talk to her now, but you won't forget, will you?'

'I won't,' I said.

There were some background voices and clicks of the receiver at the far end, and then a woman's voice, pleasant and far less excited.

'Are you the Philip Nore who rides in National Hunt races?'

'Yes,' I said.

It seemed to be enough of a reference, because she said without reservation, 'I do know where that stable is, but I'm afraid you'll be disappointed, because it isn't used for horses any longer. Jane, my daughter, is afraid you won't send her the ten pounds when you know that, but I expect you will.'

'I expect so,' I agreed, smiling. 'Where is it?'

'Not far from here. That's Horley, in Surrey. Near Gatwick Airport. The stable's about half a mile from our house. It's still called Zephyr Farm Stables, but the riding school has been closed for years and years.'

I sighed. 'And the people who kept it?'

'No idea,' she said. 'I suppose they sold it. Anyway, it's been adapted into living quarters. Do you want the actual address?'

'I guess so,' I said, 'and yours, too, please.'

She read them out to me and I wrote them down, and then I said, 'Do you happen to know the name of the people living there now?'

'Huh,' she said scornfully. 'They're a real pest. You

won't get far with them, whatever it is you want, I'm afraid. They've got the place practically fortified to ward off furious parents.'

'To . . . what?' I said, mystified.

'Parents trying to persuade their children to come home. It's one of those commune things. Religious brainwashing, something like that. They call themselves Colleagues of Supreme Grace. All nonsense. Pernicious nonsense.'

I felt breathless.

'I'll send Jane the money,' I said. 'And thanks very much.'

'What is it?' Clare said, as I slowly replaced the receiver.

'The first real lead to Amanda.'

I explained about the *Horse and Hound* advertisement, and about the tenants of Pine Woods Lodge.

Clare shook her head. 'If these Supreme Grace people know where Amanda is, they won't tell you. You must have heard of them, haven't you? Or others like them? They're all gentle and smiling on the surface, and like steel rat-traps underneath. They lure people my age with friendliness and sweet songs and hook them into Believing, and once they're in the poor slobs never get out. They're in love with their prison. Their parents hardly stand a chance.'

'I've heard of something like it. But I've never seen the point.'

'Money,' Clare said crisply. 'All the darling little

Colleagues go out with saintly faces and collecting boxes, and rake in the lolly.'

'To live on?'

'Sure, to live on. And further the cause, or in other words, to line the pockets of our great leader.'

I made the tea and we sat by the table to drink it.

Amanda in a stable-yard at Horley; Caroline twenty miles away at Pine Woods Lodge. Colleagues of Supreme Grace at Pine Woods Lodge, Colleagues ditto at Horley. Too close a connection to be a coincidence. Even if I never found out precisely what, there had been a rational sequence of events.

'She's probably not still there,' I said.

'But you'll go looking?'

I nodded. 'Tomorrow, I think, after racing.'

When we'd finished the tea Clare said she wanted to see the Jockey's Life folder again, so we took it upstairs, and I showed some of the pictures blown up on the wall to amuse her, and we talked of her life and mine and of nothing in particular; and later in the evening we went to the good pub at Ashbury for a steak.

'A great day,' Clare said, smiling over the coffee. 'Where's the train?'

'Swindon. I'll drive you there ... or you could stay.'

She regarded me levelly. 'Is that the sort of invitation I think it is?'

'I wouldn't be surprised.'

She looked down and fiddled with her coffee spoon,

paying it a lot of attention. I watched the bent, dark, thinking head and knew that if it took her so long to answer, she would go.

'There's a fast train at ten thirty,' I said. 'You could catch it comfortably. Just over an hour to Paddington.'

'Philip . . .'

'It's all right,' I said easily. 'If one never asks, one never gets.' I paid the bill. 'Come on.'

She was distinctly quiet on the six-mile drive to the railway station, and she didn't share her thoughts. Not until I'd bought her a ticket (against her objections) and was waiting with her up on the platform did she give any indication of what was in her mind, and then only obliquely.

'There's a Board meeting in the office tomorrow,' she said. 'It will be the first I've been to. They made me a Director a month ago, at the last one.'

I was most impressed, and said so. It couldn't be often that publishing houses put girls of twenty-two on the Board. I understood, also, why she wouldn't stay. Why she might never stay. The regret I felt shocked me with its sudden intensity, because my invitation to her hadn't been a desperate plea but only a suggestion for a passing pleasure. I had meant it as a small thing, not a lifetime commitment. My sense of loss, on that railway platform, seemed out of all proportion.

The train came in and she climbed aboard, pausing with the door open to exchange kisses. Brief unpassionate kisses, no advance from Monday on the doorstep.

See you soon, she said, and I said yes. About contracts, she said. A lot to discuss.

'Come on Sunday,' I said.

'Let you know. Goodbye.'

'Goodbye.'

The impatient train ground away, accelerating last, and I drove home to the empty cottage with a most unaccustomed feeling of loneliness.

Newbury races, Friday, late November.

Lord White was there, standing under the expanse of glass roof outside the weighing room, talking earnestly to two fellow Stewards. He looked the same as always, grey-white hair mostly hidden by trilby, brown covert coat over dark grey suit, air of benign good sense. Hard to imagine him high as a kite on love. Impossible, if one hadn't seen it.

As always in those areas I had to pass near him to reach the weighing-room door. He steadfastly continued his conversation with the Stewards, and only through the barest flicker of his eyes in my direction did he show he knew I was there.

If he didn't want to talk to me, I didn't mind. Less embarrassing all round.

Inside the weighing room stood Harold, expansively telling a crony about a good place for cut-price new tyres. Hardly pausing for breath he told me he'd wait for my saddle if I'd do him a favour and change and weigh quickly, and when I went back to him in colours he was still on about cross-ply and radials. The crony took the opportunity to depart, and Harold, taking my saddle and weight cloth, said with mischievous amusement, 'Did you hear Ghengis Khan got the boot?'

I paid him sharp attention.

'Are you sure?' I said.

Harold nodded. 'Old Lanky . . .' he pointed to the disappearing crony, '. . . . was telling me just before you arrived. He says they held an emergency-type meeting of the Jockey Club this morning in London. He was at it. Lord White asked them to cancel plans for a committee chaired by Ivor den Relgan, and as it was old Driven Snow's idea in the first place, they all agreed.'

'It's something, anyway,' I said.

'Something?' Harold swung towards exasperation. 'Is that all you think? It's the best about-turn since the Armada.'

He stalked off with my saddle, muttering and shaking his head, and leaving me, had he but known, in a state of extreme relief. Whatever else my visit to Lord White had done, it had achieved its primary object. At least, I thought gratefully, I hadn't caused so much havoc in a man I liked for nothing at all.

I rode a novice hurdler which finished second, pleasing the owner mightily and Harold not much, and later a two-mile 'chase on a sensitive mare who had no

real heart for the job and had to be nursed. Getting her
round at all was the best to be hoped for, a successful
conclusion greeted by Harold with a grunt. As we had
also finished fourth I took it for a grunt of approval,
but one could never be sure.

When I was changing back into street clothes a racecourse official stepped into the big bustling jockey's
room and shouted down the length of it, 'Nore, you're
wanted.'

I finished dressing and went out into the weighing
room, and found that the person who was waiting was
Lord White.

'I want to talk to you,' he said. 'Come over here into
the Steward's room . . . and close the door, will you?'

I followed him into the room off the weighing room
used by the Stewards for on-the-spot enquiries, and, as
he asked, shut the door. He stood behind one of the
chairs which surrounded the big table, grasping its back
with both hands as if it gave him a shield, a barrier,
the rampart of a citadel.

'I regret,' he said formally, 'what I imputed to you
on Tuesday.'

'It's all right, sir.'

'I was upset . . . but it was indefensible.'

'I do understand, sir.'

'What do you understand?'

'Well . . . that when someone hurts you, you want to
kick them.'

He half smiled. 'Poetically put, if I may say so.'

'Is that all, sir?'

'No, it isn't.' He paused, pondering. 'I suppose you've heard that the committee is cancelled?'

I nodded.

He drew a sober breath. 'I want to request den Relgan's resignation from the Jockey Club. The better to persuade him, I am of a mind to show him those photographs, which of course he has seen already. I think, however, that I need your permission to do so, and that is what I am asking.'

Talk about leverage, I thought; and I said, 'I've no objection. Please do what you like with them.'

'Are they . . . the only copies?'

'Yes,' I said, which in fact they were. I didn't tell him I also had the negatives. He would have wanted me to destroy them, and my instincts were against it.

He let go of the chair back as if no longer needing it, and walked round me to the door. His face, as he opened it, bore the firm familiar blameless expression of pre-Dana days. The cruel cure, I thought, had been complete.

'I can't exactly thank you,' he said civilly, 'but I'm in your debt.' He gave me a slight nod and went out of the room: transaction accomplished, apology given, dignity intact. He would soon be busy persuading himself, I thought, that he hadn't felt what he'd felt, that his infatuation hadn't existed.

Slowly I followed, satisfied on many counts, on many

levels, but not knowing if he knew it. The profoundest gifts weren't always those explicitly given.

From Marie Millace I learned more.

She had come to Newbury to see Steve ride now that his collarbone had mended, though she confessed, as I steered her off for a cup of coffee, that watching one's son race over fences was an agony.

'All jockeys' wives say it's worse when their sons start,' I said. 'Daughters too, I dare say.'

We sat at a small table in one of the bars, surrounded by people in bulky overcoats which smelled of cold damp air and seemed to steam slightly in the warmth. Marie automatically stacked to one side the debris of cups and sandwich wrappers left by the last customers, and thoughtfully stirred her coffee.

'You're looking better,' I said.

She nodded. 'I feel it.'

She had been to a hairdresser, I saw, and had bought some more clothes. Still pale, with smudged grieving eyes. Still fragile, thin-shelled, inclined to sound shaky, tears under control but not far. Four weeks away from George's death.

She sipped the hot coffee and said, 'You can forget what I told you last week about the Whites and Dana den Relgan.'

'Can I?'

She nodded. 'Wendy's here. We had coffee earlier on. She's very much happier.'

'Tell me about it,' I said.

'Are you interested? I'm not prattling on?'

'Very interested,' I assured her.

'She said that last Tuesday, sometime on Tuesday, her husband found out something he didn't like about Dana den Relgan. She doesn't know what. He didn't tell her. But she said he was like a zombie all evening, white and staring and not hearing a word that was said to him. She didn't know what was the matter, not then, and she was quite frightened. He locked himself away alone all Wednesday, but in the evening he told her his affair with Dana was over, and that he'd been a fool, and would she forgive him.'

I listened, amazed that women so easily relayed that sort of gossip, and pleased they did.

'And after that?' I said.

'Aren't men extraordinary?' Marie Millace said. 'After that he began to behave as if the whole thing had never happened. Wendy says that now he has confessed and apologized, he expects her to go on as before, as if he'd never gone off and slept with the wretched girl.'

'And will she?'

'Oh, I expect so. Wendy says his trouble was the common one among men of fifty or so, wanting to prove to themselves they're still young. She understands him, you see.'

'So do you,' I said.

She smiled with sweetness. 'Goodness, yes. You see it all the time.'

When we'd finished the coffee I gave her a short list of agents that she might try, and said I'd give any help I could. After that I told her I'd brought a present for her. I had been going to give it to Steve to give to her, but as she was there herself, she could have it: it was in my bag in the changing room.

I fetched out and handed to her a ten-by-eight inch cardboard envelope which said 'Photographs. Do not Bend' along its borders.

'Don't open it until you're alone,' I said.

'I *must*,' she said, and opened it there and then.

It contained a photograph I'd taken once of George. George holding his camera, looking towards me, smiling his familiar sardonic smile. George in colour. George in a typically George-like pose, one leg forward with his weight back on the other one, head back, considering the world a bad joke. George as he'd lived.

There and then in full public view Marie Millace flung her arms round me and hugged me as if she would never let go, and I could feel her tears trickling down my neck.

CHAPTER FIFTEEN

Zephyr Farm Stables was indeed fortified like a stockade, surrounded by a seven-foot-high stout wooden fence and guarded by a gate that would have done credit to Alcatraz. I sat lazily in my car across the street from it, waiting for it to open.

I waited while the cold gradually seeped through my anorak and numbed my hands and feet. Waited while a few intrepid pedestrians hurried along the narrow path beside the fence without giving the gate a glance. Waited in the semi-suburban street on the outskirts of Horley, where the street lamps faltered to a stop and darkness lay beyond.

No one went in or out of the gate. It stayed obstinately shut, secretive and unfriendly, and after two fruitless hours I abandoned the chilly vigil and booked into a local motel.

Enquiries brought a sour response. Yes, the receptionist said, they did sometimes have people staying there who were hoping to persuade their sons and daughters to come home from Zephyr Farm Stables.

Hardly any of them ever managed it, because they were never allowed to see their children alone, if at all. Proper scandal, said the receptionist: and the law can't do a blind thing about it. All over eighteen, they are, see? Old enough to know their own minds. Phooey.

'I just want to find out if someone's there,' I said.

She shook her head and said I didn't have a chance.

I spent the evening drifting around hotels and pubs talking about the Colleagues to a succession of locals propping up the bars. The general opinion was the same as the receptionist's: anything or anyone I wanted from Zephyr Farm Stables, I wouldn't get.

'Do they ever come out?' I asked. 'To go shopping, perhaps?'

Amid a reaction of rueful and sneering smiles I was told that yes indeed the Colleagues did emerge, always in groups, and always collecting money.

'They'd sell you things,' one man said. 'Try to sell you bits o' polished stone and such. Just beggin' really. For the cause, they say. For the love of God. Bunk, I say. I tell 'em to be off to church, and they don't like that, I'll tell ye.'

'Ever so strict, they are,' a barmaid said. 'No smokes, no drinks, no sex. Can't see what the nitwits see in it, myself.'

'They don't do no harm,' someone said. 'Always smiling and that.'

Would they be out collecting in the morning, I asked. And if so, where?

'In the summer they hang about the airport all the time, scrounging from people going on holiday and sometimes picking someone up for themselves ... recruits, like ... but your best bet would be in the centre of town. Right here. Saturday ... they're sure to be here. Sure to be.'

I thanked them all, and slept, and in the morning parked as near to the centre as possible and wandered about on foot.

By ten o'clock the town was bustling with its morning trade, and I'd worked out that I would have to leave by eleven-thirty at the latest to get back to Newbury, and even that was cutting it a bit fine. The first race was at twelve-thirty because of the short winter days, and although I wasn't riding in the first two, I had to be there an hour before the third, or Harold would be dancing mad.

I saw no groups of collecting Colleagues. No groups at all. No chanting people with shaven heads and bells, or anything like that. All that happened was that a smiling girl touched my arm and asked if I would like to buy a pretty paperweight.

The stone lay on the palm of her hand, wedge-shaped, greeny-brown, and polished.

'Yes,' I said. 'How much?'

'It's for charity,' she said. 'As much as you like.' She produced in her other hand a wooden box with a slit in the top but with no names of charities advertised on its sides.

913

'What charity?' I asked pleasantly, fishing for my wallet.

'Lots of good causes,' she said.

I sorted out a pound note, folded it, and pushed it through the slit.

'Are there many of you collecting?' I asked.

She turned her head involuntarily sideways, and I saw from the direction of her eyes that there was another girl offering a stone to someone waiting at a bus stop, and on the other side of the road, another. All pretty girls in ordinary clothes, smiling.

'What's your name?' I asked.

She broadened the smile as if that were answer enough, and gave me the stone. 'Thank you very much,' she said. 'Your gift will do so much good.'

I watched her move on down the street, pulling another stone from a pocket in her swirling skirt and accosting a kind-looking old lady. She was too old to be Amanda, I thought, though it wasn't always easy to tell. Especially not, I saw a minute later as I stood in the path of another stone-seller, in view of the other-worldly air of saintliness they wore like badges.

'Would you like to buy a paperweight?'

'Yes,' I said: and we went through the routine again.

'What's your name?' I asked.

'Susan,' she said. 'What's yours?'

I in my turn gave her the smile and the shake of the head, and moved on.

In half an hour I bought four paperweights. To the

fourth girl I said, 'Is Amanda out here this morning?'

'Amanda? We haven't got a . . .' She stopped, and her eyes, too, went on a giveaway trek.

'Never mind,' I said, pretending not to see. 'Thanks for the stone.'

She smiled the bright empty smile and moved on, and I waited a short while until I could decently drift in front of the girl she'd looked at.

She was young, short, smooth-faced, curiously blank about the eyes, and dressed in an anorak and swirling skirt. Her hair was medium brown, like mine, but straight, not slightly curling, and there was no resemblance that I could see between our faces. She might or she might not be my mother's child.

The stone she held out to me was dark blue with black flecks, the size of a plum.

'Very pretty,' I said. 'How much?'

I got the stock reply, and gave her a pound.

'Amanda,' I said.

She jumped. She looked at me doubtfully. 'My name's not Amanda.'

'What then?'

'Mandy.'

'Mandy what?'

'Mandy North.'

I breathed very slowly, so as not to alarm her, and smiled, and asked her how long she had lived at Zephyr Farm Stables.

'All my life,' she said limpidly.

'With your friends?'

She nodded. 'They're my guardians.'

'And you're happy?'

'Yes, of course. We do God's work.'

'How old are you?'

Her doubts returned. 'Eighteen . . . yesterday . . . but I'm not supposed to talk about myself . . . only about the stones.'

The childlike quality was very marked. She seemed not exactly to be mentally retarded, but in the old sense, simple. There was no life in her, no fun, no awakening of womanhood. Beside the average clued-up teenager she was like a sleep-walker who had never known day.

'Have you any more stones then?' I asked.

She nodded and produced another one from her skirt. I admired it and agreed to buy it, and said while picking out another note, 'What was your mother's name, Mandy?'

She looked scared. 'I don't know. You mustn't ask things like that.'

'When you were little did you have a pony?'

For an instant her blank eyes lit with an uncrushable memory, and then she glanced at someone over my left shoulder, and her simple pleasure turned to red-faced shame.

I half turned. A man stood there; not young, not smiling. A tough-looking man a few years older than myself, very clean, very neatly dressed, and very annoyed.

'No conversations, Mandy,' he said to her severely. 'Remember the rule. Your first day out collecting, and you break the rule. The girls will take you home now. You'll be back on housework, after this. Go along, they're waiting over there.' He nodded sharply to where a group of girls waited together, and watched as she walked leaden-footed to join them. Poor Mandy in disgrace. Poor Amanda. Poor little sister.

'What's your game?' the man said to me. 'The girls say you've bought stones from all of them. What are you after?'

'Nothing,' I said. 'They're pretty stones.'

He glared at me doubtfully, and he was joined by another similar man who walked across after talking to the now departing girls.

'This guy was asking the girls their names,' he said. 'Looking for Amanda.'

'There's no Amanda.'

'Mandy. He talked to her.'

They both looked at me with narrowed eyes, and I decided it was time to leave. They didn't try to stop me when I headed off in the general direction of the car park. They didn't try to stop me, but they followed along in my wake.

I didn't think much about it, and turned into the short side road which led to the park. Glancing back to see if they were still following I found not only that they were, but there were now four of them. The two new ones were young, like the girls.

It seemed too public a place for much to happen: and I suppose by many standards nothing much did. There was for instance no blood.

There were three more of them loitering around the car park entrance, and all seven of them encircled me outside, before I got there. I pushed one of them to get him out of the way, and got shoved in return by a forest of hands. Shoved sideways along the road a few steps and against a brick wall. If any of the Great British Public saw what was happening, they passed by on the other side.

I stood looking at the seven Colleagues. 'What do you want?' I said.

The second of the two older men said, 'Why were you asking for Mandy?'

'She's my sister.'

It confounded the two elders. They looked at each other. Then the first one decisively shook his head. 'She's got no family. Her mother died years ago. You're lying. How could you possibly think she's your sister?'

'We don't want you nosing round, making trouble,' the second one said. 'If you ask me, he's a reporter.'

The word stung them all into reconciling violence with their strange religion. They banged me against the wall a shade too often, and also pushed and kicked a shade too hard, but apart from trying to shove all seven away like a rugger scrum there wasn't a great deal I could physically do to stop them. It was one of those stupid sorts of scuffles in which no one wanted to go too far. They could have half-killed me easily if they'd meant to, and I could have hurt them more than I did. Escalation seemed a crazy risk when all they were truly delivering was a warning off, so I pushed against their close bodies and hacked at a couple of shins, and that was that.

I didn't tell them the one thing which would have saved me the drubbing: that if they could prove that Mandy was indeed my sister she would inherit a fortune.

Harold watched my arrival outside the weighing room with a scowl of disfavour.

'You're bloody late,' he said. 'And why are you limping?'

'Twisted my ankle.'

'Are you fit to ride?'

'Yes.'

'Huh.'

'Is Victor Briggs here?' I said.

'No, he isn't. You can stop worrying. Sharpener's out to win, and you can ride him in your usual way. None of those crazy damn-fool heroics. Understood? You look after Sharpener or I'll belt the hide off you. Bring him back whole.'

I nodded, smothering a smile, and he gave me another extensive scowl and walked off.

'Honestly, Philip,' said Steve Millace, wandering past. 'He treats you like dirt.'

'No . . . just his way.'

'I wouldn't stand for it.'

I looked at the easy belligerence in the over-young face and realized that he didn't really know about affection coming sometimes in a rough package.

'Good luck, today,' I said neutrally, and he said 'Thanks,' and went on into the weighing room. He would never be like his father, I thought. Never as bright, as ingenious, as perceptive, as ruthless, or as wicked.

I followed Steve inside and changed into Victor Briggs's colours, feeling the effects of the Colleagues' attentions as an overall ache. Nothing much. A nuisance. Not enough, I hoped, to make any difference to my riding.

When I went outside the nearest conversation was going on loudly between Elgin Yaxley and Bart Underfield, who were slapping each other on the shoulder and looking the faintest bit drunk. Elgin Yaxley peeled off and rolled away, and Bart, turning with an extravagant lack of coordination, bumped into me.

'Hullo,' he said, giving a spirits-laden cough. 'You'll be the first to know. Elgin's getting some more horses. They're coming to me, of course. We'll make Lambourn sit up. Make the whole of racing sit up.' He gave me a patronizing leer. 'Elgin's a man of ideas.'

'He is indeed,' I said dryly.

Bart remembered he didn't much like me and took his good news off to other, more receptive ears. I stood watching him, thinking that Elgin Yaxley would never kill another horse for the insurance. No insurance company would stand for it twice. But Elgin Yaxley believed himself undetected . . . and people didn't change. If their minds ran to fraud once, they would do again. I didn't like the sound of Elgin Yaxley having ideas.

The old dilemma still remained. If I gave the proof of Elgin Yaxley's fraud to the police or the insurance company, I would have to say how I came by the photograph. From George Millace . . . who wrote threatening letters. George Millace, husband of Marie, who was climbing back with frail handholds from the wreck of her life. If justice depended on smashing her deeper into soul-racking misery, justice would still have to wait.

Sharpener's race came third on the card. Not the biggest event of the day, which was the fourth race, a brandy-sponsored Gold Cup, but a well-regarded two-mile 'chase. Sharpener had been made favourite because of his win at Kempton and with some of the same *joie de vivre* he sailed round most of Newbury's long oval in fourth place. We lay third at the third last fence, second at the second last, and jumped to the front over the last. I sat down and rode him out with hands and heels, and my God, I thought, I could do with the muscle-power I lost in Horley.

Sharpener won and I was exhausted, which was ridiculous. Harold, beaming, watched me fumble feebly with the girth buckles in the winners' enclosure. The horse, stamping around, almost knocked me over.

'You only went two miles,' Harold said. 'What the hell's the matter with you?'

I got the buckles undone and pulled off the saddle, and began in fact to feel a trickle of strength flow again through my arms. I grinned at Harold and said, 'Nothing . . . It was a damn good race. Nice shape.'

'Nice shape be buggered. You won. Any race you win is a nice bloody shape.'

I went in to be weighed, leaving him surrounded by congratulations and sportswriters: and while I was sitting on the bench by my peg waiting for vigour to amble back I decided what to do about Elgin Yaxley.

I had grown a habit, over the past two weeks, of taking with me in the car not only my favourite two cameras but also the photographs I seemed to keep on needing. Lance Kinship's reprints were there, although he himself hadn't turned up, and so were the four concerning Yaxley. Straight after the big race I went out and fetched them.

The second horse I was due to ride for Harold was a novice hurdler in the last race: and because there had been so many entries in the novice hurdle that they'd split it into two divisions, the last race on that day was the seventh, not the sixth. It gave me just enough extra time for what I wanted.

Finding Elgin Yaxley wasn't so difficult: it was detaching him from Bart Underfield that gave the trouble.

'Can I talk to you for a moment?' I said to Yaxley.

'You're not having the rides on our horses,' Bart said bossily. 'So don't waste time asking.'

'You can keep them,' I said.

'What do you want, then?'

'I want to give Mr Yaxley a message.' I turned to Yaxley 'It's a private message, for your ears only.'

'Oh very well.' He was impatient. 'Wait for me in the bar, Bart.'

Bart grumbled and fussed, but finally went.

'Better come over here,' I said to Elgin Yaxley, nodding towards a patch of grass by the entrance gate, away from the huge big-race crowd with their stretched ears and curious eyes. 'You won't want anyone hearing.'

'What the devil *is* all this?' he said crossly.

'A message from George Millace,' I said.

His sharp features grew rigid. The small moustache he wore bristled. The complacency vanished into a furious concentration of fear.

'I have some photographs,' I said, 'which you might like to see.'

I handed him the cardboard envelope. It seemed easier this second time, I thought, to deliver the chop. Maybe I was becoming hardened . . . or maybe I simply didn't like Elgin Yaxley. I watched him open the envelope with no pity at all.

He first went pale, and then red, and great drops of sweat stood out like blisters on his forehead. He checked through the four pictures and found the whole story was here, the café meeting and George's two letters, and the damning note from the farmer, David Parker. The eyes he raised to me were sick and incredulous, and he had difficulty finding his voice.

'Take your time,' I said. 'I expect it's a shock.'

His mouth moved as if practising, but no words came out.

'Any number of copies,' I said, 'could go off to the insurance company and the police and so on.'

He managed a strangled groan.

'There's another way,' I said.

He got his throat and tongue to shape a single hoarse unedifying word. '*Bastard.*'

'Mm,' I said. 'There's George Millace's way.'

I'd never seen anyone look at me with total hatred before, and I found it unnerving. But I wanted to find out just what George had extracted from at least one of his victims, and this was my best chance.

I said flatly, 'I want the same as George Millace.'

'No.' It was more a wail than a shout. Full of horror; empty of hope.

'Yes indeed,' I said.

'But I can't afford it. I haven't got it.'

The anxiety in his eyes was almost too much for me, but I spurred on my flagging resolution with the thought of five shot horses, and said again, 'The same as George.'

'Not ten,' he said wildly. 'I haven't got it.'

I stared at him.

He mistook my silence and gabbled on, finding his voice in a flood of begging, beseeching, cajoling words.

'I've had expenses, you know. It hasn't all been easy. Can't you let me alone? Let me off, won't you? George said once and for all ... and now *you* ... Five, then,' he said in the face of my continued silence. 'Will five do? That's enough. I haven't got any more. I haven't.'

I stared once more, and waited.

'All right, then. All *right*.' He was shaking with worry and fury. 'Seven and a half. Will that do? It's all I've got, you bloodsucking leech ... you're worse than George Millace ... bastard *blackmailers* ...'

While I watched he fumbled into his pockets and brought out a cheque book and a pen. Clumsily supporting the cheque book on the photograph envelope, he wrote the date, and a sum of money, and signed his name. Then with shaking fingers he tore the slip of paper out of the book and stood holding it.

'Not Hong Kong,' he said.

I didn't know at once what he meant, so I took refuge in more staring.

'Not Hong Kong. Not there again. I don't like it.' He was beseeching again, begging for crumbs.

'Oh . . .' I hid my understanding in a cough. 'Anywhere,' I said. 'Anywhere out of Britain.'

It was the right answer, but gave him no comfort. I stretched out my hand for the cheque.

He gave it to me, his hand trembling.

'Thank you,' I said.

'Rot in hell.'

He turned and stumbled away, half running, half staggering, utterly in pieces. Serve him right, I thought callously. Let him suffer. It wouldn't be for long.

I meant to tear up his cheque when I'd looked to see how much he thought my silence was worth: how much he'd paid George. I meant to, but I didn't.

When I looked at that cheque something like a huge burst of sunlight happened in my head, a bright expanding delight of awe and comprehension.

I had used George's own cruelty. I had demanded to be given what he himself had demanded. His alternative suggestion for Elgin Yaxley.

I had it. All of it.

Elgin Yaxley was going off into exile, and I held his cheque for seven thousand five hundred pounds.

It was made out not to me, or to Bearer, or even to the estate of George Millace, but to the Injured Jockeys Fund.

CHAPTER SIXTEEN

I walked around for a while trying to find the particular
ex-jockey who had become one of the chief adminis-
trators of the Fund, and at length tracked him down in
the private entertainment box of one of the television
companies. There was a crowd in there, but I winkled
him out.

'Want a drink?' he said, holding up his glass.

I shook my head. I was wearing colours, breeches,
boots and an anorak. 'More than my life's worth,
boozing with you lot before racing.'

He said cheerfully, 'What can I do for you?'

'Take a cheque,' I said, and gave it to him.

'Phew,' he said, looking at it. 'And likewise *wow*.'

'Is it the first time Elgin Yaxley's been so generous?'

'No, it isn't,' he said. 'He gave us ten thousand a few
months ago, just before he went abroad. We took it of
course, but some of the trustees wondered if it wasn't
conscience money. I mean ... he'd just been paid a
hundred thousand by the insurance company for those

horses of his that were shot. The whole business looked horribly fishy, didn't it?'

'Mm.' I nodded. 'Well ... Elgin Yaxley's going abroad again, so he says, and he gave me this cheque for you. So will you take it?'

He smiled. 'If his conscience is troubling him again, we might as well benefit.' He folded the cheque, tucked it away, and patted the pocket which contained it.

'Have you had any other huge cheques like that?' I enquired conversationally.

'People leave big amounts in their wills, sometimes, but no ... not many like Elgin Yaxley.'

'Would Ivor den Relgan be a generous supporter?' I asked.

'Well yes, he gave us a thousand at the beginning of the season. Some time in September. Very generous.'

I pondered. 'Do you keep lists of the people who donate?'

He laughed. 'Not all of them. Thousands of people contribute over the years. Old age pensioners. Children. Housewives. Anyone you can think of.' He sighed. 'We never seem to have enough for what we need to do, but we're always grateful for the smallest help ... and you know all that.'

'Yes. Thanks anyway.'

'Any time.'

He went back to the convivial crowd and I returned to the weighing room and got myself and my saddle weighed out for the last race.

I was as bad as George, I thought. Identically as bad. I had extorted money by threats. It didn't seem so wicked, now that I'd done it myself.

Harold in the parade ring said sharply, 'You're looking bloody pleased with yourself.'

'Just with life in general.'

I'd ridden a winner. I'd almost certainly found Amanda. I'd discovered a lot more about George. Sundry kicks and punches on the debit side, but who cared. Overall, not a bad day.

'This hurdler,' Harold said severely, 'is the one who ballsed-up the schooling session last Saturday. I know you weren't on him . . . it wasn't your fault . . . but you just mind he gets a good clear view of what he's got to jump. Understand? Go to the front and make the running, so he's got a clear view. He won't last the trip, but it's a big field and I don't want him being jostled and blinded in the pack early on. Got it?'

I nodded. There were twenty-three runners, almost the maximum allowed in this type of race. Harold's hurdler, walking edgily round the parade ring, was already sweating with nervous excitement, and he was an animal, I knew from experience, who needed a soothing phlegmatic approach.

'Jockeys, please mount,' came the announcement, and I and the hurdler in a decently quiet way got ourselves together and down to the start.

I was thinking only of bowling along in front out of trouble, and when the tapes went up, off we set. Over the first, leading as ordered; good jump, no trouble. Over the second, just out in front; passable jump, no trouble. Over the third . . .

In front, as ordered, at the third. Rotten, disastrous jump, all four feet seeming to tangle in the hurdle instead of rising over it: exactly the mess he'd made over the schooling hurdle at home.

He and I crashed to the turf together, and twenty-two horses came over the hurdle after us.

Horses do their very best to avoid a man or a horse on the ground, but with so many, so close, going so fast, it would have been a miracle if I hadn't been touched. One couldn't ever tell at those times just how many galloping hooves connected: it always happened too fast. It felt like being rolled like a rag doll under a stampede.

It had happened before. It would happen again. I lay painfully on my side looking at a close bunch of grass, and thought it was a damn silly way to be earning one's living.

I almost laughed. I've thought that before, I thought. Every time I'm down here on the mud, I think it.

A lot of First Aid hands arrived to help me up. Nothing seemed to be broken. Thank God for strong bones. I wrapped my arms round my body, as if hugging would lessen the hurt.

The horse had got up and decamped, unscathed. I rode back to the stands in an ambulance, demonstrated to the doctor that I was basically in one piece, and winced my slow way into ordinary clothes.

When I left the weighing room most people had gone home, but Harold was standing there with Ben, his travelling head lad.

'Are you all right?' Harold demanded.

'Yeah.'

'I'll drive you home,' he said. 'Ben can take your car.'

I looked at the generous worry in both of their faces, and didn't argue. Dug into my pocket, and gave Ben my keys.

'That was a hell of a fall,' Harold said, driving out of the gates. 'A real brute.'

'Mm.'

'I was glad to see you stand up.'

'Is the horse all right?'

'Yes, clumsy bugger.'

We drove in companionable silence towards Lambourn. I felt beaten up and shivery, but it would pass. It always passed. Always would, until I got too old for it. I'd be too old in my mind, I thought, before my body gave out.

'If Victor Briggs comes down here again,' I said, 'would you tell me?'

He glanced at me sideways. 'You want to see him? Won't do any good, you know. Victor just does what he wants.'

'I want to know . . . what he wants.'

'Why not leave well alone?'

'Because it isn't well. I've left it alone . . . it doesn't work. I want to talk to him . . . and don't worry, I'll be diplomatic. I don't want to lose this job. I don't want you to lose Victor's horses. Don't worry. I know all that. I want to talk to him.'

'All right,' Harold said doubtfully. 'When he comes, I'll tell him.'

He stopped his car beside my front door.

'You're sure you're all right?' he said. 'You look pretty shaken . . . Nasty fall. Horrid.'

'I'll have a hot bath . . . get the stiffness out. Thanks for the lift home.'

'You'll be fit for next week? Tuesday at Plumpton?'

'Absolutely,' I said.

It was already getting dark. I went round in the cottage drawing the curtains, switching on lights, heating some coffee. Bath, food, television, aspirins, bed, I thought, and pray not to feel too sore in the morning.

Ben parked my car in the carport, gave me the keys through the back door, and said goodnight.

Mrs Jackson, the horse-box driver's wife from next door, came to tell me the rating officer had called.

'Oh?' I said.

'Yes. Yesterday. Hope I did right, letting him in, like. Mind you, Mr Nore, I didn't let him out of my sight. I went right round with him, like. He was only in here a matter of five minutes. He didn't touch a thing. Just counted the rooms. Hope it's all right. He had papers from the council, and such.'

'I'm sure it's fine, Mrs Jackson.'

'And your telephone,' she said. 'It's been ringing and ringing. Dozens of times. I can hear it through the wall, you know, when everything's quiet. I didn't know if you'd want me to answer it. I will, any time, you know, if you want.'

'Kind of you,' I said. 'I'll let you know if I do.'

She gave me a bright nod and departed. She would have mothered me if I'd let her, and I guessed she would have been glad to let the rating man in, as she liked looking round in my house. Nosy, friendly, sharp-eyed neighbour, taker-in of parcels and dispenser of gossip and advice. Her two boys had broken my kitchen window once with their football.

I telephoned Jeremy Folk. He was out: would I care to leave a message? Tell him I found what we were looking for, I said.

The instant I put the receiver down the bell rang. I picked it up again, and heard a child's breathless voice. 'I can tell you where that stable is. Am I the first?'

I regretfully said not. I also passed on the same bad news to ten more children within the next two hours. Several of them checked disappointedly to make sure I'd been told the right place – Zephyr Farm Stables? And several said did I know it had been owned for years and years by some Jesus freaks? I began asking them if they knew how the Colleagues had chanced to buy the stables, and eventually came across a father who did.

'We and the people who kept the riding school,' he said, 'we were pretty close friends. They wanted to move to Devon, and were looking for a buyer for their place, and these fanatics just turned up one day with suitcases full of cash, and bought it on the spot.'

'How did the fanatics hear of it? Was it advertised?'

'No . . .' He paused, thinking. 'Oh, I remember . . . it was because of one of the children who used to ride the ponies. Yes, that's right. Sweet little girl. Mandy something. Always there. She used to stay with our friends for weeks on end. I saw her often. There was something about her mother being on the point of death, and the religious people looking after her. It was through the mother that they heard the stables were for sale. They were in some ruin of a house at the time, I think, and wanted somewhere better.'

'You don't remember the mother's name, I suppose.'

'Sorry, no. Don't think I ever knew it, and after all these years . . .'

'You've been tremendously helpful,' I said. 'I'll send your Peter the tenner, even though he wasn't first.'

The father's voice chuckled. 'That'll please him.'

I took his address, and also the name of the people who had owned the stables, but Peter's father said he had lost touch with them over the years and no longer knew where they lived.

Jeremy could find them, I thought, if he needed to.

After I'd bathed and eaten I unplugged the telephone from the kitchen and carried it up to the sitting room, where for another hour it interrupted the television. God bless the little children, I thought, and wondered how many thousands were going to ring up. None of them themselves had ever been inside the high wooden walls: it was always their mummies and daddies who had ridden there when they were young.

By nine o'clock I was thoroughly tired of it. Despite the long hot soak my deeply bruised muscles were beginning to stiffen; and the best place to take them was bed. Get it over with, I thought. It was going to be lousy. It always was, for about twenty-four hours, after so many kicks. If I went to bed I could sleep through the worst.

I unplugged the telephone and went down to the bathroom in shirtsleeves for a scratch round the teeth; and the front doorbell rang.

Cursing, I went to see who had called.

Opened the door.

Ivor den Relgan stood there, holding a gun.

I stared at the pistol, not believing it.

'Back up,' he said. 'I'm coming in.'

It would be untrue to say I wasn't afraid. I was certain he was going to kill me. I felt bodiless. Floating. Blood racing.

For the second time that day I saw into the eyes of

hatred, and the power behind den Relgan's paled Elgin Yaxley's into petulance. He jerked the lethal black weapon towards me insisting I retreated, and I took two or three steps backwards, hardly feeling my feet.

He stepped through my door and kicked it shut behind him.

'You're going to pay,' he said, 'for what you've done to me.'

Be careful, Jeremy had said.

I hadn't been.

'George Millace was bad,' he said. 'You're worse.'

I wasn't sure I was actually going to be able to speak, but I did. My voice sounded strange: almost squeaky.

'Did you . . .' I said, ' . . . burn his house?'

His eyes flickered. His naturally arrogant expression, which had survived whatever Lord White had said to him, wasn't going to be broken up by any futile last-minute questions. In adversity his air of superiority had if anything intensified, as if belief in his own importance were the only thing left.

'Burgled, ransacked, burnt,' he said furiously. 'And you had the stuff all the time. You . . . you *rattlesnake*.'

I had destroyed his power base. Taken away his authority. Left him metaphorically as naked as on his St Tropez balcony.

George, I thought, must have used the threat of those photographs to stop den Relgan angling to be let into the Jockey Club. I'd used them to get him thrown out.

He'd had some sort of standing, of credibility, before, in racing men's eyes. Now he had none. Never to be in was one thing. To be in and then out, quite another.

George hadn't shown those photographs to anyone but den Relgan himself.

I had.

'Get back,' he said. 'Back there. Go on.'

He made a small waving movement with the pistol. An automatic. Stupid thought. What did it matter.

'My neighbours'll hear the shot,' I said hopelessly.

He sneered and didn't answer. 'Back past that door.'

It was the door to the darkroom, solidly shut. Even if I could jump in there alive . . . no sanctuary. No lock. I stepped past it.

'Stop,' he said.

I'd have to run, I thought wildly. Had at least to try. I was already turning on the ball of one foot when the kitchen door was smashed open.

I thought for a split second that somehow den Relgan had missed me and the bullet had splintered some glass, but then I realized he hadn't fired. There were people coming into the house from the back. Two people. Two bustling burly young men . . . with nylon stocking masks over their faces.

They were rushing, banging against each other, fast, eager, infinitely destructive.

I tried to fight them.

I tried.

God almighty, I thought. Not three times in one day.

How could I explain to them ... Blood vessels were already severed and bleeding under my skin ... Too many muscle fibres already crushed and torn ... too much damage already done. How could I explain ... and if I had it wouldn't have made any difference. Pleased them, if anything.

Thoughts scattered and flew away. I couldn't see, couldn't yell, could hardly breathe. They wore roughened leather gloves which tore my skin and the punches to my face knocked me silly. When I fell on the ground they used their boots. On limbs, back, stomach, head.

I drifted off altogether.

When I came back it was quiet. I was lying on the white tiled floor with my cheek in a pool of blood. In a dim way I wondered whose blood it was.

Drifted off again.

It's my blood, I thought.

Tried to open my eyes. Something wrong with the eyelids. Oh well, I thought, I'm alive. Drifted off again.

He didn't shoot me, I thought. Did he shoot me? I tried to move, to find out. Bad mistake.

When I tried to move, my whole body went into a sort of rigid spasm. Locked tight in a monstrous cramp from head to foot. I gasped with the crushing, unexpected agony of it. Worse than fractures, worse than dislocations, worse than anything ...

Screaming nerves, I thought. Telling my brain to seize up. Saying too much was injured, too much was smashed, nothing must move. Too much was bleeding inside.

Christ, I thought. Leave go. Let me go. I won't move. I'll just lie here. Let me go.

After a long time the spasm did pass, and I lay in relief in a flaccid heap. Too weak to do anything but pray that the cramp wouldn't come back. Too shattered to think much at all.

The thoughts I did have, I could have done without. Thoughts like people died of ruptured internal organs... kidneys, liver, spleen. Thoughts like what exactly did I have wrong with me, to cause such a fierce reaction. Thoughts like den Relgan coming back to finish the job.

Den Relgan's mid-world voice, 'You'll pay for what you've done to me...'

Pay in cuts and internal haemorrhage and wretched pain. Pay in fear that I was lying there dying. Bleeding inside. Bleeding to death. The way people beaten to death died.

Ages passed.

If any of those things were ruptured, I thought... liver, kidneys, spleen... and pouring out blood, I would be showing the signs of it. Shallow breathing, fluttering pulse, thirst, restlessness, sweat. None of that seemed to be happening.

I took heart after a while, knowing that at least I wasn't getting worse. Maybe if I moved gently, cautiously, it would be all right.

Far from all right. Back into a rigid locked spasm, as bad as before.

It had taken only the intention to move. Only the outward message. The response had been not movement, but cramp. I dare say it was the body's best line of defence, but I could hardly bear it.

It lasted too long, and went away slowly, tentatively, as if threatening to come back. I won't move, I promised. I won't move . . . just let go . . . let me go.

The lights in the cottage were on, but the heating was off. I grew very cold; literally congealing. Cold stopped things bleeding, I thought. Cold wasn't all bad. Cold would contract all those leaking internal blood vessels and stop the red stuff trickling out into where it shouldn't be. Haemorrhage would be finished. Recovery could start.

I lay quiet for hours, waiting. Sore but alive. Increasingly certain of staying alive. Increasingly certain I'd been lucky.

If nothing fatal had ruptured, I could deal with the rest. Familiar country. Boring, but known.

I had no idea of the time. Couldn't see my watch. Suppose I move my arm, I thought. Just my arm. Might manage that, if I'm careful.

It sounded simple. The overall spasm stayed away, but the specific message to my arm produced only a twitch. Crazy. Nothing was working. All circuits jammed.

After another long while I tried again. Tried too

hard. The cramp came back, taking my breath away, holding me in a vice, worst now in my stomach, not so bad in my arms, but rigid, fearful, frightening, lasting too long.

I lay on the floor all night and well on into the morning. The patch of blood under my head got sticky and dried. My face felt like a pillow puffed up with gritty lumps. There were splits in my mouth, which were sore, and I could feel with my tongue the jagged edges of broken teeth.

Eventually I lifted my head off the floor.

No spasm.

I was lying in the back part of the hall, not far from the bottom of the stairs. Pity the bedroom was right up at the top. Also the telephone. I might get some help . . . if I could get up the stairs.

Gingerly I tried moving, dreading what would happen. Moved my arms, my legs, tried to sit up. Couldn't do it. My weakness was appalling. My muscles were trembling. I moved a few inches across the floor, still half lying down. Got as far as the stairs. Hip on the hall floor, shoulder on the stairs, head on the stairs, arms failing with weakness . . . the spasms came back.

Oh Christ, I thought, how much more?

In another hour I'd got my haunch up three steps and was again rigid with cramp. Far enough, I thought numbly. No farther. It was certainly more comfortable lying on the stairs than on the floor, as long as I stayed still.

I stayed still. Gratefully, wearily, lazily still. For ages. Somebody rang the front door bell.

Whoever it was, I didn't want them. Whoever it was would make me move. I no longer wanted help, but just peace. Peace would mend me, given time.

The bell rang again. Go away, I thought. I'm better alone.

For a while I thought I'd got my wish, but then I heard someone at the back of the house, coming in through the back door. The broken back door, open to a touch.

Not den Relgan, I thought abjectly. Don't let it be den Relgan ... not him.

It wasn't, of course. It was Jeremy Folk.

It was Jeremy, coming in tentatively, saying 'Er ...' and 'Are you there ...' and 'Philip? ...' and standing still with shock when he reached the hall.

'Jesus Christ,' he said blankly.

I said 'Hello.'

'*Philip.*' He leaned over me. 'Your face ...'

'Yeah.'

'What shall I do?'

'Nothing,' I said. 'Sit down ... on the stairs.' My mouth and tongue felt stiff. Like Marie's, I thought. Just like Marie.

'But what happened? Did you have a fall at the races?'

He did sit down, on the bottom stair by my feet, folding his own legs into ungainly angles.

'But . . . the blood. You've got blood . . . all over your face. In your hair. Everywhere.'

'Leave it,' I said. 'It's dry.'

'Can you see?' he said. 'Your eyes are . . .' He stopped, reduced apparently to silence, not wanting to tell me.

'I can see out of one of them,' I said. 'It's enough.'

He wanted of course to move me, wash the blood off, make things more regular. I wanted to stay just where I was, without having to argue. Hopeless wish. I persuaded him to leave me alone only by confessing to the cramps.

His horror intensified. 'I'll get you a doctor.'

'Just shut up,' I said. 'I'm all right. Talk if you like, but don't *do* anything.'

'Well . . .' He gave in. 'Do you want anything? Tea, or anything?'

'Find some champagne. Kitchen cupboard.'

He looked as if he thought I was mad, but champagne was the best tonic I knew for practically all ills. I heard the cork pop and presently he returned with two tumblers. He put mine on the stair by my left hand, near my head.

Oh well, I thought. May as well find out. The cramps would have to stop sometime. I stiffly moved the arm and fastened the hand round the chunky glass, and tried to connect the whole thing to my mouth: and I got at least three reasonable gulps before everything seized up.

It was Jeremy, that time, who was frightened. He took the glass I was dropping and had a great attack of the dithers, and I said 'Just wait,' through my teeth. The spasm finally wore off, and I thought perhaps it hadn't been so long or so bad that time, and that things really were getting better.

Persuading people to leave one alone always took more energy than one wanted to spend for the purpose. Good friends tired one out. For all that I was grateful for his company, I wished Jeremy would stop fussing and be quiet.

The front door bell rang yet again, and before I could tell him not to, he'd gone off to answer it. My spirits sank even lower. Visitors were too much.

The visitor was Clare, come because I'd invited her.

She knelt on the stairs beside me and said, 'This isn't a fall, is it? Someone's done this to you, haven't they? Beaten you up?'

'Have some champagne,' I said.

'Yes. All right.'

She stood up and went to fetch a glass, and argued on my behalf with Jeremy.

'If he wants to lie on the stairs, let him. He's been injured countless times. He knows what's best.'

My God, I thought. A girl who understands. Incredible.

She and Jeremy sat in the kitchen introducing themselves and drinking my booze, and on the stairs things did improve. Small exploratory stretchings produced no cramps. I drank some champagne. Felt sore but less ill. Felt that some time soon I'd sit up.

The front doorbell rang.

An epidemic.

Clare walked through the hall to answer it. I was sure she intended to keep whoever it was at bay, but she found it impossible. The girl who had called wasn't going to be stopped on the doorstep. She pushed into the house physically past Clare's protestations, and I heard her heels clicking at speed towards me down the hall.

'I must see,' she said frantically. 'I must know if he's alive.'

I knew her voice. I didn't need to see the distraught beautiful face seeking me, seeing me, freezing with shock.

Dana den Relgan.

CHAPTER SEVENTEEN

'Oh my *God*,' she said.

'I am,' I said in my swollen way, 'alive.'

'He said it would be . . . a toss-up.'

'Came down heads,' I said.

'He didn't seem to care. Didn't seem to realize . . . If they'd killed you . . . what it would mean. He just said no one saw them, they'd never be arrested, so why worry?'

Clare demanded, 'Do you mean you know who did this?'

Dana gave her a distracted look. 'I have to talk to him. Alone. Do you mind?'

'But he's . . .' She stopped, and said, 'Philip?'

'It's all right.'

'We'll be in the kitchen,' Clare said. 'Just shout.'

Dana waited until she had gone, and then perched beside me on the stairs, half sitting, half lying, to bring her head near to mine. I regarded her through the slit of my vision, seeing her almost frantic and deadly anxiety and not knowing its cause. Not for my life, since she could now see it was safe. Not for my silence, since her very presence was an admission that could make things worse. The gold-freckled hair fell softly forward almost to touch me. The sweet scent she was wearing reached my perception even through a battered nose. The silk of her blouse brushed my hand. The voice was soft in its cosmopolitan accent ... and beseeching.

'Please,' she said. '*Please* ...'

'Please ... what?'

'How can I ask you?' Even in trouble, I thought, she had a powerful attraction. I'd only seen it before, not felt it, as before she'd given me only passing and uninterested smiles; but now, with the full wattage switched my way, I found myself thinking that I would help her, if I could.

She said persuadingly, 'Please give me ... what I wrote for George Millace.'

I lay without answering, closing the persevering eye. She misread my inaction, which was in truth born of ignorance, and rushed into a flood of impassioned begging.

'I know you'll be thinking ... how can I ask you, when Ivor's done this to you ... how can I expect the slightest favour. ... or mercy ... or kindness.' Her voice was a jumble of shame and despair and anger and cajoling, every emotion rising separately like a wave and subsiding before the next. Asking a favour from someone her father ... husband? ... lover ... had had mauled halfway to extinction wasn't the easiest of errands, but she was having a pretty good stab at it. 'Please, please, I beg of you, give it back.'

'Is he your father?' I said.

'No.' A breath; a whisper; a sigh.

'What then?'

'We have . . . a relationship.'

You don't say, I thought dryly.

She said, 'Please give me the cigarettes.'

The what? I had no idea what she meant.

Trying not to mumble, trying to make my slow tongue lucid, I said, 'Tell me about your . . . relationship . . . with den Relgan . . . and about . . . your relationship with Lord White.'

'If I tell you, will you give it to me? Please, *please*, will you?'

She took my silence to mean that at least she could hope. She scurried into explanations, the words falling over themselves here and there, and here and there coming in faltering pauses: and all of it, overall, apologetic and self-excusing, a distinct flavour of 'poor little me, I've been used, none of it's my fault'.

I opened the slit eye, to watch.

'I've been with him two years . . . not married, it's never been like that . . . not domestic, just . . .'

Just for sex, I thought.

'You talk like him,' I said.

'I'm an actress.' She waited a shade defiantly for me to dispute it, but indeed I couldn't. A pretty good actress, I would have said. Equity card? I thought sardonically, and couldn't be bothered to ask.

'Last summer,' she said, 'Ivor came one day spilling over with a brilliant idea. So pleased with himself ... if I'd co-operate, he'd see I didn't suffer ... I mean, he meant ...' She stopped there, but it was plain what he meant. Won't suffer financially ... neat euphemism for hefty bribe.

'He said there was a man at the races wanting to flirt. He used not to take me to the races, not until then. But he said, would I go with him and pretend to be his daughter, and see if I could get the man to flirt with *me*. It was a laugh, you see. Ivor said this man had a reputation like snow, and he wanted to play a joke on him ... Well, that's what he said. He said the man was showing all the signs of wanting a sexual adventure ... looking at pretty girls in that special way that they do, patting their arms, you know what I mean.'

I thought, how odd it must be to be a pretty girl, to find it normal for middle-aged men to be on the look-out for sex, to expect them to pat one's arms.

'So you went,' I said.

She nodded. 'He was a sweetie ... John White. It was easy. I mean ... I liked him. I just smiled ... and liked him ... and he ... well ... I mean, it was true what Ivor had said, he was on the look-out, and there I was.'

There she was, I thought, beautiful and not too dumb, and trying to catch him. Poor Lord White, hooked because he wanted to be. Fooled by his foolish age, his nostalgia for youth.

'Ivor wanted to use John, of course. I saw it ... it was plain, but I didn't see all that harm in it. I mean ... why not? Everything was going fine until Ivor and I went to St Tropez for a week.' The pretty face clouded with remembered rage. 'And that beastly photographer wrote to Ivor ... saying lay off Lord White, or else he'd show him those pictures of us ... Ivor and me ... Ivor was livid, I've never seen him so angry ... not until this week.'

Each of us, I supposed, thought of the fury we'd witnessed that week in den Relgan.

'Does he know you're here?' I said.

'My God, no.' She looked horrified. 'He doesn't know ... he hates drugs ... it's all we have rows about ... George Millace made me write that list ... said he'd show the pictures to John if I didn't ... I *hated* George Millace ... but you ... you'll give it back to me, won't you? Please ... please ... you must see ... it would ruin me with anyone who matters ... I'll pay you. I'll pay you ... if you'll give it to me.'

Crunch time, I thought.

'What do you expect ... me to give to you?' I said.

'The packet of cigarettes, of course. With the writing on.'

'Yes ... why did you write on a cigarette packet?'

'I wrote on the wrapping with the red felt pen ... George Millace said write the list and I said I wouldn't whatever he did and he said write it then with this pen on the cellophane wrapper round these cigarettes and you can pretend you haven't done it, because how could anyone take seriously a scrawl on wrapping paper . . .' She stopped suddenly and said with awakening suspicion, 'You have got it, haven't you? George Millace gave it to you . . . with the pictures . . . didn't he?'

'What did you write . . . on the list?'

'My God,' she said. 'You haven't got it: you haven't and I've come here . . . I've told you . . . it's all for nothing . . . you haven't got it . . .' She stood up abruptly, beauty vanishing in fury. 'You beastly *shit*. Ivor should have killed you. Should have made sure. I hope you *hurt*.'

She had her wish, I thought calmly. I felt surprisingly little resentment about den Relgan's tit for tat. I'd clobbered his life, he'd clobbered my body. I'd come off the better, I thought, on the whole. My troubles would pass.

'Be grateful,' I said.

She was too angry, however, at what she had given away. She whisked off through the hall in her silks and her scent, and slammed out of the front door. The air in her wake quivered with feminine impact. Just as well, I thought hazily, that the world wasn't full of Dana den Relgans.

Clare and Jeremy came out of the kitchen.

'What did she want?' Clare said.

'Something I . . . haven't got.'

They began asking what in general was happening, but I said 'Tell you . . . tomorrow,' and they stopped. Clare sat beside me on the stairs and rubbed one finger over my hand.

'You're in a poor way, aren't you?' she said.

I didn't want to say yes. I said, 'What's the time?'

'Half-past three . . . getting on for four.' She looked at her watch. 'Twenty to four.'

'Have some lunch,' I said. 'You and Jeremy.'

'Do you want any?'

'No.'

They heated some soup and some bread and kept life ticking over. It's the only day, I thought inanely, that I've ever spent lying on the stairs. I could smell the dust in the carpet. I ached all over, incessantly, with a grinding stiff soreness, but it was better than the cramps; and movement was becoming possible. Movement soon, I thought, would be imperative. A sign that things were returning to order . . . I needed increasingly to go to the bathroom.

I sat up on the stairs, my back propped against the wall.

Not so bad. Not so bad. No spasms.

A perceptible improvement in function in all muscles. The memory of strength no longer seemed remote. I could stand up, I thought, if I tried.

Clare and Jeremy appeared enquiringly, and without pride I used their offered hands to pull myself upright.

Tottery, but upright.

No cramps.

'Now what?' Clare said.

'A pee.'

They laughed. Clare went off to the kitchen and Jeremy said something, as he gave me an arm for support across the hall, about washing the pool of dried blood off the floor.

'Don't bother,' I said.

'No trouble.'

I hung onto the towel rail in the bathroom a bit and looked into the glass over the washbasin, and saw the state of my face. Swollen, misshapen landscape. Unrecognizable. Raw in patches. Dark red in patches. Caked with dried blood: hair spiky with it. One eye lost in puffy folds, one showing a slit. Cut, purple mouth. Two chipped front teeth.

Give it a week, I thought, sighing. Boxers did it all the time from choice, silly buggers.

Emptying the bladder brought an acute awareness of heavy damage in the abdomen but also reassurance. No blood in the urine. My intestines might have caught it, but not once had those feet, equine or human, landed squarely with exploding force over a kidney. I'd been lucky. Exceptionally lucky. Thanked God for it.

I ran some warm water into the washbasin and sponged off some of the dried blood. Wasn't sure, on the whole, that it was any improvement, either in comfort or visibility. Where the blood had been were more raw patches and clotted cuts. Gingerly I patted the washed bits dry with a tissue. Leave the rest, I thought.

There was a heavy crash somewhere out in the hall.

I pulled open the bathroom door to find Clare coming through from the kitchen, looking anxious.

'Are you all right?' she said. 'You didn't fall?'

'No . . . Must be Jeremy.'

Unhurriedly we went forward towards the front of the house to see what he'd dropped . . . and found Jeremy himself face down on the floor. Half in and half out of the darkroom door. The bowl of water he'd been carrying spilled wetly all around him, and there was a smell . . . a strong smell of bad eggs. A smell I knew. I . . .

'Whatever . . .' Clare began.

Dear Christ, I thought, and it was a prayer, not a blasphemy. I caught her fiercely round the waist and dragged her to the front door. Opened it. Pushed her outside.

'Stay there,' I said urgently. 'Stay outside. It's gas.'

I took a deep lungful of the dark wintry air and turned back. Felt so feeble . . . so desperate. Bent over Jeremy, grabbed hold of his wrists, one in each hand, and pulled.

Pulled and dragged him over the white tiles, pulling him, sliding him, feeling the deadly tremors in my weak arms and legs. Out of the darkroom, through the hall, to the front door. Not far. Not more than ten feet. My own lungs were bursting for air . . . but not that air . . . not rotten eggs.

Clare took one of Jeremy's arms and pulled with me, and between us we dragged his unconscious form out into the street. I twitched the door shut behind me, and knelt on the cold road, retching and gasping and feeling utterly useless.

Clare was already banging on the house next door, returning with the schoolmaster who lived there.

'Breathe . . . into him,' I said.

'Mouth to mouth?' I nodded. 'Right, then.' He knelt down beside Jeremy, turned him over, and without question began efficient resuscitation, knowing the drill.

Clare herself disappeared but in a minute was back.

'I called the ambulance,' she said, 'but they want to know what gas. There's no gas in Lambourn, they say. They want to know . . . what to bring.'

'A respirator.' My own chest felt leaden. Breathing was difficult. 'Tell them . . . it's sulphur. Some sort of sulphide. Deadly. Tell them to hurry.'

She looked agonized, and ran back into the school-master's house, and I leant weakly on my knees against the front wall of my own house and coughed and felt incredibly ill. From the new troubles, not the old. From the gas.

Jeremy didn't stir. Dear God, I thought. Dear Christ, let him live.

Gas in my darkroom had been meant for me, not

for him. Must have been. Must have been in there, somehow, waiting for me, all the hours I'd spent lying outside in the hall.

I thought incoherently: Jeremy, *don't die*. Jeremy, it's my fault. *Don't die*. I should have burned George Millace's rubbish . . . not used it . . . not brought us so near . . . so near to death.

People came out from all the cottages, bringing blankets and shocked eyes. The schoolmaster went on with his task, though I saw from his manner, from glimpses of his face, that he thought it was useless.

Don't die . . .

Clare felt Jeremy's pulse. Her own face looked ashen.

'Is he . . .?' I said.

'A flutter.'

Don't die.

The schoolmaster took heart and tirelessly continued. I felt as if there was a constricting band round my ribs, squeezing my lungs. I'd taken only a few breaths of gas and air. Jeremy had breathed pure gas. And Clare . . .

'How's your chest?' I asked her.

'Tight,' she said. 'Horrid.'

The crowd around us seemed to be swelling. The ambulance arrived, and a police car, and Harold, and a doctor, and what seemed like half of Lambourn.

Expert hands took over from the schoolmaster and pumped air in and out of Jeremy's lungs: and Jeremy himself lay like a log while the doctor examined him and while he was lifted onto a stretcher and loaded into the ambulance.

He had a pulse. Some sort of pulse. That was all they would say. They shut doors on him, and drove him to Swindon.

Don't die, I prayed. Don't let him die. It's my fault.

A fire engine arrived with men in breathing apparatus. They went round to the back of the cottage carrying equipment with dials, and eventually came out through my front door into the street. What I heard of their reports to the policemen suggested that there shouldn't be any close investigation until the toxic level inside the cottage was within limits.

'What gas is it?' one of the policemen asked.

'Hydrogen sulphide.'

'Lethal?'

'Extremely. Paralyzes the breathing. Don't go in until we give the all clear. There's some sort of source in there, still generating gas.'

The policeman turned to me. 'What is it?' he said.

I shook my head. 'I don't know. I've nothing that would.'

He had asked earlier what was wrong with my face.

'Fell in a race.'

Everyone had accepted it. Battered jockeys were commonplace in Lambourn. The whole circus moved up the road to Harold's house, and events became jumbled.

Clare telephoned twice to the hospital for news of Jeremy.

'He's in intensive care . . . very ill. They want to know his next of kin.'

'Parents,' I said despairingly. 'Jeremy's home . . . in St Albans.' The number was in my house, with the gas.

Harold did some work with directory enquiries and got through to Jeremy's father.

Don't die, I thought. Bloody well live . . . *Please live.*

Policemen tramped in and out. An inspector came, asking questions. I told him, and Clare told him, what had happened. I didn't know how hydrogen sulphide had got into my darkroom. It had been a sheer accident that it had been Jeremy who breathed it. I didn't know why anyone should want to put gas in my darkroom. I didn't know who.

The inspector said he didn't believe me. No one had death traps like that set in their houses without knowing why. I shook my head. Talking was still a trial. I'd tell him why, I thought, if Jeremy died. Otherwise not.

How had I known so quickly that there was gas? My reaction had been instantaneous, Clare had said. Why was that?

'Sodium sulphide . . . used to be used in photographic studios. Still sometimes used . . . but not much . . . because of the smell. I didn't have any. It wasn't . . . mine.'

'Is it a gas?' he said, puzzled.

'No. Comes in crystals. Very poisonous. Comes in sepia toner kits. Kodak make one. Called T – 7 A . . . I think.'

'But you knew it *was* a gas.'

'Because of Jeremy . . . passing out. And I breathed it . . . it felt . . . wrong. You can make gas . . . using sodium sulphide . . . I just knew it was gas . . . I don't know how I knew . . . I just knew.'

'How do you make hydrogen sulphide gas from sodium sulphide crystals?'

'I don't know.'

He was insistent that I should answer, but I truthfully didn't know. And now, sir, he said, about your injuries. Your obvious discomfort and weakness. The state of your face. Are you sure, sir, that these were the result of a fall in a horse race? Because they looked to him, he had to say, more like the result of a severe human attack. He'd seen a few in his time, he said.

A fall, I said.

The inspector asked Harold, who looked troubled but answered forthrightly, 'A wicked fall, inspector. Umpteen horses kicked him. If you want witnesses . . . about six thousand people were watching.'

The inspector shrugged but looked disillusioned. Maybe he had an instinct, I thought, which told him I'd lied on some counts. When he'd gone Harold said, 'Hope you know what you're doing. Your face was OK when I left you, wasn't it?'

'Tell you one day,' I said, mumbling.

He said to Clare, 'What happened?' but she too shook her head in exhaustion and said she didn't know anything, didn't understand anything, and felt terrible herself. Harold's wife gave us comfort and food and eventually beds; and Jeremy at midnight was still alive.

Several rotten hours later Harold came into the little room where I sat in bed. Sat because I could breathe better that way, and because I couldn't sleep, and because I still ached abominably all over. My young lady, he said, had gone off to London to work, and would telephone that evening. The police wanted to see me. And Jeremy? Jeremy was still alive, still unconscious, still critically ill.

The whole day continued wretchedly.

The police went into my cottage, apparently opening doors and windows for the wind to blow through, and the inspector came to Harold's house to tell me the results.

We sat in Harold's office, where the inspector in daylight proved to be a youngish blond man with sensible eyes and a habit of cracking his knuckles. I hadn't taken him in much as a person the evening before, only his air of hostility; and that was plainly unchanged.

'There's a water filter on the tap in your darkroom,' he said. 'What do you use it for?'

'All water for photographs,' I said, 'has to be clean.'

Some of the worst swelling round my eyes and

mouth was beginning to subside. I could see better, talk better: at least some relief.

'Your water filter,' the inspector said, 'is a hydrogen sulphide generator.'

'It can't be.'

'Why not?'

'Well . . . I use it all the time. It's only a water softener. You regenerate it with salt . . . like all softeners. It couldn't possibly make gas.'

He gave me a long considering stare. Then he went away for an hour, and returned with a box and a young man in jeans and a sweater.

'Now, sir,' the inspector said to me with the studied procedural politeness of the suspicious copper, 'is this your water filter?'

He opened the box to show me the contents. One Durst filter with, screwed on to its top, the short rubber attachment which was normally pushed onto the tap.

'It looks like it,' I said. 'It looks just like it should. What's wrong with it? It couldn't possibly make gas.'

The inspector gestured to the young man, who produced a pair of plastic gloves from a pocket, putting them on. He then picked up the filter, which was a black plastic globe about the size of a grapefruit, with clear sections top and bottom, and unscrewed it round the middle.

'Inside here,' he said, 'there's usually just the filter cartridge. But as you'll see, in this particular object, things are quite different. Inside here there are two containers, one above the other. They're both empty now . . . but this lower one contained sodium sulphide crystals, and this one . . .' he paused with an inborn sense of the dramatic, ' . . . this upper one contained sulphuric acid. There must have been some form of membrane holding the contents of the two containers apart . . . but when the tap was turned on, the water pressure broke or dissolved the membrane, and the two chemicals mixed. Sulphuric acid and sodium sulphide, propelled by water . . . very highly effective sulphide generator. It would have gone on pouring out gas even if the water was turned off. Which it was . . . presumably by Mr Folk.'

There was a long, meaningful, depressing silence.

'So you can see, sir,' the inspector said, 'it couldn't in any way have been an accident.'

'No,' I said dully. 'But I don't know . . . I truthfully don't know . . . who could have put such a thing there . . . They would have to have known what sort of filter I had, wouldn't they?'

'And that you had a filter in the first place.'

'Everyone with a darkroom has a filter of some sort.'

Another silence. They seemed to be waiting for me to tell them, but I didn't know. It couldn't have been den Relgan . . . why should he bother with such a device when one or two more kicks would have finished me. It couldn't have been Elgin Yaxley: he hadn't had time. It couldn't have been any of the other people

George Millace had written his letters to. Two of them were old history, gone and forgotten. One of them was still current, but I'd done nothing about it, and hadn't told the man concerned that the letter existed. It wouldn't anyway be him. He would certainly not kill me.

All of which left one most uncomfortable explanation . . . that somebody thought I had something I didn't have. Someone who knew I'd inherited George Millace's blackmailing package . . . and who knew I'd used some of it . . . and who wanted to stop me using any more of it.

George Millace had definitely had more in the box than I'd inherited. I didn't have, for instance, the cigarette packet on which Dana den Relgan had written her drugs list. And I didn't have . . . what else?

'Well, sir,' the inspector said.

'No one's been into my cottage since I was using the darkroom on Wednesday. Only my neighbour, and the rating officer . . .' I stopped, and they pounced on it. 'What rating officer?'

Ask Mrs Jackson, I said: and they said yes they would.

'She said he didn't touch anything.'

'But he could have seen what type of filter . . .'

'Is it my own filter?' I asked. 'It does look like it.'

'Probably,' the younger man said. 'But our man would have had to see it . . . for the dimensions. Then he would come back . . . and it would take about thirty seconds, I'd reckon, to take the filter cartridge out and put the packets of chemicals in. Pretty neat job.'

'Will Jeremy live?' I said.

The younger man shrugged. 'I'm a chemist. Not a doctor.'

They went away after a while, taking the filter.

I rang the hospital. No change.

I went to the hospital myself in the afternoon, with Harold's wife driving because she insisted I wasn't fit.

I didn't see Jeremy. I saw his parents. They were abstracted with worry, too upset to be angry. Not my fault, they said, though I thought they would think so later. Jeremy was being kept alive by a respirator. His breathing was paralyzed. His heart was beating. His brain was alive.

His mother wept.

'Don't worry so,' Harold's wife said, driving home. 'He'll be all right.'

She had persuaded the casualty sister, whom she knew, to get me to have some stitches in my face. The result felt stiffer than ever.

'If he dies . . .'

'He won't die,' Harold's wife said.

*

The inspector telephoned to say I could go back to the cottage, but not into the darkroom: the police had sealed it.

I wandered slowly round my home feeling no sort of ease. Physically wretched, morally pulverized, neck-deep in guilt.

There were signs everywhere that the police had searched. Hardly surprising, I supposed. They hadn't come across the few prints I still had of George Millace's letters, which were locked in the car. They had left undisturbed on the kitchen dresser the box with the blank-looking negatives.

The box . . .

I opened it. It still contained, beside the puzzles I'd solved, the one that I hadn't.

The black light-proof envelope which contained what looked like a piece of clear plastic and two unused sheets of typing paper.

Perhaps . . . I thought . . . Perhaps it's because I have these that the gas trap was set.

But what . . . *what* did I have?

It was no good, I thought: I would have to find out . . . and pretty fast, before whoever it was had another go at killing me, and succeeded.

CHAPTER EIGHTEEN

I begged a bed again from Harold's wife, and in the morning telephoned Swindon hospital again.

Jeremy was alive. No change.

I sat in Harold's kitchen drinking coffee, suicidally depressed.

Harold answered his ringing telephone for about the tenth time that morning and handed the receiver to me.

'It's not an owner, this time,' he said. 'It's for you.'

It was Jeremy's father. I felt sick.

'We want you to know . . . he's awake.'

'Oh . . .'

'He's still on the respirator. But they say that by now if he'd been going to die, he'd have gone. He's still very ill . . . but they say he'll recover. We thought you'd like to know.'

'Thank you,' I said.

The reprieve was almost more unbearable than the anxiety. I gave the receiver to Harold and said Jeremy was better, and went out into the yard to look at the horses. In the fresh air I felt stifled. In relief, over-thrown. I stood in the wind waiting for the internal storm to abate, and gradually felt an incredible sense of release. I had literally been freed. Let off a life sentence. You bugger, Jeremy, I thought, dishing out such a fright.

Clare telephoned.

'He's all right. He's awake,' I said.

'Thank God.'

'Can I ask you a favour?' I said. 'Can I dump myself on Samantha for a night or two?'

'As in the old days?'

'Until Saturday.'

She swallowed a laugh and said why not, and when did I want to come.

'Tonight,' I said. 'If I may.'

'We'll expect you for supper.'

Harold wanted to know when I thought I'd be fit to race.

I would get some physiotherapy from the Clinic for Injuries in London, I said. By Saturday I'd be ready.

'Not by the look of you.'

'Four days. I'll be fit.'

'Mind you are, then.'

I felt distinctly unfit for driving, but less than inclined

967

to sleep alone in my cottage. I did some minimal packing, collected George's rubbish box from the kitchen, and set off to Chiswick, where despite wearing sunglasses I got a horrified reception. Black bruises, stitched cuts, three-day growth of beard. Hardly a riot.

'But it's *worse*,' Clare said, staring closely.

'Looks worse, feels better.' A good job, I thought, that they couldn't see the rest of me. My whole belly was black with the decaying remains of internal abdominal bleeding. The damage, I'd concluded, which had set off the spasms.

Samantha was troubled. 'Clare said someone had punched you . . . but I never thought . . .'

'Look,' I said, 'I could go somewhere else.'

'Don't be silly. Sit down. Supper's ready.'

They didn't talk much or seem to expect me to. I wasn't good company. Too drastically feeble. I asked with the coffee if I might telephone Swindon.

'Jeremy?' Clare said.

I nodded.

'I'll do it. What's the number?'

I told her, and she got through, and consulted.

'Still on the respirator,' she said, 'but progress maintained.'

'If you're tired,' Samantha said calmly, 'go to bed.'

'Well . . .'

They both came upstairs. I walked automatically, without thinking, into the small bedroom next door to the bathroom.

They both laughed. 'We wondered if you would,' Samantha said.

Clare went to work and I spent most of Wednesday dozing in the swinging basket chair in the kitchen. Samantha came in and out, went to her part-time job in the morning, shopped in the afternoon. I waited in a highly peaceful state for energy of any sort to return to brain or limbs and reckoned I was fortunate to have a day like that to mend in.

Thursday took me to the Clinic for Injuries for two long sessions of electric treatment, massage and general physio, with two more sessions promised for Friday.

On Thursday between the sessions I telephoned four photographers and one acquaintance who worked on a specialist magazine, and found no one who knew how to raise pictures from plastic or typing paper. Pull the other one, old boy, the specialist said wearily.

When I got back to Chiswick the sun was low on the winter horizon, and in the kitchen Samantha was cleaning the french windows.

'They always look so filthy when the sun shines on them,' she said, busily rubbing with a cloth. 'Sorry if it's cold in here, but I won't be long.'

I sat in the basket chair and watched her squirt liquid cleaner out of a white plastic bottle. She finished the outsides of the doors and came in, pulling them after her, fastening the bolts. The plastic bottle stood on a table beside her.

AJAX, it said, in big letters.

I frowned at it, trying to remember. Where had I heard the word Ajax?

I stood up out of the swinging chair and walked over for a closer look. Ajax Window Cleaner, it said in smaller red letters on the white plastic, With Ammonia. I picked the bottle up and shook it. Liquid. I put my nose to the top, and smelled the contents. Soapy. Sweet-scented. Not pungent.

'What is it?' Samantha said. 'What are you looking at?'

'This cleaner . . .'

'Yes?'

'Why would a man ask his wife to buy him some Ajax?'

'What a question,' Samantha said. 'I've no idea.'

'Nor did she have,' I said. 'She didn't know why.'

Samantha took the bottle out of my hands and continued with her task. 'You can clean any sort of glass with it,' she said. 'Bathroom tiles. Looking glass. Quite useful stuff.'

I went back to the basket chair and swung in it gently. Samantha cast me a sideways glance, smiling.

'You looked like death two days ago,' she said.

'And now?'

'Now one might pause before calling the undertaker.'

'I'll shave tomorrow,' I said.

'Who punched you?' Her voice sounded casual. Her eyes and attention were on the window. It was, all the same, a serious question. A seeking not for a simple one word answer, but for commitment to herself. A sort of request for payment for shelter unquestioningly given. If I didn't tell her, she wouldn't persist. But if I didn't tell her, we had already gone as far as we ever would in relationship.

What did I want, I thought, in that house that now increasingly felt like home. I had never wanted a family: people always close: permanence. I'd wanted no loving ties. No suffocating emotional dependents. So if I nested comfortably, deeply into the lives lived in that house, wouldn't I feel impelled in a short while to break out with wild flapping freedom-seeking wings. Did anyone ever fundamentally change?

Samantha read into my silence what I expected, and her manner did subtly alter, not to one of unfriendliness, but to a cut-off of intimacy. Before she'd finished the window I'd become her guest, not her . . . her what? Her son, brother, nephew . . . part of her.

She gave me a bright surface smile and put the kettle on for tea.

Clare returned from work with gaiety over tiredness, and she too, though not asking, was waiting.

I found myself, halfway through supper, just telling them about George Millace. In the end it was no great hard decision. No cut and dried calculation. I just naturally told them.

'You won't approve,' I said. 'I carried on where George left off.'

They listened with their forks in the air, taking mouthfuls at long intervals, eating peas and lasagne slowly.

'So you see,' I said at the end. 'It isn't finished yet. There's no going back or wishing I hadn't started . . . I don't know that I do wish that . . . but I asked to come here for a few days because I didn't feel safe in the cottage, and I'm not going back there to live permanently until I know who tried to kill me.'

Clare said, 'You might never know.'

'Don't say that,' Samantha said sharply. 'If he doesn't find out . . .' She stopped.

I finished it for her, 'I'll have no defence.'

'Perhaps the police . . .' Clare said.

'Perhaps.'

We passed the rest of the evening more in thoughtfulness than depression, and the news from Swindon was good. Jeremy's lungs were coming out of paralysis. Still on the respirator, but a significant improvement during the past twenty-four hours. The prim voice reading the written bulletin sounded bored. Could I speak to Jeremy himself yet, I asked. They'd check. The prim voice came back; not in intensive care: try on Sunday.

*

I spent a long time in the bathroom on Friday morning scraping off beard and snipping out unabsorbed ends of the fine transparent thread the casualty sister had used in her stitching. She'd done a neat job, I had to confess. The cuts had all healed, and would disappear probably without scars. All the swelling, also, had gone. There were still remains of black bruises turning yellow, and still the chipped teeth, but what finally looked out of the mirror was definitely a face, not a nightmare.

Samantha looked relieved over the re-emergence of civilization and insisted on telephoning to her dentist. 'You need caps,' she said, 'and caps you'll have.' And caps I had, late that afternoon. Temporaries, until porcelain jobs could be made.

Between the two sessions in the clinic I drove north out of London to Basildon in Essex, to where a British firm manufactured photographic printing paper. I went instead of telephoning because I thought they would find it less easy to say they had no information if I was actually there; and so it proved.

They did not, they said in the front office politely, know of any photographic materials which looked like plastic or typing paper. Had I brought the specimens with me?

No, I had not. I didn't want them examined in case they were sensitive to light. Could I scc somconc clsc?

Difficult, they said.

I showed no signs of leaving. Perhaps Mr

973

Christopher could help me, they suggested at length, if he wasn't too busy.

Mr Christopher turned out to be about nineteen with an antisocial hair-cut and chronic catarrh. He listened, however, attentively.

'This paper and this plastic've got no emulsion on them?'

'No, I don't think so.'

He shrugged. 'There you are, then.'

'There I am where?'

'You got no pictures.'

I sucked at the still broken teeth and asked him what seemed to be a nonsensical question.

'Why would a photographer want ammonia?'

'Well, he wouldn't. Not for photographs. No straight ammonia in any developer or bleach or fix, that I know of.'

'Would anyone here know?' I asked.

He gave me a pitying stare, implying that if he didn't know, no one else would.

'You could ask,' I said persuasively. 'Because if there's a process which does use ammonia, you'd like to know, wouldn't you?'

'Yeah. I reckon I would.'

He gave me a brisk nod and vanished, and I waited a quarter of an hour, wondering if he'd gone off to lunch. He returned, however, with a grey elderly man in glasses who was none too willing but delivered the goods.

'Ammonia,' he said, 'is used in the photographic sections of engineering industries. It develops what the public call blueprints. More accurately, of course, it's the diazo process.'

'Please,' I said humbly and with gratitude, 'could you describe it to me.'

'What's the matter with your face?' he said.

'Lost an argument.'

'Huh.'

'Diazo process,' I said. 'What is it?'

'You get a drawing ... a line drawing, I'm talking about ... from the designer. Say of a component in a machine. A drawing with exact specifications for manufacture. Are you with me?'

'Yes.'

'The industry will need several copies of the master drawing. So they make blueprints of it. Or rather, they don't.'

'Er ...' I said.

'In blueprints,' he said severely, 'the paper turns blue, leaving the design in white. Nowadays the paper turns white and the lines develop in black. Or dark red.'

'Please ... go on.'

'From the beginning?' he said. 'The master drawing, which is of course on translucent paper, is pinned and pressed tightly by glass over a sheet of diazo paper. Diazo paper is white on the back, and yellow or greenish on the side covered with ammonia-sensitive dye. Bright carbon arc light is shone onto the master drawing for a measured length of time. This light bleaches out all the dye on the diazo paper underneath except for the parts under the lines on the master drawing. The diazo paper is then developed in hot ammonia fumes, and the lines of dye emerge, turning dark. Is that what you want?'

'Indeed it is,' I said with awe. 'Does diazo paper look like typing paper?'

'Certainly it can, if it's cut down to that size.'

'And how about a piece of clear-looking plastic?'

'Sounds like diazo film,' he said calmly. 'You don't need hot ammonia fumes for developing that. Any form of cold liquid will do. But be careful. I said carbon arc lights, because that's the method that's used in engineering, but of course a longer exposure to sunlight or any other form of light would also have the same effect. If the piece of film you have looks clear, it means that most of the yellow-looking dye has been already bleached out. If there is a drawing there, you must be careful not to expose it to too much more light.'

'How much more light is too much?' I said anxiously.

He pursed his lips. 'In sunlight, you'd have lost any trace of dye for ever in thirty seconds. In normal room light . . . five to ten minutes.'

'It's in a light-proof envelope.'

'Then you might be lucky.'

'And the sheets of paper . . . they look white on both sides.'

'The same applies,' he said. 'They've been exposed

to light. You might have a drawing there, or you might not.'

'How do I make hot ammonia fumes, to find out?'

'Simple,' he said, as if everyone would know items like that. 'Put some ammonia in a saucepan and heat it. Hold the paper over the top. Don't get it wet. Just steam it.'

'Would you,' I said carefully, 'like some champagne for lunch?'

I returned to Samantha's house at about six o'clock with a cheap saucepan, two bottles of Ajax, an anaesthetized top lip, and a set of muscles that had been jerked, pressed and exercised into some sort of resurrection. I also felt dead tired which wasn't a good omen for fitness on the morrow, when, Harold had informed me on the telephone, two 'chasers would be awaiting my services at Sandown Park.

Samantha had gone out. Clare, with work scattered all over the kitchen table, gave me a fast, assessing scrutiny and suggested a large brandy.

'It's in that cupboard with the salt and flour and herbs. Cooking brandy. Pour me some too, would you?'

I sat at the table with her for a while, sipping the repulsive stuff neat and feeling a lot better for it. Her dark head was bent over the book she was working on, the capable hand stretching out now and again for the glass, the mind engrossed in her task.

'Would you live with me?' I said.

She looked up; abstracted, faintly frowning, questioning.

'Did you say . . .?'

'Yes, I did,' I said. 'Would you live with me?'

Her work at last lost her attention. With a smile in her eyes she said, 'Is that an academic question or a positive invitation?'

'Invitation.'

'I couldn't live in Lambourn,' she said. 'Too far to commute. You couldn't live here . . . too far from the horses.'

'Somewhere in between.'

She looked at me wonderingly. 'Are you serious?'

'Yes.'

'But we haven't . . .' She stopped, leaving a clear meaning.

'Been to bed.'

'Well . . .'

'In general,' I said. 'What do you think?'

She took refuge and time with sips from her glass. I waited for what seemed a small age.

'I think,' she said finally, 'why not give it a try.'

I smiled from intense satisfaction.

'Don't look so smug,' she said. 'Drink your brandy while I finish this book.'

She bent her head down again but didn't read far.

'It's no good,' she said. 'How can I work . . .? Let's get the supper.'

Cooking frozen fish fillets took ages because of her trying to do it with my arms round her waist and my chin on her hair. I didn't taste the stuff when we ate it. I felt extraordinarily light-headed. I hadn't deeply hoped she would say yes, and still less had I expected the incredible sense of adventure since she had. To have someone to care about seemed no longer a burden to be avoided, but a positive privilege.

Amazing, I thought dimly; the whole thing's amazing. Was this what Lord White had felt for Dana den Relgan?

'What time does Samantha get back?' I said.

Clare shook her head. 'Too soon.'

'Will you come with me tomorrow?' I said. 'To the races . . . and then stay somewhere together afterwards.'

'Yes, I will.'

'Samantha won't mind?'

She gave me an amused look. 'No, I don't think so.'

'Why do you laugh?'

'She's gone to the pictures. I asked her why she had to go on your last night here. She said she wanted to see the film. I thought it odd . . . but I believed her. She saw . . . more than I did.'

'My God,' I said. '*Women.*'

While she did try again to finish her work, I fetched the rubbish box and took out the black light-proof envelope.

I borrowed a flat glass dish from a cupboard. Took the piece of plastic film from the envelope. Put it in the dish. At once poured liquid Ajax over it. Held my breath.

Almost instantly dark brownish-red lines became visible. I rocked the dish, sloshing the liquid across the plastic surface, conscious that all of the remaining dye had to be covered with ammonia before the light bleached it away.

It was no engineering drawing, but handwriting.

It looked odd.

As more and more developed, I realized that from the reading point of view the plastic was wrong side up.

Turned it over. Sloshed more Ajax over it, tilting it back and forth. Read the revealed words, as clear as when they'd been written.

They were ... they had to be ... what Dana den Relgan had written on the cigarette packet.

Heroin, cocaine, cannabis. Quantities, dates, prices paid, suppliers. No wonder she had wanted it back.

Clare looked up from her work.

'What have you found?'

'What that Dana girl who came last Sunday was wanting.'

'Let's see.' She came across and looked into the dish, reading. 'That's pretty damning, isn't it?'

'Mm.'

'But how did it turn up ... like this?'

I said appreciatively, 'Crafty George Millace. He got her to write on cellophane wrapping with a red felt-tip pen . . . she felt safer that way, because cigarette packet wrapping is so fragile, so destructible . . . and I expect the words themselves looked indistinct, over the printed packet. But from George's point of view all he wanted was solid lines on transparent material, to make a diazo print.'

I explained to her all that I'd learned in Basildon. 'He must have cut the wrapping off carefully, pressed it flat under glass on top of this piece of diazo film, and exposed it to light. Then with the drugs list safely recorded, it wouldn't matter if the wrapping came to pieces . . . and the list was hidden, like everything else.'

'He was an extraordinary man.'

I nodded. 'Extraordinary. Though, mind you, he didn't mean anyone else to have to solve his puzzles. He made them only to please himself . . . and to save the records from angry burglars.'

'In which he succeeded.'

'He sure did.'

'What about all your photographs?' she said in sudden alarm. 'All the ones in the filing cabinet. Suppose . . .'

'Calm down,' I said. 'Even if anyone stole them or burned them they'd miss all the negatives. The butcher has those down the road in his freezer room.'

'Maybe all photographers,' she said, 'are obsessed.'

It wasn't until much later that I realized I hadn't disputed her classification. I hadn't even *thought* 'I'm a jockey.'

I asked her if she'd mind if I filled the kitchen with the smell of boiling ammonia.

'I'll go and wash my hair,' she said.

When she'd gone I drained the Ajax out of the dish into the saucepan and added to it what was left in the first bottle, and while it heated opened the french windows so as not to asphyxiate. Then I held the first of the sheets of what looked like typing paper over the simmering cleaner, and watched George's words come alive as if they'd been written in secret ink. Ammonia clearly evaporated quickly, because it took the whole second bottle to get results with the second sheet, but it too, grew words like the first.

Together they constituted one handwritten letter in what I had no doubt was George's own writing. He must himself have written on some sort of transparent material ... and it could have been anything: a poly-thene bag, tracing paper, a piece of glass, film with all the emulsion bleached off ... anything. When he'd written, he had put his letter over diazo paper and exposed it to light, and immediately stored the exposed paper in the light-proof envelope.

And then what? Had he sent his transparent original? Had he written it again on ordinary paper? Had he typed it? No way of knowing. But one thing was certain: in some form or other he had despatched his letter.

I had heard of the results of its arrival.

I could guess, I thought, who wanted me dead.

CHAPTER NINETEEN

Harold met me with some relief on the verandah outside the weighing room at Sandown.

'You at least look better . . . have you passed the doctor?'

I nodded. 'He signed my card.' He'd no reason not to. By his standards a jockey who took a week off because he'd been kicked was acting more self-indulgently than usual. He'd asked me to do a bend-stretch, and nodded me through.

'Victor's here,' Harold said.

'Did you tell him . . .?'

'Yes, I did. He says he doesn't want to talk to you on a racecourse. He says he wants to see his horses work on the Downs. He's coming on Monday. He'll talk to you then. And, Philip, you bloody well be careful what you say.'

'Mm,' I said non-committally. 'How about Coral Key?'

'What about him? He's fit.'

'No funny business?'

'Victor knows how you feel,' Harold said.

'Victor doesn't care a losing tote ticket how I feel. Is the horse running straight?'

'He hasn't said anything.'

'Because I am,' I said. 'If I'm riding it, I'm riding it straight. Whatever he says in the parade ring.'

'You've got bloody aggressive all of a sudden.'

'No . . . just saving you money. You personally. Don't back me to lose, like you did on Daylight. That's all.'

He said he wouldn't. He also said there was no point in holding the Sunday briefing if I was talking to Victor on Monday, and that we would discuss next week's plans after that. Neither of us said what was in both of our minds . . . after Monday, would there be any plans?

Steve Millace in the changing room was complaining about a starter letting a race off when he, Steve, hadn't been ready, with the consequence that he was left so flat-footed that the other runners had gone half a furlong before he'd got started . . . the owner was angry and said he wanted another jockey next time, and, as Steve asked everyone *ad infinitum*, was it fair?

'No,' I said. 'Life isn't.'

'It should be.'

'Better face it,' I said smiling. 'The best you can expect is a kick in the teeth.'

'Your teeth are all right,' someone said.

'They've got caps on.'

'Pick up the pieces, huh? Is that what you're saying?'

I nodded.

Steve said, not following this exchange, 'Starters should be fined for letting a race off when the horses aren't pointing the right way.'

'Give it a rest,' someone said: but Steve as usual was still going on about it a couple of hours later.

His mother, he said when I enquired, had gone to friends in Devon for a rest.

Outside the weighing room Bart Underfield was lecturing one of the more gullible of the pressmen on the subject of unusual nutrients.

'It's rubbish giving horses beer and eggs and ridiculous things like that. I never do it.'

The pressman refrained from saying – or perhaps he didn't know – that the trainers addicted to eggs and beer were on the whole more successful than Bart.

Bart's face when he saw me changed from bossy know-all to tight-lipped spite. He jettisoned the pressman and took two decisive steps to stand in my path, but when he'd stopped me he didn't speak.

'Do you want something, Bart?' I said.

He still didn't say anything. I thought that quite likely he couldn't find words intense enough to convey what he felt. I was growing accustomed, I thought, to being hated.

He found his voice. 'You wait,' he said with bitter quiet. 'I'll get you.'

If he'd had a dagger and privacy, I wouldn't have turned my back on him, as I did, to walk away.

Lord White was there, deep in earnest conversation

with fellow Stewards, his gaze flicking over me quickly as if wincing. He would never, I supposed, feel comfortable when I was around. Never be absolutely sure that I wouldn't tell. Never like me knowing what I knew.

He would have to put up with it for a long time, I thought. One way or another the racing world would always be my world, as it was his. He would see me, and I him, week by week, until one of us died.

Victor Briggs was waiting in the parade ring when I went out to ride Coral Key. A heavy brooding figure in his broad-brimmed hat and long navy overcoat: unsmiling, untalkative, gloomy. When I touched my cap to him politely there was no response of any sort, only the maintenance of an expressionless stare.

Coral Key was an oddity among Victor Briggs's horses, a six-year-old novice 'chaser bought out of the hunting field when he had begun to show promise in point-to-points. Great horses in the past had started that way, like Oxo and Ben Nevis which had both won the Grand National, and although Coral Key was unlikely to be of that class, it seemed to me that he, too, had the feel of good things to come. There was no way that I was going to mess up his early career, whatever my instructions. In my mind and very likely in my attitude I dared his owner to say he didn't want him to try to win.

He didn't say it. He said nothing at all about anything. He simply watched me unblinkingly, and kept his mouth shut.

Harold bustled about as if movement itself could dispel the atmosphere existing between his owner and his jockey; and I mounted and rode out to the course feeling as if I'd been in a strong field of undischarged electricity.

A spark ... an explosion ... might lie ahead. Harold sensed it. Harold was worried to the depths of his own explosive soul.

It might be going to be the last race I ever rode for Victor Briggs. I lined up at the start thinking that it was no good speculating about that; that all I should be concentrating on was the matter in hand.

A cold windy cloudy day. Good ground underfoot. Seven other runners, none of them brilliant. If Coral Key jumped as he had when I'd schooled him at home, he should have a good chance.

I settled my goggles over my eyes and gathered the reins.

'Come in, now, jockeys,' the starter said. The horses advanced towards the tapes in a slow line and as the gate flew up accelerated away from bunched haunches. Thirteen fences; two miles. I would find out pretty soon, I thought ruefully, if I wasn't yet fit.

Important, I thought, to get him to jump well. It was what I was best at. What I most enjoyed doing. There were seven fences close together down the far side of the course ... If one met the first of them just right they all fitted, but a brakes-on approach to the first often meant seven blunders by the end, and countless lengths lost.

From the start there were two fences, then the uphill stretch past the stands, then the top bend, then the downhill fence where I'd stepped off Daylight. No problems on Coral Key: he cleared the lot. Then the sweep round to the seven trappy fences, and if I lost one length getting Coral Key set right for the first, by the end of the seventh I'd stolen ten.

Too soon for satisfaction. Round the long bottom curve Coral Key lay second, taking a breather. Three fences to go . . . and the long uphill to home.

Between the last two fences I caught up with the leader. We jumped the last fence alongsides, nothing between us. Raced up the hill, stretching, flying . . . doing everything I could.

The other horse won by two lengths.

Harold said, 'He ran well,' a shade apprehensively, patting Coral Key in the unsaddling enclosure; and Victor Briggs said nothing.

I pulled the saddle off and went in to weigh. There wasn't any way that I could think of that I could have won the race. The other horse had had enough in hand to beat off my challenge. He'd been stronger than Coral Key, and faster. I hadn't felt weak. I hadn't thrown anything away in jumping mistakes. I just hadn't won.

I had needed a strong hand for talking to Victor Briggs; and I hadn't got it.

When life kicks you in the teeth, get caps.

I won the other 'chase, the one that didn't matter so much except to the owners, a junketing quartet of businessmen.

'Bloody good show,' they said, beaming. 'Bloody well ridden.'

I saw Victor Briggs watching from ten paces away, balefully staring. I wondered if he knew how much I'd have given to have those two results reversed.

Clare said, 'I suppose the wrong one won?'

'Yeah.'

'How much does it matter?'

'I'll find out on Monday.'

'Well . . . let's forget it.'

'Shouldn't be difficult,' I said. I looked at the trim dark coat, the white puff-ball hat, the long polished boots. Looked at the large grey eyes and the friendly mouth. Incredible, I thought, to have someone like that waiting for me outside the weighing room. Quite extraordinarily different from going home alone. Like a fire in a cold house. Like sugar on strawberries.

'Would you mind very much,' I said, 'if we made a detour for me to call on my grandmother?'

The old woman was markedly worse.

No longer propped more or less upright, she sagged back without strength on the pillows; and even the eyes seemed to be losing the struggle, with none of the beady aggression glittering out.

'Did you bring her?' she said.

Still no salutation, no preliminaries. Perhaps it was a mistake to expect changes in the mind to accompany changes in the body. Perhaps my feelings for her were different . . . and all that remained immutable was her hatred for me.

'No,' I said. 'I didn't bring her. She's lost.'

'You said you would find her.'

'She's lost.'

She gave a feeble cough, the thin chest jerking. Her eyelids closed for a few seconds and opened again. A weak hand twitched at the sheet.

'Leave your money to James,' I said.

With a faint outer echo of persistent inner stubbornness, she shook her head.

'Leave some to charity, then,' I said. 'Leave it to a dog's home.'

'I hate dogs.' Her voice was weak. Not her opinions.

'How about lifeboats?'

'Hate the sea. Makes me sick.'

'Medical research?'

'Hasn't done me much good, has it?'

'Well,' I said slowly, 'how about leaving it to a religious order of some sort.'

'You must be mad. I hate religion. Cause of trouble. Cause of wars. Wouldn't give them a penny.'

I sat down unbidden in the armchair.

'Can I do anything for you?' I asked. 'Besides, of course, finding Amanda. Can I fetch anything? Is there anything you want?'

She raised a faint sneer. 'Don't think you can soft soap me into leaving any money to you, because I'm not going to.'

'I'd give water to a dying cat,' I said. 'Even if it spat in my face.'

Her mouth opened and stiffened with affront.

'How . . . dare . . . you?'

'How dare you still think I'd shift a speck of dust for your money?'

The mouth closed into a thin line.

'Can I fetch you anything? I said again, levelly. 'Is there anything you want?'

She didn't answer for several seconds. Then she said, 'Go away.'

'Well, I will, in a minute,' I said. 'But I want just to suggest something else.' I waited a fraction, but as she didn't immediately argue I continued. 'In case Amanda is ever found . . . why don't you set up a trust for her? Tie up the capital tight with masses of excellent trustees. Make it so that she couldn't ever get her hands on the money herself . . . and nor could anyone who was . . . perhaps . . . after her fortune. Make it impossible for anyone but Amanda herself to benefit . . . with an income paid out only at the direction of the trustees.'

She watched me with half-lowered eyelids.

'Wherever she is,' I said, 'Amanda is still only

seventeen or eighteen. Too young to inherit a lot of money without strings. Leave it to her . . . with strings like steel hawsers.'

'Is that all?'

'Mm.'

She lay quiet, immobile.

I waited. I had waited all my life for something other than malevolence from my grandmother. I could wait forever.

'Go away,' she said.

I stood up and said, 'Very well.'

Walked to the door. Put my hand on the knob.

'Send me some roses,' my grandmother said.

We found a flower shop still open in the town, though they were sweeping out ready to close.

'Doesn't she realize it's December?' Clare said. 'Roses will cost a fortune.'

'If you were dying, and you wanted roses, do you think you'd care?'

'Maybe not.'

All they had in the flower shop were fifteen very small pink buds on very long thin stems. Not much call for roses. These were left over spare from a wedding.

We drove back to the nursing home and gave them to a nurse to deliver at once, with a card enclosed saying I'd get some better ones next week.

'She doesn't deserve it,' Clare said.
'Poor old woman.'

We stayed in a pub by the Thames which had old beams
and good food and bedroom windows looking out to
bare willows and sluggish brown water.

No one knew us. We signed in as Mr and Mrs and
ate a slow dinner, and went unobtrusively to bed. Not
the first time she'd done it, she said: did I mind? Preferred it, I said. No fetishes about virgins? No kinks at
all, that I knew of. Good, she said.

It began in friendship and progressed to passion.
Ended in breathlessness and laughter, sank to murmurs
and sleep. The best it had ever been for me. Couldn't
tell about her. She showed no hesitation, however,
about a repeat programme in the morning.

In the afternoon, in peaceful accord, we went to see
Jeremy.

He was lying in a high bed in a room on his own,
with a mass of breathing equipment to one side. He
was, though, breathing for himself with his own lungs.
Precariously, I guessed, since a nurse came in to check
on him every ten minutes while we were there, making
sure that a bell-push remained under his fingers the
whole time.

He looked thinner than ever, and greyly pale, but
there had been no near-execution in his brain. The eyes
were as intelligent as ever, and the silly-ass manner

appeared strongly as a defence against the indignities of his position. The nurse, on every visit, got a load of weary waffle.

I tried to apologize for what he'd suffered. He wouldn't have it.

'Don't forget,' he said, 'I was there because I wanted to be. No one exactly twisted my arm.' He gave me a travelling inspection. 'Your face looks OK. How do you heal so fast?'

'Always do.'

'Always . . .' he gave a weak laugh. 'Funny life you lead. Always healing.'

'How long will you be in here?'

'Three or four days.'

'Is that all?' Clare said, surprised. 'You look . . . er . . .'

He looked whiter than the pillow his head lay on. He nodded, however, and said, 'I'm breathing much better. Once there's no danger the nerves will pack up again, I can go. There's nothing else wrong.'

'I'll take you home if you need transport,' I said.

'Might hold you to that.'

We didn't stay very long because talking clearly tired him, but just before we went he said, 'You know, that gas was so quick. Not slow, like gas at the dentist. I'd no time to do anything . . . it was like breathing a brick wall.'

Into a short reflective silence Clare said, 'No one would have lived if they'd been there alone.'

'Makes you think . . . what?' said Jeremy cheerfully.

As we drove back towards the pub Clare said, 'You didn't tell him about Amanda.'

'Plenty of time.'

'He came down last Sunday because he'd got your message that you'd found her. He told me while we were in the kitchen. He said your phone was out of order, so he came.'

'I'd unplugged it.'

'Odd how things happen.'

'Mm.'

Our second night was a confirmation of the first. Much the same, but new and different. A tingling, fierce, gentle, intense, turbulent time. A matter, it seemed, as much to her liking as mine.

'Where's this depression one's supposed to get?' she said, very late. 'Post what's-it.'

'Comes in the morning, when you go.'

'That's hours off yet.'

'So it is.'

The morning came, as they do. I drove her to a station to catch a train, and went on myself to Lambourn.

When I got there, before going to Harold's, I called at my cottage. All seemed quiet. All cold. All strangely unfamiliar, as if home was no longer the natural embracing refuge it should be. I saw for the first time the bareness, the emotional chill which had been so apparent to Jeremy on his first visit. It no longer seemed to fit with myself. The person who had made that home was going away, receding in time. I felt oddly nostalgic ... but there was no calling him back. The maturing change had gone too far.

Shivering a little I spread out on the kitchen table a variety of photographs of different people, and then I asked my neighbour Mrs Jackson to come in and look at them.

'What am I looking for, Mr Nore?'

'Anyone you've seen before.'

Obligingly she studied them carefully one by one, and stopped without hesitation at a certain face.

'How extraordinary!' she exclaimed. 'That's the council man who came about the rates. The one I let in here. Ever so sarcastic, the police were about that, but as I told them, you don't *expect* people to say they're rating officers if they aren't.'

'You're sure he's the one?'

'Positive,' she said, nodding. 'He had that same hat on, and all.'

'Then would you write on the back of the photo for me, Mrs Jackson?' I gave her a Lumocolor pen that would write boldly and blackly on the photographic paper, and dictated the words for her, saying that this man had called at the house of Philip Nore posing as a rating officer on Friday, 27 November.

'Is that all?' she asked.

'Sign your name, Mrs Jackson. And would you mind

repeating the whole message on the back of this other photograph?'

With concentration she did so. 'Are you giving these to the police?' she said. 'I don't want them bothering me again really. Will they come back again with their questions?'

'I shouldn't think so,' I said.

CHAPTER TWENTY

Victor Briggs had come in his Mercedes, but he went up to the Downs with Harold in the Land Rover. I rode up on a horse. The morning's work got done to everyone's reasonable satisfaction, and we all returned variously to the stable.

When I rode into the yard Victor Briggs was standing by his car, waiting. I slid off the horse and gave it to one of the lads to see to.

'Get in the car,' Victor said.

No waster of words, ever. He stood there in his usual clothes, gloved as always against the chilly wind, darkening the day. If I could see auras, I thought, his would be black.

I sat in the front passenger seat, where he pointed, and he slid himself in beside me, behind the steering wheel. He started the engine, released the brake, put the automatic gear into drive. The quiet hunk of metal eased out of Lambourn, going back to the Downs.

He stopped on a wide piece of grass verge from

where one could see half of Berkshire. He switched off the engine, leaned back in his seat, and said, 'Well?'

'Do you know what I'm going to say?' I asked.

'I hear things,' he said. 'I hear a lot of things.'

'I know that.'

'I heard that den Relgan set his goons on you.'

'Did you?' I looked at him with interest. 'Where did you hear that?'

He made a small tight movement of his mouth, but he did answer. 'Gambling club.'

'What did you hear?'

'True, isn't it?' he said. 'You still had the marks on Saturday.'

'Did you hear any reasons?'

He produced the twitch that went for a smothered smile.

'I heard,' he said, 'that you got den Relgan chucked out of the Jockey Club a great deal faster than he got in.'

He watched my alarmed surprise with another twitch, a less successful effort this time at hiding amusement.

'Did you hear how?' I said.

He said with faint regret. 'No. Just that you'd done it. The goons were talking. Stupid bone-headed bull-muscle. Den Relgan's heading for trouble, using them. They never keep their mouths shut.'

'Are they ... um ... out for general hire?'

'Chuckers out at a gaming club. Muscle for hire. As you say.'

'They beat up George Millace's wife . . . did you hear that too?'

After a pause he nodded, but offered no comment.

I looked at the closed expression, the dense whitish skin, the black shadow of beard. A secretive, solid, slow-moving man with a tap into a world I knew little of. Gaming clubs, hired bully-boys, underworld gossip.

'The goons said they left you for dead,' he said. 'A week later, you're winning a race.'

'They exaggerated,' I said dryly.

I got a twitch but also a shake of the head. 'One of them was scared. Rattled. Said they'd gone too far . . . with the boots.'

'You know them well?' I said.

'They talk.'

There was another pause, then I said without emphasis, 'George Millace sent you a letter.'

He moved in his seat, seeming almost to relax, breathing out in a long sigh. He'd been waiting to know, I thought. Patiently waiting. Answering questions. Being obliging.

'How long have you had it?' he said.

'Three weeks.'

'You can't use it.' There was a faint tremor of triumph in the statement. 'You'd be in trouble yourself.'

'How did you know I'd got it?' I said.

1001

He blinked. The mouth tightened. He said slowly, 'I heard you had George Millace's . . .'

'George Millace's what?'

'Files.'

'Ah,' I said. 'Nice anonymous word, files. How did you hear I had them? Who from?'

'Ivor,' he said. 'And Dana. Separately.'

'Will you tell me?'

He thought it over, giving me a blank inspection, and then said grudgingly, 'Ivor was too angry to be discreet. He said too much about you . . . such as poisonous creep . . . he said you were fifty times worse than George Millace. And Dana . . . another night . . . she said did I know you had copies of some blackmailing letters George Millace had sent, and were using them. She asked if I could help her get hers back.'

I smiled in my turn. 'What did you say?'

'I said I couldn't help her.'

'When you talked to them,' I said, 'was it in gaming clubs?'

'It was.'

'Are they . . . your gaming clubs?'

'None of your business,' he said.

'Well,' I said, 'why not tell me?'

He said after a pause, 'I have two partners. Four gaming clubs. The clientele in general don't know I'm a proprietor. I move around. I play. I listen. Does that answer your question?'

I nodded. 'Yes, thank you. Are those goons your goons?'

'I employ them,' he said austerely, 'as chuckers out. Not to smash up women and jockeys.'

'A little moonlighting, was it? On the side.'

He didn't answer directly. 'I have been expecting,' he said, 'that you would demand something from me if you had that letter. Something more than ... answers.'

I thought of the letter, which I knew word for word:

Dear Victor Briggs,
I am sure you will be interested to know that I have the following information. You did on five separate occasions during the past six months conspire with a bookmaker to defraud the betting public by arranging that your odds-on favourites should not win their races.

There followed a list of five races, complete with the sums Victor had received from his bookmaker friend. The letter continued:

I hold a signed affidavit from the bookmaker in question.
As you see, all five of these horses were ridden by Philip Nore, who certainly knew what he was doing.
I could send this affidavit to the Jockey Club, in which case you would both be warned off. I will

telephone you soon, however, with an alternative suggestion.

The letter had been sent more than three years earlier. For three years Victor Briggs had run his horses straight. When George Millace died, a week to the day, Victor Briggs had gone back to the old game. Had gone back . . . to find that his vulnerable jockey was no longer reliable.

'I didn't want to do anything about the letter,' I said. 'I didn't mean to tell you I had it. Not until now.'

'Why not? You wanted to ride to win. You could have used it to make me agree. You'd been told you'd lose your job anyway if you wouldn't ride as I wanted. You knew I couldn't face being warned off. Yet you didn't use the letter for that. Why not?'

'I wanted . . . to make you run the horses straight for their own sakes.'

He gave me another of the long uninformative stares.

'I'll tell you,' he said at last. 'Yesterday I added up all the prize money I'd won since Daylight's race at Sandown. All those seconds and thirds, as well as Sharpener's wins. I added up my winnings from betting, win and place. I made more money in the past month with you riding straight than I did with you stepping off Daylight.' He paused, waiting for a reaction, but, catching it from him, I simply stared back. 'I've seen,' he went on, 'that you weren't going to ride any more crooked races. I've understood that. I know you've changed. You're a different person. Older. Stronger. If you go on riding for me, I won't ask you again to lose a race.' He paused once more. 'Is that enough? Is that what you want to hear?'

I looked away from him, out across the windy landscape.

'Yes.'

After a bit he said, 'George Millace didn't demand money, you know. At least ...'

'A donation to the Injured Jockeys?'

'You know the lot, don't you?'

'I've learned,' I said. 'George wasn't interested in extorting money for himself. He extorted ...' I searched for the word ' ... frustration.'

'From how many?'

'Seven, that I know of. Probably eight, if you ask your bookmaker.'

He was astonished.

'George Millace,' I said, 'enjoyed making people cringe. He did it to everybody in a mild way. To people he could catch out doing wrong, he did it with gusto. He had alternative suggestions for everyone ... disclosure, or do what George wanted. And what George wanted, in general, was to frustrate. To stop Ivor den Relgan's power play. To stop Dana taking drugs. To stop other people ... doing other things.'

'To stop me,' Victor said with a hint of dry humour, 'from being warned off.' He nodded. 'You're right, of course. When George Millace telephoned I was expecting straight blackmail. Then he said all I had to do was behave myself. Those were his words. As long as you behave, Victor, he said, nothing will happen. Victor. He called me Victor. I'd never met him. Knew who he was, of course, but that was all. Victor, he said, as if I were a little pet dog, as long as we're a good boy, nothing will happen. But if I suspect anything, Victor, he said, I'll follow Philip Nore around with my motorized telephotos until I have him bang to rights, and then Victor, you'll both be for the chop.'

'Do you remember word for word what he said, after all this time?' I asked, surprised.

'I recorded him. I was expecting his call . . . I wanted evidence of blackmail. All I got was a moral lecture and a suggestion that I give a thousand pounds to the Injured Jockeys Fund.'

'And was that all? For ever?'

'He used to wink at me at the races,' Victor said.

I laughed.

'Yes, very funny,' he said. 'Is that the lot?'

'Not really. There's something you could do for me, if you would. Something you know, and could tell me. Something you could tell me in future.'

'What is it?'

'About Dana's drugs.'

'Stupid girl. She won't listen.'

'She will soon. She's still . . . saveable. And besides her . . .'

I told him what I wanted. He listened acutely. When I'd finished I got the twitch of a throttled smile.

'Beside you,' he said, 'George Millace was a beginner.'

Victor drove off in his car and I walked back to Lambourn over the Downs.

An odd man, I thought. I'd learned more about him in half an hour than I had in seven years, and still knew next to nothing. He had given me what I'd wanted, though. Given it freely. Given me my job without strings for as long as I liked . . . and help in another matter just as important. It hadn't all been, I thought, because of my having that letter.

Going home in the wind, out on the bare hills, I thought of the way things had happened during the past few weeks. Not about George and his bombshells, but of Jeremy and Amanda.

Because of Jeremy's persistence, I'd looked for Amanda, and because of looking for Amanda I had now met a grandmother, an uncle, a sister. I knew something at least of my father. I had a feeling of origin that I hadn't had before.

I had people. I had people like everyone else had. Not necessarily loving or praiseworthy or successful, but *there*. I hadn't wanted them, but now that I had them they sat quietly in the mind like foundation stones.

Because of looking for Amanda I had found Samantha, and with her a feeling of continuity, of belonging. I saw the pattern of my childhood in a different perspective, not as a chopped up kaleidoscope, but as a curve. I knew a place where I'd been, and a woman who'd known me, and they seemed to lead smoothly now towards Charlie.

I no longer floated on the tide.

I had roots.

I reached the point on the hill where I could see down to the cottage, the brow that I looked up to from the sitting room windows. I stopped there. I could see most of Lambourn, stretched out. Could see Harold's house and the yard. Could see the whole row of cottages, with mine in the centre.

I'd belonged in that village, been part of it, breathed its intrigues for seven years. Been happy, miserable, normal. It was what I'd called home. But now in mind and spirit I was leaving that place . . . and soon would in body as well. I would live somewhere else, with Clare. I would be a photographer.

The future lay inside me; waiting, accepted. One day fairly soon I'd walk into it.

I would race, I thought, until the end of the season. Five or six more months. Then in May or June, when summer came, I'd hang up the boots: retire, as every jockey had to, some time or other. I would tell Harold soon, to give him time to find someone else for the autumn. I'd enjoy what was left, and maybe have a last chance at the Grand National. Anything might happen. One never knew.

I still had the appetite, still the physique. Better to go, I supposed, before both of them crumbled.

I went on down the hill without any regrets.

CHAPTER TWENTY-ONE

Clare came down on the train two days later to sort out what photographs she wanted from the filing cabinet: to make a portfolio, she said. Now that she was my agent, she'd be rustling up business. I laughed. It was serious, she said.

I had no races that day. I'd arranged to fetch Jeremy from hospital and take him home, and to have Clare come with me all the way. I'd also telephoned to Lance Kinship to say I'd had his reprints ready for ages, and hadn't seen him, and would he like me to drop them in as I was practically going past his house.

That would be fine, he said. Afternoon, earlyish, I suggested, and he said 'Right' and left the 't' off. And I'd like to ask you something, I said. 'Oh? All right. Anything you like.'

Jeremy looked a great deal better, without the grey clammy skin of Sunday. We helped him into the back of my car and tucked a rug round him, which he plucked off indignantly saying he was no aged invalid but a perfectly viable solicitor.

'And incidentally,' he said, 'my uncle came down here yesterday. Bad news for you, I'm afraid. Old Mrs Nore died during Monday night.'

'Oh no,' I said.

'Well, you knew,' Jeremy said. 'Only a matter of time.'

'Yes, but . . .'

'My uncle brought two letters for me to give to you. They're in my suitcase somewhere. Fish them out, before we start.'

I fished them out, and we sat in the hospital car park while I read them.

One was a letter. The other was a copy of her will.

Jeremy said, 'My uncle said he was called out urgently to the nursing home to make her will, and the doctor there told my uncle there wasn't much time.'

'Do you know what's in it?' I asked.

He shook his head. 'My uncle just said she was a stubborn old woman to the last.'

I unfolded the typewritten sheets.

I, Lavinia Nore, being of sound mind, do hereby revoke all previous wills . . .

There was a good deal of legal guff and some complicated pension arrangements for an old cook and gardener, and then the two final fairly simple paragraphs.

' . . . *Half the residue of my estate to my son James Nore . . .*'

' . . . *Half the residue of my estate to my grandson*

Philip Nore, to be his absolutely, with no strings or steel hawsers attached.'

'What's the matter?' Clare said. 'You look so grim.'

'The old witch . . . has defeated me.'

I opened the other envelope. Inside there was a letter in shaky handwriting, with no beginning, and no end.

It said:

I think you did find Amanda, and didn't tell me because it would have given me no pleasure.

Is she a nun?

You can do what you like with my money. If it makes you vomit, as you once said . . . then VOMIT.

Or give it to my genes.

Rotten roses.

I handed the will and the letter to Clare and Jeremy, who read them in silence. We sat there for a while, thinking, and then Clare folded up the letter, put it in its envelope, and handed it back to me.

'What will you do?' she said.

'I don't know. See that Amanda never starves, I suppose. Apart from that . . .'

'Enjoy it,' Jeremy said. 'The old woman loved you.'

I listened to the irony in his voice and wondered if it was true. Love or hate. Love and hate. Perhaps she'd felt both at once when she'd made that will.

We drove from Swindon towards St Albans, making a short detour to deliver Lance Kinship's reprints.

'Sorry about this,' I said. 'But it won't take long.'

They didn't seem to mind. We found the house without much trouble ... typical Kinship country, fake Georgian, large grandiose front, pillared gateway, meagre drive.

I picked the packet of photographs out of the boot of the car, and rang the front doorbell.

Lance opened the door himself, dressed today not in country gent togs but in white jeans, espadrilles, and a red and white horizontally striped T-shirt. International film-director gear, I diagnosed. All he needed was the megaphone.

'Come inside,' he said. 'I'll pay you for these.'

'OK. Can't be long though, with my friends waiting.'

He looked briefly towards my car, where Clare and Jeremy's interested faces showed in the windows, and went indoors with me following. He led the way into a large sitting room with expanses of parquet and too much black lacquered furniture. Chrome and glass tables. Art deco lamps.

I gave him the packet of pictures.

'You'd better look at them,' I said, 'to make sure they're all right.'

He shrugged. 'Why shouldn't they be?' All the same, he opened the envelope and pulled out the contents.

The top picture showed him looking straight at the

DICK FRANCIS

camera in his country gent clothes. Glasses. Trilby hat. Air of bossy authority.

'Turn it over,' I said.

With raised eyebrows he did so: and read what Mrs Jackson had written. *This is the rating officer . . .*

The change in him from one instant to the next was like one person leaving and another entering the same skin. He shed the bumptiously sure-of-himself phoney; slid into a mess of unstable ill-will. The gaudy clothes which had fitted one character seemed grotesque on the other, like gift-wrap round a hand-grenade. I saw the Lance Kinship I'd only suspected existed. Not the faintly ridiculous poseur pretending to be what he wasn't, but the tangled psychotic who would do any-thing at all to preserve the outward show.

It was in his very inadequacy, I supposed, that the true danger lay. In his estrangement from reality. In his theatrical turn of mind, which had allowed him to see murder as a solution to problems.

'Before you say anything,' I said, 'you'd better look at the other things in that envelope.'

With angry fingers he sorted them out. The regular reprints . . . and also the black and white glossy repro-ductions of Dana den Relgan's drugs list and the letter I'd found on the diazo paper.

They were for him a fundamental disaster.

He let the pictures of the great film producer fall to the ground around him like ten-by-eight coloured leaves, and stood holding the three black and white sheets in visible horror.

'She said . . .' he said hoarsely, 'she swore you didn't have it. She swore you didn't know what she was talking about . . .'

'She was talking about the drugs you supplied her with. Complete with dates and prices. That list which you hold, which is recognizably in her handwriting, for all that it was originally written on cellophane. And of course, as you see, your name appears on it liberally.'

'I'll kill you,' he said.

'No, you won't. You've missed your chance. It's too late now. If the gas had killed me you would have been all right, but it didn't.'

He didn't say 'What gas?' He said, 'It all went wrong. But it didn't matter. I thought . . . it didn't matter.' He looked down helplessly at the black and white prints.

'You thought it didn't matter because you heard from Dana den Relgan that I didn't have the list. And if I didn't have the list, then I didn't have the letter. Whatever else I'd had from George Millace, I didn't after all have the list and the letter . . . Is that what you thought? . . . so if I didn't have them there was no more need to kill me. Was that it?'

He didn't answer.

'It's far too late to do it now,' I said, 'because there are extra prints of those pages all over the place. Another copy of that picture of you, identified by Mrs Jackson. Bank, solicitors, several friends, all have instructions about taking everything to the police if any accidental death should befall me. You've a positive interest in keeping me alive from now on.'

The implication of what I was saying only slowly sank in. He looked from my face to the photographs and back again several times, doubtfully.

'George Millace's letter . . .' he said.

I nodded. George's letter, handwritten, read:

Dear Lance Kinship,

I have received from Dana den Relgan a most interesting list of drugs supplied to her by you over the past few months. I am sure I understand correctly that you are a regular dealer in such illegal substances.

It appears to be all too well known in certain circles that in return for being invited to places which please your ego, you will, so to speak, pay for your pleasure with gifts of cannabis, heroin and cocaine.

I could of course place Dana den Relgan's candid list before the proper authorities. I will telephone you shortly, however, with an alternative suggestion.

Yours sincerely,
George Millace.

'It was typed when I got it,' Lance Kinship said dully. 'I burnt it.'

'When George telephoned,' I said, 'did he tell you his alternative suggestion?'

The shock in Lance Kinship began to abate, with enmity growing in its place.

'I'm telling you nothing.'

I said, disregarding him, 'Did George Millace say to stop supplying drugs . . . and donate to the Injured Jockeys Fund?'

His mouth opened and snapped shut viciously.

'Did he telephone . . .' I asked, 'or did he tell you his terms when he called here?'

A tight silence.

'Did you put . . . something . . . from your store cupboard into his whisky?'

'Prove it!' he said with sick triumph.

One couldn't, of course. George had been cremated, with his blood tested only for alcohol. There had been no checks for other drugs. Not for perhaps tranquillizers, which were flavourless, and which in sufficient quantity would certainly have sent a driver to sleep.

George, I thought regretfully, had stepped on one victim too many. Had stepped on what he'd considered a worm and never recognized the cobra.

George had made a shattering mistake if he'd wanted for once to see the victim squirm when he came up with his terms. George hadn't dreamt that the inadequate weakling would lethally lash out to preserve his sordid life style: hadn't really understood how fanatically Lance Kinship prized his shoulder-rubbing with a jet-set that at best tolerated him. George must have enjoyed seeing Lance Kinship's fury. Must have driven off laughing. Poor George.

'Didn't you think,' I said, 'that George had left a copy of his letter behind him?'

From his expression, he hadn't. I supposed he'd acted on impulse. He'd very nearly been right.

'When you heard that George had blackmailed other people . . . including Dana . . . is that when you began thinking I might have your letter?'

'I heard,' he said furiously, 'I heard . . . in the clubs . . . Philip Nore has the letters . . . he's ruined den Relgan . . . got him sacked from the Jockey Club . . . Did you think . . . once I knew . . . did you really think I'd wait for you to come around to *me*?'

'Unfortunately,' I said slowly, 'whether you like it or not, I now have come around to you.'

'No.'

'Yes,' I said. 'I'll tell you straight away that like George Millace I'm not asking for money.'

He didn't look much reassured.

'I'll also tell you it's your bad luck that my mother died from addiction to heroin.'

He said wildly, 'But I didn't know your mother.'

'No, of course not. And there's no question of your ever having supplied her yourself . . . It's just that I have a certain long-standing prejudice against drug-pushers. You may as well know it. You may as well understand why I want . . . what I want.'

He took a compulsive step towards me. I thought of the brisk karate kick he had delivered to den Relgan at Kempton and wondered if in his rope-soled sandals on parquet he could be as effective. Wondered if he had any real skill ... or whether it was more window-dressing to cover the vacuum.

He looked incongruous, not dangerous. A man not young, not old, thinning on top, wearing glasses ... and beach clothes indoors in December.

A man pushed ... who could kill if pushed too far. Kill not by physical contact, when one came to think of it, but in his absence, by drugs and gas.

He never reached me to deliver whatever blind vengeful blow he had in mind. He stepped on one of the fallen photographs, and slid, and went down hard on one knee. The inefficient indignity of it seemed to break up conclusively whatever remained of his confidence, for when he looked up at me I saw not hatred or defiance, but fear.

I said, 'I don't want what George did. I don't ask you to stop peddling drugs. I want you to tell me who supplies you with heroin.'

He staggered to his feet, his face aghast. 'I can't. I ... *can't.*'

'It shouldn't be difficult,' I said mildly. 'You must know where you get it from. You get it in sizeable quantities, to sell, to give away. You always have plenty, I'm told. So you must have a regular supplier ... mustn't you? He's the one I want.'

The source, I thought. One source supplying several pushers. The drug business was like some monstrous tentacled creature: cut off one tentacle and another grew in its place. The war against drugs would never be won . . . but it had to be fought, if only for the sake of silly girls who were sniffing their way to perdition. For the sake of the pretty ones. For Dana. For Caroline . . . my lost butterfly mother, who had saved me from an addiction of my own.

'You don't know . . .' Lance Kinship seemed to be breathless. 'It's impossible. I can't tell you. I'd be . . . dead.'

I shook my head. 'It will be between the two of us. No one will ever know you told me . . . unless you yourself talk, like den Relgan did in the gaming clubs.'

'I can't,' he said despairingly.

'If you don't,' I said conversationally, 'I will first tell the policemen investigating an attempted murder in my house that my neighbour positively identifies you as having posed as a rating officer. This isn't enough on its own to get you charged, but it could certainly get you *investigated* . . . for access to chemicals, and so on.'

He looked sick.

'Secondly,' I said, 'I'll see that it gets known all over the place that people would be unwise to ask you to their parties, despite your little goodies, because they might at any time be raided. Unlawful possession of certain drugs is still an offence, I believe.'

'You . . . you . . .'

I nodded. He couldn't find a word bad enough.

'I know where you go . . . to whose houses. Everyone talks. I've been told. A word in the ear of the drugs squad . . . and you'd be the least welcome guest in Britain.'

'I . . . I . . .'

'Yes, I know,' I said. 'Going to these places is what makes your life worth living. I don't ask you not to go. I don't ask you to stop your gifts. Just to tell me where the heroin comes from. Not the cocaine, not the cannabis, just the heroin. Just the deadly one.'

The faintest of crafty looks crept in round his anguished eyes.

'And don't,' I said, watching for it, 'think you can get away with any old lie. You may as well know that what you tell me will go to the drugs squad. Don't worry . . . by such a roundabout route that no one will ever connect it with you. But your present supplier may very likely be put out of business. If that happens, you'll be safe from me.'

He trembled as if his legs would give way.

'Mind you,' I said judiciously, 'with one supplier out of business, you might have to look around for another. In a year or so, I might ask you his name.'

His face was sweating and full of disbelief. 'You mean . . . it will go on . . . and on . . .'

'That's right.'

'But you *can't*.'

'I think you killed George Millace. You certainly

tried to kill me. You very nearly killed my friend. Why should you think I shouldn't want retribution?'

He stared.

'I ask very little,' I said. 'A few words written down . . . now and then.'

'Not in my writing,' he said, appalled.

'Certainly, in your writing,' I said matter-of-factly, 'to get the spelling right, and so on. But don't worry, you'll be safe. I promise you no one will ever find out where the tip-offs come from. No one will ever know they come via me. Neither my name nor yours will ever be mentioned.'

'You . . . you're *sure*?'

'Sure.'

I produced a small notebook and a fibre-tipped pen, 'Write now,' I said. 'Your supplier.'

'Not *now*,' he said, wavering.

'Why not?' I said calmly. 'May as well get it over. Sit down.'

He sat by one of his glass and chrome coffee tables, looking totally dazed. He wrote a name and address on the notepad.

'And sign it,' I said casually.

'*Sign . . .*'

'Of course. Just your name.'

He wrote: *Lance Kinship*. And then, underneath, with a flourish, added '*Film Director.*'

'That's great,' I said, without emphasis. I picked up

the pad, reading what he'd written. A foreign name. An address in London. One tentacle under the axe.

I stored away in a pocket the small document that would make him sweat next year . . . and the next, and the next. The document that I would photograph, and keep safe.

'That's . . . all?' he said numbly.

I nodded. 'All for now.'

He didn't stand up when I left him. Just sat on his black lacquer chair in his T-shirt and white trousers, stunned into silence, staring at space.

He'd recover his bumptiousness, I thought. Pseuds always did.

I went out to where Clare and Jeremy were still waiting, and paused briefly in the winter air before getting into the car.

Most people's lives, I thought, weren't a matter of world affairs, but of the problems right beside them. Not concerned portentously with saving mankind, but with creating local order: in small checks and balances.

Neither my life nor George Millace's would ever sway the fate of nations, but our actions could change the lives of individuals; and they had done that.

The dislike I'd felt for him alive was irrelevant to the intimacy I felt with him dead. I knew his mind, his intentions, his beliefs. I'd solved his puzzles. I'd fired his guns.

I got into the car.

'Everything all right?' Clare asked.

'Yes,' I said.

DICK FRANCIS

Field of Thirteen

£5.99

THE NEW BESTSELLER

There's a bomb scare at Kingdom Hill racecourse, where failed conman Tricksy Wilcox watches his dreams blown to kingdom come ...

At Chelthenham's glittering National Hunt Festival, protocol is rocked as a love-struck owner falls madly in love with her jockey ...

There is passion – and revenge – at the glorious Kentucky Derby ...

... and then ten other tantalizing stories to hold you enthralled from the starting gates to the finish.

Award-winning Master of Crime Dick Francis tackles a new distance with thirteen nerve-tingling tales of politics, passion, horses and crime – each one of them tied to a milestone event in the international racing calendar.

The result is beyond question.

> 'At his best, Francis can make you feel the hot
> breath of horses on the back of your neck'
> Michael Dobbs, *Express On Sunday*

DICK FRANCIS

To the Hilt

£5.99

'Another one for the winner's enclosure'
Daily Telegraph

Alexander Kinloch found solitude and a steady income painting in a bothy on a remote Scottish mountain. Until the morning the strangers arrived to rough him up, and Alexander was dragged reluctantly back into the real and violent world he thought he had left behind.

Millions of pounds are missing from his stepfather's business. A valuable racehorse is under threat. Then comes the first ugly death and the end of all Alexander's doubts. For the honour of the Kinlochs he will face the strangers . . . committed up to the hilt . . .

'The book is a cracker . . . the former champion jockey is still taking the jumps with consummate grace'
Sunday Telegraph

'Fast-moving, readable and beautifully constructed . . . a cracking yarn'
Country Life

DICK FRANCIS

10lb Penalty

£5.99

'One of the outstanding thriller writers of our age'
Daily Mail

Damaging allegations cost young Benedict Juliard his
hopes of a career as a steeplechase jockey. Instead he's
forced to join ranks alongside his father, a high-flying
businessman battling a Dorset by-election for a street level
entry into politics.

The campaign gets off to a flying start. But this time the
obstacles ahead aren't just dangerous – they're lethal.

Horses, politics, lies and treachery. They can all carry the
maximum 10lb penalty. And, as any jockey knows, a 10lb
penalty can be a killer . . .

'The Queen Mother's favourite jockey is the
world's favourite writer of racing tales'
The Independent

'How many other contemporary writers provide us with
a comparable degree of excitement and pleasure?'
Daily Telegraph

DICK FRANCIS

Come to Grief

£5.99

'This is Francis writing at his best'
Evening Standard

Sid Halley, the ex-champion jockey turned investigator
who appears in *Odds Against* and *Whip Hand*, is back.
In *Come to Grief* he faces new dangers, new deeply
demanding decisions.

Sid Halley has uncovered an obnoxious crime committed
by a friend whom he – and everyone else – has held in
deep affection. On the morning set for the opening of the
friend's trial, at which Sid is due to be called as a witness,
other people's miseries explode and send him spinning
into days of hard rational detection and heart-searching
torment.

Troubled, courageous and unwilling to admit defeat, for
Sid Halley it is business as usual.

Winner of the Edgar Allen Poe award for
best crime novel of the year.

'Dick Francis is firmly in the saddle and
leaving the opposition standing . . .'
Sunday Telegraph

DICK FRANCIS

Bonecrack

£5.99

'Excitement and sheer readability'
The Daily Telegraph

It started with mistaken identify and a threat to his life.
And rapidly became a day-to-day nightmare with little
glimmer of escape.

For Neil Griffon, temporarily in charge of his father's
racing stables, blackmail is now a terrible reality. A reality
not only threatening valuable horses but testing his nerves
to the limit.

And proving just how brittle bones can be . . .

'A classic entry with a fine turn of speed'
Evening Standard

DICK FRANCIS

For Kicks

£5.99

'Absolutely first class . . . warmly recommended'
Sunday Times

Proprietor of a stud farm in the breathtaking region of Australia's Snowy Mountains? Or muck-raking stable boy in Yorkshire?

The Earl of October persuades young Australian Danny Roke to accept the English alternative. It's the change of scene and the challenge that pushes Danny undercover, on the scent of a suspect racehourse dope scandal.

But the pain involved, dealing with vicious swindlers and the Earl's two attractive daughters, could overturn all his pleasure in the chase . . .

'Very lively, hard-bitten account . . . some jolting action scenes'
Financial Times

DICK FRANCIS

Wild Horses

£5.99

'A marvellous storyteller and an immaculate craftsman'
Daily Mail

Movie director Thomas Lyon came to Newmarket to rake
the ashes of an old Jockey Club scandal for a new Holly-
wood film. Too late, he found himself listening to a
blacksmith's dying confession. Found himself watching as
the past came violently back to life.

Capturing the shockwaves over one woman's macabre
death nearly thirty years before is drama. But a frenzied
knife attack on the set of *Unstable Times* is definitely
attempted murder. Who stood to gain from the threats?
Between truth and shadowy fiction, Thomas Lyon already
knew too much.

Following the real story could mean the difference
between life and death. His own . . .

'Still the best bet for a winning read'
Mail on Sunday

DICK FRANCIS

Flying Finish

£5.99

'Extremely exciting . . . lots of action'
Sunday Times

Lord Henry Grey was an amateur jockey and pilot. But when he decided to abandon his desk-bound job for an active career in the bloodstock market, he found there was more to couriering valuable horses around the world than he'd ever suspected . . .

Meeting Gabriella in Italy is the first, most pleasurable surprise. But a colleague's disappearance on the next Milan trip gives him a nasty jolt: for two of his predecessors have already gone absent without leave.

Thousands of feet up, in the hands of a sadistic killer, it seems that Grey has discovered the truth too late . . .

'With this book, Dick Francis takes his place at the head of the field as one of the most intelligent thriller writers in the business'
Sunday Express

DICK FRANCIS

Dead Cert

£5.99

'Fresh and exciting ... very lively'
Sunday Times

For millionaire jockey Alan York, winning is a bonus. For Joe Nantwich, victory means no cushy backhanders; and for Bill Davidson, front running on strongly fancied Admiral, triumph is an imposter. It means murder – his own.

Turning private detective, York uses Joe's underworld connections to go on the trail of the killers – only to draw a series of blanks. But when ambushed by a gang of vicious thugs, he picks up some clues, along with cuts and bruises. Bill's murder begins to make more sense. Until York finds himself in hospital, without a memory.

'As a jockey, Dick Francis was unbeatable when he got into his stride. The same is true, nowadays, of his crime-writing'
Daily Mirror

DICK FRANCIS

Enquiry

£5.99

No jockey likes being labelled a cheat. Least of all by a Stewards' Enquiry. Kelly Hughes' career looks doomed. He knows he's been framed, but finding the reason could prove dangerous. Especially with a killer on his trail . . .

Hughes' own enquiry uncovers dynamite that could blow the racing world to smithereens. Only a few powerful – and violent – mean know the sordid secret. And they'll go to extraordinary lengths to keep it that way. Murder is just one option . . .

DICK FRANCIS

Hot Money

£5.99

'A masterly plot'
Daily Mail

Malcolm Pembroke never expected to make a million pounds without making enemies. Nor did he expect his latest wife to be brutally murdered. All clues suggest the killer comes from close to home – but after five marriages and nine children, that still leaves the field wide open.

When he finds his own life in danger, Pembroke entrusts his safety to his estranged son, Ian, an amateur jockey; and through him discovers a compulsive new outlet for his financial expertise.

Soon he's playing the international bloodstock market for incredible stakes. Not the safest bet for a man on the run from avaricious relatives. Particularly when one of them's got a bomb . . .

'Dick Francis is on top form with this subtle and satisfying entertainment that saves a macabre surprise for the finish'
Evening Standard